I0831707

augury university omnibus

ROSE SANTORIELLO

Copyright 2025 © by Rose Santoriello.

All rights reserved. Neither this book, nor any parts within it may be reproduced in any form, including information storage and retrieval systems, without written permission from the author, with the exception of brief quotations in a book review.

Created with Vellum

This book is a work of fiction. All of the characters, organizations, companies, and events in this novel are either products of the author's imagination, or are used fictitiously.

Editing: A. E. Mann Editing Services

Proofreading: Heather Nix

Cover design and map: Eternal Geekery

Novella title pages (the original covers), chapter header art, and Serpentine sketches: Fallnskye Illustration

End of story art pieces: Ram (@alta.riff) and Pix Pentham

Formatting: Rae Douglas

All other graphics: Rose Santoriello

This is a limited special edition. Only 100 copies of this version (with an embossed cover and sprayed edges) of the omnibus will be sold.

This book is for 18+

 Created with Vellum

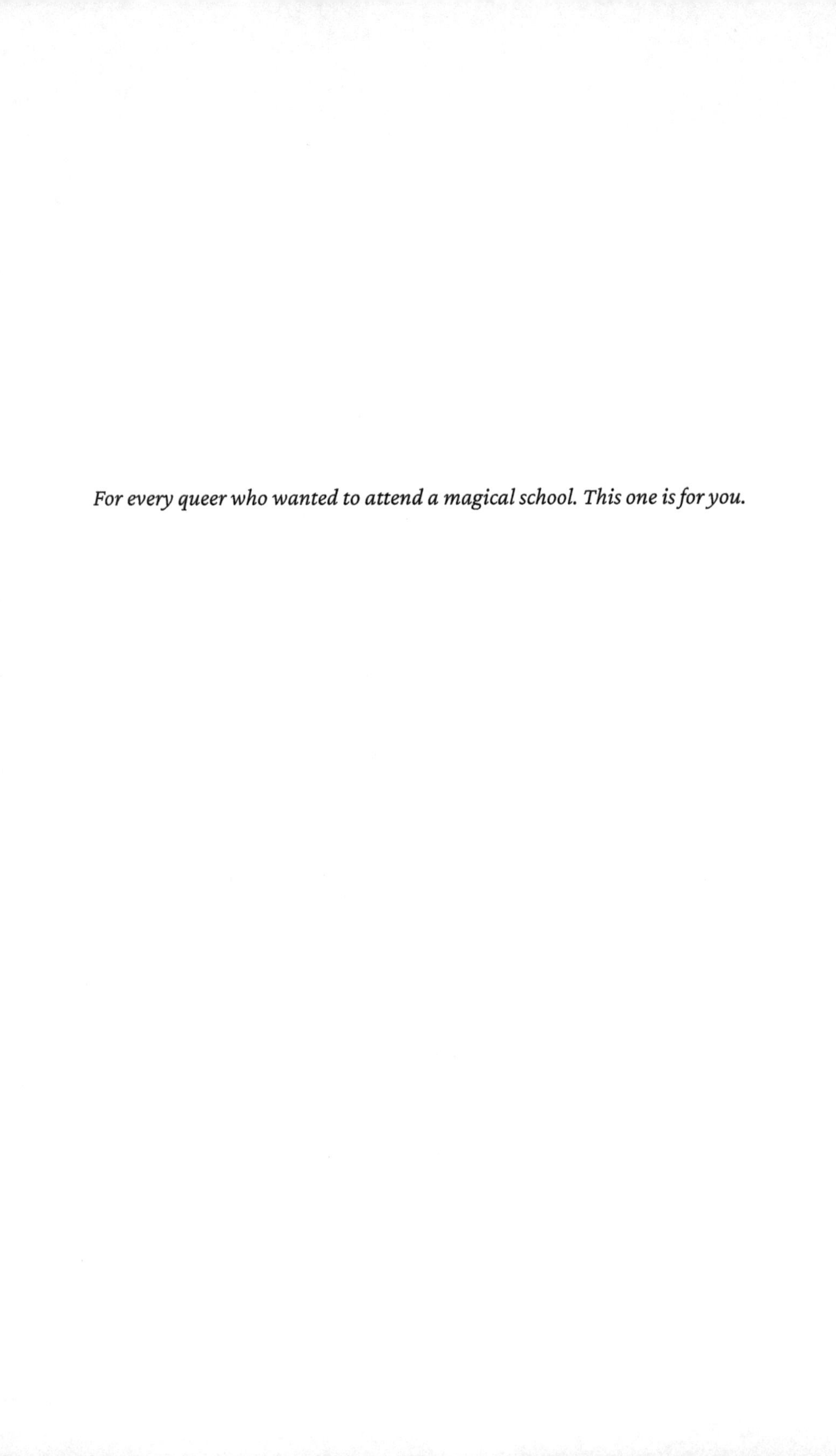

For every queer who wanted to attend a magical school. This one is for you.

content warnings

ALL STORIES

Adult language, consensual sex between adults, and mentions and discussions of mental illnesses, chronic illnesses, and physical disabilities (there are characters with anxiety, ADHD, SPD, limb differences, mood swings, depression, and endometriosis).

HOOK-UP TO HOLIDATE

Sex under the magical influence (consent received while not under the magical influence), vague and brief mention of parental and sibling death, and difficult family relationships.

STEALING ELF HEARTS

Pain play.

DISCO SPRING FEVER

Pain play, cock ring, degradation, public sex (no exhibitionism), use of a concealed toy in public, consideration of sexual blackmail (not followed through), age gap (900+ years), and taboo workplace relationships.

SWEET SUMMER SERPENTINE

Age gap (thousands of years), sexual constriction, tail play, public play, knotting, double penetration, and anal play. Brief mentions of parental death, missing family members, familial issues, and grief.

HAUNT ME, BABY

Professor and student relationship/power dynamics, age gap (5 years), sex while under the magical influence, semi-public play, double/triple penetration, and fisting.

RIDING CENTAUR'S SLEIGH

Refer to all stories' list.

ORC'S MIDNIGHT KISS

Refer to all stories' list.

SETTING UP LOVE

Impact play, pegging/anal sex, bondage, dominance and submission dynamics, and semi-public sex (unintentionally caught by coworker).

AUGURY: NEXT GENERATION

Refer to all stories' list.

SERIES EPILOGUE

Refer to all stories' list.

The Americas
Augury University
Illusionary Jungle
The Isles of Magia
Octopus Island
Sleeping Island
Sunspell City
Boca Raton
Florgia Beach
Magia Island
Naiad Island

Hook-up To Holidate

Let's Fall in Love for the Night - FINNEAS
girls girls girls - FLETCHER
IDK You Yet - Alexander 23
I'll Call You Mine - girl in red
I Do Adore - Mindy Gledhill
From Eden - Hozier
Love Is an Open Door - Frozen
Glittery - Kasey Muskgraves
Symmetrical - Allen Stone
Underneath the Tree - Kelly Clarkson

Hook-up To Holidate

ROSE SANTORIELLO

prologue

INDIGO

"A FEW THOUSAND YEARS AGO, A MASSIVE BLACK HOLE CAUSED MULTIPLE GALAXIES TO collide with one another, resulting in The Convergence. Because of this rare cosmic event, many magical races bred with humanity, which created Earth as we know it today. Some beings returned to their home planets, while others stayed. Now, in the year 6004, you can find humans, elves, orcs, serpentine, and many other races, including hybrids of all of the above. With this in mind, the leaders of Earth focused their efforts on advancing magic, rather than technology." I take in a breath, trying not to shake. This is the first class of my first week as an adjunct professor, and I want to do everything right. Augury University is the most prestigious magical college in the Americas, after all. An elfling girl waves at me, smiling wide, and I smile back. My parents were wrong. I'm not too young to be here. "Welcome to The History of Mages 101. I'm Professor Watson, and it's a pleasure to meet all of you."

Although my secret dream was always to work with potions, my mother pressured me into studying charms, just as she did, and so that's what I teach: Charms 101, History 101, and a few other history classes. I blame Eldest Daughter Syndrome. Carrying the load of my family wasn't easy, but neither was the pressure I put on myself either. I graduated high school early and went on to Augury University, where I completed an accelerated Bachelors-to-Masters program in Charms. Unlike my mother's wildest dreams though, I accepted a position here upon graduation. I love being a professor. It's thrilling to watch young mages make new discoveries about themselves and their magic, but I think a small part of her will always be disappointed I didn't follow in her footsteps to the infrastructure sector.

I teach the students an ice breaker. They're to tell me their names, their major, and to show the class a trick. One at a time, each student walks up to the front of the class and does something unique.

A tall elf named Raven, with pitch-black long hair, walks up with a dark, rainbow-feathered bird perched on her shoulder and snaps her fingers. Instantly, the bird transforms into a massive dragon, flying close to the ceiling, smoke coming out of its nose. It's just an illusion, but we all stare in awe at the magnificent creature. She smirks with amusement and snaps again, the bird falling back into place.

We clap as she heads towards her seat, and an adorable faun makes her way to the front. She has tan skin and long brown hair with flowers wrapped around her small horns.

"Hey everyone! I'm Eden, a seer. Professor Watson, would you mind being a part of my demonstration?" she asks, a happy lilt to her voice.

"Not at all," I reply, walking towards her.

"Perfect."

Her fingers are ice cold as she takes my hands in hers and closes her eyes. A few seconds go by, and they fly open, white as snow.

"You are going to spill coffee on yourself in November," she says, her voice now robotic, diluted of all its previous vibrancy. "This is all I am sure of."

What a weird vision. I mean, I know they're never certain, but that's so... odd.

"Thanks for the heads up," I say. "But I won't be avoiding coffee, especially not in November." The class laughs, everyone breaking out into different jokes.

"Pack an extra shirt!" a masculine cambion shouts. He's right, I probably should. Chances are I won't remember by then though.

Eden leans in close to me. "Your future is full of anxiety and uncertainty, but also joy and romance. Be kind to yourself," she whispers.

This exercise was supposed to be a fun little get-to-know-each-other, not an ominous warning from the beyond. Romance, huh? A girl can dream.

one

INDIGO

On my to-do list:

- Finish grading midterms
- Go grocery shopping
- Buy a portable charger

Not on my to-do list:

- The sexy orcling standing in the corner making far too much eye contact

But they say life is what happens between your plans....

"Are you gonna keep staring at her or are you gonna go say something?" Dahlia asks with one eyebrow raised.

I ignore her, trying to push down the overwhelming feeling of desire as my knees go weak, and wave a hand at the bartender. I need some liquid courage. "Could I get a lemon drop shot, please?"

He nods and grabs for the liquor. Dahlia lets out a small laugh, the pleasant sound resonating in the air. "Make it two, and you can put them on my tab."

Dahlia is my boldest friend and the only non-elfborn human I hangout with. Most folks without magic are jealous or afraid of those of us with it, but

Dahlia thinks of it as a fun party trick. It's interesting to her, but not all that we are as beings. She runs a hand through my hair, inspecting it.

"I'm so glad I used that opalescent dye. You look amazing. White with just a touch of that lilac." Dahlia smiles, impressed with herself. She's the island's top hair stylist, with some pretty intense clientele. Magia Island's main attraction is Augury University, but there are some celebrities who live here too. If it weren't for Dahlia, I'd look less like them and more like a wet mop.

"You did a great job. I wish I was in the Potions Department," I say, because it's true. I've always wanted to be a potions mage, but it wasn't in the cards. Dahlia and my coworker Alitha have been working together to experiment on different hair potions, and I'm their favorite test subject.

The bartender places both shots down on the table, and we clink our glasses together before throwing them back. The alcohol only intensifies my heady desire. My blood, like my throat, is on fire at the sight of this woman—at the look in her eyes as I shift in my seat to get another look at her. I turn around and get out my phone. I start typing out a text to Alitha when I feel a warm, towering presence behind me. Dahlia's face is like a deer in headlights, with her deep brown eyes suddenly widening.

"Well." She coughs. "I'm actually meeting someone here tonight. I'll catch you later." Dahlia walks away, her hips swaying in her orange two-piece, long dark hair flowing down nearly to her butt. She's leaving me alone with this woman? Oh boy.

The orcling sits down next to me, a mass of muscle. Her scent is intoxicating, some kind of woodsy cologne with hints of orange blossom. I love being an elfborn, however distant my lineage is, because I can make out the specific scents that cause her to smell so... *alluring*. I have to shut my mouth to stop myself from drooling. What the hell kind of mind-altering substance is in her cologne? Whatever it is, I'm addicted.

She looks at me and raises a hand, her forearms flexing as she places her thumb near her lips and licks it, seductively staring at me while motioning towards my face. "Your mascara is smudged; let me get it."

The cold wet feeling of her thumb rubbing against my skin is oddly appealing. Normally, I would feel icked by a stranger's touch, especially their saliva, but not this stranger. I'd let her do whatever she wants with me. In fact, if I knew this was going to lead to her touching me, I would have fucked up my makeup a lot sooner. The bartender comes by and nods, waiting for our orders.

"Could I get an Irish Coffee? And the lady will have...?" She gestures to me, waiting for my response.

"Oh—uh—I'll have a... sex on the beach." I'm so used to douchebag guys at the bars who order for me that this is refreshing. Still, I wish my favorite drink didn't have such a weird name. It's uncomfortable to say aloud, and I feel my cheeks heat. I don't know if other people experience the same amount of embarrassment that I do, but moments like this make me want to curl up into a ball and die. This is the kinda stuff I need to bring up in therapy.

"I'm Vega, but you can call me V, if you'd like," she says, and I take her in. She's huge. Broad, athletic shoulders lead to swollen biceps. I think she could crush my head in her arms, and maybe I'd let her. She's tall too. We're seated, but I'd bet money she's well over a foot taller than me. V has seductive golden eyes and green skin. Not green like a Christmas tree, but more of a mossy sage. Her black hair is tied back in a bun, with shaven sections on either side of her head. I could look at her for hours, counting every freckle on her body.

"I'm Indie. It's nice to meet you." Indie is the nickname only my family calls me, but I'm not sure I wanna tell her my real name. Most people don't recognize me by look or even name... better to be safe than sorry though. I reach out to shake hands before realizing how weird I'm being and flinch it back.

She chuckles, her voice much deeper than mine, and fucking hell. This woman is so hot, and I am *so* awkward. I don't know how to talk to the people I'm interested in. My latest hook-up last weekend, on Halloween, was with a guy dressed as a Mandalorian from one of the old Star Wars shows. I didn't look much different from my typical day-to-day vibe, donning a black dress as a vintage witch. He didn't wanna talk, and I was totally fine with the helmet staying on.

"You're quite cute," she says. "Tell me about yourself."

This is the part where everything goes sour. I'm going to say I'm a professor at Augury University, and she either won't believe me; or she *will,* and she'll want information on some kind of research we're doing. That, or she'll be totally normal until she finds out who my sister is, and then she'll just use me to try and get to Iris. I don't want this to be about my job or my family; I want this to be about me. Unfortunately, *I* am a nightmare. I realize I'm zoning out when the bartender places our drinks in front of us.

"Or don't. How about this, how about we give each other no specific details? Keep everything vague and just talk as... beings." She takes a sip of her Irish coffee, and the smell drowns out her cologne. Bummer. I guess I'll have to get close if I want to smell her again.

"That sounds lovely," I say, feeling as though she read my mind. No specifics. I can do that. "Do you practice magic?"

"A bit. My focus is charms," she says and leans in close. "Though I'm just as good with my hands, no magic necessary." Her breath is hot against my neck, and I squirm in my seat, pressing my thighs together.

I clear my throat. "Me too, although I'm secretly passionate about potions."

She tilts her head, and I notice the gold hoop in her nose. I'd never been into piercings much. Suddenly, I feel much different about the subject. V licks her lips. "Why not do what you're passionate about?"

"Because I'm better at charms, and because—my—it's complicated." I frown, playing with my straw. I don't know what's gotten into me. Normally, I obsess over something unrealistic, anxious over things that'll likely never happen, but this anxiety feels... warranted. I could really fuck this up and lose her interest.

She bumps me with her shoulder, her taut, bare skin brushing against mine for a split second. "It's okay. I think it's cool you do a little of both. What potions do you enjoy making?"

V sounds genuinely interested, and it makes my chest warm. Many people think magic should only be done for work, never recreationally. "I just make potions for fun, so it's nothing life saving. Mostly stuff with food and cosmetics."

"Like what?"

"Perfumes, oils. Right now I'm working on a potion that enhances an individual's pheromones," I say and take another sip of my drink.

"What's your intended goal?" she asks, her voice like honey.

I shrug. "A lot of things. It can help someone sense danger more easily, or—"

"Or attract others," V says as she finishes her drink. She stands up suddenly, the movement unexpected. She walks towards the exit and leans against a wall.

Am I supposed to follow her? Is that what she wants?

I look around for Dahlia and spot her in a corner with an elfling. He's got his thumb resting against her jaw, and I figure I should leave them to it. Assembling all of my courage, I strut up to V, and she grabs my hand, bringing me out of the building. She's intimidatingly tall, at least six foot five. Some small fragment of my instincts is fearful, telling me to run, but every other part of me wants to climb her like a tree.

Before I can even take a breath of the late night air, V pushes me against the outside wall, her lips against my neck. Something lightly pricks at me, her tusks, and I shiver. Her stature is overwhelming—I want to melt into her, for our bodies to form together as one.

"Are you wearing that potion? Are your senses enhanced right now?"

I gulp. "No. I'm not wearing any perfume or oils tonight. Though I have a vial in my purse. I considered using it...."

Her breath hitches, and I embrace our closeness, relaxing my body against hers.

"So you're just that attracted to me? Unbelievable." Vega smirks, so sure of her words.

I'm confused by her sudden cockiness. "What do you mean?"

"I'm an orcling. I can smell you, Indie. I need a taste." Her words strip me down to my bones. She can smell my desire? I must be a flustered shade of pink right now.

She nips at my neck, pushing a hand up the hem of my skirt to cup my ass. We're in public, and I don't even care if someone recognizes me. All I want is her touch. All I need is for her to use her strength against me. She raises her other hand, hailing a cab.

V rubs down my back as we get into the yellow car, easing my nerves. I don't know why I'm nervous. It appears she likes me, but some part of my brain is hyper focused on impressing this woman.

"Where to?" the man asks.

"Tropics Apartment Complex, please," she says as she rests a hand gently on my knee.

I place my head on her shoulder. "I thought we said no specifics," I tease.

She sighs. "There's really no way to get back to my place without you finding out where I live."

I lift my head and smirk. "You could have blindfolded me."

"Very true. We'll have to do that another night."

Another night. My hair raises at the thought. I could get two nights of this feeling? Sold. Sign me up. I'd've been first in line when the bar opened if I knew the night would lead me down this path.

She looks me dead in the eyes. "Now you know where I live, so can I ask one specific thing in return?"

"Of course. That seems fair."

Her mouth forms a grin as she moves in closer. "Have you ever been with anyone?"

"Yes," I say, a little affronted. I've been with a few people, thank you very much. "Less than ten, though. A few human men, an elfling woman, and even a cambion once." Is that embarrassing? Does she expect more? Less?

"Good girl. I was hoping you had some experience. I need you to be able to keep up with my adventurous spirit." One eyebrow shifts up in interest. "Have you ever been with an orc?"

I scrunch my nose. "Nope, never."

She takes the tip of her tongue, gently caressing it up my neck. "Would you like to change that, little rabbit?"

I nod and will my throat to make a sound. "Very much so."

V's apartment is clean and simple, which is exactly what I need. A few of my recent rendezvous were with individuals in grimy-ass apartments. I can't exactly get off in a place that needs more OxyClean than I need an orgasm. As I sift through her bookshelf, I notice the boxes on the floor in the corner.

"Are you moving sometime soon? Or maybe donating some old stuff?" I ask.

She's in the kitchen pouring two glasses of water. "I actually just moved in, so I haven't fully unpacked."

"Where did you move from?"

V crosses this way and hands me a glass. "Now, wouldn't that be a little specific?"

"Oh, sure," I say, remembering our rule. It's fun, though a little constrictive, trying to get to know someone without all the details.

"Far away from here, but still in The Americas. The orc half of my family comes from a few other continents overseas, but I was born here," she shares and takes a sip of water.

I shrug off my black teddy coat, tossing it alongside my purse onto the couch, and head down the hall. "Is this your bedroom?" I ask as I step inside. My heart is thumping nervously. It makes me giddy to see the room of such a majestic woman. It's the small proof I have that she's normal and just like everyone else.

There's a rustling noise coming from the living room, but I'm busy investigating. The comforter is a dark gray, and all the furniture is black and gray to match. I sit down, and V stands in the doorway, leaning.

Her arm touches the top of the door, and her shirt lifts. I can see the v-shaped muscle leading down to her pelvis. I want to lick it.

"Take off your clothes," she commands.

two

INDIGO

I NOD AND PULL OFF THE DARK FABRIC OF MY CROP TOP. STANDING, I SLIP MY SKIRT down onto the floor. In only my bra and underwear, I stare into her golden eyes. There's a controlling air to her now, one much rougher than the gentle giant she was earlier in the night. V takes off her t-shirt, revealing the sports bra underneath. Her biceps appear swollen, with thick veins sticking out, and it's sexy to watch the muscle flex with her movements. I'm pretty sure her arms are bigger than my head.

She makes a 'tsk tsk' sound at me in disapproval. "Take it *all* off, little rabbit."

As I remove my bra and underwear, I take a quick glance at us in her full body mirror that stands in the corner. We look like predator and prey, her hunky body hovering over me, waiting to pounce.

"You're going to tell me if you don't like something or don't want to do something, okay?"

It's not a question, but I nod in agreement.

"Use your words," she says. At the bar, she was so sweet, letting me pick what I wanted, listening to my scrambled thoughts. Here, she is in control of the night, and I am totally digging it.

"Yes. I will tell you," I say.

"Good. Now, flip onto your stomach and lay flat. I'm going to use that potion of yours." She pulls the small bottle out from a pocket in her cargo pants, and I shift onto my stomach, my head laying to one side against the pillow.

"Did you go through my purse?" I ask.

"Just to get the potion vial," V confesses. "Although, there wasn't anything in there... just some hand sanitizer, which I used, and your credit card, which I did not."

I fight the blush, knowing it's spreading across my face. "Is that weird?" Anxiety be damned, I did not just ask her. What if she *did* think it was weird?

"Not at all. What else could a girl need on a night out?"

I hear the click as V opens the vial and rubs it in her hands. She massages my back, kneading her hands into my bare skin. The feeling is electric. The warmth of her skin, and our pheromones mixing with the enhancement potion... I feel like I'm on cloud nine. She continues down my body, taking extra time to play with the soft skin of my ass.

I moan out, not meaning to, and I can hear her breathing deeply. She rubs my feet, and a relief I didn't know was possible happens. Her strength is undeniable, but I can tell she's holding back, like she's afraid of hurting me. With my height and size, I probably look fragile, but I don't want her to treat me that way.

"V," I say, getting her attention as she flips me over, climbing onto the bed with me.

She's biting her lip while pressing into the small swell of my breasts. "Yes?"

"You don't have to take it easy on me. I can take it." One corner of my mouth ticks up, proud of my openness.

"I don't intend to take it easy on you," she says, pouring more of the potion into her hands before rubbing it into my stomach. "As for how much you can take, we'll see, little rabbit."

She strokes my inner thigh, and there's a beauty in watching her green skin brush against the peachy tone of mine. Using one finger, she slowly circles around the apex of my thighs, purposefully teasing me with every movement. A whimper escapes my lips as I desperately cling onto my sanity, hoping she'll give in to my desires. My craving for her is potent.

With one swift motion, V cups my pussy and then slaps it with a flick of her wrist. Each love tap drives me wild, and I consider begging for more. She presses her lips against mine, her tusk gently nipping at me, and I moan into her mouth as she slowly slips a finger inside me.

The movement is slow at first, just a single digit, though her hands are larger than any I've ever experienced. Gradually, she adds another, and I melt at the pressure falling away as I open for her. I feel feral, the moment heady, and I cry out in pleasure.

"That's a good girl. You're going to come for me, aren't you, baby?" Her voice is low and heated, sex rippling through every soundwave.

V's hands are soft to the touch but strong as they flex and shift, pumping into me. I can feel the wetness between my legs, and V smiles into my mouth.

"I'm sorry," I say, not meaning to drip onto her sheets. I don't want to ruin them.

"Don't you ever apologize. I want you dripping all over my hand, and I want to taste every drop." Her words are soft and full of heat. V kisses me, her tongue swirling with mine, and her hand pressed hard against my jaw, pulling me in deeper. She lets go and shifts off from on top of me before laying flat on her back.

I sit up and notice... she's smiling. It's a wide grin, most of the top of her teeth showing, and she looks ridiculous. The expression is still sexy, but so silly, too.

"What has you grinning like an idiot?" I ask.

"Sit on my face," she instructs me.

My eyes go wide. "What?"

One of her eyebrows shifts up. "It isn't up for debate. Do it now, Indie, or suffer the consequences."

I consider I might want the consequences but move as instructed. I'm a good little rabbit, after all. I widen my legs above her face, and she takes my thighs in her hands, pulling me in closer. Her breath is hot against my skin, and I flush pink.

Lazily, she flicks my clit with her tongue, circling around it before pressing hard against it. It's torture the way she teases me, and before I can muster up my complaints, she devours me, every touch better than the last. V sucks on my most sensitive spot, suctioning it greater than any sex toy I've ever used. Her tongue is powerful, and she pushes it inside me as she uses her nose to rub my clit. The ice cold metal of her septum brushes against my skin, and I shudder.

"V, I'm—" It's too late. I'm coming into her mouth, convulsing as I reach pure ecstasy. I try to jump off, but she holds me down and continues lapping against me.

The pleasure is indescribable, and I squeal at the overstimulation. This woman knows what she's fucking doing.

I lay beside her, our fingers intertwined as she quietly hums a cheerful song and removes her pants. In just boxer briefs, I can see her thighs, which are brawny enough to crush me. I tug at her sports bra, and she removes the tight fabric. Her breasts look soft, but her pecs are still apparent. Pulling me close to her, she moans into my mouth, roughly kissing me, and after a few moments I break away so I can pleasure her. I spoon the side of her body, slipping my hand under the band of her underwear, until I feel short hair. Her arousal is apparent, and I flick her clit. I move so that I'm able to reach her supple chest and suck on her hardened peak as I dip two fingers inside her. Curling them upwards, I stroke her as I continue to kiss her breasts, and her hips buck into me. V seems to lose herself in our movements, and I slip another finger in, pumping my hand inside her.

I ride the high of her grinding on my hand—her using me for her pleasure. It's magical... downright ethereal, the way she makes me feel. I want to kiss her entire body, every freckle and every muscle, every line and curve.

"Make me come," she demands.

"Use me," I whisper.

Riding my hand like a cowboy, she bucks against me, whimpering as I watch her body tighten. She lets out the sexiest groan imaginable as she comes against me, warm wetness surrounding my fingers as I slip from inside of her.

V places a gentle kiss on my forehead and wraps herself around me, my body cradled in her arms. A small formation of stars is tattooed on her left outer-bicep, and I stare at it.

"A constellation?"

"Pleiades; it's a cluster that's a part of the Taurus constellation. My sun and moon signs," she says and gently kisses me. I haven't felt comfort like this in many years. I know I'm only twenty-four, but I spent those important years focused on school and graduating early... I forgot to live a little. The obsessive loops that played in my brain of every mistake I've ever made didn't help either.

"I'm a Pisces sun, Virgo moon. I don't really know much about astrology," I confess.

"That's okay; you don't have to. It's really important to a lot of orcs. Meaningful in the way we develop and communicate with one another."

Her body is so warm and safe, I want to burrow away and live in it forever. My sister Iris, when we were teenagers, wrote this fanfiction about two characters who developed a mating bond. It was a predestined thread-of-fate type of thing, where their magical connection clicked in their brain. I always thought it was ridiculous and teased her way too much for it, but I get it. In some crazed desperation, that's how I feel with this woman. Sex potion aside, she's just different.

The smell of hot coffee reaches my nostrils, and I stir awake. Last night was the best sex of my life, followed by the best sleep of my life, and now I'm ready for a cup of coffee. Stretching, I make my way into the kitchen, which is somehow spotless. Vega sits on a bar stool holding a newspaper, and there's a cup of coffee in front of her.

"Rude. Where's my cup?"

She puts down the newspaper, allowing a second cup of coffee and a plate of fruit to be visible. "Bon appétit, or however the French say it. How *did* they say it?" she asks, and I stifle a laugh.

"How should I know?" I sit down next to her, taking a sip. It has the perfect amount of cream and sugar, and I think I might propose.

"With your haircut, I kind of just assumed you were French... or like... a descendant of where France used to be? However the humans say it."

At that, I giggle. "I'm not French! Most of my family originates from a place called Scotland; though after The Convergence, I believe most of it ended up on another planet. I've also got some super distant heritage from the Abya Yalla as well as from... well... the elves."

"You're so cute. My mom was an orc, and my dad's Scandinavian. He's really into Viking Mythology, I know that."

Was. My heart drops at that particular word. I hope V is okay, but I don't want to pry. I take a bite of strawberry and offer the rest to her. She eats it, seductively ensuring my fingers enter her mouth.

"That's interesting. My mom made my sister and I celebrate all the elven holidays, so we never learned much about Scotland or any of our other ancestry, really. Kind of a bummer, but maybe one day I'll go off-planet and visit."

V puts her newspaper down again. "I don't know what you do for a living, but if you dream of going off-planet, you're too rich for me."

I'm cackling as I grab her pencil, answering the last word on her crossword puzzle. Irrepressible. "Don't worry, I'm not. Just a fever dream."

She stands and turns my chair around. My legs wrap around her, and she scoops me up, carrying me towards the couch. "I'll show you a fever dream."

three

INDIGO

"Why haven't you replied?!" Alitha asks, her tight black curls bouncing closely to her head. Long brown ears point up to the sky, the main physical indicator she's an elfling. Sometimes I long to be more elf. I'm barely five feet tall, and my features are painfully human. Not that it's a bad thing, but I rarely *feel* human. I'm always surrounded by so much magic. It's the most important part of who I am.

"It's been over a week. What could I say now? It'll just be weird," I pout, wanting to slam my head into the table. I wouldn't do that, as there's a waffle on my plate I intend on eating, but I'm sure thinking about it.

"You could tell her the truth, that you have an anxiety disorder and you've been freaking out over how to reply, but you've finally put on a brave face and want to see her again?" Alitha suggests.

"Or," Dahlia chimes in. "You could tell her it was the best sex of your life and that you haven't been able to walk or think all week, and you've finally healed and wish to meet up again?"

"You're both nuts."

Alitha sighs. "The logical thing to do would be to tell her the truth. Or, tell her nothing and let it go."

"Don't let it go. You rarely connect with anyone, Indigo," Dahlia says. "You *have* to see her again."

I pick at my food and take a sip of orange juice, trying to calm my nerves. "I rarely connect with anyone because nobody wants to connect with me. They all just wanna use me to meet Iris."

Alitha puts her long, slender hand over mine. "Iris is great, I get it. I mean, I'm in the Potions Department. We all worship your sister's work—"

"Not helping."

Alitha sighs. "But you're great too. This orcling would be lucky to get a second date with you. I mean it." She's kind. Both my friends are, really, and I'm lucky to have them. I just wish I had the same luck with love.

I pull out my phone, staring at her contact. It just says 'V.'

"Reply. Do it, do it, do it!" Dahlia smiles at me.

I type away....

INDIGO

V, I'm so sorry for taking forever to reply, it's been a week. I've had to pick up a lot of extra tasks at my job this week. I'd like to see you again soon... with specifics, maybe? Just let me know.

Sent. I look up at my friends. "Bleh. What if she never replies and just ghosts me like I did her?"

"Then you'll know where you stand," Alitha says with grace, per the usual. A woman of few words, I feel like she wastes all of hers on me and my antics.

Ping. My text tone went off.

"Somebody pinch me," I say, afraid to open it.

"Check your phone, or I will literally murder you, Indigo," Dahlia says as Alitha laughs.

I open the text.

VEGA

hey indie, please don't apologize. life is what happens between your plans. i want to see you again soon too. i start a new job this week and it'll likely be hectic. rain check for a date? it'll have to be a few weeks, but if you are willing to wait i'll make it worth your while.

Hell on earth.

"Hand me your phone," Dahlia says as she grabs for it. "Please don't apologize," she starts in a deep, masculine voice. "Life is what—"

I snatch the phone out of her hands. "Give me that! Don't read my messages."

"Okay, but what did she say?" Alitha asks. She turns, and we realize our server has been standing there, listening to our conversation. He's young, maybe sixteen, and has been adorably polite... why is he acting weird all of a sudden?

"Eavesdropping?" Dahlia asks, her voice coy.

He shakes his head nervously. "No ma'am, I just—are you all enjoying your meal?"

"Yes, we are. Thank you," Dahlia replies.

He pushes the brown strands of hair behind his ears. "Excuse me, are you Iris Watson?" He stares, big blue eyes staring down at me with excitement. "I didn't know you dyed your hair."

"I'm not," I say, already over this conversation. "I'm her sister, Indigo."

"Oh, I'm sorry. I thought you were—anyway, would you tell her she's amazing? I mean, really, my dad's cancer stayed in remission after using her treatment." The server is beaming with joy, and I can't bring myself to crush his spirit.

"I'll tell her a server at Sunshine & Fries said she changed his dad's life!" I say, though I most definitely won't. Iris and I don't speak these days. We didn't have a falling out. She's just too famous for little, old me, and I don't want to appear desperate. I went away to college early and stopped reaching out—it would be weird for me to contact her now. I don't want her fortune, and I am happy for her success... she's really helping people—

"Indigo?" Alitha asks, breaking me from my train of thoughts.

"Sorry, I was spacing out again." I shrug. "I'll reply to V."

My fingers shake as I type out the message.

INDIGO

I'll bring an umbrella for that rain check! Feel free to text me in the meantime ;)

Alitha quietly listens while Dahlia shit talks her ex. Meanwhile, I am just sitting here, text messages open to my chat with V, waiting for her reply. I might not be desperate enough to bother my younger sister, but I am desperate for this woman. Geeze. What's gotten into me? Lust. Pure, unadulterated lust. But there's something more here... she saw me, not my title or connections, and that was enough. Rarely does anyone ever see just *me*. It's always Professor Watson, or Iris Watson's sister, or the bite-sized elfborn... I'm never just Indigo. V and I spent a weekend where all I had to be was me, and I think she actually liked me for who I am. I don't know if this will go anywhere, but I have to try, right?

Ping. A new text from V. I stare at the screen.

VEGA

will do! i'm starting a new job this week, like i told you, and i'm essentially the... manager. any advice on getting my subordinates to like me? i can be quite intimidating, but i want to make a good impression.

I contemplate this. What would get some employees not to fear their new orcling boss? Oooooh! I type away.

INDIGO

Are you good at cooking? Or baking? Bake them a treat or something that'll show off your soft side.

VEGA

you're so good at this, indie. i'll bake some cupcakes. ty!

The server places my check in front of me, and I look up at Dahlia and Alitha, who appear simultaneously annoyed and amused.

"You missed my entire story, didn't you?" Dahlia asks as I place my card onto the receipt.

I scratch the back of my neck. "I'm so sorry. I'm being an ass."

Dahlia waves her hand in the air. "Don't be sorry, but quit acting like you're in love. What if this woman is like a serial killer? Or what if her job is for some company that scams little, old ladies out of their money?"

Alitha crosses her arms on her chest, clearly done with our shenanigans. "I don't think Indigo's new girl is secretly a bad person, but only time will tell. In the meantime, I think it's healthy to keep daydreaming about your future together."

"Thank you, o' voice of reason. I feel like you two are the devil and angel sitting on my shoulder," I say.

"Who told you?" Dahlia laughs.

I get out of my 5999 Toyota Prius, my familiar, Momiji, tucked into the crook of my arm, and head toward my office. Mondays are my least favorite day of the week, because every Monday is the same, at least ten emails from students over the weekend who want my help with something. I love teaching and am so honored to have this position at such a young age, but some of their questions are easily answered if they'd just search for it online.

Augury University differs from every other college in The Americas. Not only is it a magical university, but they built it to coexist with nature. The buildings, made of wood and glass, sit in clusters that are connected by wooden platforms. It almost looks like a village in the trees, but each building is a classroom or office. The electricity runs on solar power, though many of our resources come from employees' individual power.

When I enter my office this morning, something different awaits me. There's a cupcake on my desk.

I set Momiji down, and the white sugar rabbit flops onto his bed, lazily ready to nap the morning away. Though he's very active at dusk and dawn and is a great conduit for my magic, he's practically useless as a companion sometimes. Still, I'm glad we bonded when I matured and that he gets to be my buddy for life.

Moving to investigate the cupcake, I realize the frosting is bright green with little sparkly sprinkles on top. It looks delightful, though it's too early for this to be a Christmas gift. I pull out my phone and call Alitha.

"Hey," she picks up.

"Hey, did you leave a cupcake in my office?" I ask.

"No?"

Who else could it have been? I'm not super close with any of my other coworkers, and our boss was recently fired for inappropriate behavior. *Oh.*

"Could it have been the new Department Chair of Charms?"

She clicks her tongue. "That's probably it! Why don't you stop by and say hi?"

"That's a good idea. Thanks, love ya."

"Love you!"

She hangs up, and I open my door, heading out of the shared office building and out onto a wooden platform that leads to the Department Chair's building. I was expecting to meet my new boss today, though not first thing this morning. All I know about them is that their name is Professor Daelor, they're twenty-eight years old, and they just moved here from another smaller magical university.

Thanks to The Convergence reversing global warming, even though we're on an island right outside Florida, it's actually chilly here in November. Donning a black jean jacket, I knock on the door, now adorned with a plaque that reads "V. DAELOR Mgd."

The door swings open, and I drop my cupcake. It hits the wooden floorboards, splattering on the ground. I feel like my eyes are deceiving me, but right in front of me is V, the woman I spent one of the best weekends of my life with. And now she's my boss, and I ruined her cupcake, and oh, fuck my life.

"Oh, I'm so sorry... I didn't mean to make a mess in your new office," I say, frantically trying to wrap my head around the fact that Vega, the orcling I'm interested in dating, is Professor Daelor.

"It's okay, let me help with that." She squats down, taking a wet wipe from off her desk and cleans the floor. I throw the cupcake into the trash, guilt festering in my chest. I didn't mean to ruin the cupcake... and I definitely didn't mean to screw my boss.

"I was just coming by to introduce myself. I'm Indigo Watson, a first year adjunct in your department. I also teach one history course. Please, let me know if there's anything I can do to help." If I close my eyes and pretend my new boss has never seen me naked, it'll be true, right?

V reaches around me and shuts the door. Our bodies are now uncomfortably close to one another, and I'm unsure how I should react. What am I supposed to do when everything that comes to mind is inappropriate?

"You don't need to pretend we've never met before, Indigo," she says. Her voice is soft, like she's been wounded.

I back against the door, creating space between us, and she crosses over toward her desk. Her familiar, a hummingmouse, is sitting on a perch in its cage, watching us speak.

"I'm sor—"

"Please, stop apologizing. We didn't know."

My lips form a thin line. "But now we do."

"Do you know the university's policies on fraternization? Obviously, student-teacher relationships are forbidden, but what about cohorts?"

I frown. "We are not cohorts. Our employment contracts state that romantic relationships between employees in which one has direct or indirect authority over the other are strictly prohibited."

Vega lets out a low chuckle. "Did you memorize your employment contract?"

"More or less," I admit.

"And I am assuming you are not someone who breaks many rules?"

My heart is racing in my chest. "No, I prefer not to."

V moves around the room, searching her boxes for something, before pulling out a small paper plate. She opens the mini-fridge and takes out another bright green cupcake, handing it to me. "Here. Then at least we can be friends? I still enjoy your company, even if only platonically."

"That would be nice," I say, though I don't believe my own words. Can I handle being her friend? I have enough anxiety as it is. I'm going to be thinking of every little thing that could go wrong. What if I accidentally flirt? What if she flirts with me and I can't handle it? What will people think if I turn bright red during a meeting? The unfortunate possibilities of this friendship are endless.

I sit on my porch, Dahlia on the chair beside me, and sip my warm tea. The taste of orange blossoms sits on my tongue, gently reminding me of V.

"How did Alitha react?" Dahlia asks, taking a handful of popcorn from out of the bowl.

"She swore she wouldn't tell anyone and recommended that we discontinue contacting one another outside of employment."

She smiles with her mouth full and waves a finger. "You're not going to do that though, are you?"

I put down my tea, curling my legs up to my chest. "We have decided to remain friends, as that is not against university policy."

"You told me she has magical fingers, and you think you two can remain friends?"

I laugh. "I mean, she does literally have magical fingers... she's an orcling!"

"You're an elfborn human! But that is *not* what you meant by that and you know it. Don't bullshit me, Watson."

"Alright, Torres. It's going to be hard, but I think it'll be worth it. I really like her."

She frowns. "I'm just worried you like her too much, and you're going to get your feelings hurt. Have you texted your therapist?"

"No."

"Not to sound like Alitha, but text your fucking therapist."

I sigh, knowing she's right. Simone will probably just tell me to stay away from V since it could risk my career, but I can't explain it. I've never felt safer than how I felt in her arms on Saturday morning. She's so comforting and kind... I want to be her friend, even if it costs me my sanity.

four

INDIGO

Augury University can best be described as a series of massive jungle tree houses. There's six tall camphor trees which form a wide-spaced courtyard in the center. Each one houses a different magical discipline and their respective classrooms and laboratories. Charms, potions, illusions, sight, naturalism, including both creature crafts and botanical crafts, and lastly the histories. As an adjunct, I teach an intro level history course, as well as a few lower-level charms courses. Luckily, those trees are right next to one another, which leaves my travel light. There is also a bent tree of some species I'm unfamiliar with where the school library is kept.

Kapok trees surround the camphors, reaching up to the skies, giving cover to the university below. As I walk through the courtyard to the Histories Tree, a charms assistant helps me onto the lift. There are wooden stairs and ladders for those who want the exercise, but for anyone disabled, elderly, or just not wanting the massive trek, the school employs charms mages to run a lift system, similar to major cities' elevators.

Making my way inside the kapok, the bright morning sun high in the sky, I head down a platform until I cross the threshold into the conference room. Many professors have already taken their seats. Adeib Ali, a serpentine who heads our Botany Department, sits at the end of the table where we don't have chairs. His tail slithers around Aura Nguyen's wheelchair, and she smiles brightly at me as I sit next to Alitha. Aura is a cambion about ten years older than me, with bright red skin and leather-like wings. She uses a wheelchair from time to time, though when she's feeling up to it, she'll fly around campus bossing us all around. Aura is the Chair of the Sight Department and is friends with Alitha. One day, I'd like to consider her a friend too, but I'm scared of Adeib. Nothing seems to impress him or bring him joy. The people-pleaser in my heart cannot handle that.

Anxiety tells me that Aura's going to hate me, but I assure myself that, logically, she's warming up to me or she wouldn't have smiled. Adeib, on the other hand, doesn't smile at anyone. Nobody knows how old he is, besides Dean Archeron Bariel, and nobody asks either. Rumor has it he's older than The Convergence, but that's just speculation.

On the opposite side of Alitha and I, most of everyone else sits in a row, minus a few missing merfolk. I don't know everyone's names yet, but I'm slowly figuring it out. My other boss, Dr. Elara Lothiel, the four-hundred-plus-year-old Histories Chair, waves at me excitedly. I want to be her when I grow up. Elfborn and elflings don't live as long as full-blooded elves, nobody really does, but a girl can dream.

"Hey, any word on what this meeting is about?" I ask, quietly adjusting my pencil skirt.

"Aura told me it was legislation updates, but who knows? I wonder if they'll introduce any of the new staff members," Alitha answers. She had her hair done over the weekend, micro box braids which fall down her thin frame, reaching the middle of her back. She wears a red long-sleeve jumpsuit that compliments her long, lean frame and deep brown skin.

There are three empty chairs left. One for the dean and the other two I'm unsure of, but as I notice green skin coming through the door, an uneasy feeling washes over me.

V walks in with Malik, the other charms professor. He's a human elfborn like me; though unlike me, he's actually tall. He sits down a few seats away from me, leaving the seat next to me as Vega's only option. Shit. I mean, last we spoke I agreed to be her friend, but I didn't plan on sitting next to her at meetings. Alitha has a shit-eating grin on her face, a rare sight for her, and I tap her lightly under the table.

"Now ladies, invite me the next time you wanna play footsies?" Malik jests as he crosses one leg over the other, turning towards Dean Bariel, who is standing in front of a projector. Alitha probably wants to perish at that interaction, and frankly, I do too. V doesn't react, which irks me. I know I'm not supposed to, but I want her attention.

I didn't see the dean enter the room, so he likely entered in his barn owl form. Some beings on Earth, regardless of their magical race, developed shifting abilities after The Convergence, and passed it down to their descendants. It's rare, but the dean is one of the few. So, technically, one could say the school is run by a bird.

"Before we get started, I want to introduce the newest member of our little family, Dr. Vega Daelor," Dean Bariel says, a small grin across his face. The dean is pale, with long white hair and a thin frame. His ears are long, and he's built a lot like Alitha, but with more angular features. He's fiercer and much older.

V stands up, and I have to stop myself from shaking. It's not like she's going to get up in front of all our coworkers and yell, ''I've screwed Professor Watson, by the way!' But something about this moment leaves me teetering on the edge. She's wearing a deep green suit jacket that compliments her skin, and her hair is slicked back in a low bun. She moves with grace, gradually making her way to the front. "Hello, I am Dr. Daelor, the new Head of Charms. I previously taught at Freehold Magic University, in the mid-north of The Americas."

Everyone claps and cheers, the room bustling with excitement, but there's fear too. Orcs and orclings are strong, and sometimes they underestimate that strength; but it's nothing to fear. I'm probably the smallest person in this room, the elves and orcs towering over me, and I'm not afraid.

She moves to sit back next to me and winks. It's quick, and I don't think anyone else caught it. But Alitha does, and she flicks the side of my arm.

"Now, the reason you're all here," Dean Bariel starts. "The Council of Continents had a meeting, and there have been some legislative updates in regards to schools and time off. We have new rules we must follow about parental leave, cultural and religious holidays, and sick leave."

The Council of Continents is our new global government structure, which randomly selects individuals of specific backgrounds to serve for a limited term. From each continent, they pull a few different types of beings: a person who was born there, a person who is indigenous to the land, and a person from each prominent population of magical race. For certain issues, they also request members of different identities, including disabilities, sexualities, and religions, to volunteer as well. Each continent has an official administrator which handles all the paperwork and clerical tasks, but thanks to this process, we've gotten rid of career politicians internationally. We still have small-scale community leadership, decided upon by each community, and they're all different. Magia Island, for example, has a mayor. I know Alitha and my mother both dream of getting their names called to join the council for a session, but the thought of that level of responsibility makes me physically ill.

Dean Bariel continues droning on about new renovation projects, before getting back to the important stuff, and I'm zoning out, preoccupied by thoughts of the woman sitting next to me, about how her skin feels against mine. The way her mouth tastes.

"As professors, we must be understanding of students of different races and cultures, and how, for example, one elf might celebrate a different set of holidays than another," Dean Bariel says, interrupting my thoughts.

To me, this feels like the bare minimum. It shouldn't even have to be said. If a student needs to miss class to celebrate their heart out, so be it. But I suppose for old-timers like Dr. Lothiel, this might be a much-needed update. I can recall attending Augury University myself, and Dr. Lothiel being surprised I celebrated elven holidays as she did. I idolized her, I still kind of do, but it left a sour taste in my mouth. The world was complicated before The Convergence, but it's even more complicated now, and that's what makes it so beautiful. I love working with serpentine, cambions, and... orcs.

Dean Bariel moves on to discussing professor etiquette and dress codes, specifically about how distracting inappropriately dressed professors can be. In the year six-thousand-and-four, you'd think we'd be over this nonsense, but no. My eyes drift shut, my body tired from a night of restless sleep. I couldn't stop thinking about Vega and how badly I want her. How much I crave her. This is ridiculous, right? Surely I can't be losing sleep to sex dreams over my boss?

Something bumps my shoulder, and I realize it's V. She scooted her chair closer to mine.

"Wake up, rabbit," she whispers, and I see something flash in her eyes, almost like hunger, before they shift back to normal. "I know he's boring, but we've gotta get you and Malik to associate professor positions."

Me and Malik. If it were just me, I would think it's because she likes me, but maybe Vega is just a good person—a good boss. I can't mess this up. I have someone who actually cares about their subordinates, and here I go screwing up everything because of one fun weekend of fucking.

Alitha gives us a look with her ocean blue eyes and then focuses back on Dean Bariel's speech. If anyone in this world is more of a goodie-two-shoes than I, it's Alitha. She's just always been a perfectionist, and I admire her whole-heartedly.

As much as I feel like I'm going to scream if I have to keep listening to Dean Bariel, I have to hand it to him. He could probably win a world record for longest speech ever. I glance around the room. Aura is watching him intently, an irritated look on her face. Feather McNab is taking notes, seated next to Adeib, who is scowling at his phone. I'm just glad I'm not the only one over this meeting.

"Last announcement," the Dean says, and I hear us all take a breath of relief. "Within the next year, we plan on working towards opening a second campus. It will be off the coast of Naiad Island, in a cave system nearby. This way, our merfolk and kraken students and staff can attend university without discomfort or danger."

Well, at least that's something. I know I would remain at our main campus in the Illusionary Jungle, but it would be cool to visit. I can imagine Professor Rios and Dr. Martino would move to the secondary campus, which is closer to their families anyway. Very exciting.

"That is all for now, everybody. Please do your best as we finish up the fall semester." Dean Bariel walks out of the room. Meeting. Fucking. Adjourned.

V and Malik are talking, and Alitha has already snuck out, likely avoiding having to converse with the others. I honestly don't want to discuss the meeting either. If I'm being honest with myself, I wasn't paying attention. I need to get better at adulting... My attention span is great with people I care about, but Dean Bariel talks just to hear the sound of his voice.

Stepping out the door and onto a wooden platform that leads to a breakroom, I take in the fresh, chilled air. In the winter months, these islands can get down to zero degrees Celsius, and in the summer, up to thirty. It doesn't snow naturally here, but zero is cold to me, especially since it's wet-cold. Most of the birds have migrated farther south, closer to the equator, so the jungle is quiet. I can hear every step as I make my way across, dipping my head into the adjacent space.

Nobody is in here, so I start brewing some coffee. Opening a lower cupboard, I root around for the pumpkin syrup I stashed when October hit and can't find it. I climb up onto the counter, hoping someone moved it up here and didn't throw it away. This is one of those moments where I hate being short. My knee touches something hot, and the coffee machine gyrates, sputtering around, creating a mess.

Did I knock something loose? Stepping down, I take the machine in both hands, trying to stop it from moving. It sprays hot coffee water all over my white blouse, burning me in the process. I should've charmed the taller cupboard to open, preventing this entire disaster, but I did not. I, like a two-year-old, climbed onto the counter and likely broke the coffee machine. This moment is going to loop in my brain over and over again for weeks.

Crossing to the staff bathroom, I open the door and unbutton my blouse. Scrubbing the soft fabric with soap and water, I pray to the gods, or who*ever*, this coffee stain comes out. One of the few articles of clothing I own that isn't black and a staple of my work wardrobe, this top was a gift from my mother, and I refuse to let it fall victim to my dumbassery.

I stare into the mirror, fixing the smudge of my purple lipstick, and give myself a once over. My black bra covers what little boobage I have going on, and I decide I feel cute. I am cute. And worthy of love—just not with my boss.

The door swings open, and I realize I neglected to lock it. Golden eyes meet mine, and I see Vega struggling to stay calm. Her muscled pecs are heaving through her shirt, and her eyes are brighter than I've ever seen. There's something in them, like smolders of fire, as she unleashes herself onto me. Shoving me against the wall, the orcling dominates me with her body as she breathes hot air into my neck, lightly nipping my skin with her tusks. It all happens so fast, I haven't even taken in a breath before her lips are on mine.

"Do you think it's okay to stand around like this with the door unlocked?" she says between hungry kisses. "Anyone could have come in here and seen what's mine. What *should* be mine."

Whoa there. She's being a lot more possessive than she was when I said we should just be friends. I turn my head to the side to stop myself from going too far. I know Vega cares about this job just as much as I do, but her instincts don't; I've got to make the hard decision to save us both.

Her arm presses into the wall next to my head, her mass of muscles hovering above me. Orange blossoms and honey fill my nose, drawing me in to her. Why does it have to be this hard? Why couldn't I have the hots for a chiropractor or a mechanic—a situation without so much baggage.

V's nose, with its cute bump at the bridge, touches mine as our lips brush against each other's, and the door swings open once more. Vega backs away, scratching the back of her neck.

It's a satyr. He's an intern here. I've seen him walking around making folks coffee, but I have yet to learn his name. He's precious, closer to my height and size, but he's only nineteen or twenty. He stares at us, wide-eyed and awkward. "Professor Watson, you're—" His face is turning pink. "I'm so sorry—the door wasn't locked."

Shit, that's right. And I don't have a shirt on.

"I spilled coffee on myself. I'm so sorry for the indecency," I say, embarrassed as all hell.

He smiles, looking away. "It's fine, sorry there's two people in here. Dr. Daelor and I will be leaving." He turns around, heading out the door, and coughs at Vega when she fails to do the same. Our eyes remain locked until he grabs her by the arm and pulls V out of the single-use bathroom. I can barely contain my laughter as I put back on my sopping wet shirt. Sweet summer child.

As I walk outside of the building into the cool air, V follows shortly behind me, her footsteps loud as they hit the wooden platform. I fight my body, refusing to shiver, and step onto a bridge that connects to the Charms 101 building. I'm hopeful there's an extra shirt in my office, but I doubt it.

Opening the door, I dip into my office, which is a building in the Charms Tree that has rooms for every charms professor. Vega, as the new chair, has her own office in a separate adjacent building, and for that I am grateful. I can't deal with how badly I want her, or her body heat right now.

Soft fabric lands on top of me, and I pull the dark brown article off, investigating it. A sweater. V stands in the doorway, leaning against it with her forehead creased.

"Borrow my sweater. You're probably freezing. Why didn't you stick your shirt under the dryer?"

I shrug. "I didn't wanna traumatize the intern anymore than we already did."

"I promise you he had no idea what was going on, but I understand. Your concern is both sweet and valid."

It *is* valid. We could lose our jobs. "I'm sorry, but what happened back there was—"

"Inappropriate? Unacceptable?" She grins. "Don't be sorry; you're right. I should be the one apologizing. I lost control. It won't happen again... unless you ask me to."

"Thank you," I say. "It cannot happen again."

Ping. I touch my phone screen to see a text from my mom. Great, just what I needed today—to disappoint not only myself but also my mother.

"Have a good day, Indigo. Let me know if you need anything," Vega says as she walks out my door.

I don't think I will. I need a Xanax after saying no to that ass.

five
VEGA

Indigo Watson will be the fucking death of me. She is the reason for every urge I'm having to fight. Typically, when a fox chases after a bunny, the bunny runs away... this rabbit might as well be seasoning herself, waiting to be devoured. Between the scent I sense coming from the apex of her thighs, to the way she stares at me in meetings like she's stripping me in her mind, I'm going to lose it. What can I do? Yesterday she said she wasn't interested in breaking the rules, and I respect that... so if I cannot get my act together, I'll quit. I'll quit and move out to the sticks somewhere with no cellular service and become a bog mage, never to be seen again.

It *cannot* happen again, I repeat to myself as I splash my face with cold water. Orcs experience mating frenzies. It's a real, scientific phenomenon. It stems from our difficulties getting pregnant, long gestation cycles, and struggles with giving birth. We *have* to want each other a lot, otherwise orcs will cease to exist. But I don't want to give birth, or date men, so why am I feeling this way? I'm only a half-orc... so is this a half-frenzy? Jeez.

Walking back to my office building, a tiny creature stops on my shoulder, and I take a deep breath when I realize it's my familiar, Freja. Familiars are an important part of a mage's journey. Given to us when we mature, they're magical animals that are blessed with the ability to live out the same time as their mage's lifespan, and in return, they give their bodies to be used as conduits for magic. When we use our magic, it wears them out like exercise would. Most familiars don't complain. However, my familiar is a sassy, whiny little shit. Orcs and orclings usually have giant beings as our familiars:

winged-bulls, amphibious elephants, dragon whales. Yet, somehow, *I* got stuck with a hummingmouse? An animal created in The Convergence. She is half-hummingbird, half-mouse. With my genetics, I suppose it's fitting.

Entering the building, I sit at my desk and sort through the tall stack of paperwork I've been procrastinating. Freja jumps down and climbs over to her cage, chirping a happy little song. For me, it's paper after paper after paper. Complaints from students, ideas from staff, many absurd requests, you name it! I didn't realize taking a job in the middle of a semester would come with so much unfinished paperwork. I don't know my predecessor personally, but boy did he suck at the admin side of this. Best to get some if it done before I fall further behind.

Freja squeaks at me, trying to get my attention. I've been at these administrative tasks for a few hours, and I'm sick of it. I look up at her, and I swear she is giving me her best attempt at a reprimand. Her long beak pecks at my chest, a grumpy expression on her face, and it clicks. I keep her snack in the pocket of my sweater, which I gave to Indigo. Well... that might be a problem. Freja gets hangry quickly, so I'll have to go find her something. I look up at the clock. Indigo is teaching a history course right now, and class will be over relatively soon... I could just go ask for the bag?

I'm walking out the door, Freja resting on my shoulder, before I even think of how this might go down. I mean, it'll probably be fine. I just hope I'm not disrespecting her wishes by bothering her. We're friends... and friends help friends... and it's my sweater anyway.

History 101 is held in the History Tree, which is a bit of a walk, but it's beautiful outside. There's greenery all around me, and I breathe in the fresh air. According to my research, Earth was doing pretty horribly prior to The Convergence. Nature was dying, and the air pollution levels were high. Now? It's healthy and full of vegetation. I climb up to the building that currently houses Indigo and her students. I can just listen to the end of her lecture and catch her after everyone else has left. That's the most respectful thing to do.

Placing my ear against the door, I hear muffled noises, and that pretty sing-song voice of hers. "To understand the history of mages, you must understand the history of Earth, but especially The Convergence. We've covered a lot of grounds so far this semester, and I know most of you did well on your midterms; but the real question is... do any of you remember anything from our first few lessons? Remember, finals will be on all modules. Let's test, and potentially refresh, your knowledge."

She really is brilliant. To teach at Augury University is notable enough, but at Indigo's age? It's downright impressive. Indigo is the only person working here that teaches more than one subject. And not only does she teach charms and history, but she could totally cover a potions class as well. When I used that potion of her own creation the weekend we met, it was *highly* effective, my hormones going wild. Even now, I'm not one hundred percent sure the effects have completely worn off. Or maybe they have, and I just wish I had an excuse for my little obsession with my subordinate.

"After The Convergence, the Earth looked geographically different. What changed?" she asks.

I peer through the window, trying not to be seen. The entire class has their eyes directly on Indigo, all wanting to be the first to answer her questions.

A white haired cambion raises their hand. "Land masses split worse than my parents' during the divorce."

Indigo looks as though she's suppressing a giggle.

"Some places squished together. I heard one country even ended up on the orc planet," a faun-girl adds, smiling wide.

A masculine orc rolls his eyes. "The planet's called Barac."

"Sorry!" the faun squeaks.

My mother had books about the crash, written by our ancestors. A country known as Scotland ended up on Barac, the orc planet, and it moved many other places around. For a while, each magical race sort of stayed to themselves, but as time moved on, we all intermingled.

Indigo rests her thumb on her jaw. "When the new magical races practically fell onto Earth, we worked alongside them to rename lands. Can anyone tell me what The Americas used to be called?"

A tall elf with long, pin straight dark hair raises her hand. "North and South America, which is goofy. I'm so glad they changed it back to Turtle Island and Abya Yalla."

"Not that I disagree, because I'm glad they paid homage to the land's indigenous roots, but why do you think North and South America are silly names?" Indigo asks, a smile creeping across her face.

"They needed a tool to even tell what direction they were going," the elf says.

"Hey, full-blooded humans still use those," an elfborn reminds the room. "It's not humanity's fault they don't have an innate sense of direction."

"No, but it's kind of embarrassing," a serpentine jests.

Not that I disagree, but I try not to pick on humans for their lack of magic. They've got other things going for them, like normal human courting, sans mating frenzies. Human births are a lot shorter than orcs, and are statistically safer, so they didn't develop these pesky, amorous instincts like we did.

Indigo coughs, trying to change the subject. She probably takes the human jokes a little personally, since she considers herself one. She is a human, but she is also an elfborn. They are often at odds with one another, even though the two halves create a beautiful whole. "How many continents were there before The Convergence?" she asks the class.

"Professor Watson, that number didn't change. We had seven, and now we have seven, it's just different." The same faun from earlier says with a joyful confidence.

"You're right! Can anyone name them?"

The tall elf girl with long hair jumps out of her seat as if she were avoiding the world's most venomous spider and shouts. "Alkebulan, Arabia, Asia, Europa, Ice Lands, Levant, and The Americas!"

"Good job, Raven. You all really know your stuff." Indigo beams. "Consider this your exit ticket. Enjoy an early dismissal!"

I want to kiss her. I want to kiss her big brain and her small breasts, and I want to kiss them every day, for as long as she will let me. Right now? She is not letting me. Ugh.

I wish she didn't want me. If she didn't want me, this would be easy. I don't do unrequited love, or lust, so I'd simply move on. It's the idea that she desires me so badly while I equally desire her, yet some rule is preventing us from acting upon our natural instincts. On Barac? This would never happen. Someone would call us into a room and say, "We can smell how both of you feel, please mate and be merry."

But this is Earth, and I have to follow the rules, even though human rules feel silly to me. I was born here. I am part human, but I don't *feel* human. They are small and anxious. Correction, Indigo is small and anxious, neither of which I know what feels like. I seek to understand her... the fear that eats her up inside, that causes her to shake, to blush. Can a friend do all that? Is that what she has Professor Taylor for? Does she even need me?

The door to the classroom building swings open, and a small crowd of youthful faces come out, venturing off to their next class. There are cambion, orclings, satyrs, elflings, humans, hybrids, and more, and it's an exciting sight. I may not always feel completely home on Earth, but I do feel at home in this jungle, with these jovial mages who yearn to improve.

Indigo stands at the front with her arms around herself, giving herself a hug. "Hey, I saw you out there watching the class. Is there something you need, or are you just bored and brushing up on your history?" Her violet eyes bounce around the room, and I can tell she's nervous. When she's comfortable, she tends to lean her body to one hip, but when she's anxious, her body shifts the energy back and forth from leg to leg, like she's doing now. It's awkward yet adorable.

"Something like that. Could I have the item that's in the pocket of that sweater?" I ask, and Freja squeaks, her little green body gyrating with excitement.

Indigo's dark, thin eyebrows draw together as she pulls the bag of treats out of the pocket, and Freja goes flying towards her.

"Freja, let her hand those to me," I say, but it is too late. Freja has ripped the bag out of her hand, flown over to the nearest podium, and is chomping away at the cheese crackers.

Indigo lets out a loud, giggling laugh. It warms my cheeks, and I chuckle. "It's been a day, hasn't it?" she asks.

"It sure has," I answer. "Freja." I click my tongue. "Let's get going."

Three days. I haven't spoken to Indigo in three days, and I cannot stop daydreaming about her. I want to put my hands into that white hair of hers and force her to arch her back as I use a toy to fuck her from behind. That, or I want to hold her and let her cry on me. The worst thing is? I can't decide what sounds better. To be her pleasure, or her comfort and protector. In my wildest dreams, I am both, but in reality, I am neither.

I have never experienced emotions like these, nor am I sure I ever will again. I form a box in my mind, shoving those thoughts inside, before locking it and chucking the box straight into my metaphysical ocean.

As I grade charms student's essays, trying to clear my mind of all things Indigo, I am grateful to be here. Turtle Island is a beautiful place, but I am glad to have transferred here from Freehold University. After my mother passed away, alongside my infant baby brother, the place I had learned to love was no longer my home. My father moved back to the Scandinavian region of Europa, and I got stuck picking up the pieces of my life. I spent nearly ten years in a cold, lonely ghost town, and now I am here. This island is a fresh start—a new beginning. I want to find friends, and someone who will love me and won't leave... But for now, I will just find an open bar. Placing the stacks into my 'completed' folder, I wait for Freja to fly onto my shoulder before heading out of the office.

The moon hangs high in the dark gray sky as I make my way towards the parking garage. It's a pavilion covered by solar panels that protects our vehicles from nature. Efficient and effective, I couldn't have designed it better myself.

Heading to my SUV, a purple prius pulls up to me and rolls down its window. Hold on a second, is that Indigo?

"Hey, can we talk?" she asks, voice shaking.

"Yeah?" I offer. I'm trying to hide the grin that wants to form on my face at the sight of her, but it's not working. She makes me feel light and giddy, like I could walk on air.

"Hop in."

I look at her and open the backdoor. I will not fit in the front seat of a prius. Squeezing in, my head brushes against the ceiling.

"Sorry, probably not much leg room for you," she says and pulls into a parking spot.

Not much arm room either, geeze. There's something off about her. She looks too... plain. Her bangs are clipped out of her face, and her hair is pulled into a claw clip. All the clothes I've seen Indigo don are flowy tops and form-fitting bottoms, with lots of black. Right now she's wearing a beige sweatshirt with black leggings, and it's a little odd. There are circles under her eyes, and she's missing her signature dark lipstick.

"It's all good," I respond, looking into her eyes using the rearview mirror. "Are you okay? You're as beautiful as always, but you look... tired."

"Honestly? I'm not doing great this week. That's actually part of the reason I came to find you. That, and I wanted to return your sweater." She points to the brown fabric I'm sitting on.

"Alright, what's up?"

She turns back to face me, her cheeks flushed pink. "I have a proposal of sorts. It's very odd, and I know you'll say no, but I really think it's a great idea."

My brows scrunch together. "What kind of proposal?"

"I would like you to be my holidate," she says. My heart beats a little harder.

"Your what?" I ask. If I were drinking something, I would have spit it out.

"Holidate. My date for the holidays. A temporary arrangement."

I shake my head. This woman wouldn't go on another date with me because of our employment contracts, but now she wants to... temporarily date for the holidays? What the fuck? Alright, Vega, don't look a gift horse in the mouth.

"Hear me out," she starts. "You want me, don't you? That moment we shared in the bathroom showed me you feel exactly like I do."

"I want you," I admit. It rolls off my tongue like the sweetest sin.

"Realistically, we can't be together, but at least this way we can get it out of our systems before spring semester."

Unbelievable. I mean, could that be enough time to convince her it's worth the trouble—that I am worth the trouble? This might be my chance.

"Why? There has to be something else," I say.

She plays with her cuticles repeatedly, not making eye contact with me. "There is."

"Indigo."

"My sister Iris will be home for Gratefulness Week, and I just can't do it alone. I can't travel back to Octopus Island by myself. If you went with me, I could show you off, and it would make me feel safer," she confesses.

Well, now I understand why she didn't think I'd go for it. This is strange. "Am I hearing this right? You want me, your boss, to pretend to be your girlfriend to your family?"

"No. I want you, Vega-who-totally-doesn't-work-at-Augury-University." One of Indigo's eyebrows raises before she continues. "To pretend to be my girlfriend for my family so that I don't have to listen to my parents go on about how perfect and amazing my little sister is and how I'm twenty-four with no international awards or even a partner."

"It is perfectly acceptable for you to have zero awards and zero partners at twenty-four. Frankly, it is acceptable at any age. Why do you let them dull your shine?" I ask, not intending to let the last question slip from my lips. I don't want to be harsh with her, but I'm struggling to understand how someone so brilliant could let such petty things get in the way of her happiness. It is her life, not her parents.

"Are your parents hard on you?" she asks, and suddenly I am at a loss for words. "...or were they?" she corrects.

"No, they were not. My mother was incredibly patient, and my father left the continent when I was barely an adult. They never pressured me to do anything I didn't want to, so no, I don't understand what it's like for you. I will help you, little rabbit," I offer. Selfishly, it's more for me than it is for her, but she doesn't need to know that.

"Really?" Her violet eyes light up like fireworks.

"I have nobody nearby to spend Gratefulness Week with anyway, so this works out in my favor. I'll go on one holidate trip with you, and you'll go on one with me, and then we can stop this madness and go back to being friends."

"It's a deal!" Indigo shouts, raising a hand to shake mine. "We're going to need to leave Mond—" I grab the top of her sweatshirt and ball it with my fist, pulling her into a kiss. Her lips are soft as they melt against mine. I wish I could freeze time. I let go of her top and give my brain a second to reconfigure itself.

"I'll see you Monday, holidate," I say and wink, exiting the car.

What did I just sign myself up for?

six

INDIGO

THE PHONE CONTINUOUSLY RINGS AS I TRY TO REACH DAHLIA ON THE CAR RIDE HOME. She must be with her new boyfriend. I'm happy for her, but that doesn't help me in this panic. My finger hovers over Alitha's contact. I still haven't decided if I'm going to tell her about this whole holidating thing. Alitha and Dahlia are my best friends, but Alitha is also my coworker; I don't want to make her uncomfortable. We signed employment contracts, and we know the consequences. Alitha would want me to follow through with what I promised the university. She's got strong values, even stronger than I do, and I respect that.

"I guess I can talk to myself out loud." I look over at the car next to me, and there's a blonde lady just staring... Nevermind, I can just keep my thoughts in my brain. That's fine, too.

It drizzles, the gentle rain splashing against my windshield as I drive home. My plum purple bungalow is in the heart of Sunspell City, where most people on the island live. There are a select few who reside in the Illusionary Jungle, but I like the bit of separation this gives me between work and home. My house is a safe space for my own personal brand of clean chaos.

Momiji is in the backseat, a paintbrush in his mouth, as he works on his latest masterpiece. Sugar rabbits are notorious for being lazy, but, for a few hours a day, Momiji is like a kid in a candy store. He flies around rooms, white fluffy wings fluttering through the air, completing as many tasks as possible. It reminds me of when my mom would tell my sister and me that company was coming over and we'd rush to clean our rooms. That's Momiji every night.

Pulling into the driveway, I park, open my door, my familiar following closely, and head into the house, locking my car behind me. There are crystals and magic books lining the shelves, all meticulously placed in color-coded order, just as I like it. I can't remember if I locked my car, so I walk outside and click the button, hoping it'll ease my anxiety. It does, but the relief is only temporary. Logically, I knew I had locked my car... or at least it was more than likely I did, but my brain won't settle down until I make sure it's certain. It's frustrating, but it's probably my brain's way of protecting me.

I walk over to my sofa and flop onto it. Momiji flies to me with a blanket in his mouth, and we cuddle as I turn on the TV. There's a streaming service dedicated to documentaries, and it's my absolute favorite. I wonder what Vega's favorite thing to watch is...

I won't have these thoughts much longer. V is just a temporary distraction from the hard parts of my life, like my family, and once I get her out of my system, I'll be able to let this go. On the bright side, Iris will lose her shit when she sees her. Someone hot who's more interested in me than in her? That'll be a first. I never wanted to play these games with my sister, but I'm not the one who started this.

I wanted to be a potions mage, but our mother pressured me into following in her footsteps instead. Iris knew this, and what did she do? Suddenly became interested in potions. We were just kids, so I forgave her—but she didn't stop there. In high school, I liked an elf named Terranova, so what did Iris do this time? She went out with him. My life has been a series of steps that I've worked hard to climb, only for my younger sister to push me down on her way to the top. And the worst part of it all? I don't think she cares. She's so absorbed in herself, I'm not even sure she realizes how much she's undermined me our entire lives.

The room is dark, and my eyes drift shut to the sound of a man from Europa describing bird migration patterns...

Dahlia stands in the middle of my living room, holding up two different brand-new lingerie sets from my drawer. One is a firetruck red bodysuit and completely crotchless, the other black and lace matching bra and underwear.

"Watson, you've gotta bring one of these," she says, lifting the bodysuit a little higher.

"I'm pretty sure you bought me that one, and I love you, but it is *not* happening." I shake my head, walking back to my carry-on. We're only going to be gone a week, but Dahlia is acting like I'm spending a month in Europa. I'm so proud of every woman, or person, who feels sexually confident... but that isn't me. I like sex. I *think* I'm good at it, but talking about it and dressing up for it makes me feel so painfully awkward. Lingerie tips the awkward scale. No, thank you.

"Did you or did you not rent a condo for the two of you to stay in instead of staying with your parents because you, and I quote, 'don't need the folks hearing me get fingerbanged into oblivion,' end of quote," she teases.

I cross my arms. "You cannot get me wine drunk and then use my words against me!"

Dahlia sits on my couch, and Momiji flies over for pets. Traitor.

"Did you tell Alitha that you're gonna fuck your boss again?"

I blow my bangs out of my face. "No, Torres, I did not. I don't know how."

Dahlia shrugs. "If you're really going to end it after the holidays, maybe don't, but if things keep progressing, you're going to have to tell her."

"I know," I say. I'm terrified of disappointing Alitha. And of losing my job. "What if she tells Aura or someone else at Augury and one of them tells the dean?"

"Alitha is a square, as are you, but she's not a chismosa. She hardly talks to anyone anyway. Quit worrying. Barbara from HR isn't going to read Alitha's mind, nor is she going to fly down to hell to tell the devil to wait for your arrival."

Dahlia is right, but I still hate it. I hate lying. I've never lied this much in my life. I'm hiding things from Alitha, I'm essentially having Vega fake her identity for my parents, and worst of all... I think I might be lying to myself. Nope, no thanks. No time to unpack that.

One of Dahlia's thick brows raises as I toss the black lingerie set into my suitcase. "I'm not packing the red bodysuit, but I'll pack these just in case."

"Just in case you accidentally slip and fall and land in her pu—"

"Dahlia Torres, what is wrong with you?!" I shout, and we both cackle. I walk over to the couch and sit beside her.

Dahlia smiles and turns her head, her long high ponytail flipping with the movement. "Elorthiel has my mind in the gutter, doesn't he?"

"Alright. You have *thirty seconds* to gab about how hot you think your new boyfriend is," I say. "Go."

"I mean you've seen him, he's the hottest elfling around," she starts.

"Alitha is definitely hotter than that man," I say.

"Alitha and you are the most beautiful beings alive, but you know I don't do femmes. Anyway, he has an eight pack!"

"Is that even anatomically possible?"

Her forehead creases. "Well, I've seen it, so yes. You're the one who teaches at a fancy university. Shouldn't you know this?"

"I study magic, not abs."

"You say that, but I'm pretty certain you've licked your boss's abs. Back to my original point—he has a tongue piercing... that vibrates."

My mouth drops open. I *have* been wanting to lick V's abs. Wait, did she say what I think she said? "Vibrates?"

"Yeah. Like a vibrator in his mouth. I may or may not have gotten to experience it on Friday."

Oh wow. So that's why she didn't answer the phone. Damn, the things I could do to V with something like that. The things she could do to me. Fucking hell, I need this week.

"I've never seriously considered getting body modifications besides like... basic ear stuff," I confess. "Iris has all sorts of tattoos and piercings, and that made me shy away from them... but Vega has a septum ring, cartilage piercings, *and* a tattoo of stars. I'm starting to get it."

Dahlia rubs my upper arm. "You're so cute."

Dahlia's new man has two full sleeves and a chest panel, so she probably thinks I sound ridiculous right now, but these are big steps for me. I wear a lot of black, and my house is a deep purple—but that's about as dark as it gets. I'm like a dark cupcake. Moody on the outside, sparkly on the inside. I've always wanted tattoos, my younger sister Iris is covered in them, but needles are on the top of my list of things that trigger an anxiety attack. Oh well. Maybe one day! I've always liked when people get their wedding rings tattooed on their bodies like a permanent thread of fate.

Dahlia waves her hands in front of my face, her tan wrist covered in golden bangles. "Earth to Indigo—I've got a client first thing tomorrow morning, so I've gotta head out soon. Are you ready to see your parents?"

"Not in the slightest, but I'm not sure I'll ever be," I say. I moved here for school, stayed for work, but ultimately I think I just didn't want to go back. The island itself has done nothing wrong, but it's home, which means it's also the origins of all my trauma. I should be grateful that my life is good, but sometimes existing is so... hard.

"Try and enjoy being home, but if you don't, just sneak away with your new fuck buddy," Dahlia says with a wink. She pulls me in for a hug, and I accept it. She gets up off the couch, grabs her bag, and heads out my front door.

I rub my hands in my face. What have I got myself into?

Vega and I sit on the ferry, the morning mist rising above the sea, and run through our backstory as if we're two actors rehearsing our lines. V rolls up the brown sleeves of her sweatshirt, and my eyes wander to her exposed skin. Her hands are pressed against the bench, causing the veins in the crook of her elbow to emerge in prominent lines.

"I'm still Vega Daelor, twenty-eight years old, and I'm still from Freehold, a community in the central north-east part of Turtle Island. What can't they know?" she asks. My brain is still running through hundreds of things I wouldn't want them to know that'll never come up, like the way she sounds when I touch her.

"They can't know you work at Augury University," I remind her. Our thighs are close enough to touch, though hers are much larger. Even through the fabric of her dress pants, I can see the prominence of her quads.

"Should I even share that I practice magic?"

"Yes. My mother is an experienced charms mage, who works as an engineer. I want her to be impressed with you and to know you're skilled."

Vega purses her lips. "Is that why you're a charms professor?"

"Huh?"

"You did what would make your mother happy, not what would make you happy."

How did she figure that out? V's golden eyes stare into mine, and it's like she's seeing me. All of me. Her gaze is shattering the glass box I built around my heart, reading me like a book that's begging to be opened. She takes her time, caressing every page, and I feel so vulnerable.

I cough, desperate to change the subject. "So, what job should we say you have? It needs to be something you can discuss in great detail. I'll do my best to make sure they don't pick our story apart."

"The only things I can discuss in great detail are charms, stars, and how badly I want to take your clothes off. You choose." She bites her bottom lip, one eyebrow raising, and I swear my entire body was just set on fire.

"You're into working out. Could we choose something like that?" I say, refusing to give in to my desire.

"Sure. I'll say I design and work on fitness equipment."

"Perfect." I turn away from her, shifting my body and staring out into the sea. The water is crystal clear, and there are small octopi scattered throughout these depths in every color. We must be nearing Octopus Island.

seven

VEGA

Indigo looks like a pile of nervous energy. One of her hands is clasped over the other to hide her shaking, and she's lost her beautiful smile in this anxious daze. I want to wrap my body around hers, skin on skin, but we're in public, so instead I pull her legs over mine and rest a hand on her thigh. It's a little romantic in gesture, but nothing too far. I just need her to know I can anchor her and all the big emotions she's experiencing.

The ferry docks, and we get in line to exit, both of our familiars in tow. Octopus Island is only a few hours from the Northern part of Magia Island, where we departed from. I've never been, but it seems to be a popular destination. There's tons of humans and elves as we get off, even an orc. He stands nearby, and I nod at him in recognition.

The people traveling to Octopus Island all look like they're going home or visiting a loved one, just as Indigo does, and I get the feeling it isn't exactly a tourist destination. Sleeping Island, which is another island in the Magia Archipelago, is. I've heard many great things about their events and celebrations. It's honestly a bit odd how little I've heard about Octopus Island in comparison.

Indigo widens her violet eyes, jolting me from my chain of thoughts.

"I have a lot of baggage," she says, and I look at her with my eyebrows furrowed. The line is moving forward.

"All you brought was that little suitcase," I say, half-teasing. I'm pretty sure that's not what she meant, but I say it anyway to ease the tension. We step off the platform and onto the dock.

Indigo smiles and tilts her head, giving me a funny look. "No, V, I mean emotional baggage. You're going to witness a lot of it this week. I love my family, but you'll see all the bad stuff too." She rubs her hands down her face. "My own anxiety, my mother struggles with her mental health, my father has no backbone, and my sister and I can't seem to fucking get along. *That's* why I never visit home. It's a lot." There's the faint welt of tears in those violet eyes, and my blood boils. If her family manages to make her feel this awful when they aren't around, it's going to be a struggle to hold my tongue when I meet them.

"You made a good choice in bringing me with you. I can carry you through this week, and I'm strong enough for you and all your baggage, no matter how much it weighs you down." We walk towards a line of cars, looking for our rental.

"You think you can handle a week with a walking, talking anxiety disorder with mommy issues?"

"Do you think you can handle a week with a lonely orc who's got a dead mom and daddy issues?" I retort. I'm not afraid of her mind or her pain. I've weathered just as bad of storms myself.

"Jeez, Vega," she says, her bright eyes wide with shock.

A tall, lanky human approaches us with a set of keys. "Indigo Watson?" he inquires, and she nods, pulling out her I.D. He hands her the keys, and she pops open the trunk of the silver SUV. Placing our bags inside, I close the trunk and get into the passenger side.

Indigo is in a knee-length black dress with long sleeves. She presses the start-up button, the car pulling energy from its magi-battery, and I buckle my seatbelt, ready for the week ahead. It's a week of service, a week of convincing her family that their daughter is good enough, when the reality is that she's better. It is also a week to convince her that I am worth the trouble. A week for *my* brain to figure out how we can continue seeing one another without *her* brain falling apart, scared everything will be ripped at the seams. Here's to hoping nobody from work spots us.

I won't let this woman go without a fight. Sometimes it's impossible to even approach women... they see a massive orc approaching them and balk. Afraid of the big bad magical wolf. Orcs are massive, sure, but that doesn't make us dangerous. To be fair, men have a history of being dangerous towards women for thousands of years, and it's only recently gotten better. If I were a small woman without magic, I'd probably be afraid of a big muscled being, man or not, too.

But I've rarely felt a connection like this. I've been so busy picking up the broken pieces of my life that I forgot to find someone I want to use my strength to protect. That is, until now. I sound ridiculous… I'm not in love, we barely know each other, but something tells me Indigo is worth falling for.

Pulling into the complex of the condo we rented for the week, Indigo's face is turning red as she parks in the garage. Momiji and Freja are asleep next to one another in the backseat, and I try my best not to wake them.

"Everything okay?"

"Yeah! Everything's fine." Her voice is chipper. *Too* chipper.

I unbuckle the seatbelt, open the door and get out to stretch. "Pop the trunk, and I'll get our bags," I say.

"You sure? I don't mind grabbing mine."

"I'd be mildly offended if you did," I jest. I wouldn't, she's free to do whatever she likes, but I love doing things for her. I want to do everything for her, she can even make me a honey-do list. I know she loves to-do lists. I spotted one in her office, and if it wasn't at work, I would have added my name straight to the top.

I grab our suitcases and follow her short but delicious legs as they take us to an elevator. Indigo is holding a blanket, carrying both of our sleeping familiars within it, like a magical burrito. It's a little after noon, early for a nap, and I theorize Freja is faking being asleep so that she can be with Momiji. Whatever.

We get inside, and, right before the door closes, a man steps in. He's human with short blonde hair. There isn't even the faintest scent of magic on him. Donning some sort of human sports jersey, beer in hand, he looks like every man your mother warns you about as a child. "Hey sexy," he says, words slurred, in Indigo's direction. "You look like you'd sound as pretty as you look underneath me." What the fuck kind of drunken pickup line is that?

"Huh—no—" she stutters, and I can feel the adrenaline coursing through me, waves of anger racing to reach the surface of my tongue.

I'm pretty certain Indigo would hate me if I went full protective asshole mode on this man, but I don't know what else to do. I have to fight the snarl that wants to escape my lips as he takes one stumbling step closer to her. He takes another, and I flick my wrist, magic spraying out of me, clipping his clothing to the wall. Legally, we're not supposed to use magic to harm others, but I didn't use any on *him*. I simply charmed his clothes to the wall. He struggles, confused at why he can't move, and I laugh.

Indigo looks at me like a sad little rabbit, and I consider hitting him for good measure but decide I've got better things to be doing. We get off the elevator and she pulls out her phone, typing in a code so we can enter the condo. "Is he stuck in the elevator?" she asks, voice quiet as we walk inside. She looks simultaneously relieved and concerned, and I feel bad. My goal was to protect her, not upset her. The prick deserved worse.

"It'll wear off in a few hours," I say, putting the bags down.

Walking through the condo, it's nice. A little more vibrant than either of our styles, but it'll be a great vacation stay. I go searching for the bedrooms, only to find just one. That's odd. Heading back into the kitchen, I spot Indigo, who is leaning against the counter table. "Hey, I'm going to head downstairs and talk to the front desk to get our condo changed," I tell her.

"Wait, why? I got this condo through an app; the front desk can't help us. What's wrong?"

"There's only one bedroom and only one bed."

Her cheeks flush pink almost instantly, and she scratches the back of her head, looking down at the floor. "I picked the condo myself."

"Pardon?"

"I... I—you don't want to do this? I thought—hooboy, this is awkward; I'm so sorry." Her voice is all stutters and slurred words as she apologizes, and she drops her face into her hands.

"Don't apologize; what is there to be sorry for?" I know she's anxious, I get that, but I actually don't know what about this time.

"I asked you to be my 'holidate' and you agreed, which was very kind of you, but I thought you wanted to come along because... well, we were going to get each other out of our systems. Now I'm realizing maybe you don't struggle with the same desires for me as I do for you. I might've misread the whole bathroom lack-of-shirt event." She thinks I don't want her? How? I've been working so hard not to appear desperate for her.

"Do you think I don't want you?" I ask in earnest.

She shrugs. "I mean, separate bedrooms...."

This woman needs a fucking confidence booster, because fucking hell. Who wouldn't want Indie? I strut towards her, and she gasps as I pull her into a kiss. It's deep, and I slide my tongue into her mouth, relishing in her warmth. I break, placing her face in the palm of my hands, and open my eyes.

I stare at her for a moment, our eyes transfixed on one another's, and press our noses together. "I want you. Ever since we met, you've invaded my every thought. I can't get you out of my head, so please tell that part of your brain, the part that says you're not wanted, to kindly fuck off."

She smiles at me. It's small, but I know she believes me. I take one hand, gliding it up her dress, and use the other to grip her hair at the nape of her neck. I pull her head back, baring her throat to me, and suck on it gently. As my left hand reaches the fabric of her underwear, I consider how I should ask to go further.

Ring. Ring.

What is that?

Ring. Ring.

Fuck me. Indigo shifts, and I let go of her as she runs over to the couch to grab her phone, clearly trying not to wake Momiji and Freja, who are still sound asleep. She presses a button, and the phone stops ringing, but she's staring at it for what feels like eternity. Sliding her finger across the screen, she answers it.

"Hello, Mother; how're you?"

There's a long silence, and I can visibly see Indigo's tension grow. She's standing, stiff as a board, her shoulders tight.

"Yes, we can be there for dinner tonight. Yes, I'm glad you're excited to meet her."

There's another long pause.

"Five p.m. We'll be there. See you soon!"

Indigo hangs up the phone, and her body relaxes. She looks at me with big, doe-like eyes.

"Dinner... tonight? I thought we weren't supposed to see them until tomorrow," I say, breaking the silence.

"We weren't, but my mother decided to cook and that means we have to go tonight."

"We don't *have* to."

She shakes her head. "No, we have to."

"Do we have time for a quickie?" I jest. I don't mean it. Though I haven't known Indigo for very long, I feel a connection to her that's borderline cosmic. From what I do know, I'm pretty sure she's shut down, her body giving in to the waves of anxiety that are passing through her.

My guess is confirmed when she just stares at me blankly.

"I was kidding," I say, in hopes it'll pull her out of this catatonic state. She stands there, body immobile. I pick her up, and she's a statue in my arms as I carry her to the bedroom and throw her onto the bed.

"I thought you were kidding," she mumbles, waking out of her fog, but still distressed.

"I need your help picking out what I should wear," I say, grabbing a vest and a jacket out of the suitcase. I hold them both up, and she scrunches her brows.

"What shirt are you going to wear?"

"Uh, a white one?"

"Meh. Go with the jacket then. Black vest and white top kinda give off flight attendant or server vibes, and that'll just make my mom act weird."

I frown. "Is your mother one of those awful people who are rude to service workers?"

"No, but like... she's a snob, so it's better to avoid anything that could cause her to look down on us," she admits, and my skin chills. I'd rather have the ashes and memories of a wonderful mom, than a living breathing monster for one.

Sometimes I forget that *I'm* a monster. I mean, I'm not... at least not in the brutal, evil villain way from old human folklore, but I am in the sense that I am bigger and stronger than humanity could ever hope to be, but I like that about myself. Indigo's safe with me because I can confidently say that I could beat up any man that comes near her, with the exception of an orc, and orcs wouldn't touch her. Not unless my scent was off of her, but that'll take months. Months I won't allow to go by. I want her to reek of me indefinitely.

Putting on the black suit jacket and dress pants, I lift her off the bed, throwing her body over my shoulder. Indigo squirms, fighting to be let down, but it's all a ruse. She's magical. If she wanted to get down, she would, but I think she enjoys the fight. She grabs for my ass, and I think if she could reach, she'd try and take a bite.

"Where are you taking me?" she yelps.

"To your parents house."

eight
VEGA

INDIGO'S CHILDHOOD HOME IS PAINTED WHITE WITH CUTE, SIMPLE DECOR. IT'S NOT *overly* lavish, but it does sort of look like something out of a home decor magazine. We pull up to the driveway, where three luxury cars are already parked. The car we rented is a simple baseline SUV, which I manage to squeeze into the remaining space. Stepping out, I run over to open the door for Indie. I'd open it for her anyway, but I make a show out of it in case her family is watching through the window. I've made it my mission this week to show them that if they won't care for their daughter and make her feel appreciated, someone else will.

We walk up, hand in hand, and she knocks on the door. It's a soft knock, and for a moment I'm not sure they can hear it. The door swings open, but nobody is there.

Did Indigo's mother seriously charm the door open?

"Mom, Dad, I'm here," Indigo says, her voice shaky. She's nervous, and I'd do anything to make the emotion go away for her.

I've only met a few of my ex-girlfriends' parents, but I don't remember feeling nervous. Holidating or for real, what are they gonna do, tell a grown woman no? Besides, I'm great at winning people over.

As we cross through a corridor, I note the pictures on the wall. There's wedding photos of Indigo's parents—Mr. Watson is a tan white man with brown eyes and chestnut brown hair, and Mrs. Watson, a beanpole of a woman, with bright white hair and violet eyes, just like Indie's. They look happy, but stuck up. Almost like they're too good for their own wedding.

There are a few family photos of the four of them, and Indigo's sister mirrors Indigo well, just with darker features. As we continue down the hall, the dynamics change. All of the pictures are of Iris. There's a damn-near shrine to the girl. A screen is mounted to the wall, presenting a slideshow of online articles and social media posts about Iris and her accomplishments. *Shit.* Iris Watson, Indigo's younger sister, invented the potion that stopped cancer cells from recurring. The pieces are all falling into place, and now I get why Indigo is so nervous. Those are impossible shoes to fill. I can't believe I hadn't put two and two together.

Crossing over a lip in the floor, we enter a living room. There's a big sign in cursive that says "it's a good day for a good day," and I decide the only thing worse than that would've been "Live. Laugh. Love." I mean, what the fuck does that even mean? Isn't every day a good day to be... a good... I don't have the mental energy for this ridiculousness. The only saving grace for this room is that there's a corner of beautiful art from different cultures. Scotland, I think is one of them, and Elven culture, as well as a quilted piece of art in bright colors. It's all so unique and lovely, and each part of it represents a fragment of who Indigo is. Who her family is too.

"Your girlfriend must be mesmerized by our house or something," a man whispers from the corner.

I cough. I didn't realize they were all sitting there waiting for my introduction. "Hello, I'm Vega."

"Hi, Vega, nice to meet you," Mr. Watson says, standing up to shake my hand. His grip is firm, but mine is firmer.

Mrs. Watson stands and smiles, but it doesn't meet her eyes. She's wearing gray slacks and a white blouse. If it weren't for her hair and eye color, which are the same as Indigo's, I wouldn't think the woman was of elven descent. She's thin, as most elves are, but she isn't tall, which is rare for an elfborn. She's only a few inches above five feet, and her husband only an inch or two taller than that. I'm not complaining though; I love how much smaller in stature Indigo is to me.

"Why don't we have dinner, now that we're all here," Mrs. Watson says, heading out through another corridor.

Something moves on the couch behind me, and Iris comes out of nowhere. Her body was sinking into the sofa, being absorbed by the many decorative pillows. She looks a lot like Indigo, though she exudes more confidence. Tattoos cover her arms and some of her legs, and her outfit is a lot bolder, a black romper with a low v that exposes her cleavage. She's not what I expected. I try not to look, try not to notice her at all. I thought Indigo's 'perfect' younger sister would look less... punk rock.

"Hey, Indie," Iris says. I try to read Indigo's expression, attempting to guess what she'll say, but I haven't a clue.

"Hey." Her voice is a whisper. "I hope you're doing well. Mom says you won another award."

"Yeah, I'm okay," Iris replies, smiling wide.

We follow the Watsons until we come into a vast dining room. The table is a deep, red mahogany, with legs which spiral down in a decorative pattern. It's classical. To my surprise, the table is empty.

"Please, have a seat," Mr. Watson instructs us.

Mrs. Watson tucks her long, white strands behind her ears, and I can see they come to slight points, unlike her daughters'. "Vega, is it?"

"Yes ma'am," I say.

"Would you be a dear and help set the table?" she asks, and I nod, standing up.

She shakes her head. "No need, just use your magic."

I nod, understanding her meaning. Magic is complicated. Any mage can technically utilize any kind of magic, but it won't come naturally to them. Instinctually, when completing day-to-day tasks, you'll lean towards the magic type you're inclined to. I am truly a charms type, but I don't use my magic for frivolous things. Sex? Sure. An emergency? Absolutely. But setting the table? That feels like a waste of my and Freja's energy. Still... This is a test, and I'm not one to fail.

I flick my wrist, and my magic seeps out. Using my senses, I scent the cupboards which house what we need to set the table. A long table cloth flies out, alongside fine dining wear. The objects dance through the air, and as I neatly set things down, Mrs. Watson uses her own magic to bring in the food from the kitchen. It looks like a scene out of an old classic Disney movie I remember seeing as a child, and Iris and Mr. Watson look in awe of our show. Indigo, on the other hand, is glowering at us, and I fear I've made a mistake in passing this test.

"Excellent. Indigo would always drop something when we attempted that," Mrs. Watson says.

Fuck me. I didn't mean to one-up my girlfriend. *My very temporary holiday girlfriend*, I remind myself.

Mr. Watson pours himself a glass of wine and gulps it down in one sip. He must know something we don't.

Mrs. Watson clears her throat. "It's a wonder the most prestigious magical school in the nation hired her. She was never very good at charms—"

"Mom, that's enough. You know damn well that Indigo was hired because of how good she is at teaching. She might not be the best charms mage, but she's likely creating the best charms mages, some even better than you," Iris interrupts.

My blood boils at the way Indigo is being discussed. I'm glad Iris stood up for her sister, because if she hadn't, I was surely going to get myself in trouble. I knew there was going to be family drama, but I wrongly assumed it would take a few days into the trip. I don't want to make this worse for Indie, but the best way to protect her right now is to get her the fuck out of here.

Indigo looks at me, tears welting in her eyes, and I pull her hand, eyebrows raised. She nods, and I help her rise from her seat. Her hands are shaking as one intertwines with mine. Looking at the table, I go to speak, but nothing comes out. I've never been stunned into silence before; this is a first.

As we make our way out of the snobbish, cold house, I open the silver door of the SUV and help Indigo inside. Kissing her forehead, I lift my hand and wipe away a single tear.

Indigo sits on the balcony of the condo we're staying in, a plush white blanket wrapped around her body. My heart aches for hers. I thought she just wanted me to join her on this trip to get me out of her system, but she actually needed me here. She needed someone to be the rock while these harsh waves crashed around her. I'm realizing now that there's a lot I don't know about her. I know her body, the way she talks and moves, and the way she ticks. What I don't know is all the history that made her this way, and I desperately seek all of it.

Stirring the two cups of hot chocolate that sit before me, I take both in hand and head onto the balcony, handing one to Indigo.

"Thank you," she says and takes a sip.

I sit on the chair beside hers. Indigo's usual glow to her skin is gone, and she looks paler than normal. The fluffy white blanket which was wrapped around her slides off shoulders. Her emotions are tangible, physically affecting her appearance, and it makes my chest burn.

"Can I ask you a personal question?"

She sips on the hot chocolate before taking a deep breath. "Yes."

"Why do you keep in touch with your family when they're so cruel to you?" I inquire.

"I don't know," she admits, and that surprises me. How can you not know?

I rest a hand on her thigh, gently caressing it. "You know you don't have to put up with that, right? You could cut them off and nobody would think less of you for it."

"I know, but I seek their approval. I seek *her* approval. And it's not always so bad. My mom started going to therapy recently, and although she still has outbursts, she's gotten better."

I frown. "Just because she's trying to do better, doesn't mean you need to put yourself in unhealthy situations while she works on herself. You're her daughter, not her punching bag."

"I know, I know. Alitha and Dahlia tell me all the time."

"You should set some boundaries," I tell her.

"Okay, Simone."

"Huh?"

She laughs and places her cup down on the glass table. "My therapist. She's always talking about boundaries. I started going to her because I think I have an anxiety disorder, and she agrees, but we're still not certain which one yet. It's kind of a new thing."

I smile at her transparency, and she scrunches her nose.

"I graduated from therapy a few years ago," I confess. It's not something I'm sure I've ever told anyone, but if there's ever a time, it feels like it should be now.

"*You* went to therapy? And *graduated*? Damn, I must be in the kindergarten phase."

My brows scrunch. "What—did you not expect that? All graduating therapy means is that I've learned the strategies necessary, and at least for now, I don't need a clinician."

"I guess that makes sense. You just seem so... perfect? Hot?" she says teasingly.

"There's a reason the phrase is hot and bothered," I say with a smirk.

She punches my shoulder. It's barely a tap, but it's cute.

"Don't think that I'm perfect. I mean, you *can* think that, but I hope you know that I come with my own set of baggage too," I say. "I'm obsessive, addicted to working out, and my sex drive is naturally higher than humans."

"I know, I know. But literally nothing you listed was negative. Try again." She giggles and rolls her eyes. We're speaking in jest, but she's still guarded. Arms crossed, there's a level of openness I can't seem to get her to reach with me. Maybe if I open up more, she'll feel comfortable enough to do the same. I want to be that person for her.

"I used to struggle with depression. And abandonment issues. That's what I went to therapy for." I shrug. I still struggle with the abandonment part, but that truth remains unsaid. I don't want to pressure Indigo into making this real because she feels sorry for me. I want her to make this real because she can't stand the thought of me being with someone other than her. Because I can't stand that thought right now either.

"I'm sorry." She places her hand on my cheek, softly cupping it.

"Can I hold you?"

"Please."

Beige limbs tangle with mine as I hold Indigo closely, her face resting against my chest. She snores softly, and I kiss her forehead as my eyelids grow heavy. *Goodnight, little rabbit.*

nine

INDIGO

Stretching out my arms, I look down at Vega, who is still sound asleep. She's drooling on the pillow, but in a sexy way? In the sexiest way that someone can drool.

I need to fucking text the Unholy Trilogy. Snaking my arm over V, I grab my phone off the nightstand, unplugging it from the charger.

INDIGO

Hey, okay, so... I asked Vega to be my holidate for Gratefulness Week.

DAHLIA

Mmmhmmm.

ALITHA

Dahlia told me...

INDIGO

TORRES?!

DAHLIA

In my defense, she was going to find out anyway.

INDIGO

Urgh, whatever. Okay, is there a way we're like... destined to be?

DAHLIA

Cosmically or biologically?

INDIGO

Both? Either?

DAHLIA

Do you know her chart????

INDIGO

Not really. I know she's a Taurus sun and moon.

DAHLIA

Hmmmmmmmmm.

INDIGO

This whole thing feels like an illusion, except she never dissipates. She's toooo perfect for me.

ALITHA

I could do some research in the lab. See if there's a scientific explanation for all of this.

DAHLIA

Omg, YES!!!

ALITHA

I just need a small sample of her DNA.

DAHLIA

Is she sleeping now? Pull out a strand of her hair or something.

INDIGO

...

ALITHA

It would be much less risky to just get some from her hair brush.

DAHLIA

True, true.

INDIGO

I'M NOT GIVING YOU BIZZARE BITCHES A HAIR SAMPLE.

ALITHA

That's Dr. Bizarre Bitch to you.

DAHLIA

I just snorted.

I lock my phone and carefully get up, not wanting to wake Vega. She looks like a green cherub, her skin shimmering in the early light of the rising sun. I grab my toiletries out of my suitcase and head for the bathroom. Reaching one arm into the shower, I turn the water on and undress as I wait for it to get hot.

Nobody texted me. Not my mother. Not my father. Not my sister. The Unholy Trilogy replied, of course, but nobody from last night, my own family, dared to see how I'm doing or apologize for their awful behavior. Whatever. I can't let them ruin this week, or let the panic take me. There's a gorgeous woman in the bed I got to sleep in last night, and I won't let anyone ruin that for me.

The warm water washes away my troubles, as it always does. I regret not packing purple shampoo. Dahlia is gonna kick my ass by the end of this week. Maybe I could get some at a store nearby? I'll put that on the to-do list, which was recently updated.

On my to-do list:

- Decorate for Christmas
- Get Vega out of my system
- Buy purple shampoo

Not on my to-do list:

- Developing feelings for my boss
- Waiting for an apology from my mother that'll never come

I'm not doing a great job at the not-list, but I'm trying.

I brush through my hair, detangling it gently. It's Gratefulness Week, dammit. Instead of being miserable and spending the day sulking about my family, I'd rather find something to be grateful for—like fucking the sexy orc that's lying down in the other room. After giving my body a solid 3 rounds of scrubbing, I turn off the water and look at myself in the mirror. It's time to put on the ritz.

Getting out my blow dryer, I consider making a potion that would permanently render it silent, but decide to charm it quiet instead. Butt-naked, I stand there, drying my bob. Throwing on some winged eyeliner, I add the final touch of my signature deep purple lipstick, and shimmy into the bra and panties that Dahlia made me pack. They're lacy and black, and I think now's a better time than ever to put them to good use.

I exit the bathroom and cross towards the kitchen, where I dig around for ingredients. We don't have much here to make breakfast, so I add that to my mental list. Turning, I suddenly feel her warm body behind me.

"You moved so fast, I hadn't even realized you woke up," I say.

"I was slow until I saw what you were wearing," V whispers in my ear, her voice still groggy from recently waking.

She turns me around, pushing me onto the kitchen counter. The morning sun settles in through the window, lighting the space, and I close my eyes as she nips my neck with her tusks. Vega leaves a trail of wet, heady kisses, before putting her nose up to mine and looking me straight in the eyes.

"I brought you a surprise; do you trust me?"

"Yes," I say, my voice coming out breathy.

She moves away from the counter and crosses towards the bedroom. As she walks away, I get the best view of her solid ass and thighs. She's all muscle, yet somehow has the most delightful bubble butt I've ever seen. It's too perfect. I'm practically drooling as I wait for her to return.

"Close your eyes."

I smile and obey. "Closed them."

Her footsteps come closer, until she's right up against me. Her deeper, sultry voice comes out again. "Open your legs, little rabbit."

A shiver hits my entire body at those words, and I do as I'm told. I'm hoping I'll be rewarded for how good I've been about following her orders.

She places something against my underwear, right on my clit, and I hear a click.

Zzz

Is that a fucking vibrator?

Zzzzzzz.

"Oh my god," I gasp out in pleasure, allowing the feeling to take over me. Vega's tusks run against my neck, and she sucks on my skin, her wet warm mouth dissolving any semblance of control I ever had. I have been stuck in this limbo between wanting to get her out of my system and not wanting to catch feelings, and at this moment I've decided I don't fucking care.

One of V's hands strokes my thigh while the other grabs my hair, exposing my neck further. I'm moaning and enjoying myself when my brain starts doing the math. What's holding up the vibrator?

I shift my head, looking straight into those pools of gold she has for eyes. "How're you doing that?"

"Magic," she says with a wink. Oh my—she can use her hands for other things.

Vega licks all the way down my neck and unhooks my bra. She places my breast into her mouth, sucking on the hard peak of my nipple.

"I can use my tongue," she says, swirling it around again. She flicks one wrist out, pointing up with her finger, and the vibration increases in intensity. "Or I could use my magic."

I'm on the edge when she lowers the setting of the vibrator to almost nothing. I whimper, wanting the pleasure to return.

V kisses me deeply. "Can I charm your body? I have something I want to try on you."

"Right now? You can use me as you see fit."

"Good girl." She kisses me once more, and parts from between my legs. Slipping off her shorts, I can see the short, trimmed black hair and her plump, perfect lips, fully exposed.

Forget anything I ever said about purple. Green is my favorite color.

Vega steps away, rooting for something in one of her bags, and I get a look at her ass. It's the hottest thing I've ever seen. A roundness like a lot of women I've seen, but with the muscle of every star athlete. I can never fuck another human again, knowing what lady orc ass looks like. She places a green dildo onto the counter. It's a deep, fleshy green with olive undertones, similar to the shade of her skin.

Is that for me?

Vega moves her hands, swirling them through the air, and then my hands are locked down onto the counter. The pressure of her magic isn't painful, but it would be incredibly hard to move my arms right now. If I weren't magical, it would be impossible. Even still, her magic greatly outweighs mine in this department. She deserves her title of Department Chair of Charms. *Don't think about work, Indigo.*

I blink, watching as Vega climbs onto the island in the middle of the kitchen. Her hair has been thrown into a bun, and I can see the shaven parts that wrap around underneath. Everything about her is painstakingly sexy. From the nose piercing, to the tattoo on her arm, to the muscles sparkling in the morning sunlight. Everything.

Opening her legs, V puts herself on full display before me. She places two fingers into her mouth, sucking on them before slowly drawing them out and moving them down her lips. She trails down her chin, past her sports bra, and down her chiseled stomach, until she reaches her pussy.

Vega teases at her folds before finally pushing them inside. She moans out in pleasure, and I would do anything to touch her right now. To be touched by her.

As if sensing my need, she uses her other hand to fling her magic out, driving the setting of the small, bullet shaped vibrator all the way up. My legs are shaking, hanging off the counter across from her, but my arms won't move—can't move.

"Vega," I say as she dips her fingers in and out. The sounds of her body opening up is driving me mad. I'm so incredibly close when she snaps her fingers, and the vibrations come to a complete stop.

"You bitch," I say, out of breath and overwrought. I half-mean it.

"Tsk tsk. Talk to me like that, and you'll get nothing, little rabbit."

She reaches back, grabbing the dildo. It is thicker and longer than any I've ever purchased, with a suction cup at the end. She sticks it straight onto the black and white marble she's seated on, and gets up onto her knees. As she lowers herself onto the cock, I watch, mouth agape and watering.

Her body takes it so well. Every muscle in her leg flexes at different moments as she moves herself up and down. Her hands grasp her knees, and I squirm, desperately trying to move my hands out from the force of her magic so I can touch her—touch myself, really.

She moans, biting her lips as she stares into my eyes, and I realize this is the most intimacy I've ever had with someone. I've fucked, I've been fucked, but I've never shared this type of vulnerability, or experienced this level of unadulterated lust, with anyone.

V bounces, the movements quickening, and I whimper, needing to chase the high of my own pleasure.

"Beg for it." It is not a suggestion, but a command. Her voice is liquid gold. "Beg, and I'll let you come."

I almost laugh, but when she stares at me with those fierce, lust-filled eyes, I choose to do as I'm told. "P-please."

"I said beg."

"Vega, I want to come," I say, not sure if I sound awkward or sexy.

One of her eyebrows shifts up, and the vibrator starts again for a split second, before shutting off once more.

Were it not for her magic, my body would cave in on itself, my thighs rubbing against each other, craving friction.

"Please, Vega," I start, before realizing I already said that. I pause briefly, my mind sifting through information until I land on the perfect thing. "Dr. Daelor." Her eyes go wide at that. "I need you to make me come. Fuck me, punish me, do whatever you want with me. I'm yours, please let me finish."

She climbs off the counter, grabbing me and throwing me over her shoulder. My body goes limp as her magic ceases its hold on me, and I let her toss me onto the island countertop. Can I add "being thrown around" onto the list of things I'm into?

Vega climbs up onto the island, and I'm suddenly thankful to past-Indigo for renting the fancier condo with the massive kitchen. Spreading my legs open, Vega uses one hand to hold her body up, while she uses the other to tease my opening. The pink, little vibrator is still charmed, pressed against my clit, and she gradually ups the vibration.

V pushes my underwear to the side before curling one strong finger inside me, I experience pure bliss as Vega fucks me with her finger. When I'm alone, I always require at least two, but with Vega's massive and muscled six-foot-six body, one finger is plenty. She bounces backward onto the dildo, fucking herself as she finishes me off.

"Vega, I'm so close," I say.

"Me too," she replies, bouncing with more fervor than ever.

The overwhelming feeling of her muscles body hovering before me, convulsing as she comes. The combined feeling of the curve of her finger and the pulsing vibrations against my clit send me toppling over the edge.

Slowly, she pulls her finger out of me and moves to kiss me. Her lips are soft, and I smile against them.

"It's still early; can we go back to sleep?" I ask.

"Of course, my rabbit." Vega kisses the top of my forehead, and I nuzzle against her chest.

Not *little* rabbit, but *her* rabbit. How I desperately wish that could be true.

ten

INDIGO

I unwrap myself from Vega, and she laughs as I put on a fresh pair of underwear.

"Two pairs in one day, is that a record?" she teases.

"No, definitely not. I think the record is four. I can't wear the pair I had on this morning because *someone* got them soaked."

"*You* soaked them; I just helped," she says with a smirk.

"Anyways. We need lunch and to run a couple of errands."

"Sure thing. What do you need?"

I start counting on one finger. "Groceries, purple shampoo, new parents."

"Can't help you with the last one. Let's grab a bite, get your shampoo, and hit up groceries last. If I go grocery shopping on an empty stomach, I'll buy everything in the store."

"I feel that."

V's smile is addictive, and I savor her toothy grin. I put on a pair of black leggings, and a black peplum top with wide flared sleeves. Vega is wearing beige cargo pants and a brown sweatshirt with the Augury University logo on it. The embroidered AU is gold, with a dainty golden wreath wrapped around it in a circle. Underneath the AU, are two hands performing magic. It's beautiful, really, I can't think of another University with a cooler logo, but it's a bit on the nose? We're supposed to be hiding that we work there, not making it more obvious.

"Should you change?" I suggest, unsure of how she'll react.

"Meh. Alumni wear this kind of stuff all the time, plus my hair will be up.

Nobody is going to think either of us are professors, we're a bit young," she says with utter certainty.

I wish I could live in her head. Curl up next to that pretty brain of hers and cease to feel the anxiety that spirals within my own.

I forget that we're young. I mean, I know I'm young, but Vega is also only twenty-eight. Alitha is twenty-nine, and I believe Malik is in his late twenties as well. Many of the other professors are in their thirties and forties, but some are literally hundreds of years old. We're infants in comparison. My sister's accomplishments made my job at Augury University look frivolous, but I have to remember how amazing this opportunity is and that I cannot fuck it up. I will not get fired because of my unbridled lust for my boss. This week will get her out of my head for good. This is just an itch I have to scratch.

Kissing Momiji on the head, we turn on the TV. The white, fluffy sugar rabbit has his wings wrapped around Freja, who stares intently at the screen. I didn't know hummingmouse were such big fans of reality TV, but I guess if you're going to watch trashy television, Magically Mine is where it's at.

Hopping into the car, we drive towards the center of Octopus Island. The Isles of Magia are all unique in their own ways. Magia Island is full of magic, and the people there are one with nature. We didn't destroy jungles to make our buildings, we built them in the trees, or on open planes. Naiad Island has its own vibe as well, comprised of merfolk cultures from all over the galaxy. Sleeping Island is a quieter place, and a more tight-knit community. They've dedicated a lot of resources into archiving and preserving humanities' culture from before The Convergence. Octopus Island is the odd man out. The name derives from the creatures that lurk in waters around it, but the island itself is anything but friendly to nature. On Turtle Island, in The Americas, there is a region in the west known as the Valleys of Silicon. It's a hyper-technological space. Octopus Island is similar, utilizing more technology than magic.

After The Convergence, humanity had to rebuild. Most of our ancestors banded together with the magical races, combining nature with magic, magic with science, and science with technology to forge a new world. There's a balance we've carefully struck, but some pockets of the globe have decided other methods were better. They allowed technology to take over. I think it's one of the ways that humans, the ones without magic, feel in control. Either way, there's a lot of debate in the political sphere on how much of that technology is safe, but ultimately we cannot govern communities that are not our own.

I watch Vega as we drive to the main city, her brows remaining furrowed the entire time. She's seeing it too—seeing what I hate about this place. How clear it is that they cut down trees and manipulated the Earth to create this place.

Though I was raised on Octopus Island, I spent my entire life dreaming of anything else. It felt... uncomfortable. There's something about feeling the grass against my feet that is so natural and grounding, and Octopus Island is nearly void of that. There is grass, sure, but it is perfectly contained in little suburbs.

As we drive past pristine house after pristine house, the anxious feeling in my gut heightens. I am being reminded of how much I hate it here—reminded of how much Magia Island has become my home. I've been living there for eight years now, ever since I was accepted to Augury University after I graduated high school early. I thank my lucky stars for Augury, for it has become my home.

We park the car on a side shoot of Main Street, and I hop out of the car. Tapping my phone against the meter, I pay the four dabloons it costs to park for the day.

Vega looks at me with a peculiar expression. "It costs money to park here?"

I shrug. "Yep. This place sucks, dude."

"Okay, okay. Take a deep breath," she says, and so I do, letting out a deep sigh. "I know you hate it here and you want to be miserable and for me to commiserate with you, but I don't want to. You invited me to come out with you. Let's treat this like we're random tourists. Ignore all the capitalist-technological-hellscape parts of this island, and let's just enjoy the holiday and each other's company."

"I'm sorry. You're right," I say.

"It's okay. You have bad memories from this place, and it isn't as magic-friendly as you'd prefer. I get it, I really do, but let's make the best of it. Focus on the good stuff, like the fact that they're decorating this place for all the winter holidays," she says, taking my hand in hers.

We walk down the busy street, and it reminds me of why I love this season. There are people putting up Christmas lights, wreaths for Winter Solstice, and light fixtures shaped into the Star of David. As we pass a family, I see a poster in a woman's arms that reads "POETRY READING FOR YALDĀ NIGHT." So many cultures, so many planets, and yet nearly all people have their own way of celebrating winter.

We walk towards a hair supply store... Vega goes to open the door, when a small crowd of people come marching towards us holding pamphlets.

Are they all... religious? Is this a cult? Some type of spell? I honestly have no idea what is going on, but they're all wearing funny outfits that remind me of old movies.

Vega's eyes widen, and her eyebrows scrunch like she's just deciphered what's going on. "They're Christmas Carolers... in November."

The party of people, mostly human but a few cambion, elves, and hybrids take in a collective breath.

"Dashing through the snow," a woman's voice sings out.

"In a one-horse open sleigh," a man joins.

"O'er the hills we go." Each line is like a solo, and I can't help but grin.

"Laughing all the way."

A child jumps out from behind their parents. "Ha. Ha. Ha."

I take Vega by the hand and lead her into the store as the singers continue down the street, coming up to all who pass.

"That was... prematurely festive," I say with a small laugh. Vega and I continue down the aisles until we find the one dedicated to white hair. Every section is broken down by hair color, then texture, then product. "What was that?" I ask as I grab the purple bottle. Though my hair is naturally white, if I don't use a special shampoo, it often looks brassy. This shampoo helps the lavender tint to last longer.

V tilts her head at me. "The Christmas Carolers?"

"Is there some kind of event going on?"

She shrugs, not answering as we approach the checkout counter. An employee rings me up in polite silence, and we cross the threshold to exit the store.

Vega looks at me. "This is your hometown, you tell me. Is there usually some kind of event during this time?"

I roll my eyes. "I haven't lived here in forever. I just think it's weird that they'd celebrate so early."

Vega laughs as we continue down the street towards a sandwich shop. "People always celebrate Christmas early. I think it's hilarious. It's humanity's thing, I don't know. Did you not celebrate Christmas growing up?"

"We do. My dad loves Christmas, but my mom was always more into Winter Solstice. I think she just likes the aesthetics of Christmas, since none of us are religious."

"That's funny. My mom celebrated a Barac holiday called Jul—"

"God rest ye, merry Gentlemen," a caroler sings, interrupting Vega.

What is going on?

"Didn't we just fucking see carolers?" I whisper through gritted teeth.

People walk by and stop to watch. There's a mother orc carrying her toddler son, and he watches in awe of the vocalists.

"I think these are the same people too," Vega whispers back. She takes me by the hand, snaking me out of the small crowd that's forming, and we head back down the street.

"God rest ye, merry mouths," I say once everyone is out of earshot.

Vega lets out a grunt of a laugh, and my cheeks turn red.

The carolers are continuing this direction, and I'm getting rather annoyed by them. "Why don't we go somewhere else instead of the sandwich shop?"

"That's fine with me," Vega says. "Anything you had in mind?"

"There's a ramen and boba place two streets over," I suggest and she squeezes my hand.

"Lead the way."

Crossing Main Street towards Token Bubbles, there are workers putting up holiday decorations at every corner. Lots of specialized screens that flash different designs for a multitude of holidays.

"You were telling me about Jul? It sounds like Yule," I say, passing a bookstore and a crystal shop.

"It's similar in many ways. Orcs would eat these animals... similar to boars, and we'd light candles and tell stories around a fire. When I was young, and my mother was still around, we did an earthly version of it with hot chocolate. I can recall sitting in her lap, snow on the ground, and we were bundled up around the fire pit," Vega shares, and my heart sinks. Although my family is awful at times, they're alive. They are a phone call away.

I pull her hand up to my face and kiss it gently. We continue walking until we're at the doors of Token Bubbles and step inside.

There is a beautiful mural of a wave painted on the wall as we get in line.

"Could I please get grilled chicken ramen with extra chicken? And a brown sugar milk tea," Vega says. Her voice is smooth and warm, with a deep timbre.

I order the same, without all the extra chicken, and some kind of passion fruit drink with popping pearls that sounds appealing.

Walking up to the machine to pay, Vega bumps me out of the way with her hip and places her phone on top of the machine.

"As the person who gets to decide if you deserve a pay raise, you deserve a fucking pay raise *and* a free meal" Vega whispers to where no one can hear, and I flush.

"Vega, I make the base adjunct pay, which is not bad at all. I can pay for myself."

"You are doing more than any other adjunct, and frankly more than many of the other professors. Don't argue with me; I'm paying for your food."

I sigh and accept. I hate to say this, but I love it when she's bossy. When men tell me what to do, it makes me want to scream, but when Vega does it, something melts inside me. I immediately want to abide. Maybe I should bring this up in therapy too. Bisexuality is strange. Sometimes it feels like my personality alters a little, depending on the gender of my partner. But Vega isn't my partner.

The server calls our number.

"Do you want to sit outside? The weather is really beautiful out," I suggest.

"Not as beautiful as you."

I roll my eyes. "Has that line ever worked on *anyone*?"

"It just did." She winks. "Yeah, let's eat outside."

Grabbing the tray, Vega and I open the door that leads to the patio outside. The air is slightly chilled, and it's refreshing. We sit down, and I watch as Vega takes a massive bite of chicken.

"Can I ask a silly question out of ignorance? I'm just seeking to understand you better," I say nervously. I hate asking people—monsters, humans, anyone—of different cultures or from other planets questions about why they do things. They don't owe me anything, but I want to know everything about everyone. It fascinates me. Admittedly, I'm also terrified I'll come across as rude or insensitive.

"Go for it."

"I've noticed... orcs eat a lot of meat? Like, a lot more meat than humans. Is there a reason for that?" I ask.

Vega's golden eyes shimmer back at me. "That's not something we're sensitive about, so don't worry. Our bodies simply demand more protein. It's one of the reasons orcs are naturally more muscular."

"Deck the halls with boughs of holly, fa, la, la, la, la, la, la, la, la." There is a group of voices singing, and the sound of marching footsteps from around the corner.

"Are you kidding me? Did you pay these people to follow us?" I ask V as they get closer to the restaurant.

Vega smirks, one corner of her mouth perking up. "No, but I wish I orchestrated this. It would make this one hundred times funnier."

They continue singing as they walk, until the carolers are standing directly in front of the patio. There's only a few other people on the deck, and everyone seems to be amazed by the singers. Everyone but me, apparently.

I don't know whether to laugh or scream when they all open up their coats and take out a plethora of hats. From Santa hats to elf ears, everyone sticks something on their head.

"Isn't it kind of weird that people still dress up as Christmas elves, when actual elves exist?"

"Yeah, a bit. I think they call them something else now... Santa's fae? Something like that," Vega says as the carolers continue. "Most elves are so tall, they don't look anything like Santa's helpers."

"Except my elfborn family. We inherited so many elven traits, except the height."

Vega's smirk widens into the biggest grin I've ever seen on her. "They should cast you guys next time."

"I'm going to kill you."

"Sh!" A human woman shushes me, and I look at V with wide eyes.

We continue eating our ramen in silence, the sound of Christmas music grating in my ears. There's no place I'd rather be than here with Vega, being tortured by Christmas carolers, day dreaming about a future we might never have together because of stupid fucking work policies. I wish I didn't love my job so much.

Maybe in another life I'm an assassin, or a restaurant worker, or an engineer like my mother wanted me to be. Vega could still work as a professor. Maybe in another life, I'm hers.

eleven

INDIGO

Ping.

"What was that?" I say with a yawn.

Ping.

"It's your phone; it's been blowing up for like a half-hour," Vega says as she turns in bed to face me. I'm bleary eyed and groggy, but I'm awake. Vega's face is stiff, like she slept with it smushed into a pillow the entire night, and I giggle.

"Should I check it?"

I unlock my phone to a plethora of texts from my mother.

MOM

Indigo, will we be seeing you today?

I'm so sorry

Indigo, I have to apologize for the other night. My medication had worn off and I've been very stressed lately. I know it's not an excuse, but my therapist and I talked about it, and I wanted to tell you I really didn't mean most of what I said. I mean I did, but I didn't. I usually mean what I say, but not how I say it.

We are getting the Christmas tree this morning at 10. Do not miss it.

That sounded very bossy, but it's family tradition. Your father would be very upset if you weren't there.

I'm not trying to be annoying, but could you answer the phone? What if something happened to you? Don't make your poor mother worry.

"Fucking hell on Earth, what is her problem?" Vega says from over my shoulder.

I sigh, typing up a single response.

INDIGO

We will be there to get the tree.

"Is she always like this? Or did something recent make it worse?" Vega inquires.

"I mean, yes, and yes. The holidays are especially triggering for her, but this is pretty much the norm. She has good days and bad days—times where she hurts me, and times where she helps."

Vega's mouth twists to the side, and her septum piercing moves as her nostrils flare. "I don't even know how to respond. How do you deal with this all the time?"

"Not sure. I think it's easier because I moved away. Sometimes I just mute her number for a few weeks. Other times, she's so busy with Iris that she forgets to text me. It's a weird dichotomy."

Vega sits up, pushing the blanket off of her. "So, where are we going?"

"Raemond Hill—it's a plant nursery that imports Christmas trees. We go every year. We're supposed to be there in forty-five minutes, so we better hurry up and get dressed."

"Do you want me to make breakfast?" Vega offers, standing up in just her boxer-briefs and a sports bra.

"I don't think we have time. Maybe we can get smoothies on the way back and then I'll make us lunch?"

"I'd like to cook for you," Vega says.

"Okay," I say, cheeks flushed pink. She always wants to take care of me, and if I'm being honest with myself, I always want to let her.

Momiji and Freja are flying across the room, racing one another, when I put out a bowl of lettuce and carrots for them to chomp on. Freja is significantly faster and makes her way over to the bowl, reaching it before Momiji even lands on the table.

Heading back into the bedroom, I open my suitcase and take out a black sweater and matching leggings. The sweater is knitted, and there are holes in the sleeve where I've shoved my thumb through.

"Vega," I shout.

"Yes, love...ly," she shouts back. There was a long pause between *love* and the *ly* sound at the end, and I can't help fixate on it. Part of my brain wants to ball it up and toss it into a fire and burn it, never to be uttered again. I can't be her love, not now. The other part of me wants to hold it close to my heart. I blink away the thought before an anxiety spiral seizes me.

"Do you think my mom will be mad at me if I show up in a sweater with holes in the sleeve?" I ask.

Vega walks into the room, brows furrowed, and shrugs. "I don't know, and frankly, I do not care—*we* do not care." Vega stops and points to her and I. "Stop caring and wear what you want."

"It's just... it's so comfy."

"You don't have to explain yourself to me. Wear the sweater."

"Alright," I say. "Let's go see my family."

The plant nursery is just as I remember it. There are large black metal gates leading into a wide open space, with lots of potted plants lined up on tables and the ground surrounding them. There is the old section where they keep imported trees, as well as a new section of some sort of pine which is actually growing out of the ground. Magic must be required to grow these trees on Octopus Island.

Entering through the gates, I spot Iris standing next to our parents, who are all in their own unique outfits. Iris is wearing short, orange corduroy overalls on top of a tight, black top, which is so typical for her. If I wore something like that growing up, I'd have been scolded for showing too much leg, but our mom always let Iris wear whatever she wanted. Mom, who always dresses more conservatively, is wearing a long, flowy black top over pants, and our dad is in a t-shirt and jeans. At least dad's outfit is practical. We all look like we're attending different events, and it makes me chuckle a bit to myself.

"You good?" Vega asks as we get out of the SUV and head towards my family.

"Yeah, just thinking."

As we reach my family, my dad pulls me into a hug and kisses my forehead.

"I'm sorry, sweet girl. I should've defended you the other night. You know how your mother can be sometimes," he whispers, and I smile, forcing myself not to let out the tears that threaten to fall.

"So, do we want an imported one, or one of those weird experimental ones growing out of the ground?" Iris asks. "I hear a potion mage created them."

"Well then, in honor of you, our little potion mage, let's get one!" My mom says and starts walking. We all follow after her, crossing by tall trees coming out of the ground, and we head towards the back of the nursery. Vega holds my hand, rubbing my pointer finger with her thumb in an attempt to soothe me.

Coming up the pathway, we stop at a little shack. There are axes hanging from the outer wall, and a short cambion leans against their desk reading a book. The cambion, who I'm almost certain is Raemond in disguise, has massive breasts that are falling out of their shirt. Their high-waisted leather pants lead to chunky black heels. It's ridiculous how sexual they're posed, with their tail waving back and forth.

"Raemond," Iris says with a cough.

The cambion shifts into their usual form, wearing a sweatshirt and biker shorts. Raemond has pinky-red skin and white straight hair cut into a bob. They have short black horns that are spiked, growing out of the top of their head. Although some cambion have wings, Raemond does not.

"Is this more... family friendly?" they ask Iris, who laughs.

"Yeah, who the fuck were you dressed up for anyway?" Iris's smile is wider than I've seen in years, and it sends a pang to my heart.

Raemond adjusts their square-shaped glasses. "There's a guy who buys a lot of his plants here. I don't know his name, but he's very tall and hunky. I saw his car drive by and was hoping to catch his attention, but I guess he didn't stop. Oh well, maybe another time." Raemond lets out a deep sigh. "Or maybe I'll just die alone."

My mouth opens, unsure of what I should say in response to that, but Iris just laughs. Maybe this is an inside joke? Vega's expression is amused as she witnesses this all unfold.

"Was that an illusion?" my dad asks Raemond, breaking the awkward silence.

"It was!" they say, unbothered by their previous statement.

I start to think that my mother is being oddly quiet, when I realize she's no longer standing with us. Looking around, I see she's already investigating the new experimental trees.

Iris, Raemond, and my father head over to Mom, while Vega stands with me by the shack.

"How come you all get your tree here every year?" Vega asks.

"Before Raemond inherited the family business, I think it belonged to their aunt... uncle... ancle? Cambion all have a different thing with gender. Some of them like gendered terms, others don't, but generally they're all what we'd consider genderqueer."

"I feel that." Vega smiles wide. "I'm what they'd call... a little queer."

"A *little*? You're really gay *and* really tall, there's nothing little to you." I shake my head. "Anyway, I think it was their aunt Roxana. We always got our trees here growing up, it's just kind of a tradition. Maybe one day Iris will have a kid, and they'll come here too."

"Vega, would you be a dear and grab an ax?" my mother yells in our direction.

"No need," Vega shouts. "I'll just use my magic."

Raemond snaps their fingers and is suddenly next to us, staring up at us with golden eyes, more yellow than Vega's. "You cannot use magic to cut down these trees; you have to do it by hand."

"That takes so much effort," my dad says, walking our way.

"It takes the same amount of effort it took humans to cut down trees before The Convergence. I'm not trying to be a dick; it's just a rule from the mage who created these trees. You have to do it the old-fashioned way," Raemond explains.

Vega grabs an ax off the wall and throws it over her shoulder, heading back towards my mother and the tree she's selected. My father follows suit. Raemond transforms, their body shifting into a tall, lean and muscular figure. They grab an ax, and we all head to the tree. Although I've known Raemond for a long time, this illusion skill is new, and it's impressive.

Iris is sitting on the ground, watching videos on her phone. I know twenty-four and twenty-two isn't a massive age gap, but she looks like a child to me right now, the way she's so enamored by whatever she's watching. She'll always be my little sister, no matter how hard she tries to be bigger than me.

Vega swings the ax, chopping at the base of the tree. The muscles in her arms flex with every swing, shown off thanks to her tank top. I know that my whole family is next to me, that Raemond is here too, but I don't care. As V chops down that tree, it is just me and her in this whole wide world. I stare at her beautiful lady orc ass and remember how she looks without the sweatpants on.

I am, once again, reminded that green is my new favorite color.

Vega and Raemond carry the massive tree onto the roof of my dad's luxury SUV. You can see my mom wince at every branch which scratches against the top of the vehicle, but my dad doesn't seem to mind. He stares at Vega in awe.

"Dude, I think Dad is more in love with your girlfriend than you are," Iris jests. *More in love with my girlfriend.* I let the words settle in my mouth, but I don't utter another sound.

Once the pine is secured, my mother pulls out her phone and sends Raemond the dabloons she owes them for the tree. Raemond walks back through the gate and waves their hand and tail simultaneously, saying goodbye.

"Are you two close?" Vega asks Iris.

"Yeah! Raemond is in my book club. We read a lot of smut together," Iris says without an ounce of shame. It's kind of amazing how much she's unapologetically herself.

My mom is sneakily trying to take pictures as the three of us are talking, when my dad starts the car. "Come on Ilona, we've got to get home to decorate the tree for Gratefulness Dinner. We only have a few days to prepare the house," he shouts.

"Coming, dear."

She gives Iris and I wet, sloppy kisses on the cheek before hopping into dad's car. *Ick.*

Iris drove herself here, and she gives us a small wave before jumping into her own vehicle. "See ya in a couple days, love birds."

We hop into the car, and Vega looks at me with fervor in her eyes. She leans over my body, her arm hovering above me as she locks my car door, and then grabs my face in her hand and kisses me.

The kiss deepens before I break from it. What is she doing? "Vega, we're in public."

"Did we not just see a half-demon bent over reading smut?" Vega asks, and I stifle a laugh.

"Yes, but there are children who come here, Vega."

"Ugh, fine. You're right." Vega gives me a look, one eyebrow raised. "Smoothies?"

"A smoothie sounds great right now."

The next morning, I was slow to wake, slow to get up, and slow to start the day. Vega and I spent hours in bed snuggling, watching a Christmas movie from every millennium of humanity. We started with the 1900s, and went all the way up until recently, which ended with a movie about a satyr and a cambion falling in love over the holidays.

I didn't ask Vega to take a photo with me this week, mostly because I didn't want to have something to stare at late at night when I'm missing her in the weeks after this trip. I don't want to wallow in what could be. I did, however, sneak a photo of her with Momiji and Freja resting on both of her shoulders. It's from the back, and it's a little blurry, but it's mine. My little keepsake.

I flip to my texts with the Unholy Trilogy and type away as Vega uses the bathroom.

INDIGO

Can someone remind me of why I like my job more than I like Vega?

DAHLIA

Because it pays your bills!! And you get to work with Alitha doing fun magic stufffff?

INDIGO

Yeah...

ALITHA

I'm not sure you do.

INDIGO

:/

twelve

VEGA

Indigo has been brushing her teeth for *six* minutes. I don't know what kind of anxious state she's in, but I think her brain is convinced the more she brushes, the less likely it is that dinner will go poorly.

If anyone ever made me feel this bad, I would probably punch them in the face, I lie to myself. In reality, I'd just block their number. But Indigo, as kind hearted as she is, remains in contact with everyone that hurts her. She's *too* kind. I don't know much about Indie's dating history, but I can imagine if one of her awful exes came knocking on her door asking for help, she'd let them right in too.

I admire it though, really. When my mother and little brother passed away, my father died along with them. He gave up on me when I needed him most. I could never see Indigo doing that to her family, not even to Iris. As much as the two seem to have issues, I truly believe Indigo would do anything for her sister if it came down to it.

"Indigo, we've got to get going. Dinner is in less than an hour," I say into the crack of the bathroom door.

"I'm coming." Indigo's words are muffled and coated with toothpaste. "Wait in the kitchen for me."

I head into the kitchen, leaning against the island as I adjust my suspenders. I'm clad in solid black, dress pants and top with suspenders and loafers. I look... really fucking good. I hear the pitter patters of what is either Indigo's footsteps or my heart. Maybe both. Typically, I don't get anxious or nervous, but whatever I'm experiencing now is something similar—*butterflies*—as I wait for Indigo to enter the room.

Damn. Besides that time she borrowed my sweater, this is the first I've ever seen her in any color other than black. A deep green velvet, the dress cuts low on her petite chest. Embossed with roses, it's absolutely gorgeous. There's a sort of twisted wrap effect to it, pulling at her hips, accentuating their curve. Indigo is lean-but-hippy, and it shows off her frame well. It's stunning—*she's* stunning.

Mouth agape, I stare at her in awe.

"Well, don't act so shocked," she says. "You make it seem like I look unkempt most of the time."

"I've just never seen you wear anything other than black."

"Oh." She twirls in the dress, showing off. "Green is my favorite color."

I thought it was purple. "Since when?"

"Since you."

Our eyes meet, and there's so much unsaid between us. Her words have implications; they give me hope. I still have a chance at changing our fate.

As we pull up to the Watson house, it's different this time. The eaves and gables of the roof are lined with bright white Christmas lights, and the yard is covered in decorative blow-up snowmen. I can't tell if we're about to walk into a Christmas movie or a Christmas catastrophe. I'm hoping for the former.

Indigo interlocks her fingers with mine as we walk inside. The door swings open to Iris, who invites us in. She's smiling wide, like she always does, and I realize how different she is from Indigo and their mother. Indigo is happy and bubbly, but there's a hesitation in her voice and movements at times. The anxiety leaks out of her, and, while it's endearing, it's also clear that it hurts her. Similarly, there's a sadness in Mrs. Watson. Her smiles don't seem to reach her eyes. But Iris doesn't come across this way. There's no anxiety or melancholia bubbling at the surface. If she has any, she must keep it locked deep down, like I do.

Inside the living room is the pine we picked out together the other day, now covered in lights and ornaments. A few are clearly from when Indigo and Iris were children, and I can't help but stop and stare at the white-haired child with big purple eyes in some of the photos. She was always adorable.

“Come sit at the table, everyone; dinner's almost ready,” Mrs. Watson shouts from the kitchen. There’s a cinnamon smell coming from her direction, and it’s enticing me to want whatever she’s cooking. I’m practically drooling, I’m so hungry.

We all walk into the dining room and take our seats. Indigo’s father is dressed up, just as we are, but Iris didn’t get the memo. She’s in an oversized anime t-shirt and a black mini-skirt. To each their own, but I can’t imagine wearing something like that in front of my own father. I’d receive a lecture, even at twenty-eight.

“Did you get Mom anything for Christmas yet?” Iris whispers to Indigo, who is seated next to me.

“Not yet; why?” Indigo whispers back.

“I was thinking we could go halfsies and get her and Dad a cruise.”

Indigo stares at their father, then back at Iris. “Dude?”

Iris rolls her eyes. “He already knows. The surprise is for Mom, dip-ass.”

I try not to interject their sisterly bickering, though it pains me. I guess it’s something I’ll never understand.

“So, Vega, tell me about your job,” Mr. Watson inquires.

My job? Fucking hell, they don’t know I work at Augury. Job—what did we say I do? I have zero memory. Play it cool, Vega. “Well, I get to use my magic quite often.”

“Oh really? How so?” he asks.

I remember my conversation with Indigo. Her parents can’t know that I work at Augury, but I need to impress her mother with my magic... but what did we decide I do? “It really comes in handy. Of course, anyone can work in almost any field, but my magic definitely makes it easier for me.”

I’m an idiot. I really just mage-splained the usefulness of magic to a human married into a magical family. Jeez. I’ve never been off my game more than today.

“Not to be weird, but I’ve always wondered this. Do people’s sweat make the equipment fall apart faster?” he asks, and I blanch. Sweat? Equipment? Did we tell them I design sex toys for a living?

“I’m not sure,” I say, seeking an out from this conversation. By the looks of Iris’ tongue sticking out and Indigo’s snarl, I’d say they’re still getting into it with one another.

“With a body like yours, I’m sure your customers believe you know what you’re doing,” he says. “You’ll have to give me pointers sometime. As you can see, I’m rusty.”

That’s... so incredibly perverted. And strange. Why would he say that? Indigo is so lucky that I adore her, because otherwise I’d walk out.

"I—"

"Yeah!" Iris interrupts. "I never really thought Indigo would be into a muscle mommy, but here we are."

Muscle mommy? *Oh.* I really am an idiot.

"Who better to design gym equipment than an expert at working out?" Indigo says with a grin, leaning closer to me.

I have never been so embarrassed in my life. I'm so flustered, I think my ancestors on Barac can feel it in the past. If my skin weren't green, it would be flushed bright red right now.

"Everything okay?" Indigo whispers, her lips brushing against my ear.

"Just peachy," I say and place a hand on her thigh. I can never tell her about this, she wouldn't let me live it down.

"Dinner's ready," Mrs. Watson says jovially, carrying a tray with one hand, while using her magic to carry in the others. All at once plates come down onto the table. There's turkey, mashed potatoes, salad, and even lasagne.

Mr. Watson cuts into the meat, passing it around the table until everyone's plate is full of food. I love food, and as excited I am to eat all of this, I can't help wondering where the cinnamon scent went.

"I'm so glad you could join us, Vega, truly," Mrs. Watson starts. I can visibly see Indigo tense up at the statement. "Sometimes we worry that Indigo and Iris won't find love, but I'm happy to see she's having some success in her romantic life."

"Huh?" Worried for what? They're both beautiful, both young, and both successful. How would Indigo or Iris have any problems dating?

"Indie hasn't had a serious partner since undergrad. You're the first person she's brought home to us in years," Mrs. Watson shares, and my heart throbs.

First person she brings home, and it's not even real. Well, it's real to me, just maybe not to her.

"Iris has never really had an interest in anyone." Mr. Watson frowns. "At least not anyone real."

"Why would I set myself up to be disappointed? Fictional men are better anyways," Iris jokes, but I get the sense that she's not exactly kidding.

"As you can see, they're both worrisome," Mrs. Watson says and takes a big bite of turkey.

I think the problem I have with people like Mrs. Watson is that Indigo and Iris don't need to find love. I want them to, especially Indigo, if that's what they want, but it's not required. You can live a full life without romance.

Without sex. Everyone's needs and desires are different, and it's weird of her to push her personal expectations onto her daughters.

Mrs. Watson flicks her wrist, and Christmas music starts to play. Some recently released popular Christmas melody comes on, and the singers take it away. Indigo stares at me, completely frozen, until I snap my fingers in front of her eyes.

Coming out of it, she shakes her head. "Sorry, I was thinking about those Christmas carolers."

"Christmas carolers, are you talking about the group that walks around Main Street? I've been thinking about joining them. Maybe next year," Mrs. Watson shares, and I take a bite of lasagne. The flavors are rich, and I'm glad, because I was about to open my mouth when I shouldn't.

"Of course," Indigo says. "You would join the most annoying group known to man."

"C'mon, Indie, you and I both know the most annoying group ever was that craft club Mom ran when I was in middle school," Iris shares.

"Craft club?" I ask.

"It was an arts club." Mrs. Watson crosses her arms, appearing humorless.

"They really created art. One time, Mom cut our sandwiches to look like dinosaurs." Iris laughed. "Except mine fell apart—"

"And mine looked like a dick. Everyone made fun of me, and I had a panic attack and went home crying." Though Indigo is sharing something that sounds awful, her smile and laughter is genuine, which warms my heart. I've been a little afraid to joke about trauma with her, but she seems to be opening up to it.

Mr. Watson scratches the back of his neck. "I had to pick her up early from school that day. I couldn't understand why she was crying until she showed me my wife's dick sandwiches."

"Alright, alright. Thanks a lot, Emilio. I get it; I'm terrible at arts and crafts," Mrs. Watson says, her tone defeated.

This is a normal amount of family drama. A healthy amount. I hope all of Indigo's future Gratefulness Dinner's are like this, and I hope I get to see them....

"Did you guys know that although Gratefulness Week is a tradition the satyrs brought over from their planet, humans used to celebrate a similar holiday called Thanksgiving Day?" Mr. Watson shares.

"Yeah, but wasn't it like... a colonizer holiday? Or like, it had some kind of awful origin story," Iris says.

I shrug. I actually don't know. I've never heard of 'Thanksgiving.'

"Yeah, the origins were definitely not favorable. The holiday, alongside the Fourth of July, were pretty much wiped away with The Convergence, especially since Turtle Island and Abya Yalla came together to form The Americas," Indigo explains. I love her brain.

"Well, then I'm glad the satyr holiday took over. It's a whole week long too! Which is great. A nice break from school and work for everyone," Mr. Watson says. Indigo makes a funny face, but I think she decides to let it go once her mom gets up.

"Who wants apple pie?" Mrs. Watson offers, and I just about leap out of my seat.

"Before dessert, let's all share something we're grateful for." Mr. Watson looks around the room, and there's a plethora of reactions. I probably look like I want to strangle the man, Indigo is a polite-neutral, and Iris is beaming.

"I'll start," he says. "I'm grateful for my beautiful wife and our two lovely daughters."

There's a pang in my chest. I wonder if my father is thinking of me.

"I'm grateful for fanfiction, chocolate peanut butter cups, and wifi," Iris says. "Oh, and my... magical discovery."

Mrs. Watson looks full of pride. "I'm grateful for Iris, who has stopped cancer from coming back after it goes into remission." She takes a deep breath. "And for Indigo, who is making her own discoveries at her own pace."

Can this woman say one nice thing without making it a slight against her poor daughter?

"What about you, Vega?" Mr. Watson asks.

That's too easy. "I'm grateful for apple pie and Indigo Watson."

thirteen

INDIGO

The ferry home is a quiet trip. I lean my back against Vega, whose arms wrap around me as we silently watch the sunset at the edge of the waters. The sky is a bright red, and I recall the old adage my dad used to say to me. *Red sky morning, sailor's warning; red sky night, sailor's delight.*

I've missed home. On Octopus Island, the stars aren't visible. There's too many lights everywhere. But on Magia? Almost every star in the sky can be seen, especially in the Illusionary Jungle. I'm glad to be back, truly, but the reality dawns on me that our week of holidating is over. We can't remain lovers, so are we friends? Does she just become my boss now? I thought I was getting her out of my system, but now that feels like the furthest thing from the truth. I'm addicted to her.

Images of every scenario possible flash through my mind. The two of us dating, only to be caught and forced to break up. Dean Bariel finding out and firing me—firing Vega. There are a hundred terrible ways this could all play out.

Exiting the ferry, we head towards the parking garage in tense silence. Once you give so much of yourself to someone, it's hard to reel it back in.

I pop open my trunk, and Vega places my suitcase inside.

I face away from V. I can't look her in the eyes right now. "I guess I'll see you at work tomorrow," I say, not wanting to let the emotions out. If I say anything more, I might tumble down like a house of cards.

She grabs me by the hips and gracefully spins me around, pulling me close. Our lips collide, and I allow my muscles to relax, my body melting into hers.

Vega takes her mouth off mine, but keeps her hands on my waist.

"We're not done," she says quietly. It's not a warning, but a promise.

"Vega, the university's policy—"

"I know the policy, Indigo. I'm not saying we should break the rules, I'm just reminding you that we agreed to holidate, which is not dating. We're simply each other's plus ones for this holiday season."

My forehead creases as I try to wrap my brain around her implications. "So, what now? Gratefulness week is over."

"And it's going to be December," she interrupts me. "Christmas and Jul and Winter Solstice—all of the best holidays—are coming. I went on a whole trip for your holidate, allow me one holidate of my own."

"You want one date?"

"*Holidate*," she corrects me. "I want one final hoorah. You said you needed to get me out of your system. Let me course through it properly, first."

"Okay," I agree, because she's right. This week did *not* get her out of my system, but maybe we just weren't trying hard enough. I'm deluding myself into thinking one last date, or fuck, might just do the trick. My mind spins through everything that could go wrong again, but I shove that feeling back down. "When?"

"Saturday?" she suggests, and I nod.

"Saturday."

We have to unloop our familiar's, who are wrapped around one another, refusing to separate, before saying goodbye. Her tusks brush against my skin as she kisses my forehead and then turns back to her car.

Unlocking the front door, Momiji and I enter the house, my suitcase heavy in my arms, but not as heavy as my heart feels. I fumble with my keys, almost dropping my bag, but use my magic to stop it from hitting the floor. My body is exhausted; this past week was a mess. Between my mother's mood swings and the lack of permanence between Vega and I, I think this little vacation only made me feel worse about everything. And I can't forget about Iris. I still feel like we haven't resolved anything either.

Slouching on the couch, I get out my phone to text the Unholy Trilogy.

INDIGO

Just got home!

I turn on the TV as I wait for their reply. Momiji flies over to me, his white fluffy body in contrast with the dark purple of the sofa, and we snuggle up to one another.

Ping.

DAHLIA

How was it?

INDIGO

Eh. My mother was having a really rough day the first time we saw them, but everything was fine for the most part.

DAHLIA

What kind of rough day??

INDIGO

She was kinda a bully :/

DAHLIA

I'm sorry, Watson. I'll kick her ass if you want.

INDIGO

I wish, lol.

ALITHA

How was Dr. Daelor?

DAHLIA

OHYMGOD don't call her that.

INDIGO

She was great. Toooooooo great. We're going on one final date this Saturday.

ALITHA

Sure you are.

It really will be the final date. I have to draw a line in the sand, I can't lose my fucking job over a hot woman. A brilliant, emotionally intelligent, wonderful fucking woman... but still.

This week is finals week at Augury University, and I can't help but wonder how my students are going to do. I taught history during grad school, and, while the students did well, this is my first year as an adjunct where I'm also teaching charms.... If I'm being honest with myself, I don't feel very confident in the subject. I've always been better with potions, as crazy as that sounds. I try not to dwell on the past more than my silly brain already requires, but sometimes I regret not majoring in potions. I think if my mother was going to be disappointed in me no matter what, I could have at least made it count.

My eyes flutter until they close, and my mind drifts into darkness.

Crash.

What the fuck was that?

My body flings itself off the couch, and I race towards the kitchen, where I find nothing. Coming back into the living room, I finally see it. There's broken glass on the floor behind the couch, liquid coating the floor. Momiji is sprawled across my potion shelf with not one fuck to give.

"Why would you knock off one of my potions? You're lucky that was one that's easy to reproduce," I say in a stern voice.

Momiji moves his foot towards another potion, and I move to grab at him. His wings shoot out, pushing potions over in their wake, and he flies around the room. I somehow manage to catch three potions, the fourth stopped mid-fall by my magic. What a little shit. Did I do something to piss him off? He must be hungry or something...

Putting the potions back on the shelf, I cross towards the kitchen where I open the fridge and get out the carrots. We're almost out, and some of the lettuce looks bad. I'll have to go grocery shopping after work tomorrow. I place a carrot onto my cutting board and reach for the knife drawer. Turning back, Momiji is seated in front of me, one potion between his paws.

"What is your problem?" I shout in frustration, and the sugar rabbit makes a pouty face at me. "Do you want to drink the potion or something?"

He shakes his head.

"Do you... want me to work on my potions more?"

Momiji nods, and I get a little choked up. Even my familiar can feel how much the path I've chosen is draining on me. He probably just wants me to do what makes me happy. My magic and life force and Momiji's are directly connected. I don't think he feels my feelings, but I know he feels my exhaustion. He knows that charms doesn't come naturally to me, and he likely wants me to practice potions just as much as I do.

I scoop him up and put him over my shoulder, hugging him closely to my chest. Maybe we're both exhausted.

Ping.

I check my phone to see a text from my dad.

DAD

It was really nice seeing you this past week. Don't be a stranger. Love u.

INDIGO

It was nice to see you too, love you.

However complicated my family can be, it really was nice to see them. Maybe next time my mother will show me more kindness. As it stands, I only visit home for Gratefulness Week. Iris visits during Christmas, Spring Break, random days over the summer. I know, because my mother gloats to me about it, trying to use it to make me feel guilty for not visiting more often. I wish she'd stop to think that maybe I'd visit more if I felt more welcome there—that maybe it's her that keeps me away.

As I start to doze off again, my mind is a maze of emotion. I try to tether myself to reality, that I need to focus on my job, bettering my relationship with my family, and maintaining my friendships, but I am so attached to my dreams. Dreams of working with potions everyday, of coming home to a girlfriend, maybe even one day a wife, and her having green skin. Green skin... and black hair... and a septum piercing... and a tattoo of her favorite constellation. If a shooting star flung itself across the sky right now, that is what I'd wish for.

Beep. Beep. Beep.

What the fuck is that awful sound? Oh right, my alarm.

Beep. Beep. Beep.

My eyes will hardly open as I snooze my alarm for the third time. Wait, third time? Oh shit... it's Monday. I have work today.

fourteen

INDIGO

I've always hated Mondays, but this Monday feels different. There's a tension in the air, with students buzzing about the school preparing for finals, but there's also a note of excitement. It's subtle—the early Christmas gifts exchanged between friends and the cookies for Hanukkah. Though some of the staff will be here during the break between fall and spring semester, the students will not, so many of them celebrate their holidays early.

Being such a young teacher has its ups and downs. It's annoying to constantly get mistaken for a student—and I believe some mages and staff members take me less seriously—but overall, it's a blessing. I relate to my students on a level many of the other professors won't understand, because I was literally one of them a few years ago in undergrad. And even just last year, I was attending Augury for grad school. Many of the professors here went to other universities around the world. For people like Adeib and Dean Bariel, regardless of where they attended, it was so long ago it might as well have been another lifetime. So here I stand, grateful I'm recognized in our cafeteria. A perk of being a favored professor of the freshman class is that I get to cut in line.

I'm here because I heard the special dessert of today was cranachan, and it would be an offense to my ancestors if I didn't try some. Composed of cream cheese, oats, raspberries, whip cream, and honey, the Scottish dessert is delectable. I've only had my father's rendition, and he was never the greatest in the kitchen.

My favorite satyr and elf duo, Eden and Raven, let me cut them in the astronomically long line. I usually only see them in my history class, so it's fun to see how they are outside the classroom. They're doing their nails, which amuses me. I never knew there were portable nail kits. I rarely get my nails done, as I've always had too much anxiety about it, scared of all the choices I'd have to make at once. The color, the style. It makes my brain hurt. I turn back around, facing forward.

Emilia, a pink-haired mermaid from one of my charms classes, is in line in front of me. She's not the kind of merfolk that can shift, so she uses a portable tank that runs on magic. The upside of having a tank is that there's room for advertising and decorations. Emilia has decked the backside of her tank with infographics on different political causes she supports, and it amazes me to read them all. Merfolk want their own school, as well as a tubing system so they can swim through Sunspell City without needing a tank. I scan the QR code and sign the petition.

Her phone beeps, and she looks back at me. "Professor Watson? Thank you!"

"Of course," I say, not realizing she'd get an immediate notification.

The line moves quickly, and I get my treat. I snap a picture, meaning to send it to my Dad, but accidentally press Daelor instead. *Shit.*

VEGA

getting a treat?

INDIGO

Yeah. It's sweet, but not as sweet as you!

I want to punch myself in the face the second I send the text. I hope she doesn't reply, because I don't know what I'd say next.

Crossing towards the Potions Tree, I meet Alitha in the lab. Though I'm not a potions professor, I like to play around with them from time to time, working on personal experiments of my own. Alitha and I have been testing some new concepts. I throw the bamboo cup away and put on a pair of gloves. I would've brought a treat for Alitha, but I don't think they make vegan cranachan.

"How close are you to achieving your desired results?" Alitha asks, watching me rip pieces of fabric and pour the potion onto them.

"I'm close. It works on natural fabrics, but not synthetic blends. I think it needs some sort of honey or honey-like element," I say.

Basic potions are easy. Basic potions that get an object to start or stop doing what it already does are the easy part. Other concepts, like permanent alterations that have nothing to do with the object's intended purpose, are much harder. You can use a simple potion to make a carrot round, or a different color, but you'd need a lot more practice to turn a carrot into a cucumber. This potion has taken me *months.* It is anything but basic.

She hands me a bottle of honey, and I pour a generous amount in, mixing the substances. I pour my new concoction onto the synthetic fabric, and the fibers immediately grow together, fixing the rip I had made.

"We fucking did it," I shout, and Alitha gestures for me to quiet down with her hand. She grabs me into a tight hug, holding me against her tall, lean form and I wrap my arms around her.

"*You* did it," she says.

Tuesday and Wednesday go by in a blur of review packets, study halls, and office hours. Despite how busy I am, all I can think about is this weekend.

A few of my students sneak me little gifts and treats. I think, for some of them, they just want to be nice... for others, this is very clearly a bribe that won't help them on their finals.

Just a few more days until my final date with Vega, I think to myself on the drive home. *Just a few more days until it ends.*

With finals happening tomorrow, today we're having a little study party in my History 101 class. All of my students pitched in. Raven and Eden brought punch and chips. Kwon, a masculine cambion, made a holiday-winter playlist with songs like All I Want For Christmas Is You, Frosty the Snowman, Feliz Navidad, and A Moonflower Solstice. Everyone wants to study in different ways. Many brought textbooks, flashcards, and even tablets.

"What if I put on a game? It'll quiz you about our history, and whoever wins will get ten points of extra credit," I say.

"Yes," shouts two of my students at once. I look over to see Wren, an androgynous-looking cambion, and Zinnia, a feminine satyr, jump out of their seats.

Wren and Zinnia are polar opposites. Wren is thin with red skin and long straight white hair and seems to prefer darkness. From their fluffy sweater, to their mini-skirt and lace-up combat boots, everything is pitch black. Even the curved horns on the top of their head are onyx. Zinnia, on the other hand, is like a cloud. Her skin is a light tan, her hair a sage green, and her clothes pastel pink. She's much more curvaceous, with softer lines to her figure. Somehow, through all their opposition, I always see them together, even outside my classroom.

"Get out your devices then," I say with a smile.

Frantically, Wren and Zinnia get out their phones and swiftly join the game while the other students type their names at a normal page. Zinnia taps her foot, impatient as we wait for everyone to get logged in. It's loud—too loud—but I don't say anything. She's just really competitive.

"Could you please quit tapping? It's vexatious at best," Wren says to Zinnia, who crosses her arms.

"Buttercup, I do what I want—and I want to win," Zinnia has a soft, southern accent as speaks. Her voice is somehow sweet yet... there's a sinister note to it. Why is she making such a big deal out of this game?

"What is their deal?" I ask a few students sitting in row behind them.

"I don't know, but they're like this in *every* class," a serpentine, whose name I *think* is Alya, says. Another student rolls his eyes, clearly annoyed at the two. I would find it annoying if it wasn't so entertaining. It's like watching two cats fight.

"Wren, Zinnia, you know this is just for fun, right?" I ask.

"It is most certainly not," Wren says. "You offered ten points extra credit to the winner. If I'm going to be number one and beat Zinnia, I need those points."

Oh gosh... should I have offered candy instead?

The game begins and everyone seems to be having fun—everyone but Zinnia and Wren, who have furious looks on their faces as they type away. They keep trading first and second place, and I have no idea who will come out on top. They're equally brilliant.

Anxiety fills me as I consider what could happen next. What if one of them wins and it causes the other one to have a meltdown... couldn't that be bad for their finals? I can prevent this. I sneak Dahlia a text as I watch what might as well be an olympic-level competition. The entire class is half-assing their answers, solely focused on Zinnia and Wren.

INDIGO

Hey, if I send you an answer key, can you sign up for this game? It's on qahoot.earth, code is 14157.

DAHLIA

Heyyyy Watson. Yeah I can do that but like why?

INDIGO

Long story. Trying to prevent a meltdown in one of my classes. Answer key is: CCDABCDDBAA.

DAHLIA

Gotcha, on it.

Someone with the username HumanGirlyy joins the game, and I know it's Dahlia. Quickly, she pushes Wren into second place and Zinnia into third, claiming first by the end.

"Who is human girly?" Zinnia says with a kind of rage I didn't know was possible. Her vibrant eyes are now violent.

Wren crosses their arms. "I would have won anyway, so just sit down."

"Anyone want to claim human girly?" I ask the class, but everyone shakes their head no. Perfect, just as I had hoped. "It must've been a bot. Sorry, Wren, maybe if you have me next semester."

"I'm a charms minor, so I think I'll have you for one class," they say, running their fingers through their long white strands.

"What did you say?" Zinnia says, and their rivalry is starting to make sense. I don't think either of them have any other friends, so maybe this is the way they developed a friendship—through competition.

"I'm a charms minor?"

"No, I'm a charms minor," Zinnia says, as if only one of those can be the truth.

"It's not mutually exclusive," I say. "You can both get a minor in charms."

"Okay, but we can't both be number one," Wren says with fervor. "That *is* mutually exclusive."

An elfborn human stands and walks over to the speaker, turning the music up so loud that I can no longer hear Wren and Zinnia argue. I'm going to miss this group of freshmen, just maybe not all the arguing.

On the drive home Friday afternoon, Momiji curls up in the passenger seat, snoozing away. My students all did fantastic on their finals; I only had to fail one girl, but she skipped nearly every class... that's not my fault.

I'm excited for the much needed break from classes, from responsibility. Unfortunately, Dr. Lothiel requested I plan our legendary Augury University Christmas Party. It's not technically a Christmas party, as we encompass many holidays, but it might as well be with the amount of Christmas lights and spiked eggnog there is every year, as told to me by Alitha.

I'm the one running it; I want it to be next level epic, but I'm also afraid. What if it sucks and someone else gets to do it next year? Or what if I'm so amazing at planning it becomes my new responsibility?

I decide to turn off that part of my brain to the best of my abilities and just listen to the soft violin playing through my radio. Tomorrow is my date with Vega, and I'm going to allow myself to enjoy it. I deserve this, and so does she. *Just one last time,* I tell myself. I'm not sure I'm very convincing.

fifteen

INDIGO

It's finally Saturday. Having spent the entire week trying to ignore how quickly this day was coming up, nervous energy still tumbles around in my belly. Vega had texted me telling me to dress for the cold, so dress for the cold I do.

Pulling my tight black pants up my legs, I pick out a purple long sleeve top to go with it and put it on over my head, tucking the bottom into the pants. I decide to keep my makeup light, topped with a glossy black lipstick. The final touch to complete the look? A long scarf. I yank on my boots and tuck a pair of gloves into my purse, alongside all the other goodies I have stuffed in there. Emergency potions, chapstick, mints—you name it.

Ring.

The doorbell. Already? I open the door to find exactly what I expected. Vega. She's wearing tight black pants as well with a form-fitting jacket in a fuschia color. We practically match, and I giggle with excitement. Blowing a kiss towards Momiji, I shut the door.

"Where to?" I ask. I want to know what we're doing so bad, but she insisted it be a surprise.

"Boca Raton," she informs me. "But first, this." V gets out a black piece of fabric and moves behind me, wrapping the fabric around my head, blindfolding me. I feel my face flush as she takes me by the hand and escorts me to her car.

It feels like we've been driving forever. I know it's only been an hour or so, but without knowing where we are, time moves strangely. There's Christmas music playing over the radio, and I listen as Vega quietly sings along. She's actually kind of good, which only adds to my long list of reasons I find her attractive.

V's hand rests on my leg, and I suddenly wish I had worn shorts so I could feel the warmth of her skin against mine. Her cologne—perfume—whatever it is... it's woodsy, with hints of cinnamon and peppermint, and it goes with the energy of the day. It's really December.

The car comes to a stop, and I move to remove my blindfold when Vega stops me. "Not yet," she says. "First, we've got to walk for a few minutes."

She gets out of the car and opens my door, taking me by the hand, leading me to who knows where. There's Christmas music playing, and I can hear the bustle of a crowd in the near distance.

"Vega, can I take this thing off now?"

"Yes."

Untying the blindfold, I look up to see Vega smiling down at me, but when she moves, my mouth opens in awe. There's a colossal fucking snow globe behind her. A small-theme-park-sized snow globe. *Holy shit.*

"How? What is this?" I ask, shock still lingering on my face.

"It's called Winter Wonderland. A bunch of illusionary mages got together and designed a theme park that feels like you're inside a snow globe. Let's go inside," she says, interlocking our fingers and leading me to the entrance.

There's a door on one side of the base, and a cambion dressed as one of Santa's helpers takes our ticket stubs. Entering the park, it's ethereal. Bright white and pastel Christmas lights are everywhere. A tiny snowflake falls onto my shoulder, and I turn to Vega, the corners of my mouth ticking upward.

"There's snow?"

She grins wide. "That was the big reason I wanted to bring you here. I know it's not real snow, but—"

"It's perfect," I interrupt. "Just perfect. I've never seen snow, real or fake, so it doesn't make a difference to me." This is one of the sweetest gestures anyone has ever made towards me, and I could just about cry if I weren't filled with so much joy.

I've never really gone out with anyone who showed me this much kindness. Terranova and I never dated, as he caught feelings for my sister instead of me. Thomas, my only long term partner, broke up with me after being accepted to a trade school in The Americas. There was Amber. And Walnut. And Mai. But those were all short college flings. Sexy and meaningless. This is the first connection I've felt in years, and however fleeting it might be, it's real.

"Have you ever been ice skating?" Vega asks, and I scrunch my nose.

"I've been a few times, but just at one of those skating rinks in a mall, nothing fancy."

We cross towards the rink, which is interesting. It's as if a frozen lake and a skating rink had a baby. It's outside in the open air, but there's a glass wall with a railing surrounding it. There are couples skating around, and mothers with their children. There's even a faun spinning and performing jumps.

Walking up to the counter, a centaur wearing a bright green polo greets us with a mustache-covered smile. "Greetings, I'm Larry with Winter Wonderland. How can I help you two lovely ladies?"

"We'd like to go skating. Can we rent two pairs?" Vega asks, tone jovial and polite. Her hair is down, but she pushed all of it to one side so it looks like half her head is shaved. I stare at her long, pretty strands.

"What size?"

"Size eleven and size... five?" she says, though she doesn't sound confident.

"Close. I'm a six," I correct her.

"That'll be twelve dabloons."

Vega puts her phone against the reader, and it beeps, accepting her e-payment. The man goes over to the shelf and picks up two pairs of skates, one black and one white, and hands them over to us. Sitting on a nearby bench, we put them on. I wore fluffy white socks, and the tops hang over the skates.

Vega pulls out her gloves, and I do the same, excited to skate with her. I've never been super into ice skating. Iris really enjoyed roller skating; she was on a derby team when we were kids. Me? I tended to prefer things that didn't have high chances of me falling on my ass. Skating with Vega would be different though.

Getting onto the ice, I'm a little wobbly, rocking back and forth to try and not fall. Vega, on the other hand, is smooth as silk, gliding beside me. She takes me by the hand and helps me balance. At first, I'm completely leaning against her, but after a while, we only have to hold hands.

I look into Vega's golden eyes. "Can I make a confession?"

"Always."

"When I was a kid, I was super jealous of the girls who could do skating and dance tricks. I was never talented or flexible enough, and of course I never trained hard enough for it because for so many others it came so naturally."

"I'm sorry, little rabbit. Do you want to try a trick right now?" she asks, and I blanche.

"I don't think that's a good idea."

"Sure it is. Trust me, I'll charm your skates."

Vega pulls me in close and lifts me from my hips. Without any work, my legs lift up and swing back, and it feels like I'm flying beside her. When she puts me down, she keeps control of my skates so that I safely land.

We skate around some more until our legs grow tired, and Vega pulls me over to the sidelines. "Do you want to go get a bite to eat?"

I nod, my stomach growling. "It's a little late to be grabbing lunch, so maybe there won't be a huge line?" I say.

"Huge line or no line, doesn't matter to me. We've got all day."

We get off the ice and trade the skates for our boots.

"I think there's a restaurant on the other side, let's head there," Vega says.

We walk through the park, passing a group of Christmas carolers. There are children taking photos with a man dressed as Santa Claus, and a performer is juggling toys. There are smaller rides, and lots of little stands with snack food.

"Are you sure you don't want to just get something from one of the stands?" I ask.

"No, let's go inside and sit down. There's something I want you to try," she insists, and so I follow.

We get to a building which looks like an actual gingerbread house. The roof is lined with fake icing, and there are people-sized gumdrops sticking out of the top. A hostess wearing a candy cane-esque dress brings us to our table and hands us two menus. As we wait for our waitress, Vega holds the menus, not handing one over, and I look at her funny.

"Can I look at the menu?"

"Nope," she says and winks.

I want to be mad, want to demand she hand it over, but I'm not. It's super sexy when she does stuff like this, and so far, I've never been disappointed with the results.

Our waitress comes over, and she looks like a Christmas tree. Her green dress has light up bulbs that sparkle as she walks. "What can I get you two?"

"We'll have the hot chocolate flight, an order of the Christmas charcuterie board, and a large side of sweet potato fries. Oh, and two waters, please,"

Vega says with more confidence than I've ever mustered in my life. I have a tendency to stutter and mumble when I order food; anxiety really is a bitch.

"Thank you," I whisper as the waitress takes our menu and walks away.

When she returns, she's got a tray with two waters and a piece of wood covered with mugs full of hot chocolate. Prior to today, I'd only heard of flights of beer and liquor. She places everything on the table, and I notice each mug has a label in front of it. Peppermint. Dark Chocolate Raspberry. Caramel. Cinnamon. S'mores. It all sounds so good.

"Which one do you want to try first?"

"Hmm. I'm not a big fan of caramel. The rest all sound so good, you pick," I say.

Vega picks up a spoon and dips it into the whip cream, then the cinnamon hot chocolate. She places one hand under my chin, and I open my mouth, allowing her to place it on my tongue. The richness of the cinnamon mixed with the chocolate is delectable, and I can't help but make a little sound of appreciation.

"I usually hear that sound in a different context," V says, and I snort. I touch my nose, shocked that hot chocolate isn't coming out of it.

We take turns feeding spoons full of hot chocolate to one another, and I'm incredibly grateful to be in this moment. Partially because of how wonderful this moment is, but also partially because we must look incredibly cringey and love-stricken in this moment, draped over the table, romantically sharing a flight of hot chocolate. This is like something out of one of those bad Christmas romance movies my sister would watch every year. I love it. I'm the main fucking character—I might as well move to an abandoned farm and try to revive it by selling Christmas trees with the help of the town's mysterious sexy lesbian lumberjack, Dr. Vega Daelor.

When our food arrives, everything is perfect. One half of the charcuterie board is meats, crackers, and cheeses. The other half is pumpkin bars, sugar cookies, and peppermint bark. Vega stuffs her face with meat and cheese, while I wholly consume the sweet potato fries. The vibes here are immaculate, and I feel like I'm in Christmas heaven.

After we finish eating and pay, Vega takes me outside. The snow is falling harder now, and there's a big field with piles of it to the left of us.

"Can we build a snowman?" I ask, and the childlike grin that spreads across her face is priceless.

"Of course we fucking can."

sixteen

VEGA

I BEGIN WORKING ON THE BODY OF THE SNOWMAN, WHILE INDIGO COLLECTS STICKS and rocks to form its arms and legs. We should've saved a sweet potato fry for his nose, but we'll figure something out. As we work on our masterpiece, Indigo seems to take notice with a couple walking by.

"Shit. Uh—Vega—I... that's Malik," Indigo whispers.

"Malik Hills, as in our coworker?" I ask.

"Yes, let's go." She grabs me by the sleeve of my jacket, dragging me towards some bushes.

My pants get caught on a branch, and as she pulls me forward, they rip. It's nothing crazy, but I can feel the chill air on my thigh now. We huddle on the ground behind a bush as Malik and his girlfriend walk by. I didn't even know he had a girlfriend. She's cute—clearly a faunborn—and they pass us quickly, holding hands and kissing one another.

"I ripped my pants," I say, showing her the tear in the fabric. She opens her purse and digs out a small vial.

"I don't know why, but I just knew this would come in handy," she says as she pours some of the liquid onto my pants, the fibers instantly growing back into themselves.

"You're fucking with me," I say aloud. Where did she get that? Magical potions can't be mass produced because nobody has enough magic to do so. If you have a magic potion, it's either because you made it yourself, or you were gifted it from someone else. "Did Alitha give that to you?"

"No actually," Indigo starts. "I made it. It's one of the main projects I've been working on."

"That's amazing," I say, grabbing her head between my hands and kissing her on the forehead. "You're amazing, Indigo."

"Thank you. Also, I think we're safe to get up now," she says, and I help her stand. "What's the next plan, Dr. Daelor?"

I almost blush every time she calls me that. She's the only one that has that effect on me. "Well, we're going to watch a movie on the lawn, but that's not for a couple more hours...."

"And?"

I clear my throat. I'm not nervous, it's more like excitement bubbling within me. "I heard there's a part of the park that's closed off for construction."

"Closed off like... nobody will be over there?" Indigo's cheeks flush.

"Precisely, little rabbit," I whisper. "Because the noises you make should be for me and me alone."

We move towards the back of the park where they're working on a small theater, as well a mini-Christmas village. Passing through the small cottages that presumably belong to Santa's helpers, I dip my head as we enter one that looks more complete. Once we're both inside, I realize there's nothing here except a few tools on the floor and a little portable heater. Perfect.

I shrug off my jacket, placing it on the floor. Indigo looks up at me with those big violet eyes, and I can barely help myself. Shoving her against the wall, my head ducked down into the crook of her neck, I kiss her soft skin as I use my knee to create friction, right where she likes it.

"Vega," she moans out as I suck on her throat.

Indigo takes one finger and pushes it underneath my jaw, bringing me into a kiss. Our tongues collide, and I keep rubbing my knee, doing my best to make sure I'm hitting her clit through her pants. She whimpers, kissing me harder before going silent. She shudders with release and pushes me back with an undeniable force that I've never seen from her. "Oh, what is this? Do you think you're in control?" I ask, licking my teeth and tusks.

Indigo wraps her leg around me and kicks the back of my leg, toppling us down to the ground. Now on top of me, she grins as hard as she's blushing. "No, but I can sure try. Let me give you what you want." Her voice is like a plea—like a song, and I give in. I'd give her anything she asked for, even my heart.

She wriggles my pants completely off, and I shimmy out of my longsleeve shirt. Pulling off my boxer briefs, Indigo takes in a deep breath before crawling up between my legs, and I rest my back onto the hard ground.

The slow, soft drag of her tongue is simultaneously everything I need, and nowhere close to enough. My leg twitches as she swirls her tongue, dancing it around my clit. My back arches as she digs her fingers into my thighs, further pushing my legs apart.

I love looking down and watching her between my legs. My thighs are strong enough to crush her, and yet like a good little rabbit, she stays there. Perfect prey.

"I want your fingers," I say, voice low with desire. She slowly trails them up towards my swollen lips. "Now." Two fingers gently enter my opening, and as I moan out in pleasure, practically whimpering, she drives them deeper inside me. Thrusting her fingers while sucking on my clit, Indigo gives me everything I could have ever asked for.

But when has she not?

Toppling over the edge, my body twitches as I let out a long, staccato breath.

"Good gir—"

"Don't," I interrupt. "Or I'll stick a vibrator in your panties and control it while we walk around."

"You'd have to have one with you," she teases.

"Who says I don't?"

Once my skin is no longer slick with sweat, we put our clothes back on and exit the construction zone, careful not to be caught as we sneak out the doors, back into the main part of the park. There's a little stand selling popcorn, and I send the man five dabloons for a bucket. The sun is setting in a cotton candy sky, and our fingers intertwine as we make our way to the field. There's a big screen with a projector, and we sit down as the opening scene of Elf comes on.

"Honestly, the main actor looks more like an elf than all of those tiny people. Elves are usually tall," Indigo whispers to where only I can hear.

"Yeah, but the smaller elves remind me more of you," I whisper against her ear. Sometimes Indigo explains elves to me like they aren't the majority of the population of the Isles of Magia. Although it's usually stuff I know, it's still cute to see her so interested in her magical origins. Perhaps I should get to know the human part of me too.

Her eyebrows scrunch, and she frowns for a second before giving out a small giggle. Snuggling up to Indigo, we watch the movie with my arms wrapped around her.

I don't play music on the drive back to Sunspell City. Indigo is curled up in the passenger seat, snoring away. This isn't the last time I'll see her—hell, she's my subordinate; I can see her everyday if I want to, but this is the last time I'll get to be with her.

I have to be the one to end this. She doesn't have the strength to do it. I know that we both value our jobs, I know that we both have feelings for one another, but I think it's too much for her. If I told her to drop it all and go with me to live in The Americas or—or even off-world on fucking Barac, she'd probably go. She wants someone to make that decision for her, but I can't let her.

Indigo allowed someone to control her for her entire life. Her mother was the puppet master, pulling her strings. Indigo went to Augury University and cut those strings, but now she's desperate to hand them over to someone new. I won't let it be me, and I sure as hell won't let it be her mother again.

We stop at a light, and I take a mental snapshot of her cute little body, all huddled up against me as she sleeps somberly. I make note of the sound of her voice. Her laugh. And the look she gives me when she smiles—when she comes. I try to record it all, tuck it into my heart for later. She may not get to be mine in this lifetime, but maybe in another.

Once we're in the city, I drive really slow. I could get ticketed for going this far under the speed limit, but I don't fucking care anymore. All I want is more time, something I'd never valued much until recently. Pulling into her driveway, I stop the car. I don't wake her up... No, not yet. I just brush my finger against the soft skin of her cheek and try not to let out the tear threatening to fall.

Am I really getting teary-eyed over a goodbye with someone I'll see in a few weeks? Man. This screams abandonment issues, doesn't it? A big screw you to anyone who has ever called me a player. Clearly I'm not very good at playing.

I lightly brush Indigo's shoulder, and she makes an eyes-half-closed hand gesture for me to carry her. Getting out of the car, I go over to the passenger's side and scoop her up into my arms.

After entering the house and removing our boots and coats, I lay her down onto her bed, before kissing her cheek and crossing to the door.

"Vega, will you stay with me?" she whispers, voice weak.

I don't know how to say no to her.

Crawling into bed, I snuggle up behind her, basking in her natural scent. Before I know it, she's snoring, and I drift alongside her.

Indigo stirs, barely awake as I give her one last kiss goodbye; her lips are as soft as clouds. I walk over to the door and wave at Momiji, who makes a whimpering noise.

"I know you'll miss Freja, but you can see her at school," I say.

The white little rabbit frowns. Little rabbit—that was Indigo's nickname before I ever knew about her familiar. It truly is like we were meant to be, at least one day. I just wish that day was today.

seventeen

INDIGO

I WAKE TO AN EMPTY BED. NO WARM, GREEN, MUSCLED BODY SLEEPING NEXT TO ME. Just a cold, lonely gap where Vega was. I worried she was going to leave in the middle of the night. I actually didn't expect her to stay, but she did. I need coffee. Walking into the kitchen, I find Momiji moping on the dining room table, staring down at a scrap of paper.

She left a note?

indie,

i care about you so much that i have to say goodbye. be kind to yourself. i am so glad i got to experience this with you, however short it was. thank you. i'll see you around.

-v

It's really over. I mean, it had never truly begun... we always knew this wasn't allowed, that it wouldn't work, but we gave into our whims and desires. She is an obsession. A fixation. I should be able to move on soon, I just need a little time.

What if nobody ever wants me like that? Or what if nobody ever makes me feel that good again? I shake my head, pushing away those thoughts, and wipe the tears that are falling down my face.

It's been a week since I've seen Vega. An entire week without her sultry smile, a week without the deep notes in her voice. Without work to distract me, I've been an anxious mess. I decide to text the Unholy Trilogy.

INDIGO

I am fucking sad, friends.

They both reply instantly.

ALITHA

We know.

DAHLIA

What did you do all day?

INDIGO

...

DAHLIA

Watsonnnn

INDIGO

I cried into a bucket of ice cream.

The next thing I know, I've got an incoming call from Torres.

"Hello?" I pick up.

"Indigo, Alitha, can you hear me?" Dahlia asks.

"I can hear you," Alitha replies.

"I'm here. I can hear you."

"Perfect." Dahlia pauses to take in a deep breath. "This is broken-off-engagement level relationship mourning for a holiday fling. I know you fell hard, but it's get your shit together time, Watson."

As harsh as it is, she's right.

"Why don't we all go out together tomorrow night?" Alitha suggests. "I've got news to share, anyhow. What about that one bar—"

"Not the best idea. That's where they met. Why don't we go to dinner; how's Italian food sound?"

"Perfect," I reply. Besides grocery shopping and long walks with Momiji, I've barely left the house. "Tomorrow at six?"

"Great," Alitha says.

Dahlia makes kissing sounds into the phone before hanging up.

Plans. Alright, now I have plans. At least that'll give me something new to spiral about instead of my forbidden relationship.

I pull up to the restaurant in a sweater dress and tights. They're the kind that look transparent but actually have a fleece lining on the inside. I wonder if they make them in green or red. I've seen them from the fairest white to the deepest brown, but I'm not sure I've seen them for non-human, non-elf skin tones. I wonder if Vega has ever gone to buy a pair.

Dahlia is in an off-the-shoulder, sexy sweater dress with heels, and Alitha in a long white dress that hugs her tightly, with knee-high boots to match.

The three of us walk into the Italian restaurant and every head turns. I know my friends are gorgeous, but damn, even I feel good tonight. The hostess seats us at a booth in the corner; Alitha and Dahlia slide in across from me.

"Okay history person, why do we call it Italian food?" Dahlia asks.

"There's a region in Europa called Italia, named after the country Italy that used to be there. Countries may have disbanded their governments after The Convergence, but most of the cultures are still alive," I explain.

"Oh, so it's like how my mom says we're Puerto Rican and Portuguese, even though those aren't countries anymore, but more so regions within their continents?" Dahlia asks.

"Yeah!" I confirm.

"I guess I'm just confused on why us humans are so obsessed with the past. I feel like most of the magical races don't give a shit about what happened prior to The Convergence," Dahlia says.

The waiter interrupts us to take our orders. Dahlia orders herself and I margaritas. Alitha orders a glass of white wine.

"I think the majority of people without any human blood don't care because Earth prior to The Convergence really has nothing to do with them," I say. "Whereas we're tied to the past through culture, blood, and history."

"See, I try to learn about both Earth's history, as well as Loria," Alitha chimes in.

I smile. "I try to learn everything. I'm like a sponge."

Dahlia grabs a piece of bread and dips it into the olive oil and spices. "Enough about history. Alitha, what's your big news?"

"Laurel Gilbert, Chair of the Potions Department, is leaving Augury University," she says, blue-eyes wide. "And they offered me the position." Alitha's hand moves to cover her mouth. Her nails are white with little blue snowflakes, and they contrast beautifully to the deep brown of her skin.

My jaw practically unhinges itself as I finally process what she just shared. There's a new availability in the Potions Department. Holy shit.

Dahlia looks at us with eyebrows raised. "I was going to say congrats, but you both look concerned. This is a good thing, right? You'll be making way more money."

"And I'll have a lot more responsibility," Alitha shares. "But this also means I'll need to hire my replacement."

A grin spreads across Dahlia's gorgeous face. "You could hire Indigo. That's like her dream!"

Alitha's mouth forms a thin line. "I can't just hire my best friend, there's a whole process involved, and they'd likely accuse me of nepotism."

"Okay, fine. But you should still apply," Dahlia says, looking at me.

"I'll think about it."

We all order pasta and stuff our faces with bread as we wait for our meals to come out. Alitha recommends her new nail tech, and I write the name down, though I'm still unsure I'll ever get the courage to go get mine done. Maybe if someone went with me.

"I have a new client," Dahlia says, her voice full of mystery.

I place my fork on my plate and put my elbows up on the table and rest my head in my hands. "Tell us more."

"She's an elf. Her hair is like twelve feet long, but she usually wears it in a bun," Dahlia shares. "It took me two days to give her highlights and trim the dead ends. I charged her a few thousand dabloons."

"That's intense," Alitha says.

"Yeah. She wouldn't stop talking about history, which I think is why my brain keeps thinking about it."

"Wait," I say. "What was her name?"

"Elia? Elara?"

"That's Dr. Lothiel, one of my bosses," I say with a laugh, trying not to think of my other boss. "Her hair is twelve feet long?"

"Something like that. How did you not know?"

"She's never worn it down," Alitha shares. "Ever. It's always in a bun. We knew it was long, but not that long." She takes another bite of her cheeseless pasta.

"Honestly, I kind of just assumed her hair was really thick, that's so funny." I crinkle my nose. "I wonder if she'll wear it down now that it's all fancy."

"We'll see at the Christmas party," Alitha says.

Sitting at my desk in my little house, I hover my mouse over the submit button on my application. I had gotten an email from Augury University suggesting anyone can apply, but that they'll be looking at applicants from outside the organization as well. I know what's going to happen. I'm going to get my hopes up, they'll hire some potions professor with years of experience from somewhere else, and they'll probably even give them relocation assistance.

Why would they hire me? I'm an adjunct with no formal potions training. I majored in charms and minored in history, much to my own dismay. If I could go back in time, I would. I'd be a potions professor working alongside Alitha, and I'd be dating Vega. Everything in my life would be perfect.

But it's not. So here I am, paloma in hand, crying and drinking my feelings. Simone told me I have to stop using sugar and alcohol to make me feel better, and although I agree, I can't heed that advice tonight. I've been thinking about this for days—ever since Alitha told me. Dahlia has been hounding me to put in my application before it's too late, so screw it. Here goes nothing.

Click.

I want to feel relieved, but all I feel is nervous. What if they interview me? What if I'm actually given a chance, will I fuck it up?

The Christmas party is just a week away. I load up my car with all the projects I've been working on. I've got fake present boxes, strings of snowflakes, and even giant paper poinsettias. Iris would always find new hobbies she wanted to try; every year it was something new. One year, it was arts-and-crafts, and she decided she wanted me to try it with her. We made a whole scene, a room of decorations. There were houses and flowers and all sorts of things. I don't know if she does arts-and-crafts anymore, but it's something I'll always be fond of.

Getting into the car, Momiji in tow, I head towards the Illusionary Jungle. This is going to be a party to remember.

eighteen

VEGA

I do laundry once a week. From my bedsheets to my winter jackets, I wash everything. I think it's one of the things she liked about me—she liked how clean my apartment was.

The first week, I could still smell the remnants of her. It was faint, barely there, but my orc nose allowed me to notice.

The second week, it was barely a note. Maybe I once had my arms around a woman, and this was that smell—but maybe not.

Now, the scent is gone entirely. As is the sound of her laugh, and the look in her eyes. It's pathetic how much I miss her. She wasn't a craving I could manage; she was my every desire wrapped up in a neat little bow, just in time for Jul and Christmas.

After I left Indigo's house, I spent an hour sifting through our employment contracts for the third time, just to be sure. Nope. Still not allowed, not unless one of us switched departments.

I spent the following few weeks working out, drinking protein shakes, and meditating. I ignored the lack of texts from my father, ignored work emails, and ignored Freja's whining for me to practice my magic.

I gave myself time to mourn and mope, but now I've got to pull myself back up onto my feet and be the strong independent orc that I am. Opening my laptop, I check my emails.

Spam. Spam. Last minute holiday sales. More spam.

An open position. This email is from the dean.

Once I finish reading the email in its entirety, I jump out of my chair, throw on a vest and a pair of pants, and haul ass towards my car. Freja follows, trying to keep up with me.

"Freja, I've fucking figured it out. I know exactly what I need to do so that Indigo and I can be together." I just hope it's not too late. He sent that email days ago.

I drove so fast that even with my windows rolled up, my hair likely looks tousled, but I don't care.

Augury University is a massive campus. Besides the six large camphor trees, there's also fields, fallen logs, and courtyards galore. I sprint my way to the History Tree, climbing up a series of stairs and ladders. Freja flies next to me, taking breaks to sit on my shoulder. I could've waited to be escorted up, but I don't have the time for that. Finding Dean Bariel's office building, a decent sized hut that sticks out of the side of the History Tree, all the way at the top. I can see him speaking to someone through the three glass window panes, and I cross my arms. I can wait. Being rude won't help Indigo's chances.

The elf woman leaves, and I calmly knock on the door, trying not to seem frantic. The Dean opens the door.

"Dr. Daelor, come in." He's tall, though not as tall as me. His body is extremely lanky, and his features are angular, bird-like.

"How has your winter vacation been so far?" I ask in an attempt to make small talk.

"It's been quite nice. Winter Solstice is only a few days away, as you probably know."

"I hope it's everything you wish for," I say. He gestures for me to sit down, and he sits behind his desk, which is a hurricane of paperwork. Freja nuzzles herself against his hand, and he gently pets the top of her colorful little head.

"Thank you. What brings you this way?"

"It's about the job opening—"

"Oh?" His forehead creases, ocean blue eyes squinting at me.

"I think you should pick Indigo—I mean, Professor Watson."

He crosses his arms. "Your charms adjunct? She's an applicant, and I was considering interviewing her."

"Choose her. She's an amazing mage, sir. You will not regret it."

"If she's so amazing, why do you want her out of your department?"

I clear my throat. "She's... she's better at potions. She's not a bad charms mage, that's not what I'm saying, but I've seen her do potions. She created one that fixed a hole in my pants, she's got another one that can help women sense danger; she's truly something."

"So why did she specialize in charms?"

"Familial pressure. It's been great having her in my department, and she works well with Professor Hills and I, but I think she would be better suited replacing Dr. Taylor," I say, and it is brutal honesty. She has been great, not a single student complained about her... but potions is where she belongs. It's what brings her joy, and it'll allow her to be with me. A fucking win-win if I've ever heard one.

"Can I see some of her potions? I'd like to witness this mastery myself," he says, and I scratch the back of my neck.

"I'm not sure where she keeps them, but Dr. Taylor could probably tell you."

"I'll check with Alitha. I make no promises, but I will heavily consider Professor Watson. Thank you for your recommendation. It's been a pleasure having you join our team."

We shake hands, and Freja hops onto my shoulder. Exiting, I step out and make my way down the History Tree. I stop in my tracks when I smell Indigo.

Standing on a ladder on one of the platforms, Indigo is hanging string lights all around. Dressed in her usual-all black, she's got billowing sleeves and tall chunky boots on. Not ideal for what she's doing, but she looks damn good doing it. I cross towards her, even though I know I shouldn't.

As I get closer, I realize she's accidentally wrapped herself in the lights.

"Indie, are you okay?" I ask.

She yelps, falling off the ladder, and I dart towards her. Catching her in my arms, Indigo looks down at me with her bright violet eyes. I hold her for just a moment, not wanting to let her go.

"Hi," she says, before wiggling. "You can put me down."

"I know—"

"Vega," she says sternly.

Placing her down onto the platform, I help her untangle herself from the lights. "Doing some decorating?"

"Yeah! The Christmas party is Friday," she says. "You would know if you ever checked your email."

"How do you know I don't check my email?"

"Because I know you," she says, and there's a small sprinkle of sadness in her tone. "And because you never RSVP'd."

"Well, I'll be there." I back away from Indigo, and Freja lets out a little squeak.

"Momiji is at home, baby, but you can see him at the party," she says and then looks me straight in the eyes. "I'll see you there."

I turn. Unlike the ancient myth of Orpheus and Eurydice, I don't look back.

Two days until the Christmas party. I sift through my sweater drawer, looking for anything to wear when I see Indigo.

Knock knock.

Someone's at my door?

Knock knock knock.

Someone impatient is at my door. Willing my legs to carry me faster than I have before, I sprint to the front of my apartment, opening the door. Indigo launches herself at me, grabbing my face and kissing me harshly. Her face is wet with tears, and I wrap myself around her pulling her onto the couch with me.

"My little rabbit, why are you here? Why did you kiss me?"

She wipes away a tear and looks at me with the biggest smile. "I got the job. I'm not your subordinate anymore; we can be together."

"Really?" *This isn't a dream?* I cup her face in my hands.

"Oh, don't act like you didn't know. The Dean said you practically begged him to kick me out of your department." She crosses her arms.

"I did *not*. I specifically said you were amazing, but that you'd be better suited as a potions professor," I say. "Also, I didn't know. I simply made a recommendation. I wasn't sure it would work."

"V, this is all I've ever wanted."

"Wow, I'm flattered."

She pushes me lightly. "Not just you, asshole. All of it. This is everything I've ever dreamed of—everything my mother told me I couldn't have."

"But you can have it," I tell her.

"Because of you."

I shake my head. "No Indigo, you did this. You're the one who graduated early and got a job at Augury University at the age of twenty four. You're the one who took a chance with me at that bar—the one who manages to teach charms and history and practice potion. You're the one who has done all this work, allow yourself to take credit for it. You deserve this."

She kisses me again, this time deeper, and I allow her to take control. "Do I get a reward?"

"Of course," I slowly drift my fingers up her thigh.

"Have I made the naughty or nice list?" she asks, voice full of sin.

"Obviously naughty." I move to unbutton her pants. "What do you want Santa to bring you this year?" I ask with a wink.

"A girlfriend."

My heart grows ten times in size. "I think I can arrange that."

"Wake up sleepy orc," Indigo says, and I roll over.

"Sleep."

"I've got to get going."

At that, my eyes shoot open. "Going where? It's like eight in the morning."

Indigo, already dressed and ready to go, stands over me. "I've got to set up for the party tonight. I'll see you there."

"Are we not going together?" I ask, holding her hand so she can't go yet.

"I don't think it's the best idea to hard launch our relationship at the annual holiday party."

"Fine. We'll drive separately, but I'm spending the entire night by your side."

"Deal," she says and kisses me on the cheek.

I should probably wrap her gifts. She wanted a girlfriend for Christmas, but I already gave her that. A pair of earrings and a strap-on will have to do.

nineteen

INDIGO

Everything is perfect. Alitha and Aura showed up around three to help me finish setting up. We discussed what classes I'll be taking over from Alitha, and I told Aura about some of the sight students she should expect to meet soon. Augury University truly feels like home to me.

As the clock strikes five, people start to make their way in. The trees are covered in lights, sparkling bright so all can see.

Don't stress, I remind myself. *It's going to be awesome.*

To get into the meeting room, guests have to enter through an archway covered in fake Christmas presents. There are shimmery snowflakes dangling from the ceiling, and a gorgeous tree in one corner for everyone to place their gifts under. Dr. Ali and Dr. McNab are the first to arrive. Adeib brought tabbouleh, and Feather brought a large vat of mac-n-cheese. Others trail in not long after, carrying their gifts and treats. There's white chocolate lemon truffles, lasagne, and more. Our librarian, Chak Rokismith, brought a whole turkey.

"You did a fantastic job, Professor Watson," Dr. Lothial says, hovering over me. "I couldn't be more impressed. I mean the poinsettia photo wall? This whole thing is effortlessly charming."

"Thank you. It definitely took a lot of effort," I reply.

Vega is almost the last to arrive, walking in with a decent-sized box covered in purple wrapping paper and a grocery bag. I'm honestly surprised she read the email far enough to know we're playing Dirty Santa.

She comes up to me in her green, chunky knit sweater, and quickly kisses my forehead. Freja flies in after her, practically crashing into Momiji before the two make their way to the charcuterie board to steal cheese and crackers.

"I brought this as a treat," Vega says, and I open the paper bag, which includes a box of hot chocolate packets and a bag of marshmallows. Very Vega.

After all the food is on the table and all the gifts are under the tree, we start a line and get to eating. I make sure to get a scoop of everything, and Vega gets two.

Seated between Vega and Alitha, munching on some delicious food, I watch the dean stand and raise his glass. "I wanted to make a toast for Professor Watson. Though she may not be a charms professor anymore, she sure knows how to throw a charming party. I cannot wait to see what you and Dr. Taylor do with the Potions Department"

Everyone raises their glasses, and I could cry—I could, but I've cried enough in the last few weeks. A grin spreads across my face, as well as a flush of pink.

Transforming into an owl, he flies around the room before landing on our table, winking, and shifting back.

"Did he just wink at me in owl form?" I ask the table. I didn't know owls *could* wink.

"I don't know, but I don't believe I've had enough spiked eggnog," Aura says.

"I remember seeing an owl at a previous meeting, but I didn't put two and two together," Malik says. "Archeron is a bird?"

"Dean Bariel is an elf with the rare ability to shift forms," Alitha explains. "Your eyes did not deceive you."

"Everyone, move your chairs into a circle," I say, and they all follow along. Furniture is being shifted around left and right until we make a circle in the center of the room.

Though not all our staff is here, there's a good group of ten of us. Vega, Alitha, Malik, Aura, Adeib, Feather, Dr. Lothial, Chak, Dean Bariel, and myself. Each one brought a different, uniquely wrapped gift.

Vega's golden eyes are wide as she looks over towards the pile in the center. "Indigo," she whispers in my ear. "What is going on?"

"Dirty Santa," I explain. "Didn't you read the email?"

"I did not."

"Oh, well. What was the gift for?"

"For you," she says, her tone stern. I don't know what she's so riled up about, but she's got to let loose.

I shrug. "Guess you'll have to win it back."

She goes to say something else, but I shoo her away, ready to start the game. “Alright everyone. Is anyone confused about the rules for Dirty Santa?”

“Same rules as White Elephant?” Chak asks.

“Same rules.” I nod, and he gives me a thumbs up. When nobody else says anything, I continue. “Alright. Alitha, how about you open the first gift?”

Alitha walks over and grabs a small blue box, the one Aura had brought.

“Go ahead and open it,” I say.

Alitha unwraps the gift to reveal a small golden ornament. It’s Augury University, or at least the six camphor trees.

“Wow, someone outdid themselves,” I say.

One by one, everyone goes about selecting and opening gifts. There’s a small violin that plays music, a mini waffle maker, and other fun items.

As each person makes their selection, Vega’s leg shakes faster and faster, the stress emanating off of her.

“Are you okay?” I ask.

“Not in the slightest,” she confesses. I’m really worried about her. Maybe the gift she got me was expensive, and she’s worried she won’t have anything to give me now? I mean, that’s silly, but I chose myself to go last for a reason. I’ll just steal it from whoever opens it.

Dean Bariel does a little dance as he shimmies his way over to the pile and grabs the purple box that Vega had brought. Sitting down, he slowly starts to unwrap the gift.

“Wait,” Vega shouts, standing up. This is so unlike her. “I’m afraid I might have accidentally switched that gift with a different one; can I open it privately first?”

“Absolutely not, that would ruin all the fun,” Dean Bariel teases. God, he’s insufferable. He continues to slowly take off the wrapping, purposefully taking his time to torture Vega.

“It’s nothing bad,” Aura says to Vega, but the tension doesn’t leave her body until he opens the box to reveal a much smaller velvet box.

“Another box. This better not be the gift, Vega.”

“Open it,” I say, now curious.

Dean Bariel opens the jewelry box to reveal a pair of earrings. They’re little white rabbits, with purple gems for eyes. That’s so cute.

Vega lets out a deep sigh of relief. Just a few more turns.

Malik stands up and walks over to the pile, carefully making his pick. He grabs a small yellow box and carries it back to his seat. Opening it, he reveals a hundred dabloon gift card to a local eatery.

“Vega, it’s your turn.”

"She's definitely going to take my gift card," Malik says, holding it up to her, but Vega moves past him and right towards Dean Bariel.

"Earrings, please," she says with a smirk.

Dean Bariel hands over the earrings and then looks at Adeib, who is holding fuzzy socks. "Only because I pity the feetless."

It goes on like this for a while, people stealing one another's gifts, until finally it's my turn. I walk up to Vega and gesture for her to hand it over. "Earrings, please," I say, just as she did.

She grins and presents the earrings to me. I take out my hoops and put them in. I'm wearing a tight, purple, crushed velvet dress, and they match perfectly. Doing a little spin, everyone hoots and hollers as I show them off.

"Thank you," I say and lean down to kiss her.

It's already too late when I remember that everyone else is there too.

Alitha shakes her head, smiling.

"Surprise!" Vega says, as if we had the entire thing planned, and we all start laughing.

Dr. Lothial tells us a story of when she played a similar gift exchange game years ago with some friends that resulted in two brothers getting into a fist fight. Everyone continues eating and laughing, and Aura tells us about the meanings of the songs she picked for tonight's playlist. Dean Bariel gives us another update on the secondary campus, and we all have a jolly good time.

After a while, things start to settle down, and people go home. Most of our coworkers with kids didn't come, and I think about how maybe next year we could do something more family friendly, or have a separate event for families. Vega and Alitha stay behind to help me clean up.

"You really went from having your future-girlfriend as your boss, to your best friend being your boss," Vega says suddenly.

"What can I say, I like who I work with." I giggle.

"Good luck though; I'm sure Alitha is a lot tougher than me."

"I think I'll be okay," I look at Alitha, who smiles.

"I hope next year I have someone to bring," Alitha says, and I realize something... I've never seen her date anyone.

"I'm sure you will," I assure her.

"Just not any from Augury."

Standing in the Illusionary Jungle, we watch Alitha drive away. I go to move, but Vega stops me.

"Nuh-uh. Look up," she says, and I do.

There's a little bunch of greenery with white berries, wrapped in a bright red bow. Mistletoe. Vega grabs me by the hips, pulling me into her warm embrace. She dips down, kissing me fiercely. I'd pity how bad she has to crane her neck to reach me if I didn't know how much she enjoyed our height difference. A pink flush spreads across my cheeks, and I swear I can see some in the green of hers too.

A singular snowflake falls, and I put out my hands to catch it.

"I learned a trick or two from the illusionary mages," she says with a wink.

"Did you get your Christmas wish?"

"Better," I say as Momiji and Freja finally fly down to be with us. "I got you."

epilogue
INDIGO

Sitting in Vega's lap on my living room floor next to the Christmas tree, we open our gifts. Vega starts with the big box I got her, unwrapping it to reveal a machine that makes both coffee and hot chocolate.

"You love it so much, I figured you could make it at home too," I say, turning to kiss her on the cheek. "Okay, open the other one."

"So bossy," she teases as she reaches for the smaller box. Unwrapping it, she sees the snowglobe. It's from Winter Wonderland's gift shop. "Indigo, it's perfect."

"I think it might make music, but I can't remember. You should check the bottom," I lie.

V flips it over to reveal a golden key. "What's this for?"

"My house, silly."

She presses her forehead to mine, and I close my eyes. This is what love is supposed to feel like.

"Thank you," she says. "Now open the other one I got you."

I grab the box and pause before opening it. "Is this what had you freaking out during Dirty Santa?"

"Fucking yes." She puts her face into her hand, rubbing it. "I neglected to label the two boxes, and I wasn't sure if I had brought the one with earrings or... this one."

Holding up the box, I let out a laugh. "If you lifted it up, you would've realized the weight is totally different."

"Yeah well I'm a dumb ass, so."

"Alright, let's see what had your panties in a twist."

"I do not wear panties."

Unwrapping the box, it's obvious it's a sex toy from the logo. What toy, exactly, is what I'm looking forward to finding out. I open the box, and there's a bright green dildo attached to a black harness... oh my. That's a strap on.

I hold it up to my body and let out a giggle. "I can't wear this, it's way too big."

"It's not for you to wear. It's for me," she murmurs, taking off my tank top. We bought matching pajama sets in a deep green plaid. V strips me of my little shorts before removing her shirt and pants as well.

She picks me up, throwing me onto the couch. "Wanna watch me put it on?"

"Yes please," I say, practically foaming at the mouth.

Vega takes a minute to get herself into the harness, the black straps going around her muscular thighs and overtop her tight fitting boxer briefs.

"Lube?" I ask, and she nods, grabbing a small tube from out of the pocket of her pajama pants. "Oh, so you had this *planned* planned."

"Obviously," she says and licks her lips. She leans a knee onto the couch, while the other leg remains planted to the floor. "Now turn around."

She uses a finger to stimulate my clit while the other plays with my opening. I can feel myself getting wetter as she toys with my body, sucking on her finger before dipping it back into me. She takes the head of the strap and plays with me, teasing me with the tip.

Vega stands and grabs me by the ankles, dragging me over the arm of the couch until my ass is up into the air. Ever so slowly, she sinks the dildo into me. Her strokes start out long and slow, but gradually she works it deeper into me, picking up the pace of her thrusts.

"V-V-Vega," I stutter, relishing in this pleasure. It isn't the largest toy I've seen, but it's pretty damn big—and she uses it to fill me wall to wall.

She pulls my hair, right at the nape of my neck. "Come here," she says, pulling out of me. Turning me around, she kisses me. It's hot and wet, our tongues clashing as we touch each other with such fervor.

"I want you to fuck me," I say.

"Request approved," she says with a chuckle.

Pulling me up and wrapping me around her body, she holds me as I sink back onto the bright green cock. I moan as she uses her arms to bounce me up and down, kissing me while she does.

Vega finds a rhythm I enjoy and continues bouncing me, thrusting the dildo inside me until I go silent and still for a moment. She kisses me, moaning into my mouth as she watches me come, and I shake and shudder as

I reach my release. My muscles continue to spasm as she puts me down, gently kissing me.

V wipes me down with a towel and then covers me in a soft blanket, wrapping me up like a burrito. She pulls me onto the couch, and we snuggle up to one another, rubbing our noses together.

"I love you," I say without planning to. There's no anxiety as I watch her eyes go wide and wait for her to react, because I know she feels it too.

"You fucking better," she teases, pulling me in for another kiss. "I love you more, little rabbit.

Stealing Elf Hearts

stealing elf hearts

DAHLIA

Impulsively deciding I need a big tattoo on my thigh is pretty on brand for me, but it's best I don't tell the group chat. *Or my parents.* My best friends are busy tonight, anyway. Indigo is going on a picnic with her girlfriend, Vega, and Alitha has a tendency to hide in her house every Valentine's Day, having sworn off love entirely. I don't need to bother them with my antics. Besides, I'm riding the high of the honeymoon phase—and riding on the back of a motorcycle.

"Dahlia, did you bloom just for me?" Elorthiel whispers in my ear as he parks the bike. I roll my eyes, scrunch my nose, and smile. *He's so cheesy.*

We hop off and head out of the parking garage towards his shop. The wind is howling, and the Earth has given us a rose-colored sky, just in time. There's the faint smell of flowers in the air, and I swear it feels like I'm walking on clouds. As I strut hand-in-hand with Elorthiel, I can't help but smile. I'm dating this elfling. Tattoos, piercings, muscles and all—he's mine. And somehow I manage to make this tough looking man say the sweetest things.

There's a big, blue, neon sign in front of his shop which says *tattoos*, and as he opens the door and invites me in, I nearly stumble. There are petals lining a walkway to one of the black benches, with a heart-shaped box of chocolates sitting atop it. I'm a glass-half-full kind of gal. A bold, do what I want when I want it type of gal. And yet, I never get what I want when it comes to love. Not until recently, at least. I'm going to bask in this love, because I have no idea how long it's going to last. I hope a long, long time.

On the walls of the shop are different concepts he's drawn—there are striking snakes and fascinating flowers—all illuminated by the bright light shining onto the chair. "Be a good girl for me and have a seat," he says, walking me to the bench. I do as I'm told for once in my life. Only because he called me a good girl; that's my kryptonite. I open up the box of chocolates and take a bite before moving it to a nearby table. Dark chocolate is my absolute favorite, and I'm honestly a little impressed he remembered.

Elorthiel stands in a corner as he puts on black gloves and gathers his supplies. My mind goes fuzzy at the sight of it. Why are black gloves sexy? I want to feel them against my skin. As if catching my stare, Elorthiel takes his shirt off. Right here, in the middle of his shop, he stands in nothing but his black jeans. How am I supposed to sit still now? His lean muscle is on display as he moves towards me, carrying a stencil. Elorthiel quietly sits beside me, ever so focused, as he prepares my skin and places the design on my upper thigh. The rubber of his gloves is cold against my skin, and I picture him pumping those same fingers inside me. I shake my head. *Stay fucking focused, Dahlia.*

The hum of the needle starting is louder than I expected. I've only heard it when I've entered the shop to drop off a treat for Elorthiel, never this close. I can feel the adrenaline rush coursing through my veins.

"This is going to hurt a little, my flower," he says before he makes the first line. I think hundreds of tiny needles just hit my skin, but I barely felt a thing.

I shrug. "I think I can handle it just fine."

"You know the old adage thick thighs save lives? Well, yours also makes for perfect canvases." Elorthiel kisses my right thigh, goosebumps trailing down me as he continues the outline of the flower.

I considered a couple of tattoo designs. A note in my abuelita's handwriting, a tiger, or even something geometric. A million different things crossed my mind before I decided on a Dahlia. I want this tattoo to commemorate me. My success and confidence, my self love; it's taken a long time to get here, and I want this to be a little celebration for it all.

An hour or so of outlining goes by, and he starts shading it in. The needle feels different, the vibration pressing into my skin. I like the pain—it's thrilling, and I can't help but get a little turned on as Elorthiel's red eyes stare into mine. Wait...

"Shouldn't you be watching what you're doing?" I say, cheeks flushed.

"I'm watching *who* I'm going to be doing... later tonight." *Ah.* I press my thighs together, hoping he can't smell my affection. Mages seem to all have this sixth sense, and, unfortunately, it's being able to tell when the rest of us are horny. *Fucking obnoxious.* I'd like some privacy, please.

My attraction to Elorthiel is tangible as he cleans me up and applies the adhesive wrap to my fresh tattoo. Standing, he goes to take the supplies into the other room. Now's my chance. Feeling bold, I slip off my jean shorts and panties and toss them onto the floor. Spreading my legs on the bench, I rub my clit until I hear his footsteps. Slowly, I dip one finger in, gently teasing myself as I wait for his return.

Elorthiel walks in and drops everything he's holding, metal clanging against the floor as he stares at me in shock before rushing towards me, red eyes wide with heat. He kneels and grabs the side of my thighs and slides me towards him. His hand grips my jaw, aggressively pulling me into his kiss.

He releases me from his grasp and whispers, heated breath against my ear, "You couldn't wait to get back to my apartment, could you?" He lightly kisses down the side of my neck and then removes my shirt, unhooking my bra as he kisses me. "I'll have to devour you right here."

Elorthiel makes his way down my body, ever so slowly, until I ache. His tongue glides as he creates circles, headed straight for my center. He puts his mouth on me and sucks, tugging at my clit. My pussy throbs as I writhe with pleasure.

His touch is all-consuming, his tongue as sweet as his whispers. I hang on by a thread as I allow myself to experience his devotion to me, and before I know it, I'm falling off the edge. He releases me from his grasp, and, before I can say a word, flips me onto my stomach. There's a light pressure against my freshly tattooed skin, and the pain invigorates me. Arching my back for him, he grabs a hold of my ass, and then I hear the crisp crackle of the condom wrapper opening. Face against the bench, I wiggle excitedly as I wait for him to fill me.

"You're such a fucking tease," he says as he stands and pulls me against him.

Elorthiel thrusts into me in one swift, hard motion. There is nothing gentle or nurturing about the way he pulls my hair, making my neck bend back as he pounds into me. I love it. I think I might even love him, but right now I just love the feeling of his cock inside me. I hope nobody else on the strip can hear my moans; that would be *super* embarrassing.

My elfling flips me again, and I get a full view of him enjoying himself. His pointed ears are perking up, and sweat drips down the muscular panes of his tattooed chest. Elorthiel's hands grip my hips, ensuring he goes deeper. *Heaven.* I've died, and this is my eternal bliss.

"I love how soft you feel, inside and out," he says, dragging me closer to him, still drilling me. I moan, unable to stay quiet as the intensity of his thrusts increase. By the look on his face, I don't think either of us can hold on for much longer.

My pussy clenches as we both crash on an orgasm, his body shaking as much as mine. After we catch our breaths, I sit up, and Elorthiel pulls me into his chest, wrapping his arms around me.

"Let's clean you up and get to dinner," he says and kisses the top of my forehead. He grabs a small towel and dries us both before putting on a t-shirt. I go to put my shorts back on, but he stops me. "Go into the bathroom. There's something waiting for you in there. Don't wear anything underneath."

The bathroom of the shop is clean and dark, with black fixtures and dark red roses sitting in a vase. Closing the door, I find a red dress hanging off the back. I slip it on, and it fits like a glove, effortlessly falling off my every curve.

When I open the door, Elorthiel is in a sports jacket waiting for me. I swear if we were in a cartoon, his eyes would be popping out of his head in the shape of hearts. "Perfect, my flower," he says, taking my hand and kissing it.

"How'd you know what size to get?"

"I took your measurements while you were sleeping and had it custom tailored."

"Damn." I laugh. This man might be as obsessed with me as I am with him.

He locks up his shop, and we head back to his bike, our matching helmets hooked to the back. He picks mine up and kisses me before placing it on me. Once he helps me on, we ride off to dinner. I can feel the seat against my most sensitive parts, but I don't even care. It's that much hotter. The sky is now dark and full of stars, and warmth fills my chest. Elorthiel turns and snakes his hand up my dress to rest on my thigh, and I think it's true:

This is what love feels like.

Disco Spring Fever

one
ARCHERON

Ring. Ring.

Although it's not a school bell, my alarm going off feels just the same. Spring break. Finally, I can rest.

Being the dean of Augury University has its perks. I'm truly one of the most influential men on Magia Island. I control who attends and how the school is run. The future of powerful mages, at least in this part of the world, is in my hands... I'm a little over it. I get no reprieve. I've lived so many lives, and yet I find this one to be the most exhausting.

During the summer, there are still classes and practices going on. Research projects and internships. Winter break, if I can even call it a break, I spend worrying about Solstice and how to please the other elder elves in my community. Spring break is the only time I get to relax or be me—just Archeron Bariel, no titles attached. So what do I do every year? Rot on my gods damned couch.

This year is going to be different. I don't know what I'm going to do yet... adopt a dog, maybe? Host an orgy? The possibilities are endless, but I'm going to make this week count. It's a shame practically everybody on this island is off-limits to me. Perhaps I should take a vacation. Opening a new tab on my computer, I type "nude beaches near me" into the search bar.

Knock. Knock.

"Come in," I say, quickly closing the tab. I'm not embarrassed, but I'd rather not traumatize Daffodil.

Daffodil Langstrom—my assistant—can be described as strawberries and.... I shake my head. *What is wrong with you, Archeron? You sound like a weirdo.*

It's just that I spend most of my time trying *not* to notice her beauty. Or speak to her. Or even look at her. Daffodil is quiet and sweet, with red hair and blonde chunky highlights which compliments the bright green of her eyes. I have a healthy crush but nothing more. I would never want to use my position against her, and besides, she's great at her job. No need to scare her away.

"Is there anything you need before I leave?" she asks, her usually floppy ears perking up.

"Not that I'm aware of. Thank you, Daffodil," I answer.

She takes off her wide-framed reading glasses and smiles. "Enjoy your break."

I watch as she walks away, her orange corduroy pants showcasing the round curves of her—nope. Back to searching for getaway locations.

A few hours go by where all I do is scroll through vacation vlogs, trying to select the perfect spot. Ugh. Nothing is interesting to me; I've done it all before. That's what happens when you get to be my age. A thousand years go by and everything blends together. It's quite a bore.

Getting up, I grab my briefcase and head towards the door when I nearly slip on a piece of paper. These loafers might have been expensive, but there's no traction. I gather my bearings and pick up the flier. *Sleeping Island's annual Disco Spring Fever*, it reads in big bold letters. *Bring your best pair of skates and join us for a roller dance off!*

On the flier is an image of a bunch of people, all different magical and non-magical races, all wearing wild outfits which remind me of the Disco Renaissance. I believe the style originated prior to The Convergence, and I'm a big fan. The metallics, the denim, and most importantly... the tight pants that flare. Simply delightful. Bell-bottom jeans are the key to my heart.

Walking out the door, I place my briefcase into my mouth and shift. The breeze feels nice against my feathers as I fly home. In the depths of the Illusionary Jungle rests Augury University. It's not far from Sunspell City, but I don't want anyone in my business, so my house is deep in the jungle. Flying past the dorms, I try to remain out of sight. Most students have gone home for the break, but the medicinal mages usually remain put. When I spot my neighbor's condo, Dr. Ali, I know I'm close. Adeib is my only neighbor and a quiet one at that. We rarely see one another. Once, I asked him to borrow sugar just to see how he'd react, but he seemed... annoyed. I may be his superior, but I'm not his boss, nor his elder. He's an anomaly I've yet to decipher.

Where the buildings and structures of Augury are in the trees, my house is on a mass of stone, originally taken out of a cave near a cliff on the far edge, propped up in the center of a more open area. Though most of the jungle is filled with thickets of trees, the land around my home is more barren, making it easier to fly around. My house is made of wood, with a small circular door in the front which only opens via magic. My barn-owl form fits nicely inside, but almost no one else can enter. There is a hidden door in the back that most races, elf or not, can fit through... It's rarely used.

I believe that is why I talk so much. Spending so much of my time alone in my house, or my office, causes me to crave attention, so when I'm put in front of someone... I usually want to get it all out. My thoughts, concerns, confessions. I just want someone to listen, to care. Not because they're forced to, but because they really want to, and that is something rare to me—something I'm hoping to find in a short fling on Sleeping Island.

Shifting back into elf form, I walk toward my office. When I was very young, I lived in an elven village on the planet Loria—the elves' home planet —and we had lots of windows. I had to learn to shift back into human form fully clothed, or at least giving the appearance of being fully clothed. With a combination of illusion and charms, I managed to make it happen. Luckily for me, I don't need to waste the energy doing it here in my home. I'm completely isolated, which is both a blessing and a curse.

I head to grab my laptop, feeling the velvety carpet against the bottoms of my feet. I pull my computer onto my lap as I splay across the couch. Emailing the contact on the flier, I type:

Hello,
My name is Archeron Bariel and I would like to participate in the "Disco Spring Fever." Please let me know what I need to do to prepare.
Thank you,
Archeron

Ten minutes go by in the blink of the eye.

Ping.

Archeron Bariel,
We are pleased to invite you to take part in Disco Spring Fever. The registration fee is 500 dabloons, which includes your stay at the resort. This event is put on by the island's cultural museum. The grand prize

`for 1st place is 10,000 dabloons. May the best skater win!`
`Sincerely,`
`Miss Meadow Miles`

All of the Isles of Magia have a specialty–magic, technology, the merfolk. But Sleeping Island? Surprisingly, not sleep. Their focus is culture. When The Convergence came about, many countries and pieces of planets were combined or destroyed. Sleeping Island was created with part of Turtle Island, specifically a section which held an Indigenous reservation, and part of Ireland. The result after a few thousand years? An island buzzing with Indigenous and Irish culture, as well as the new culture that formed. The people of Sleeping Island decided to not only dedicate their efforts to conserving their own traditions, but other cultural phenomena and traditions globally as well. It makes sense that they'd put on a roller disco, because they are trying to preserve the past.

I have never purchased a ferry ticket so fast in my lifetime.

As I walk out onto the dock, I'm greeted by the beauty of Sleeping Island. Magia Island has segments that are one with nature, but Sleeping Island somehow takes it a step further. Everything is in perfect harmony—nature alongside humanity. I checked the population of the island before I left, and very few mages or magical races reside here. They're welcome to visit, yes, but this island is overwhelmingly human. Honestly? Good for them.

It's Sunday evening, and the sun hangs low in the sky. I packed a small, hard suitcase full of clothes with a duffel bag tucked over the handle. In it are the essentials: a toothbrush, toothpaste, my phone charger, and of course... my centuries old roller skates. I refused to pack my work laptop or anything that would distract me from the competition. This isn't about winning—it's about relaxing.

The Oovoo driver calls my name, and I get into the backseat of the small sedan. Big, beautiful light fixtures line the streets, except I realize they are not lights at all, but clumps of fireflies eating worms from bird-feeder-like containers. As long as I've been alive, I've never been anywhere like this. It's almost magical, except it isn't.

We pull up to the resort, and there's disco themed decor everywhere you look. Some stylized like the 1970s and 1980s, and some from the Disco Renaissance in 5605. It was 400 years ago, but I remember it like it was yesterday. I would go out dancing and skating every night, bringing a different partner home each time. A wild decade, but a memorable one.

Walking into the building, there is a large banner which says "Disco Spring Fever Competition" in sparkling letters. A woman, most likely an elfling, donning a cream-colored headscarf greets me with a wide smile.

"Welcome! You must be Archeron Bariel, our final competitor," she says, waving me towards where she stands. "My name is Gray Majidi, and I am one of the judges." She waves down a staff member, and they hand me a card with a QR code. I scan the code with my phone to download the resort's app and access my room key. "There's a meet and mingle tomorrow morning with brunch before you're all free to go practice. Come down to the lounge around 10 AM to join us," she says.

Meet and mingle. Perhaps another competitor can become my spring fling.

I take the elevator down to the lounge, only mildly nervous about my outfit. Tight black pants and a vest, no undershirt. It's nothing like the loose trousers and sweater vests I don at work, but I'm trying not to be *him*. I'm vacation Archeron. I want nothing but sex and salt and vinegar chips this spring.

The elevator doors open to a spacious room with couches, chairs, and tables. On a table in the very back sits a transparent case displaying a shiny gold medal. A large, colorful balloon arch frames the wall behind it. I'm not positive, but I'd bet that medal is made of real gold, the way an older man hovers around it like a bodyguard.

In a corner by the elevator stands a tall, beautiful woman with endless, wine-red hair, drinking a glass of champagne. Her ears are long and pointy, and her eyes are like two unique ecosystems: one green and one blue.

"Petunia Picard. It's a pleasure to meet you," the elf says, reaching out a slender hand.

There's a certain smell to her. It's like my own. Fowl.

"Archeron Bariel. Not to be invasive, but are you able to shift?" Shifting was a rare ability on Earth, and I was one of the few people on the Isles of Magia capable of such things.

"Yes. I'm a peacock," she says, as if it's no big deal.

"That's amazing! I'm a—"

"Barn owl."

My brows draw in. "How do you know?"

"Everyone knows who you are, Dr. Bariel," she replies.

I frown. I was hoping for the opposite. "That's unfortunate."

"Don't give me that look. I'm an elf, of course I know who you are. The humans and other species likely don't, and I won't say anything. Now, how long have you been skating?"

The change in topic is welcome, and we share our experiences during the Disco Renaissance, as well as the special powers we have from being shifters. The conversation is interesting, but my mind keeps wandering as a familiar voice resurfaces in the background chatter.

Turning my head, I see big green eyes I know all too well.

Daffodil?

two
DAFFODIL

THE DEAN TOOK THE BAIT AFTER ALL. AMAZING. I'M NOT AN EVIL PERSON, BUT I MIGHT just be an evil genius. I applied for the job at Augury University hoping I could learn magic from the dean. Dr. Bariel is one of the best mages in the world, but he doesn't teach magic classes anymore, only history.

After graduating from Sleeping Island University with a bachelor's in Magical Studies, I realized I wasn't particularly good at anything. Yikes, I know. That's when I hatched my plan. I researched, maybe even stalked a little, and found out what the dean is into. I showed up for my interview in a Disco Renaissance era outfit. It doesn't hurt that my boyfriend, Moss, also loves disco. Getting the job was easy, but getting the dean to like me enough to where I felt comfortable asking for him to mentor me was harder.

Dean Bariel has a reputation for enjoying the sound of his own voice. He never shuts up, according to everyone I know. Except around me. I can hardly get a few words out of the man. He's so reserved, it drives me nuts and forces me to act reserved as well—I just have one of those chameleon personalities. I prefer to match people's energies.

We're halfway through second semester, and I still haven't cracked him. So I came up with part two of my brilliant plan: plant the seeds for him to come to Moss' roller disco competition, and get to know him better here. As his eyes lock with mine, his pupils dilate, and I know I've hooked him. We're going to be best fucking friends by the end of this week, and then I'll ask him.

Dean Archeron Bariel stalks towards me, ignoring the other contestants in the process. I'd never seen his bare arms before, but he's got strong, lean biceps which flex as he walks. His long white hair falls down his back, and I can't help but stay fixed on his eyes. Gorgeous pools of blue.

"Daffodil, what are you doing here?" he asks, tone serious.

"I'm competing in the roller disco. What are *you* doing here?" I retort, as though I'm surprised to see him.

"I saw a flier at work, and I—I wanted to compete as well. It reminded me of a time long ago that I quite enjoyed. The Disco Renaissance was one of my favorite seasons of my life," he replies, and it's the most he's ever shared with me. "Enough about me. Have you ever been to Sleeping Island before?"

I nod. "Yes, my boyfriend is actually from here."

"Boyfriend. Right. Is he coming to watch the competition?" The dean's face is now depleted of its previous glow.

"He's actually—" Moss comes towards us before I can finish my sentence.

"Moss O'Flaherty. It's a pleasure. I've heard so much about you," he says, and I swear I see the dean gulp.

My boyfriend is a handsome man. With a prominent nose, high cheekbones, and deep reddish-black, straight hair which billows past his shoulders, he's ethereal. Moss is broad, substantially broader than Archeron, and I wonder if he could lift us both up at the same time.

"About me? Oh no, that's never a good sign."

Moss gives us a winsome smile, his golden-tan skin making his teeth appear that much whiter. He sits down onto the red corduroy couch, and the dean and I follow suit. I'm almost sitting on Mosses lap, but I still feel too close to my boss. The couch feels... intimate. There are other contestants sitting on neighboring couches and chairs, though nobody seems to pay us any mind. Everyone is lost in their own conversations.

"All good things. How you're one of the world's greatest mages. She thinks quite highly of you," Moss says.

That makes my skin flush red.

"Okay, well, I'm going to go get some orange juice or maybe a mimosa. Do either of you want anything?" I offer.

They both shake their heads. Making my way toward the buffet table, I take a long look at the other contestants. There's an older woman, a cambion with red skin and wings, standing next to a tall elf woman whose hair is the same shade of red. They appear to be two of the oldest players here. I don't want them to break a hip or anything, but I hope they're slow. I really want Moss to win.

Grabbing a glass, I go back to the couch. Moss and the dean are deep in conversation, something about the history of Sleeping Island.

My boyfriend enjoys some interesting things. Obsessed with human culture, Moss double majored in Turtle Island Indigenous Studies and Gender Studies, and minored in Irish Gaelic. He almost earned a dance minor as well. Moss wanted to learn about the world prior to The Convergence. He celebrated the culture but also listened to the darkness. I've never paid much attention to human history, but I've heard it was grim. The looks on their face tell me they aren't discussing the grim parts but the joy. The dancing, the music.

"History is so fascinating, which is why I teach it," the dean shares as I take a seat. "Every moment in time that passes affects the next."

"Is it history for you though, or is it just memories?" Moss ponders aloud.

"Ouch. I'm old, but I'm not as old as The Convergence," the dean says and then chuckles.

Ring.

Tintinnabulation fills the air as a sweet-faced human woman shakes a bell, drawing our attention to her. "Greetings contestants. My name is Mrs. Phoenix White, and I am one of your judges. We have many plans in store for you all. Practice hours, fun events, et cetera. Before we get started, can everyone introduce themselves?"

Everyone stands, and I stretch my doe legs before getting up, the tile hard against my hooves. She nods to a centaur, and the masculine person looks down.

"Hi, I'm Azure Morris," they say, voice quiet. They've got on blue lipstick and a sparkly top, with long locs in their hair. Their upper body is incredibly muscular and their lower body is well... horse. They mumble something I don't quite catch, and then gesture to the next person.

"Petunia Pecard. I'm a doctor, although there are many doctors here. I'm the medical kind. A medicinal mage, to be precise," the tall elf-woman says and shakes as if she is fluffing feathers. *Weird.*

"My name is Professor Plumb. I work at Sleeping Island University and am head of Geology," a human man says. He's staring at Mrs. White... It's an intense sort of stare that makes me uncomfortable. He continues staring at her, and the room falls uncomfortably silent.

"Heyo! I'm Daffodil. Daffodil Langstrom. I work at... as a secretary of sorts," I say, distracting everyone from the nervous energy in the room. I want to talk about Augury as little as possible while I'm around the dean. "To be honest, I'm not very good at skating, but I'm here to have a good time."

A few members of the crowd sigh in relief. They're probably glad they have a little less competition.

"I'm her boyfriend, Moss O'Flaherty. I'm a museum educator who hopes to be a curator one day," he says, and a smile makes its way into my features.

Light of my life. "And I'm good at skating," he mumbles under his breath. There's the ego.

Everyone continues to introduce themselves. The cambion lady's name is Lavender Sue. There's a young satyr woman named Ella who seems like a total ditz, and then—

"Scarlett Safar. My line of work is nobody's business," the woman says. She is... a hybrid? Her S's remind me of the serpentine, and I think I see the forking of her tongue, but her legs— They're concealed under her jeans, but they almost look like mine. Faunborn? Or perhaps she's satyrborn? Mixed with some human and serpentine. I know I shouldn't speculate about strangers, but hybrids are becoming increasingly more common with every new generation, and I want to learn about them. I wonder how strong her magic is.

"What is she, a spy? A princess?" Moss jests, and the dean laughs, a low chuckle that vibrates in my bones.

I shake off the feeling. Why is my body betraying me now of all times?

"Hi hi hello. I'm Emerson Green, and I use they/them pronouns. I'm a banker," the short elfling says. Their cheeks are bright red with delight.

The dean clears his throat. "I'm Archeron. That's all I'd like to share right now, but I'm elated to be here. Let's have the best week ever."

"I'll cheers to that," Moss says and lifts up my glass of orange juice. The rest of the group joins in, toasting to this joyous occasion.

I feel... *odd.* There are so many different personalities, so many different behaviors. I find it hard to acclimate. Should I be happy? Competitive? Reserved? I guess I'll just try to have fun.

Today's practice is in an outdoor rink with lots of ramps. The judges instructed us there won't be many ramps available during the competition, but that they're good practice for harder tricks.

Unfortunately, I don't know any tricks. I'm athletic, a decent skater, and I've even taken some swing dancing lessons with Moss, but I'm no pro. Sitting on the sidelines, I watch as Moss and Archeron interact, their bodies in sync with the music.

"Oh my, this is ABBA!" Moss shouts.

"I've heard of them! Pre-Convergence, right? They're a classic," Archeron shouts back as they sway to the groove.

I almost bite my fist at the sight of them. Drenched in sweat, both men remove their shirts. Moss' chest scars on full display, he proudly skates around, faster than anyone else here. Archeron is all smooth, pale skin with washboard abs rippling down his front.

If someone scanned me using infrared, I'd probably show up magenta right about now. The feeling below my abdomen scares me. It doesn't scare me that I'm attracted to someone other than Moss; we haven't been monogamous in a while, but as my boyfriend's small black eyes widen to a size I've never seen as he looks Archeron up and down, I realize I'm fucked. My mouth is agape as I feel the tension fill the air. I'm never going to be able to stop the fantasies of my boss from circulating in my horny little brain. Yep. I'm totally fucked.

"I would like to propose something," Moss says as we cross the threshold of the hotel door. We plan to invite Archeron out to the club with us tonight in hopes I can get to know him better.

"Go on," I say, curiosity getting the better of me.

Moss smirks. "I think we should invite Archeron to bed with us."

If I were drinking something, this would've been a television-worthy spit take. "You think we should sleep with my boss?"

"He's incredibly attractive, and you want to get to know him better. If we sleep with him, you could use it as leverage to get him to mentor you."

"Moss! I am not going to blackmail him," I whisper-shout as we make our way into the elevator.

I press the close-door button before anyone can join us.

"I don't mean it like that. He mentors you in magic, you mentor him in... orgasms. The man's clearly in a dry spell. I can see the lust in his eyes when he looks at us," Moss says and waggles his eyebrows.

Fuck. Maybe he's right? It's not like I'd be sleeping with him to get a raise or a promotion. I just want some training... that's not a crime.

"And you *want* to sleep with him?" I ask, though I already know the answer.

"Did you seriously just ask me if I want to shag one of the strongest mages on this part of the globe? Of course I do. Imagine the things he could do to us."

With that statement, my mind was made, busy wandering off to all the things Archeron could make me feel—could make Moss feel. Good thing I wore the shortest shorts I packed.

Knocking on the door, I patiently wait for the dean to come out. When the door swings open, I have to avert my eyes from the slight bulge in his pants. Note to self: the dean definitely has a cock, not a cloaca.

Archeron's face lights up. "What do I owe the pleasure?"

"Come out with us," Moss says, his voice low and charming. It's not a request, but a quiet command.

"Should I change?" Archeron asks, gesturing at his silky button-down and grey sweatpants.

Absolutely not. If he changes, I might cry.

"No, your outfit is fine. This place is pretty chill," Moss says and arches a brow.

"I'd love to."

Although Moss has a car, we decided to take an Oovoo, just to be safe. The entire ride over, there was a charged energy in the air circulating around me. It threatened to swallow me whole. I was drowning in sexual tension.

When I took the job at Augury, I never planned to fuck my boss. He was undeniably attractive, sure, but that was it. I liked the looks he gave me when I wore something more showy. I even enjoyed seeing him flirt with my boyfriend. Still, I never pictured I'd be at a raunchy club envisioning myself and Moss taking turns riding the dean.

"Three blue lagoons, please," Moss says to the bartender. He's holding me by my ass, my cheeks close to making an appearance, and I catch Archeron staring.

"My eyes are up here, sweetheart," I say. "But maybe you can get a better look at my body later."

His cheeks flush, and I wink before grabbing my drink and slurping it down. I need a healthy dose of liquid courage if I'm going to continue to be this bold.

A song I love comes on, and I dart onto the dance floor, making sure I shake my ass right where the guys can see it. Another man makes his way towards me, but both Moss and Archeron block him before he's within even a foot.

My eyes lock with Moss', and we make our move.

I sway my hips back into Archeron. He puts his hands on my hips, and I lace my fingers with his, keeping us close. Leaning back into him I whisper. "I notice the way you look at me. At school. You think I don't, but I do."

He scoots us back, and I can feel the moment he realizes Moss is behind him. At first, the dean's muscles stiffen, but after a moment, he relaxes into our touch.

"Are you two open? Or ENM?" I hear him whisper to Moss.

"We're whatever you want us to be, baby."

"Yes, we're open," I say, giving him a clear answer.

I continue to grind back into Archeron, feeling his length harden behind me. Turning around, I grab him by his balls and pull him into the nearest corner. One that's shielded by an out-of-service bar top. Archeron yelps a bit, but I can see by the look in his eyes that he's enjoying it too.

"Do you like a little pain with your pleasure, professor?" I say and feel his cock strain even harder.

"Y-yes," he says, his breathing heavy.

"Good, because by the time this week is over, I'll have you torn to pieces," I say and mean it.

I grab Archeron by the face and kiss him, our tongues swirling deeper into each other's mouths. Moss lowers himself to the ground and tugs at Archeron's pants. As Moss bobs up and down, Archeron moans into my mouth, bucking against Moss' face. I put Archeron's slender hand down my shorts and guide him to my most sensitive parts.

"You're going to make me feel the exact way he's making you feel," I say, unable to control the fierceness of my demand.

Archeron nods and uses his thumb to make small circles on my clit. I writhe at the sudden boost of pleasure. Putting my hands underneath Archeron's shirt, I use my nails to claw down his back. He's hot and panting as I feel his skin break, a tiny drop of blood trickling down his skin.

Moss looks up at me, eyes wide as he engulfs Archeron's long length with his mouth. *Simply bliss.*

Two fingers slip inside my opening, and I practically lose it, Archeron's thumb still making circles. "I want you to make him come before I do," I say to Moss, my voice low and breathy.

Archeron cups my ass with his other hand, and I wonder if he likes my fur. I know Moss does. As interesting as he finds humanity, he is sexually interested in anything but. I can't blame him... I, too, like the adventure that comes with magic. The things you can utilize it for. I'm picturing Archeron creating shadow hands that play with my ass while his cock is inside me. He could even charm a dildo and use it on Moss, or I could take care of Moss. Maybe in our magic lessons, he could teach me how to—

Before my thoughts can continue, I'm almost toppling over when Moss steadies me with one hand, his other still gripping Archeron's cock as he comes, too.

"Someone's coming," Archeron says abruptly. I can't hear anything over the sound of Moss swallowing, but I rush to fix my shorts and help Archeron pull up his sweats. Moss wipes his mouth and a devilish grin spreads across his face.

"But I wanted to ride his disco stick," Moss says and sticks his tongue out. His voice sounds half-whining, half-teasing.

I stifle a laugh at his sudden shift from sensual to humor. "Oh don't you worry; we're returning the favor tomorrow," I whisper as we disperse from the corner, hoping we're not too conspicuous. "You should be scared."

"I welcome whatever you throw my way, darling," Moss says and kisses Archeron on the mouth. "Thank you for joining us."

three

MOSS

My girlfriend is the most bonkers person I know. I truly believe once she gets Archeron to train her, she should leave Augury and pursue a career in the film industry. She's an incredible actress, the way she's pretended to be a put-together professional, when in reality she's an unhinged mage on a mission to make her boss her mentor.

This morning's skating session was gruesome. They had us doing drills through cones to the beat of certain songs. I'm exhausted, so we came back to the room to get in an early nap and a shower.

"Here, put these on," she says, handing me a suspiciously heavy pair of boxer briefs.

As I slip on the underwear, I feel something hard, hidden underneath a pocket. It's got to be a vibrator. "Daffodil," I say sternly.

She crosses her arms, still naked, water droplets falling down the light brown fur of her legs, and I pause.

"Daffodil," I say again. "Why did you put a sex toy in my underwear?"

"Don't question it."

I watch as she shakes her legs out, her damp hair flowing down her back in pools of red and blonde. I fucking love this woman. She grabs a green floral dress with long flared sleeves and puts it over her head. More modest than her usual—oh *fuck.* It's not modest at all. Daffodil's dress is completely cut out in the center, exposing part of her under-boob, as well as the top of her abdomen above her navel. It's also *extremely* short. I'm done for.

"Are you going to get dressed, my love? We're running late."

I furrow my brows. "Late? It's almost two. The other contestants had lunch around noon."

She smiles, and I know that smile all too well. "Archeron will be joining us."

Of course he will. Listen, I like Archeron. I'm the one who suggested we fuck him. But if she's having him meet us for lunch, and I'm supposed to wear these underwear...this isn't good. I'm going to be next-level tortured.

Archeron joins us for lunch. It's a buffet-style restaurant, so we wait in line, and I'm so hungry, I consider cutting the little old lady in front of us but decide not to. That would be such an asshole move, and she looks precious in her little luncheon outfit.

Archeron does not look precious. Where I decided to wear loose trousers and a flowy short-sleeve button down, Archeron chose the opposite. Tight pants and an even tighter dress shirt. We can see the contour of his every muscle.

I feel a slight tingle begin in my underwear and see Daffodil's face light up. She must've taken out the remote. It's barely vibrating, but I definitely feel it.

Making our way out to the outdoor patio, which is practically empty, we take our seats. Daffodil must have clicked a button, because the vibration has increased immensely.

"So," Daffodil says, seated across from us. "How are you feeling about the competition?"

Archeron shrugs. "Fine, I suppose. I didn't really come out to win, and I don't expect to, but I don't think I'm the worst skater here either."

He is right. He's most definitely not the worst skater here. Archeron is a decent skater, though it is clear he is out of practice. Where he excels the most is actually his dancing. Roller Disco isn't just about speed and agility, but creativity too.

"Who do you think is the worst skater here?" Daffodil asks as I stifle a moan. She lowers the vibration level, and I'm simultaneously glad and displeased.

"The little old lady, a cambion? I believe," I say, my voice thick.

"Lavender. Yeah, she's pretty rough," Daffodil says. "But she's a super sweet person! When she met my familiar, Pickles, she offered me a jar of pickles she packed with her. I *love* pickles."

"Everyone knows you love pickles," I laugh.

She eyes me ferociously and whispers, lethally soft, "Don't make me change the level again."

Archeron scratches the back of his neck. "I actually think Professor Plumb is the worst one here... that, and his personality kind of sucks. Emerson, Azure, Scarlett, they've all got entrancing personalities. Patrick is blander than white bread."

I let out a soft laugh that mixes with the oncoming orgasm when an overly-perky satyr comes into view.

"Did somebody say Professor Plumb?" the blondie asks, taking a seat next to Daffodil. I think her name was Stella or Ella or something.

Don't ask me why, because I could not tell you, but I do not like this woman. Daffodil thinks she's stupid, but I think she's self-important. There's something off with her.

"Why, is he your lover?" Archeron asks boldly.

Daffodil must hate me because she turns the vibrator all the way up, and I have to push my already touching thighs together as hard as I can muster. I'm strong, but I'm unsure anyone could survive this.

"No, he's my professor," she says. "What, do you know him or something?"

"I don't believe any of us know him," Archeron says, and I watch in agony as Daffodil tries not to laugh. I lightly kick her under the table, hoping she might drop the remote, but it's no use.

Putting my fist in my mouth, I try to think of anything to turn me off. Dead puppies. Naked grandmothers. Human men. It's all atrocious, but as she abruptly turns the vibration off from full speed, I'm swallowed whole by my own pleasure. Teetering on the edge, she yanks me back before I fall.

I let out a quiet whimper at the sudden lack of feeling against my cunt, and one corner of Daffodil's mouth ticks up. This satyr lady needs to go away. Archeron takes a fist full of cheesy fries and shoves them in his mouth, his cheeks flushed pink. I think he knows, somehow, that this was happening. Maybe he hears the vibrator.

"One of the judges knows him!" the satyr says, interrupting the silence.

That got all our attention.

"Yeah, I heard him tell another competitor that Mrs. Phoenix White was his ex-wife and that he's here to win her back," she tells us.

"Bold move for someone who looks like he shits his pants once a month," I mumble under my breath, and Daffodil cackles.

"Well, good luck to him," Daffodil says. "Hey, do you want to join us?"

"Sure!"

Archeron shakes his head. "Actually, I need assistance. I was talking to Petunia the other day and needed to ask her something, but I have no idea where she is. Could you help me locate her?"

Ella looks at us and flips her blonde locks. "Of course. Come here, Magic." She pats her shoulder and a small purple rat comes climbing up her arms. Must be her familiar.

Archeron winks at me before following Ella towards the main building of the resort. Saved by the sexy professor.

Daffodil stands and takes a seat next to me. She crosses her arms grumpily before she re-ups the vibration, licking up my neck as she finally allows me to fall into fulfillment.

A few days of practice goes by, and we're almost to competition day. Sergeant Mustard, one of the judges, sent us all emails with instructions on where we were to go for dinner. All ten of us are here, nervous and excited for the big day tomorrow.

I'm seated between Archeron and Daffodil. On Daffodil's other side is Scarlett, the hybrid, and Petunia, the other elf, is next to Archeron. The rest of the contestants are filed around the large round table, and I feel like a juror at court.

Professor Plumb is acting like he's had fourteen beers when he's only had four, which I suppose is a lot for someone his size and stature. I'm not a big drinker, but I'm a pretty big guy. That many beers isn't going to have me sharing my deepest darkest secrets, but it's sure happening to this guy. Apparently, his wife left him because she said he wouldn't shut the fuck up about rocks. Now, she's married to an astronomer named Rusty who never shuts up about the stars. At least, that's what Petunia told Archeron.

"Scarlett won't say a word to me," Daffodil whispers. "This isn't fair! Why do you two get to be a part of the gossip train?" She pouts, her big green eyes glowing like twin moons.

"I came on this trip for disco vibes, relaxation, and in hopes of a good fuck. I don't want to hear this lady discuss the elders in her community; I barely want to learn about the elven elders from my own island," Archeron whispers pointedly.

From the look on Petunia's face, she heard at least some of that. Whoops. I was really looking forward to getting some elven dick, but at this rate I might just be attending an elven funeral.

"Don't you have supersonic hearing or something?" Daffodil asks Archeron, her warm body leaning over mine.

"No, but I can hear things up to ten or so miles away." Archeron smiles.

Daffodil furrows her brow. "So do some listening! I want to know what everyone's been talking about."

There's another round of whispers as food is served. Some meals are chicken, while others are vegetarian. I'm more of a salmon guy myself, but this will do.

Taking a big bite, I try to listen in, but can't hear anything. Daffodil and I quietly witness the information make its way around the table, our ears filling with the sound of soft voices and abrupt gasps. Archeron's face is strained as he leans over towards Petunia, trying to catch the gossip for Daffodil. As Azure whispers something to Petunia, her and Archeron's faces contort, now aghast.

Petunia smashes her chest into the table, nearly knocking over her drink as she shouts, "Scarlett apparently threatened to beat up Emerson."

Why would she say that? Why would *anyone* say that?

Horrified expressions cascade across some of the other contestants' faces.

"Okay, okay. What is happening?" I say, loud enough so that the entire table can hear me.

"What?" Scarlett asks, sounding genuinely confused.

"Everyone is freaking out, and I have a feeling we're playing a giant game of telephone," I say. "Petunia, what did you just accuse Scarlett of?"

"Apparently, she said she's going to beat up Emerson," Petunia shares. Scarlett's face turns unamused.

"Eat. I said she was going to eat them," Professor Plumb corrects.

"Why would you say that? She said Emerson was going to be a treat," Ella shares, her little rat sitting in the crook of her neck.

Familiars, the being that provide mages their source of magic, were supposed to be kept in our rooms, as magic was forbidden during the competition. Ella and her rat didn't seem to get the memo.

"I'm sorry, but I didn't say anything fucking close to that," Scarlett hisses. "I said I was going to defeat Emerson, you dense idiots. Defeat. It's a competition."

The old cambion frowns. "I heard deplete."

"And I heard obsolete," Azure whispers.

Emerson shakes their head. "I don't really care what anyone heard, but I really don't like this. This is not a fun game at all."

"How would I eat you? I'm a hybrid, but I'm mostly human," Scarlett says, matter-of-factly. And she's right. She's tall and mostly lean—there's no way an elfling would fit in her stomach.

I chuckle at the absolute absurdity of this situation. Ten adults just sitting around a table talking shit about one another. I should talk about this the next time I give an adult-only presentation at the museum.

Tomorrow is going to be a riveting day. Everyone's so distracted, it'll give me the chance to really succeed.

four
ARCHERON

It's competition day! I'm excited to see everyone's performances, especially Moss, but I'm also sad. Once the competition ends, everyone will go home. I will go back to being Dean Bariel, Moss will return to the museum, and Daffodil will continue being... my assistant? I can't fathom ever being able to look at her again and not immediately picturing her naked.

Last night was fantastic. We snuck out to the competition rink after hours and tried to see if Moss and I could fuck while skating. I was able to fill his cunt, but I wasn't able to stay like that for long. We all ended up bent over the bleachers, taking turns on one another.

I've been in love before, had many partners, but nothing felt like this. It's like our three varying bodies all connected in some way. We were like a chord—three notes creating a new sound.

I stayed the night in their room, and now we're all getting dressed. Daffodil just put on the cutest orange and pink two-piece outfit, the fabric showing off the curves of her furry legs and ass. Her ears flop in the most adorable way, and I feel absolutely smitten.

Moss is somehow just as sexy. He's soft and muscular. He's wearing nothing except tight red bell bottoms. It's so human of him, and that made it even more hot.

I went for a different vibe with my all white three-piece suit. We were a trio not to be reckoned with.

"You boys ready?" Daffodil asks. "Afterward, I've got a special treat for the two of you." Her voice is as sweet as honey, but something devious lies hidden beneath.

"Ready as I'll ever be, darling," Moss croons.

"I'm ready to watch Moss take first place," I admit.

Down the elevator we go.

Roller Disco is about a few different things: overall balance and agility, tricks, and dance/creativity. The grand prize medallion hangs from a stand on the judges' table, reminding us of what we're competing for.

Professor Plumb goes first and completely bombs. He almost trips twice, and his face looks more sad than anything. The man weirds me out, so I don't feel bad. Moss whispers commentary the whole time to Daffodil and I, filling us in on where Plumb went wrong and how he could improve for the future.

Next up is Lavender Su, who is doing fine. Just okay. She's slow–as slow as the annual magical university dean mixer and trivia night. I feel kind of bad... Lavender is so kind. I hope she at least had fun.

Azure Morris skates like I couldn't have imagined. I thought having four legs would put him at a disadvantage, but he crushes it, gliding across the floor with grace.

I can't keep my eyes off of Daffodil when she takes the stage, so to speak. She's not an incredible skater, but she's an incredible person. If my brother was still alive, I would be calling him up to give him a play-by-play. The sight of Daffodil's thighs alone would make any man weak in the knees. She is probably the best dancer of the entire group.

As Daffodil makes her way back to us, she kisses Moss on the lips before planting one on my cheek, and I consider how grateful I am magic is banned from this competition. Sight may be my strongest discipline, but it's a pain in the ass. Do you know how hard it is to get someone to kiss you when you just saw them kiss you in your mind yet you aren't sure what you did to get there? It's not ideal.

Petunia, Ella, Scarlett—they are all really good. If I didn't know the skill Moss contains, I would assume these three women would all place top three. Their impressive skills make me nervous for my performance. Petunia gives me a little wink before she has a seat, and I'm not sure how to react, so I don't. I let the nervousness consume me for a moment.

I go on and do my best. I chose the song *You Should Be Dancing*. It's a human song from before The Convergence, and Moss' face lit up when the music came on. My skating is fast, but I'm more off-balance than usual. I did a little dance move with my arms and hips and then started skating backwards. It's not something I had originally put in my routine, but everything is going so well. I don't want to win—I just want to make Moss and Daffodil proud.

Emerson goes on after me, and they do alright. I could barely watch, still coming off the high of my own adrenaline.

Moss O'Flaherty. My heart grows ten times in size at the sound of his name. Daffodil grabs my hand and interlocks it with hers as we wait until the lights dim and the music comes on.

It feels electric. *He* is electric. He moves with such fervor and groove, it's mesmerizing. If someone asked me to show one clip of what it means to be good at Roller Disco, this would be the moment I would want to share. He sways along, giving us the disco finger, before getting close to the ground. Moss shifts his body weight onto one foot and lifts the other in the air before accelerating. Backwards. There's a small crowd of people watching the competition. Most are relatives of competitors, and a few are fans of disco or human culture. All of them gasp as he slides on his knees towards the judges, stands up, and does one final twirl.

Moss earns himself a standing ovation.

"Competitors, please line up below," Sergeant Mustard shouts from the judges' panel.

We all line up, one after another, and I place myself between Moss and Daffodil.

"In third place, earning an eight point five, is Ella Peach," Miss Meadow Miles says, her voice beaming with joy.

Ella Peach was an annoyance. When I rescued Moss from Daffodil's orgasm-torture lunch, I got trapped listening to her share how she broke her nail while attempting skating tricks for twenty minutes. Good for her, I guess.

"She doesn't look very happy," Daffodil whispers.

Gray Majidi stands up. "In second place, earning a nine point three, Scarlett Safar."

Everyone claps except Emerson, who I don't think likes Scarlett very much. Scarlett's absolutely beautiful, her long dark hair flowing past her shoulders. It's a shame she's such a hardass.

"And finally, in first place, scoring a perfect ten... Moss O'Flaherty," Sergeant Mustard shouts. "Congratulations, you've won ten thousand dabloons, as well as the grand prize medallion!"

Daffodil squeals and jumps up for joy, grabbing Moss and practically climbing him like a tree.

“Wait!” Mrs. Phoenix White shouts. Everyone turns back to the judges' panel. “The medal. It’s gone.”

five
DAFFODIL

"ANY ONE OF YOU COULD BE A SUSPECT," SERGEANT MUSTARD SAYS TO US ALL. "Nobody leaves until we find the medal."

"How do we know it's not one of you? I mean, the judges sat closest to Mrs. White," Moss says, the joy of his win quickly fading.

"Moss has a point. The three of you had ample opportunity," Archeron says to the other judges.

"I say we pat everyone down. Nobody can leave until everyone has been searched," Sergeant Mustard suggests, an off-putting grin spreading across his face.

"Absolutely not," Scarlett says.

Ella shakes her head. "No, thank you. That makes me super uncomfortable."

Okay, so that makes both of them potential suspects.

"Let's make it a game," I say. "Someone pat me down and prove that I don't have the medal, and then I'll help us figure out who took it. No other sergeant pat-downs necessary."

Sergeant Mustard looks hesitant, but nods in my direction. *Is he a creep or something? I don't have time to figure it out.*

After an uncomfortably thorough pat down, I'm ready to play detective. Everyone, judges and contestants, is seated in chairs, one after the other. Moss hovers, leaning on the back of Archeron's chair. I remain standing, going up and down the aisle of suspects.

"Does anyone have any weapons on them?" I ask, and Emerson shakes their head.

"I got one after the threat on my life by Scarlett—"

"I didn't fucking threaten you. Give me a break."

Not this again.

As I pace back and forth, I hear Lavender whisper to Azure something about the judges. Their brows are furrowed as they stare at Sergeant Mustard.

"Sergeant, how do we know it isn't you? Do you have some sort of vendetta against my boyfriend?"

"Your boyfriend?" he asks, tone curious.

I shake my head. "Yes, Moss is my boyfriend."

"I thought the elf-guy and Moss were together," Sergeant Mustard says frankly.

"We're still working out all the details," I say. "Anyway, do you have a vendetta?"

"No, I have a vendetta with Gray Majidi because—"

"Nope," I interject. "That's all I needed to know. Hash out your personal drama somewhere else."

Miss Meadow Miles lets out a loud chuckle, and Gray frowns. "Can we hurry this up? I need to go home and feed my cat," Gray says, pulling on the long sleeves of her shirt.

I stare back down at the line of people. "Petunia, you've been awfully quiet," I say. Petunia is full on glaring at Archeron, and I'm realizing she might have had a thing for him. Could they have been together in the past? I feel like Archeron would've told us, but their past is a lot longer than mine and Moss'. Whatever the case may be, she's clearly pissed.

"I did not take the medal, and I do not want to speak to you any further."

Okay, grouchy lady.

Moss gestures for me to come closer with his hand."What about Professor Plumb? Could he be doing this to get back at his ex-wife?" he asks, his voice hushed.

"Yes. I believe his ex-wife is actually Mrs. White," Archeron replies.

Ella raises her hand.

"Yes, Ella?" I eye her suspiciously.

"Professor Plumb had a complete mental breakdown when they got divorced. I think it had to have been him."

Professor Plumb stands and walks toward Mrs. White. "You have to understand, I came here for you."

An audience member comes down from the bleachers. A human man, not someone I recognize.

"Patrick?" the man shouts as he comes and joins the group. He and the professor look like different brands of the same person.

"Hey, Rusty," Professor Plumb says.

Mrs. White stands and hugs the man, giving him a big kiss on the cheek.

"Did you take the medal?" Rusty, who I'm realizing is Mr. White, asks.

Professor Plumb shakes his head. "No."

"Then why are you here, Patrick? It's been three years," Mrs. White says. Sadness laces her eyes, and her skin has turned as grey as her hair.

"I wanted to win you back," Professor Plumb confesses, his voice pained. "I thought if I won, maybe that would be enough."

Honestly, I kind of feel bad for him. I look over at Moss and Archeron. Everyone's eyes are the size of their heads.

"She's never going to be yours again. She grew tired of you," Rusty says.

"And you think she won't grow tired of you? I wouldn't stop with the rocks, and you won't stop with the stars. She'll never be satisfied until she's the single most important thing in somebody's life," Professor Plumb yells.

The two men are almost nose-to-nose, their breaths heavy as they argue.

"Phoenix is the brightest star in my sky," Rusty says.

Professor Plumb looks as if he's going to punch Rusty in the face. Moss moves from behind Archeron and gets between the two men. "Don't be unreasonable. You two still have to work together."

Wait–Wait a second. The cogs in my mind start to turn. Three years?

"I'm sorry, did you guys get divorced three years ago?"

"Yes," they all say in sync.

Hmm. The cogs are moving full-speed ahead, now. "Stella, didn't you say Professor Plumb had a breakdown over the divorce in class?"

"It's Ella, and yes, I did," she spews.

"Aren't you *currently* his student?"

"I am."

I move towards her, grabbing the small lump beneath her sleeve. It's Magic, her familiar, and in its mouth is a shiny, golden medallion.

"Unbelievable," I say and snatch the medal from the creature's mouth. I could have never get my little dandehog, Pickles, to do something like that.

"So wait—why did blondie do all that?" Moss asks, and even Archeron looks surprised.

"I signed up for the roller disco so that I could win the grand prize, but when I saw Moss practicing, I knew he'd beat me," she admits. "That's when I devised the plan to have Magic steal the ring. At least I could sell it as gold and pocket the money."

"But why'd you blame it on your poor professor?" Archeron questions.

Ella shrugs. "He gave me a C on my mid-term, and it was pretty convenient given his ex-wife was a judge and all."

Wow. And I thought my plan to convince Archeron to tutor me in magic was genius. This was next level.

"Congratulations," Sergeant Mustard shouts at Ella. "You are banned from this competition. For *life*."

She rolls her eyes and stomps out of the building.

Well, that was dramatic.

When Moss, Archeron, and I get back to the hotel room, I hand Moss a box and tell him to go put it on and nothing else. Archeron sits on the couch, and I place myself on his lap, lavishing in the kisses he places down my neck.

Moss comes out in nothing but a crown, and I feel Archeron harden underneath me.

"A crown for our king," I say. "Now get on your knees."

I hand Archeron the second box. "Now you two are going to make it to where this is the only thing he is wearing."

Archeron opens the small box to reveal a cock ring. It's got an extra loop for his balls, and I watch as Moss struggles to make him fit. Once they've got it on, I sit on the couch.

"I'm going to watch you fuck him from behind," I say as I remove my shorts. I dip my fingers into my already dripping pussy and play with myself. Curling two fingers up, I feel for that extra sensitive spot as I watch Archeron use one hand to prepare Moss, and the other to stroke his own cock.

When Moss is ready, Archeron pushes inside him, their bodies on full display for me. I let my mind wander and my fingers do the work. Pleasure radiates through my body. I want to try everything with these men. I've tied Moss up, we've had all sorts of fun, but Archeron makes me more devious. In my wildest fantasies, I'm wearing tall black boots and stomping on his cock and balls. *Fuck.*

I continue to touch myself, to feel my own desire as I watch Archeron plow Moss into the next realm. The next lifetime. Moss screams out in pleasure, his entire body shaking.

"Now come and fill me," I say, kneeling onto the ground and bending over, my face touching the carpet.

Archeron comes up behind me and shoves his cock inside. He pounds into me, and my head spins, the feeling of him consuming me.

"Daff, can I teach you some magic?" No words have ever made me hornier. I'm melting.

"Yes, baby," I say, trying not to show my excitement.

"I learned how to use my shape shifting abilities in tandem with some of my other magic types, just let me show you," he says and pulls out of me.

Archeron lays on his back. Moss and I watch as his cock changes shape. There are now ribbed lines near the base of his shaft, and soft spikes towards the top. *What the fuck?*

I bring my legs over Archeron, slowly sinking my way onto his cock, facing Moss instead of Archeron. Moss comes up and kisses me, licking down my neck until he reaches my nipples and sucks. I feel like I'm on fire. The texture, the friction, I feel like I'm going to melt into a puddle of flowers.

I have never experienced such heightened pleasure. Archeron is grabbing my ass as I bounce on his cock, feeling the soft bristles he adapted to just for me. Moss is sucking on my breasts, twisting my nipples, and he's still wearing his crown. I'm panting and sweating as I moan, a scream threatening to leave my lips.

"Archer—Moss—Fuck," I whimper as I come, my body writhing with pleasure. These two men would worship me, and that makes my orgasm all the more stronger.

epilogue
MOSS

I lay sprawled out on the hotel room bed, Daffodil curled into one arm, Archeron tucked under the other.

"What happens when we go back to Magia Island tomorrow?" he asks, and my heart drops in my chest.

"I don't know," I say. And it's true. Daffodil and I never discussed what the plan was for after spring break. Her and I would always be together, no matter how far apart, but we never discussed what would happen with Archeron. I've grown fond of him—long white hair and all.

"I have a question to ask you. It's a big one," Daffodil says.

"Anything," Archeron replies.

I can feel her breathing, feel her pulse racing. "Would you mentor me in magic?"

Archeron lets out a deep sigh. "Of course. Let me know what discipline you want to focus on, and we'll get started right away."

"Really?" She sits up, and I join her, my back leaning against the bed frame.

"Why do you sound disappointed?" I ask, hoping my voice sounds more curious than accusatory.

"Because I thought she was going to ask me something else."

"What?" Daffodil asks.

"I thought you were going to ask me to be your boyfriend. Or your boyfriend's boyfriend. Or both," Archeron says with a shrug.

"Do you want to be our boyfriend?" she asks, and we lock eyes. I give her a nod and a small smile. White freckles dance across her skin, and I want to kiss them all.

"More than you could imagine."

"So do it," I say. "Say yes."

"I—what about Augury?" he says, fear lacing his words.

"We don't have to tell anyone, but I could quit. I don't care. This was one of the most fun weeks of my life," Daffodil says, and I feel the same. Having a partner I can dance with and a partner I can talk about history with? That's the dream.

"Okay," Archeron says.

"Okay."

Silence lingers in the air as we all lay back down, basking in each other's embraces.

"I want it to be just us three," I say, ending the quiet.

"Polyfidelity?" Archeron asks.

"Yeah, I want it to be just us. All we need is one another."

Daffodil kisses my forehead. "Just us three, then."

Sweet Summer Serpentine

Too Sweet - Hozier
New Girl - FINNEAS
Sake Pase - Michaël Brun, Saint Levant, Lolo Zouaï
Sokkar - Elyanna
Mr. Alwaysright - Pictures of Vernon
Habibi - Tamino
Love - Allen Stone
Meet Me in the Woods - Lord Huron
She - Dennis van Aarssen, Jeff Franzel
sun and moon - anees

Sweet Summer Serpentine

ROSE SANTORIELLO

one

IRIS

My vibrator stopped working in the middle of the greatest orgasm of my entire life. *Okay*, perhaps that's a slight exaggeration, but I'm still pissed.

The momentum dies, buried in my disappointment. I go to plug it in, but the cable is nowhere to be found. I get up and search through every drawer yet find nothing. A strange sensation creeps across my body, like I'm moving through syrup, my eyes heavy-lidded and tired as the faint sound of an alarm goes off.

Forcing my eyes open, I rub my face and look over at the nightstand, where the little black bullet safely sits on its charger. *What a strange fucking dream. I need to find a hook-up and stat.*

Standing, I walk over to the bathroom and turn on the shower. When it's hot enough to nearly melt my skin off, I get in. Today I will be reassigned to a new position—or laid off. *Who knows?*

Ever since I graduated from Octopus University, I've been working as a medicinal mage for MagiPharm X, one of the world's leading medicinal magic companies. They put the *Big* in Big Pharma. I have no clue what I'm fucking doing, and I'm terrified for the day MagiPharm X figures that out.

I scrub my body with a loofah, which was harvested nearby from an actual luffa plant, not that fake shit they sell on Octopus Island.

Hiro—my familiar—and I have gotten used to life on Sleeping Island. The people here live more slow, quiet lives. I'm a fast talker—fast thinker, fast mover, fast everything. It's the unmedicated ADHD mixed with the culture of the island I grew up on, but I've come to deeply respect the way of life here.

I'm not ready to leave. The Isles of Magia are all so different. There's no telling where I'll end up. Technically, they could send me anywhere in the world if they really wanted to.

Turning off the water, I get out and dry myself off. I slip on my softest loungewear set and open my laptop. The email is sitting in my inbox, begging to be read. *Do I fucking dare?* Hiro sits on the floor at my feet, his fuzzy green body nuzzled comfortably in his bed. The bed, which was definitely meant for dogs and not small moss-sheep, is a light gray and covered in little bones. He makes faint, snore-like noises as I move my computer mouse at an agonizingly slow speed.

Click.

Dear Iris Watson,

Thank you for your hard work and dedication this past year. We are excited to inform you that your process of preventing cancer remission patients from relapsing is being utilized by many of the medicinal mages at Augury University for their experiments and research, and with great success. We applied for a grant, and The Council's Department of Medicine approved the project. MagiPharm X and Augury University will be collaborating with the goal of eliminating certain types of cancer altogether.

What the fuck? I mean, I'm glad this is helping people, but I never approved of my processes being used at Augury, of all places... yikes. I wonder if my sister has used them? She's a potions professor, but not in the medical department, so she probably hasn't—at least I hope she hasn't. I'd be so embarrassed if she saw my research prospectus. She could probably figure out I'm a fraud just by reading it.

My eyes continue to scan the email.

You will be on a three-month contract at Augury University, working with the Department Head of Botanical Magic, Dr. Ali, to test different plants for properties that could be useful in relation to cell division and manipulation. With his knowledge base, and your potion processing, we are confident you will make a great team. When the three-month term is over, your contract can be renegotiated, but you will then be partnered with one of our head Cellular Mages at the MagiPharm X research center in Florgia for an eighteen-month contract.

I can't help but flinch at this email. I get no say—no control over anything? They expect me to do what they say and go where they tell me to go.

You will receive an email shortly with your ticket and itinerary for your ferry ride over to Magia Island. Your departure date is May 18. Thank you again for your dedication to this cause and to MagiPharm X.

Best of luck with your new project,

Signed, The Department of Development.

Best of luck to the person who wrote this email if I ever figure out who they are. It's my fault that I'm stuck in this mess—stuck with this job—but it doesn't stop me from being pissed off that they control my life. Grabbing my phone, I press the video call button under my best friend's contact.

Raemond's pinky-red face flashes across my screen, and I lean my phone against my laptop. Their eyes are wide, and their smile broad. "What's up, cutie patootie? You look like you've seen a ghost."

"I'm about to create a ghost."

"*Create* a ghost?"

"Kill somebody. I'm going to fucking kill somebody," I shout at my phone.

"Okay. That seems a little dramatic. What's going on... did you get fired?"

"Worse."

"Babes, I'm not sure there are a ton of things that are worse than getting fired here."

I rub my face with my hands. "They're sending me to work at Augury."

"Oh shit. That might be worse." Raemond's nose scrunches as they assess the news. "Are you going to be working with your sister?"

"I don't think so. Indigo works as a professor, and I think my mom said her doctorate project involves a cosmetic lab? Nothing with cancer or botany."

"Botany. What do you mean, botany? Are you going to be working with plants?" They beam. My best friend Raemond only really cares about two things in life: sex and plants. And friendship. And books. Okay, they care about a lot of things, but plants are like their *thing*. They own a nursery on Octopus Island, which is how we met.

"I'm being paired with a botany professor. I don't know all the details yet. Dr. Ali is his name," I reply. "I leave May 18th."

Raemond's eyes widen. "That's tomorrow."

"Fuck me."

Trying to pack my life into two big suitcases and a tote bag is even more difficult than I initially thought. One suitcase is dedicated entirely to my clothes. *Just* my clothes. I never knew how many pairs of shorts and tank tops I had until today. I pack my dresses and skirts, a sweater in case I get cold, and lots of socks.

Opening another drawer, I take two fistfuls of underwear and throw them into my suitcase. As though I'm channeling my sister Indigo, I can't stop my mind from wandering to all the worst-case scenarios.

What if I shit myself twice in a day? I need to be as prepared as possible.

I can fit everything else into the other suitcase. Family photos, my sketchbook, anything I need. Maybe Makeup? Or jewelry. In all honesty, I'm not sure *what* I need. I never thought MagiPharm X would send me to Magia.

Octopus Island, Sleeping Island, and my favorite fanfiction websites are all I've ever known. They're my home. I'll be honest, I took the easy route to adulthood. Thanks to a fluke college experiment, I got my first big girl job. I never had to apply and interview, never even had to handle getting my first apartment, or hiring movers. MagiPharm X did everything for me.

MagiPharm X is like my mother. They apply the same pressure for me to outperform everyone, the same drive for perfection, and yet they baby me, doing everything for me.

I just wish I knew how to do everything they expect of me. All I know how to do is pretend.

The Watson women have two things in common: purple eyes and a love of lists. I cross my to-dos off, one by one, and triple check my bags.

Movers are taking the rest of my belongings back to my childhood home. The bustle inside my apartment is even louder than the never-ending sequence of noises that circulate through my head.

The inside of my mind is a metro station: it's not loud, but it's also never silent. There's always a dull roar, always another train coming in. Sometimes I wish I could turn it off and cut the wire, but I'm afraid I'd somehow keep going. I don't think I know how to stop.

For whatever reason, I secretly hoped I stayed here. I miss home, yes, but not for the right reasons. I miss meeting with my book club in person. I miss my favorite gluten and dairy-free ice cream shop. What I don't miss? My family.

When I look at my mother, all I can think about is how close I am to failing her—to failing everyone. I am one mistake away from being caught, one statement away from losing everything I didn't work to get.

I came close to sharing my truth—but everything happened so fast and I panicked.

I was screwing around with potions in a medicinal magic class. I wasn't even pre-med, I was just a potions major, but I took a class for fun. We were assigned a project involving clearing the ducts in breast tissue and preventing them from getting clogged. When my lab partner realized one of our samples was cancerous, I decided to throw a bunch of potions together for shits and giggles. I didn't know what I was doing, it wasn't something I planned, but it worked. It allowed us to control those cells, and in doing so, allowed us to cure the cancer.

Everything spiraled from there. My lab partner told my professor about my so-called discovery, and he told every academic and news source on the island. At some point, it was too late to come clean. I'd fallen too deep into a bed of lies that I didn't even create.

I didn't discover anything. Yes, I created a potion that was helping prevent breast cancer from returning, but I couldn't tell you why.

I'm a fraud. And now here I go, solidifying my path of deception even further.

Closing the door to my apartment, I walk down the stony path to my oovoo ride. It's time to go.

The ferry ride is peaceful, and I spend a few hours of the trip staring out into the water instead of on my phone. Hiro naps on my lap, and his presence comforts me as I try not to focus on the tasks that lay ahead.

Passengers get off the boat in waves, and when it's finally my turn, I grab my luggage and head down to the bus stop. Sitting on the bench, I smile at a sweet-looking old orc lady.

"Where are you headed?" she asks. "I'm visiting my grandson in Sunspell City."

"Augury University," I say. "Does this bus have a stop in the Illusionary Jungle?"

She shakes her head, her green skin wrinkled around her eyes and mouth. "No, honey. You'll have to get an oovoo or rent a car."

Rent a car? I don't know how to do that. Am I even old enough to rent a car? I thought they charge a premium until you're twenty-five. Something about not wanting us to drive their rentals until our frontal lobes are fully developed.

Fuck being twenty-three.

I tap the screen of my cell, but it's black. Pressing the *on* button, I realize my phone died.

Shit.

"I don't have a way to call anyone," I say to the woman. It's not her problem, but I'm just speaking out loud.

"Here," she says and pulls out her phone. "Call someone to come get you."

There is only one person on Magia Island whose number I have saved to memory. Dammit. I have to call her.

An SUV pulls up to the bench and rolls down the window. *Who is that?*

Golden eyes meet mine—Vega, my sister's girlfriend. She gets out of the car, pops open the trunk, and puts my luggage inside without a word. Indigo opens the passenger door and walks towards me, pulling me into a tight hug.

"It's good to see you," she says.

I hope she means it. I never wanted to distance myself from Indigo, but I did what I had to. Hiro and I enter Vega's vehicle, and I buckle our seatbelts.

"I'm surprised you called me," Indigo confesses. "I figured my bigshot little sister has contacts everywhere."

I shrug, knowing I'm no bigshot. "You're the only person I know who lives here."

"Well, here, so you can charge your phone." She hands me a charger, and I plug in my cell, grateful for their help.

The car ride across the island is quiet. We pass through some smaller suburbs before entering Sunspell City.

"Our cottage is down that street," Vega says, pointing a green index finger while maintaining her grip on the wheel.

What feels like an eternity passes, and we cross through the Illusionary Jungle. Flowers line the dirt path we're driving on, and there are massive trees everywhere I look. Clusters of pod-like treehouses come out of different branches. There are big open fields of green where the sun shines brightly, followed by pockets of jungle where the sky isn't visible.

Vega parks the car in front of where the email stated my apartment was located. She lugs my suitcases up to the door, and I load the app that my key is in. Bless my sister for dating an orcling. Their strength is amazing.

"Make sure you charge your phone from now on. You don't want to get locked out. Actually, if you come see me sometime at work, I can give you one of my extra portable chargers. I'd hate for you to get stranded," Indie says, and heat encircles my heart.

"Thanks. This was a pretty dumb move on my part, so I appreciate you two saving my ass."

"No problem," Vega says, one arm wrapped around Indigo. "Looking forward to seeing the work you do at Augury."

That makes one of us.

two

IRIS

I walk past a thicket of kapok trees that border the main segment of Augury. Six large camphors surround a wide-spaced courtyard, and I head towards the tree one of the follow-up emails described.

There's a mage standing outside what I think is a magical elevator, and there's a set of stairs nearby. There's also a rope ladder hanging from above. I grab onto the rope, but Hiro makes an ungodly sound that I cannot ignore. He uses his head to gesture to the staircase, and I sigh. We ascend the busted-up wooden stairs.

Creak. Creeeaak.

Abso-fucking-lutely not. Not only are these stairs rickety, but they're *steep*. I'm not looking to sweat my ass off right before meeting one of the world's most influential elves. Or fall off a century old staircase to meet my most untimely demise.

I awkwardly step down, Hiro following closely behind, and make my way to the little mage I passed, who is standing there with their arms crossed, blue strands of hair flowing down into their face.

"May I take your... elevator?" I ask, unsure of what to call this device. It's almost tube-like, but there's nothing electric or even a pulley system visible. What does this thing run on?

"Of course, step into the lift," they say with a soft smile.

I hop onto the platform, Hiro at my side, and the glass door closes. It starts to move, slowly at first, but then shoots me into the skies.

I'm dead. I'm a goner. The mage killed me with just a brief wave of their hand.

Oh fuck. I'm—I'm fine.

The door opens, and I step onto the wooden platform. The lift runs on... magic. Honestly? If it wasn't terrifying, it would be super cool—like a free roller coaster ride to get you to class. I wonder if they went fast because it was my first time, or if they like making people's lunches reappear.

A satyr greets Hiro and me, bringing us to the very top of a cluster of buildings up within what he calls the History Tree. He opens the front door, and we step inside, where there is another set of doors. One reads *Dean Archeron Bariel*, and I turn the handle.

The Dean's office is a large cottage, covered floor-to-ceiling in trinkets. It resembles the inside of my brain more than it does an astute elf's place of work. There are piles of papers, gemstones, and other odd magical devices covering his desk. The Dean, however, is nowhere to be found.

"You—you probably shouldn't be in his office while he isn't here," the satyr says in a gentle tone, backing away as I step towards him. Does he think I'm going to bite him or something?

"Oh. My bad!" I say, not wanting to stress the guy any further. There's an odd-looking chair in the corner, almost like the pods peas grow in, and I take a seat, curling my legs up under me. Hiro sits down beside me.

Opening my backpack, I take out my Nintendo and boot up my village, which exists on the planet Floria. It's the newest game, and I'm eager to start it. Before I can even visit my neighbors, the door swings open.

"Good luck with your meeting; I'll ask Moss if he's still down for us to visit next week," a faun says as she walks through the door. She's stunning in a tight pencil skirt and a top with fun, flowing sleeves.

"Thank you, Daff," the tall elf says.

That must be—

"Ms. Watson! It is a pleasure to finally meet you. I've heard so much about you from my medicinal mages. You've helped them greatly with their research," the dean says, holding out a slender hand.

"Dean Bariel, the pleasure is all mine," I say in a chipper voice. It's forced, but I don't think he notices.

Actually, I don't think the dean notices much at *all* as he spends the next ten minutes talking about some adventure he went on recently. Something about disco dancing. I don't really listen. If I'm being honest with myself, I'm a poor listener.

It's not that I don't care about what anyone has to say, *I do*, but if I don't have a relationship with someone, or they don't have some cool fact to share, I don't really give a shit. Blame the ADHD, but small talk is my enemy.

Tell me you believe that dark matter is actually our souls gathering in the furthest depths of the universe, but don't tell me what you had for lunch or that your son, little Johnny, learned how to do a cartwheel—because it's *boring*. Unless little Johnny is my nephew, or you're my best friend, I'm not interested. Is that wrong? Probably. But it's true.

"How about we go into my office to continue this conversation? I have some things to share that require confidentiality," the dean says, interrupting my distracted daze.

"Sure," I say. If it were anyone else, I'd be a little weirded out, but the dean seems... dorky? *Too* dorky to be hitting on me.

We enter the dean's office, and I slouch down onto a chair, Hiro laying on the floor beside my feet. The room decor borders on psychedelic, and it's incredibly distracting. I don't know where to look.

"I want to tell you something, but you cannot repeat it," the dean says, taking a seat behind his desk.

Cone of silence. Got it.

I nod. "Of course."

The dean tucks a white, long strand of hair behind his ear. "Your research partner is a... difficult man."

"Okay?" I mean, I'm not the easiest person in the world to work with.

"I just—I don't want to deal with you reporting him over something that is expected. If he did something heinous, of course, but I don't have time to handle things involving his prickly personality."

"Is this your way of politely saying he's an asshole?"

The dean smiles. "Precisely."

I stifle a laugh. "Assholes? I can handle them all day. I was raised by one."

"Good to hear. I just didn't want you to come in blindsided. I ensure you, he's the best of the best when it comes to magical bot—"

Knock. Knock.

"Speaking of. Come in, Dr. Ali," the dean says and stands.

I turn to meet my new research partner and the breath is stolen straight from my lungs in one sudden whoosh.

Fuck. Me.

Over six feet of tan skin, muscular arms peeking through fitted fabric, and... scales. Black and gold scales trailing down to a sharp, curved tail. He's a serpentine. An unbelievably sexy serpentine. I've met a lot of hot men, women, and enbies, but I don't think I've ever gawked this hard. This dude looks like a statue, for fuck's sake.

"Ahem," the dean coughs. "Are you two going to continue staring, or are you going to introduce yourselves?"

"I am Dr. Adeib Ali," he says. His serious tone combined with the low depths of his voice is making me think of things I most definitely shouldn't be. "And you are?"

"I'm-Hi-I—" I stutter. My brain is flying in fourteen different directions, clarity thrown to the wind. I don't know my name or why I'm here, but I know what I want.

"This is Iris Watson. She's an employee of MagiPharm X and will be partnering with you on the research project this summer," the dean says, bringing me back to reality.

"Assisting me," Dr. Ali corrects. "I am heading this project."

Geeze. Someone takes their job too seriously. "Nice to meet you!" I say with a flushed smile.

"Is there a reason you called me down here? If it was to meet my research assistant, I would have met her on Monday when we started work," Dr. Ali says coldly, not looking at me.

"No, I'm not that ignorant of your attitude towards greetings and small talk. I called you down here to meet regarding your magic," the dean states.

Dr. Ali audibly groans. "Can we discuss this in private?"

The dean nods. "Of course. Ms. Watson, you are dismissed."

And just like that. Chopped liver. So much for a tour of the grounds. I'll just have to go investigate myself.

I'm only a few hundred feet away from the main part of campus when I hear loud noises coming from the direction of my apartment. Augury University is made up of camphor trees in a circle for the main part of campus, followed by a few buildings and sports fields, and then finally the dorms. The student dorms are first, then the grad school, medical, and research apartments.

Smack dab in the middle of the medical and research apartments is a series of fratremity houses. These so-called siblings, or fratrem, live together and throw giant parties under the guise of friendship or volunteer work. It's bullshit. In my experience at Octopus University, they're all just obnoxious.

The building I'm staring at now, rattling with sound so loud its windows are vibrating, is covered in spray paint and streamers. I approach the door, which has a bright yellow sheet of paper taped to the front that reads "FINE: Ecological and aesthetic destruction. 40d will be taken from your accounts and donated to charity."

Okay... that's pretty cool. Using the money from destruction for charity? A+ decision on whoever's part.

"Hey, you're not a fratrem, are you?" a masculine voice calls out toward me.

I twirl around, not wanting to be associated with this bag of dicks. "No, no. I was actually going to bitch at them for the noise," I confess.

"Don't bother. They don't care, and it won't go anywhere. I'm Fern."

"Iris!"

"Nice to meet you," Fern says.

"He's an ass," someone calls out from inside the building.

"No, I'm a centaur," he corrects while chuckling. Fern moves towards me and reaches out a hand, and I shake it.

Fern *is* a centaur. His hair is a ginger color, but his horse-half is a tan brown. Muscular, long legs lead to a tail that matches his head, and I smile. Raemond would say he's a cutie patootie.

There were other magical races where I grew up, but they weren't as common as they are on Magia Island. It's comforting to be around people with similar capabilities as myself, though I wish I looked more the part. Unlike my sister Indigo, who has stark white hair, the only thing that really gives away my heritage is my eyes. These pools of purple are anything but human.

"Are you touring the campus, then?" he asks.

"Sort of. I'm working for the Botanical Magic Department this summer, and I was supposed to tour the campus with the dean, but something came up."

"Naturally. Well, I'm a third-year med student. Medicinal magic. I'm usually busy studying, but if you need a tour, I'm free now," he says.

I shrug my shoulders and nod. "Sure. I'd love to."

Fern gestures away from the frat house, and we cross the distance to the multitude of fields and stadiums. Fern points with a pale, freckled hand, explaining each one.

"This is our ice rink, where our illusionary ice skaters practice. Over there is the enchanted soccer field, and then there's the track field."

"Just regular track?"

"In a way. There's an annual triathlon where athletes compete in running, swimming, and flying," he shares. "I don't compete, as you could probably guess."

"Don't feel bad, I won't be competing either," I say with a laugh.

Fern is fun and easy to talk to as we make our way across the lush, green campus.

It's humid, and I'm thankful I packed mostly shorts and tank tops. The ones I'm wearing today end right below my ass, and I'm a little surprised Fern hasn't taken a peek. Dr. Ali and Dean Bariel definitely did as I was leaving. I could feel their stares piercing through the fabric of the denim.

I mean, listen, I'm not full of myself, but I'm not an idiot either. Any red-blooded creature wants a chance to get a look at a nice ass, but maybe Fern's not into women, or at least not me. Only one way to find out.

"So, do you have a partner or something?" I ask, curiosity getting the better of me; I'm nosy by nature.

"Nope. I was dating this girl, a cambion, in my medical class our first year, but we broke up because I wouldn't let her cheat on one of our exams," he admits, sitting down on some grass. I take a seat on the bench beside him, the camphor trees circling us and the courtyard.

"Ooooof. Anyone you have your eye on now?"

He flushes bright red. "There's this guy who recently graduated Augury's paramedic cert course," he says, not maintaining eye contact.

"And why isn't he your boyfriend?" I inquire. Fern is cute. He might not be my type—*too sweet*—but he's definitely plenty of people's type.

"Honestly? I'm not sure he knows I exist. I was a simulated patient in a few of their scenario practices, but he was too in the zone to pay me much mind, and now he's gone," Fern shares with a shrug. "Guess I should move on."

"I am totally down to play matchmaker!" I squeal.

"Alright, bet. I'll give you the rules of the road for surviving at Augury, and you help me find some fun hook-ups," he says, and we shake hands.

I'm making friends already. My besties back home would be so proud.

three

ADEIB

That same day

Iris Watson more or less skips out of the room, long brown hair falling down her back in elegant waves, and I cannot help but stare. I did not want a research assistant, but Archeron Bariel insisted it was necessary. MagiPharm X has a lot of information we need, which left me agreeing to their requests, and now here we are.

"Did you look into any alternative methods of magic conduction?" I ask.

Archeron nods. "Yes, I've looked into everything. On the planet Hel, they use this green crystal called magicite. We don't have any on Earth, and it will be a year or longer until we get a shipment, if they'll even part with one."

"Unfortunate."

"Couldn't you go back to search for more tea leaves?"

"I do not wish to go back. It is too different." *Too* different from the home I once loved. I am afraid if I go, I will stay to search for more than just tea.

My ukhti. My twin.

My mind unravels images of the past, laying them out before me. My sister, The Convergence, and the dunes I once knew and loved. It is my most painful truth, and I blink away the memories.

"I understand. Really, I do," he shares, though I know he does not understand.

Grief is too personal an experience for anyone to truly empathize with. They might sympathize, but they cannot feel what you feel.

"I think of what life would've been like if I were born on our home planet," he says.

I remember what life was like before The Convergence. When Earth was just Earth, and there were no pieces of Floria, Barak, Hel, and other planets scattering our globe.

"So, what do you propose?" I ask, changing the subject.

Archeron smacks his hands down onto the desk. "I got you a familiar!"

"I am well past maturity," I scoff.

"Obviously, Adeib, but you need something to replace your saharshay."

"Saharshaay," I correct.

"Without those tea leaves, you might as well be a human, unless you find another conduit."

"I know." He does not need to tell me that my time has run out. I have been counting the leaves. I have been wrapping my head around a life without magic. A life unlike the one I have always known.

"Just give it a try," the dean says and stands. "Daff, bring her in!"

I cannot explain the sight before me. Flying towards me is the oddest little creature I have ever seen. The being is a gecko with leopard-like spots... except she has the bright orange wings of a monarch butterfly.

She sticks her tongue out and wags her plump tail. Absolutely not.

Daffodil, Archeron's pain-in-my-tail assistant, snickers in the corner. "Is her size linked to Dr. Ali's magical capabilities?"

Archeron shakes his head. "On the contrary. I chose a familiar with strong magical capacity. I thought I'd earn bonus points because she's from Adeib's part of the world. Or at least, half her ancestry is. She's a leopard geckfly."

The faun smiles, enamored by what the dean is saying.

The little creature flies over to me, landing on my shoulder with a quiet thump. She might just be my best option—my only option to continue being a mage. We are incredibly close to so many medical discoveries. We have eradicated STIs. Next is cancer.

"Fine. I will take the creature with me," I say, giving in.

I slither, crossing the threshold of the door.

"Hey Adeib," Archeron calls out.

"What?" I do not turn back to look at him.

"You should really consider giving her a name. She's a being with feelings, just like you."

I enter my condo, the little creature following behind me. There is not a lot of furniture in my home, as I prefer to give myself a wide berth. She flies from object to object, panting heavily once she gets to the countertop.

"I have to name you," I say, looking over at her. "How about Arsh?"

She shakes her head and frowns. The geckfly actually frowns.

"Hmm. That is a good name. What about Nasira?"

She stomps her feet, angrily turning away from me.

"Alright. Not Nasira, either. Asma? It is quite a complimentary name," I suggest.

The geckfly flies towards me and grabs the neck of my tunic with her claw. Slowly, I slither out of the living room as she tries to drag me into my office. I am not sure why I am following her, but I suppose I am curious enough to see what she wants.

She lets go of my shirt and perches herself onto the keyboard of my desktop. She taps the spacebar, and my log-in screen comes up. I unlock the computer and click on a word processing application, hoping that will satisfy whatever she requires.

Tap. Tap. Tap. Tap. Tap.

"F-L-O-R-P," I read aloud. "Florp?"

She turns towards me, tail wagging and all, and nods.

"You want me to call you... Florp?" I ask.

She nods again, this time even more ecstatic.

I am not doing that.

Leaving the room, I head down the hall towards the shower. My condo is a lot like my classroom and greenhouse. Plants are coming out of every direction, growing onto walls and hanging from ceilings. I tend to keep mostly non-magical plants here. They are easier for me to grow and maintain. Magical plants require more... well, magic.

I keep one magical plant in my house, however. The rosa aeternitas, given to me by a previous elven elder, Asopus Bariel. I see his face when I look at the dean, but none of his humorless personality.

I turn on the shower, and the hot water melts the stress off my skin and scales. Hanging from the shower head is a bundle of lavender and eucalyptus, and I delight in the scent.

Scent is the strongest sense of the serpentine. I can smell with both my nose and tongue, though it is different. My tongue can smell chemicals—pheromones, hormones, among other things. I could tell you what is in something by scent alone. The eucalyptus clears my senses, allowing me a fresh start.

When I am finished, I turn off the water and grab a towel. Drying off, I make my way back to the office. The little creature sits perched on my desk. My computer screen is open to a document, and I read it in a flurry.

FLORPFLORPFLORPFLORPFLORPFLORPFLORPFLORPFLORP
FLORPFLORPFLORPFLORPFLORPFLORPFLORPFLORPFLORP
FLORPFLORPFLORPFLORPFLORPFLORPFLORPFLORPFLORP
FLORPFLORPFLORPFLORPFLORPFLORPFLORPFLORPFLORP
FLORPFLORPFLORPFLORPFLORPFLORPFLORPFLORPFLORP
FLORPFLORPFLORPFLORPFLORPFLORPFLORPFLORPFLORP
FLORPFLORPFLORPFLORPFLORPFLORPFLORPFLORPFLORP
FLORPFLORPFLORPFLORPFLORPFLORPFLORPFLORPFLORP
FLORPFLORPFLORPFLORPFLORPFLORPFLORPFLORPFLORP
FLORPFLORPFLORPFLORPFLORPFLORPFLORPFLORPFLORP
FLORPFLORPFLORPFLORPFLORPFLORPFLORPFLORPFLORP
FLORPFLORPFLORPFLORPFLORPFLORPFLORPFLORPFLORP
FLORPFLORPFLORPFLORPFLORPFLORPFLORPFLORPFLORP
FLORPFLORPFLORPFLORPFLORPFLORPFLORPFLORPFLORP
FLORPFLORPFLORPFLORPFLORPFLORPFLORPFLORPFLORP
FLORPFLORPFLORPFLORPFLORPFLORPFLORPFLORPFLORP
FLORPFLORPFLORPFLORPFLORPFLORPFLORPFLORPFLORP

Florp… over and over again. She must have done it a few dozen times, and I stare at her in utter shock.

"Alright," I say, conceding. "I will call you Florp."

The little creature smiles and happily flies out of the room.

I am unsure how I will go to events with influential mages and introduce my familiar as Florp, but I will have to figure it out.

Before I shut off my computer, I decide to do some sleuthing. Googling Iris Watson pulls up dozens of articles about her miraculous cure for cancer. From the research I received, it is no cure at all. It helps prevent cancer from returning, but does not completely eradicate it.

Her socials are pretty clean. All are private or blank; at least the ones that use her legal name. I am sure she has a secret account somewhere I am not finding.

There is a post with her full name in the caption by some elf called Terranova. The photo he posted looks old. She has fewer piercings in it, but he shared the picture a few months ago. His arm is slung around Iris, her expression screaming discomfort. The image makes me feel oddly protective. She has such a sweet demeanor here, meanwhile he looks downright villainous.

I cannot find much else about my new research assistant, but I am sure she will tell me all about herself. Hopefully, she is as interesting as she looks. I am bored with talking to basic, simple scientists.

Slithering into the kitchen, I go to make my favorite tea. Noomi basra. Opening the container of dried limes, I pull some out.

Florp flies over and lands on the counter. She takes a giant bite out of the dried lime.

"Hey, do not do that," I say, scolding her. "Those are sour."

She takes another big bite of dried lime. I try pulling it out of her mouth, but she drags it away from my hand.

What is wrong with this creature?

Florp eats the last bit of the dried lime I had on the counter, and I flinch as she chomps away. The taste is too strong... somehow both sour and woodsy. I am unsure how or why she enjoys it in this form. I need lots of sugar for my tea, and that is diluted by water.

Laying on her back, Florp rubs her belly to tell me she is full.

This is my life now.

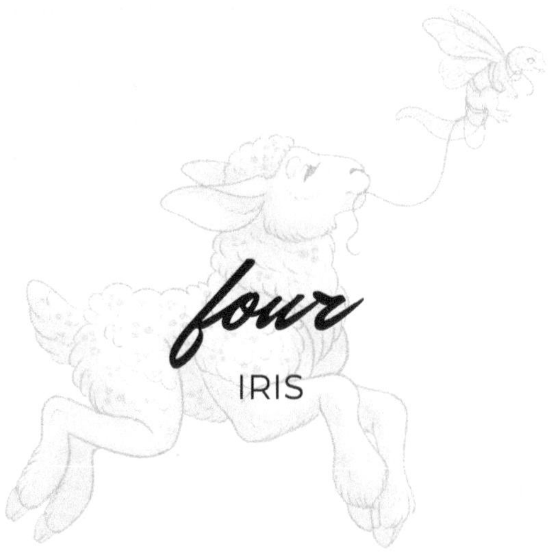

four

IRIS

How did humans survive before GPS?

Yesterday Fern showed me the Augury University app, which has an interactive map. Dr. Ali's greenhouse isn't listed, but since I know what building it's near, I'm able to find it. Walking past a series of medical buildings, I make my way towards the greenhouse, which sits on the west edge of campus. Hiro follows beside me, quietly trotting by my side. I think he's just glad to be out in the clean, fresh air.

Tall, clear glass panels showcase the massive volume of plants that grow inside. There are dark green vines cascading down the back exterior wall, and I walk the smooth path, which is lined by small yellow flowers. I open the door to find Dr. Ali waiting inside, rearranging beakers on a table. He's facing away from me, and I take my time absorbing his figure. The broad expanse of his back is covered by a purple jacket which falls past his hips. It's not a bad view.

I'm sure it's not called a jacket. I'm sure it's called something beautiful that I'm going to fail to pronounce, but his clothes are to die for. Embroidered and embellished in these golden swirls that line the edges—his top hugs his chest and arms perfectly.

As my eyes travel down his body to his tail, I realize I've never seen a serpentine in person before meeting him. There's a famous movie star—Mohammad Al-Aziz—who I used to have a crush on, but I never met him. I never got to see the shimmering scales or the sheer size of his tail in person.

It's otherworldly. Which is funny, because they're from our world. I'm the one with ancestors from another planet.

Dr. Ali turns, and I force my gaze off of him and gasp when I notice the other sight before me. Hundreds of flowers and plants fill the space. Hanging from ceilings, coming out of fixtures, growing in potted plants and out of the ground, there is life everywhere.

"Wow," I say, not sure how else to describe it all.

"What?"

"That's a lot of plants."

Dr. Ali and I lock eyes, irritation setting in to his features. "Yes. It is a greenhouse."

"I know that, I just... there's so many," I say, my mind still unraveling the beauty of nature. I get why Raemond loves plants so much.

"Congratulations," he says in a condescending tone. "You have working retinas and cognitive function. Glad we could share this moment together."

Ouch. I mean, I know the Dean said he was going to be a dick, but I figured I'd have to do something to set him off first.

"Okay, grumpy. What's the first order of business?" I'm not going to give him the satisfaction of reacting. I refuse to let a man bother me. Hiro lays down on the ground nearby, but his eyes are wide as he watches us interact.

"You may call me Adeib or Dr. Ali," he states coldly, not breaking my stare. His eyelashes are different from mine, almost like they are facing downward.

"Okay, *Adeib.* I'm guessing you don't want to have a get to know me chat, so what would you like me to do to start?"

"I am sure I will get to know you plenty while we work. You seem to do a lot of talking," he says and slithers past me. "Follow me, I will show you what plants we have here."

I hate that he's attractive, but I'm not sure if I hate that he's an asshole. I wanted an easy summer job, but working in the medicinal magic field is everything but. At least the bickering will make things a bit more interesting.

"There are obviously more plants here than we have time in the day, but I will show you some of the ones I believe will have the properties we are looking for," he says, gesturing to a specific section.

There's a magistera by the table, a plant I recognize. I majored in potions, and it's a common ingredient we used. It looks like the average monstera, but there's a specific sheen to the leaves that allows mages to tell them apart.

"That's a magistera," I say.

He nods. "We are looking for plants that have properties which involve redirection. If, when put in a potion, a mage is able to deteriorate or reconstruct something, the same property applied to a cell might be able to reproduce what we are looking for," he explains.

"Are there any plants you're hopeful will work?" I ask, gesturing to the heap of flowers and greenery growing before us.

"Yes, but we will need to do more research. There are a few here, but even more that we do not have."

"Why not?" This is the great Augury University, after all.

He shrugs. "Some plants are rare, and others require higher quantities of magic to grow and maintain. I... had something going on with my magic, and have needed to be more... particular with how much I was using."

I cock my head, unsure of what he means. Is he being vague because he doesn't know me yet, or is it unimportant to share and therefore a waste of his time?

"And what if we research these plants and find we do need them? What'll we do then?"

"I will grow them," he states directly. "My magic situation has been resolved."

Wait—where is his familiar? I didn't see one when I came in, but I was highly distracted, per the usual. Could it be so small I can't see it? Like a bug?

"Do you have a familiar?" It's a stupid question, honestly. There are very few mages on this planet without familiars. The only one I'm personally aware of... is well, the Dean.

My arms are crossed as I stand beside him, and I wonder how it feels to be upright like he is. Do serpentine ever slither flat on the ground like a snake? Could they use their arms to go even faster?

"I do," he says. "Her name is Florp."

Something comes flying towards us, so fast that I can't even make out what it is. The wings remind me of a butterfly, but the body is—is that a reptile?

"Florp? What origin is that name from? Is it orc?" I ask.

"It is... a name of her own doing." He frowns, almost scowling, as the little creature lands on his shoulder.

"Does she speak?!" I say excitedly. Hiro is my other half. I can understand his emotions and he mine, but I didn't study creature crafts. Mages can technically do any kind of magic, but at around an elementary level. To be able to communicate with creatures other than your familiar, you have to practice for years. It's possible Adeib double majored in Botanical Crafts and Creature Crafts.

"No, but she can type on a keyboard. She made it very clear this was the only name she would accept."

I smile. "May I touch you?" I ask, and Florp nods. I take my index finger and rub the back of her head, and she leans into it.

I can see the rise and fall of Adeib's chest in my peripheral vision, and I freeze. I was so focused on Florp, I didn't think about how close I was getting to him. If it weren't for our height difference, our faces would be touching right now. He smells good. Like, incredibly good. Deliciously, incredibly good. His cologne must be some combination of citrus and oud.

I back away, made uncomfortable by my own lack of spatial awareness, and put my hands against my thighs. "Sorry, I didn't mean—"

"It is fine. Can we continue the tour?"

"Sure."

Adeib shows me every plant imaginable. So much so, I literally don't think I'll remember any of them. Maybe ten percent, if I'm lucky.

We head back to the table where Hiro is laying. Adeib pulls out a blue plastic box and opens it. The scents of lemon and garlic hit me, causing my stomach to growl.

"I am going to eat lunch now. Feel free to do the same," he says nonchalantly.

"Okay, thanks."

I'm not going to bother telling him I forgot to make myself food. Or that I forget to make myself meals most days. If I didn't set an alarm on my phone, I might forget to eat. I get so busy and my mind is so preoccupied by every little thing, my hunger cues get thrown to the wayside. I want to remember to eat just like I want to remember to wash all the conditioner out of my hair, yet I don't. I can't.

Sitting down, I watch him eat. He brought hummus and pita, and a salad I don't recognize. When he pulls out a vanilla protein shake, I'm officially fucking jealous.

Adeib has a short, thick beard that frames his face nicely. I think without it, his jaw would be too sharp to handle. Almost everything about him is sharp. From the angle of his brows to the bridge of his nose.

He looks over at me and frowns. "Why are you watching me eat? Get out your lunch."

Oh boy. "I didn't bring a lunch."

"Why?"

"I forgot," I admit.

"How do you forget to bring your lunch?"

"I just moved here and now I'm in a new apartment and I don't know. I forgot, okay?" It's a half-truth, though he doesn't need to know that.

"Here," he says and gestures to his food. "Have some of mine."

"You don't need to do—"

He shoves a spoonful of salad into my mouth.

"Just be quiet and eat. You won't be a very good research assistant if you run out of energy or pass out on your first day."

"Research partner," I say after swallowing. Whatever this is, it's delicious. "What is that? It's so good."

"Tabbouleh. Here, have some more." He scoops another spoonful, this time handing it to me. His forearms flex, and I watch his veins as he hands me more food. "Have some pita, too."

I think I'm in love. Not with Adeib, but with his tabbouleh.

"Not to be stupid, but I just moved here. Is there like a Mediterranean market you get this from?" I ask.

"Yes. It is called my kitchen."

What a weird—oh. "You made this?"

"From scratch."

"How?" I'm amazed.

"Farfora, this is the most basic of foods. It is salad and bread and hummus. People were making bread thousands of years before electricity was even invented. Do you not know how to make *bread*?"

I frown. "No, I'm not really the cooking type." And it's true. I tend to get frustrated with things I'm not instantly good at and give up on them. Cooking was unfortunately one of them.

"Everyone has to eat, therefore everyone is the cooking type."

"Not me," I argue. "I just order out or make PB&J."

"There is no way you are getting enough nutrients," he says and puts his container down, crossing his arms.

"I take a multivitamin," I say. Or at least I *try* to. I usually forget.

He squints his big brown eyes. "You would not need a multivitamin if you ate properly." His tone is serious and cold, sending chills down my spine.

"Okay, okay. Save the lecture. Don't we have work to do?"

"Apparently, we have more work than I thought."

five

IRIS

Hiro rests his head on my thighs as I stretch my arms out and yawn. The prospect of helping cancer patients, of doing important work, is exciting. What weighs me down is my own inadequacy.

I *know* potions. I understand how potions can create things. I'm not brilliant at it, but I'm pretty damn good. Medicinal magic is entirely its own craft. Usually performed by those of us whose focus is potions or botany, medicinal magic intertwines human and non-human biology with magic. Specifically, the biology of diseases and illnesses. The focus is on healing, not just on transformation.

Hiro jumps onto the ground as I shift my weight, slowly climbing out of bed. My mind is so jumbled from all the recent changes, and I feel out-of-place. After a quick shower, I blow-dry my hair and pick an outfit. The weather app says it's going to be hot today, so I throw on a crop top and shorts. They keep me cool *and* show off my tattoos. I grab my funky, thigh-high fishnets to go with my boots. Looking in the mirror, I do a little spin. *Outfit complete.*

I check my phone before I leave. Six notifications from my mother. An all-time *low* record. I quickly shoot her a text, keeping her up to date with my work at Augury. She's ecstatic I'm near Indigo again. She's hoping I can help them mend their relationship. I will not be doing any of that. The things our mother has said to my sister are unacceptable, and, frankly, I wouldn't blame Indie if she found them to be unforgivable too.

The walk to the greenhouse is longer than I prefer, but it's not unbearable.

I think, maybe, I'll invest in a bicycle while I'm here. A cute one with one of those little baskets on the handlebar. If the basket is big enough, I can put Hiro inside it.

My familiar doesn't seem to mind all the walking. I like walking in theory... if the theory was that it was cool out, the sun was shaded by clouds, and I was wearing more comfortable shoes.

I've never really been an exercise girly. Hiking tires me out, sports are not my thing, and lifting weights makes me nauseous. Growing up, my version of exercise was cleaning the house with my sister. Now, as an adult, it's sex. Especially sex with individuals with non-human appendages. I get a workout trying to fit my body around them. Everybody has their own preferences. Kraken ladies are a fun time. A lot of orcs won't sleep with elfborn because of the size difference, but I've had my fair share. I think the only magical race I haven't fooled around with is... serpentine.

Hiro and I pass the sports fields, and I know we're close to the greenhouse. My heart rate accelerates as we approach, and I can't really be sure of why. The anxiety I had around this fake narrative I webbed myself into has subsided, and now all that's left is guilt. I don't feel anxious, I feel awful.

Maybe it's not my guilt that's got me sweating. Excitement can raise your heart rate. Adrenaline. Perhaps I'm just really into working with a snarky snake.

I push open the glass doors and enter the greenhouse, Hiro by my side. Adeib is standing at our workbench, his arms crossed. I walk towards him and push his set of beakers further back on the bench before plopping down onto the table.

Adeib stares at me for a long while, his eyes like sunlight shining through a glass of whiskey. He places a hand on my face, holding me by my jaw.

"You are late," he says in a temper. His voice is low and menacing, making goosebumps rise on my arms.

"It's six past nine," I say, looking up at the clock. "That's hardly late."

"The reason we start at nine, even though my contracted hours typically start at eight, is because Magi Pharm X informed us their little princess cannot wake up that early. Hence, your start time is nine." He looks at me with the kind of fury that would make any person cower—any person but me, apparently.

"Oh, cry me a fucking river, Adeib. Are you seriously complaining about an extra hour of sleep?" I spit back.

"Except I do not get extra sleep. I arrive here at the same time I did before you and begin working, waiting for you to arrive. And when you do finally show up, you are half-naked and begging for an OSHA violation."

My brows furrow, and his grip on my jaw loosens. "What the fuck is OSHA?"

"Nevermind. I forget they disbanded after The Convergence." He removes his hand and rubs his face.

In this exact moment, I decide that whatever game he's playing, I'm playing too—playing to win. "You said I was half-naked and begging, is that a position you often think of me in?"

He looks speechless, skin red and flushed. Game over.

Adeib slithers away from me towards a group of colorful plants. I hop off the table and follow him, my legs struggling to keep up. I'm not short by human standards, but by every magical race, I'm puny.

"I do not think of you much at all. I just met you. Unfortunately, I see this changing with how often you manage to piss me off," he shares. It's not his best work, but my last retort was a hard act to follow.

"Is pissing you off another ocean violation?" I ask. The only ocean I know is the water, but I'm sure this sounds sarcastic enough.

"Pretty much." He shrugs. "I need you to cut a few samples of magistera for us to source for a potion."

Adeib hands me some small shears and holds a bag open for me as I carefully cut off some stems and leaves. If you cut a magical plant the wrong way, the entire thing can wither in an instant. There's a process we learned in beginning potions, a specific angle that enables me to do it with ease.

"Can I ask a question?" I just need to know why he says the weird things he does. That, and I'm hoping to ease some of the tension.

"You just did, farfora."

I roll my eyes. "I know serpentine live longer than most, but how old *are* you?"

"Old," he says, sealing the bag. We cross back towards the workbench.

"Do you ever get ID'd at bars?" I inquire.

"No, they generally think I am in my thirt—"

"For your senior discount?" I interrupt.

Adeib sighs and mumbles something under his breath.

"What was that?"

"Charming. You are quite the charmer."

I'm going to need to learn arabic if I'm ever going to keep up with this man's insults, because he did *not* say charming the first time. I'll add that to the never-ending list of shit I want to learn.

Adeib hands me a large bag of dried flowers and places a mortar and pestle onto the table. "The bag has a few different flowers another researcher recommended. The magistera will act as the active ingredient. Once we have the potion made, we can send it off to the laboratory for further testing," he explains as I grind the flowers.

As he talks, I watch Adeib's tongue move. It's thin and forked, much like a snake's. I wonder what it would feel like entangled in mine. *Nope. Next thought.* Why does Adeib always talk like he knows about life from before The Convergence? Could he really be that old? Maybe I should ask him.

"What was the Earth like before The Convergence?" I say, still grinding the flowers.

"At what point in time?"

I cock my head curiously. "Right before The Convergence."

"It was awful, actually. I think The Convergence might have saved the world," he confesses. "Earth was beautiful and messy. Humanity fought and progressed, while the serpentine and merfolk remained hidden, continuing with our own separate societies. Over time, humanity got selfish."

"Selfish?"

"Fighting over land was the big thing. And religions. And race, nation, ethnicity. The whole thing disgusts me. Everyone was too hungry for power," he shares. "The Convergence brought a lot of pain, but a lot of good too."

I look into his eyes. "What did it feel like?"

"The Convergence?"

"Yeah."

Adeib slithers closer, only a few centimeters away. "I did not know if I was going to live or die."

Nothing he's saying is sexy. It's all surprisingly truthful and raw, but there's a tension in the air I can't seem to break. I'm fixated, hooked on his every word.

"I'm sorry for your loss," I say, not knowing what else to do in fear I'll do something crazy like kiss him.

"How do you know I lost someone?"

"Everyone's lost someone. If you've been around since before The Convergence, you've had time to lose plenty."

He backs away, and I'm half-grateful, half-disappointed.

"We should eat lunch."

Whatever moment we just shared is going to be ruined when I tell him I forgot to pack a lunch again.

"I'm actually not hungry," I lie, sitting on one of the chairs near the workbench. The seating in this school needs a makeover. Almost nothing is comfortable, and I find myself curling my legs up to my chest.

"I do not believe you."

I shrug. "You don't have to. They don't pay you to believe me, just to work with me."

"I am the Head of Botanical Crafts. I oversee our magical botany courses and ensure our plants are thriving. If anything, you are being paid to work with *me*."

"Weren't you just bitching about power hungry humans?" I tease.

"Good thing I am not human. I do not have to fight to prove I am powerful—I *am* powerful," he says and opens his lunch container.

I'm not going to address the feeling tingling down my abdomen towards my thighs. Nope. Nope. Nope.

The smell of his lunch is alluring, and my stomach grumbles loudly, revealing my lie. Adeib hands me a fork, and I realize he brought two. His lunch is also significantly bigger than yesterday's.

I take a bite, enjoying the flavors. It's chicken biryani, which is a favorite of mine. There are so many different foods on Earth now, some from different cultures, but others from whole other planets. It makes it hard to keep up. Some things, however, everyone knows about. Waffles, caesar salad, tacos, neenos, and chicken biryani. All the best stuff.

"I will cut you a deal," Adeib says, breaking my train of thought. "If you agree to wear more appropriate clothes, I will make your lunch every day."

I don't know whether to cry tears of joy or punch him. I would love for someone to make me lunch—it would help my executive function issues immensely. But I also don't want to let a man control what I wear.

"Why do you have such a problem with what I wear? Why do you even care?" I'm pissed. I don't care that his offer was sweet, it was laced with control.

"I have a problem because what you wear is a safety hazard, Iris. I do not care if you show your skin in your free time, but while you are in the greenhouse or the lab, I would rather be safe than sorry."

"And you care if I get hurt?" I ask, putting my fork down. If there's one thing I can't stand, it's disingenuity.

"I have fed you. I have shared things with you that I have told very few people. So yes, I care if you get hurt. You are my assistant, and therefore, my responsibility."

"Partner," I correct. "I am your research partner."

"So act like an equal and dress appropriately."

I cross my arms. "All you're wearing is that jacket. That doesn't look like a lab coat to me."

"This coat is made of a special synthetic fabric that protects me. I wear a different coat while I am in the lab, but this is what I wear for my day-to-day life, including my time at the greenhouse."

He always has to have a fucking answer for everything.

"Fine. I will wear long sleeves in exchange for lunch, but I want a cool light-weight robe or something pretty. Can I get the contact info of the person who made yours?"

"No need, I will handle it," he says, and my heart skips a beat.

I follow Adeib as he cares for the plants, giving some medicine and others water. He takes better care of this greenhouse than I do myself.

"Do you have a favorite plant?"

His eyes widen, pupils dilating as if he's taken aback. "No." His tone is sharp.

"Have you ever thought about it?"

"Why, are you going to kill my favorite plant?"

My brows furrow, and I give him a look. "I'm not a monster. I'm genuinely curious. Someone who works with plants this heavily *has* to have a favorite."

"Roses," he says, his tone soft. "There are so many unique types. All are beautiful, and all equally delicate."

six

ADEIB

Iris is both La Belle et la Bête. She is frighteningly brave and breathtakingly beautiful. I want to strangle her, and I want to choke her—and no, those are not the same thing.

Every part of this elfborn is a work of art. From the ink that lines her arms and thigh, to the jewels that elevate her already angelic face. There is a piercing above her lip, two gems connected by a chain across her nose, and a plethora of different jewels and metals in her ears. Everything is silver, and, for whatever reason, I deeply want to swap it all for gold. She deserves gold.

Last night, I put in the order for her lab coat. I got her one that is black with faint red irises embroidered onto the back. I am not sure why I went with red; I think her favorite color is something else, but it suits her. The designer said it will be ready in a few weeks, and I smile at the thought of giving it to her.

There is a small, air-conditioned building next to the greenhouse with a bathroom, refrigerator, and a microwave. I put our lunches into the fridge before heading back to the greenhouse to wait for her.

Florp sits on my shoulder, still snoozing away. She has become a helpful little thing, allowing me to regrow the magistera we trimmed yesterday. You cannot even tell we took any, which is how I prefer it.

I sit at the workbench and stare at the potions Dr. Taylor provided me. I think, had I not chosen botanical crafts, I would have considered potions. But botany is like coming home. It is the connection to every land I have ever lived on. Magia Island, Europa, Arabia. The cultures and experiences have been different, but botany has been my constant.

Iris walks in, her familiar trailing behind her, and I nearly sigh in relief. She is wearing a long sleeve top that flows down to her knees. There are slits on the sides, all the way up to her hips.

At this moment I am envious of the leggings that get to hug the curves of her body. I am not even sure I like her, but the lust I'm experiencing is undeniable. It borders on insatiable, and as her eyes dilate, I am positive my lust is not unrequited.

"Good morrow," I say, keeping my tone cool. Light.

"You don't always have to speak like you're in a Shakespeare play, you know?" She blows a strand of hair out of her face. "Morning."

"I was going for Donne, not Shakespeare, but I will take the compliment," I retort.

"It's far too early for snobby, multi-thousand year old literature references. What's the plan for today?" she asks and sits down beside me.

The corners of my mouth quirk up. "What do you read, then?" I gesture to the six young hibiscus trees sitting in a pot on the workbench. Adjacent to the row of trees is a small pile of specimen bags. "We are going to run a little experiment."

Her face turns bright red. "I read a lot of things."

"Do you?"

"Yes."

"Like what?"

"A lot of different genres," she says, frustrated. I can feel her body heat, even though we are a meter apart.

"If you read a lot of genres, why do you refuse to name any?"

"Can you just tell me what to do?"

"Gladly, mon chéri."

"With the *plants!*" She freezes, every muscle in her body going stone still. "Did you just speak French?"

I shrug "من زبانهای زیاد حرف" میزنم."

"That wasn't Arabic. And it definitely wasn't Serpenia. What was that?!"

"Farsi," I say. "I speak a lot of different languages."

"Well. Didn't realize you were a fucking polyglot. That's weirdly cool."

It would be embarrassing if I did not speak multiple languages after this many millennia.

"I know you tried to change the subject, but I did not forget. Tell me what you read. I am curious," I confess. It is true. She fascinates me in a strange, infuriating way.

"Ohmygoodness, fine. I read romance, mostly." Her cheeks flush.

"What kind of romance?"

"Nothing you'd know."

I sigh. "I have been around for a long time, Iris. What kind of books do you read?"

"I don't read a ton of books."

"You just said you read a ton!"

She frowns and looks the other direction. "I do. Just not *books*."

"Well, what are they then? Subtitles? Instruction manuals? Pornographic magazines? Stop evading the question."

"I read a lot of fucking fanfiction, okay?"

"Oh," I say, almost relieved. I really thought she was going to confess to reading something heinous like self-help books. Those are by far the worst books I have ever read. Fanfiction is normal. Fun, if you are into those kinds of things. "Do you have a favorite fandom?"

"You did not just ask me that."

"What?" My brows furrow.

"You're a bajillion year old serpentine with a doctorate degree, the fancy head of the plant magic department, and you know what fanfiction and fandoms are? I was expecting judgment."

"*Not* a bajillion years old, and that is precisely why I know of these things. It is a huge part of human and elven cultures." Her hand moves faster than I react, and she pinches my forearm. I almost hiss, but decide to feign pain instead. "What was that for?"

"Just checking if you're real. Now, can you please tell me what to do with the plant?"

"We are using the hibiscuses as test subjects. Go collect six plant samples," I explain. "We are not looking for anything too specific, just ones you think could create any sort of cell adaptation."

"Plants for cell adaptations, got it."

"Oh," I say, stopping her. "The greenhouse is a non-sterile site, so do not worry about how you collect them."

"Okidoki." She flashes me a devious grin. "By the way, I read omegaverse," she whispers and walks away.

Why did she sound flirtatious when she said that? And why did I like it?

I grab a watering can and water the hibiscus, trying not to think about the last twenty minutes. I do not tend to a lot of non-magical plants, but I still care about them. Every being serves a purpose.

Florp flies over to a small patch of murrseae and chomps down. I would stop her, but the grass can regrow. She deserves it; she has been working so hard to conduct all the magic I have used this week.

The elfborn returns, brown hair swaying as she walks back to me carrying a bundle of stems and flowers. She looks cute like this, so joyful and full of energy. I envy her demeanor.

Wait a second.

"Iris. Why are you carrying them like that?" I ask.

"You said not to worry about how I collect them, so I just grabbed them like this," she says and plops them onto the workbench.

Wallah, this woman is going to kill me.

"I meant you do not have to wear gloves. I did not mean you do not have to put them in separate bags. Always collect samples separately," I say through gritted teeth.

"Whoopsie. Sorry. Anyway, it's not a big deal."

"It is a big deal. How will we know if the hibiscus reacts because of the sample itself, or if something happens thanks to cross-contamination?"

"I guess we can redo it if something like that happens."

"Go back and collect the samples again," I demand, crossing my arms.

"No," she says and crosses her arms in mockery of me.

"Are you leading this project?"

"Fuck you, Adeib," she says and stomps off.

I thought we were doing so well.

Walking off, I exit the greenhouse and go to heat up our lunches. The chicken and rice smell delightful as they circle around in the microwave.

There is a picnic table outside the greenhouse. I decide, since the workbench is hosting our test subjects and samples, we might want to have lunch out here. Crossing the threshold into the greenhouse, I go to find Iris.

"I made you lunch," I say, hoping that lures her out. She is sitting at the workbench, organizing the samples in what appears to be alphabetical order.

"Are you angry with me?"

"Yes, you're a dick."

At that, I snap. "I did not—I—you were the one who collected the samples incorrectly. You should be a responsible adult and fix your mistakes without throwing a temper tantrum."

"Maybe I don't know everything. Maybe I'm the research *assistant* for a reason, and I need proper guidance," she says, throwing my previous words back at me.

"World renowned Iris Watson is not actually as perfect as she acts on camera? Who would have thought?" I looked into Iris when they informed me she was going to be my assistant. Tabloids, papers, and talk shows all over the world shared her so-called miracle. She is beautiful... thrilling, even. But the brilliant scientist? Has yet to make an appearance. I almost believed they had confused her with her sister, Indigo.

Iris stands like she is going to run off somewhere, and we cannot have that. "Listen," I say, softening my tone. "I am not trying to be harsh—"

"But you *are* being harsh."

"Have you ever considered that everyone else has been too gentle? That maybe you need something else?" I ask and gesture to the door, trying not to show her the heat that laces my stare. "Come on, before the food gets cold."

Fifteen minutes and a mouth full of Machboos later, suddenly I am no longer the villain in Iris' story.

"Mmmm." She swallows another bite, moaning as it enters her mouth. "This is so fucking good."

There is something about the way she says it, and the sensual way she is eating. I cannot stop thinking about what it would feel like for her mouth to wrap around my cock. So much so, I fear it will spring out at any moment.

"Iris," I say.

"Yes?" she asks.

"I have to go. We will reconvene tomorrow morning. I am glad you enjoyed the food." I nod, collect my things, and hurry out the door.

The second I get home, I take off my coat and head to my bedroom, shutting the door behind me. I sprawl across my bed, my tail slithering down, the tip touching the floor.

Finally alone, I allow my cock to spring out from its pocket. It is tense and throbbing, and I slowly rub up and down my shaft, gradually increasing speed and pressure.

As I continue pumping, I cannot help but wonder if Iris has ever fucked someone with a cock like mine. Long and red with lots of texture. Would she enjoy the dextrous fins that cover my shaft? I picture her riding me, my second cock springing loose to stimulate her clit. I want to rip her to pieces—to watch her crumble around me as I drive into her, tearing her in two, only for her to fall back together in my arms.

I want to be the only name she can remember. The only face she cannot forget.

After what she shared about her reading habits, I want to knot her too. I dream of filling her until she is a wet, sopping mess. Most of all? I want her to smell like mine, and for every serpentine on planet Earth to know she is untouchable.

I would never commit murder, so to speak, but I would do unspeakable things to the next man that thinks he can have Iris Watson.

Cock in fist, I allow these fantasies to take over. The rage. The lust. My unadulterated desire. I ride the high until I come toppling down, climaxing all over my sheets.

"Fuck," I say out loud.

I am not supposed to want to fuck my research assistant. I never cared much about rules or forced politeness, but I have stayed out of unnecessary trouble. And yet everyone at Augury University seems to be fraternizing with their inferiors, so why should I be any different?

Besides, the only thing that will fix this feeling that is festering inside me... is her.

seven

IRIS

Have you ever considered that everyone else has been too gentle? That maybe you need something else?

Adeib's words from yesterday circle my mind in a constant loop. I understand what he means—that I've lived an easy, privileged life compared to many. I didn't have to deal with poverty or cosmic crises, but not everything has been easy. Not *everyone*, I should say. My mother's expectations weigh heavily on my heart.

When I matured and developed my magic at an early age, everything changed. I had to fit in the tightest of molds. My mother had dreams for what she wanted me to be, but all I wanted was to be more like, well, Indigo.

Indigo wore whatever she wanted. She cut and dyed her beautiful white hair. Indie was quiet and demure, while I was loud and obnoxious. Everything got worse when I made my discovery. The expectations only heightened. Suddenly, the weight on my chest was too heavy to bear.

Shaking my head, I force myself into the moment. I'm sitting in the middle of the university's food court, which is a conglomerate of food from all over the world. I grab a Caesar salad and a brownie from the buffet-style restaurant. Working with Adeib this week has been... exhausting? Exhilarating? It's fun flirting with him, and I'm learning so much—but he knows exactly how to fillet me open and see every tiny mistake, every minute flaw.

Whenever I screw something up around Adeib, it feels like his stare presses into me, burning holes through my lies. Nausea creeps its way into my stomach as I recall the sheer embarrassment I felt when he corrected me. My throat constricts at the memory, and tears well in my eyes.

I take in a deep breath and try to steady my shaking hands.

Hiro sits on the bench across from me, eating the pile of greens I got for him. Sometimes it feels like it's Hiro and me against the world. He's my one constant, and the only being in my life that follows me wherever I go.

I pull out my sketchbook and ink pen and just allow my mind to wander aimlessly. I could draw anything, but right now, all that I keep envisioning is a snake creeping down a feminine spine.

Tattoos are one of my favorite art styles. There's something so undeniably beautiful about permanence. Yeah, you can laser them off. There are even mages that're working on potions to completely remove them, but what's the fun in that?

A familiar voice, much like my own, rings in my ear.

"Iris?" Indigo asks, looking as beautiful as ever.

"Oh, hey Indie. What're you doing here?"

She takes a seat on the bench next to Hiro, who is snoozing away. Momiji flies towards me and I scoot over, quickly closing my sketchbook.

"We had an all-staff meeting about the new campus opening," she shares. "Everyone was required to be there."

"Oh? Where's Vega, then?"

"She and Professor Mills have some powerlifting meet tonight."

Powerlifting. I think I'd rather die.

I give a curt nod. "Cool!"

"Adeib was in the meeting too," she says, eyebrows raised. "How's it going working with him?"

Oh man. Did he tell her I'm a certified dumbass who doesn't even know how to collect a sample?

"It's been... fine."

Indie gives me a look like she knows I'm full of shit. "He can be a total ass. You can always vent to me about it. Vega actually has a decent relationship with him, so she could probably give you some pointers."

"That doesn't count. Vega has a good relationship with everybody. Not a single soul alive dislikes that woman."

Indigo blushes, and it warms my heart. "I mean, she is the best."

I decide to ask the hard question, because it's easier for me than talking about myself any longer. "Have you spoken to our mother lately?"

"No." There's a sadness in Indigo's eyes that guts me, ripping me apart.

"I get it," I say, not trying to pry any further.

She shakes her head. "You don't, but that's okay. I know being the favorite isn't easy either."

"What do you mean? It's super easy as long as you don't have any hobbies or opinions of your own, don't cover yourself in tattoos and piercings, and fulfill her every demand," I say sarcastically.

We both chuckle at the much needed brevity.

There's a long stretch of uncomfortable silence before either of us speak again. It's not that I don't want to talk to my sister; it actually physically pains me that I can't, but it's not worth the risk.

My mother might be all starry-eyed when she looks at me, blinded by the fame and fortune. Adeib just thinks I'm young and stupid. Everyone's fallen under this spell—this curse that I didn't cast. Everyone but Indigo. I know that if anyone can see right through my facade, it's her.

"Do you want to go out with me and my friends on Friday night?" she asks, breaking the silence. "It'll be me and Vega, Dahlia and Elorthiel, and Alitha."

I would do anything to say yes, but then Alitha or Indigo would ask me some basic medicinal magic question and the guilt would eat me alive. Like a sinner in the confessional, I would tell all. The lies, the deception.

"Sorry, not this time. It's been a long week, and I just want to rest," I say. Another untruth.

I swear Indigo's mask slipped, pain flashing in her eyes, but it was gone in a second. I can't be sure. Maybe she was secretly hoping I said no.

"That's okay. Another time then."

"For sure."

She stands and shrugs. "Well. It was nice seeing you."

And with that, Indigo and her familiar exit the building.

"Dammit, Hiro," I say, rubbing my face with both hands. "This fucking sucks. How did I end up here?"

"You're wearing the black sparkly dress," Raemond says over video chat.

I think I've officially tried on everything in my closet for them tonight, but what else are best friends for?

"I guess," I say with a pout, and shimmy back into the short dress. I've never really been a tight-dress girl. With a flowy skirt, I can at least wear something underneath so it doesn't restrict my movement. Bodycon dresses are too much, but I'll admit, I look *good.*

Knock. Knock. Knock.

"Looks like Fern's here. Bye, I love you," I say and stick my tongue out.

"You look gorgeous. Love you," they reply as I hang up.

When I open the door, Fern is waiting by his car for me.

"You look stunning," he says as he kisses my cheek.

He's wearing a white vest, which matches his pearly white SUV. Centaur vehicles have more space, and I stretch my legs out as we head to the bar to meet his friends.

Once we arrive in Sunspell City, everything is buzzing with lights and music, and I try to shrug off my difficult week as we walk into the bar.

I fuck up a lot. For a while, I could use the excuse that I was young, or that it was because of my inexperience. That doesn't really work with Adeib. He doesn't understand why I do the things that I do, or why I'm wrong about every protocol. And besides Indigo, he's probably the last person I'd want to know that I'm a fraud. I think I'd even rather tell my mother.

The bartender snaps his fingers to get my attention.

"What can I get you, gorgeous?"

"I'll have a sex on the beach," I say without hesitation. "And an extra shot of vodka."

"You look like you've had a rough week. I'll make it two," he says and winks.

I think that was supposed to make me feel better, but all it did was make me feel like I look tired.

Fern's friends are nice, but they're an odd bunch. Chrysanthemum and Basil are Fern's classmates in medicinal magic school, Daffodil is the dean's assistant, and Saga is an incredibly tall freshman that Basil does sports with. I think she might even be taller than Vega.

I take both shots as Daffodil is sharing her crazy plans for summer, and the whole group gives her suggestions on different places she can travel to. Except me. I'm trying not to talk too much, because I have a tendency to take over conversations if other people don't balance me out. Luckily my friends back home do this, but I don't know these people like that.

Now that I think about it, I guess my friend group back home is somewhat eclectic. Raemond owns the plant farm, Jessie is a hacker, Rutherford owns a marketing company, Kat is an event planner, and Gail is an apothecary. We're all different magical races, but we come together for one thing: book club.

This group, however? I think they only come together for drinks and gossip. Which, like, more power to them, but I'm more of a get-matching-tattoos-then-movie-marathon kind of friend.

"I'm bored, let's play truth or dare," Daffodil suggests.

"I'm game," Basil replies.

Fern and Chrysanthemum make out, Basil orders a cocksucking cowboy, and the night just gets crazier from there.

"Truth or dare?" Fern asks.

"Dare," I say. I'm not a big fan of truths, apparently.

"I dare you to do a bodyshot off of Saga's abs."

Oop. I'm usually into people older than me, but I wouldn't mind giving this hybrid a lick. The muscular panes of her deep-red stomach are in full view beneath her crop top.

"Let's do it," I say, speech mildly slurred.

Daffodil pours the shot onto Saga's stomach, and I lick it up. She's got a lime between her teeth, the pulp-side facing out, and I suck on it.

"I'm more into blondes, but that was hot," Saga says, and I let out a giggle.

"Alright bitch, truth or dare?" I say to Daffodil. This is the most juvenile shit I've done in a while, and I'm having a blast.

"Dare, obviously."

"I dare you to dance topless on a table with me," I say.

Daffodil and I are stripping off our tops in the blink of an eye, standing on the table of the bar. Everyone is singing a pretty popular song at the top of their lungs, and we hold onto each other as we sway to the groove.

That is, until strong muscular arms scoop me up and throw me over their shoulder.

Adeib? No, there's no way. Who the fuck grabbed me?

"Archeron needs to put a leash on you," Vega says to Daffodil, her tone is playful but angry.

"Is Indigo here?" I ask, and she puts me down outside.

"Yeah, when we saw you taking off your shirt, she went to go get the car."

Yikes.

Vega escorts me down the street and opens the door for me. "Thought you were too tired to go out."

"Vega, drop it," Indigo's voice rings clear as my vision goes dark.

Stretching my arms, I turn off my Wednesday morning alarm and check my text messages.

RAEMOND

Bitch, are you dead??

IRIS

only on the inside

RAEMOND

You haven't texted me since SATURDAY. How's your week going?

IRIS

oh you know.. dealing with plants and shit. honestly you're more suited for this job than I am

RAEMOND

How's plant daddy?

IRIS

he's been a total diiiiiiick this week. tbh, in all fairness, I suck at this job.

RAEMOND

The self deprecation isn't cute, Iris.

IRIS

i'm not trying to be cute !!!! i'm trying to not perish

RAEMOND

Man. Did something else happen?

IRIS

YEAH OKAY SO MY SISTER FUCKING ASKED ME TO GO OUT AND I SAID NO I DIDN'T FEEL UP TO IT BC I DIDN'T WANT TO HANG OUT WITH HER AND HER FRIENDS AND THEN I WENT OUT WITH MY NEW FRIEND FERN AND HIS WHOLE FRIEND GROUP. THE ONE I TOLD YOU ABOUT THE CUTIE PATOOTIE CENTAUR. ANYWAYS I GOT SOOOOOOO DRUNK AND I SAW INDIGO AND I WAS APPARENTLY BEING A LITTLE WACKADOODLEDOO AND HER AND VEGA DROVE ME HOME. PLS KILL ME !!!!!!!!!

RAEMOND

Fuck, dude. I'm sorry.

IRIS

YEPPP :(

RAEMOND

On the bright side, she probably won't invite you out again?

IRIS

:(

RAEMOND

:(

I put down my phone and decide it's time to get ready for the day.

Whatever progress Adeib and I had made as research partners died the second I accidentally poured acid on one of his precious test subjects. It was a plant! Not even a magical one, and yet he acted like I killed a member of his family. It's not like I did it on purpose.

"Are you going to ignore me like you did yesterday?" I ask.

"I did not ignore you, I simply had nothing to say," he retorts.

I sigh. "Are you still mad about Tuesday?"

"I am not mad, just disappointed."

Ouchy. I'm pretty sure my mom has said that to me once or twice.

We continue working in silence. Adeib is now collecting the plants, while I make potions. This is much more of what we're accustomed to, and we work better this way.

Crunch.

I look back to see Hiro eating some grass and smile. He's laying down, enjoying himself, and I'm grateful. He deserves some joy.

I need to find my own source of joy.

Adeib slithers back to me, plastic bags full of samples in hand. He looks over to Hiro, who is chomping away, and gasps. Within an instant, Florp flies over and smacks Hiro with her tail.

"What is your familiar doing? Stop him!" Adeib demands.

"Excuse me? Your little shit just smacked Hiro in the face," I say. What the fuck is their problem all of a sudden?

"Shoo, shoo from there," Adeib says, waving his arms. "That is murrseae. He cannot eat that."

"Why? I've seen your familiar take a bite?"

"Yes, and look at the difference in size between our familiars. If Florp takes a tiny bit, I can regrow it, but Hiro will consume the whole thing."

"That doesn't seem very fair."

"Life is not fair, Iris," he shouts, his hands expressive. "But I need to conserve my magic for this experiment, not to regrow murrseae your familiar eats."

"I don't get you."

"This does not surprise me," he says, crossing his arms. "Someone who has been alive for thousands of years is going to be a lot more complex than someone in their twenties."

"First of all, you're an asshole. Second of all, that's not what I'm saying. I don't get how you pick and choose what rules to follow," I say. "You don't follow basic politeness, but you're a hard ass about everything involving this project. Is it me?"

He lets out a deep, low sigh. "This is my life, my livelihood. I care about botany. I care about helping people live longer. I would think you, the girl who worked on cancer preventatives in her free-time at college, would understand that."

"I—"

"Most college students go out and party, but you chose to try and make a difference, so fucking act like it. Follow protocols, because they are here for our safety and for the validity of our experiments."

The guilt settles back into my chest, pushing on my heart. I was the girl who partied all through college. That stopped when I got the job with Magi-Pharm X, sure, but not because I wanted to. If it were up to me, I'd be living an average life, and one of my own volition.

I hate this week. I know Adeib is trying to teach me how to be a better scientist, but what he's really taught me is that I can't keep the charade up much longer.

eight

IRIS

Fern and his friends said they have to study this weekend, so I'm on my own. I've never been the type of person to stay in on a Saturday night, but I think it's time.

Last weekend was super embarrassing, anyway. I can't believe I ran into Indigo after telling her I wasn't going out. Even worse, I can't believe she and Vega had to take my drunk ass home. I'd like to crawl into a hole and never come out.

Thankfully MagiPharm X put me in a nice on-campus apartment with a shower and bathtub and not one of those shitty tiny dorms Augury places freshmen in. Or worse—a frat house.

I shiver at the thought.

Last Christmas my friend Kat gifted me a kadoodle, and I've been obsessed with it ever since. Kadoodles are these fancy e-readers that look like physical books, except you can download anything onto them. You even get to flip the page.

I give Hiro a treat, settling him down for bed and grab my kadoodle and a towel. Turning on the water, I let it run until the bathtub is full.

This month's book club pick is a vampire-werewolf romance Jessie chose. Settling into the bath with my kadoodle in hand, I let the warm water envelop me, and relax my muscles.

Thump. Thump. Thump. Thump. Thump.

That sound isn't coming from my door... what the fuck is that?

Boom. Cha Boom. Boom.

Is that music?

The loud music continues for some time, distracting me from my romance novel. Fifty percent of me wants to scream, and the other fifty percent wants to order overpriced earplugs on instant delivery.

Actually, I doubt they do instant delivery to the middle of the jungle.

Getting out of the bath, I wrap myself in a towel and go to grab some clothes. I wish I were better about laundry, but it's my least favorite task. If Adeib thinks me forgetting to pack a lunch is bad, he would probably die at the endless piles of laundry to wash and put-away.

The only unwrinkled and clean article of clothing I have is a pale yellow sundress. It's short and flowy, with a cinched waist and a cute wench-style bustier. Way too cute to be wearing to tell a neighbor to shut the fuck up, but maybe my cleavage will entice them to listen. Probably not. I throw on a pair of sandals and head out the door.

To no surprise, it's the frat house making all the racket. I feel bad for the poor medical students, who probably can't study in these conditions.

Walking up to the house, I knock on the door. I'm not sure anyone can even hear me knock. It's so loud the walls are shaking. If they turn up the volume anymore, I'm not sure the structure would make it.

Knock. Knock. Knock.

I try again, this time more forcefully, but nobody seems to give a shit. Whatever. I'll find somewhere I can sit and relax without all the noise. Maybe if I go deeper into the jungle, I can get some quiet there.

Passing through thickets of trees, it's clear that my apartment sits at the most northern edge of campus. There's nothing but animals, plants, and the calming orange light of the setting sun.

Adeib would probably love it out here. So would Raemond. Indigo and my mother would not. They'd probably complain about spiderwebs or something, and Vega and my dad would be stuck clearing their path.

When it feels like I've walked a mile, I spot a large modular condo mounted atop a boulder. There are vines growing over the side and a ramp that comes down to ground level.

Nope. Not going there. I don't even want to think about who—or what—might live in the middle of the jungle. Continuing my trek, I pass a tree that has bird feeders hanging from every branch.

Weird.

I don't experience fear at the average level. Most people's brains have a switch that tells them to stop, or to not continue in case of danger. Not my brain. If curiosity truly killed the cat, I'm dead.

I keep walking. I'm just going to call this my exercise for the week.

Although I wish I had worn something other than sandals. It's nice out, the summer air is starting to cool with the evening breeze. Had I brought snacks, my kadoodle, and a hammock, I could stay out here all night.

There's a *thing* in this tree that resembles a birdhouse. I think it *is* a birdhouse, but a mega-sized one. However, the hole to get in is still only large enough to fit a regular bird. Whatever bird does live here is a lucky duck.

Well... it's probably not a duck. I bet it's a parrot. Or maybe an owl. If I were a bird, I'd want to be a parakeet.

A drop of rain falls onto my shoulder, breaking me from my bird-filled thoughts. *Shit.* I should probably head back to the apartment before I get soaked—or before it gets too dark out.

I walk towards the apartment, and the rain is coming down harder. It was drizzling only a second ago, but now it's full-on pouring. The wind is howling, and every animal seems to be fleeing for shelter.

That's not a good sign.

I can't help but think about how I feel lately. This rain and its rapid increase has me feeling introspective. Once, I was able to bottle up all the guilt and lies, and everything I felt was just a light drizzle—but now I'm practically drowning. I've gotta get out of here; I'm a mess.

Lightning strikes a nearby tree, and a branch falls to the ground, splintering and coming towards me.

I try to run, but my sandal gets caught on a branch, causing me to trip, hitting my knee on the ground. Blood trickles down my leg, and I struggle to stand. A halo of rain clouds my vision, water dripping into my eyes as I desperately try to find my way back.

The rain is cold, and I'm so, *so* tired. Tears stream down my face, but I blink them away along with the pain. I don't know how I'm supposed to keep going like this.

Passing another round of brush, I spot the condo again. The weird one on the rock that gave me the creeps earlier. Barrelling up the ramp, I bang on the door.

"Please let me in!" I shout, unsure of what'll convince the owner to allow a soaking-wet stranger into their house. "Please," I say, knocking again.

The door swings open to the most unexpected of sights. Adeib.

I was thinking it was going to be some person who owns land near the jungle, or even maybe the dean or another staff member, but I had never even considered this could be Adeib's home.

I'm kind of glad, kind of mortified.

"Hey, it's you," I say with a smile, and he grabs me by the hand and drags me into his home. I'm woozy from the sight of blood. In the race of what'll kill me first—ADHD or anemia—I'm afraid my anemia might win this round.

"What happened to you?" he asks as my eyes go blurry, everything fading in and out of frame.

I open my eyes again, and I'm being carried through an unknown space. A beautiful space, but still an unfamiliar one. There are plants everywhere, and the rooms are spacious and pristine.

A strong, tan arm is visible in my peripheral, and I turn my head to the other side. Adeib is carrying me. I am in Adeib's home, and he is carrying me.

"Oh, good. You are conscious," he says, though he doesn't sound very happy about it. "I am going to ask again. What happened to you?"

He puts me down on a table, and I instantly feel the absence of his warmth, his touch.

"I was getting really overwhelmed by the noises some of the neighbors were making, so I decided to go on a walk," I share.

"Noises?"

"Yeah," I answer.

He starts to walk away. "Keep talking. I am listening."

"They were throwing some sort of party. Super obnoxious. Anyway, I just left."

"Without thinking?" he scolds me. "You did not consider checking a weather app before you left?"

"No. I didn't even bring my phone with me. I'm sure you think I'm stupid—"

"I did not say you were stupid," he says pointedly and pours something onto a cotton pad and dabs my knee with it.

It stings, but he quickly bandages me up and places the first-aid kit on the table beside me.

"And then?" His tone is serious

"I had a nice walk, it started raining. I then tripped and fell, busted my knee, and ended up here."

"I will get you something dry to wear and perhaps a blanket."

"I'm sorry. I wasn't trying to bother you. This was just the only house around, and I didn't even know it was yours," I share.

There's a gentleness in his eyes that wasn't there before. "Who says you are a bother?"

"Adeib. You don't have to pretend you like having me around. I piss you off all the time at work."

"You frustrate me, yes. But you also make things more exciting—"

"How?" I interrupt. "I'm just a stupid, young elfborn."

"You are not just a person, but an experience. One I look forward to every day."

I think my heart might just pound right out of my chest.

Adeib slithers away, and I remain on the table, waiting for him to come back. I've never seen him like this. So doting and concerned. I mean, he makes me food, sure, but this is a new level. And I kind of like it.

He returns, white fabric in hand, and my pulse is suddenly a racehorse again.

"Here, you can put this on, and I will throw your clothes into the washing machine," he says, handing me the shirt.

"I—" I don't know what to say. "I'm not wearing anything underneath this," I gesture down to my soaking wet dress and realize my nipples are peeking through.

Adeib's brows raise for a split second before his neutral demeanor returns. "Just put on the tunic so you can be comfortable. You will be here until at least morning."

"Morning?!"

"There is a tropical storm," he explains. "I am not letting you go back out in this weather."

I let out a heavy sigh before realizing he's right. That, and there's no point in arguing with the world's most stubborn serpentine. "Where's your bathroom?"

"Down the hall and to your left."

I follow his instructions, passing by a snoozing Florp along the way, and slide open the double-wide door. What lies inside, however, is not a bathroom.

Adeib's bedroom.

It's dark, the only brightness being the tiny bit of moon coming in from the skylight. So many images flash through my mind at once. Adeib peacefully sleeping, resting his pretty head on a pillow. This is probably where he brings people to fuck, and a different, more sour feeling settles into my gut as well.

"The bathroom is through the other set of doors," he calls from outside the bedroom.

Entering his bathroom, it's massive. There is both a shower and bathtub, each big enough to fit more than one serpentine. The tiles are beautiful, shiny dark gray, and everything is covered in luscious green plants.

I strip off my still-wet dress and toss it onto the floor. Putting on the white shirt Adeib provided me, the thin white fabric comes down to my knees. There is a slight collar with an opening, and it reveals a lot of my chest.

I cross the threshold back into the bedroom. There's a book sitting on his dresser, and it's one I recognize. His field journal.

I flip through the pages, noticing the different plants he's observed.

His sketches are messy and raw—but beautiful. I had no idea he liked to draw. Adeib's art is so full of passion, it makes my heart sing. I continue flipping until I stop on a specific page.

Are those...

Those are *my* eyes.

Adeib reenters the room, and I slam the book shut before sitting down on his bed. He looks me up and down, and I notice he's now holding a cup.

"Here, I brought you tea," he says and hands me the mug. "Drink. It will promote faster healing."

"Oh! It's a healing potion," I say, and take a sip. The liquid is warm and minty. I take another big gulp.

"No, it is not a potion. There is only one ingredient. I just know my way around plants, as you have already learned."

Sounds like a potion to me. I place the mug down on the nightstand and stare at him, just allowing myself to take in his waves of hair that curl down past his ears, and the vast brown of his eyes.

Heat culminates in my lower abdomen, and I can't shake the feeling wrapping around my chest. *I want him.*

"You can sleep in here, I will sleep in the living room," Adeib says and crosses towards the door.

"Wait," I say, unsure of what to say next.

"Yes?" he looks at me, confusion and curiosity etching his features.

"Don't go."

"Why?"

I walk towards him, inching closer and closer. "I—"

Our noses touch, and his lips brush mine with the softest of contacts. He looks me in the eyes, and I give him a silent plea to kiss me.

He does.

Adeib's hand caresses my jaw, and he envelops me with his mouth, his forked tongue tangling with mine. Our bodies tango to the insatiable rhythm of our beating hearts, and before I know it, Adeib is taking off his tunic.

"Someone could do laundry on your abs," I say before thinking.

Adeib lets out a soft chuckle and kisses the side of my neck. He actually *laughed.*

He pushes me onto the bed, continuing our dance until his body is on top of mine, his tail trailing off towards the floor.

"I take contraceptive—"

"Who said we were doing anything like that?" Adeib whispers into my ear, his voice dark and mischievous. "But for the record, I do too."

His tongue trails down my ear and past my neck before he lifts our bodies and pulls my shirt off. He cups my breasts, sucking one into his mouth. The way his tongue snakes around my nipple is driving me mad.

"Adeib," I moan.

"Every day I add to the running list of all the things I want to do to you," he says between kisses.

I let out a nervous laugh. "I love lists."

"Farfora, are you going to let me touch you?"

"I want you to do whatever you want to me. Tonight, I'm yours."

nine

IRIS

ADEIB OPENS A DRAWER AND GRABS A POTION VIAL, POURING IT OVER HIS FINGERS. HE reaches a hand down and gently rubs my clit, slowly working me. Using one hand to hold himself over my body, and the other to touch me, part of his weight rests on me. I'm not complaining one bit.

"You are so wet," he says as he sticks two recently trimmed fingers in and starts pumping. Whatever magical lubricant he's using works, because I open right up for him.

I pant through sloppy kisses, and he works his way up to three fingers, my body convulsing with every movement, until finally he puts in a fourth.

"So wet and ready for me," he practically purrs into my ear.

I'm not used to partners preparing me this much, or using magic in the bedroom, and it makes me wonder how big he is. I've spent every day since I met him wondering what it's like down there. What it would feel like to touch, to suck. To *ride.*

As he fingers me, I picture it being his cock instead. How it would feel to be so close to him, our hearts beating the same rhythm. I never thought I'd actually find out, but there's a first for everything. I leap over the edge of ecstasy, allowing the orgasm to take control of me.

Something shoots out of Adeib's body, and a big, heavy weight presses against my abdomen. There are tiny objects prickling against me, and I have to fight the urge to laugh. It tickles.

Is he... are there little thorns on his cock?

"Iris," he says, his fingers still inside me.

"It's really big. Yadda yadda. I have toys bigger than you, I can take it," I lie. I have no idea how big he is, but from the weight of his member on my stomach, my toys don't even *compare.*

"No. I mean, yes, but no. I have—"

"Thorns on your dick?" I interrupt him, giggling.

"No. Can you stop talking for two seconds?"

"Probably not."

He sighs and removes his hand from my sex, placing it over my mouth. "At least you are honest. Those are fins, not thorns. They will not hurt you. And again, no, that is not what I was going to mention."

I try to speak, but the sound is muffled by his hand.

"I have a knot."

My eyes grow as wide as my head.

I bite his hand, and he releases his hold on my mouth. "A knot?!"

Man. Dreams really do come true.

"I can pull ou—"

"Don't," I beg. "Please don't."

"Fine, but do *not* try to remove yourself too early," he says, his voice serious.

Oh, don't worry. I won't.

Adeib pushes his cock inside me, little by little, and I scream. It's part-pain, part-pleasure. I've enjoyed people of all sizes. People with dicks. People without. I own many toys too, but nothing has ever been this *much.*

It's wonderful and horrifying, and I think he might literally rip me in two. What a beautiful way to die.

"Are you still mine to do with what I please?" he asks in a breathy voice.

"Yes," I pant, feeling him stretch me further.

"Good, because I don't think I can hold back any longer," he says and pushes all the way inside me.

Adeib's hands take mine as he pulls my arms up over my head while forcing himself inside, filling me to the hilt. The way he stretches me, the way he caresses me, it's all too much. My mind is normally an endless spiral of information and thoughts, but all I can think about right now is him.

His fins shift back and forth with every thrust, moving and flexing. Everything he does is my undoing.

My devastation.

There's something about seeing someone who is always so poised and put together at their dirtiest, most natural state that is so thrilling to me. The grumpy man who never even smiles laughed for me and now he's moaning my name, telling me how good I take him.

His breath is hot against my skin as he licks down my neck and pounds into me. I want to wrap myself around him like a blanket and never let go.

The way our bodies move with one another's rhythms is primal. Instinctual.

I let the waves of pleasure crash over me as he moves faster and faster until he grunts, deep and guttural, and I feel what has to be his knot pop inside me. It swells, pressing against my inner walls, filling me more than I even knew possible. The feeling is so good—on the outer edge of pain, but not quite there yet.

Adeib's muscles spasm and he holds onto me, clawing my hips as he pushes me into the bed. He seems desperate to bury himself deeper. There's nowhere else to go.

A hot liquid pools inside me, but it's trapped inside me. It's a strange sensation, though not an unwelcome one. I feel satisfied. *Full.*

Adeib flips us over, my head now resting on his chest, and his knot keeping his cock buried in me. He smoothes a hand over my back, brushing my hair with his fingers.

"How long are we going to be stuck like this?" I ask. I'm not complaining, moreso curious.

"My body will release you when it is ready," he says, his voice hot with lust. It's so strong, it almost sounds like rage. I know it's not. I know the only thought crossing his mind right now is desire, and that makes my cheeks flush a rosy pink.

We're quiet for a long moment.

"What's the difference between cuddling and snuggling?" I ask, ending the small stretch of silence.

"How should I know?" he says and kisses my forehead.

"Aren't you supposed to be an expert in everything in your ripe old age?"

"Ouch."

"I'm just teasing you. But I thought maybe you learned about etymology while you learned those million different languages." I stick my tongue out.

"Six. I speak six languages, and I am not an expert in anything except magical botany," he admits.

"Okay, but like, do you have a theory?" I ask.

"I think snuggling can be done alone, but cuddling is done with someone else. We are currently cuddling."

I smile. "So snuggling is like masturbation, but cuddling is like sex."

"You are insufferable," he responds as one corner of his mouth ticks up.

His knot releases, my body suddenly empty, and warm liquid slowly drips down my legs. He gets up and grabs a towel, gently cleaning me off. My heart is as full as I was as he climbs back into bed and wraps himself around me.

"Goodnight," I say and nuzzle into his chest.

"Goodnight, farfora."

The most delightful scent hits my nose, and I open my eyes to an empty bed. Is Adeib making breakfast?

Crossing out of the bedroom towards the kitchen with nothing on but my birthday suit, I am met with the most delectable of sights. Adeib is standing in the kitchen, shirtless and leaning against the counter, drinking tea.

"Not a coffee guy?" I ask.

"Coffee stains one's teeth," Adeib explains.

"So what are you drinking?"

"Here." He passes me his cup. "Take a sip."

I put the cup against my lips and sniff before drinking. The tea is warm and sweet, with a strong flavor of cinnamon.

Adeib grabs a piece of white fabric that's hanging from a hook and wraps it around me, tying it in the back.

"What're you doing?" I ask, giggling at the apron and the fact that I'm naked in his beautiful kitchen.

"I am going to teach you how to make bread. I am currently waiting for the dough to rise."

Adeib shows me what ingredients he used for the dough, and he helps me divide and shape the pitas. His large hands cover mine, guiding my every movement.

"We can bake some in the oven and cook a few on the stove, and you can tell me which you prefer," he whispers in my ear, his breath hot on my neck.

I decide to make a batch for the oven, while Adeib cooks some on the stove. His arms flex as he flips the bread, and, unable to explain why, I just want to take a bite out of him. I want to taste him, to consume him and learn everything about him.

"So, was Arabic your first language?" I guess asking him questions will have to do.

"No, technically Arabic was my third."

"What was your first?"

"Serpenia, the language of the serpentine. That's the English translation.

Before the Convergence, my homeland was located in modern-day Arabia, underneath the desert between two countries called Kuwait and Saudi Arabia. It was called a name in our ancient language, a language humans cannot hear. We translated it to Old Arabic, but it is not the same," he explains.

"Can elfborn hear it?" I'm genuinely curious.

He opens his mouth, his forked tongue sticking out, but nothing comes out.

"Okay, I guess not. So was Old Arabic your second language?"

"Yes, and then Arabic, Farsi, English, and lastly French."

The corners of my lips curve up. "What's next?"

"The language of your body, of course," he says and kisses my temple.

I am no longer a person. I am a puddle.

When the bread is done, he puts the stovetop ones in a container, and the baked ones in another.

"Try mine," I say, tearing off a piece from the oven.

"Mmm." He grabs a piece from the stovetop pile and shoves it in my mouth. I half-laugh, half-gag before I grab some flour and throw it onto him.

He comes at me, and I dart down the hallway, my feet sliding on his smooth floors, as he chases me. Adrenaline pumping through my veins, I run as fast as I possibly can, but it's no use.

Serpentine are faster.

Adeib picks me up by my waist and carries me. I kick and try to wriggle out, still laughing, and he undoes the apron, pulling it off me before throwing me over his shoulder.

"Put me down!" I shout, even though that's not what I want.

"Gladly," he says and tosses me onto the bathmat.

Adeib starts the bath, and water comes down into the massive clawfoot tub.

I don't know where the boldness manifests from, but I spread my legs open wide and begin touching myself, reveling in what I already know is about to occur.

He comes toward me, but I reach out my other hand in protest.

"Stop, I did not give you permission to approach me," I say in the brattiest tone I can muster.

"Permission?" Adeib's eyes flare with a kind of heat I've never seen more. "You think I need your permission?"

"Maybe," I say through a moan, my fingers knuckle deep in my pussy.

"You said you were mine to do with as I pleased," he reminds me.

I smirk. "That was last night, and this is today."

"Keep it up, farfora, and I will have you begging for my cocks."

What? "I'm sorry, did you just say *cocks?!*"

"You heard me." His grin is downright devious as not one, but two spring out from their pockets. The second one is shorter and less-girthy. It's missing the dextrous fins of the top one, and I thank my lucky stars. I don't think I could handle it if they were both like the one I had last night.

Adeib picks me up and slips me into the water, following me in. He turns off the faucet and pushes me forward. My upper body hovers over the tub, my legs struggling to find something to hold onto. Normally, I could use the back of the tub for balance, but this one is serpentine-sized, almost like a small pool. Adeib takes me by my hair and pulls it back, keeping me upright.

He pulls harder, bringing my back in contact with his chest, and I feel his cocks pulsing against me. "What do you need, Iris?" His voice is low and guttural.

"Please."

"I want you to beg for it."

"Adeib, please."

His grip on my hair tightens, and my neck cranes back. "Please, what?"

"Fuck me. Fill me. Do whatever you please with me."

"Gladly." And with one thrust, I am completely undone.

Adeib fills me, stretching me in every direction, and I realize I missed it. It's been less than twelve hours, and I felt empty without him. What am I going to do when summer ends?

He pounds into me, and I no longer remember what I was thinking, or who I am. All I feel is our bodies melting together.

Adeib grabs me by the throat, wrapping his strong hand around my neck, and pulls me back towards him, his cock buried inside me. His second cock, which is covered in little textured bumps, rubs against my clit. This is the most deadly combination of sensations I've experienced, and I don't know if sex with anyone else will ever compare. He's ruined me.

I want to tattoo this feeling into my skin so that it's always with me. In this moment, Adeib is my damnation and salvation wrapped into one. He impales me, pumping in and out as I scream in pleasure, seconds away from climaxing.

Suddenly, Adeib pulls out from me, and I whimper at the loss of contact.

"I just wanted to torture you a bit," he says and slams into me one final time, his knot pressing against my walls.

I could stay in this bathroom for eternity.

ten

ADEIB

Once, I told Iris my favorite flower was a rose. As of late, I find myself thinking of Irises instead.

In all my years living on Magia Island, nobody has ever asked me about my people. Not about Arabia, nor the serpentine, nothing. I am unsure if they do not care, or avoid the subject so as to not seem rude.

I want to tell someone. I want someone to look at me with genuine curiosity. Iris is the first to do so. She is the only person who is not put off by my icy exterior, and she is melting it into an oasis.

My only regret in regards to my weekend with Iris was that I did not taste her—did not allow my tongue to roam her body, basking in the smell of her pheromones.

I will not idle away time on what could have been, but instead, focus on making it happen.

Opening the doors to the greenhouse, I wait for her to arrive.

The clock strikes nine, but I do not fret, she is always late.

Nine-fifteen.

Nine-thirty.

Nine-forty-five.

This is unlike her. Even Florp appears concerned. I should shoot her a text message and see if she is alright. Except, I do not have her number.

ADEIB

What is Iris' address?

ARCHERON

Why do you ask?

ADEIB

Do not beat around the bush. Send me her address.

ARCHERON

Surely you realize I can't send confidential information without reason.

ADEIB

Archeron.

ARCHERON

Adeib.

ADEIB

She did not show up for work and I am worried about her.

ARCHERON

That's a first. She's in the researcher's apartments, they're next to the med student housing on the edge of campus. She's the corner apartment, ground floor.

ADEIB

Thank you.

Now that my boss thinks I have lost my marbles, time to go see if Iris is okay.

I hope she is not avoiding me.

I lock the doors and slither to where Iris is staying. I pass her every day on my way to work. We could walk together, though it would make me late. Florp rests on my shoulder and makes a little squeak when we arrive at our destination. Corner apartment. This must be where Iris is staying, except there is a centaur outside her door.

"Who are you?" I ask, not caring about the harshness of my tone.

The centaur's eyebrows furrow. "You must be the infamous Dr. Ali."

Merde. Wait, does she talk about me?

"And you must be her... what?"

"Don't worry, I'm not her boyfriend. I'm just a friend," he says and pats me on the back. I try not to, but I stiffen out of reflex.

"Is she alright? She did not show up for work."

"She's got a nasty cold, but I brought her a potion. She should be brand-spanking-new in a day or so."

I fight to hold back a hiss. I hate that my mind is angry that he used the word spanking in the same sentence he referred to her.

"Thank you for letting me know," I say. I try to will some semblance of politeness into my voice. This centaur did not do anything wrong, but his presence irks me nonetheless.

I want Iris all to myself.

Walking past her apartment and towards my house, I dial in a favor.

"Hello," I say into the phone.

"Adeib?" the cambion asks.

"Obviously. I am going to text you an address, would you deliver some food there—some soup or something? I will wire you money."

"Sure thing."

"And do not tell her where it is from."

When I first met Iris, I found her to be a nuisance. A sexy, talkative nuisance. But she has grown on me, and honestly? I miss her presence when she is not around.

Yesterday was lonesome without her and that silly little lamb. Hiro is such a unique creature. He seems to be quite intelligent, as well as gentle. I think he balances Iris' personality perfectly. Also, the fact that his fur is actually moss makes the flowers in my heart grow.

The clock strikes ten, and I hold my breath, hoping she is still going to walk through the door, but I know it is no use.

I am dispirited by her absence, but even more so, I wanted to give her a gift. Her smile is the brightest part of my days lately. The protective robe arrived early from my seamstress last night, and it is absolutely beautiful. Almost as beautiful as the woman who will wear it.

Maybe I am losing my mind. I have spent so much of my life being completely task oriented, I never allowed myself to stop and reflect. I told myself I had no time to spare, that I am better off not dwelling on the past, or trying to find temporary love.

I rest my eyes, allowing myself a moment to feel and reflect.

Iris has shown me that perhaps I was wrong. She spends so much of her time daydreaming. Her mind is a clock that keeps ticking. But even Iris, consumed by her own thoughts, is still so full of joy.

I, too, was full of joy once. My twin Aida and I used to play in the cave systems, snooping around into others' homes and places we had no business in. We were inseparable. With my botany and her sight, we were a powerful duo. I blink, forcing myself not to remember those times. Whenever I think of the past, I become more callous, shutting myself out from the world.

I choose not to remember my sister, because remembering her means remembering losing her too.

Serpentine are the keepers of memories–the archivists of history, because we age at a substantially slower rate than humans and even elves. This is what enabled my sister and I to enjoy our mischievous youth for a long, long time. The Convergence stripped us of that in an instant.

I miss Aida. I miss ‘umi. I miss my entire clan. Yet, life keeps going, and the Earth keeps turning. Without any of us.

Perhaps I should keep going too.

Florp would not stop pestering me today. All day, nonstop, she dragged me towards the second building with the refrigerator. And all day, every time I would open it, she would act disappointed. *Dramatically* disappointed.

This creature is responsible for conducting all my magic. Me, a powerful mage. How did I get stuck with such a little diva?

"What is it? What do you want?" I yell in frustration.

She makes a sound. It is something I have heard before, though I cannot quite place it.

She rubs her belly, making the odd sound again.

If food is what she wants, I could take her to a restaurant, or perhaps a grocery store.

"Would you like to go to the store?"

She nods, flying up and down with excitement.

Alright. We are onto something.

I scoop her up, though she barely weighs a thing, and place her on my shoulder. Locking the door to the greenhouse, we head for Sunspell City.

Once we have arrived, we head through the doors of the grocery store. Florp flies up to look me in the eyes.

"Is there any possible way you can tell me what you want?"

She makes the strange sound again.

"What are you doing?" I whisper-yell.

She repeats the sound, and I realize it reminds me of when a can runs out of air.

"Oh, ya Allah, you have got to be kidding me," I say and slither towards the dairy aisle.

Once we reach what I believe Florp is imitating, she does gymnastics in the air, flipping repeatedly, clapping her paws with excitement.

Whipped cream. Really?

We cross towards the exit, and I have to shake Florp away from the can as she tries to pry off the cap in the middle of the store. I send the cashier three dabloons, and we head outside.

I take off the cap and watch as Florp nearly unhinges her jaw, ready to receive the whipped cream. Spraying it into her mouth, I glare at her in both amusement and disgust.

Where has she even had whipped cream before?

Love has carved a geckfly shaped hole directly into my heart. I am going to kick Archeron's ass for doing this to me.

eleven

IRIS

I CAN'T BELIEVE I CAUGHT A FUCKING COLD. MAYBE THIS IS A SIGN FROM THE GODS that Adeib is too much for me to handle.

Or maybe being out in the rain compromised my sorry excuse of an immune system. Whatever the case may be, I am sick. Thankfully, the gash on my leg healed, but my sinuses didn't seem to get the memo.

I text Fern, and he's on his way over to deliver me a medicinal potion.

Knock. Knock.

Oh thank goodness.

"Hey."

"Hey Iris, here's the potion you requested."

I take the paper bag and place it on the entryway table. "Thank you. I don't wanna get you sick, so I'm going to text you some shit," I say, blow a kiss, and close the door.

IRIS

okayyyy

Fern isn't replying yet. Weird.

Ping.

FERN

Hey, sorry. Your research partner was outside your door asking about you.

IRIS

Adeib?

FERN

Yeah.

IRIS

i'm going to call you.

He picks up after the first ring.

"Okay, so he was here?? He's not here now," I say, panting into the phone. Being sick makes everything exhausting.

"Yeah, and he was super duper jealous," Fern shares.

"Of *what*?"

"Me. I think he thought I was your boyfriend, or we were hooking up or something."

"Okay, that's what I wanted to talk to you about."

"Iris, you're stunning, but I don't want to sleep with you."

I burst out into laughter. "No, idiot. Cone of fucking silence."

"What's that?"

"Just don't tell anyone what I'm about to tell you."

"I promise," he says, tone serious.

I take in a deep breath. "I fucked Adeib this weekend."

"You did *what*?"

A knock sounds from outside my door.

"Wait a second, someone's here," I say and put the phone down. Opening the door, there's a big bag on the ground. I pick it up and carry it into the apartment.

"Okay, I'm back," I say into the phone. "Someone dropped off a package." I start unraveling the brown bag and notice multiple food containers. Some look like soup, others noodles. "Did you send me food?"

"No?"

Hmm. "Could my sister have sent me this?"

"Did you tell her you were sick?" he asks.

"No." I shake my head. "I haven't spoken to her since the other weekend."

I take a swig from the potion vial and then crack open one of the containers of soup. It smells delightful, and I grab a spoon and have a seat on the couch, cellphone on speaker. I'm a mess.

"Maybe it was your new boytoy?" Fern suggests.

"It could be. He is always trying to feed me," I say and drink another spoonful of soup.

"Are you going to see him again?"

"I work with him, I have to."

"No," he pauses. "I mean, are you going to sleep with him again?"

"Hmm." I think about it. We are probably breaking some sort of rule, not that either of us give a shit. "I think so? If he wants to."

"Oh, he definitely wants to."

"I'm gonna go eat and watch some anime, but I'll see you later this week? Let me know if you run into that paramedic guy again."

"Will do."

I open my laptop and load up my favorite streaming services when I'm quickly distracted by a series of ads. There was a snakeskin corset, and, with everything that happened this past week, I think I *have* to have it.

Click.

Teasing Adeib has become my favorite pastime, after all.

"I have the most beautiful daughter in the world," my mother's voice rings from behind me in the mirror.

Indigo looks at me, stunning in her bridal gown, and smiles. "You do look beautiful, Iris." A single tear falls down her face, and I scream.

My mother's face melts away like hot clay, morphing into Jamie Snow.

The hiring director of MagiPharm X.

"What's going on?" I ask as I realize Indigo's wedding venue has shifted into a meeting room.

Jamie's seated at the end of a long, long table. She's so far now I can barely make out her features. The temperature is ice cold. I shiver, goose-bumps trailing down my arms and legs.

"You're going to find us a cure." Her movements are robotic as she stands and comes towards me. "Our perfect Ms. Watson will save the world."

I shake my head, but am unable to speak. Looking down, I realize I'm completely naked. It feels like I'm swimming through sludge. Reality sits at the posterior of my mind, completely out of reach.

Everything wobbles and shakes until I'm in Professor Douglass' office. My throat feels like it's closing as he looks me in the eyes. "Chelsea showed me your findings. I went ahead and sent your findings to a few experts in the medicinal magic field. You have an interview with Octopus News 9 tomorrow morning at seven," he says. "I told your mother, and she is so proud! You're making a real difference, Iris."

You're making a real difference, Iris.

Everything goes black, and I wake up, covered in sweat. Hiro sits at the edge of the couch, staring at me. Lazily, I rise and make my way towards the bedroom.

Guilt is an infection, and mine has started to affect me, even in sleep.

Opening my eyes, I stretch out my arms and take in a deep breath. I feel a lot better, although I still can't breathe out of my nose. I grab my phone off the nightstand and unlock it. I swipe away the notifications from my mother, and click on my text thread with Raemond.

RAEMOND

WAKE UP. We rescheduled book club just for you!

IRIS

aww, you didn't have to do that.

RAEMOND

Okay, but we did, so hop on video chat.

I open the app to five beautiful faces. Our book club, nicknamed Slut Shack, used to be bigger, but some of our members moved to other time zones. I still lurk at them on socials, rooting for them and their lives from afar.

"Luckily, I don't have any meetings today, but the kiddos are off from school, so don't mind the background noise," Rutherford says with a laugh. He recently shaved the sides of his head, and it shows off his pointy brown ears.

"Same," Jessie responds.

"Not a mood," Raemond says and points to the trees, their nursery in the background.

The tips of Kat's horns are visible from the tiny corner of my phone screen.

"Is Kat at work?" I ask, noticing the background.

"Yeah, she's in a meeting, but we're muted. She'll join back in a sec," Gail says.

Gail missed the last few meetings, and I've missed their spotted face.

"Gail, are you at work?" Jessie asks.

They give us a wide-grin. "Absolutely. My clients don't care, and if they do, good riddance."

"Okay, I love you guys, but can we talk about the book?" Jessie asks. Her tail, adorned with purple scales, swishes back and forth.

"Don't kill me, but I did not love it," Raemond says, and I dramatically gasp.

"Shocker not shocker," I say teasingly.

Jessie laughs. "Let me guess, he wasn't enough of a simp?"

"I needed him to adore her; I wanted obsession."

Kat unmutes her microphone. "I wanted her to have more than one love interest, honestly," she whispers before muting herself again.

This is exactly what I've needed, a distraction from the endless work and guilt. I can just laugh with my friends and talk about smutty books.

"Honey." A small elfling comes into view on Rutherford's screen. "Get out of here, dad is working."

"*Working,*" Jessie snorts while doing air quotes, and Raemond lets out the world's loudest cackle.

Kat unmutes again. "I think I'm the only one *actually* working today."

"You're always working," Gail points out. "What were your favorite scenes? I loved everything involving the cat."

"Okay but, the feeding scene. They're *so* hot," Jessie says.

Gail waggles their eyebrows. "The *marking* scene."

"The marking scene was everything to me," I share.

"I want to be marked," Rutherford says. "Or knotted."

Simply the best. "Wouldn't that be the dream?!"

Raemond leans super close to their camera. "Plant daddy could knot you."

"Plant daddy?!" Jessie asks.

Gail scrunches their brows. "Her research partner? I don't think he'd have a knot."

"I slept with a serpentine once, and I am ninety-nine percent sure he had a knot," Raemond shares. "I don't remember, though. That feels like a lifetime ago."

"Serpentine definitely have knots," I let slip. "Okay! Anyway, moving on." I try to change the subject.

"Iris," Raemond squeals.

Rutherford and Jessie's eyes widen, while Gail just smirks.

"We expect all the details," Gail replies.

"Later," I say. "I'll text you guys about it later. I think I'm going to go take a nap; I still don't feel well."

"Boooooooo," at least three of them reply at once.

My friends *and* my body are against me.

twelve

IRIS

Today is the first day back at work after my weekend with Adeib, and my stomach is full of butterflies. Typically, I spend my energy crushing on fictional characters, not real people. That isn't to say I don't have flings, but I tend to avoid anything serious. This *isn't* serious, but it feels like it could be, if I play my cards right. Or wrong. I'm not exactly sure what I'm hoping for.

What would Adeib and I even be considered? *Fuck buddies* is too vulgar. He's not my boyfriend; you can't call a multi-thousand year old serpentine a boyfriend. Lover? Maybe.

Whatever we started on Saturday, I need *more.*

I walk into the greenhouse and Adeib is seated, writing something in his field journal. My mind flashes back to the sketch of my eyes. and my heart skips a beat.

Leaning over the workbench, I pose in front of him. "Hey professor," I say flirtatiously.

"How are you feeling?" he asks, standing to observe me. He looks me up and down, putting his hand under my jaw and lifting my chin. His fingers are human, but his nails are claw-like as he grasps my skin. Adeib moves my head up and down, back and forth, inspecting me for injuries.

"I'm good, really," I say with a smirk. "I'm more than good."

Gently, he releases my jaw. "And your leg?"

I'm wearing black jeans, my wound covered by the denim. It's cute that he's worried about me. "Completely healed."

"Good," he says and sits back down, continuing to count the petals of the hydrangigus.

"How were the last few days?" I ask, hoping they were agony.

"Everything was fine. I believe hydrangigus will be our best bet for utilizing some of its magical qualities. We just need to figure out the perfect plant to blend it with," he answers. His tone is genuine, and it irks me just a tad.

I want him to suffer. I want him to beg for it. For me.

We work in silence for a while, and I write down qualities of the hydrangigus I think would be best. He corrects half of my choices.

"Oh, how could I forget?" he says and opens his briefcase. He pulls out a black pile of fabric and unfolds it. "I had this made for you. Here, stand up."

Adeib places my arms through the holes, and I spin. It's a black coat with red irises embroidered in a repeating pattern. It's breathtaking.

"I don't know what to say. It's beautiful."

"Do not say anything," he says and approaches me. We're only a fingers length away from each other, and I think he might kiss me.

I want him to grab me and pull me into his embrace. I want his mouth on mine and his hand around my throat, but I don't speak. We just stare into each other's eyes...longingly.

"It suits you well." He grabs a small pile of sample bags and hands them to me. "Now, get back to work."

Once I collect the samples he requested, I sit down and pull out my sketchbook. I begin drawing a tattoo design I've had bouncing back and forth in my head. I think of the lines of the art and the sharpness of the blade.

I can feel the weight of Adeib's stare pressing into me. He crosses over to where I'm seated, the look on his face downright menacing, and I freeze.

"If you are going to draw instead of work, will you at least allow me to look at your sketches?"

Not at all what I expected, but I dig it. "Sure," I say and nervously hand it over.

He looks over the dagger through the heart piece I've been working on, inspecting it, before flipping through the book.

Adeib stops when he gets to a certain page, and I stand, trying desperately to see what's captivated his attention so attently. When my eyes finally reach the piece, I snap the book from his hands, closing it shut.

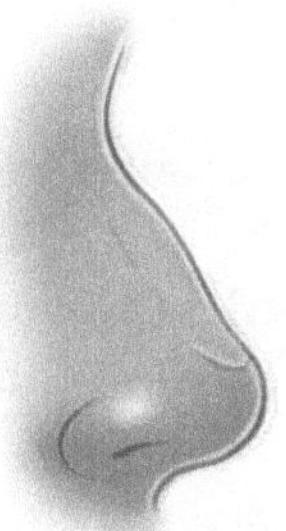

Walking into the greenhouse this morning, I decide to start what I'm calling Operation: Make Adeib Admit He Wants Me Again. Today is day one. After the things this man did to me last weekend? There's no way he doesn't want me again. I think he's just playing hard to get.

I cross towards him and dramatically collapse. I don't know what parasite took over my body, but in this moment, it's the only thing that makes sense.

My hand comes up to my forehead, and I let out the most histrionic sigh to ever come out of an elfborn's body.

Adeib catches me in his arms and dips me. For a second, I think he'll take the bait, but instead he lifts me, helping me back onto my feet.

"Oh, *Dr. Ali,* thank you for saving me," I say theatrically.

"Iris." His tone is sharp.

"Yes?"

He furrows his brows. "I did not *save* you. Quit being a drama queen; we should get back to the project."

Booooooo.

Adeib slithers away, and I watch as Hiro and Florp pass a large leaf around. Hiro hits it with his nose, and Florp flies up to catch it, bringing it back.

I giggle, watching as Hiro almost falls backwards. Florp does figure eights through the air, whirling around to catch the leaf. They're both utterly adorable.

"I think we should try adding magnamint to a potion with the hydrangigus," Adeib says, crossing towards me, holding a sample bag with magnamint leaf.

"I think not."

"Excuse me?"

"Magnamint can't be added to most potions without turning the entire thing invisible," I remind him.

"No, that is not true," Adeib tries to argue.

I cross my arms. "This is like potions 101. I promise you, magnamint is not a solution."

"Magnamint was used in a trial to help manage muscular dystrophy," he shares.

"I think you're confusing it with another plant," I say with a smirk. "It's okay to be wrong."

"Except I am not wrong, and I do not mix up plants." There's this authoritative tone to his voice; it's sexy, but it also pisses me off.

"I won't pretend to know more than you about... anything, really, but I swear on my favorite book boyfriend's life that I'm right this time."

"Book boyfriend?"

"It's like a fictional crush. I've got book girlfriends too."

Anger laces his features. "You have a boyfriend?"

"No. Adeib, just shut the fuck up and trust me."

He points one finger into the air. "I am going to look it up."

I snort as he pulls out his phone and searches for magnamint.

"Honestly, I thought you were going to pull out a three-hundred page encyclopedia," I say.

He glares at me before looking back down at his phone. Adeib scrolls. And scrolls. And scrolls some more, until I am sitting, nearly falling asleep.

"You were right," he admits.

I am unable to contain my smugness as I stand and do a victory dance. "I told you so. Me, the silly twenty-three-year-old mage, told you so."

A wide grin spreads across Adeib's face.

Why is he so happy about being wrong?

To end my busy week, Fern and his friends practically drag me out of my apartment to try this new speakeasy that's hidden away in the heart of Sunspell City.

We get to the address, and there's only an old mini-van in the middle of an abandoned parking lot.

"It's a puzzle. You have to solve it to get in," Chrysanthemum explains, her flamingo-pink hair flowing in the wind.

"This reminds me of those old escape rooms," Moss, Daffodil's boyfriend, says.

"Human thing," Daffodil explains, and we all laugh.

Moss is a fun guy. He's a human from Sleeping Island. He works at a museum, and he's obsessed with historical human culture—specifically Irish and Indigenous cultures. I can't tell if it's the shots we pre-gamed or his personality, but I want to be his best friend.

"Tell me about it," I say.

"Humans used to pay money to be locked in a room and forced to solve puzzles so that they could leave."

"That's so weird."

I just realized that almost everyone here has red hair. Fern is a ginger, Daffodil's hair is orange and blonde, Basil has strawberry-blonde locs, and Moss has long, reddish-brown hair. Chrysanthemum's hair is pink, but that's close enough. The only person who doesn't, besides me, is Saga, but like... her *skin* is red. That's so interesting. I wonder if that's why they all became friends. Red fan club.

I love hair. Growing up, I hated that mine was a boring brown. I've always wanted to dye it white like Indie and our mother, but I never got around to it.

Lost in thought, I realize Basil and Moss have been playing with the car, trying to find something. They open doors, try to pop the trunk, but nothing seems to work.

I walk over and press a button on the back of the vehicle, pulling off the gas cap, and the car doors pop open, allowing us entrance into the jazz bar. *Neato.*

A few of them give me congratulatory cheers, but Basil and Moss look less-than-pleased about their failure.

The inside is otherworldly, with diamond chandeliers hanging from the rafters. Everything is dark and noir, with floor lights illuminating the path. Moss and Daffodil immediately make their way onto the dance floor, grooving to the funky electric-piano pieces that are playing, while the rest of us take a seat.

"There's a saxophone solo in a minute with a really cool call-and-response," Basil says to Fern, who nods.

I think Basil likes Fern a lot, but Fern has feelings elsewhere. We'll have to find Basil his own match.

"I'm going to go get shots, I'll be right back," Chrysanthemum says.

Saga is quiet as she leans against the bar.

"How come you don't have a girlfriend?" I ask.

She shrugs. "There's a girl—a dancer—I'm interested in, but all her friends are bitchy."

"Get her alone," I suggest. "Maybe she needs to be shown how she should be treated."

A long, black and gold snake tail slithers past me, and I gasp, nearly stumbling off the barstool.

What the ever-loving-fuck is Adeib doing here?

I stand and get ridiculously close to Saga, whispering in her ear. "Can you help me make someone jealous?"

"Of course." Saga smiles and winks. "It would be my pleasure. But, you'll owe me one."

"Deal," I say and take her by the hand, leading her onto the dance floor. We cross the room, ensuring to stop right before the table Adeib is seated at. There's an elf with a monocle and pretty short white hair sitting across from him, and I have to fix the nasty expression that wants to settle into my face.

I face away from Saga and grind my body back into her, swaying with the music. She puts both hands on my hips and follows my lead, kissing down my neck.

Operation: Make Adeib Want Me is turning into Operation: Make Adeib Jealous. I'd feel bad about it, except I've spent the entire week trying to get a read on the serpentine, and he gave me... nothing. This will show me exactly how he feels. It's toxic, but I don't really give a fuck.

I run my fingers through Saga's hair before opening my eyes. Adeib is almost on top of us, his nose nearly connecting with mine.

"What are you doing here?" he asks.

"I'm hanging out with my friends. What are you doing here with that guy?" I ask. Saga backs away, giving us space.

"Not that it is any of your business, but I hired a private investigator a few years ago to help me search for my sister. We like to meet in neutral locations," he shares.

"Your sister?" I ask, my heart tearing in two. I had no idea.

He nods. "Who is that?" he asks, gesturing to Saga.

"She's just a friend," I say, and it's the truth.

"You two sure looked *friendly*."

I shake my head. "No, Adeib, really. It's not like that. I was messing with you on purpose."

"If you like your friend, you will not do that again. Understand?" The coldness in his voice sends shivers down my spine. This man worries about the lives of plants, but for some reason I think for me, he might commit murder.

I am not complaining.

"Noted," I say, my cheeks turning red. "I'll see you Monday?"

He gives me a heated look that says more than words ever could.

thirteen

IRIS

I HAVEN'T SEEN ADEIB SINCE OUR RUN-IN ON SATURDAY NIGHT. FOR WHATEVER reason, I seem to be making a habit out of running into people. At least I used it to my advantage.

Today we're finally doing research at the campus library, and I'm super excited about it. Although I'm not really good at being quiet, I am an avid lover of books. I want to smell them all.

I'm also excited because today is Operation: Make Adeib Want Me, day three, and I am wearing the shortest skirt I own and the snakeskin corset I ordered. This will be fun.

The library is close to the main part of campus. Located at the base of a tree, it is a large building with multiple floors and sets of winding stairs. I left Hiro back at the apartment today to enjoy some time off, but I almost wish I hadn't. He has to see this place.

It feels like I've walked onto the set of a movie. Books are everywhere, and vibrant monarch butterflies soar through the air. Everything is deep brown wood except the skylights, which reflect ethereal tones of gold and blue. I have never seen anything quite like it, but if I moved to this island permanently, I would come here every day.

When I don't spot Adeib, I decide to take a few snapshots to send to Raemond.

IRIS

look at this library!!!!!!!

RAEMOND

Holy fucking Hel! That's so cool.

I head down a stairwell, unwinding into a darker section of the library. There are dictionaries and reference books lining the shelves, and I pick up one on potions.

"What is *that*?" A dark, almost ominous voice calls out. Adeib.

I spin on my heels and nearly crash into him. We're nose to nose. "Oh this? Just a little something I picked up. Made me think of you."

"Take it off," he demands.

"Oh, so now you want me, huh?"

"I said... Take. It. Off." He lets out a short hiss. There's a flame of rage in his eye, like he's seeing red.

I start untying the underbust corset, undoing it before him. He catches it as it falls, glaring at the strip of fabric.

Did I offend him?

"It's not real. I would have never purchased real snakeskin. It's definitely not serpentine," I explain.

"I do not care whether it is real. Somewhere out there is a man slithering around with that exact tail. You look like you belong to him," he says through gritted teeth. "This is a problem."

"Wh—why?"

"You belong to me."

Adeib grabs me with the greatest force possible without snapping me in half. He pulls me to him, crushing his mouth against mine. My nipples peek against the thin fabric of my black top as they press into him.

He throws the corset onto the ground, tossing it to the side.

"Good. Now you look like my whore," he says, and my eyes widen.

Dickhead.

"Excuse me, what did you call me?" I say, wriggling out of his grasp.

Adeib pulls me back towards him, forcing me into his embrace.

"Let me go, asshole," I say loudly. He puts a hand over my mouth, muffling my voice.

"I did not call you *a* whore. I called you *my* whore. Because you're mine." He smacks my ass, aggressively grabbing at it, and I feel... primal. My heart is racing, conflicted by his words. I never previously would've allowed a man to talk to me like this, but the thought of being *his* whore turns me on.

Whether it's instinct or lust, something inside me shifts, and I give in, allowing our bodies to tangle as his hand comes off my mouth and our tongues collide. His tail wraps around me, putting pressure as it constricts my movement.

It's constricting my movement. *Constricting*.

"What kind of serpentine are you?" I ask between kisses.

"A constrictor."

"Oh!"

"Why, did you want me to fill you with venom?"

"No," I say softly. For the first time, I think ever, I realize just how strong he is. How he could suffocate me in an instant. My heart thumps a million miles a minute, my head feeling light.

"Did you wear that little skirt for me?" he asks. Adeib licks down the side of my neck, caressing me.

"No, I wore it for someone I'm seeing later," I tease.

His tail squeezes around me even tighter, my feet now off the ground as he suspends me in the air.

"Did I not warn you what would happen to your friend if you did that again? Or was I too vague? I can provide the gritty details of what would happen to her," he warns me.

I... I almost want to know. Of course I don't want anything bad to happen to Saga, or any innocent person, but I like the image that's forming in my mind. Adeib towering over someone, his face splattered in blood.

There's something so attractive about someone with the means to kill almost anyone with their bare hands choosing softness.

His words may be violent, but his actions are gentle. Except in bed. Or in this case, the library.

Adeib tosses me onto a table, and I look around, worried someone will hear us. Or worse, see us.

"Do not worry, ya fo'aadi. Nobody comes down here, and I told the librarian we need privacy for our research." One of his eyebrows ticks up as his tail releases me, wrapping only around my middle.

My skirt is lifted, my body leaning back as he kisses down my neck, his tongue moving in circular motions.

"I have dreamt of your taste, your smell," he says, hissing in a low growl. "How it would feel to drown in your wetness."

He places my nipple between his teeth and lightly tugs, the sensation sending me into overdrive. He repeats the movement on my other breast, and I become undone.

Legs spread, using my arms to hold myself up, I watch as his mouth kisses my inner thighs, slowly grazing towards my center.

Adeib sticks out his tongue—his forked tongue—eyes drowsy and cheeks heated, and flicks it against my clit. I moan, my hips bucking towards him.

He sucks me into his mouth, and I have to fight not to make a sound. I bite my lower lip and tip my head back as he performs a symphony on my body, his tongue working magic.

When he releases his tongue, I whimper.

"Ssh," he says and covers my mouth with his hand. His tail constricts even tighter around my body, locking me in place.

Adeib takes his other hand and slaps it against my pussy, my clit throbbing with the sensation.

"That was for wearing the corset," he says, his tone honeyed.

Slap.

"That was for Saturday." He flips me over, my ass now bared to him.

Smack.

He hits my ass much harder. I gasp, my body convulsing. I wait, holding my breath, but he doesn't move.

"Please," I beg. I'm aching for him to touch me again.

"What do you want?" he asks as he turns me onto my back, his clawed hands creeping up my legs, gently caressing my skin.

"Ruin me," I say. It's both plea and demand.

He moves, razor sharp, until his lips are nearly touching mine. "I will. I will ruin that pretty little cunt of yours until no one else can satisfy you."

Adeib works his tongue back down my body and flicks it over my clit. My eyes shutter close, my body relaxing with pleasure. His tongue oscillates rapidly, increasing in speed.

Something hard and wet touches my ass and I stiffen. Opening my eyes, I notice his briefcase is unfastened on the table beside me, a potion bottle clearly out and opened.

Lube?

His tail makes its way towards my hole and slowly pushes me open, stretching me little by little.

"Adeib," I rasp, biting back a moan.

"I want my name burned into your skin, heating your body for days," he growls, his mouth still buried in my cunt.

I start to unravel.

The fullness of his tail, the quickness of his tongue, it's all too much. *He's* too much. The way he cooks and cares, even though he'd probably deny having even an ounce of feeling for me. His venomous words and yet gentle touches. I feel like I've been empty my whole life, and Adeib has finally come in and filled me.

He continues devouring me as I explode. I scream, seeing stars as I crash with the waves of my orgasm.

My muscles spasm as Adeib pulls me close, and I nuzzle my face into the base of his neck, basking in the salty smell of his sweat-slicked skin.

"Here, I brought a towel," he says and grabs it from his bag. "Take this." He wipes away the sweat on my forehead before running the towel up my thighs, patting my vulva.

"I can't believe you brought a fucking towel," I say, laughing. "Oh my goodness, you *planned* this?!"

"That short skirt, no undergarments, and you are claiming you did not *plan* this?" His eyebrows raise, his lips forming a thin line.

"Okay, so maybe I did plan this, but seriously, a towel and lube?"

"You had a fantastic time." He smirks.

Cocky bastard. I just can't believe no one heard us. Although, had we been caught, we could've quit and ran away together. I shake away the thought.

"Your... your cocks are still inside your—"

He nods. "Yes, I am fully in control of my body."

"Well, that makes one of us. Do you want me to—"

"Another time," he interrupts. "Today was about you."

My heart does seven backflips in a row. Everyone I've ever been with made it about them. Adeib is so different; selfless.

He kisses my forehead, and I hop off the table, adjusting my skirt.

"We have research to do. Tomorrow will be our first day in the lab," he tells me, and I gulp.

My mind is torn between the ecstasy I just received and the pit in my stomach at the reminder of tomorrow. I'm a walking contradiction, unable to decide how to think or feel.

Deep breaths, Iris. You're just embarrassed at how bad you are in the lab. It's not a big deal, we'll get through this.

How will we get through this? I'm not sure.

fourteen

ADEIB

Iris and I have yet to work in the laboratory together, and I am not looking forward to it. Every day with her is a new adventure, but these are uncharted waters.

We both suit up, putting on gloves, goggles, and long white lab coats. It is not my most attractive attire, but Iris looks adorable. Her freckles dance across her face. I push a strand of hair behind her ear and then triple check to ensure everything fits her properly.

Protocol states that familiars are not welcome inside, so Florp and Hiro sit in the other room, staring at us through a wide window.

"Have you ever dreamt that you had superpowers?" Iris asks as we set everything up.

"I have not. We have magic; we do not need superpowers. I mean, look at us, we are trying to cure cancer," I say proudly. Because frankly, I am proud. Of myself, of her. Of everyone at Augury University who is trying to make a difference. I may have not gotten enough time with my family, but others deserve to.

"Right," Iris says nervously.

Thanks to our own experiments, as well as research I completed in the library, we believe hibiscae and hydrangigus can be spliced together to create a potion that will prevent cancer from ever occurring inside the breast ducts.

No magnamint here.

Those tested and found to be predisposed to breast cancer will be able to take this and prevent it. Anyone who is not tested, and develops breast cancer, can take Iris' original potion once they go through treatment and are in remission.

It is amazing to see how much medicine and magic have come together. Humanity should be grateful for The Convergence, and the new life it provided Earth. I would be grateful, had The Convergence not torn my family apart.

"So... what are we doing here? I know we're splicing some DNA, but can you explain everything to me in great detail? I don't want to miss anything."

"We are going to blend the hibiscae cells and subsequently separate the DNA from the intracellular fluid using a centrifuge," I say, placing the samples into the machine with the necessary counterbalances. "We will set it to the ideal rotation per minute, using the same speed you did in your original trials."

"Um. You should do it, you're the one running this project. I'm just the assistant, remember," she says.

No? She has fought me tooth and nail, insisting that she is my partner. The Iris I have become fond of over the last few weeks wants to do everything, even if she does it totally wrong. Why is she passing off every task to me?

"That thingy." She points to the centrifuge. "It separates them by density?" she asks.

"Yes." *Obviously.*

"And after that's complete? Please, I'm trying to remember everything."

What is with these intern-level questions? Is she stalling? I groan in frustration. "We will use a polymerase chain reaction to isolate and replicate the RNA."

Iris' purple eyes are wide but empty, like she does not understand a single thing I am saying.

Something is definitely off, but I decide to keep going. "The goal is to take some of the magical genes and add them into the genetic code of the hibiscae, while removing some of the non-magical genes from the plant."

"And then we'll make the potion," she says. Her hands are shaking.

"Exactly. This hybrid-plant DNA, in combination with a potion base a different research group was tasked with developing, will allow us to manipulate the breast duct cells as we please," I explain. Surely she will not have any additional questions.

"Adeib," Iris says, her voice soft and distant.

"Yes, farfora?"

"I don't know what I'm doing." Tears line her eyes, and something in me breaks. I have no clue what is going on, but I hate to see her hurting.

"It is okay," I say and take off my gloves. We can do the experiment another time, clearly something is bothering her. "You do not have to remember how to splice DNA. I can do this part."

"No," she says, her face buried in my chest. "I don't know how to do any of it."

I take her by the shoulders and push her back, looking her in the eyes. "Do not be so hard on yourself."

"No, Adeib, you're not listening. I'm a fraud."

"What do you mean?"

"I never figured out any sort of cure. I was just fucking around in a class I took and happened to stumble upon a miracle. Seriously, I wouldn't have even noticed if it weren't for my lab partner," she confesses. Her skin is paler than normal; she looks sickly.

"How? How is that possible?"

"I majored in potions in college, but I needed an extra class, so I took a medicinal magic class. They were doing trial experiments on cancer cells around the same time, and our class was accidentally given the wrong samples to use for a project. I, being the asshole that I am, started throwing random shit together and injected it into the cells, and they changed," she explains. "That's when my partner realized the sample was cancerous."

"Why did you pretend you discovered it?"

"I didn't." She frowns. "My lab partner told my professor, who then informed the dean, the news, my parents, and just about everyone else on the planet."

"When the company you work for hired you, how did you duplicate your original mishap?"

"I had a friend hack the cameras in the lab, and I rewatched the footage," she confesses.

All the missing pieces are falling into place. The way she dressed at the greenhouse, the way she collected samples, and the mortified look on her face when I said we were finally going to be working in the laboratory.

"So, you lied to all of us?"

"I—"

"Do not try to backtrack now. You lied."

Tears are streaming down her face. "I didn't want to lie, Adeib, but I had no choice."

"Does your sister know?" I doubt Indigo would have allowed her sister to work here if she knew.

"No," her voice comes out raspy and desperate. "And please don't tell her—don't tell anyone."

This is ridiculous. "We are not going to continue this experiment. I will not allow your name to be written next to mine, discrediting me and everything I have worked for. Iris, I care about you, but I will not lie for you."

"I understand."

"Do you?" I cross my arms, brows furrowed. "Did you ever stop to think about the consequences of your lies? That someone might be relying on you for a fucking cure, while you are out here playing scientist?"

"It's not like I wasn't going to try; I just don't know what I'm doing. I still want to help people," she says, as if that makes a difference.

"So you were going to make tons of money assisting while myself and other hardworking mages do the real work?"

"No—no, it was never like that. I didn't intend for it to go this far."

"Impact matters more than your intent. You may think this was okay, because you did not mean to hurt anyone, but you have been lying to all of us. Taking money and interviews you did not earn," I say. "You should be ashamed of yourself."

"I am."

Iris stands and quietly packs her things. She walks out of the lab without a word, her long, shiny hair flowing behind her as she steps out the door.

Was I too hard on Iris? I wonder as I slither towards her apartment. What she did was wrong, but I also know all too well the pressures of family and society.

When The Convergence happened, I went from having zero responsibilities, to being one of the key members of our village. I became responsible for locating those we lost, whether that be by finding them, or their corpses.

I could not handle it. When I was unable to find my sister, I decided not to return. I took the coward's way out and spent many years of my life living in shame, the guilt eating away at me.

While I do not appreciate Iris' untruths, I think I can forgive her for them and help her make amends.

Knocking on the door, I wait for her to answer.

For someone whose life is quadruple the span of most, it goes by quickly. *Usually.* Right now, it feels like forever has gone by.

The door cracks open just a peep. "Hey, you can come in," she says, tone sullied.

She gestures to the paisley couch in the middle of the room. This apartment is not very stylish, and it is obvious Iris has not made it her own.

I sit down next to her, taking note of the bags that line her normally vibrant eyes.

"Thank you for giving me space," she says. "But I've missed you."

I would have waited an eternity to hear those words.

"Of course. Have you thought about what your next steps are?" I ask.

"I don't know. I can't continue lying and working jobs I'm unqualified for. It's not right, and it's eating me alive."

"I agree."

She shrugs. "But I also don't know what I want out of life."

"That is okay," I say and take her hand in mine, bringing it to my lips and planting a soft kiss. "You do not have to know, and you can always change your mind."

"Did you ever have other dreams?"

"'Ummi owned a farm, so I always presumed I would take over one day," I share.

"Did you ever have dreams that were *yours*?" Desperation lines her features.

"*This.* I wanted to be a botanist... or a poet."

"That's amazing, I'm glad it worked out for you."

I run the back of my hand across her cheek. "It can work out for you too. You just have to know what you want out of life."

She leans into my touch, a single tear streaming down her precious face. "What should I do?"

I contemplate this. "There is nothing you should do, but many things you can do. I am not a medicinal magic expert, but I could help you learn things. Maybe your friend, the centaur, could tutor you too. You will probably never cure cancer, but you could assist others in their attempts."

"Yeah."

With everyone, even Florp, I have to will gentleness into my tone. But with Iris? It comes naturally.

"Next week I have to go on a trip for a few days. Think about it, and when I get back, we can figure it out," I say, remembering I have to visit Naiad Island.

"Okay."

Gently, I plant a kiss on her cheek and leave the apartment.

fifteen

IRIS

This is the third pint of ice cream I've had this week. I even had regular ice cream—dairy and gluten included. The stomach ache that followed was not even remotely worth it.

I feel like I deserve a little pain right now. I'm not a perfect person, I've never claimed to be one, but I always intended on being a good person.

I've failed my goals. I became exactly who I despise. Adeib was right. There are people out there waiting on me to find a preventative. A treatment. I have been stringing them along, and the guilt of that gnaws at my heart. The consequences of my actions were more significant than I ever pictured, and I hurt people.

Without realizing it, I hurt everyone I care about too. I lied to Adeib, failed to meet my mother's expectations, and pushed away my older sister in the process.

The worst part of it all? This isn't what I love. I really put myself in a den of lies for a career that makes me stressed out and miserable. Potions are part of my passion, but not *medicine.*

I want to create. Growing up, I wrote fanfiction and drew pictures and made silly potions that did fun stuff. I never dreamed of curing cancer or playing around in a lab.

Now, I have to face reality. If I'm going to come clean, I need to find a clear path to follow. What am I even good at? Art. Potions.

I could become a graphic designer or a tattoo artist. I could create potions for fun and do something mundane. Forging a new future will be hard, but it'll be so worth it when I feel like I'm being my authentic self again. *Right?*

There's got to be a job out there where I can create wonderful things and make my schedule; I need to do things on my own time. I ponder this.

Where will I even live? I could go back to Sleeping Island. Octopus Island doesn't feel right; it's home to a version of me I've shed, letting go of.

Knock. Knock. Knock.

I cross the living room, making my way to the door. I expect Fern, or maybe Adeib is here to say goodbye again before he leaves.

Opening the door, I'm met with white short hair and purple eyes that look a lot like mine. Indigo.

"Hey, Indie," I say, a smile spreading across my face before I force it to dissipate. "Come in."

Something akin to surprise lines her features, like she didn't expect me to let her inside. It sends a pang to my heart. I never wanted to avoid my sister, but she is the one person I'm afraid I've failed the most.

"Feel free to have a seat. Do you want water or something?" I ask.

Indigo sits down, as elegant as ever, and shakes her head. "No, thank you."

I hate to say it, but I don't know where to start. The last time I saw her, I was shit-faced drunk. I'm not ready to tell her I'm leaving the research project. Not yet.

Wow. I guess I have solidified my decision. I hadn't even realized until the thought flew across my mind like a shooting star. I'm not going to keep this act up much longer. I can't.

"Vega and I are taking a trip to Naiad Island for the grand opening!" she says, voice laced with excitement.

"Grand opening?"

"The grand opening of Aquatica Academy: An Augury University Affiliate. It's our Naiad Island campus," she beams.

"That's so cool. Is it specifically for merfolk?"

"Yeah. And other water-friendly races. Augury University has developed a lot of accommodations, but with how many merfolk attend, the dean and the elven council wanted somewhere specifically catered to them."

Images of mermaids and krakens swimming around with textbooks fill my mind, and I wonder what this new school will look like.

"Are you excited?" I ask.

"Of course. I was actually wondering if you'd like to tag along? Vega and I both get a plus one, and since we don't have to take each other, I thought it would be nice to take you. It's free."

It's free. Why is she still so kind to me? After I've spent so long avoiding her, I can't comprehend why she still tries. I consider saying yes, but I can't.

"I have a lot going on with this project, so I don't know if it's a good idea," I lie. It feels like the lies just keep piling on, but I'll free myself from this toxic loop soon enough.

She gives me a look. "Well, Adeib is also going to be there, so you won't be getting much of the project done if you stay here."

Why is Adeib going to—*oh.* He said he was going on a trip, but he never said where or what for. I assumed it was personal stuff about his sister again. Nevermind, I definitely *can* go. The deep need to be with him overshadows my want for isolation.

"I'll be there," I say without another thought.

One long car ride and one short ferry ride later, we're on Naiad Island. This place is otherworldly. Every map I've ever seen paints this island to be a regular mass of land, no lakes or rivers listed on the key, but that couldn't be further from the truth.

The island has tons of water. Most of the citizens live on the edges, many merfolk living in the cove systems themselves, but there are others who can shift, or have human legs and walk on land. Despite the mostly empty streets, the island's warm and tropical vibe makes it less eerie.

We walk down the pier and onto a street, heading for the Lesgod Hotel, the island's top resort on the western side. It's only a few miles from Aquatica Academy, and I look forward to seeing the new school.

Hiro walks as if he knows where he's going, and Freja, Vega's little hummingmouse familiar, sits on his back. Momiji flies above them, his rabbit tail swishing back and forth. The three musketeers. Vega and Indigo are inseparable, walking hand-in-hand in the peaceful silence. I stay back, directly behind them.

This is the quietest I've been around people in a long time, but it's nice. I can't manage like this for long though. Adeib has to listen to me yap every day.

We head into the resort, and Vega pulls out her phone, letting us into our room. There's a kitchen, a living room, and two separate bedrooms, each with their own bathroom. I don't know how I ended up agreeing to sharing a hotel with these two lovebirds, but I did.

I place my duffel bag onto the bed and try to figure out what to wear. This afternoon is the big beach kick-off party, and tomorrow is the formal dinner where they cut the ribbon. I zone out, my mind numb after these hectic last couple of weeks.

Grabbing black swim shorts and an orange sports bra, I get dressed for the beach. I cross into the living room to find Indigo and Vega waiting for me.

"For a minute, I thought you might've fallen into the toilet," Vega jests.

"What?" I ask on a laugh. "Oh, did I take longer than I thought? Sorry." I have a tendency to lose track of time.

"It's totally fine, let's get going though. Indie will have a panic attack if we're late," she says and kisses Indigo on the cheek. Indigo is wearing a deep purple tennis dress that matches Vega's swim trunks. It's so cute it makes me want to tie myself to train tracks.

Our familiars are lucky they don't have to wear clothes, and they all follow us out of the resort and back down the street as we make our way to the beach.

The beach, which is the dreamiest place I've ever seen, is practically empty. There are cutesy magic decorations everywhere, from signs with potions doodled on them, to banners with common familiar-breeds etched into the design.

People I recognize, and people I don't, are all crowded in different groups, drinking and playing games.

Is that—? My mind puts together the pieces like a puzzle. The cambion who brought me food when I was sick is sitting in a 3-wheel mobility device, fitted with two larger back wheels that allow her to move around different types of terrain. Adeib must have been the one to ask her to make the delivery. When Fern told me he saw Adeib and the food arrived, I knew in my heart it was him, and realizing he sent his coworker just confirms it.

So where is Adeib? He should be here too.

"Iris," I hear a familiar voice call out. The dean's tall, lanky body comes towards me. "Good to see you, how have you been? Are you looking forward to the big reveal tomorrow night?"

If there is one person who talks more than I do, it's Dean Bariel.

"Yes, this is so exciting. Congratulations!"

He's wearing a thin green t-shirt and cargo shorts, and his pale skin practically sparkles in the sun. He looks more vampire than elf, though vampires don't live on Earth. The Convergence never took them this far.

"Thank you. It is most exciting. Would you like to play volleyball against Vega and I?" he asks, and I freeze.

"I'm not really a sporty person. And besides, who will be on my team?"

A warm presence lingers behind my back, and I feel a hand brush my hair off my shoulder. "Me, of course," Adeib's voice rings through the air like my favorite song.

We cross over to the net and Vega serves the ball. At first, I feel bad that Adeib has such an inept teammate, but I quickly realize I'm just there for show.

Adeib absolutely wipes the floor with them. Vega is incredibly athletic, and Archeron is no slowpoke, but the two of them can hardly keep up as Adeib slithers through the sand.

"Foul!" Daffodil shouts from the sidelines, her boyfriend Moss standing with his arms wrapped around her.

Moss has a tattoo of a moon underneath the scar on the right side of his chest, and I realize it matches the sun on Daffodil's sternum. The dean looks at the two of them all starry-eyed, and I wonder if there's something deeper there.

"Foul for *what*?" I ask when I realize I'm staring.

"Adeib used his tail. No tail play allowed," she remarks.

I definitely enjoy when Adeib uses his tail, but I get it. My cheeks flush pink, and I look back at Vega and Archeron.

"Alright, you heard her, no tails allowed," I say and serve the ball. Vega immediately bumps it back, but luckily Adeib slithers forward, sending the ball spiraling towards Archeron.

We go like this for some time until Malik steps up to the net. "Alright guys, wrap it up. Some of the rest of us want to play, and *not* against Dr. Ali."

"I am going to go get a drink, if you would like to tag along," Adeib says and nods towards the cooler.

I walk beside him, and he grabs a bottle of water, handing it to me. We continue down the beach and slowly shift closer and closer, until I am leaning against his shoulder.

"Am I something to you?" I ask, unsure of if I want an answer.

"What do you mean?"

I sigh. "Am I... a girlfriend, a friend? What am I to you?"

"You are whatever you want to be, farfora," he says, and I cross my arms.

"What does that mean? I tried looking it up, but I think I must have spelled it wrong," I admit.

"It is a nickname, a diminutive. I am calling you... in English, it would be like saying you are my little mouse. My soft mouse."

"Are you calling me a rat?"

He shakes his head. "I did not call you a *rat*; I called you a mouse. It is a term of endearment."

Adeib wraps his arms around my waist and pulls me close, kissing me softly. He smells of sweat, sand, and the ocean, and I breathe him in, allowing him to invade my senses.

We have to go back to where everyone else is, but for this moment, it is just him and I in this world.

sixteen

IRIS

The heat of the sun lingers on my face, and I'm sure I'll have more freckles by morning. I'm not sure where Adeib is sleeping tonight, but we walk back to the resort separately, so nobody gets suspicious. Indigo likely already senses something is up between us, but she doesn't mention it.

Vega unlocks the door to the hotel room. "I am going to run out and get some water and snacks, I'll be back in a bit," she says. "Text me if there's anything specific you two want."

"Oooh! Chocolate. Get me whatever looks good. Iris likes peanut butter cups," Indigo says, her voice chipper.

We slouch onto the couch next to one another, Indigo flipping through the TV channels, her stopping on some historical movie, as she always does. Hiro and Momiji nuzzle up together like two old friends.

"Are you working on lab trials when we get back to Augury?"

"No," I say before I can think. *Fuck.*

Her brows furrow. "No? Why not? I thought Dr. Ali said you guys had started them."

I had asked Adeib not to tell my sister the truth, and now it's come back to bite me in the ass. It's time to face the music, as dissonant as it may be.

"I'm quitting."

"What do you mean?" Indigo looks borderline horrified.

"This doesn't make me happy, Indigo. I'm quitting to pursue other things."

Her voice sounds shaky. "What other things?"

"I don't know, but I feel like my life isn't my own. I spent so long trying to impress our mother, my professors, and even you... I lost sight of me," I confess. It's not everything, but I'm working my way up to the whole truth.

"I'm sorry, I don't mean to sound like a bitch, but how does this have anything to do with me?" She turns her body to face me and mutes the TV. I watch as Hiro and Momiji crawl under the couch together.

"I spent so much of my life idolizing you. I wanted to be the perfect sister, someone you could be proud of."

Indigo's brows knit together, her lips forming a thin line. "Iris, I've been compared to you all my life. *Your little sister matured early. Your little sister is dating, Indigo. Your sister is on TV. Iris grew out her hair. Iris calls me every week.* Over and over again, like clockwork, our mother hounded me."

"I—"

"I never faulted you for it. It wasn't your fault that she preferred you, so I worked to never make you feel bad about it. That being said, whatever pressure she put on you to be perfect, it has nothing to do with me. I would've rather you been flawed... like me," she says, and I swear tears are forming in her eyes, but she blinks them away.

I stand and walk into the kitchen, grabbing a glass and filling it with water. I take a sip before speaking again, giving myself time to formulate my next words.

"I always wanted to be just like you, Indigo."

She turns back to face me. "A failure in our mother's eyes?"

"No," I shake my head. "*Delicate.* You are petite and poised, your voice soft. Nobody ever scolds you in public for being too loud. I'm always too much for everyone." My voice is breaking, but I continue. "Too loud, too talkative, and too clumsy. My thoughts never stop, my mind is constantly going, and it physically pains me to keep it all locked inside."

There's a sadness in Indigo's eyes as she hears my words.

"But I do," I say. "I keep most of it inside. Everyone thinks I'm obnoxious, but none of you have any idea how hard it is to be in my head. If I didn't babble on for hours, I would implode. I wanted to be like you. I wanted to be pretty and likable, without the rough edges."

"Do you think it's easy being me?"

Yes, I think. But I don't respond, because there's no kind way to answer.

"Because it's not. This isn't a competition to see whose life is harder, but for the record, I'm not perfect either. Yes, I'm more quiet, but that's because I'm scared, Iris. I envy your boldness. I live my life in constant anxiety," she shares.

And I know that. I know that Indigo struggles with anxiety, but my brain is so flustered. I have done so much to make her and our mother proud, and she doesn't ever acknowledge it. Maybe she never will.

"At least people never make you feel like you take up too much space. Like you need to dim your light for theirs to shine brighter," I say, regretting it before the words leave my mouth. It's not her fault, even if I'm looking for someone to blame.

"Nobody gets the opportunity to dim my light, because I dim it myself," she bites back.

Vega enters the hotel room quietly, as if she can sense the tension in the room. She hands Indie a chocolate bar and passes me a bag of peanut butter cups.

"Should I leave?" Vega asks.

"No," Indigo and I say in unison.

"Okay, what's up with you two?"

I take a deep breath. "I was just about to apologize to Indigo for lying."

Vega's golden eyes widen, and she shifts her weight onto one hip. The movement is something my sister does often, and it heats some of the coldness lingering in my chest.

"My college experiment was a fraud. I discovered the potion completely by accident," I confess, and it feels like an elephant has been lifted off my chest. "I can't keep living this facade, so I wanted to come clean. About everything."

"Are you two punking me?" Vega asks, but I shake my head.

"No. When my professor told the local news, and other scientists, and worst of all, our mother, I was too embarrassed—too afraid to disappoint everyone, so I lied. I went along with it." Like ingredients going into a potion, everything comes together. The emotion I've been tortured with, it's not embarrassment. My racing heart, sweat-slicked nightmares, and the pit in my stomach. I had never felt anything quite like this before, but I understand now. This sickening feeling I cannot seem to rid is my guilt and worry mixing to form the worst concoction. Anxiety. Fear.

Vega opens and closes her mouth.

"Iris. You're good at potions; it always came naturally to you," Indigo says, tears streaming down her face. "How could it be fake?"

"I might be a good mage, but I don't know anything about medicine. And honestly? You were always better than me," I say. And it's true. Our parents never noticed how talented Indigo was because I was too busy stealing the spotlight. "I'm sorry it took so long for everyone to notice. I'm sorry it's my fault you never got the recognition you deserve."

"Stop apologizing," she snaps, her tone full of ice. It's so unusual for

Indigo that it shocks me to my core. I kind of thought she would accept my apology, we'd hug, and everything would be okay again.

That's what I need right now, but this isn't about me. I swallow hard.

"Okay. I just—"

"I spent my whole life living in your shadow, my hero of a little sister, only to find out the entire thing was a farce. How did you expect me to react!?"

I try not to respond. She is allowed to feel her feelings, even though I don't know what to do about them. I want to comfort her, to make everything okay, but I can't. I made this mess, and I have to suffer the consequences. *Fuck.*

Vega moves to sit on the couch, rubbing a hand down Indigo's back, and I'm grateful. I should give them space.

I cross into my room and unzip my duffel bag, opening the contents onto the bed. Clothes spill out everywhere, and I grab a short, ruffled black dress and throw it on, removing my bra and swapping the shorts for underwear.

I check the weather app, remembering Adeib's words, before deciding it's the perfect warm summer night to go on a walk.

Hiro enters the room, and I rub the back of his ears. "I'll be back in an hour. I just need to go clear my head," I say.

Opening the door, Indigo and Vega are no longer in the living room, and I sigh in relief. I exit through the front door and make my way down to the hotel lobby.

Unlike in Sunspell City, or even on Octopus Island, there's hardly a person in sight here on Naiad. The normal hustle and bustle of a city is replaced by quiet, hot summer sounds. Cicadas. Sea gulls.

I'd actually prefer the noise. Something, anything to get my mind off of what I've done. I think I can forgive myself, but I have to be patient and wait to see if everyone else can forgive me, too.

I continue walking further and notice a mural across the street. It's vibrant, with gorgeous shades of red and orange. I shift to move towards it when my foot gets caught in a grate. Metal clangs, and I'm suddenly falling.

What the fuck just happened?

Darkness surrounds me as I fall deeper and deeper underground, the loudest sound being my thundering heart. I try to grab for something, but there's nothing within reach.

Splash.

seventeen

ADEIB

Knock. Knock.

Thump. Thump. Thump.

Someone is pounding on my door. My eyes shoot open, and I grab my phone, checking the time. One o'clock in the morning. Who would disturb me in the middle of the night?

I slither to the door, opening it, expecting to see a stranger, or even Iris. *What is Vega doing here?*

"What is going on?"

"I woke up to Hiro whimpering and realized Iris hadn't come back," she explains.

My heart drops. "Come back from where?"

Vega scratches the back of her neck. "Indigo and Iris got into a huge fight, and I guess Iris left after. But she didn't take Hiro, and she hasn't returned. I'm worried about her," she says. "Indigo is too, but she's exhausted from all the big feelings and passed out in the rental car."

"What kind of a car is it?" I ask.

"SUV. Specialty kind, it's able to fit centaurs in the back if need be."

"Perfect. Let us get going."

Vega explains the fight that went down between the two sisters as Indigo sleeps in the front passenger seat. She states everything neutrally, and I am impressed. I do not think I would be able to do the same. I favor Iris too much, and I am not nearly as level-headed as this orcling.

We drive up and down the empty roads, searching for any sign of Iris. A business that looks like something she would enjoy, an article of clothing that reminds us of her, nothing. Not a single sign.

Worry, which is not an emotion I experience often, settles into my bones, radiating through my body. I want to hold Iris close and keep her safe; I cannot stand the thought of something happening to her.

"Stop here," I say when we are down the street from the resort again. "I am going to get out and search by myself."

"Is everything okay?" Indigo asks, yawning.

"Hey, little rabbit. Everything's okay, we're just searching for Iris," Vega says, soothing her.

"Okay." Her eyes flutter back closed.

"I can track her by her pheromones if I am out in the open air. I will call you when I find her." When, not if.

Vega nods and I open the car door, slithering out into the night.

At first, I smell nothing. Not a single recognizable scent. Something hits my nose, and I spring forward, flying my way towards her. When I reach where it feels the strongest, I groan in frustration.

Where is she?

I look down and notice an old steel grate tossed to the side of a hole in the ground. *Oh fuck.* She is underground. Sickness envelops me, swallowing me whole.

For someone who spent most of his early years playing in cave systems, you would think I might be comfortable searching through one for the person I care most about. I *will* go down there and find her, but I am not happy about it. Sadness, terror, and guilt mingle in my stomach, reminding me of my past. Of my childhood, my sister. I still do not know what happened to Aida. Though I never found a trace of her, she could be dead. Or she could be alive, thriving on another planet.

Whatever is happening to my sister, the past is the past, and I have to do what I can to help Iris. *My farfora, ya hayati.*

Lowering myself into the ground, I drop until I hit water with a loud splash. It is only a few feet deep, but I can tell it eventually leads into a larger cavern.

The underground tunnels of Naiad Island are not sewers, but an old, unused cave system. This lightless space expands through the entire island. I feel like I am in the catacombs, except no one is here to steal my flashlight. I do not have one, nor do I need it. Infrared vision is on my side.

It is not often I am grateful for being a serpentine. We live long, lonely lives. But when it comes to the senses? We are the most powerful beings on Earth.

I continue through the wet, never ending darkness, following the trail of Iris' fear. I have to find her. After I lost my sister, I did not have anyone to protect, or any reason to care—any reason to keep going. That was until her.

Her scent dissipates, and I feel a dropping point. There is a deep cavern down here. She is either trapped down there, or on the other side. I bite back any remnants of other emotions, dedicating my mind solely to protecting Iris, and dive in.

Snaking my way through the water, I catch a whiff of her scent again and cross through. I have no idea how Iris got down here, but I need to see her. I need to feel her beating heart and see the rise and fall of her chest before I will be okay again. The water is ice cold, and my muscles tense as I continue on.

I see a leg with a birdcage tattooed on the thigh and leap towards it. Iris' upper half rests on some rocks, her lower body dangling in the water. I grab her and hold her to my chest before diving back in.

She shakes at the impact of the water, and I hold her even closer, wanting to bury her in my skin, making her a part of me.

When we get to the other side, I carry her in my arms, and she coughs out water, her eyes flickering open as she slowly wakes.

"What happened?" she asks, her voice faint.

"Great question, I wish I knew," I say in earnest.

She opens her eyes and looks at me. "I—I fell. Oh, goddess. I tried to find a way out, but fell deeper into more water. I don't remember much after that."

I pass the hole we initially came down in search of one with a ladder. Emotions pass through me in waves. Gratefulness that Iris is safe, melancholy towards the past. I am not used to feeling this much without shutting it off, turning away from it.

Iris looks up at me, shifting in my arms, and I feel the weight of her stare. For the first time in a long time, I do not want to hide my emotions.

"What's wrong?" she asks, her voice still rough from swallowing so much water.

"I am fine. Everything is okay, now that you are with me," I say to comfort her. It is the truth. I am fine, even if my mind tries to tell me otherwise.

"You don't have to pretend to always be okay," her voice trails off, and she moves the back of her hand down my jaw, brushing through my beard. *She* is comforting *me.* "Grumpy old serpentine can feel things too."

I sigh, settling into the idea of sharing my deepest truths and my closest secrets with someone else. I want to share everything with Iris.

"This place reminds me of my twin, Aida," I tell her. "She was the other half of my soul, and when The Convergence took her from me, I was not sure I would ever be whole again."

She does not reply.

"I found it hard to care about anything, even living." I am never this vulnerable with anyone, but in the dark and the unknown with this woman so full of light, I feel like I can finally free myself from this burden. "Truly, I believed I did not deserve to enjoy life until I found her. I refused to go back to my village until after 'ummi, our mother, died."

I can see, even in the dark, Iris is looking at me, listening intently.

"But I have learned I cannot punish myself for my history, and neither should you. We have to leave it behind."

"Adeib, I'm so sorry," she says and kisses my jaw.

"There has always been a lantern, a little spark of fire hidden deep inside me. I have been holding on to the light, grasping the small ember, as I search my soul for answers on how to keep burning. I have had to struggle to keep the fire alive, to not allow myself to dim, but you, farfora, have set me ablaze."

On the wall up ahead, I spot a ladder, and I haul us towards it. I use my tail to hold on, carrying us back up to the surface.

"How did you even find me?" she asks.

"Your scent. I could smell your fear."

She blinks slowly. "Wouldn't the water make it hard to track?"

I shake my head. "No. I am a serpentine, not a simple bloodhound. I could track you from the other side of the earth if I had to. Iris, I will always find my way back to you."

She nuzzles her head into the crook of my neck, and I get out my phone, calling Vega to come pick us up. I stand there, Iris sleeping in the crook of my arms, and wait.

Vega is quiet when they arrive, Indigo barely awake in the passenger seat. We enter the vehicle, and Indigo's eyes soften at the sight of her sister.

Good. Hopefully their fight is over. They should feel lucky to have one another.

When we get into the hotel, I place Iris down and let her walk. Her dress, still wet, clings to her body like a lover's caress, revealing her hourglass frame.

"Do you want her to go back with you, or us?" Vega asks and I cock my head to the side.

"Hmm?"

"Adeib, it's okay. It's clear you two have developed a... strong bond. You can even stay with us, whatever you think is best," she explains, and Indigo nods, dozing off.

We go up the elevator and somehow I find myself in bed next to Iris, Indigo and Vega just on the other side of the wall.

I am seated at a table with Iris, Indigo, Vega, Alitha, Aura, and Malik. Archeron is giving a presentation on who the staff will be for Aquatica Academy. Some staff members will be from Augury, while others are completely new. Everyone is dressed to the nines and either dozing off or drinking too much alcohol. My table included.

Iris, who insisted we come out tonight despite my best efforts to convince her otherwise, watches intently as they call Alitha up to the stage, congratulating her on her most recently published piece.

"Remember when you asked if you were something to me?" I whisper in Iris' ear.

"Yes, Adeib, that was yesterday," she teases me, and I bring her hand up to my lips, kissing her soft skin.

"You are everything to me, ya hayati."

eighteen

IRIS

Indigo sits across from me at the cute coffee shop we started frequenting in Sunspell City. Although the Illusionary Jungle has become like home to me this summer, there's not much there besides the university and a bunch of trees. Her hot chocolate and my coffee arrive, and I sip it to make sure it's almond milk.

"I quit MagiPharm X. Told them I was not only leaving the project, but the company as well," I say.

She gives me a small smile. "I think this will be good for you. A fresh start."

"I think so too," I say and take a larger sip of my drink. "I told mom."

Indigo's eyes widen. I almost think she's going to drop her cup, but she holds it steady. "Oh boy. How'd she take it?"

"She cried. Told me I was a failure, and hung up the phone," I share. I thought it would hurt, but I honestly feel relieved. I know she's just being dramatic, and that she doesn't mean the cruel things she says and does. It doesn't make it right, but it lessens the sting.

"Iris, I'm so sorry—"

"Don't be. Really, I'm better than I've been in a while. Dad texted me directly after telling me he's proud of me," I say.

"We really do have the world's sweetest dad and the world's bitchiest mom," she says, and I laugh.

"Truly."

"What are you going to do now?" she asks.

I shrug, because I honestly don't know. I love the life I've started building here. Being close to my sister, hanging with Fern and my new friends, the university itself, and of course, Adeib. I'll miss Raemond and my parents, but I haven't lived on Octopus Island for some time now. It doesn't feel like home anymore.

"I would like to do something with potions, or maybe art," I share.

"What about working in the cosmetic lab?" she suggests.

Augury University has a cosmetic lab that Alitha runs. Indigo works at it as well, and they've created different potions for things like hair dye and perfume. They make beauty magical too.

"What could I do there?" I ask.

Indigo furrows her brows, but she's still smiling. "Anything you like. You could develop something! Or help us with our ongoing projects. I could write you a letter of recommendation. I bet Adeib would too."

"I would love that, thank you."

"Think about what kind of projects you'd like to try," she says and a smile, purple-lipstick-and-all, spreads across her face from ear to ear.

I walk into the dean's office with a stack of paper in hand. Letters of recommendation from Professor Watson, Dr. Adeib Ali, Dr. Vega Daelor, Dr. Aura Nguyen, and Dr. Alitha Taylor. It's weird to see their names like this, so formal.

Daffodil sits at the front desk and grins when she sees me. "Iris! What're you doing here?"

"I'd like to see Dean Bariel," I say. Nervous energy flutters in my chest.

Dean Bariel's door flies open, and he waves. "Ms. Watson, come in!"

The door shuts behind me, and I have a seat. His office is still as messy as ever, but I don't mind. It's chaos, but it's consistent.

"It's nice to see you. I was sad to hear you were dropped from the project with MagiPharm X," he says.

Dropped. That's a funny way of putting it, but what should I expect from a big corporation?

"Yeah. I've really enjoyed my time at Augury," I say. I still live in the apartment, but I received an email telling me my move out date. "That's actually why I'm here."

"Oh?"

"I would like to apply to work in the cosmetic lab. I know I failed you with the big project, but that's because medicinal magic isn't what I'm good at. I'm good with potions, and that's what I'd like to be doing." My voice is fast but steady as I drone off my qualifications and reasoning. "There are so many cosmetic opportunities the lab has yet to explore. I would be focusing on more alternative beauty, specifically tattoos."

"Tattoos, huh? I just recently got one," he says.

"Ooh! Can I see?"

The dean unbuttons the top two buttons on his shirt, revealing a star. It's the same style and detailing of the tattoos I saw on Daffodil and Moss, and my heart warms. *I knew it.*

"I think I want to get more, though I'm not sure what," he shares.

"I love that for you!"

I place my short stack of papers on his desk. "I have some recommendations, as well as a formal proposal for my first product. Please look it over and let me know if you think I'd be a good fit."

Archeron waves his hand in the air, shooing me, and my heart climbs up into my throat. *How can he disregard me so quickly? I thought this conversation was going great.*

"I don't need to see it. You're hired," he says. "'I'll have Daffodil send you a contract once it's drafted."

And just like that, I'm in a new career field, and one I'll actually enjoy.

Once I'm out of the history tree, I head towards my apartment, pulling out my phone.

IRIS

I GOT A NEW JOB

RAEMOND

Congrats!!! What will you be doing?

IRIS

i'm going to develop a potion to animate tattoos. after that, i don't know. i'll just see where things take me.

RAEMOND

So you're staying at Augury?

IRIS

that's the plan

RAEMOND

I'm so happy for you!

IRIS

thanks!!! you'll have to come visit

RAEMOND

Brb, booking my flight now.

"Did you blackmail the dean into hiring me?" I ask as I walk into Adeib's condo.

He is shirtless, sitting on the couch reading an old poetry book titled *The Adam of Two Edens*. On the coffee table beside him sits Shakespeare's *The Taming of the Shrew*, another book written in Arabic, and a newly published smutty dark romance I've been trying to convince him to buddy read with me. I've never been into nerds, but there's something about this hot, muscled scholar that really gets me going. The tail is a plus too.

"I did not," he says, turning another page.

"I don't believe you," I tease. I cross over to him and sit on his lap, the book instantly falling onto the coffee table alongside the others.

He places his hands on my hips and plants a trail of kisses down my neck. "Perhaps he recognizes your talents."

I let out a staccato, breathy sigh. "I highly doubt that."

"And perhaps I... recommended you," he says and gives me a look. "I know of a way you can return the favor."

The larger of his cocks springs out of its pocket, and I shift to straddle him, grinding it against my already swollen clit. Adeib grabs my tank top and pulls it off of me, exposing my tender nipples. He tugs my skirt over my head until I'm naked and bared for him.

"Already so wet for me," he whispers into my ear, his breath hot against my skin.

The fins on his cock rub against me, and I writhe in pleasure until I sit up, placing the tip of his head inside me. Slowly, I work my way up to a faster rhythm, and Adeib uses his hands to help guide me, bouncing me up and down his shaft until he's completely in.

"More, I want more," I plead, needing our bodies to be fused together. When I was trapped in that tunnel, I had no idea if I was going to get out. All I could think about was Adeib. His touch, his voice, his heart.

In an instant, Adeib's tail flicks around us, wrapping around and grabbing something off the end table. His second cock comes loose, and I can hear as he opens a cap.

Cold, slick pressure hits my other entrance as he gradually stretches me, filling me completely. I sit back onto his cocks, rocking back and forth. The flesh between my openings feels so thin, both dicks practically against each other as I grind on him.

I can feel every bump, every fin. The texture is sending me skyrocketing towards pleasure.

Adeib moves his tail, bringing it above my leg and swings the tip towards my clit. I continue rocking, every nerve in my body on edge as he uses his tail to stimulate me.

"Is that what you needed?" he says against my lips, and our tongues collide, dueling in each other's mouths. He releases for air, but I suck his bottom lip back into mine and bite down.

Slap.

He uses his tail to flick my clit.

Slap.

Another, harder flick comes down, my body pulsating in reaction. I am shaking, practically convulsing as I undulate against him, his tail slapping my sex over and over again until I come toppling off the edge. His second cock comes out of my ass, receding back into his body, and I moan as he pounds back into me.

"Adeib," I scream. I can feel his knot swelling.

"Just reminding you who this pussy belongs to. Who gets to fill you," he says and delivers one final thrust, his knot pushing inside me, pressing on my walls.

We stay like this, my body coiled around his, our heartbeats singing the same song. His knot loosens, and I feel his fluids drip out of me, spilling down my legs. I sigh with content, loving the feeling, like I'm being bred.

Adeib unravels himself from me and makes his way towards the kitchen. I follow closely behind. I sit on his dining room table, still naked, and smile when he doesn't complain.

"I am going to make some baklava. Do you prefer walnuts or pistachios?" he asks.

"Pistachios."

"Good girl," he says and turns on the oven.

This is what home feels like.

epilogue

ADEIB

Getting out of the shower, I slither over to the sink, where make-up and jewelry sits messily on the counter. I make a mental note to buy Iris some organizers for her items. I also make a mental note to remind myself that I will likely have to be the one to organize them, but that is okay.

There was not much thought put into Iris moving in with me. We did not have a long, drawn out conversation, nor did we make rules or stipulations.

Not that she would follow my rules any way.

Iris' apartment lease ended, and, while she was in the lab working on her new potion, I grabbed all her things and brought them to my condo. I was expecting a little bit of push back, but when I showed her and Hiro, they happily settled in. Florp is the happiest of all; she loves having a friend to spend her evenings with.

I put on a tunic before crossing into the kitchen. Grabbing a bowl, I open the fridge and get out yogurt and fruit.

Florp flies around me, and I throw a raspberry. To my surprise, she catches it, chomping down on the juicy fruit. I throw another one, and she catches it again.

We play this game for a while. I take a few bites of my yogurt and throw a raspberry. Florp flying around, beaming with joy. She even does a few tricks. I chuckle, grateful she is my familiar.

I was hesitant to acquire a familiar, as it is not something my people have ever done. But traditions change just as people do, and I needed something new. Otherwise, I was going to lose my magic. Botany is deeply significant to me, and I refuse to let it slip away, especially due to my stubbornness. It is the one thing that ties me to my past and to every place I have ever lived. The connection to my family and our ancestors before us.

No one will ever replace my mother or sister, and nothing will make me stop searching for Aida, but now I have a reason to smile again. Florp and Iris have revitalized my life, giving me things to look forward to.

I exit my home, Florp following closely, and we head to the cosmetic lab, lunchbox in hand. Today is the first test on live skin Iris will be performing with her animated ink prototype. I want to see how it goes, as well as bring her lunch. Summer is almost over, classes starting in another week, and I will miss all the extra time I have with her.

Entering the building, I find Alitha seated at a table, searching her computer for something.

"They're in there," she says.

I cross into the laboratory where a tan woman is standing outside the large window, watching them work inside. Her hair is long and dark, with perfect curls flowing down her back.

"Hey, I'm Dahlia," she says, her voice loud and excited. "I'm best friends with—"

"Indigo and Alitha. Yes, I have seen the three of you around together," I interrupt. "Who is that?" I point to the white-haired elfling who is covered in tattoos.

"That's my boyfriend Elorthiel. Isn't he handsome?"

"Yeah, he sure is," I say. It is true. A different Adeib, the one before Iris, would have hit on both of them.

"He's going to tattoo Indigo and Vega using Indigo's little sisters' potion," she explains, not realizing I already know.

"What are they getting done?" I ask, watching as Iris' face lights up with excitement as the elfling preps his equipment.

"Matching snowflakes that sparkle. Iris told us this prototype can make tattoos shimmer and glow. The next one will make them move, but she hasn't figured out how yet."

Indigo and Vega lay on adjacent reclining chairs, their fingers intertwined. Elorthiel is seated on Indigo's left, tattooing what I think is her ring finger.

Did they get engaged? No, surely Iris would have told me.

Will we get engaged? I think one day, I would like to marry. Serpentine outlive every other race, magical or not, by a longshot. It is unwise for us to fall in love outside our species, because that love will inevitably end in great loss. Between that, and our long gestation periods, serpentine have become a rarity on Earth. Our hybrids even moreso. Sometimes, I like to imagine there is a planet out there that belongs to us—that maybe Aida is there too.

My twin is not the only secret I have kept from others all these years. An image of the rosa aeternitas, given to me by an elven elder, flashes across my mind. It is hidden in my condo, in a place not even Iris knows of.

I could use it. I could take the rose and create a potion, which is something I have heavily researched. It would shorten my lifespan, allowing me to grow old with her. I am almost positive it would work.

Elorthiel lifts the tattoo needle off of Vega and places it down, wiping her skin clean with an antiseptic.

Indigo and Vega's snowflakes sparkle, the black ink shimmering a blue-white in waves across the pattern. Iris beams, jumping up and down, her big, beautiful smile making an appearance. She looks through the window, and her eyes widen as she darts out the door.

"It worked! I did it, it worked, Adeib," she says and wraps her arms around my neck.

I pull her in close, breathing in her scent. My heart is so full. I have finally found a flower that does not mind all my thorns.

bonus chapter

IRIS

A rustling sound is coming from the other side of the condo, and I stand, crossing the living room to investigate the noise. Could it be an intruder? Wait, no. Adeib is home—he would've likely already strangled the guy. R.I.P. to anyone who tries to break into the home of a constrictor.

CRASH.

"What the fuck was that?" I shout as I speed towards the kitchen.

"Nothing, ya hayati, go sit back down," Adeib says, his voice deep and yet full of mischief.

I enter the kitchen, and it's not what I expected. Popcorn litters the floor, Hiro snacking away as he picks up the pieces one by one. He looks at me as if to say *please don't be mad,* and I give my familiar a small smile.

That's when I notice he's covered in butter.

"How did this get all over his coat?" I ask, raising a brow. As a moss-sheep, his fleece should be green! Not a buttery yellow. *Ick.*

Adeib scratches the back of his neck. "I believe Florp may have—"

"Of course it was Florp," I interrupt and point a finger at the geckfly, who looks guilty as ever. "You're always getting Hiro into trouble."

"Do not blame her."

I cross my arms and stomp my foot. "Are you kidding me?"

"She is an innocent, little creature who could do no wrong," he says, though I know he isn't serious. Adeib and Florp had a rocky start, with Adeib being so used to having his own methods for using magic, but I think now he's grateful for his conduit. Loves her, even.

Florp looks at me with big, pleading eyes and flies towards the paper towels, grabbing one with her claw and flying down to where Hiro rests on the floor. She tries to wipe some of the butter off of him, but it's no use. It's everywhere. Seeping into his moss and even coating the kitchen floor.

I stifle a laugh as I try to pretend I'm still mad at the little being, but I just can't be. She's too cute and sweet, and I know she didn't mean to make such a mess.

I let out a sigh. "C'mon, let's go get a bath," I say.

Adeib slithers across the house as the three of us follow, making our way for the bathroom. I can already hear the sound of water filling the tub, and as we enter through the doorway, Hiro jumps right in.

I'm so glad my familiar isn't a cat. If it was, it would've probably chased Momiji, and my sister Indie would've strangled us both.

Once I finish scrubbing the top of Hiro's head, Florp flies over and sits on him like a plover on a crocodile. I grab a bottle of bubbles from under the cabinet and decide to make this bath a little more fun.

Adeib gives me a look as I pour the concoction into the water. "What happened to watching a movie?"

"We'll get to the movie after we bathe our babies," I say with a smile as I sit on the bath mat and watch them play with the bubbles.

"Babies? I do not want babies, nor is—"

"Stop taking things so seriously. They're our fur-babies."

He gets down beside me and looks at Florp, then back at me. "Except neither of them have fur. Hiro has... *wool*, and Florp has scales," Adeib says in protest.

"It's a figure of speech!"

Florp suddenly jumps off of Hiro and dives headfirst into the clawtooth tub. When her leopard-printed body reemerges, she blows a bubble out of her nose and I snort laugh.

"Did you—did you just snort like a little pig?" Adeib asks, chuckling.

I push his broad shoulder. "Don't be an ass."

"Oink oink," he says, trying his best to imitate the sound of a pig.

"Imagine being a multi-*thousand*-year-old serpentine and making fun of your girlfriend for snort laughing," I say, glaring at him. "Couldn't be me."

"Imagine being the most attractive elfborn alive and yet laughing like a hog sunbathing in mud. That *could* be you, though."

"You are literally a snake-man!"

"Serpentine," he corrects me.

The dichotomy of Adeib will never fail to surprise me. He's so serious and stern, but there's more layers underneath. He's passionate and poetic, snarky and full of wit. Anything more than dry humor is rare from him, but when he does let his comedic side shine, it's like a gift from the beyond. Whatever that might be.

We dry off Florp and Hiro, wrapping them in towels, and make our way back towards the living room. *Our* living room. I'm still not used to living in a place quite so grand, or calling it mine, but I have enjoyed every minute of it. From the smooth floors which allow Adeib's tail to easily glide, to the plants lingering in every corner, this condo is ours.

He clicks the remote, and our familiars tuck themselves into the crooks of our bodies. The movie starts as we sit in comfortable silence, snuggling under the blankets together, and watch the projector screen.

I make a mental note not to talk through the entire film, but that's definitely hard for me.

Rain is falling as Spider-Man suspends himself in the air with his web. Mary Jane pulls down his mask, revealing only his jaw and lips and as they kiss, butterflies fill my stomach. It's such a romantic scene—kissing in the rain after being saved by a masked superhero—and yet devious thoughts fill my brain. Adeib in a mask, Adeib shooting out something *other* than a web, and finally it lands on my most devious thought of all. We could recreate the Spider-Man kiss!

I reach over the muscled panes of his chest and fumble for the remote, pausing the old film. Only movies that were burned onto DVDs and VHS survived The Convergence, and I'm so thankful this was one of them.

"Do you trust me?" I ask, and Adeib's face turns suspicious.

"I am hesitant to say yes, but yes," he answers candidly.

"Perfect."

I gesture at Hiro and Florp to skedaddle, and to my surprise, they actually do without any fuss.

Languidly, I strip off my sweater and shorts as Adeib remains seated on the couch. He places a hand on my tattooed thigh, rubbing down the side of my leg.

"Nuh-uh, not yet. You can look, but you can't touch," I tease as I unhook my bra.

I practically moan at the comfort of removing the death contraption. You'd think a thing that was invented thousands of years ago would be comfortable, but alas. We're still wearing what might as well be boob prisons.

His vision lingers on my chest until I take a finger and push his jaw up, forcing his eyes to meet mine. I stare into those pools of whiskey like they're a lifeline as I gradually lower my panties onto the cool marble floor.

The tension in the air is tangible as I stand there, completely bared for him, already dripping with excitement. He's in for quite the treat.

"You can touch me, but only with your tail," I say, explaining the rules of this little game I conjured up.

"Where may I touch you?"

A thousand possibilities swirl around my brain before I land on the right response. "Only my ankles."

His brows furrow with confusion, but he follows my instructions all the same. Usually Adeib is the one in control, but I'm having a grand time taking the lead for once. *I can't always be a fuck puppet. As fun as that might be, I've gotta diversify my portfolio, y'know?*

His cold scales wrap around my ankles, and as if he can read my mind, he flips me upside down, my head facing his body. Reaching my hands in front of me, I let my fingers dance across the deep tan skin of his torso before making my way towards his seam. The black scales of his body hide it, but I know all-too-well where to find his cock now.

I caress him until his hard member shoots out from its pocket. His dick is warm in my hands as I slowly stroke down his finned shaft. The texture will never stop making me giddy inside.

Adeib lets out a low moan as I take him into my mouth, allowing him to hit the back of my throat. I suck his cock like its oxygen and I'm underwater, desperate for release. My tongue swirls around the head, twirling through the dextrous fins as I make my way up and down his throbbing length. Blood pools in my head, giving me a rush, my fingers and toes tingle from being upside down so long, but I refuse to not see this through.

I revel in the fact that I'm pretty much the only person alive who can make such a serious, cantankerous man come completely undone. I make him blush, I make him laugh, and I make him come. As I squeeze his bulging knot, I remind him of this.

Adeib moans, his body contracting as I continue bobbing up and down, my hands gripping his knot, trying desperately to pull it into my mouth. I'm here to take the Spider-Man Kiss to an all-new level. As I feel him start to come, there's a swift motion, and I'm suddenly being dropped onto my knees. It's so fast I'm surprised at how gentle I land.

Before I know it, Adeib is coming onto my face, cum dripping into my mouth and down my body. I am wearing not only a necklace, but an entire dress made of his seed. He grabs onto my neck, pushing my head back, and I lick my lips before swallowing.

This serpentine allows me to play out my every fantasy, and I love him for it.

"I do not appreciate your lack of self-preservation while I am in the middle of an orgasm, farforra," he says, his voice stern yet full of sex and sin. "You do realize you could have been hurt if I knotted your mouth? You could have choked on my cum."

"And what a wonderful way to go!" I tease. I wasn't trying to hurt myself —just live on the edge a little. "What are you going to do to punish me, Dr. Ali?"

Fire ignites not only in his eyes, but under my skin as he grabs me and lifts me up as if I'm light as a feather.

"I am going to remind you that no other being can satisfy you as I do."

Before I can even protest, he's sitting down with my knees resting on his shoulders and my legs hanging over the back of the couch. His arms wrap tightly around my thighs, locking me in place. Adeib's long, forked tongue laps at my pussy, and my body practically vibrates with need.

Adeib Ali is not just a scholar of Botanical Magic, but of my body as he swirls his tongue against my clit, undoing any semblance of put-togetherness I'd ever managed to muster.

"Pressure, I need more pressure," I say on a shaky exhale. "Fill me, please Adeib."

And he does exactly that. My thighs clench around his head, but he doesn't seem to notice as he tongue-fucks my cunt. He thrusts into me with a strength I've never felt from a tongue before. He eats me out like I'm a craving to fulfill, and I shake, toppling over the edge of pleasure.

Adeib doesn't stop.

"Adeib," I scream, my leg muscles convulsing as he continues, this time sucking on my swollen clit. "Adeib," I moan.

But I don't ask him to stop, because I could ride this high for the rest of my life. And I think I will.

Haunt Me, Baby

Consider Me - Allen Stone
Obsessed With You - The Orion Experience
Her Body Is Bible - FLETCHER
After Hours - Kehlani
Inarticulation - Rio Romeo
we fell in love in october - girl in red
Sunlight - Hozier
Wrong Places - H.E.R.
Till Forever Falls Apart - Ashe, FINNEAS

Haunt Me, Baby

La Perle

ROSE SANTORIELLO

prologue

ALITHA

"Welcome back from summer break!" President Bariel's voice booms, vibrating off the walls of the small conference room.

Indigo and I didn't get a summer break, as we were busy managing the cosmetic lab, but President Bariel knows that. I'm not sure why he pretends our schedules line up with the students'. Dr. Adeib Ali and Dr. Aura Nguyen were preoccupied as well. Honestly, everyone I know had something going on this summer, but that's life. There's no rest for the wicked.

"I have many updates in store for you all," he says and takes a theatrically dramatic pause. "Which include the return of Dr. Aloe."

Dr. Destiny Aloe, one of my only four friends, was out for the last year to take care of her dying mother. I thought of her nearly every day, but I never spoke about the situation to anyone. Nobody else knows why she was out, and I promised to keep her secret. She gives me a thoughtful smile as she waves hello to the room.

"As well as Professor Volkova, who is back from parental leave after the birth of his son," President Archeron shares. He clicks a button on his remote and the slide show behind him reveals a photo of an adorable baby.

Professor Volkova is a pompous asshole, but at least his kid is cute.

Aura snaps her fingers at Adeib, who is smiling down at his phone, most likely texting Iris. He comes out of his love-crazed fog and looks back up at the president. Hiring the younger sister of my best friend was a *choice*, one I hope not to regret, but if Adeib likes her this much, she must be something special.

Archeron drones on about his recent promotion from Dean Bariel to President Bariel, a change my father most definitely did *not* play a part in. My old man tries not to speak ill of my boss, but let's just say Archeron hasn't won the hearts of everyone on The Elven Council. Not yet, at least.

Two new professors are introduced—Dr. Stella Flowers and Sara Al-Mutairi. My nose scrunches when I hear their departments and roles. We've been needing a new Head of Illusionary Magic, but why is there a new sight professor?

Chatter fills the space, and I get the slight urge to flee from all the noise.

"With the opening of Aquatica Academy, Dr. Marino and Professor Rios will transfer to the new campus, as it should better serve them and their families' needs. A few Augury University graduates will be heading there as well, including Emilia Morrigan," President Bariel explains.

All these changes rattle me. I just want to teach here with the same people until I'm old and dead. I know that won't happen, because I'll outlive many, but I sure wish it could be the case.

President Bariel shows off pictures of the new Naiad Island campus, and we all *ooh* and *ah* until he's satisfied.

"As for the position of dean—" he starts, and my heart races, the fast-paced rhythm beating up into my throat. "—applications for Augury University will open shortly. Dr. Guarav Singh, former Head of Creature Crafts at Sagan University, accepted the position for Aquatica Academy."

And just like that, President Bariel changed the trajectory of everything I've been working on. I thought becoming Department Chair would be enough for me. Then, I thought running the cosmetic lab would satisfy, but now... I want more. I'm going to become the Dean of Augury University. No one can stand in my way.

one

ALITHA

A few weeks later

I've been so busy overseeing everyone else's projects, I've barely had time for my own. Indigo is still perfecting her pheromone perfume line, Iris is in the testing phases of her magic tattoo ink, and I still don't know how I'm going to make hair curl into the shape of a heart.

The last potion I created in the lab gives an iridescent shimmer to any hair product, and it was a complete success. Indigo now permanently includes it in her routine. The catch? We've made it a Magia Island exclusive. To receive this product, you have to go to Dahlia's salon. People have actually started traveling to get this hair treatment. I'm proud, really, I am. This is what I said I wanted—to use magic and make beauty projects for my best friends. I'm just afraid this won't ever fulfill me.

I thought this was all I needed, but now I'm hungry for more. My dad nudged me to apply for the dean position, which I did, but I made him promise not to pull any strings for me. If I get this job, I want it to be fair and square. Though my parents are two of the most successful elves on Magia Island, I want my success to feel like it's mine.

"Y'know, for someone who has sworn off love, you sure like to make cutesy romantic shit," Indigo says, peering over my shoulder as I stare at the 3D model of the heart-shaped curls on my computer screen.

I turn in my chair to face her, crossing my arms. "I haven't sworn off love;

I'm just not actively looking for it," I say, but my tone isn't convincing even to myself.

"Sure, yes, and I'm not anxious all the time. Pigs can fly. The sky isn't blue," she says with the uptick of an eyebrow.

"Sometimes the sky is beautiful shades of pink and red, and other times dark shades of gray. It's not always blue," I correct her.

"Your language arts teachers must've had a field day with you, huh?"

"I think my philosophy professor freshman year actually asked me to transfer out," I say with a grin. "He suggested I take psychology instead."

"What an ass. I'd kill to have you as my student," she says and wraps her pale arms around me. Indigo and Dahlia are the truest friends I have ever had. I don't know what it's like to have romantic love—at least not romantic love that doesn't end in tragedy—but my reservoir of platonic love is full... so full. It overflows.

"Dinner tonight?" I ask.

"Yes please! I'll text Dahlia."

"Perfect."

Ping.

I click on the notification. There's an email from the president asking me to come to his office. This is almost never good, but maybe...

It *could* be about the dean position? I push down that thought, not allowing myself to feel excitement or nervousness. This is simply a meeting; it doesn't have to mean anything. I can't get my hopes up. For all I know, this could be him telling me he gave me a different classroom or something else that could have easily been an email. Archeron Bariel has a propensity for melodrama, after all.

Pulling my wrap out of my bag, I twirl the fabric around my body until Serenade gets the hint we're leaving and jumps up onto my calves. I pet the white scruff of her fur, running my fingers through the little flower stems that grow out of the top before I scoop her up and place her into the wrap.

My familiar is a snow ferret and quite literally the opposite of me in every way. Where I am warm, she is cool. I am collected and calm, analytical and firm. She is utter chaos. Everyone around me—all my friends, coworkers, they're all chaotic. The only people who are like me are my parents and Dr. Ali. With his recent decisions, even that's debatable.

I don't want to toot my own horn, but there's a sense of pride in my put-togetherness. It gives me purpose. Serenade, the conduit of my magic, is kind of the antithesis to everything I represent. And yet I love her. Not only that, but I *need* her.

Exiting the front door of the cosmetic building, I make my way down the path that leads to the main segment of campus. The sun is high in the sky, illuminating the humid jungle. Sweat beads on my forehead, and I wipe it off with the back of my hand.

I wish it were winter.

Six camphor trees circle the courtyard, and I walk down the path to get onto the lift. A mage sends me up the history tree, and I stop before Archeron's office building.

I walk inside, and Daffodil greets me with a smile. I don't *dislike* Daffodil, but I don't like her either. She's often sassy and clipped, and she's most definitely screwing President Bariel. That alone has earned her infinite judgment from me. Not because she's sleeping with her boss, I mean, everyone I know but me is doing that. It's that it's... well, Archeron. *Yuck.*

"He's waiting for you, whenever you're ready," she says, and I form my mouth into a thin line.

Here goes nothing.

"President Bariel, it's so nice to see you," I say, willing genuineness into my voice. My dad taught me to play the game, and play it well. Be what people want from you, and you'll reach the top, eventually.

"Thank you, really. Everyone's been calling me *Dean Bariel*, and it's been driving me crazy," he says.

Is he serious?

"Well, didn't your promotion—which by the way, well-deserved—go into effect like... a week ago?"

"Honestly, they should really be calling me President *and* Dean since we haven't found my replacement yet."

What a weird thing to say to someone who *applied* for the position. I struggle not to let out a frustrated groan. "Right. Is that what we're here to talk about?"

He shakes his slender, bird-like head. "No. I have something more pressing. Dr. Scuttleton, a new hire at Aquatica Academy, is... pregnant."

"Okay?" *Is he about to confess to being the father?!*

"She's going on parental leave in a few weeks to give birth and won't be returning until spring semester," he explains.

"Go on." Oh, thank goodness. Seriously, get to the point, Archeron.

"The students have been informed of their professor's upcoming absence, as she is the Head of Potions over there and teaches the upper-level potions classes. Many have requested your skills and area of expertise to replace her this semester."

I give a small smile. It's nice to feel acknowledged. "How many requests have you received?"

He scratches the back of his head, his expression uneasy. "Well... one... but even just one is many to some! And her argument was *very* convincing."

My smile fades almost as fast as it arrived. Uproot my life for a semester? No, no thank you. Change is not my thing. "I'll think about it," I lie.

"When you're thinking, consider it might be wise for you to work with Dean Singh, and see how you two get along," he says, and his eyebrows raise.

Oh. Oh. *Oh*. This must be some sort of test.

My eyes widen at the sudden realization. "You know, I have always enjoyed the water."

"Then it's settled! I'll be curious to see how the cosmetic lab fares without you."

Not nearly as curious as I am. "Who will cover my classes?" I only teach a few upper-level and graduate potions classes, but someone has to do them.

"Professor Watson has already agreed to take them on, and I'll handle your graduate students. I've been meaning to get back into potions anyway," he says nonchalantly.

This is all easy, as though he knew I'd say yes. What would he have done if I declined? What if I didn't care? But I suppose he knows I do. He knows how badly I want this. I wonder if he's using the applications to manipulate me, or if he genuinely wants to see how I'll handle it. Or maybe I'm his only hope. My mind sifts through all the possibilities.

"Pack your bags, Dr. Taylor. You're going to Naiad Island!"

Indigo and Vega sit across from Dahlia and me at Sunspell Diner, their snowflake finger tattoos glistening in the fluorescent lights. This restaurant has retro seating and decor, with red stools and booths amidst bright teal walls. It's precisely the kind of place Dahlia loves, and that's why we started coming here. Bonus points for the ball pit our familiars get to play in while we eat.

"Sorry Elorthiel couldn't make it. He has a client," Dahlia explains.

"That's totally okay," I say.

Indigo's brows crease. "How come you didn't invite Aura or Dr. Aloe?"

I take a pause, considering her question. If I'm being honest with myself, I'm kind of avoiding Aura until the dean position gets fulfilled. I know it's between her, Feather McNab, and myself... and I'd rather not let this damage our friendship. Anyway, Destiny has her own things to deal with.

But I don't want to say any of that. "I just wanted it to be me and my main girls."

Dahlia smiles broadly. "The Unholy Trilogy reigns supreme."

"Ahem," Vega says on a cough. "I can go?"

"No, no." I shoot my hands out. "You're an honorary member at this point."

The waitress, who is some sort of faun-cambion hybrid, swings by and takes all our orders.

"Could I get extra chicken?" Vega asks the server, who politely nods before collecting our menus. Vega flexes her big green arms and waggles her eyebrows. "It's almost Enchanted Rugby season, and this coach needs her protein."

Indigo says something under her breath that I don't catch, earning her a surprised look from Vega.

"By the way," Vega starts. "I've always wondered why you three are the Unholy Trilogy."

"Oh, this is a great story," Dahlia says excitedly. "In the Bible—"

Vega interrupts her, laughing. "Dahlia, I know what the Holy Trinity is."

"Oops." Dahlia shrugs. "You're an orc, so I assumed you didn't have Catholic ancestors like I do."

"Orc*ling*," Indigo corrects.

"Yeah, meaning I'm also half-human. Although I'm pretty sure my ancestors were Pagan, not Christian."

It's sometimes hard to remember Vega really is half-human. I'm technically half-human, too. Unlike Vega, I don't have one parent of each. Both of my parents are elflings, which makes me an elfling. Indigo is an elf*born*, so her heritage is more distant, but elven magic clearly runs through those veins. You can see it in the light hues of her purple eyes.

"Back to my original point," Dahlia says, pointing a tan finger at Indigo. "This one thought I said Trilogy and started calling us as such."

Pink blush spreads across Indigo's cheeks. "I misheard her!" she says defensively.

"Why didn't either of you correct her?" Vega asks, chuckling hard.

I let out a giggle. "We didn't have the heart to. We've been the Unholy Trilogy ever since."

Vega rubs Indigo's shoulder. "Don't be embarrassed, little rabbit. We're only teasing you."

Dahlia makes a disgusted sound, feigning like she's going to puke. "Leave your weirdo pet names in the bedroom, *please*."

That causes me to let out a genuine cackle. I'm going to miss these girls so much. I don't know what's scarier—the thought that my friends and coworkers can't succeed without me—or that they can.

The waitress brings out our food, and everybody digs in. Dahlia tells us about a nasty client who won't be invited back into the salon, and Indigo and I go over some of the candidates for the professors-in-training intern program.

"You are going to call me every day to keep me updated," I tell Indigo as we clean up and get ready to head out.

"She is probably going to call you seven times a day," Vega says, and there's some truth to her words. Indigo is already an anxious bean, I feel bad leaving her to fend for my classes and the cosmetic lab on her own, but I believe in her. She's an incredibly hard-working elfborn. She'll figure it out like she always does.

Our bill generates on the little computer monitor, and Dahlia snatches it before any of us get a chance.

"Can you receive calls underwater?" Dahlia asks, and I give her a look.

"No, I'll be too busy drowning," I say sarcastically as we get up out of our seats.

"*Taylor*, that's not what I meant, and you know it."

I shrug. "I'm sure there's a special adapter I can get for the cave system, *Torres*."

She gives me a tight hug before whispering in my ear. "Try to let loose while you're in this new place. It'll be good for you."

Smiling, I turn to Indigo and Vega and give them a meaningful nod. I hope Indigo realizes I really do believe in her. I think she's going to handle the cosmetic lab just fine while I'm gone.

After I finish saying my goodbyes, I head out the door and onward towards this new, albeit temporary, chapter of my life.

two

CORDELIA

Ping.

I reluctantly click on the email from Dr. Pease, one of my sight professors this semester.

Dear Ms. Tremblay,

I apologize for taking a few weeks to get back with you. I am quite a busy individual. As for your concerns, I'm afraid we don't see eye-to-eye.
You may see faults with Aquatica Academy and the construction of the campus, but it is incorrect to claim that it was built in a way that is not inclusive of all bodies and magical races. Anyone on Naiad Island can attend Aquatica Academy. My coworkers include merfolk, jellyfolk, krakens, and elflings alike. I myself am not the average joe you'll find on the island. You may not have realized, but I'm a hybrid. I find Aquatica Academy to be exquisite, and anyone who does not is simply not trying hard enough.

I am so grateful for the opportunity to move here and be a part of this staff, so unfortunately I am going to have to deny your request for assistance in contacting the Dean or President of the school.

I wish you all the best, and may you find a solution to your problems within.

Sincerely,
Dr. Daniel Pease

Fucking asshole.

I fight the urge to punch a hole directly through my computer screen. A few weeks after fall semester began, I sent an email to one of my professors in regards to some concerns I have about the structure of the brand new campus. Having spent my first two years at a local community college and then one year at Augury University online, I was elated to see Aquatica Academy open. I was front row at the ribbon cutting ceremony and supported this school since its conception, but it hasn't been so kind to me.

As a kraken, I've found it really hard to fit my tentacles through some entryways. Dr. Pease thought I didn't know he was a hybrid, but I purposefully emailed him *because* of who and what he is. I didn't want to guilt a fellow kraken or even a jellyfolk into having to stand up for us. I chose someone with a merfolk tail, but someone I had hoped would understand the plight of not being the typical person on Naiad Island, which is overwhelmingly merfolk.

I thought he would understand... but clearly I was wrong. Maybe he fears jeopardizing his position, and I empathize with that, truly I do. At the very least, though, he should have been more sympathetic and validating about how I feel.

Whatever. I'm not really angry, just disappointed.

I click out of my email and onto my favorites list. There are tons of articles and websites bookmarked, but my favorite video imaginable is right there at the top.

"Every living being—magical or not—deserves a life of liberty and equity. One of passion and comfort. We have progressed far as a society, but we must not give up until *everyone* has an equal chance of success... and more importantly, joy," Dr. Taylor's voice rings through my headphones for the hundredth time.

There's something so captivating about this speech she gave a few years back as a speaker at an Augury University graduation. It's justice oriented and yet warm. I want to wrap myself in her words like they're the softest blanket, cushioning me from the cruel realities of the world.

Earth has improved deeply since The Convergence. All these planets crashing and colliding forced us to rethink our governments and to make room for new species. Species like krakens—like me. But we're still flawed beings. All of us. The elves run the show, as they live the longest and are really the middle ground between humanity and the other magical races, but even elves make mistakes.

I wonder what kind of mistakes Dr. Taylor makes. I bet they're silly, like putting too much sugar in her coffee or accidentally stepping on gum.

Knock. Knock.

Using my sight, I watch as the image of my step-sister coming into my bedroom plays across my mind. I try not to use magic on the people I love without their consent, but figuring out who is about to enter my bedroom feels like fair game. I take off my headphones, placing them onto the mantle above my desk. "Come in," I shout.

The door opens to reveal Nahla, who swims towards me. Most krakens and merfolk are mammals, at least on Earth, and so our homes are built in shallow waters. There are some people who can shift and typically live on land, but they have tanks to rehydrate their tails or tentacles. Neither my mother nor my step-family shift, so we live towards the shore in a cave-like cottage.

"Are you seriously rewatching that video of Dr. Taylor?" Nahla asks, judgment lacing her tone.

"I would think you'd agree with and enjoy her speech."

"I agree with it, *obviously*." She looks down at her prosthetic fin. "But it's boring once you've seen it more than once."

"I still like it," I say, crossing my arms across my chest.

She shakes her head. "That's because you're obsessed with her."

Obsessed. Obsessed makes me sound like a weirdo. I'm just... appreciative of her works. I'm a fan.

"Why did you interrupt me?" I ask, trying to change the subject.

"I wanted to let you know I plan on applying to Aquatica Academy next year!" She beams, her deep purple eyes practically glowing.

Nahla and my stepfather Marwan are practically foils to my mother and I. Nahla is self-assured, whereas all my confidence is a facade. A mask to hide what's bubbling underneath. Marwan is sweet and gentle; my mother is not. She is harsh and stern, instilling strong morals while also terrifying me. We're a topsy-turvy family, neither of us knowing much about our other biological parents, but we're happy. *Usually.*

"Oh my goodness. I'm so happy for you!" I lie. It's not that I'm *not* happy for her, I would be, but Aquatica Academy isn't the great school it was advertised to be.

As an extension of Augury, I would assume that Aquatica Academy would have the same accommodations or thoughtfulness in its design, but it's clear that isn't the case. Every day, I struggle on campus to fit through some of the entrances and exits. I'm soft and have big muscles, but that isn't even why. It's my fucking tentacles. Krakens have a wide berth, seeing as we have eight long appendages sticking out of our lower-half. Whichever piece of shit architect designed this school did not care about us.

Nahla isn't a kraken, but she's also not an able-bodied mermaid either. She needs something to hold on to sometimes and places to rest. I'm horrified by the idea of her working up excitement over a *dream school* and being crushed by what she finds. And then being stuck there for four years? Absolutely not.

She embraces me in a tight hug, and I rub the warm, tan skin of her back. She's tiny in my arms, still so young and full of light, and I want to protect her forever. I need to find a way to get someone to make changes to the school. It's one thing for me to be uncomfortable, but it's another for this to affect my little sister.

"Do you have any idea what you want to major in?" I ask.

She shrugs. "I'm not sure. Probably Botanical Crafts," she answers, and a grin spreads across my face. She's always had a fondness for plants.

"I think that would be good for you!" I say, and I'm grateful it's true.

"Do you want to watch the latest episode of Love Underwater with me?"

I might be crushing on a big-wig in magical society, but Nahla is much worse than me when it comes to obsessions. Her bedroom is covered in posters of cute pop singers, and she watches every episode of her coveted reality TV shows the second they come out.

"Sure." I follow her into the living room, where we both lay across the couch. It's made out of a specialized fabric which can withstand the salt water, and it's extra soft.

My mom chose a tacky color, though. Bright red.

Click. Nahla flicks on the TV.

A sexy woman walks onto the screen in stiletto heels, and I drool a little at her long, lean legs. She shifts in an instant, disregarding her clothes and jumping into the water.

"She's hot," my sister says as I strain to close my unhinged jaw. A shirtless merman swims onto the screen, and Nahla squeals almost as loud as the mermaid shifter on TV. "He's even hotter," she practically shouts. Man, was I this obnoxious at seventeen? Probably. Shit, I'm obnoxious now.

"He is not hotter than her, dude," I say.

Nahla shakes her head, long purple waves flowing with the movement. "I'm a better judge of this than you. You don't like men, so of course you think she's hotter."

"It's not that I'm a lesbian, it's that I have eyes. And my eyes are telling me she's objectively hotter!" I argue.

"Beauty is inherently subjective!" Nahla shouts back, and I can hear Marwan's tail swish before I see the front door open.

"Good evening, girls. Are we arguing about something silly or something intellectual today?"

Nahla crosses her arms over her chest. "Intellectual! We're arguing about whether or not beauty is objective or sub—"

"We're arguing over whether this dude on TV is hot," I interrupt.

Marwan puts his white coat on the rack and comes over to where we're both seated. "Which dude?"

Nahla points excitedly at the six-pack abs on screen.

Marwan shrugs and undoes his tie. "He's okay."

"Yes!" I shout. "Mom, did you hear that!? I won!"

"I believe Charlotte is at the grocery store picking up supplies for dinner."

"Ugh. Whatever. A win is a win," I say. Our mom is a stay at home mother and wife, except now that we've all grown up, she's more like a stay at home activist-philanthropist. She does charity work with all sorts of organizations and runs galas to raise money. It's really cool and keeps her busy.

I think I'd enjoy doing that some day. Being some lucky ladies' stay at home wife. I'd run a cat or catkoi rescue or something. I glance over at Torzu, my familiar, who is sleeping peacefully on his bed. For a conduit of magic, he sure does spend most of his time sleeping.

You'd think with my aspirations I'd have majored in Creature Crafts, but I actually think Sight was a better choice. Not only am I pretty good at it, but I can actually use it to rescue animals. I'll use my magic to envision their next potential moves, which it'll make it easier for me to capture them. I've got it all planned out... I just need the wife part.

Everything comes with time.

When the episode ends, I head back to my room and check my computer, which has a little notification waiting for me. I open my email, and the squeal I let out practically shakes the whole house.

`Cordelia Tremblay,`

I have some exciting news for you! I've read your multitude of emails and have an update. Starting this Monday, there will be a new professor in Potions 401. I hope she is up to your standards.

Sincerely,
President Bariel

Could it be her? I asked the President to select Dr. Taylor as Dr. Scuttleton's replacement this semester, but I didn't think he'd actually listen. My cheeks heat, and my heart races in my chest as I take a deep breath.

Welp, no use in sitting around in despair as I wait to find out if it's her. *Might as well make the most of this week,* I mumble to myself before grabbing my gym bag and heading out the door.

three

ALITHA

"Yes, mom. No, tell Aunt Jasmine I want to keep my hair appointment. Explain to her I'm not moving here, I'm just covering for someone for a semester. I'll be visiting often to check on the cosmetic lab anyway," I say into the phone.

I've been on Naiad Island for only a day, and my mom is already losing it with anxiety, assuming I'll be living here forever. I will not, and even if I were, I would still come back to visit. I love my family, especially my parents, but I'm an only child. A perfect, never-done-anything-wrong, only child. And sometimes they forget their fancy careers and circle around me like twin helicopters.

"How's the latest case?" I ask, and she sighs into the phone.

"Oh, you know. Just another client who was way too young to be signing the contract she did, and now the situation is... less than ideal," my mom says into the phone, though I know that translates to *the case is not going well.*

We continue chatting as I walk to the nearest grocery store from the dorms. Naiad Island is different from anything I could have imagined. Most of the center of the island is empty—I shouldn't say empty, but it's more wildlife than city. All of the people live on the coasts. Humans, other magical races, and shifters live in homes right before the shore, while merfolk and the other water-bound people live directly on the water. We finish up our conversation as I find the nearest grocery store, and I hang up on my mom.

The majority of stores and facilities were built to be swum into, but there are some hybrid and *land dweller* places as well. I get out my phone and type a text to the Unholy Trilogy.

ALITHA

The grocery store here is called Legs' Lagoon.

DAHLIA

What the fuck?

INDIGO

That's toooo funny. Imagine if we had a store in the water called 'Scales & Skirts.'

ALITHA

We honestly probably do.

DAHLIA

I'd go there, but I'd want a skirt made out of scales.

ALITHA

I don't think anyone here would appreciate that.

DAHLIA

Oh my god! Not MERFOLK scales, fish scales!!!

INDIGO

They eat fish, so I think they'd be fine with a scale skirt.

ALITHA

Oh good! I'll pick up some salmon and hummus while I'm at the store.

DAHLIA

Miss you already!!

INDIGO

Vega told me to say you should hook-up with a random person and hope it's your coworker so you can fall in love like we did!

DAHLIA

LOL

I couldn't roll my eyes harder if I tried.

Walking into Aquatica Academy is a surreal experience. I packed a wetsuit because it was unclear to me whether or not I'd have to spend my time halfway in the water, something my skin is not designed for. Elflings are *land dwellers,* as the merfolk call us.

Thankfully, I am greeted at the door by *who I believe is* Dr. Quilen, a dark-skinned elf who's standing on a moving platform. There's an empty one beside it, and he gestures for me to hop on.

"Welcome, Dr. Taylor." His voice is deep in pitch and smooth in timbre.

"It's a pleasure to meet you," I say in earnest as I get onto the platform. I am particularly interested in learning why this man chose to work at Aquatica Academy rather than Augury's main campus, but I decide not to lead with that. "Do a lot of professors utilize these platforms?"

He shakes his head, his long white braids swaying with the movement. "Not many, but there's a few of us. Let me know if you run into any trouble, and I'll get yours fixed up right away."

Unlike Augury University, which is a grouping of trees with separated pods for buildings and classrooms, Aquatica Academy is one long, almost tube-like structure. Probably-Dr. Quilen leads me to a conference room where I'm greeted by familiar faces. Professor Rios, Dr. Marino, his daughter, as well as a mermaid I recognize are all seated next to the rest of the Aquatica Academy staff.

Dr. Singh, the dean of this new campus, is treading at the front of the room. His energy is in stark opposition to what I'm used to with Augury's previous dean. Archeron Bariel is loud and silly, frivolous and unpredictable. I like Archeron—well, *sometimes* I like Archeron, but he's not exactly what you'd expect from someone in such a high-ranking position. Dean Singh embodies the qualities of a Dean—confident and reserved.

"Good morning," he says, his voice quiet but firm. "Before we get into today's meeting, I wanted to inform everybody that Dr. Alitha Taylor, Head of Potions at Augury University main campus, will be joining us for the remainder of fall semester. She is to substitute for Dr. Scuttleton while she is out."

I nod to everyone, not wanting them to see I'm not exactly pleased to be here.

The rest of the meeting goes fine, with many professors bringing up concerns about athletic competitions and their lack of arts programs, as well as other issues which don't pertain to me. I listen in and try to workshop solutions, but I don't hold any real power here.

There are, however, many things I'll be bringing up with President Bariel. Especially if I become dean. Aquatica Academy is a great addition to the AU conglomerate, but they're severely lacking in many categories. We hold all athletic events, we host every arts program, everything is attached to the main campus, and that has got to change.

My familiar follows me down the road, and I watch her little legs as she trails behind me, eager to make our way back to my apartment. Seeing as she's a snow ferret, it's obvious that if it were up to her, we wouldn't be living on tropical islands.

On Magia Island, I think she was used to the jungle and all the rain, but here is something entirely different. Everything is wet. Not just the air, but the ground, too. The buildings were made for merfolk and krakens alike, ready to swim into, and I think she's struggling to get used to the change in atmosphere.

As I walk down the street, I pull out my phone and check for text messages from Indigo or Iris. None to be found, which means the cosmetic lab is still standing. That's a good sign. I almost wish they had a problem, just so I could be of use and solve it. I know it's not right, but I want them to need me. Putting my phone back in my pocket, I look back and see an empty street.

Where is my pesky little familiar?

Retracing my steps, I look across the street and decide to sift through the brush, hoping to spot Serenade. There are mangrove trees growing near the water, but my snow ferret friend is nowhere to be found. Worrying thoughts fill my head. I open a trash can to find empty nothingness, and decide I finally have to do what I didn't want to. I'm going to have to jump in the water.

Chucking off my jacket to avoid a trip to the dry cleaners, I remove my shoes and take in a deep inhale.

Alright Alitha, you can do this. 1. 2. 3.

Diving in, I don't see much, but as my eyes adjust, I swim around, searching for some clue that'll lead me towards Serenade. Nothing. Swimming up for air, my body won't budge. There's something wrapped around my ankle. I squirm, desperately trying to free myself, but it's no use. Thanking the universe that I'm somewhat flexible, I curve my body and chew on the long piece of kelp that has attached itself to me like an aquatic parasite.

This is possibly the most embarrassing thing I have ever done. I am gnawing on a piece of kelp like a rabbit would a carrot. Finally getting free, I make my way up to the surface and take in a big gulp of air.

I climb up over the rocky edge, standing back on the street and shiver. I slip on my jacket and start to put back on my heels when I notice a little white tail peeking out from the top of a rock, squirming back and forth.

Serenade lifts her head out of the water to reveal a small guppy, carefully perched between her teeth. Oh good, at least she caught herself dinner.

I reach down to scoop her up by the tail when my ankle twists, and I feel my body begin its descent. I flail out my arms, trying to catch my balance, but it's no use.

The universe is playing a cruel joke against me.

four

CORDELIA

Nervous energy bubbles in my chest as I swim towards my next class. Having to see Dr. Pease at eight a.m. after that abhorrent email was criminal—but attendance matters, and I need the credit hours. Potions 401 is an okay class. I'm a sight major getting a minor in potions, and although I like the topic, I don't exactly find it riveting. That could change today.

I uncomfortably contort my tentacles to fit through the entryway into this wing, and have a seat at the front of the class. The room is set up in a proscenium shape, with our seats curving around where the professor teaches.

Except there is no professor.

Dr. Scuttleton left for parental leave when she got close to her delivery date, and our new professor is nowhere to be found.

Ah. I really hope it's Dr. Taylor.

I turn my body to ask one of my fellow classmates if they've seen the beautiful elfling woman when I remember I don't really have friends here. Most of my friends from community college went to schools in other parts of the world, and I didn't make any friends at AU Online.

The door swings open to reveal a thin figure with long, deep brown ears and even longer limbs standing on a moving platform. It allows her to float above the water.

It's her. Dr. Alitha Taylor.

I can't believe I'm in the same room as Dr. Taylor. This woman is more than just a silly crush to me; she's an academic icon. She permanently changed the hair dye industry. She also works hard promoting diversity and inclusion. For sex and gender, sexuality, race and skin tone, disability, and even magical race. Alitha Taylor has worked hard to combat negative complexes about other people in the elven community. And for all of that, I have fallen hard.

It could be worse. My sister is in love with reality TV stars and pop singers. At least I get to meet my crush in person.

Dr. Taylor's hair delicately dances in thick, long twists that reach past her chest. Between her tall stature and the fact that she's standing on a platform, she appears like a goddess. She's above us—*beyond* us, as she makes her way to the board and writes her name in a beautifully angelic script.

I wipe my face, afraid that I'm drooling.

"Can someone confirm this group left off on module seven before Dr. Scuttleton had to take her leave?" she asks the class, and a merman raises his hand.

"Yes. She was about to assign us a research paper on transformative potions," he says, and I hear someone audibly groan.

"Perfect," she says, smiling wide to reveal her pearlescent teeth. "Let's review before we get into it."

Grabbing my textbook out of my favorite waterproof backpack, I flip to the right chapter while listening to my classmates' whispers.

"He pretty much told her we have homework," one girl groaned.

"Who is this woman, anyway?" a kraken whispers to one of his friends.

One of them scoffs. "Who cares? It's weird of them to send an elf here."

Do not go off on your classmates. Do not go off on your classmates, Cordelia.

Dr. Taylor reviews the chapters in module seven with us, carefully ensuring that everyone feels comfortable with the research paper we're about to write. She takes her time, answering everyone's questions as she goes through the different components of transformative potions. She even shares lesser known tips she's learned through her own failures.

I think I'm in love.

Class ends, and everyone rushes out, ready to bitch about our course load, or get started on their papers. Everyone except me. I'm slowly packing my bag, taking my time as I come up with a game plan on how to talk to her.

"What was your name?" Dr. Taylor asks, breaking the silence.

Oh, this is really happening.

"Cordelia Tremblay," I say with confidence. It's fake confidence, but it's there. She squats down on her platform, long legs nearly coming up to her neck as she reaches out to shake my hand.

"Ms. Tremblay, it's nice to meet you."

Her eyes are an almost-white blue, brighter than anything I've ever seen before. They're like twin diamonds shining down on me.

"I have a question," I start. I really hope she doesn't see me as some giant weirdo that's snooped at her old work. "It's in regards to your research on visionary potions."

"Sure, of course." Her eyebrows scrunch in what appears to be both confusion and something akin to fascination. I can't be positive, but I think she's genuinely curious about what I want to ask.

"Prior to your focus on cosmetics, you were researching the effects of certain potions on sight mages' visions, and I noticed you stated you were unsure if any mages have ever consumed a potion that led to an inaccurate change to their visions."

One corner of her mouth ticks up. "I did state that, yes."

"Well I have," I share, and those pools of blue grow wide. "I consumed a potion last year that created false visions for a few hours. Every time I went to use my sight, it was wildly incorrect in its predictions."

"Are your visions usually correct?"

I shake my head. "Not always, no, but they're never this off. Sight, as I'm sure you know, shows the most likely possibilities. This was almost the opposite—it felt as though I was being provided the *least* likely scenarios."

"Interesting," she says and scratches her chin. "Did you record these findings by any chance?"

"I did. I have a log of the entire experience."

Her smile reaches both corners of her mouth now. "I would love a copy! If you don't mind sharing with me."

"Of course," I say. My heart is practically pounding out of my chest.

"That paper is grad-school level research and beyond. What inspired you to read it?"

"Oh, uh." I scratch the back of my neck. *Keep it cool, Cordelia. Don't be a dork.* "I'm a sight major with a potions minor. I don't know. I guess I just thought it would be interesting."

"I hope you enjoyed."

"I did!"

Dr. Taylor nods and stands back up at her full height, towering over me above the water.

I am somewhat tall, at least I think I'd be if I had legs, but Dr. Taylor is *tall* tall. She's probably close to six feet, and it makes my cheeks flush.

Everything about her makes my cheeks flush, if I'm being honest with myself.

I cross the threshold, narrowly making it out of the small doorway, and head to my next class. Professor Pease was a bust, but maybe Dr. Kalu can help me.

When sight class ends, I swim up to the front. Dr. Kalu turns to face me, their orange tentacles shifting with the movement.

"Hey Cordelia, how're you?" Their voice is quiet.

"I'm okay," I say. "How're you?"

"Just peachy," they reply awkwardly, their hands sifting through papers..

"Can I ask you something kind of personal or weird? I don't know how to word it."

Their brows draw in. "Of course." One of their papers begins to fall into the water, but I quickly catch it..

"If you were a kraken—"

"If?" Dr. Kalu gestures to their body. Deep brown skin leads to eight bright orange tentacles that match their short, cropped hair.

"Of course I realize you're a kraken, but just follow along the hypothetical," I say.

"Okay," they laugh nervously.

"Let's say you went to a wonderful university you were super excited to attend, but you didn't fit in through some of the doorways, and you noticed some other issues that could affect disabled and plus-sized students."

They nod.

"Who would you talk to? I've already spoken to another professor, and I'm afraid nothing's going to get done," I admit.

"I agree, I think the structure of this school was badly designed, but—"

"But?"

"I'm not the right person to take this on with you," they say with a frown. "I am an incredibly nervous person, and I'm not a good speaker. You need someone who will talk to Dr. Singh for you, or better yet, someone who knows President Bariel. Maybe one of the professors that transferred from Augury? Try Professor Rios or the Marinos. Or even Professor Morrigan."

A little bulb goes off in my brain as I race back to my dorm. *Or Dr. Taylor.*

I quietly enter the small dorm I share with Brittany Greensleeve. Brittany has decided to make herself the official Aquatica Academy party girl, much to my detriment. I'm not a total nerd, but I don't do parties. I'm what you might call an introverted extrovert. Someone who loves people, but one at a time, and preferably deep and meaningful conversations. *That* is what energizes me. Not getting drunk, staying out late, or getting straight Cs on my midterms.

I'm not trying to be a judgmental bitch, but Brittany isn't exactly prepping to become top of our class either. Whenever I've asked her to keep it down because I'm studying, she scoffs at me. Or she tells me I'm a *fuddy duddy*. What the fuck does that even mean? Are those real words?

Whatever. We just have different priorities, and it's fine, but I don't like her. There are kind party girls. *Probably.* She just isn't one of them.

"Oh, you're actually here?" Brittany says from inside the open bathroom. She's doing her makeup, which she's quite good at. "I thought you'd be back at your family's house again."

"Nope, I've got classes all this week," I say, not wanting to have this conversation.

I came back to forward the emails to Dr. Taylor and then hide in my room and prep for tomorrow.

"Well, I'm going out, but I wish you luck with whatever you're up to," she says and rolls her eyes. "Going out with my girls tonight. You wouldn't wanna join; it's probably just going to be merfolk."

And there it is. I know she's not intentionally being rude. She's a mermaid, her friends are all mermaids, but there's something icky about the way she says it. The land dwellers have their shit more together than us. With the magical races on land, there's a hierarchy. Elves pretty much rule in tandem with humanity, but it's balanced. The magical races all have one another.

In the sea? It's not like that at all. Merfolk rule, but they don't rule fairly like the elves. They don't ensure jellyfolk and krakens are treated equally, and that's fucked up. We probably descended from other planets, hence the smaller numbers, whereas merfolk can be traced to pre-Convergence, but that isn't our fault. We didn't ask to end up on Earth. I'm so sick of magical politics.

I remember my History 101 professor telling me that politics were worse before The Convergence, and that humans were so vile, the merfolk had to remain completely underwater. I'm glad things have progressed, I really am, but sometimes it feels like they've only progressed on land. In the waters, we're still centuries behind.

Swimming towards my bedroom, I get out my laptop and search for the files I want to send to Dr. Taylor. There are multiple logs of my experiences with the negative effects of potions, and I forward each one her way. I won't lie when I say I'm eager for her response. I'm not sure if any of this info is helpful, but she'll be reading my thoughts. It's a glimpse into my brain—my soul, and I'd love to show her how I think.

I'd love to help her in any way that I can. Dr. Taylor may have put a pause on this research, but imagine if I'm what sparks her to go back to it. I would be honored.

Swimming down the halls of Aquatica Academy, I search for Dr. Scuttleton's name on the doors. Wherever her office was is where Dr. Taylor is sure to be, and I desperately need to speak with her. I'm going to ask her to help me speak to President Bariel. I believe if anyone can do it, it's her. Not only has she worked with him for many years, but she will believe in my cause.

I'm sure of it.

As I make my way towards the S's, Dr. Taylor is nowhere to be found. The lights are off in Dr. Scuttleton's office. Reaching for the handle, I feel that it's locked.

Fuck.

What am I supposed to do? I could wait until our next class to reach her, but this is one of those things that I'm stuck on. If I don't get the information out, my mind will stay fixated on it. I need to speak with her now.

Swimming past the HR department, I have an idea.

five

ALITHA

I open my laptop to an email from Cordelia. There are sixteen attachments, all diligently labeled with time stamps. The logs themselves list other potential factors: what she ate that day, her mood, as well as which potions she consumed. She shared her vision results after every potion. The final file includes her accuracy guesstimates of her typical, unaltered visions, and it makes my heart sing.

Not just my heart, but my mind and body as well. I need to get a grip.

I cannot think about how much I find intelligence, discipline, and structure incredibly sexy. Not here, at least. Indigo and I discuss this regularly, but a well-organized filing cabinet is probably the horniest thing a woman can showcase. In my youth, I got my heart destroyed by a mermaid who didn't even bother to label any of her computer folders. Everything just said Untitled, Untitled 1, Untitled 2, so maybe she did me a favor?

I continue reading Cordelia's logs, and there's something unique about them. People who are loud and bold often come across as attention seeking, but Cordelia's writing is confident. She's not saying how she feels because she thinks she's better, she's just telling you how it is. Her words flow with a sort of transparency that isn't common in our field of study anymore. Every mage and researcher alike want to be the next big thing. I developed some cool potions for hair. Indigo and Iris have made developments of their own as well. Everyone wants to be us—everyone wants to be at Augury, but nobody wants to put in the work. It's all fluff.

But this isn't. Cordelia isn't overblowing her discovery to try to get fame or fortune, she's just sharing her geeky processes with her professor. For a moment, as I'm reading these findings, it feels like I'm sharing research with a colleague. Cordelia's words are as good as something I'd read from Indigo and Iris, but there's more underneath that I refuse to analyze further. She's my student, I'm her professor, and there is no alternate reality where this isn't the case. At the very least, I've got to keep these fantasies right up here in my brain, never to be seen by another soul.

Still, intellect is sexy, and I am in trouble. *She's* trouble.

Passing through the halls of Aquatica Academy, I head for my office. Unlike most professors' offices, mine is on the other side of the building. They were going to give me Dr. Scuttleton's office, as that is who I'm covering for, but opted for this room instead, since it has regular floors and is above sea level. Although it's cramped, I must admit I like the fact that I feel grounded here. Elves have a natural inclination towards nature, and sometimes this island makes me feel like I desperately need to touch grass instead of more water.

Sifting through computer files in search of an older research project of mine, I stumble across a folder of old photos. The day I graduated from grad school, the first time I was photographed with Indigo and Dahlia. There's old pictures of my parents and even a photograph of me and Victoria.

I click out of the folder, blinking away any bad memories that threaten to resurface.

Knock. Knock.

"Come in," I say, wondering which professor needs help with what frivolous task now. I swear, some of the professionals in this building are lacking all self-sufficiency.

"Hey, Dr. Taylor?" Cordelia enters, her tentacles floating through a cloud of water which moves with her body as she trails down the hallway and into the small office space.

What is she doing here?

"Oh, good!" she says, big blue siren-like eyes staring into mine. "I was having a hard time finding this place. Glad I was able to find you."

"Hi. Cordelia Tremblay, right?" Surely I cannot let her know I've been thinking about our conversation since she swam out of my classroom. Or that her emails sent my mind through a whirlwind of inappropriate thoughts.

"That's me."

“The magic you’re using, it’s different. Do a lot of folks on Naiad Island possess this capability?”

“Yes,” she answers. “It’s a special potion that allows a user to charm water, while also attaching it to ourselves. My tentacles are the point of contact, so the droplets remain connected to them. It’s called vitacloud.”

“That’s amazing!” I gaze at Cordelia’s face, taking in her round cheeks and pouty, supple lips. Silence stretches between us for a beat too long before I process that we both forgot the original reason for this interaction. “So, what did you need?” I ask, wondering why she’d come find my office.

“I need help contacting President Bariel,” she says frankly.

President. The title sounds strange to my ears; almost as strange as Dean Taylor is to envision. "I could get you President Bariel's contact information for you easily," I say with a smile. I feel nothing but unease at the moment, though that isn't Cordelia's fault.

She shakes her head. "I would like you to help me write a formal proposal on physical adjustments that must be made to Aquatica Academy campus. It's one thing for me to contact him. He might refuse or say he'll fix the issues, but who is he to fix it? He doesn't know the comings and goings of merfolk, kraken, jellyfolk, or other sea dwellers. We can't expect him to understand our plight or the accommodations we need to make the campus better.."

"That's a fair point," I concede.

Cordelia tucks a cobalt strand of hair behind her ear and bites her lip, staring off in thought, and I feel something tingling in my abdomen. A feeling I deeply wish to avoid right now.

"What if we wrote something up and got Dean Singh's approval before we present it to President Bariel?"

I ponder this. It would help the cause deeply, although I could always ask for my father's support. It's not something I want to share with Cordelia, but it could be my backup plan. "I think that's exactly what we should do."

She grins, a pinky flush reaching her cheeks. "Okay! When should we meet up? And where?"

"We can meet up tomorrow morning," I say, eager to get out of this conversation. If I’m going to talk more with Cordelia, I’ve got to mentally prepare myself for it. I’ll need to think of things like paint drying or dead flowers. Whatever will crush this mood she puts me in.

"Here? Or at your place?"

My eyes go wide, and I shake my head. *We’re not meeting at my place. Ever.* "At a coffee shop or something."

"Sure, of course." She nods, her cobalt orbs staring up at me as I escort her towards the door. "Email me the details?"

"Will do. We can also discuss those logs you sent over. I have many questions about your findings," I say, forcing my tone to remain neutral.

Her blue tentacles inch closer to the door. "I look forward to meeting with you."

Hopefully, I can help her out tomorrow, and then that will be that. Her plan will be set in motion, and she won't need to speak to me anymore. Even though I'd like nothing more than to continue to pick her brain.

I have to do what's right.

six

CORDELIA

I have no idea what just happened. One minute I'm searching for Dr. Taylor's office, and the next minute I'm standing there as she stares at me like a shark watching its prey. I just hope the charged energy I felt sizzling through the air wasn't a figment of my imagination.

But yay! She's actually going to help me. Of course she is; Dr. Taylor is an amazing person. We're going to fix Aquatica Academy, and my little sister will have a wonderful college to attend. This is what I want to do with my life. Raise money for charities, make buildings more accessible, and improve people's quality of life. No idea what career I can have doing those things, but I'll figure that part out later.

Swimming away from the school, I head towards my gym. I'm going to go lift some weights and clear my mind.

I put down the barbell and move towards the mirror, my tentacles brushing against the ocean floor. I am neither solid nor completely soft. Muscle shows through layers of squish, and I smile at my reflection. For many years, I wished I had legs or a fishtail, but I love my tentacles now. I am going to find someone who will love them too.

My only dilemma is that I very-much-so wish that person was Dr. Alitha Taylor.

Nahla teases me, but it's true. I don't know if I believe in soul mates, but I know we have a connection. I just need to strengthen it, and then maybe one day when she goes back to working at Augury University, I can ask her on a proper date.

Walking back to the bench, I decide I'll do two more sets and then go home. I don't live far from Aquatica Academy, but I got a dorm for the experience. That, and it was free. My mom and step-dad wanted me to make friends other than my sister, but so far that hasn't happened.

Curling my arm, the tension makes me feel strong. I love the way my body feels when I lift weights, like I could take on any challenge. Whatever chemicals release in my body make me feel like I'm on top of the world. When I finish, I take a wipe and clean off my weights, carefully putting them back where I got them, and head out the door.

"Where have you been all day?" My mom asks, sitting with her laptop at the kitchen high-top. She looks frustrated, and I don't want to poke the bear.

"I went to school to ask for some help on an assignment," I half lie. "And then I went to the gym." It's not that I have to lie to my mother, she would one hundred percent support me in this endeavor, it's just that I want to reveal it to her after it's complete. I will be so embarrassed if I don't succeed.

"Good. The gym is a good place to get out pent up aggression. I'm thinking about going to MMA classes again," she says through gritted teeth, ice-blue eyes still locked on her computer screen.

And that's my cue to leave. Whatever problem my mom is having, it's none of my business. Probably another diplomat trying to do something shady, or maybe it's someone who is embezzling money from a non-profit again.

Swimming towards my bedroom, I stop when I see Nahla's tail coming from around the corner. "Hey, baby sis. What's up?"

"Oh! You're home. Perfect. Take me to this haunted house," she says, holding up a flyer. It's not a question, but her voice pitches up at the end. Nahla isn't very demure; she wants to go to this event, so she's telling me to take her. There's no pleading or beating around the bush, just a polite demand.

I take the flyer and inspect it. It's next weekend. "Yeah, let's go." It'll be a healthy distraction from Dr. Taylor and everything else going on at Aquatica Academy. An excuse to just have fun.

"We could go to the mall that morning and get cute matching tops too!" she says, face beaming with excitement.

"That sounds great."

I cross out of the hallway and into my bedroom, where I plan to spend the rest of the evening preparing for tomorrow. Coffee with Dr. Taylor. We'll discuss my suggested changes to the Aquatica Academy campus buildings, and we'll enjoy each other's company.

Torzu is resting in his bed, and I come up to him and pet his fur, brushing down until I reach his scales. He purrs, and I let the familiar sound soothe me, freeing me from the nervous energy bubbling in my chest.

The morning sun sits high in the sky, brightening up the entire island. Standing outside the doorway to the coffee shop, I wait for Dr. Taylor.

What if she doesn't show? Or worse, what if she *does* show and is disappointed in my ideas, or doesn't agree with them? I hate to admit it, but I desperately want her approval, almost as much as I need her assistance.

If one of Augury's most brilliant minds can't help me with this campus accommodation redesign, who can? We might have to get an architect involved, but I think we can at least get down the basics. What needs to be improved, what are the best ways to improve it, and how fast can it be completed?

The coffee shop she sent me the address of last night is a little ways from the coast, so I used my vitacloud to allow me to travel on land. There's a yellow bicycle with a basket full of flowers leaning against the glass underneath the welcome sign, and I picture Dr. Taylor riding it along the busy streets of Magia Island.

Long, deep brown legs come walking down the pavement, and I realize Dr. Taylor is wearing shorts. They're not super short, but they're shorter than anything I'd expect to see her in. They're a deep navy blue, and her top is white with matching blue stripes. She looks like an adorable sailor, and I have to refrain from biting my fist, opting for playing with my septum piercing instead.

"Dr. Taylor, thank you for meeting me," I say, and she gives me a wide smile.

"Of course. It's early; let's get our caffeine fix."

We quietly wait in line, and I realize I am standing far too close to her. Yet she doesn't seem to mind, or at the very least, she doesn't say anything. When we get up to the register, Dr. Taylor orders a regular green tea and a small black coffee, and then asks me what I want.

"I'll have an ice blended mocha," I say. I'm not really sure what that is, but the picture looks great.

"Our blender is down, do you want a regular iced coffee with syrup?" the cashier replies, an apologetic look lining her features.

Every restaurant has a machine that's down, I swear it's a requirement. "Oh, sure. What kind do you have?"

The woman sighs. "Vanilla, French vanilla, mocha, mint, strawberry, blueberry, raspberry, caramel, marshmallow." She pauses and gives me a look, but I'm not sure what to say. "Cinnamon, chocolate, cheesecake, cinnamon brown sugar—"

"That! I'll take that. Cinnamon brown sugar, please," I interrupt, not wanting her to have to continue.

I really need to frequent more coffee shops on the island, but I've always been more of an energy drink kind of gal. I know it's going to be the death of me.

Dr. Taylor holds up her phone and transfers the dabloons to the cashier, and we take a number before heading to a little booth in the corner.

"You didn't have to pay for me, but that was very kind of you."

"Of course I did. I make good money as a professor, and you're already having to deal with attending a college that doesn't accommodate your needs. It's my treat, really," she tells me. Everything she says is so frank, yet so caring. I've never met anyone like this woman. It's as if she thinks through every thought before saying it, which is not something I'm always able to achieve.

"Well, thank you."

She opens her duffel bag, pulling out a leather binder. She unzips it to reveal a legal pad and fancy pen, and she titles the page something in cursive.

Cursive has never been my strong suit, I can hardly read it, but I think it says *Aquatica Campus Modifications*.

"Alright, before we get started, I wanted to let you know I think we should come up with a proper proposal before we contact anyone or get anyone else involved. I'd also like to run this by Dean Singh before we pitch to President Bariel. Do you agree to these terms?" Her tone is serious.

"Sure, yeah. That sounds good to me," I say, trying and failing not to show my age. "You know, you'd have made a great lawyer."

Dr. Taylor visibly flinches. "Never say that again, thank you." I scrunch my brows, unsure of what I shouldn't have said, and she shakes her head. "You didn't know, but my mother is a lawyer. I, like most people, tend to not want to follow in my parents' footsteps."

Is there something wrong with following in your parents' footsteps, though? Am I less creative than most, or less of an individual? I contemplate asking her, but I think we should probably just focus on the topic at hand. I don't need Dr. Taylor's approval to know I'd be a good philanthropist and community organizer. That shit is something I feel in my bones; it speaks to me.

"That makes sense. My bad," I say.

The server swings by, dropping off our drinks with a wide grin. "Let me know if I can get you two anything else."

"Thank you," we both say in unison.

Dr. Taylor picks up her mug of tea and blows on it before taking a small sip. Her lanky fingers wrap around the cup, overlapping each other, and I stare at them for a little too long. "What are the main things that need fixing?"

"The entryways are far too small," I say.

"How big do they need to be?" she asks, and I let the cogs of my mind start turning.

"At least as big as a plus-sized kraken, I'd say. Or an incredibly tall kraken. Actually, both."

She looks off into the distance for a moment before staring back into my eyes. "They cannot make the entryways taller, but they could definitely make them wider, taking space from inside the classrooms, which are plenty spacious enough. What if we had them nearly match the hallway width?"

"That would work."

"What else?"

"Hmm." I take a sip of my *cinnamon brown sugar* iced coffee. It's incredibly sweet, almost candy-like. "We need rest spots. People like my sister Nahla, who have prosthetic fins, need a place to rest for a bit sometimes. It could be a bench, or even a literal bar on the side of a wall to hold onto."

"How about both? We could alternate every other stop."

"Yeah!" I say, my heart beating with excitement.

Her blue eyes, which I see now are not icy, but beautiful clear pools, stare into mine. "Have you thought about accommodations for disabilities and situations other than your family and your own?"

"I have," I say, unsure if she's accusing me or just trying to be helpful.

"Good girl." Her voice drips like honey. Did she just—? My mind malfunctions, unable to form a coherent thought. I have to force myself to tune back into what she's saying. "I was thinking we could have a refrigerator and cabinet with migraine medication, sugar for diabetics, salt for POTS, and maybe water bottles in case anyone gets dehydrated."

I. Um. My brain continues to malfunction for a moment before I can muster a proper response. "That would be amazing! I also think the entrances should remain open for longer. Jellyfolk have incredibly long oral arms. I don't want anyone to get stuck in a door," I say, and she nods.

"Good thinking!"

Fish on a stick, this elfling doesn't have a clue about what she does to me. I'm such a stereotype. Hot women make all cognitive function go out the window.

"So," she says, taking another sip of her tea. "I think that's all we need for now. How about I contact an architect and we have them draw up some plans? We can discuss the rest of our ideas at a later date."

"You mean, meet up again?" I ask, swallowing hard. I don't know why, but I assumed this would be a one and done situation.

"Yes. We'll meet up in another public setting like this, maybe here or somewhere else, but let's avoid campus locations. We don't need anyone spotting us together or overhearing our conversation. I'd like to be the one to tell Dean Singh about this," she explains.

"Of course," I say with a smile. "Thanks for everything."

"Anytime," she says and stands. Grabbing her drinks, Dr. Taylor walks out the door.

My eyes remain fixated on where she was for a long time.

seven

ALITHA

Cordelia Tremblay drives me up a wall. Actually no, she drives me to want to shove her into a wall and place my lips on hers. She's so calm and collected, even when facing difficult situations.

Sure. Yeah. Thanks.

Her chill demeanor and subtle confidence are thrilling to watch. People have a tendency to be cocky, but Cordelia is just self assured.

Walking into Aquatica Academy, I hop onto the small platform and make my way to my classroom. Serenade is perched on my shoulder. She's not the biggest fan of water unless it's frozen, and I can't say I blame her. Our earlier mishap in the water has reframed my thoughts on it too.

The architect said he would reach back out to me in the next few days, and I'm eager to see his plans. I made sure to hire a kraken, hopeful that he would be more considerate to their needs. An elf, elfling, or even a human was likely who created the original plans, and we're all seeing how that went.

Whoever designed Augury University all those years ago handled it with care. Aquatica Academy deserves the same; it is an extension of us.

Crossing through the admittedly small doorway, I turn back and watch as the door quickly shuts behind me. Cordelia is right; jellyfolk would almost definitely get stuck in there. Students swim through the doorway, familiars in tow, and I watch carefully and make note of the different ways people are affected. A jellyfolk has to hold up her oral arms to ensure she doesn't get stuck. A mermaid with an elongated eel for a familiar holds the doorway open to ensure her familiar doesn't get hurt. My students are all different, with different bodies and abilities and familiars, and the longer I watch, the bigger I realize the problem is.

I'd be disappointed in myself for not realizing sooner, but how could I know? This is why it is so important to listen to all voices. Really hear what people have to say. That's the only way to make sure society continues to improve. We have to want to do better.

A familiar set of tentacles comes through the entryway, and it feels like all oxygen in the room has been depleted. Cordelia is wearing a tank top. It's October, and I'm positive the water is cold, but here she is in a tank top, the soft curves and large muscular planes of her body on full display. I probably look like a cartoon character with the way my eyes feel like they're popping out of my head.

Cordelia is a young woman, sure. I knew that. But I am more focused on the brilliant things she says and her cool demeanor to really look. Now I can't do anything except look at her. She's gorgeous. Blue has always been one of my favorite colors, and she wears it so well. A walking, talking ocean.

"Good morning, Dr. Taylor," Cordelia says, the warmth in her voice filling my ears.

Dr. Taylor was always such a normal phrase for me. Everyone calls me it at work besides my friends; it's the proper thing to do. Cordelia manages to make it sound improper. I'm probably imagining things, but she says like it turns her on, which makes me want to go places I shouldn't go.

As all my students settle into class, I grab my brain from out of the gutter and wipe it off, hopeful I can remain focused on today's mission: teach these students the taxonomy of potion making.

Projecting the presentation I made over the weekend, I go over the different levels of potions. Basic potions are the ones most people can perform, but there are intermediate and advanced potions as well. I list off examples, and the students assign each potion to a level.

"What about the vitacloud?" I say, and a mermaid with straight yellow hair raises her hand.

"Advanced."

"Good," I tell her. "I would classify the vitacloud potion as an advanced level potion."

There's a movement from the corner of my vision, and I turn to see Cordelia shaking her head. "Is there a problem, Miss Tremblay?"

"There is," she says boldly. "I don't think vitacloud is an advanced level potion. Basic potions can be performed by anyone, intermediate potions require some studying and knowledge, but advanced potions are rare."

"Not necessarily. Rare isn't a requirement for advancement, though it's common," I correct her, walking towards where she sits. "The potion has to be incredibly hard, demanding years of practice."

"And yet I learned it in just a few months."

I squat on my platform, making myself eye level with where she rests on a desk. "Did you ever consider you might be just *that* good?" I ask.

My eyes trail down, stopping at her lips while I wait for her response. They're pink and plump and pillow-like, and I ache to touch them. Shaking my head, I snap myself out of it.

"Wouldn't that make taxonomy subjective? If a potion can be advanced for most but intermediate for some."

I nod. "Ultimately, yes, you're right. It is subjective. But we base these classifications off the majority, not off of magical prodigies and rare exceptions."

A fiendish smirk makes its way onto her features. "Are you calling me a prodigy?"

There's something maddening about this girl. She unravels me in ways that haven't been unraveled in a long, long time. Smoothing my hands down the length of my pencil skirt, I ignore her question and continue with my lesson.

The other students seem to agree with my classifications of potions for the most part, everyone taking three column notes as we discuss my reasoning for classifying each potion and level. When the class ends, I unplug my laptop and turn around to see Cordelia staring at me. She's floating above water on a vitacloud, our bodies no longer as distanced as they are in class.

"Can I ask you a question?" she asks, her tone coy.

"You just did."

"Whenever someone gets an answer right, you tell them good or excellent," she points out.

"Okay?"

"But whenever I say something right, you've called me a good girl. Is there a reason for that?"

Suddenly, my throat isn't wide enough to let the oxygen in and out. Oh no. I have to be more careful. I didn't even realize I was responding differently to her than other students. Racking my brain, I try to remember when I called her a good girl.

"I—" I fumble for words before grounding myself. I'll just explain that I didn't mean anything by it. Her eyes are so vast as they stare into mine, and I fight not to fold under the weight of them. "I apologize if I've made you uncomfortable, Miss Tremblay. I didn't mean anything by it."

"That's a shame, *Dr. Taylor*. I was hoping you did."

And there it is. She says my name like it's dirty. I want to jump into the water with her, if only to make myself clean again. Does she feel this energy surging between us?

Cordelia turns to exit. I'm not positive what takes over me, but I grab her by the wrist and pull her back towards me. I'm not very strong, but I overestimated my own strength and our bodies are now pressed together, her ample chest pushing against my small frame. My back is against the projector screen, and she lifts her arms up, leaning them against the wall as she boxes me in.

I look at her lips as she leans towards me, her breath against my neck. "I was hoping—"

Ring. Ring.

My phone vibrates against the podium. In one sudden swoop, Cordelia backs away from me, her familiar following close behind as I check my phone to see Indigo Watson's name and phone flashing across my screen.

“I have to take this. I'll let you know when I hear from the architect,” I say curtly, and she nods, her eyes now like a deer in headlights as she sprints out of the room.

Pressing the accept button, I place my cellphone against my ear. “Alitha speaking.”

“Alitha, oh my goodness, hi," Indigo says on the other line, her voice distressed.

“What happened?”

"Nothing, everything's totally fine."

"Indigo, do not lie to me," I say.

"Okay, everything is not totally fine, but everyone is fine," her voice shakes as she speaks.

"What did Iris do?"

"Nothing!" she says strongly.

If it wasn't Iris, it had to be someone else. Indigo doesn't make big mistakes like this very often. Even when Indigo makes mistakes and freaks out over them, they end up working out for the best. That is, everything except her family life.

"Was it Wren?" I ask. Wren is one of our students and a new intern in the cosmetic lab. They are extremely diligent and organized, so I would be surprised, but mistakes happen.

"No, Alitha. I don't—"

"Just spit it out, Indie," I hear Vega say in the background.

"The cosmetic lab caught fire last night."

My heart stops. Reaching my hands out, I grasp the podium to keep my body upright. "Who did this?"

Indigo sighs. "See, that's the thing. We don't know. It started externally. The lab is fine, just some damage to a wall. Archeron and Adeib get alerts to their phones when the smoke detectors go off, so they were alerted immediately. And Adeib was able to put it out."

Of course it wasn't *President Bariel* that came to our rescue. Thank goodness for Adeib Ali. "Can I speak to Vega, please?" I ask.

"Speaking," her low voice comes through the phone.

"Pull the cameras. I'm emailing you access now. Go through all the footage and notify campus security. The elven council can decide how they want to proceed with this. Maybe they'll have the culprit pay for the damages, or we could give them supplies and they fix it themselves."

"On it. I hope you're enjoying Naiad Island."

"I am," I say, a blush creeping onto my face. "Keep me updated. And Indigo, stop worrying. This is not your fault, you couldn't have prevented this."

"Okay. Love you, bye."

"Love you," I say before hanging up.

Serenade and I make our way back to the apartment, walking down an empty street on Naiad Island. There's a light pole with lots of posters on it, and one has fun Halloween graphics that catch my eye.

Haunted House. Be there if you dare, it reads. I grab my phone and shoot a text to the Unholy Trilogy.

ALITHA

This week has been hard on everyone. How about you two come visit me on Naiad Island this weekend? I can take you to this fun haunted house, as well as show you my apartment and the new Aquatica Academy campus.

DAHLIA

OMG! That sounds amazing. Count me in.

INDIGO

I could definitely use a break.

ALITHA

Is it okay if it's just us three?

DAHLIA

Sounds good to me. Frankly, I need a break from Elorthiel. He's getting on my nerves this week.

INDIGO

Let's fucking goooooo!

ALITHA

Perfect.

eight
ALITHA

I know that logic and reasoning are my best friends, but those qualities of mine have gone out the window since coming to Naiad Island. Besides, Indigo and Dahlia make for much better company. They're both funnier, at the very least.

Although this is a haunted house, it isn't Halloween yet, so the three of us are opting for sort-of costumes. We're not going full out, but we're definitely making things a little fun. Dahlia stands in front of me in a short dress with black spiderweb leggings underneath, her curvaceous figure filling the outfit nicely. Indigo is wearing her typical all black witchy vibe, but with purple eyeliner shaped to look like a bat. I'm in orange.

A sheer orange long-sleeve top and black bra with black slacks, to be exact.

"You should cover those bright blue eyes with black sparkly liner all the way around. It would look killer," Dahlia says with excitement, her golden tan skin practically glowing against the red fabric of her dress.

"Yeah, maybe."

"Here." Indigo reaches towards me and starts applying the eyeliner.

"I know how to do my makeup!" I say, but she's already pushing me towards a chair, sitting on my lap and finishing the job. While we have heavy boundaries on the job, both because of our levels of professionalism and because of our outward queerness, my friends and I don't have many boundaries at all in private.

I mean... all girl friendships are homoerotic to some degree, am I right?

Besides, if I wasn't affectionate with my friends, I would never be touched. My parents are busy, my love life is abysmal. I can't have the only physical interaction I receive be my hairdressers and doctor. Hugs and silly moments like this with friends will have to do. I don't know if or when I'll ever find love, and I've never been very good with hook-up culture, but friendship is enough. Or at least that's what I've started telling myself.

"Are you seeing anyone?" Indigo asks and waggles her eyebrows as she finishes up on my makeup. I frown, not wanting to admit that the only things I've been doing are working and crushing on one of my students.

Her violet eyes brighten when I go to speak, but immediately dim with my simple reply.

"No."

"Hmm. That's okay, but maybe you'll meet someone tonight."

"Highly doubt it," I say blandly.

Dahlia tsks me from the couch. "Not with that attitude!"

The thing is, I'm unsure I want to meet anyone. Romance comes with a plethora of things: validation, affection, and intimacy, but it also comes with heartbreak and betrayal. Which I'd never like to experience again. My mind flashes back to my youth and a dream of being high school sweethearts with a girl who proceeded to leave me high and dry. It's ridiculous that I'm still terrified because of a relationship from ten years ago, but it painted my entire experience. Victoria ruined me. I'm a crumpled up wad of paper, and no matter how hard you work to remove my wrinkles, I'll never be back to the blank slate I once was.

Some people are just built differently. Immune to heartbreak. I'm not one of them. I care deeply, so deeply that I have to reserve my love for a select few. My family. Serenade. Indigo Watson. Dahlia Torres. Destiny Aloe. Even Vega and Iris have grown on me, but that's it. That's my list. So then why am I so hung up on this girl?

"I'm so excited to see the haunted house. I love the whole vibe Naiad Island has going on right now," Indigo shares as we exit the threshold of my apartment and start walking down the street. Naiad Island was a pretty, tropical-looking place when I first arrived, but it has gone into full-on Halloween mode. Fake cobwebs hang between light fixtures, with pumpkins outside most doorsteps. I have to wonder if they decorate underwater, too.

As we meander down the street, I take in a deep breath, trying to clear my head of all distractions. This is just going to be a fun night with my girls.

"Do they do everything on the shore?" Dahlia asks.

"For the most part," I answer. "Although there are shifters, humans, and elves living on this island, the majority of folks require water to survive. It's hard to walk on land when all you have are fins, tentacles, or oral arms."

Indigo scratches her chin. "What about everyone on the weird floating water clouds?"

"Oh. Those are called vitaclouds. A lot of mages here know of this potion-charm combination they're able to perform. It allows them to float on water as they travel through spaces without it," I explain, desperately trying not to envision a certain mage who frequently uses it.

Mermaids, kraken, and other individuals filter into one of the three line options that lead to different entrances to the adjacent haunted houses. One seems to be themed like a dollhouse, another a house of mirrors, and a third is a... dark lagoon? Seeing as that one requires entrants to fully immerse themselves under water, I think we'll try one of the other two.

"Dollhouse or hall of mirrors?" Indigo asks as we walk around, basking in the energy of the night. Everything is exciting and new and *should* be fun.

Emphasis on should be. Except the music is too loud and the space too unfamiliar. That, and my mind keeps ping-ponging between Cordelia and the campus accommodations, the fire at the cosmetic lab, the dean position at Augury, my parents expectations of me, and my general loneliness by my lack of a love life. Life is complicated, and I know that everything will work out for the best, or whatever anyone would spew at me the second I voice my distress and concerns, but man. Can't an elfling catch a break? Can one thing in my life just be normal?

I think I control every aspect of my life so heavily because control is precisely what I crave. I like to make the decisions, to be the one to have the final say, and I need the berth to do so.

Dean of Augury University must be mine. I will manifest it into existence, one way or another. A crush on Cordelia and an accidental fire are only wrenches in my plan. However, fixing Aquatica Academy might prove me to be a better candidate than whoever else President Bariel is considering.

I just have to play my cards right.

"Let's do the hall of mirrors. We look sexy, might as well enjoy the view," Dahlia says on a laugh. She's not wrong. Dahlia and Indigo are two of the most beautiful women I know, and I'm not bad looking either.

Before we get in line, Indigo grabs a hot chocolate while Dahlia and I purchase a bag of candy corn. Snacking away, we wait for entry.

“Did you guys ever figure out what happened with the cosmetic lab fire?” Dahlia asks.

I nod. “There’s a report in my inbox explaining the entire situation, but I haven’t read it yet.”

Shock lines Dahlia's rounded features.

"You haven't read the report yet? Anxiety would drive me up a wall," Indigo shares, her purple eyes wide with surprise.

I shrug my shoulders. "I'm not anxious about it because it's going to be fine. They've found the culprit, and I'm confident it'll be fixed."

"Do you wanna know what happened?" she asks, and Dahlia nods excitedly.

"Go for it."

Indigo's expression turns sour. "Someone was smoking a cigarette."

"Aren't those like super illegal on Magia?" Dahlia asks. The line moves forward, and I watch as patrons come in and out of the entrance and exit, some dressed completely average while others don costumes.

"Incredibly so. He put it out on a bush growing beside one of the walls. The elven council decided he'll pay for the damages, as well as assist in fixing the structure—repainting and all," Indigo explains.

"Was this one of our coworkers, or perhaps a student?" I can't imagine anyone working or attending Augury University would be so stupid, but wilder things have happened.

"It was a TA." Indigo frowns, her eyes moving back and forth between us. "It was Elara Lothiel's new TA."

"Oh boy," Dahlia says. Although Dahlia doesn't work for Augury University, as she runs her own hair salon and is the island's top color expert, she knows all the ins and outs of Augury thanks to Indigo and I. "Dr. Lothiel's probably going to burn his house down in return."

"Welcome, come one come all, to the famous Hall of Mirrors," a performer says. There are pointed horns growing out of his face and fake blood trickling down his chest.

We enter the space and are immediately met with three separate tunnels. "Which one should we enter?" I ask.

"Let's all go down one and share at the end," Dahlia suggests, excitement shining in her big brown eyes.

Indigo shakes her head, her petite frame appearing even smaller in this room. I squeeze her hand. "It's okay. You can go with one of us—"

"If you're a chicken. Bock. Bock. Bock," Dahlia teases.

"I'm going down this one," Indigo says, storming off through the far right entryway.

Dahlia salutes me before heading in to the left entrance. That leaves me the middle.

Entering the tunnel, there are bright lights and an unfathomable amount of mirrors. It's probably a trick of the eye, but it looks like there are thousands. I walk through, staring at my reflection.

My body is tall and slender, my features long and angled. I'm beautiful, but not in a human way. I'm beautiful in an elven way, and that makes my chest warm. Closing my eyes for a moment, I allow myself to dream.

Dream myself as Dean Taylor. Dream that I am not alone. And even dream that Cordelia is beside me. As I stare into the mirror, I envision her coming up from behind me, her tentacles snaking their way around my body to bring me pleasure.

I'm really not sure why this kraken is so different to me. I've met krakens before, and I've met beautiful women before. Working at Augury for years now, I've met many brilliant minds and taught lots of lovely people.

She's just stuck on me like glue.

Crossing through the mirrored corridors, I make my way outside. The smell of popcorn fills my nostrils, and Indigo and Dahlia are waiting on a bench near the exit.

"Did you get lost?" Indigo asks, her voice earnest.

"No?"

"You were in there for a hot minute," Dahlia states, as if their confusion is obvious.

Was I?

"I'm sorry; I didn't realize." It feels like someone's watching me, but there's nobody nearby.

"It's okay! Let's get in line for the other house," Indigo says and pulls us by our arms towards the crowds of people.

This event is essentially a Halloween carnival, with fun games to play and clowns walking around making balloon animals for children. We get in line for the dollhouse, and I still, the hairs on the back of my neck standing at attention.

Turning my head, I still don't see anyone. I shake it off, refusing to let the overstimulation from all the noise get the better of me.

"Did I ever tell you two about the time I was invited to a costume party but was sent the wrong theme?" Dahlia asks, and we shake our heads. "They told me everyone was dressing like fruit, but when I got there, all the girls looked like Playboy Bunnies. I wanted to die."

I continue listening to Dahlia, but as the feeling of being watched increases, I scope out the entire area around me. A familiar pair of ocean eyes meet mine, and suddenly Cordelia Tremblay is moving towards me while using a vitacloud, a young mermaid on her arm.

I cross towards her, not wanting Indigo and Dahlia to hear our conversation, but the mermaid remains by Cordelia's side. Fifty percent of me is incredibly jealous of this purple-haired beauty, and the other fifty percent of me is concerned that Cordelia's girlfriend is far too young.

"Oh hey, Dr. Taylor," Cordelia says, and one corner of her mouth ticks up. "What are you doing here?"

"Enjoying the upcoming holiday with some friends, you?"

"My sister Nahla wanted to come here, so I promised I'd take her," she says, gesturing to the mermaid on her arm.

I'm so stupid. Of course it's her sister and not her girlfriend.

"How very kind of you," I say, trying my best to remain as professional as possible. "I sent our ideas to the archite—"

"Well, it was nice seeing you," Cordelia interrupts me mid-sentence. "You look beautiful, by the way," she whispers before leaving with her sister.

I stand there, stunned for a moment, before Indigo and Dahlia break me out of my trance.

"Who was that?" Dahlia asks.

"Just one of my students," I explain. "She had a question about class."

Indigo eyes me suspiciously but doesn't say another word.

nine

ALITHA

Indigo and Dahlia sit on the couch of my apartment living room, their bags piled by the door, giving me pointed glares.

"I avoided bringing it up again last night, but we're both dying to know, what was up with that blue-haired kraken last night?" Dahlia asks.

"Nothing, like I said, she's one of my students," I reiterate.

"Sure, we get that," Indigo says with a sigh.

"Why was she giving you bedroom eyes? And what did she whisper in your ear?" Dahlia's voice is loud and accusatory.

I put my face in my hands and groan. "She told me I looked beautiful."

"That's so sweet!" Dahlia replies with excitement. "Wait, why were you afraid to share that with us? Girl, it's fine. So your student has a little crush. No biggie."

Indigo coughs slightly, stifling a giggle. "I think the student isn't the only one with a crush."

I pin Indigo with a glare. "Listen. I'm trying not to—"

"Save it. We all try not to, but we're a little bit human. You're both adults, and she's not even really your student. Maybe you can just..."

"I swear to God if you say *get her out of your system*," Dahlia says, laughing. "That didn't work for you and Vega, it's definitely not going to work for Alitha. Just make her like your sex fantasy and never act on it like a man would."

"Except I'm not a man, and I actually like her, guys. It's not just attraction.

It's mental," I say. "Oh my goodness. I'm acting mental." I sit down on the couch beside them, and Indigo touches my arm.

"Want me to discreetly find out if you're allowed to pursue her? Maybe there's a special rule since you're on a special assignment, or maybe it doesn't matter because you work on a different campus normally," Indigo offers, and I nod.

"I'm going to try not to get entangled with her, but I'd appreciate the information, nonetheless."

"I love watching the two of you battle your morality with your humanity," Dahlia says. "I know, I know. You're both elven. But you're also both human, and this is such a human dilemma."

"Take it away, please," I say, my voice pleading. "Take my humanity with you."

"I'm going to miss you," Indigo says as they both stand, grabbing their bags before heading out the front door.

Okay, I ordered a dildo. So what? I've never been around so many beautiful women. Mermaids, jellyfolk—frankly, everyone on this island is sexy. My mind wanders to the krakens I've come into contact with. Dr. Som, Ms. Tremblay...

Bad thoughts, Alitha.

This is not the time to be lusting after coworkers, or worse, students. This is a time for safe exploration in the comfort of my own home—err—in the comfort of the Aquatica Academy apartment I'm temporarily being housed in.

I unwrap the large phallic object and realize it's almost *blue*. I thought I had ordered a bright purple, but they sent me a purple that borders on blue. My mouth waters as I coat it in lube. Placing the dildo onto the spot on the tile, which I've freshly cleaned, I start removing my athletic shorts. Slowly, taking my time with it, I strip and lower myself until I'm hovering over the toy.

I've never had anything this big. My ex-girlfriend was a mermaid, and my last fling was an absolute pillow princess. Honestly, I guess I haven't had much outside of those two. My friends live these fun, adventurous lives, while I've been trapped in the past. Stagnant.

Lowering myself onto the tentacle, I can feel every ridge and bump. The suction cups don't actually suction, but the textured feeling they create has my eyes rolling into the back of my head.

Thanks to my tall stature, I'm able to fully move up and down the long toy. It's skinnier at the top, making me feel almost-empty as I lift myself up with my hips and thighs, just to be filled once again when I come back down.

I allow my mind to wander.

I crave suction. Not *just* the suction, but also how many tentacles krakens have. Having eight appendages at my disposal for my satisfaction sounds like a dream.

I picture Dr. Som, and her beautiful brown skin. Tentacles fill my fantasies. Deep blue tentacles wrapping around me, holding me down by my wrists and ankles as they fill me.

Except, Dr. Som's tentacles are red. *Cordelia's* are blue. I could picture Dr. Kalu; their tentacles are a vibrant orange.

I shake my head before allowing myself to give in to this darkness in me. Just for a moment. I can have these desires for Cordelia. It might not be ethical, but as long as I don't act on them, this feeling is natural. She's a beautiful woman—a beautiful kraken, and I want her. Her brilliant mind and the way she thinks. My body craves her, but that's all. It's carnal.

Continuing to ride the toy, I can practically taste her body on my tongue. I imagine it's salty yet sweet. Her natural scent would mix with the water, creating an irresistible aroma. My body is long and lanky, and I think I'd perfectly fit next to her supple curves. She'd hold me with those muscular biceps, and we'd balance each other out.

I chase the high of this dream, my pussy pulsating with every movement.

Knock. Knock.

I freeze. *Who could possibly be at my door?* Uh, this isn't my home back on Magia, I should actually answer; it could be Dean Singh. I scrounge to get my shorts back on and throw the tentacle dildo into the kitchen sink before making my way down the meager hallway.

Opening the door, I stifle a gasp before plastering on a smile.

"I wasn't sure if this was the right apartment. I'm glad it's you," Cordelia says, as if it's perfectly normal that she showed up where I'm staying.

"Hey Cordelia." Surely I cannot let her find out that our interaction at the haunted house made me horny enough to order a dildo on next day delivery.

"Yes! I'm sorry to barge in like this, but your office hours were closed, and I have a sorta pressing request for you."

"Come in." The words fall out of my mouth before I can reel them back in, and I instantly regret it. She's my student; if someone else witnessed this, it could be perceived poorly.

Cordelia enters, her tentacles floating through her vitacloud as she enters into the small living room.

"Did you have fun last night?" *Oh no. That's not good.* My words come out as a half-shriek as I come to realize Cordelia has a straight line of vision to the kitchen.

The dildo is still in the kitchen sink.

I shift my body, or at least try and do what I can to block the sink from her line of vision. I just hope to the gods it works.

I look into her eyes, which are as deep as the ocean. I could get lost swimming in them, and I almost do as she tells me how she came to find my apartment.

"What's this pressing issue?" I ask. There's got to be a good reason she'd show up to where I live on a Sunday morning.

"Did you send our concepts to the architect already?" she asks, stress lining her features.

"I did," I say, and watch as she paces back and forth, her visible anxiety filling the space.

Cordelia doesn't usually come across as anxious. The Cordelia I know has always been cool and calm. This version of her is both endearing and jarring.

"Can we amend them? I realized last night that we didn't put in anything for the blind or for chestfeeding or pumping individuals. How could I be so inconsiderate?"

"Well, Cordelia, you're just one person. I will ask the architect to include braille and raised pathways, as well as a chestfeeding room, but you can't beat yourself up over not thinking of every possible situation."

"But what if someone comes to the school and has a terrible time, and I could've solved it?"

Her words tug at my heartstrings, and I give her a small grin. "We can come up with an idea for that too. How about some sort of suggestion box? Where students and staff can anonymously air their grievances, or make suggestions on ways to improve the campus," I suggest.

"That's so brilliant, I could kiss you!" Cordelia says, moving close to me. She's smiling from ear to ear, her face flushed pink with excitement, and her words hang in the air.

I could kiss you.

"Thank you profes—Dr. Tay—"

"You can just call me Alitha, now. When we're working on the project. In class, I'm still Dr. Taylor," I interject.

She blinks slowly at me, her body facing the kitchen, and my heart jumps up into my throat. "Thank you, Alitha. I'll see you next week."

"Good luck on your exams," I say, opening the front door.

She crosses the threshold, and I sigh in relief. Maybe, just maybe, she didn't see the giant tentacle dildo in my kitchen sink. If she did, I'll have to quit my job and move to another continent, never to be seen again. I wish I could tell the Unholy Trilogy about this embarrassing moment, but then I'd have to explain both the tentacle dildo and the massive crush on my student.

So much for never meeting at my place. I don't curse, but this is the closest I've come in a long time.

ten

CORDELIA

Did Dr. Taylor have a giant tentacle dildo in her kitchen sink?

It's been a week since I saw the toy, and I legitimately don't know how to react to this whole thing. I can't believe I told her I could kiss her; I'm so embarrassed.

This week was midterms, and she behaved as though everything was fine. Fine, but not normal. Her voice was so monotone, and I honestly felt like she didn't want to speak with me. She was curt and unenthusiastic, avoiding eye contact with me during all of class.

Was this whole thing a coincidence? Did she just happen to have a sex toy that looks eerily similar to my tentacles? Or did she buy it because of me?

Oh no, what if she bought it because of someone else?

I feel like I'm panicking, and I cannot panic right now. It'll serve me no good, but man. At the very least, she has a thing for tentacles. This could be my in. I could ask her on a date? No, I couldn't. She probably thinks I'm too young for her. She's not even thirty, but I bet she dates sexy older mascs. Silver fox vibes.

Whatever. It doesn't matter.

Although I usually spend weeknights in the dorms, I'm at home today getting ready thanks to the holidays. Classes are out today and tomorrow to give us a little break after midterms, as well as in honor of all the different October celebrations. Diwali, Samhain, and Halloween, to name a few.

Today is October 31st, and I don't have any plans other than my gym's yearly costume contest. We all come in, work out, and whoever has the best costume-pump-combo wins one hundred dabloons.

I won a few years back when I dressed as this popular cthulhu-esque character from a film, but this year I'm going simple. Sexy pirate.

Torzu sits perched on his bed as he watches me do my makeup in the vanity mirror. I slip on a white top that shows off both my chest and my biceps, and throw on a pirate hat that Nahla found for me at a costume shop. Swimming out of my bedroom and into the kitchen, I open up the cupboard and get out my pre-workout.

Scooping up the powder, I throw it into my mouth and swallow as quickly as possible.

"Yuck. I still can't believe you dry scoop that shit," Nahla says.

"It's not pleasant, but it's fast," I cough out. "Any plans for today?"

She shrugs, dressed like a combination of two Disney princesses. "Going to watch movies and video call some friends. You?"

"Gym."

"Have fun!"

The gym is not far from home, and I'm already starting to feel the itchy jitters from the pre-workout. I use my sight to try and envision the results of the costume contest, but I see something else entirely. I'm turning a corner, and a familiar figure is walking up ahead.

Entranced by this vision, I follow my gut and swim underneath a walkway and around a corner. There she is.

Alitha Taylor, dressed up like a skeleton in a skintight purple-colored suit with high-heeled boots. She's extraordinary.

I know that I should turn around and swim back to my gym or home or dorm. Or maybe I should say hi. But something takes over me, and I do none of those things. I duck down low, trailing her with my eyes. Every few moments I swim forward, keeping up with her while remaining a few paces behind.

The public transport system on Naiad Island is unique. We have trolleys that are partially in water, where you hold onto the railings or strap yourselves in, and they take you faster than you could swim yourself. There's also an upper deck of the vehicle that land dwellers can use. As Alitha climbs up the stairs onto the top cart, I quietly get into the bottom, obscured from her view.

As I ride the trolley, I feel like I've *maybe* taken things too far. It's not okay to follow people around just because you think they're lovely, yet nothing has made me want to stop either. I would never hurt Dr. Taylor, or push her to admit feelings for me, but I know there's something there. I'm simply conducting research to find out for myself.

Field research.

The trolley stops, and I realize we're fairly far from Aquatica Academy. Long legs climb down the stairs and head down the dimly-lit pathway. Split seconds away from taking off, I bolt out the door and follow her, swimming close by.

Alitha is headed straight for La Perle, and my cheeks heat at the thought.

I've only been to La Perle once. I had just turned twenty-one and entered the sex club in hopes of some fun, but most of the attendees were a lot older. I left before ever really participating in much of anything. Clubs, whether it be for dancing or sex or kink, I've learned, are not my thing.

I'm surprised to see they might be Alitha's thing, but I guess you never know. I wait for her to pay the admission fee and step inside and count down the seconds before I enter.

Flashing my ID, I pay and swim through the club. The few land dwellers in the building, Alitha included, are all on platforms, while everyone else sits on rocks or clamshell shaped beds and couches. There are neon lights and loud music everywhere, and I take a seat and wait. I should probably get a drink, but I'm afraid I'd lose sight of Alitha in the busy buzz of the club scene.

I watch as she gets increasingly and increasingly more uncomfortable, her hands coming up to cover her long, pointed ears. Following her through a doorway, she loops around the building until she's in the private room, and I wait a few minutes before following her in.

Alitha is sitting on a clamshell bed, watching as colorful fish swim by through a tank in the wall. She looks angelic. Some of her twists are up in a bun, while others cascade down her back.

I quietly swim through the space, electronic music filling my ears, before I perch myself on the back of the clamshell.

There's some kind of mist in the air, it smells almost like magic, and I waft it in, enjoying the sweet aromas.

Alitha remains facing the other way, though I'm positive she can sense my presence. It feels like energy is soaring through my bloodstream, pushing me to make a move. I might be crazy. Dr. Taylor calling me a good girl and having a tentacle dildo might be all some wacky coincidence, but what if it's not?

What if she feels this connection, a pull towards me like I feel for her? I can't live my life for the what-ifs.

Slowly, I shift one of my tentacles, tiptoeing it towards where her hand rests against the bed. The movement is gentle as I brush against her fingers and watch as her entire body shivers.

"Are you cold?" I ask, though I know that isn't it. Alitha is wearing a full-body skeleton suit, her bare feet and fingers exposed since she removed her boots and gloves.

Just one glimpse of her skin, and I'm desperate to see more—to feel more.

"Cordelia," she says, her voice breathy. "Did you follow me here? Oh my goodness, and the haunted house. And my apartment. Are you *stalking* me?"

Shit. Am I stalking her? I don't think I am. "No." I shake my head. "The haunted house was a coincidence. I came to your apartment because I really did need to speak with you."

"And tonight?" she asks.

"I followed you, though I considered it more of a friendly Halloween haunting," I jest, hoping she'll laugh.

Thankfully, she lets out a half-breath, half-laugh of a sound. "Why did you follow me, Cordelia?" Alitha turns her body, crawling across the bed on her hands and knees and my entire body melts at the sight.

"I don't know," I confess, staring at the luscious curves of her lips. Alitha is all sharp angles, but her nose and lips are different. They're softer, and I want nothing more than to feel them pressed against me. "I feel drawn to you."

Alitha lays down on her chest and runs her fingers through my hair, the movement causing goosebumps to form on my arms. "I want to kiss you," she says.

"Then kiss me," I whisper. She sits up onto her knees, her hands touching the sides of my shoulders. I feel somewhere between floating and feeling like the room is spinning.

"I can't."

My eyebrows furrow. "Why not?"

Alitha shakes her head, but her face moves closer, our lips almost grazing. "I can't be the one to start this."

"Well I can't kiss you, either," I say boldly, placing my hands on the small of her waist.

Alitha looks sad but understanding. "And why is that?"

"Because it won't be just once. If I kiss you, Alitha, I'll need to kiss you a thousand times more."

"Please." It's all she needs to say to make me come completely undone.

Pressing my mouth against hers, I take in her soft lips, opening my mouth to allow our tongues to glide against each other. Tugging on the zipper of her jumpsuit, I help Alitha out of her costume as we deepen the kiss.

I freeze when I feel down her waist and realize she isn't wearing any underwear.

"Dr. Taylor," I gasp. A devious smirk makes its way onto my face. My eyes instinctively trail down her body, and I push her onto her back, carnal desire filling my every thought.

I'm hovering on top of her, my tentacles resting above and next to her bare legs, and I use an arm to lower myself close to her face.

"Tell me what you want me to do," I say. I'm trying not to show that I'm nervous, feigning a sort of sexy confidence, but I'm scared.

Alitha Taylor is one of the most brilliant and sexy people I've ever met, and I'm a little terrified I'm fucking all of this up. I'm also confused, because I'm so incredibly horny. All of the itchy need-to-work-out feelings I was suffering through earlier have completely dissipated, and now all I want is to pleasure this elfling.

"Be a good girl and make me come," Alitha whispers, her voice a little raspy.

Licking down her body, I stop when I reach where her thighs meet her little pussy. Using my fingers, I part her soft brown folds and suck on her clit.

I move two of my tentacles up her body and attach suction cups to her nipples. Alitha writhes against me, the suction of my mouth and tentacles overwhelming her with pleasure.

Gently, I push a finger inside as I continue to lick her soft cunt. Alitha's body is long and thin, much harder and more angular than mine, but this part of her is so soft and sweet. I could bury myself inside her forever, basking in her warmth.

"You're so wet for me, beautiful. So very wet," I say, pushing another finger inside. She moves her body with the rhythm of my fingers, riding my hand as I make circles with my tongue.

I want to do so much more to this woman. I want to fill her with my tentacles and ride her face. Most importantly, I want to share ice cream with her while talking about academic research and kiss her goodnight.

But that can't happen, at least not yet, so for now I ride the high of how good she takes my fingers and the breathy moans that escape her lips as I eat her out.

I devour her, lapping up every drop as her muscles contract and she comes on my tongue and hand.

Alitha nestles into my lap, her bare skin against my tentacles as I draw figures on her back.

My mind starts to clear from the foggy, sex-driven craze it was just under. Fucking shit, I just—

"Cordelia," Alitha whispers, breaking me from my thoughts. "We can never talk about tonight."

And with that, my heart splits in two.

eleven

ALITHA

What was I thinking? Actually, I know what happened. I wasn't thinking. Last night with Cordelia was lovely and wonderful in the moment, but I woke up feeling dreadful. If I'm being honest with myself, I felt mortified the second her mouth left my body. Talk about post-orgasm clarity.

I pace my apartment back and forth, feeling the cold wooden floorboards against my feet, as I decide my next step. Do I call my friends? Or perhaps I should just quit my job and move to a remote island off of the Arctic Circle? Although I like winter, I decide I'll take my chances with Indigo.

She picks up on the first ring.

"Indigo speaking."

"Hey, do you have a second to talk?" I ask, my voice shaky.

"Of course. What's up, buttercup?" There's some rustling in the background, and it sounds like she puts something down before sitting.

"Are you positive?"

"Yes," she sighs. "Alitha. Tell me. Now."

"I decided to go out clubbing last night for Halloween, except I've never been clubbing before, and I accidentally picked a sex club. I've been doing some research into it—La Perle—but essentially they use a magical aphrodisiac in all the private rooms. The whole place is... really different. It's like nothing I've ever seen before."

"That sounds super fun. What's the catch?"

"I fucked Cordelia there last night. Or rather, she fucked me."

"You what?" Indigo takes in a deep breath, calming herself. "How did that occur?"

"She followed me into a private room," I say, pacing the room again. "I didn't realize this, but the admissions form included a consent form about the magic."

Indigo gasps. "I can't believe you didn't read the terms-and-conditions."

"I know. It's so unlike me, but this girl has me acting all sorts of strange," I explain. "It's like my logic switch was flipped."

"Did you want to sleep with her?"

I consider this. "Yes and no. Physically, yes. Mentally, of course not. That's a terrible idea."

"Did you feel forced?"

"No, no. Gosh, no. I just... couldn't control myself? All logic went out the window. I've been looking into the specific ingredients of the potion, and it looks like it only works if there's prior attraction and desire."

"Sounds like you've got some things to think about," she says.

"Yeah." I'm embarrassed to share all of this with her, but it also feels like a weight has been lifted from my chest.

"If it's any consolation, Vega and I weren't technically allowed to be together at first either, and she's the love of my life," she says, and I let out a small laugh.

"I'm happy for you guys."

"Be happy for *you*. I fear it's more than just her being your student that's holding you back," she says, and I let a few beats of silence pass.

"I've got to get ready for the week. I'll chat with you later," I reply, and hang up.

Serenade sits in my lap, and I run my fingers through her soft, white fur. Indigo is right; it is more than just her being my student that's holding me back.

Sure, I'm a stickler for the rules, but rules can be bent or amended even. I'm not just afraid of losing my job; I'm afraid of losing focus. I have worked so incredibly hard that I can practically taste the dean position. It's mine. I've just got to take the leap. A girlfriend or lover would just get in the way.

That's what I tell myself, at least. A small part of me knows I'm also just terrified of another broken heart. I know it seems silly to most, but I've almost come to terms with dying alone. It makes sense to me. I was an only child to two incredibly loving but busy parents. My first brush with love ended in betrayal and heartbreak. Every other attempt I've made has failed miserably. I've been stood up, told I'm too serious, that I'm not serious enough, and even that I'm too tall.

Not much I can do about that. I just don't understand why it has to be this hard; I am smart and attractive, and I have my shit together—my standards aren't too high. Reasonably, I should've found someone by now. Indigo and her sister have. Dahlia has. I'm the oldest of the trio, and the most painfully alone.

Serenade nuzzles into me, her soft fur bringing me some comfort, reminding me I'm not completely alone. At least I have her.

Walking into the classroom, a sinking feeling hits me in the core. Whether it's trepidation or excitement, I'm not sure. Perhaps it's a bit of both, but I don't enjoy it. I don't know what to say or do about Cordelia, and my mind is swirling in a million different directions, all with entirely unique outcomes.

Will she confront me about this? Will she let it go and find someone else to fool around with, or does she have legitimate feelings for me? It's hard to tell where her mind is at. Everything she says, she says cooly. It's like she doesn't have a care or worry in the world, and it makes it hard to read sometimes. I'll get random bursts of her, what makes her tick and causes her fear, but they're few and far between.

It's probably for the best if she lets this go and never brings it up to me again, but some masochistic part of me hopes she says something. *Anything.* I just need her to throw me a line and I'll catch it.

I want to learn her mind, body, and soul. Even if I know I shouldn't.

Students meander in, settling in their desks. There are eager mermaids, distressed looking jellyfolk, and yet one missing person threatens to haunt me.

I start my lecture. We have only a few classes left before Gratefulness Week, and then once we return, it's finals. This is one of my last opportunities to teach these young adults all they need to know about potions, and I'm determined to get it right. I won't let anything distract me.

Fifteen minutes go by, and I internally applaud myself for staying on topic.

The doors open to reveal a familiar face swimming in, her upper-half barely covered. I gulp but continue the lecture.

It's odd that Cordelia was late. She's not an over-the-top student, not like I was. Indigo and I have taught a few of those. They're seniors now, one is even an intern of ours at the cosmetic lab. They're early for every class, beg for extra work, always strive for one hundred percents. No, that's not Cordelia, but she has a genuine lust for knowledge. She values intellect and does legitimate research on the things that interest her. It's unlike her to show up to class nearly twenty minutes in.

Once I finish the lecture, I assign a reading and inform the class that there may or may not be a quiz the next time I see them.

I wink and all but one of the students collect their belongings before filing out, leaving me alone with Cordelia. Her features are so different from elves and so many other magical races. She is soft, with rounded cheeks and a button nose. Her face is almost doll-like. Her body is different too, the supple curves of her breasts contrasting with the strong lines of her muscular biceps. I want to consume her whole.

I'm standing on my platform, hovering above where she sits, and it's not helping the shirt situation. The low cut of her tank top combined with the angle is allowing me to see everything she has on display.

Maybe that's what she intended.

"Aren't you cold?" I ask, gesturing to my sweater.

"It's a little chilly, but my body is different. It adapts to the weather. Like, my nerve cells will just change to accommodate the cold," she explains, and suddenly I want to study her. Or octopi. Or both.

I cut to the chase. "About last week."

"You asked not to talk about it, so I'm respecting your wishes. Actually, you demanded it."

"I know, but that was unfair. There's more left to be said," I say, and her eyes turn wide with surprise.

"Oh?"

"We were... manipulated. There was an aphrodisiac potion in the air."

She nods, her full lips now pursed. "I know."

"You knew the whole time?"

"No." Her voice is hurried, sounding desperate. "I didn't know, but I know now. I did a little digging after the weekend."

I bend my knees and squat down, wanting to be closer to her. "Me too. I did a little research myself and discovered all sorts of things. Honestly, I had no idea it was a sex club."

Cordelia full-body laughs at my admission. "What the fuck did you think it was?"

"A night club? I don't know. I've never really been clubbing. It was a holiday, and I was alone on an island where none of my friends or family live—I honestly just wanted to feel something."

"Did I make you feel something, Dr. Taylor?"

My blood runs hot at her disorienting question. I can feel my pulse in my neck, my fingers, and elsewhere. It thrums, reminding me of what I could have again. But I can't. For a million reasons, I cannot keep pursuing this girl. Whether it be because of my position in the Augury University system, or for deeper reasons I refuse to admit to myself, I have to shut this down.

"We should hear back from the architect soon," I say, swallowing my lust. "Do you feel comfortable going to Dean Singh with me once we have the plans?"

"Sure," Cordelia replies, all emotion leached from her voice.

"We can meet at my office. I'll text you when the blueprints are ready," I say. "I'll see you later, Cordelia."

I get out my phone and type the dreaded text.

ALITHA

I may require your assistance.

DAHLIA

Indigo filled me in. Oh this is BAD.

INDIGO

DID YOU SEE CORDELIA?

ALITHA

Yes.

DAHLIA

And???!!!!

ALITHA

We had a brief discussion about the sex potion and then I changed the subject to discuss logistics on the Aquatica Academy remodel plan.

DAHLIA

Urghhhhh. Alitha...

INDIGO

Did you ask her what you two are? Whether she wants to be something more?

ALITHA

Of course not. What if she wants to be TOGETHER together?

INDIGO

You don't want that?

ALITHA

I want to become Dean of Augury University, and I never want to be heartbroken again. That's what I want.

INDIGO

I looked into our code of conduct, and you can technically be with her once you're no longer her professor. That's in just a month!

DAHLIA

Okay, so become fuck buddies???? Nobody's asking you to marry her.

ALITHA

Good, because I don't plan on ever marrying. Also, that's wonderful news for whoever needs that, but I don't. I don't need to know that it's okay in a month, because it isn't okay right now.

I let out a breath of relief knowing that there is a way to pursue this ethically, even if I don't plan on using it.

DAHLIA

Ohmygod stop being so serious! For ONCE can you just allow yourself to enjoy something??

ALITHA

Probably not.

INDIGO

What if you just asked her out on a date? Nothing serious, no grand intentions. Just a cute little date.

ALITHA

Fine. I will try this and report back to you guys.

I cannot believe I just agreed to this, but maybe they're right. Maybe this is what I need.

twelve

CORDELIA

Two days ago I was knuckles deep in Alitha Taylor, and now I'm sitting on my couch drinking a protein shake and trying not to cry because of how easily she brushed me off.

Dr. Taylor flicked me away like an unwanted piece of lint, and I don't get what I did wrong. We had an incredible evening together. I know we were both pretty much drugged, but the potion didn't invent our feelings. It just subdued our anxieties and increased our horniness enough so that we'd both finally go for it.

Fuck.

Marwan walks in from the kitchen and sits down, holding a tub of ice cream and two spoons. Mom and Nahla are out on a swim, and it's just the two of us and our familiars.

"I need more protein," I say, gesturing to the shake. "I'm trying to hit a new PR."

"You need the smile to return to your face, Cora. Take a spoon," he demands, his voice stern. A smile spreads across his face as I grab the spoon and pop open the lid.

"Neapolitan?"

He smiles. "They were out of strawberry. What's bothering you?"

"I don't know what to do with my life," I say. It's a lie of omission, but I don't want to talk about my love life with my stepdad, no matter how old I get.

"That's understandable. I became a doctor because I didn't know what I wanted out of life, and that's what my parents expected of me."

"That's kind of sad," I say. "What about your dreams?"

He shrugs. "I didn't have any. Not everyone has a dream to chase, sometimes people just let life take them on a journey. Life is a river, learn to go with the flow of the water."

I take my spoon and dig out another scoop of ice cream, and Marwan does the same.

"What do I do next?"

"Get a job," he laughs, and I give him a subtle glare. "No, but seriously. Finish university and go work somewhere, or even work with your mother. Do something fun, something that gives you purpose. You'll figure it out later."

"Yeah. You're probably right," I say as Torzu lays on one of my tentacles. Marwan's familiar, a seahorse dragon, rests on one of my adjacent tentacles, and the two creatures stare at each other admiringly.

If there's one thing I love about familiars, it's witnessing their relationships with one another. They all know their place in magical society, but they also have fun and build bonds of their own.

Taking another bite of ice cream, I get under a blanket as Marwan turns on a documentary.

DR. TAYLOR

Meet me in my office in an hour. I have updates for you.

My heart feels like it's beating out of my chest as I reread her text over and over again. Grabbing my bag off the chair in my bedroom, I sprint out the door, my tentacles moving into overdrive.

Our last class, Dr. Taylor and I didn't speak. She gave her lecture, I quietly listened, but there was no after-class discussion. The time before that, she made it obvious that she didn't want to pursue anything more. With only a couple classes left before we break for Gratefulness Week, I'm worried I'll never get to experience her again. I want to show her more of what I'm capable of.

Swimming into Aquatica Academy, I'm met by the quick-closing doors that I vehemently despise. Groaning, I pull my tentacles into my body and quickly cross inside. I make my way towards the tiny room that is Dr. Taylor's makeshift office, desperation clinging to my chest as I try and think of things to say.

Act cool, Cordelia. Don't pressure her.

I need her to know that the connection she feels—I feel it too.

Opening the door, I pull out a premade vitacloud potion and cast out my magic, charming the liquid to attach itself to my tentacles. Making my way up the steps to her office, the magical, moving water allows me onto her solid floor. Alitha is seated with a blue-gray sweater on, drinking what looks like a cup of hot black coffee. I want to taste her lips to confirm, but I just stand here, silently waiting.

Alitha puts down her drink before looking up at me, and our gazes meet in a fervorous stare. The coldest, iciest blue eyes have the capability of melting me into pure liquid.

"The architect completed the blueprints. He's made a lot of changes, but they're actually not too expensive or major. I believe if we get approval soon, they can be completed before spring semester begins," Alitha says, smiling at me. "Would you like to see them?"

I nod. "Of course."

Crossing closer to her, I feel Alitha's body heat as she opens up her tablet, tapping on the correct file. Maybe it's not her body heat, maybe it's just the warmth from the apple-cider scented candle on her desk, but the feeling is pleasant.

The blueprints are stunning. It's the same beautiful campus, but with wider entryways and lots of extra features. Metal bars hang on walls to allow for people to take a break. There are benches, emergency kits, and chest-feeding rooms. The list goes on. It's everything I dreamt of and more, and I beam with pride, knowing we're the ones making it happen.

"It's beautiful," I say. "Thank you. What's our next step?"

Alitha stands at her full height, her long, lean body towering over mine. "We're going to ask for Dean Singh's approval."

Alitha exits the small office, but her platform doesn't move. She pushes it with her foot, but it still won't budge.

"Is something wrong?"

Her brows are furrowed as she stares down at the floor. "My platform seems to be malfunctioning. I'm not sure if I should just jump into the water, or call Dr. Quilen to help me fix it. I'm not a super technical person. I'm an expert at magic, not mechanics," Alitha explains.

Considering this, I use my sight to decide my next steps. Mystical visions flood my senses, one of which is of me carrying Alitha in my arms. “I could take you there using a vitacloud,” I say, eager to make that vision reality.

“Would that be alright?” she asks, and I scoop her up. Thanks to all those sessions in the gym, she’s light in my arms as I carry her towards the Deans’ office.

Luckily it’s Friday, so there’s not too many people on campus other than employees. Otherwise, I’d have to awkwardly explain to my classmates why I’m carrying our professor.

“The individuals who work here are smart. They can likely deduce that you’re carrying me due to my circumstances as a land dweller,” Alitha says, as if reading my mind.

“True. But I’m still glad it’s a ghost town today.”

Alitha smells like citrus and amber, the aromas intoxicating as they fill my nostrils. I want to record every detail of her into memory. Once, Dr. Alitha Taylor was just a beautiful mind on a screen. An intelligent voice of reason. Now, she’s so much more than that to me. She’s so real. I know what her touch feels like. Her smell.

Her taste.

And now that I’ve gotten to wholly experience her, I can’t get enough. It is so much more than a crush. It’s an obsession.

We enter a large room where Dean Singh is treading at a podium, typing away on his computer. His deep maroon turban matches the scales of his tail, and I smile. Whether merfolk, krakens, or jellyfolk, we all love for our hair and headpieces to match our tails and tentacles. It’s rare to see otherwise. It’s almost like how humans match their purses with their shoes.

“Dr. Taylor,” he says, his face scrunching at the sight of me carrying Alitha bridal style into his office.

“I’m sorry. Her platform broke and we needed to meet with you urgently. This was the quickest solution I could come up with,” I explain, and he nods.

He swims over to a cabinet and takes out a platform, pressing a switch on the underside before placing it on top of the water. “You can borrow this while you’re here, but Miss Tremblay will need to take you back.” It glides towards us, and I gently place Alitha down.

“Thank you. Both of you,” she says before making her way to him. “Would you open up the email I just forwarded to you?”

Dean Singh does as requested and clicks on the email attachment of the blueprints. He begins scrolling through them before he looks up.

“We would like to formally propose modifications to the Aquatica Academy campus,” Alitha says. “Many issues with the accessibility of the campus have been brought to my attention, and I would like your approval before bringing this up with President Bariel."

"Of course. Can you briefly explain some of the issues you've noticed?" he requests, genuine interest lining his features.

"Unfortunately, much like you, I didn't notice many of the issues. Cordelia Tremblay was kind enough to inform me of them; she can explain it better," Alitha says, giving me the floor.

I clear my throat. "Aquatica Academy is a lovely campus, but it was built with able-bodied, standard size merfolk in mind. There are many issues with the structure itself. For plus-sized beings, krakens, and jellyfolks, it can be really difficult to pass through the entryways. And for those with disabilities or that need to chestfeed, there's not a lot of space for breaks or privacy to handle those sorts of issues," I share, and he nods, actively listening.

"There are going to be metal bars and benches in hallways to allow for rest or breaks," I say.

Alitha nods. "And we'll keep stock of emergency kits—ones that might be different than the typical emergency you'd go to the clinic for. Water bottles, tampons, migraine medicine, et cetera."

"I think those are all incredibly valid points. It impresses me that you two would go out of your way to have blueprints designed before even bringing your proposal to the president," he says.

"You both have my approval." A wide grin spreads across his face. "And Dr. Taylor."

"Yes?" she asks.

"I hope you take up the mantle as the new Dean of Augury University. It would be a pleasure to continue working with you."

Alitha gives him a small smile. "That would be wonderful."

Heading down the long, winding hallway, we make our way back to Alitha's office. Crossing through the entryway, my body is a livewire. Nervous energy and excitement flutters in my chest, snaking its way down to the tips of every tentacle. Her eyes bore into mine, and I realize I'm still holding her.

I place her down, a red flush coating my cheeks. She doesn't move. Chest-to-chest we stand there, excitement filling the tiny space.

I'm about to thank her or congratulate her when she presses her lips to mine and fireworks go off in my mind.

Holy fuck.

I don't believe in religion or a god, my ancestors hailing from other planets likely had beliefs completely separate from this world I know, but I know in this moment I'm a sinner.

I'm a sinner, and I do not care because I would get down on my knees any day of the week for this elfling.

Her fingers dig into my short, straight hair, and I groan, releasing my breath. I press her against the wall, her legs circling my waist, and I'm suddenly thankful that she's tall and lithe.

Our bodies fit together perfectly, moving in sync as she grinds against me. I push up her sweater and cup one of her breasts in my hand, burning with need as I move to unhook her lacy bra. Her kisses are heady as our tongues collide, our mouths crashing against each other.

Water fills my vision, and I blink up in confusion. It's raining from the ceiling and a high-pitched sound blasts our ears.

Shit. Shit. Shit. It's sprinkling?!

Alitha sighs loudly, our eyes both trailing to the candle that is letting off more smoke than normal. Our bodies unravel as I put her back down. "Oh goodness, I didn't realize I left it burning. The candle must've set off the smoke detectors. It's probably better we don't do this here."

"Okay," I say, but doubt starts to rear its ugly head again, creeping into my mind to tell me she doesn't want me.

"I have to see you again," Alitha says. My heart stops. Or maybe it just beats so fast my mind can't keep up with it. My vision is hazy, water still coming down from the sprinklers, but I think she just made my year.

Wait. Not want. *Have.* She said she *has* to see me again.

"Do you have plans for Gratefulness Week?"

I shake my head, my hands still resting on her hips. "I don't. My family isn't super into the holiday."

"Let's do something then."

"That's the week after next—"

Alitha leans in and kisses me softly. "I'll text you with details later. I've got to go dry my hair so my twists don't unravel. And change clothes. And—"

I kiss her again, squeezing her body with my hands. "Go. I'll see you around, Dr. Taylor," I say, my voice smug.

We did it. *I did it.* Not only are we going to fix the campus, but I might get the girl too.

thirteen

CORDELIA

ALITHA

Pack a suitcase, enough for a week. Meet me at the trolley station at 7 PM.

NAHLA SWIMS INTO MY ROOM TO FIND ME WAIST DEEP IN PILES OF TOPS AS I TRY TO decide what to pack.

"You should be grateful we're not land dwellers. Then you'd have to decide on tops and bottoms," Nahla teases. "Who is this mysterious woman you're going on vacation with anyway?"

"She's not a mystery, I'm just choosing not to share details about her with the family until it's serious, and it's not a vacation. We're not even leaving the island," I say, though I'm not positive that's true. Alitha gave me minimal details, and I didn't ask for anything more for fear she'd change her mind.

Nahla rests on my bed, her purple tail covering my comforter. "Semantics, Cora. I can't believe mom and dad are just going to let you go and fool around," she says.

"That's because nobody lets me do anything. I'm twenty-two years old. You have to ask permission to do everything because you're a minor," I explain, and she sticks her tongue out at me. "Point proven."

"Be careful. Don't let a grimy man put his hands on you."

"Lesbian, remember?"

She shrugs. "I don't know. Don't catch anything and don't get your heart broken. Oh! And don't get kidnapped or murdered."

"I'll try not to," I say, glaring at her. "Are you going to help me pick out cute tops or what?"

"Sure!"

Torzu lays there, watching as we try to shove everything into the small bag. Nahla sits on top of it while I try the zipper for a third time, and it finally closes.

"Don't have too much fun without me," she says and pulls me in for a hug.

Oh, I will.

One trolley ride and two oovoos later, Alitha and I are standing outside what feels like the combination of a resort and an inn. It's not overly corporate, but it's big. I see pools and hot tubs, separate buildings for dining and sleep, a built-in spa.

A giant sign covered in palm fronds reads *Naiad Paradise.*

This place is a vacation destination. Land dwellers come here to enjoy the best of what Naiad Island has to offer on dry land. The pro is that it's safe for us, since nobody from Aquatica Academy will be here. The con is I'll be making a lot of vitacloud potions this week. Poor Torzu is going to have to put in the work to conduct my magic.

We check in at the front desk before bringing our bags upstairs where the most lavish room awaits us. The hotel staff even formed the towels into pumpkins.

"Look, it's like our own little personal pumpkin patch," I say, gesturing to the bed.

Alitha gives me a small smile. "We could go to an actual pumpkin patch, you know?"

"Oh yeah?"

"Yeah," she shakes her head, hanging her purse over a chair. I carried all the heavy bags. "There's a seasonal section of the resort that rotates different activities year round. I heard right now there's a pumpkin patch."

"I'm down. We can take cute pictures and bob for apples," I say.

"You'd definitely win at bobbing for apples."

"Why, cause I'm good with my mouth?" I tease.

She crosses her arms and raises a brow as I inch towards her. "Or because you're better under water."

"I might be better under water, but you did just fine getting wet," I say. I'm not sure what's come over me, but I'm enjoying the little innuendo game we've got going.

I lean in and lick my lips before letting her mouth consume me.

This is going to be an amazing week.

Serenade rests next to the large tank Torzu is swimming in. Alitha was kind enough to request a tank for my familiar to save me the trouble of having to create double the amount of vitacloud potions on our trip. The little ferret stares at me, her fur like fallen snow, and I scratch the back of her head.

"I have a surprise for you," Alitha says as she opens the bathroom door. "I picked out a special restaurant for dinner tonight."

"Good, because I have a surprise for you too. I want you to wear the dress that's hanging in the bathroom," I say, voice coy. "Don't worry; it's from your suitcase."

I feel giddy with excitement as I envision her in the gown, fighting with myself not to use my magic to see it early. Originally, I debated between the short black one and this one, but the vibrancy caught my eye. *And the cut.*

I put on a white dress shirt, the fabric tight against my taut muscles, and button up until the top three buttons. Just enough cleavage to hopefully drive Alitha wild. I grab a black corset belt to cinch my waist, allowing my tentacles to sprawl out from underneath.

Desperately waiting, I lean against the bed as I wait for her to come out of the bathroom.

"Close your eyes," Alitha says from the other side of the door. I do exactly as I'm told.

"Eyes are closed." I hear the door creak, nervous at the anticipation. "Can I open my eyes now?"

"Yes, but only because you've been a good girl."

I open my eyes, and my mind goes many places; they're anywhere but good.

Alitha's dress is long and red with an incredibly low v cut at her chest. The brightness of the red balances beautifully with the deep brown of her skin, and I swear I'm experiencing what must be heart palpitations.

"Do a little turn for me, Dr. Taylor," I say, my voice pleading.

She spins, and I melt. The tight fabric clings to the soft curves of her ass, and my body suddenly feels too hot. The back is low, even lower than the front v, adorned with a silky bow.

I want to tear at it with my teeth and spread her open. We should skip the restaurant. Alitha can be my dinner.

"Down, dog," Alitha jests. "You look like you're about to pounce."

"And what if I am?"

"After the surprise."

We walk into the restaurant arm-in-arm, and I feel like a professional athlete sporting around their trophy wife. Everyone stares at us, and for once I don't think it's my tentacles or muscular biceps—it's her.

Alitha's beauty is tantalizing. She's like a siren calling everyone to meet their tragic ends, and I would swim in those icy pools of blue a million times if it meant getting to be with her.

The restaurant is cute, but being the land dweller vacation destination that it is... it's a little kitschy. There are wooden boats hanging upside down from the ceiling with light fixtures inside. Nets drape down different areas, and everything is wood and navy blue. It's fun, but it's painfully nautical.

There's a bunch of tables grouped around a dance floor with an emcee booth, and a guy stands behind it holding a microphone while scrolling on his computer. A hostess seats us, and I realize this is freaking trivia. I love the concept of trivia, though I've never been.

"Okay, so how does this work?" I ask, staring down at the blank answer sheet the host handed to us.

"It's couples trivia. Instead of the typical group of four to eight, there can only be two people per team," Alitha explains.

"No, I got that part. What kinds of questions are they going to ask us?"

"Have you ever seen Jeopardy 6000? Or Trivia Bonanza? It's a lot like those shows. They'll have specific categories picked out, but you really have no idea what kind of question you'll get."

"Oh cool! Okay, what should I order?"

"What are you in the mood for?" Alitha asks.

I shrug. "I'm not really that kind of person. All food is good, but I have like—please don't judge me."

Alitha narrows her eyes, waiting for the punchline. The thing about fitness and nutrition is that it's hard to talk to people about it. Luckily I'm not a bodybuilder, because that would be even worse, but I have recently gotten into powerlifting. I don't want to talk about my food choices and accidentally trigger someone who has a negative relationship with food, or a history of eating disorders, or who thinks it's just... weird. All these thoughts tumble through my mind before I finally form the words I'm looking for.

"I do powerlifting, and I have specific goals, though I don't need to bring them up to you unless you're comfortable," I explain.

"Of course. Are you looking to find something with a lot of protein?" she asks.

My heart flutters. "Yeah, actually."

"They have a well-reviewed grilled chicken dish here. It's topped with cheese and bacon. Why don't you try that? I looked into their different restaurant menus before we arrived."

I love my family, but they often roll their eyes at my antics, spouting that I'm already strong enough. It makes me feel unsupported. Alitha, on the other hand, is full of support. Not just to me, but to everyone she meets. I saw it in the way she spoke to my classmates and during her speeches. She's like a light at the end of a tunnel.

A server comes by and takes our orders, and a grin spreads across my face.

"My mom wasn't super happy with me powerlifting," I share, and Alitha's face turns serious.

"Was she worried you'd get injured?"

I scratch the back of my neck. "Not exactly. She was afraid it would make me too masculine."

"Nonsense. You've got a doll-like face, and your body is all feminine curves—how could you be too masculine? What does that even mean?"

"I don't really know. Do you match up with what your parents expect of you?" I ask. I'm curious. Someone as smart and hardworking as her, her parents must have high expectations.

"Aesthetically, yes. My parents didn't have any gripes with how I came out; I look exactly like the two of them," she laughs. "But success wise, maybe not always. My mother, as I've shared, is an incredible lawyer. And my father is the first elfling to join the elven council, so there's a lot expected of me."

I blink. Of course she doesn't want to be seen out in public with me—a scandal would tarnish her family's reputation.

"Okay, folks," an emcee's voice rings across the loud speaker. "Our categories for tonight are magic, science, pre-Convergence times, and pop culture."

Pre-Convergence? I don't know shit on shit about life prior to The Convergence.

"First question. Make sure to write down your answers. What is the least common magic type on Earth?" the emcees asks. "And remember folks, do not use magic or the internet to get your answers. No cheating and no blurting!"

Alitha looks at me, and I nod. "Sight," I whisper, confirming her suspicion.

I love that my magic type is less common. I think it makes life more interesting. Potions are the most common, but that doesn't negate Alitha's talent with them.

The emcee, who I'm now realizing is a serpentine, asks a science question, and Alitha immediately jots down the answer, her beautiful handwriting scrawled across the page.

"What pre-Convergence soap was famously used to clean oil off of small animals?"

"Dawn," Alitha shares, and I write it down, my handwriting nowhere near as eloquent as hers.

"Why do you know that?" I ask, trying not to stare at the deep v of her dress.

"I took a human anthropology class, and it was briefly mentioned."

"Do you memorize every fact you hear?"

"I try to. Do you not?" she asks, her tone honeyed.

"You make it hard for me to remember anything," I whisper.

Servers come out with everyone's food, and I realize I am the only sea dweller in the room. There are a few centaurs, a handful of humans, and every once in a while I'll glance and spot a cambion or faun or satyr, but most of everyone appears to be elven.

The next question is about pop culture, which we both have no idea about, and it's followed by another round of questions. To my surprise, we get them all correct.

Celebratory music plays on a speaker as the emcee announces the team rankings so far. The game is only halfway complete, but we're second out of seventeen different groups.

A server blows into a trumpet, and an entire big band comes out. Trumpets, saxophones, double bass, and then some. People are heading to the dance floor to show off their moves, and I'm realizing this is almost like a trivia intermission. It's fun and silly, energy exploding through the place.

Alitha looks less than pleased. Her eyes track back and forth between all the different sources of sound. She holds her hands tightly to her body, squeezing them.

Maybe she just really hates jazz, but I don't know—she looks... pained.

This isn't the Dr. Taylor I fantasized about, or the Alitha I've come to know, this is someone full of what can only be described as a look of pure anguish.

I reach for her hand, but she doesn't react, her eyes dull of all previous brightness.

"Alitha," I say, and she comes out of her trance.

"Yeah." Her voice sounds numb.

"I'm really tired. I hate to ask this, but why don't we head back early? We can snuggle and watch a movie?"

Her shoulders visibility relax. "That sounds great. Let's do that." She sighs.

Alitha opens up her payment app and pays the check before we stand, crossing to exit the restaurant. We move, hand-in-hand, as we head towards the main building of the resort.

"Thank you," Alitha says after a few beats of silence.

"No problem, but really, I didn't do much of anything."

She squeezes my hand. "Well, it meant a lot to me. I have sensory processing disorder—it's usually associated with something else, like autism or ADHD, but as far as I know I just have SPD."

I laugh. "As far as you know, huh?"

"Let me live. I'll figure out what else is wrong with my brain later," she laughs.

"I didn't know you have SPD. I just noticed your discomfort. That's all," I explain. I had never seen Alitha talk about her disorder publicly. Not in speeches or in published papers or articles. It didn't seem to be something she advertised, and I can't say I blame her.

Giving out pieces of yourself to the world can be terrifying. You never know who will support you or who will judge you.

fourteen

ALITHA

Every rule I've ever invented for myself magically dissipated from my mind the second I locked eyes with Cordelia during that first class. I tried to resist, truly, I did. I know that I should be mindful of my position as her professor, however temporary that may be.

But the problem is? I no longer care.

I want her. And I'd want her in every scenario. A random meet-cute at the grocery store, a blind date set up by my best friends, she's an attendee at a speech I'm giving who asks good questions, whatever the path might be, I'd take it.

And now we're here, at a resort in the middle of nowhere, and I'm sunbathing on a chair while I watch her swim laps in the pool.

I blame the Unholy Trilogy for this; it was practically their idea. Dahlia suggested we "get it out of our systems," but we all saw how that went for Indigo and Vega.

I don't think this will get Cordelia out of my system, but it'll be more like a taste of what I could have. A wonderful beginning and ending to our forbidden fling. I am supposed to be calm and logical and put together, and yet this beautiful woman turns me into something entirely outside of myself. This behavior of mine is passionate and borderline irrational.

Cordelia comes up from under the water, her short hair slicked back against her head, coming to a point at the back of her neck. She rests her chest on the edge of the pool, her breasts spilling out of her midnight blue swimsuit top, and it takes every ounce of control to not stare straight at them. I think they might be as large as my head, and I like them.

A lot.

So much so that it causes cognitive impairment.

Cordelia cocks her head, a big grin spreading across her face. "Did you know that sound waves generally travel faster in warmer weather?"

"I did not. Where'd you learn this?"

"Possibly from a book. Or a documentary. I'm not sure. I've memorized a plethora of facts that I've double checked, but they're all pretty useless," she laughs. "Random tidbits here or there about certain topics, but nothing too vast."

I smile. "I can't believe you've never been to trivia before. It's perfect for you. We'll have to go again sometime."

"For sure, maybe somewhere more quiet?"

"That would be nice," I say, but I realize I'm lying. There won't be another time because we can't keep doing this. A few more days, and then Cordelia and I are through.

I blink the bad thoughts away, refusing to let despair or sadness take control of me, and just force myself to experience the joy of this moment.

To just appreciate the beautiful kraken in front of me.

We're halfway through the week when I realize we haven't once stepped foot on the balcony. We've been poolside, to two different restaurants, and Cordelia and I even enjoyed the sauna, but our balcony remains untouched.

"I'm going to go see what's out there," I say, pointing to the balcony. I kiss Cordelia on the cheek before I get out of bed.

We've spent the evening watching scary movies, as there's a ton I didn't see growing up that are *must-watches* according to Cordelia.

I open up the frosted-glass sliding doors to reveal a massive outdoor balcony. Beautifully ornate metal bars protect us from falling, and a giant hot tub sits directly in the center.

"Cordelia, come out here," I say. "And bring the navy blue lunchbox."

I packed an emergency kit of sorts. Inside it are water bottles, a protein bar, and lube. I don't know what kind of emergency I was preparing for, but it feels relevant right now.

Quickly, I strip off my pajamas before climbing into the tub. My muscles relax upon contact with the warm water, and I adjust the temperature, making it hotter.

My hair is up using a thick, large claw clip, and I turn my body so all she can see is my bare back.

A guttural sound comes from Cordelia's throat as I hear her enter, and before I know it, she is in the water with me, her tentacles peeking over the side of the tub. I turn and move forward, bringing our chests together. Her gaze and the silver hoop adorning her nose sparkle in the light of the moon.

Cordelia looks at me, her deep blue eyes appearing sex-craven, and I process the fact that I haven't made her orgasm. She's always been the one to make a move, to go down on me, but I've never offered in return.

My cheeks flush hot with embarrassment.

"Cordelia, do you want me to touch you?" I ask, unsure of what she likes. She could be a stone top, or maybe she's just been waiting for me to make a move. I haven't yet, but that's mostly been out of fear. There are power dynamics between us. We might only have a five year age gap, but there's no denying the fact that me being her professor changes things. Even if I'm just substituting.

"Yes." Her voice comes out breathy.

"I'm not particularly experienced with kraken anatomy," I confess.

"I'm not *particularly* experienced with anything," Cordelia shares in return. "I think I've only been with two women before you."

"Were they both elves?"

"No. One was a human and the other was a mermaid. You?"

"A mermaid, a few humans and an elf. You know how it is," I say.

"I do now."

I laugh against her lips, my hands trailing down her body before I reach her waist and freeze.

"Teach me," I say, pleading. "Tell me how you like to be touched."

She places her hand above mine, pushing my arm underneath the water, and her tentacles part. "It's not a slit. You'll know it when you feel it. It's a vulva, similar-*ish* to elves and humans."

Languidly, I run my finger down the underside of her tentacles before I find frilly, wavy flesh. Gliding my finger across it, I press into her opening.

Cordelia gasps, her pale cheeks turning a rosy pink. Using my other hand, I push her against the side of the tub. Her back arches over the edge, and I place my mouth on her chest, flicking her nipple with my tongue.

I continue to finger fuck her, her pussy pulsating against my hand as I work another finger inside, and then a third.

Her body is more beautiful than anything I've ever seen. Strong arms lead to a supple chest, followed by a soft belly. My eyes continue to trail down to her tentacles and sweet cunt.

"Be a good girl and let go, Cordelia," I whisper.

She moans as she rides my hand. Always so chill, so carefree, and now I've caused her to come apart.

I remove my fingers, and she stares down at me, her deep blue eyes now representing the hottest flames.

Cordelia's going to melt me until there's nothing left.

"Sit on the ledge, Dr. Taylor," she demands, her voice now low and domineering. Completely different from the high-pitched cries I heard just a few moments ago.

Moving, I take a seat on the lip of the hot tub, where there's a small bench-like step.

Cordelia's strong hands force my legs apart, a tentacle coming up to brush against the apex of my thighs. One of her suckers latches against my clit, suctioning itself completely. She tugs and pulls, sucking against the sensitive spot, and my legs jerk. I'm hardly able to contain my reaction to the new, intense feeling.

"Cordelia," I moan.

I'm soaking wet, my body aching for more of her touch.

"What do you want?"

"More," I say, my voice barely audible.

"Beg for it then."

Her smirk is devious as she uses a second tentacle to play with my opening.

"Please. Be a good girl and fill me," I whimper.

Cordelia pulls her suction cup off and slaps my clit, and my body braces. She repeats the movement, alternating between sucking and flicking.

"Cordelia, I can't. Please, my pearl," I say, my body overcome with want.

She pushes a tentacle inside, stretching and filling me as another one sucks on my clit. Working my body, she pushes me closer and closer to a high I've experienced a thousand times, but never quite like this. There must be clouds further up than cloud nine.

She kisses down my neck as I come on her tentacle, but she doesn't release me. "Do we have any lube?" she asks.

I point to the lunchbox, and she flicks it open with one swing of her tentacles. My head tilts back, eyes fluttering closed as she continues pumping into me when I feel something press against my back entrance.

Ever so slowly, Cordelia pushes her tentacle into my other hole, filling me completely. I am all feeling and nerves, so very full, yet I crave more.

"I want to fill every one of your holes until all you know is my touch. I want the only thing you remember to be my name, my taste," Cordelia says, her voice heady.

"So do it," I plead. "Fill me."

As if that was the confirmation she needed, her tentacles move in quick succession. One sucking on my clit while the other two fill my holes. A fourth and fifth tug on my nipples. A final appendage enters my mouth, threatening to snake its way down my throat and choke me, but she lets it linger.

My body climbs for ecstasy until I can't take it any longer. My skin is on fire, and all I know is fullness. Her thick tentacles threaten to rip me apart at the seams, and yet she remains almost tender, gentle in the way she plows into me. Everything is too much.

I'm at the peak, and I come toppling down, my muscles convulsing as I come over the edge.

"Fuck," I cough as her tentacle exits my mouth.

"Did you just curse?" Cordelia asks as removes her tentacles from all of my entrances.

"Quite possibly for the first time," I admit, my heated cheeks burning even hotter.

"Say it again," she says with a grin.

"Fuck? We just fucked," I say, high off my release.

The grin spreads from ear to ear, her eyes lighting up and face beaming. "I feel like a gold medalist now."

At that, I smile back. Cordelia lifts me into her arms, carrying me back to bed. I nuzzle at her chest, the familiar scent of sea salt and water lilies entering my nose.

Cordelia Tremblay might just make my list of favorite people after all.

We lay on the rooftop, a place I didn't realize we had access to until today, and count the stars. Thanks to the low light pollution of this area, we can see so many more than usual.

Cordelia points to all the different constellations, explaining to me their myths and legends. She's a walking, talking fun fact, and I enjoy every minute of it.

The midnight air is cool against my skin, reminding me that even though we're on a tropical island, it's fall.

"Alitha," Cordelia says, her voice pitched up.

My head rests against her stomach, her tentacles sprawling out every which way, and one of her hands rests on my chest.

"Yes?"

"I hope this question isn't like... rude to elflings, but why is your name Alitha Taylor and not like—"

"Archeron Bariel or Elorthiel or something?" I stifle a laugh. "That's not rude at all. My parents are both elflings."

"So."

"So, they both have one elven parent and one human parent. My mother, Lauren, named me after her human mother, Alitha."

"Aw, that's cute," Cordelia says.

"My father, Geladorial, gave me his human father's last name, Taylor. Hence, Alitha Taylor."

"Does it make you feel like less of an elf?"

"I'm nearly six feet tall with massively long ears. I've also got almost white-blue eyes. No, I almost exclusively feel like an elf. I mean, I'm human too, but I'm an elf," I state.

"That's totally valid. Krakens and merfolk get told we're part human, but none of us *feel* particularly human either."

"Yeah. Your beauty was blessed by Aphrodite herself. You're more likely to be a goddess than a human," I say, referencing one of the myths Cordelia shared earlier.

Her cheeks flush. "If I was blessed by Aphrodite, you were blessed by Athena. You're the perfect balance between beauty and wisdom."

Moonlight streams down onto us, illuminating Cordelia's glistening body, and I can hear the pitter patter of our hearts beating in sync.

fifteen

CORDELIA

Alitha stands there, leaning against the doorway in a hunter green cable-knit sweater, her other hand in the front pocket of her denim overalls, and just smiles at me. She's silent, and yet her body speaks a thousand words. A million maybe. She likes me. She really, *really* likes me.

And I like her too. I mean, in more ways than one, I'm her biggest fan.

I got to not only meet my idol, but truly get to know her. The way she thinks, details of her past, the taste of her lips. I got the opportunity of a lifetime, and I seized it. I just hope this was enough time to show her we could be something more.

It's silly and cliché. The college senior thirsting after her young professor. Nahla would probably remind me that life isn't like the movies or reality TV, but I don't care. I know that we're going to make things work.

Alitha and I are just beings—beings that belong together.

"Are you going to stand there and stare at me all day or are you going to get dressed?" Alitha asks, and my heart skips a beat.

I could stare at her all day, if I was being honest with myself. Her rich brown skin, angular face, and blue eyes the color of lightning. She's perfect. Ethereal, even.

Alitha's twists cascade down her back, looser than they were when we first met. I ache to scoop her up and hold her in my arms again. But if I do that, we'll never make it to the pumpkin patch.

Grabbing my sweater from inside my suitcase, I throw it on over my head.

It's a dark gray with a band of ghosts circling the collar, and Alitha beams even brighter.

"You look adorable."

My cheeks flush as I grab her hand.

We take an elevator and cross down the wide, aquatically decorated resort hallways until we're outside. The chilly fall breeze whirls around us, and Alitha clings to me for warmth.

"Your parents are pretty great, right?" I ask, seeing if she'll let me pick her brain.

"Yes. I love my parents," she says. "What about you?"

I furrow my brows. "Hmm. I guess my parents are pretty great, nix my biological father. He left. But it's okay, because my mom found Marwan, and I got Nahla out of the deal. She's the best little sister ever."

"That must be so nice. Having a sister. I don't have any siblings, though I have a lot of cousins."

"Having a sister is like having a best friend you're not afraid of losing," I explain. "She's never going to dump me or find someone better, y'know?"

"I will say, I feel like I have that, at least with my two best friends Indigo and Dahlia. I know they're not going anywhere."

"Yeah, but they could." I shrug.

She shakes her head sternly. "No, they would never do that to me. No."

Oof. I did not mean to bring up a touchy subject, fuck. "Sorry, you're probably right. I don't have a ton of friends, so I don't know what it's like."

We continue walking until we find the field of pumpkins and people. There are drink vendors, carnival-esque games, and even a few small rides.

"It's okay. I'm just very confident in the Unholy Trilogy."

"The what?"

"Long story, but that's the name of my friendship trio. You met them! At the haunted houses."

"Oh yeah! The curvy human and the tiny elfborn. I remember," I say, proud of myself. Between Nahla's chaos and the blood rush of running into Alitha, I'm surprised I actually can recall her friends.

We get in line at a drink booth, still holding hands, as Alitha continues. "That was Dahlia and Indigo."

"How'd you all meet?" I inquire. I want to know everything about Alitha. If I were to go to grad school, she'd be my course of studies.

"It was truly a chance encounter. I was on a ferry to Octopus Island for a research project a few years ago while working on my doctorate," she says, her body leaning close to mine, and I nod, actively listening.

"Indigo was visiting her family, and I believe Dahlia was going on holiday. We were all seated next to each other. I know it's going to sound odd, as this is statistically improbable, but we were all actually reading the same book too," she shares.

"What book?"

Alitha looks down, her expression one of true embarrassment. "Promise not to laugh?"

"I promise," I assure her.

"It was this... smutty romance book—"

"Romance books are nothing to be ashamed of," I state, thinking of all the things my sister reads.

She giggles, the sound music to my ears. "No, no. I know. It's not that. It was pre-Convergence alien smut. They thought people from other planets were blue with—" She leans in closely and whispers, "—vibrating dicks."

I stifle a laugh, remembering my promise, and she kicks me lightly on the tentacle.

"I mean, I'm blue-ish."

"Do you *vibrate*?"

I waggle my eyebrows. "I can sure try."

The line moves forward, and we make our way up to the counter.

"Dahlia had the paperback, and then Indigo showed her that she was reading the same book on her e-reader. When I saw them comparing, I took off my headphones and revealed that I was listening to the same story via audiobook. It was absolutely bonkers, and I'll never forget it," she shares, elation etching her features.

"What can I get you?" a human asks, a fake smile plastered across her face.

"I'll have a plain hot coffee and a pumpkin donut," Alitha says. "Cordelia."

"I'll have an apple spice spritzer," I answer in turn.

Alitha pulls out her phone and sends the cashier the dabloons. I feel bad that she's funded this entire getaway, but I'm also just a college student. I make money when I assist my mom with philanthropy work, though that's few and far between. I mostly spend my time volunteering.

Grabbing our drinks off the counter, we sit down at a nearby table. Everything here is adorable, and it's nice to be at a section of the resort that doesn't remind me I'm an octopus-person.

"Did you know that the human heart beats over one hundred thousand times in a day? Our hearts don't beat as fast, so the same doesn't apply to krakens and elves," I say.

"I did not know that. I wonder how fast my heart rate is."

"We could test it."

"The data would be skewed," Alitha says with a laugh. "It's always faster when I'm around you."

My cheeks flush as I take another sip of my drink. Alitha finishes her donut, and we stand, ready to move to the next event. There's apple bobbing, pumpkin carving, and other cute stations set up.

"Do you want to carve pumpkins?" I ask.

"Honestly, I find the look and feel of pumpkin guts to be repugnant, but I'll do it if you want to!"

That might've been the most brutally honest sentence I've ever heard come out of Alitha's mouth.

"No, that's okay. What if we took a photo at the photo booth?" I offer, and she kisses me on the cheek.

"I'd like that."

We make our way to the pile of hay, which is adorned with pumpkins and other fall decor, and have a seat while the photographer takes our picture. He hands us the image, and my heart threatens to burst when I take a peek. Laughter lines my features, and Alitha is shining brightly, too. The two of us make a lovely couple.

"You ladies should try our corn maze. It's gotten raving reviews all week," the photographer suggests.

Alitha and I lock eyes, and I already know she's down. Hand-in-hand, we cross towards the entrance and are met with the quietest, most empty corn maze I've ever seen.

Not that I've seen many, but still.

"Have you ever successfully completed a corn maze before?" Alitha asks as we turn into another dead end.

"Well, I'm here, aren't I? So, somehow I would've gotten out," I tease.

"Yes, but you could've been found via helicopter and rescued. I wouldn't call that a success," Alitha teases back.

I shake my head. "Technically, I have not, but I have successfully completed a coral maze, which is our equivalent."

She nods, seeming to assess the situation.

"I wish we had a pen and paper so we could take notes. It would make it a lot easier to analyze and search for patterns."

"Just track them in your mind," I suggest.

"I can't."

We turn another corner. This one seems to have an edge that leads elsewhere, and we follow it down.

"What do you mean, you can't?"

Alitha shrugs. "I don't have a mind's eye. I have to write it down."

"That must be wildly inconvenient."

"Sometimes," she says. "Most of the time it's fine."

I quirk a brow. "So if you were to say you're picturing me naked, you actually couldn't be?"

"Correct, but it's easy to get you naked." Alitha's tone is heady as she pushes me against the wall of corn stalks.

My eyes go wide as I feel her fingers trail underneath my tentacles, gliding towards my most sensitive area. She brushes against my clit, languid and teasing.

"Do you want me to fingerfuck that sweet little cunt of yours right here in public?" she asks, and I swear I feel myself opening.

Alitha is never usually so vulgar, and the switch-up in itself turns me on.

She kneels down before me. "Or how about I have a taste?"

"Ah," I can only sigh as Alitha squats and spreads my tentacles, lapping at my pussy.

One of her fingers gently pushes inside me as she continues, my entire body fidgeting due to the pleasure.

A moan escapes me, but I tamp it down, not wanting anyone to hear. I turn back and forth three times to confirm there's nobody around us, but I still don't want to be loud. It could draw someone to our direction.

With each additional finger, Alitha intensifies her movements, her mouth still sucking on my clit. The warmth of her mouth envelops me.

There's a sound nearby, and she halts.

"Alitha," I whimper. "Please."

It's all I need before she starts both movements back up, her fingers and tongue moving in tandem to push me over the edge. I come apart, pleasure filling my senses.

"Good girl," she whispers. "Now let's get out of here."

After our rendezvous in the corn maze, Alitha and I headed back to the room where we now rest, relaxing on the bed.

Some garbage reality TV show Nahla would love comes onto the screen, and I grab my phone to ask if she's seen it when a phone starts ringing.

Ring. Ring. Ring.

"Dr. Taylor speaking," Alitha says, picking up her cell.

She sits up, her body fully alert as she excitedly listens to the phone. My mind wanders to all the possibilities. At first I thought somebody died, but there's a spark of joy in her eyes that doesn't match that vibe. Alitha doesn't seem like the type to play the lottery, but this is giving big *lottery winning* energy.

A few minutes go by of attentive listening before Alitha speaks again.

"Congratulations, I love you so much. This is wonderful news," she says, her grin spreading from ear to ear. "Text me all the details about the party. You deserve this, seriously."

She hangs up the phone and looks at me. "Indigo's girlfriend proposed to her at a picnic in the park today. Dahlia and I helped plan it months ago, but kept it a secret because Vega wanted to wait for the perfect time. Something about the alignment of stars in the sky needed to be a specific... I'm not really sure, it's an orc custom, though."

"That's adorable," I say.

And it was for some people. I never personally thought about things like weddings and engagements, and I definitely didn't care about dresses or jewelry. I don't think I'm better for it or anything like that, it's just not my thing. All I care about is the person I want to spend my life with one day, not all the silly frilly extras.

However, I fully expect Nahla to care about those things, and I cannot wait to help her with all the extravagant details.

Everything will happen in due time.

sixteen

ALITHA

Our bodies relax, the warm water of the hot tub covering us completely, as we enjoy our last night at Naiad Paradise.

"Your friend Indigo is marrying an orc, right?" Cordelia asks, ending the peaceful silence. It's not that I don't want Cordelia to speak, I do. I love all her fun quips, but I really just want to be in this moment with her, not talking about my friends.

"An orcling, but yes," I answer. "Why do you ask?"

"I took a class in high school that talked about customs from around the globe as well as other planets, and orcs were covered in one unit."

"Huh."

Her deep blue eyes light up as she talks. "On their planet, constellations and star placements are vital to their decision making processes. It's almost like a religion."

"Interesting," I say, genuinely intrigued. I knew Vega's tattoo of the pleiades constellation held significance to her, but I had no idea how much.

"That cluster of stars right there," Cordelia says, pointing to a constellation above us. "That's Argo Navis."

"Okay, nerd, what's the story?" I tease, and we both chuckle.

"Jason, an ancient Grecian hero, in his search for the golden fleece, had a ship called Argo. That's what it represents."

"It's interesting that we can see it from here, on Naiad Island."

"Fitting, isn't it? Given all the tales of mermaids and ships."

"Quite," I say and lean closer. "Now quit talking about mythology and kiss me."

The adjustment back to normal life was not an easy one. Returning from breaks is always hard on professors and students because we lose our routines, but this time especially so.

I feel weirdly off-kilter. I mean, it makes sense. I'm on a still somewhat unfamiliar island, with coworkers that I don't fully understand. They're polite, but it's different from the colleagues I've worked with for years, some of which taught me.

It's also odd to be without Cordelia now. I'll get used to the quiet loneliness of my day-to-day life, but I can't say I'm happy about it. Part of me aches for a love I know I'll never have.

I've emailed Dean Bariel asking for a time to set up a video conference with Cordelia and I, and his assistant, Daffodil, replied letting me know it would have to be sometime after finals.

Working hard or hardly working? The phrase echoes in my mind as I think of President Bariel.

Every day this week was the same. I woke up, pet Serenade, and went to work at Aquatica Academy. I administered an exam, which students moaned and groaned about, and I went home. The only day that was different was the one where Cordelia took and aced her final.

Even then, it's not like we could say anything to one another in front of all her classmates. The main difference was the fast-paced beating of my heart as I watched her enter my room, and the empty feeling in my chest when she left.

Now I sit here, listening to the sounds of the ocean coming through my open window, as I pack my bags for home. I've missed my friends, my apartment, and the school I love so dearly.

I can't wait to get back into the cosmetics lab and finish the hair potion I'd been tirelessly working on before I left. Mulling it over these last few months, I think I finally know the last step I need for it to work as I intended.

I leave for Magia Island tomorrow morning, and there is just one thing I have left to do here.

ALITHA

Can we meet in the library this afternoon, 3 PM?

I send the text to Cordelia. I don't want to do this—I don't want to hurt her, but it's something I have to get off my chest before I leave. One final goodbye.

We'll still talk. We have to finish the Naiad Island campus project, and I'm sure we'd both like to stay in touch regarding research. But this might be the last time I see her in person.

CORDELIA

Of course. I'll see you then :)

Underwear, check. Socks, check. Tops, check. Pants, check. Diligently, I make sure everything is accounted for. I check every drawer and every nook and cranny, ensuring I don't leave something valuable behind.

My eyes linger on the clock each time I walk by, the time dwindling down until it's finally 3 PM.

"Hey pretty girl," I say, wanting to kick myself immediately after the words exit my mouth. I need to communicate where we stand with her. I have to tell her that we cannot continue like this.

Sitting down at the booth across from her, I take a look at the book she'd been reading. It looks like an Iliad or Odyssey retelling, but it's hard to tell with all the damage to the front cover.

"Alitha, hi. I've missed you," she whispers, the cutest small smile on her lips.

"How've you been?" I ask.

"Good! I feel like I really did well on my finals," she shares. "Not all the grades are in yet, but I'm confident."

"Of course you did." I'm dancing around the topic at hand, not wanting to get to the punchline. "I enjoyed myself the other week."

"I did too."

"But I'm moving back to Magia Island now that the semester is over. I'll still help you with the Aquatica Academy campus project though. I just needed to tell you that." As I wait for her reply, it feels like my heart is in my throat.

Her smile fades for a moment before returning again. "I totally get it. You've got to focus on becoming dean."

"Yeah, I do. Thank you for being understanding and allowing me to make this break—"

"It's not a problem, really. I always knew things would change when you had to go back, but I only have a semester left, and then things will change for me too," she says, interrupting me. "Thank you. For everything. You were exactly the person I needed you to be."

"Of course," I say, though I have the gut feeling that we're on two entirely different wavelengths.

As she leaves, I take one long and hard final look at Cordelia. From her flippy blue hair to the depths and shades of her tentacles, she's gorgeous. No one will ever hold a candle to her luscious curves and beautiful brain. Not in my eyes, at least.

I think Cordelia and I are textbook examples of right person, wrong time.

Stepping into my apartment feels like drinking cold water on a hot summer's day. It's exactly what I need right now. I want the comfort of familiarity, and honestly, I want a hug from my mom. I know she's busy dealing with court cases, and I'm a grown woman who can handle herself; I just want that maternal love and comfort right now.

I'm not even sure why. Everything is fine. I am Head of the Potions Department, as well as in charge of the cosmetic lab here at Augury University. I am making connections at our sister school as well as working my way up to becoming dean. My friends are great. I have a cute apartment and a fantastic familiar. What is wrong with me?

Romance? No. Absolutely not. I can live a completely and utterly wonderful life without needing a relationship. I can, but I'm not positive I want to. Pocketing that thought, I put it away for a rainy day. There's no time for fluff now; I've got to remain focused.

Putting up my things, I walk downstairs and hop into my car. Driving with the windows down for once, I allow myself a moment to take in the sounds of Sunspell City before my SPD kicks in and I can't handle all the noise.

The drive to my mother's firm is short, and I easily find a parking spot.

Walking up, I open the door to her waiting room, and the receptionist gives me a wave. She trots over to the phone, her mane swishing back and forth as she dials for my mother. They talk for a brief moment before the door opens, and I head for her office. My mother's building is quite drab and bland. I prefer simple things, but I like a little more color than this. I lean towards pinks... and blues, not the grays and browns and whites of this space.

She's standing, waiting for me when I open her door.

"Sweetie, I've missed you," she says as her arms come around me, enveloping me in a hug.

When she lets go, she gestures for me to have a seat, and I feel a little too much like I'm a client right now, about to defend my side.

"Tell me everything; what did you learn from your experiences?"

I inform her all about Dean Singh, the other staff members, and the set-up of the university. She asks me a ton of questions about Naiad Island, and I explain the ins and outs of semi-aquatic life. I even tell her about the campus modifications proposal, which I state is pending.

She beams at me, a proud look in her icicle-blue eyes, but there's no warmth in my chest. All I feel is a strange sort of emptiness.

"Why do you look so sad?" my mother asks, confusion lining her features.

I wave my hand at her, wanting to brush it off. "It's nothing. I'm just overwhelmed."

She shakes her head. "We don't get overwhelmed, Alitha. We're fixers. Doers. This isn't like you."

"I'm fine."

"Are you sure?"

"No," I finally let out. "Mom, I've watched you and dad build each other's success. You two have accomplished all that you have because you did it together. Can I do the same without love or a relationship?"

"Of course you can," she sighs. "You don't need a relationship to be happy or find success. And you can be in a partnership without needing to ever get married. There are a multitude of paths you can forge for yourself, Alitha."

"Do you feel like you needed to be loved, though?"

"It's not about needing to be loved; it's about wanting to be loved and allowing that love to expand you—"

"But what if you've built up walls?" I ask, not meaning to cut her off.

Her eyes widen. "Take them down."

"I can't."

"Build a door."

"What?" My brows knit, unsure what she means.

She smiles. "If you can't take down the walls you've built around your heart, build a door. Give someone you love the key."

Build a door. The line repeats in my mind over and over again until it cements itself.

Between shopping for engagement party outfits with Indigo and Dahlia, deep cleaning my apartment, and restocking my fridge, the first few days of winter break go by in a blur.

Sitting on the couch watching a documentary with Serenade, my phone buzzes and I pick up before reading the caller ID.

"Dr. Taylor speaking," I say.

"It's President Bariel. I have time on Friday to discuss your proposal with... Miss Tremblay?"

"Yes," I say, nervous and excited emotions bubbling in my belly. If there's one thing I was certain of, it was that I'm going to help Cordelia get these changes done. It's not only the right thing to do, but if it's a success, it'll guarantee I'm the best candidate for the dean position. "Do you want to meet with me in person and she join via video call?"

"No," he says, the short word drawn out. "I would much rather see you both in person. Pay to sail her here, and I'll reimburse the costs."

"Will do. Thank you," I say and hang up.

I click through my recent messages until Cordelia's name pops up and begin drafting the text. More emotions, ones I'm not ready to confront, threaten to appear, but I push them down.

I'll deal with those feelings later, I remind myself.

seventeen

CORDELIA

Cold ocean waves splash against the sides of the ferry as we make our way to Magia Island. The morning sky hasn't fully shed the darkness of night, and I yawn, not quite ready to start the day.

Nervous energy flutters in my chest at the thought of seeing Alitha again. I know we're on a break because of the distance and because we both have things to be focusing on, but she's still the woman I want.

At the very least, we can make this trip sexy and fun. We'll get the approval from President Bariel, and then we'll celebrate to our hearts' content. It'll be great.

I watch as the sky turns bright shades of pink and red, thinking of how these stolen weekends will one day be our forever.

A couple of hours go by, and the boat docks at the harbor. Getting off the boat, all I have in tow is a duffel bag, the vitacloud attached to my tentacles, and Torzu. My poor familiar sticks his head out of the tank-like backpack, his tail swishing in the water. I suppose I'll stick him in the bathtub when we get to Alitha's apartment.

Standing by the road, I wait until a sleek, simple sedan pulls up. I open the backdoor and place my things inside and hop in the backseat.

I would love to sit up front, but I don't think my tentacles would fit.

"Hey," Alitha says, her voice quiet.

"Hey," I say as she starts driving us away.

It's silent for a while as we drive out of Boca Raton and head towards the city Alitha lives in.

"How's winter vacation treating you?" she asks.

"Good. I'm ready for this last semester to be over."

More silence hangs in the air, and a sinking feeling fills my stomach. She's acting really strange. Polite, but strange.

She turns up the music, and an orchestral symphony quietly plays.

"Did you know that catgut, a rare and expensive type of string used for instruments, is not actually made of cat guts?" I say, looking at poor Torzu.

He's only half-cat, but I still feel a little guilty bringing it up. It's such a cool fact though, I have to share it with Alitha.

"I did not. What are they made of?"

"Animal guts! But not cat. Sheep, cow, buffalo, those kinds of animals. They're almost never used these days because of how far we've advanced other string types, like nylon, but it's a fun little part of history," I share.

"I don't know what's more odd: the fact that they called them catgut or the fact that they used animal guts at all," she says, a horrified expression on her face as she looks back at me in her rearview mirror.

"To be fair, they *were* byproducts."

"I play Symphony No. 5, and your first instinct is to share facts about animal intestines? You're truly an anomaly," Alitha laughs, and I smile.

There it is. That silly, funny, wonderful feeling.

We drive for another hour or so, playing games utilizing license plates, which Alitha almost always wins.

"This is Sunspell City, my home." She gestures to the windows, which show a busy and buzzing cityscape full of skyscrapers, hotels, and... nature. Vines grow on many buildings, and it's as if much of the island was built around its natural environment instead of in spite of it.

We come up to a tall hotel building, and Alitha parks in a nearby parking lot.

"Is this your apartment complex?" I ask, perplexed. I thought Alitha lived in a nice apartment that was a drivable distance from the Illusionary Jungle. I'm not quite sure what this place is.

"No, I got you a hotel. My apartment is only one bedroom, and I didn't want things to be weird now that we're not together," Alitha says, and the sinking feeling in my gut hits rock bottom.

"Now that we're not together?"

"Sorry. Not that we were ever officially together, but you understand my meaning," she corrects. "Now that we have gone our separate ways."

"Ah," I say, getting the bigger picture.

Alitha and I were apparently having different conversations the last time we spoke. I thought she was asking for a break until I graduate so that she could focus on becoming dean, and I could figure out what I wanted to do. I'd likely have to move to Magia Island, but I'd find something. Now I see the bigger picture.

I debate on what to tell her, before I decide that silence is probably for the best. If she can break my heart like it's nothing and move on with her life, then I can do the same.

Or at least I can try.

When I get up to the hotel room, I go in and close the door. There's a massive tub just for Torzu, and I get in with him before the tears fall down my face.

This fucking sucks.

An order of takeout, a sob-ridden phone call with my little sister, and one terrible night of sleep later, and I am on my way down the escalator to meet Alitha. Today's the big day. Months of hard work and planning have gone into this, and we'll finally get to present our proposal to the President of the Augury University System.

I get in the car with just my phone and body, and Alitha doesn't greet me this time. There's no classical music, no fun facts or funny jokes.

Painful silence is all I have as we drive into the jungle.

Augury University is one of the most unique places I've ever seen. Located in the heart of what my research said is called the Illusionary Jungle, Augury is an amalgamation of a bajillion different styles crashing and blending together. The buildings look like modular huts, nestled into the branches of six giant camphor trees. The entire campus is one with nature, everything natural and non-destructive.

I'm torn between my fascination with this beautiful place and the pangs of pain hitting my chest in random intervals. My body is having some sort of physiological reaction to the emotional pain I'm currently in, and I am not here for it.

Nerding out wins for a moment, and my brain enjoys the tiny boost in serotonin. Not only is this place in tune with nature, it's also in harmony with the beings that attend it. There are lifts and other helpful tools to provide accommodations to those who need them, something that wasn't considered when Aquatica Academy was designed.

Aquatica Academy is one long tube-like structure, with not much space for change or growth. This place is expansive, its fields and other facilities sprawling out into farther depths of the jungle.

Alitha's last minute request to have me join her came at a surprise, but it wasn't an unwelcome one until last night. Now I'm not sure what the future holds for us, if anything, and it's tearing me apart.

My heart aches.

But at the very least, we can present the new campus accommodations to President Bariel and hopefully get the approval we need to make Aquatica Academy a better place.

Alitha and I cross towards a mage standing by a lift system. We step onto the platform, our bodies so close and yet miles apart, and the assistant uses his magic to move us upward.

Exiting the lift and moving down a wooden pathway, I almost feel like I'm going to lose my balance as she brings me to a building that is nestled a little farther up from the other structures.

We open the door and are greeted by a ginger-haired faun. She smiles, her bright and colorful outfit a much needed momentary distraction. "Archeron is waiting for you inside."

The door wooshes open, and a very strange man is sitting at the edge of the conference table. He takes his feet off the table before standing to greet us. He's tall, a little taller than Alitha, with long white hair and pointy ears. His ears aren't as slender and long as Alitha's, but other than that he looks entirely elven.

"Hello, nice to meet you, Miss Tremblay," the man says. "I'm President Bariel." He sticks out two finger guns, and I cringe.

"Hey." Alitha's tone is casual.

"We've definitely missed you here, Alitha," President Bariel says, his eyes expressive and genuine.

"Glad to hear it."

I connect my phone to the projector and pull up a 3D model I had rendered for the presentation. It shows Aquatica Academy with all the new accommodations installed.

President Bariel takes a seat as I go over the reasoning behind every change, including medical and other life experiences that could cause these changes to be necessary. I even adlib some points about how I've seen a lot of similar attributes in my short visit at Augury.

After I'm done explaining the structural changes and other necessities, Alitha switches into going over logistics. She shares quotes from contractors she's gathered and even goes into timelines and how the university will pay for it.

"Additionally, I wanted to let you know that Dean Singh has given his approval for these changes," Alitha says, wrapping the presentation up in a nice little bow.

"That was lovely, thank you both," President Bariel says. "Alitha, I will meet with you later this week to discuss which contractors we're going with, as well as new changes to Augury as well."

"Sounds great," she tells him and starts for the door.

"I'm sorry, what? You don't have any further questions?" I ask, perplexed at how easy this was.

"Your presentation was fantastic, but I get a little bored after a while. I don't need any more details; I trust Dr. Taylor wholeheartedly."

I'm not sure if I'm elated, or if I want to punch this man. Maybe a bit of both.

"Great," I say, not trusting myself to say anything more.

"We should get going," Alitha says, gesturing towards the door.

Grinning ear to ear, I beam as we take the lift down and head for the car. Alitha hasn't said a single word to me since we left the president's office, but surely she has to be thrilled?

It's obvious she's going to be the next Dean of Augury University.

We get into the car, and I stare at her side profile, assessing her.

"Alitha, we did it! Aren't you proud?"

"I am, you were a really good—you did really well, Cordelia. Seriously. You should be proud of yourself," she says, and her words immediately flood my chest with the warmth I've been so desperately craving from her.

"Thank you. I can't wait to tell my parents and Nahla, of course. This was all for her," I say. My eyes are watering, and I'm overwhelmed with a deep sense of satisfaction.

Nahla will get to go to a university basically built for her. With her body in mind, and the body of any friend she'll make. Aquatica Academy will truly become a place worthy of being proud to attend.

"Where do we want to go to celebrate? Do you have a favorite restaurant?"

Alitha shakes her head and gives me a look in the rearview mirror. "I actually can't. Tonight's Indigo and Vega's engagement dinner," she explains, and my heart stops.

"What?"

"Yeah, I'm sorry. That's tonight. But you should definitely do something that brings you joy; you deserve it."

"We could do something tomorrow!" I suggest.

"Your ferry home leaves first thing in the morning," she reminds me, her tone cold.

It feels like I'm being tossed aside, thrown away like forgotten garbage. We have accomplished so much together and brought each other so much joy, and she doesn't even care. If she were Orpheus and I, Eurydice, she wouldn't look back. She could easily hear me scream her name or cry, and she wouldn't bat an eye, her heart as cold as ice.

"Why are you doing this to me?"

"What?"

I take a deep breath, willing myself enough courage to confront her. It's now or never. "We have spent months working on this presentation. Not only that, but we spent an entire week together where all we did was nuzzle into each other's arms and make love all night, and you don't even care."

"I do care," she tries to assure me.

"No you don't. If you cared, you wouldn't have put me in some hotel and ordered me the first ferry back on a Saturday morning when we could've spent the whole weekend together," I argue, staring out the window.

"Cordelia, you're my student. I can't just be with you."

"That's a bullshit excuse, and you know it. You're not my professor anymore. I read the code of conduct, and I'd bet money you have too. We both know that there's no red tape stopping us anymore; it's just you. You and your cold words and your empty heart."

"Cordelia," she says, pain lacing her words.

"That was fucking mean, I'm sorry. I'm just hurt. I worked so hard to prove to you we were meant to be. That we could be together, and it still wasn't enough. I don't know what I did wrong." Tears start to fall that I try my damndest to reel back in, but it's no use.

"What did you think was going to happen when you pursued me? We live on different islands. Frankly, we live in different worlds, Cordelia. Did you expect me to jump into the ocean to live with you?" she asks. I stare at her furrowed brows through the rearview mirror.

"I'd have figured it out for you. Just like I have this whole time. Every meetup, and even our week-long trip, I worked without complaint to create vitaclouds. You said it yourself in your lecture, that potion isn't easy. But I made sure we could be together. I would've done it forever if it meant being with you," I say, the tears now streaming down my cheeks, droplets falling onto my top.

She frowns, pain etched into her features. "I don't want you to have to do that. You shouldn't have to change or move for me—"

"I would have been happy to," I say as she parks the car in the hotel parking lot.

And it's true. I would've moved mountains to make it happen, but she would rather keep being comfortable. Stagnant.

"You have so many excuses, but have you ever looked into yourself and thought that maybe you're just afraid to feel something? That what's holding you back isn't rules or logistics, but you?" I ask, opening the door. "Have fun at the party." And I slam the car door shut.

eighteen

ALITHA

MAYBE YOU'RE JUST AFRAID TO FEEL SOMETHING?

Cordelia's words ring in my head like an alarm clock, screaming at me to wake up. Except I'm not dreaming, and although it feels like it, this isn't a nightmare either.

This is the reality I forged.

I knew that our end was inevitable. But I listened to my friends' advice, and I allowed myself to enjoy the stolen moments. We got to experience a week of pure bliss. And now it's all toppling down. My house of cards has fallen in on itself, and I am left to clean it up.

I'm happy, I lie to myself. I *should* be happy. Archeron accepted our proposal, I am back on the island I love so much, and I have a bubbling suspicion I'm about to be named Dean of Augury University.

So why is it all I feel is emptiness?

Heading inside my apartment, I pet Serenade before scanning the invite, finding the word *formal,* and changing into a blue gown. I throw on some lip gloss and mascara and run out the door. I'm not usually one to be late, but this meeting was necessary.

When I get to a longer red light, I shoot a text to Dahlia. It's rare any of us text outside the group chat, but I don't want to stress Indigo out with my problems.

ALITHA

> Cordelia and I had a massive fight. She didn't realize we weren't together.

DAHLIA

Alitha. How could she not realize???

ALITHA

I don't know. I think I wasn't clear enough in our conversation, but she was pretty hurt and combative. She told me it isn't rules holding me back from being with her, but myself. I left her at the hotel.

DAHLIA

I love you, but I mean, is she wrong, though?

ALITHA

...

Anyway, I'm on the way now. I'm sorry for being late.

DAHLIA

It's okay, it's been pretty chaotic so far.. Just drive safe!

If anyone on Earth deserves happiness and love, it's Indigo and Vega. I drive fast, faster than usual, heading farther into Sunspell City until I find the old, purple Victorian-style mansion from the invite.

I head up to the door but hesitate. Every part of me knows that I should head in and greet my best friends and celebrate their big day, yet some small fragment of my mind is screaming at me to turn around and head back to that hotel. I blink it away and turn the handle.

Walking into the space, I am immediately greeted by a fusion of spooky Victorian furniture and cute holiday decor. I scan the room, searching for my favorite beings, and am greeted by many familiar faces.

Iris and Dr. Adeib Ali are cuddled up to one another in a disgusting public display of affection while Aura points, laughing at someone on the dance floor. My eyes scan until I lock onto the humorous guest, only to find Mr. Watson doing the limbo as Mrs. Watson desperately gestures for him to get off stage.

I never imagined I'd see Adeib so happy and full of joy, but it warms my heart. I also never thought I'd see Mr. Watson drunk, clearly having *pre-gamed*, as my students would call it, his daughter's party, but here we are.

Continuing my search, I pass by a table covered in Vega and Indigo themed cookies. There's bisexual flags, lesbian flags, constellations, and other fun reminders of my friends. There's even sugar rabbit and hummingmouse shaped cookies to represent Momiji and Freja, their familiars.

I snag a lesbian flag cookie, ignoring the sinking feeling of missing a girl whose eyes light up like stars as my finger passes the constellations, and head back to the tables. Elorthiel is seated at one in a corner, and I cross his way.

"Hey," he says, his shirt sleeves rolled up to reveal a plethora of tattoos.

"Hey," I reply, taking my seat.

"It's been a while," he says. "The girls missed you."

"It's been too long. Where are they?"

He shrugs. "Don't know. Probably the bathroom."

"Thanks," I say and quickly stand, darting across the dance floor.

Turning the doorknob, the bathroom is locked.

"Who is it?" a loud voice asks from inside the bathroom.

"Dahlia, open the door," I command.

The door swings open. The inside of the bathroom is massive, with lots of counter space and a huge clawtooth tub. Indigo sits on the edge of the counter, her legs swinging down to Vega, who kneels before her. They both look adorable, donning matching black outfits. Vega's jumpsuit shows off the contours of her muscles, and Indigo's dress is the perfect sparkly little number. It's a shame though, because her face is streaked with tears.

"What's wrong?" I ask to Dahlia, who stands with her arms crossed.

"Mr. Watson got drunk, and it caused Indigo to have a panic attack about how she's going to be perceived at her own engagement party," she explains. "He's a total dick."

"I cannot believe her mom is the good guy in this scenario," I say, dumbfounded.

"What if we left?" Vega asks, wiping Indigo's tears.

"What?" she says, and my heart hurts.

"Let's walk around and maybe dance for another hour, and then we escape through the backdoor or something. I doubt anyone will even notice," Vega says, grinning at her brilliant plan.

Indigo nods, still sniffling as she gets off the bathroom counter and throws her arms around me. "And you. Don't leave us for that long ever again."

We cross back onto the main dance floor, and the DJ plays a slow song. Vega and Indigo sway to the music, Vega's tall frame towering over everyone around her. Dahlia gestures with her hands for Elorthiel to come join her, and I move to exit the floor when my wrist gets caught by someone's grip.

"Alitha," Dahlia says, her tone firm. "Go get your girl."

That was all the push I needed to leave. I blew Indigo and Vega a kiss before racing out the door.

I spent so much time convincing myself I didn't need her and could simply live without her, I forgot to ask myself if I *wanted* to.

Driving down the highway, I'm going speeds I'd never feel comfortable driving on a normal day, but that's what Cordelia does. She pushes me, for both better and worse. I want to do all sorts of wild and outlandish things if it means making her smile.

I park my car and dart through the parking lot, entering the hotel.

People used to assume I was an athlete due to my tall stature, but tonight I am reminded of my lack of athleticism as I run down the corridor of the hotel, desperate to see Cordelia. It doesn't help that I'm in a long gown and heels either. Opening the door to the stairwell, I barrel my way up to the third floor.

When I get to Cordelia's room, I knock on the door with fervor.

No answer.

I knock again, my fists slamming against the wood, but there's no one there. My heart is pounding, but I choose to calmly walk to the escalator. Maybe she's at the hotel gym or something. I take a long lap around the building, checking every option. The gym, the pool, the restaurants and bars. Cordelia isn't in this building.

Pulling out my phone, I go to call her but stop myself. Cordelia made it clear that she always has to go out of her way for me. I want to prove to her that I can do the same.

Opening maps, I search for the nearest beaches. Florgia a half hour or so west of here, and Boca Raton around two hours east. I could flip a coin and guess where she'd go, but that wouldn't be romantic, now would it?

Florgia is closer, but it has more light pollution. Boca Raton is where her ferry is leaving out of tomorrow, and it's also closer to her home and the waters she's used to.

Walking to my car, I turn on GPS and head for Boca Raton.

After two hours of painful silence, I arrive in the city. When I get to the beach, I turn my car off and start walking in the sand. The shore is surprisingly empty, except for the bright blue hair bobbing in the distance. I take off my heels, chucking them, alongside my purse, onto the sand before walking into the water.

The only sounds I can hear are the crashing of waves and the thundering of my heart in my chest as I swim towards Cordelia. She's at the sandbar and I slowly make my way towards her.

When she turns to face me, it's the first time I'm greeted by darkness instead of her usual joy. It pains me, and I desperately wish to make it stop.

"Hey, sweet girl," I say, my voice shaking.

Cordelia's brows furrow. "How did you find me? Shouldn't you be at the party?"

I inch closer to her. "I had somewhere more important I needed to be."

"Oh yeah?" There's a harsh sadness lining her eyes. "What are we doing, Alitha?"

"Apologizing."

Her expression softens. "You don't need to do this. I don't need you to apologize for not loving me."

"I'm not apologizing for not loving you. I'm apologizing for not loving you enough—for not loving you out loud," I say, and it's the first time I've admitted it, even to myself. My words spill out without my usual filter in place.

Cordelia's eyes widen, and little tears glisten against their blue depths.

"At first, I avoided a relationship with you, whether romantic or platonic, because it was questionable at best. I didn't want to abuse the power I had as your professor, and I didn't want to get in trouble."

She nods, giving me a look of understanding.

I continue, "But then I didn't care. I knew that if I wanted to, I was smart enough to not get caught."

"So what about now? Now that the semester is over and there's no rules to stop you?" she asks, cocking her head ever-so-slightly.

"I'm scared," I confess. "Not of trouble, but of love. Of you. I said it before, and I meant it, we live in different worlds, Cordelia. And the last time I tried this with someone was nearly ten years ago."

"Your ex girlfriend?"

"My *only* girlfriend. The only other person I've ever loved like this offered to do long distance and then cheated on me and broke my heart." I didn't realize I had been on the brink of crying until I feel a single tear fall down my cheek.

"But she's not me," she says, raising her voice.

"But that's all I've ever known. That's my only real lived experience with romance. After that, I put up a wall. I trained myself to live my life without needing a relationship to find satisfaction or success," I explain.

"What changed?"

You. "I built you a key."

"What?"

I shake my head. "Not a key, a door. I built you a door. Forget it. My mom had this brilliant metaphor, and I'm messing it all up. It doesn't matter—"

"I can't believe you got into the water, gown and all, only to stumble on your big speech. C'mon now," Cordelia cackles, the sound heavenly, and she wipes the tears from my face.

"I wanted you to know that I'm willing to meet you halfway—I'm willing to meet you all the way, if that's what it takes."

She kisses me, and it's nothing like our usual torrid ones. It's soft, her pouty lips so gentle as they graze mine.

"I don't know when or how I fell, but I did," I whisper. "You haunt my every thought and there isn't a single thing anyone can say or do now that would keep me from you." Our noses touch, her chest pressing against mine. "That is, unless you don't want this anymore."

She shakes her head. "Of course I still want you. I have loved you since before I met you."

epilogue

ALITHA

"What should we name it?" Cordelia asks, gesturing to where we lie.

When the dean's position became official, I used my savings to purchase us a houseboat off the southern shores of Magia Island. Cordelia will go back and forth between our house and her parents' home, while I'll still spend the majority of my time at my apartment. Vacations and breaks will be exclusively spent with Cordelia on the waters, which was something we agreed upon shortly after officially getting together.

"We just finished unloading the U-Haul, we're not even done unpacking, and you're worried about naming the thing? You do realize it doesn't sail?" I say with a laugh.

"I know, but it's cute. What about the S.S. Persephone?"

"Am I Hades?"

Cordelia shakes her head. "No, I'm Hades. Persephone had to split her time between her mother and the underworld. You're obviously Persephone."

"Obviously," I tease.

Her eyes go white for a moment before she snaps back to reality. "You're going to kiss me now."

One corner of my mouth ticks up at her vision. "Oh, am I?"

"Yes," she whispers against my lips. Cordelia grabs the sides of my head in her hands, and our mouths collide, the taste of her tongue sweet against mine.

"Remove," she demands, tugging on my top.

"As you wish," I say, and pull the shirt over my head.

She unhooks my bra and licks down my neck until she reaches my already hardened nipple.

I arch my back as she sucks and nips, her tentacles trailing up my body to remove my shorts.

I lay here, entirely naked on the deck of the home we now share together, and bask in the winter sun as Cordelia trails kisses up my body until we're face to face again. Desire ricochets through my entire body.

A tentacle slithers up my thigh, and she uses one of her suckers to latch onto my most sensitive spot, the suction driving me mad with pleasure. Another tentacle follows suit, snaking its way up until it presses against my entrance. Cordelia gets on top of me, holding herself up with her arms, pushing her tentacle deep inside.

"Your pretty little pussy is already dripping for me," she says as my body opens for her.

I moan, my body slick with sweat and the heat of my own pleasure. Cordelia's fair skin glistens in the sunlight, her cheeks flushed pink as she plows into me.

This is everything I could've ever wished for. I needed this kind of love. Obsessive and all consuming, I know this ray of moonlight would do anything for me, and I feel exactly the same way.

I want more of her. I want the only thing I can remember to be her name.

"More," I beg, my voice coming out hoarse.

She gently pushes in another tentacle. Suddenly, all I can feel is her. The suction on my clit, the tentacles pounding in and out of me. It's anything and everything all at once.

"Dr. Taylor, you take me so well," she purrs as my muscles begin to fidget and shake at her unrelenting pace.

Cordelia presses her mouth against mine as I come, my body practically convulsing with my release.

I look up into those ocean depths she calls eyes and smile, a wicked grin cresting its way across my features.

I want to do to her exactly what she does to me. Pushing Cordelia's shoulder, I force her onto her back.

"Be a good girl for me and spread those tentacles," I say, and she squeaks, the dominating kraken completely reversed.

Parting her already swollen flesh, I swirl my tongue around her folds before making my way to her clit. I lick and suck harder and harder as her moans increase.

Gently, I take her clit in my teeth and bite down ever-so-slightly. She squeals in pain and pleasure, her hips gyrating against the ground.

"Fill me. Please," she begs, breathless and panting as I slip a single digit inside.

Curling my finger into her, I continue lapping at her sweet sex, the feeling of her against me so hedonistic. Her body is much different from my own and anything I've ever experienced, but it's perfect. It's soft and frilly, strong and muscular. Her cunt is as lovely as her.

"More?" I ask as she squirms against my hand.

She nods, and I push another finger inside, slowly quickening my pace. I pump in and out, delighted by the sound. She's so wet for me.

Pushing in a third, she gasps.

"More. I want all of it," she begs. "Give me your entire hand."

My eyes widen with surprise. "Are you positive this is what you want?"

"Yes," she answers swiftly.

There's nothing I've wanted as much as I want her, desperate and completely undone.

I click my tongue. "You're so greedy, asking for more when you're already so close to coming for me."

She whimpers, the sound music to my ears.

"Be a good girl and beg."

"Please," she cries, her eyes watering. "Please, I can't. I need—"

Four of my fingers are inside as I feel her stretch around me, her body pulsing with need. I slowly fill her to my knuckles, and she whines, still wanting more.

She's dripping, her face depraved as I take the final push and fuck her with my fist. Her eyes seem to roll back into her head as she stretches and opens around me, my arm her puppeteer. Her tentacles curl more with every movement.

Cordelia's cunt contracts, and my hand continues working in and out. "That's it. That's my girl. Come for me, beautiful."

Her back arches, tentacles moving every which way as she screams out.

When Cordelia comes down from her high, her smile is laced with satisfaction.

"Just giving you a taste of your own medicine," I say as I kiss my girlfriend, relishing in the fact that she's mine.

Walking back into the bedroom, a sleeping Cordelia rests in our bed. We had one custom made with an extended bottom with a filtered tank. Cordelia's tentacles drape into the water, allowing her to be with me, while also sleeping comfortably.

She quietly snores, her hand tucked underneath her head, and I kiss her cheek before leaving for work.

Today is the first day I return to Augury as Dean Taylor. College classes start back up next week, but professors go back a week earlier so we can set everything up and host meetings and trainings.

Cordelia decided to spend her last semester at Aquatica Academy before moving here to the houseboat full time. She plans on opening a vet rescue for familiars who have been abandoned or are having magical issues. It'll be a safe haven, and something I know she'll be excellent at.

Walking from the parking lot and through the jungle to the Potions Tree, I climb up the ladder and head to my office. Archeron requested to keep the dean's office, transforming it into the president's office, and I obliged. I liked being in the Potions Tree. It's where I belong.

Coming up to my building, warmth floods my chest. Love and a partner are not necessary for my success, but I desire them. I desire her. The dean position isn't necessary for my happiness, but I managed to achieve it. Although it's cliché, I've realized I can do anything I put my mind to.

Crossing to my office, I raise my arms and push the new placard in place, satisfaction resonating within me.

It reads *Dean Alitha Taylor.*

Opening the door, I walk inside and place the picture frame I've been holding onto my desk. In it is a photograph of me and Cordelia at the pumpkin patch, her face lit up with laughter, and I smile.

That's my girl. Haunt me, baby.

Riding Centaur's Sleigh

one

FERN

I never thought I'd see the day that Santa Claus is played by a red-headed centaur, but as I look into the makeup artist's mirror, I realize it's here.

Dahlia's, a luxury hair salon in the heart of Sunspell City, is hosting a charity benefit for children with juvenile arthritis. I've been 'hired' on as Santa, with a plethora of my friends as my helpers. When Iris originally pitched the idea to me, I told her she was crazy, but one of my medicinal magic professors said it would be good to put on my resume before residency. Dahlia Torres, the salon owner, apparently has a cousin with juvenile arthritis, hence her involvement in the project. Dahlia is best friends with my friend Iris' older sister, who is also a professor at my university. It's a small world.

Once our costumes and makeup are in place, we make our way to the front of the salon, where a giant throne-like chair sits, adorned with holly and Christmas lights.

I have a seat, Iris and Chrysanthemum flanking me to my left and right, and I watch as Daffodil crosses to the door, holding it open for the families and children who walk in. As kids walk, clomp, and stomp in, they stand in front of me and take pictures.

"You're such a pretty elf!" a human boy shouts at Iris, who is now feigning the biggest smile I've ever seen.

Being an elfborn—a distant descendant of elves—her costume is probably problematic, but she's wearing it like a champ for these kids. Actually, elves have more power than most magical races, so maybe it's fine. I don't have time to think about the societal dynamics of magical beings as I am forced to listen to a little serpentine ask for a life-size monster truck for Christmas. The funniest part? He demanded it be a BMW.

I'm fake Santa, not a freakin' miracle worker.

I watch as Iris and Chrysanthemum talk to the kids, and I have to stifle a laugh at how absurd we all look. Iris is covered in tattoos, her face adorned with more piercings than I can count. Chrysanthemum has hot pink hair and a trans flag pin on her collar. Are we Froot Loops, or Santa and his crew? The world may never know.

Out of our friend group, Basil and Saga are the only ones not here. Basil went home to his parents, who live across the world on Alkebulan. Saga doesn't have an excuse, though I'd bet anything she's walking around our empty campus trying to *accidentally* bump into the girl she likes.

I don't like anyone these days. Chrysanthemum and I have had a few drunk make outs, but it's clear we're better as friends. Iris thought Basil was interested in me, yet he never made a move.

I don't want my friends, though. At least, not romantically. I want something fresh and exciting.

Last semester I was really into this guy named Oak, but he's long since graduated medic school. That'll be me soon. Not a paramedic, but a full on Doctor. Capital D and all.

If only I could get some capital D for myself. Or V. Honestly, I don't have a preference, I just want someone to hold my hand and kiss me under the mistletoe, y'know?

Sweat coats my gingery brows as I plaster on another smile for the next family. I look over to Dahlia, who is grinning ear-to-ear, but there's a level of anxiety in her features that I didn't expect from her. She, much like Iris and Daffodil, is usually confident and loud.

She crosses over to us and pulls Iris close, whispering something before returning to where she was previously standing.

"Mr. Claus, you might want to wipe your face with a towel or something," the white-haired elfling says after he takes another photo. I go to use my shirt sleeve when Chrysanthemum stops me, dabbing a tissue against my skin.

Where she conjured the tissue from, I have no idea.

Iris leans close to me. "Fern, we have a problem," she whispers in my ear.

"What is it?" I ask through gritted teeth.

She frowns. "The air conditioning is out. That's why it's getting so hot in here."

Although it's December, Magia Island is not exactly cold. On some days it's chilly, but it doesn't snow naturally here. It's a tropical island, not the

North Pole. Wearing a Santa outfit in these conditions is not ideal, especially when my legs are already covered by my coat.

I steel myself, mentally preparing for the next hour. I can do this. So what if it's a little hot? I've been through worse.

More families come inside, all making note of the warm interior, but still excited and ready to pay for pictures with Santa. People tell Dahlia how kind she is for putting on this event, and they compliment my helpers on their beauty. Overall, everyone seems to be enjoying themselves.

Everyone but me.

My head throbs, my heart galloping in my chest, and I am slicked with sweat. I probably smell disgusting, but thankfully, none of the children seem to notice.

"Why aren't you preparing for Christmas?" a little girl asks, her big purple eyes shining up at me.

Why would I be preparing for Christmas? Oh, shit. I'm Santa Claus. That's right. "I," I start to say, but my voice comes out strange. "I was—I went." My words are slurred as I struggle to respond.

"Mr. Claus, are you feeling alright?" Chrysanthemum asks. I try to respond, but the warmth of the costume is overwhelming me. It feels like I'm spinning in a cloud of heat.

Everything starts to go blurry as Iris shouts. "Fern!"

Opening my eyes, I wake up in heaven. I didn't believe in a god before now, but I'm grateful for whatever religion was correct as I stare up at the absolute angel hovering over me. His face is soft, his chestnut hair draping down in front of him in one long braid.

I want to—oh fuck. That's not an angel.

"Oak?" I ask, my eyes finally able to fully focus.

"Yeah, you remember me?" he asks. His voice is gentle and sweet, like he's afraid if he's too loud, it'll hurt me.

Of course I remember you, I think to myself. I have had a total of maybe four interactions with Oak, but each one was more unforgettable than the last. The first time we met was in undergrad. We were freshmen, and he had turned to me to ask if he could borrow a pencil. I told myself I'd never seen someone with such big, beautiful eyes.

We continued randomly seeing each other on campus but nothing substantial. That was, until medical school. I never really left Augury University, but Oak did. I'm not sure what he did for work during that time, but when he came back, he was different. Testosterone had deepened his voice, and his eyebrows were thicker. He was still thin, but there was clearly a bit more muscle under his uniform than he had before.

And I still could not stop staring into those oxblood-colored eyes. They were hypnotizing, convincing me I needed to be near him.

The paramedic program requested other medical students volunteer to be patients in their scenarios to allow the future medics to experience the 'real deal', or close to it. I volunteered, and without fail, they always paired me with Oak. I didn't complain.

Actually, I think that's why I kept volunteering. I wanted any excuse to get closer to him, even if I fumbled the ball every time. Not once did I ask for his number, or offer him mine.

I'm an idiot.

And now here we are. And I'm his patient. Except this time, it truly is real.

"How long have I been out?" I ask as I look down at my abdomen to see only a white undershirt. "And where are my clothes?"

"Your friend, Iris, said she couldn't get the Santa suit off of you, so I cut it off myself. As for how long you were out, maybe six minutes? We were only down the road," he says as he adjusts the blood pressure cuff.

"Is Iris okay? What about the other girls? And the kids?" I ask, worry filling my chest. If it was hot enough for me to pass out, surely it was hot enough for someone else to fall ill.

"Everyone else is fine, I promise," Oak says. "Besides, if they weren't, I wouldn't tell you anyway." He winks, and I swear I see stars in his eyes for a moment.

I sit up, my four legs folding underneath me as I look at this beautiful elfling. He's all long limbs and lean features, and I could eat him up. Glancing around the room, it seems everyone has been sent out of the building, and guilt pangs in my chest at the thought that I may have ruined this event.

"Do you know what your name is?" he asks, going through the steps he should to confirm I'm okay.

"Fern Hallowhoof," I answer.

"What month is it?"

"December," I say, my eyes still scanning the room, avoiding his.

"I need to do a 12-lead. I'm going to have to have you lift up your shirt," he says, and our eyes finally lock.

I blow a silent kiss in my mind to Saga and Basil. Although they're not here today, it's thanks to them I've gotten this muscular. They both play rugby, and they made me join their morning workouts in preparation for their next season. At first I moaned and groaned, but now I couldn't be more grateful.

I look damn good.

Oak gets onto his knees, a sight I'd only ever dreamed about, and starts applying the electrodes to my chest and core. The coldness of his gloves touches my stomach as he sticks them on and runs his next test.

"Seeing how much I'm still sweating, I don't think it's heat stroke," I say, and one corner of his mouth ticks up.

"No, I think it's just heat exhaustion, but you were pretty dang close." Oak's eyes linger on the muscular panes of my abdomen for a beat too long, and I flush.

"No need to blush; I see shirtless men every day on the job," Oak says boldly as he unhooks me from the EKG machine. "Though none as pretty as you," he whispers.

If I was blushing pink before, I'm fully crimson now.

The other medic, which I had honestly forgotten about until this very moment, is a blonde satyr with thick muscular arms. She leans against one of the walls of the salon, holding a small cooler.

She hands Oak the blue box, and he gets out a cold towel, wrapping it around the back of my neck. Crossing over towards us, she gets out a water bottle and forces it to my lips.

"You should drink something," she says, her voice stern.

She's definitely my type. I love mean women. I also love himbo men, and witchy non-binary folks, but I barely glance her direction as I stare at the wall, trying not to act weird around Oak.

"Hey, look at me," he says, and I follow his calm instructions. "Do you want to go the hospital?"

I shake my head. "No, I'm okay."

"Are you sure?"

"Really. I'm good," I say. Because I am. I just need a few hours in some nice cool air conditioning, and I'll be fine. Physically, at least. Emotionally, that's another story. The embarrassment of today mixed with my general loneliness stirs in my belly, making me nauseous. I crave affection and physical contact, more than I've been wanting to admit.

Oak runs a few more tests in silence before he and his partner pack up, my last chance at starting something with him fading before my very eyes.

I'm unsure if it's the exhaustion, or the fear of rejection after this many years of pining, but I just can't bring myself to say anything more than a polite goodbye.

The ambulance takes off, and my friends, alongside the owner, return to this section of the building and crowd around me.

"I'm so sorry," I tell Dahlia, whose brows furrow at me.

"Sorry? Sorry for what? Honey, I'm sorry my air conditioning broke. I feel terrible," she says, her loud voice echoing through the room. "Let me know if I can do anything to compensate you."

Iris and Daffodil move closer while waggling their eyebrows at me.

"That blonde paramedic girl was cute," Iris says boldly.

"Really? I thought the other one looked more like his type," Daffodil says. "Although, he kinda stared at Fern like a deer in headlights when he first showed up. Almost like he didn't know what to do."

"He was just surprised to see me," I say, defending Oak.

"Do you two know each other?" Iris asks, and Daffodil's eyebrows shoot up.

Chrysanthemum crosses her arms. "Where have you two been? That's the guy he had a crush on last year."

"I knew I recognized him." Daffodil grins at me, and although all three of these women are shorter than me in stature, sitting here like this, I feel small.

"Well, it's too late now. I didn't even ask for his number."

Iris looks as if she's about to growl. "For a medical student, you're such a dumb ass sometimes."

I sigh. "Yeah, yeah. Now help me up."

two

OAK

College was hard for me. I figured out *who* I was, but not *what* I wanted to do. After spending some time in boring office jobs, I realized I wanted to help people.

The moment it clicked for me was actually when my coworker, Heather, went into anaphylactic shock. I had never seen someone look so scared in my life. I sprang into action, stabbing her with the epinephrine injector we kept in our emergency first aid kit. It literally saved her life, as well as mine.

The rush I felt giving her the medicine mixed with the pride I had knowing I helped someone combined and transformed into sheer determination. That night when I went home, I applied to Augury's paramedic program, and the rest is history.

Fern has a weird part in my story. In undergrad, Fern was just a nice guy. Snarky, funny, and cute, I'd bump into him on occasion, or we'd have a class together. Nothing crazy. But when I returned for paramedic school, he helped me more than he'll ever know.

Somehow, Fern was my patient for almost every scenario. The entire time, he'd quietly root for me, whispering to tell me how good of a job I was doing, or giving me hints with his body language of what I needed to do next. He made me feel like I could do this job. It was that extra push—that little bit of support from a near-stranger, that helped me ace my scenarios and exams.

When medic school ended, I regretted not reaching out to him to say thank you. I had the speech planned in my head. *Hey, Fern. I just wanted to thank you for being my partner for all those scenarios. Could I take you out to dinner sometime? Y'know, to say thanks.* I had repeated it again and again, but on the last day I saw him, I froze.

I'm great on the job and at school—scenarios where there's a script I can stick to, or specific goals in mind, but small talk is my kryptonite.

I am just shy, I guess. A product of two very introverted parents, one elf and one human. That's me.

It's not like I hate talking to people, it can be quite fun. But it's also exhausting.

And now, as Lily drives us away, I am filled with a deep sense of regret. It's two-fold. My first regret is not taking Fern to the hospital. Although he's almost a doctor, it would've been good to get him checked out by one, and it would have granted me a bit more time with him. My second regret is not asking for his number.

I stare at my computer screen, realizing I can just pull it up. It would be ethically wrong to do so, I remind myself.

But! What if I was doing it to check on him? I'm just a diligent paramedic, trying to confirm my patient got home safe. If caught, my sergeant would say that's utter bullshit and I'd most definitely get a write-up, but wouldn't it be worth it?

While Lily's eyes remain fixated on the road, I quickly pull up his address and type it into my notes app. I'll just drive by after work and confirm his car is there. Centaurs have specialized vehicles, so it'll be obvious if he drove versus a friend.

Continuing my shift after seeing Fern had been difficult at best. Now, our truck is completely restocked, and I watch as Lily waves goodbye before plopping Fern's address into my GPS.

He lives in the middle of the Illusionary Jungle. *How?*

Logic hits me like a train as I recall Fern is still in medical school and likely lives on campus in the dorms. *Shit.* I just hope he doesn't have roommates.

The drive through the jungle is a peaceful one, though my nerves ruin the luscious view. Kapoks follow tall camphor trees as my car winds through the greenery until we reach the trees which contain the medical dorms. It doesn't look like December, but the chilly breeze fills my lungs as I force myself to breathe in deep. I love driving with my windows down.

What will I even say to him? *Hey, I'm here to see if you're still breathing and also because I think about you all the time.* Yeah, that's gonna go over well.

Walking up to the dorm, which really just looks like a giant treehouse, I timidly knock on the door.

Seconds feel like hours as my heart lurches in my throat, waiting for someone to open up. I really hope it's him.

The door swings open to reveal Fern in a tight-fitting white t-shirt, and my eyes fixate on his hardened nipples peeking through the fabric.

"Oak Eildre. The heck are you doing here?"

I flinch. *Oh no.* Maybe this was a horrible idea, and he's going to tell my job I stalked him and everything's going to go to shit.

I shrug. "I—"

"Well, come in. It's a bit cold out there," he interrupts, gesturing me inside.

His dorm is nice, decorated somewhat simply. There's a bulletin board with pictures of him and his friends, a trophy shaped like a horseshoe, and an old stethoscope. There are also ferns. Everywhere.

One corner of Fern's mouth ticks up, and he gestures for me to sit on the couch. I oblige.

"I wasn't expecting to see you again," he says.

"I wasn't either," I admit. "But—please don't be upset. If this makes you uncomfortable, I promise I'll leave and never bother you again, just please don't tell my job. I wanted to check on you and make sure you got home okay."

Fern's smile widens, his face flushing a vibrant peach, the color beautiful against the constellation of freckles that sparkle across his cheeks and nose.

I want to count every one with my fingertips before I kiss every inch of his body. Blinking, I center myself back in the moment.

"That's very kind of you, but you didn't have to do that."

"I wanted to," I blurt out. "I've meant to say and do a lot of things to you —" I stop myself, realizing that sounds much more sexual than I intended. "I meant...."

"No, I get it. Every time I see you, I think about asking for your number, but chicken out. I know this isn't the most romantic situation," he says, gesturing to the newest rendition of The Grinch playing on his TV. "But I'd love to take you out sometime. What do you say?"

I wasn't sure what I was expecting. I mean, of course I was hoping that he felt the same as I, but I wasn't sure. Warmth fills me, my heart thumping at a quick pace. "I'd like that."

He gets out his phone and hands it to me, and I type in my number, texting myself a fern emoji.

We both stand, and he trots towards the door, the tan browns of his coat contrasting beautifully with the paleness of his skin. He looks otherworldly, and I want to kiss him. We're standing far too close, his chest nearly touching mine. *Fuck it.*

"I'm going to kiss you," I say and lean into him.

Our lips collide, and it feels like the weight of the world was just taken off my shoulders. His scent is intoxicating, all woodsy pines, and his fingers grip the sides of my jaw as he deepens the kiss.

Fern releases me, his lips still grazing mine. "Are you off tomorrow?" he asks, voice low and full of unsaid thoughts.

"I am," I whisper and kiss him again, this time softer.

"Then I'm taking you out tomorrow," he says and turns. "See you later, Oak."

Fuck. Fuck. Fuck. Fuck. Fuck. Fuck. Fuck.

three

OAK

Beep. Beep.

Fern honks to let me know he's here, and butterflies fill my stomach as I make my way to the door. My outfit is simple—a thin, red sweater and loose black trousers. I tuck the sweater into my pants and belt before exiting my apartment.

As I open the pearly white car door, Fern greets me with a handsome smile, the green fabric of his shirt clinging to his muscled chest and biceps. He looks positively delectable. I stretch out my long legs in his spacious SUV. Centaur cars are super comfy, and I'm excited to be here with him.

Even though dates, and hanging out in general, makes me immensely nervous, I really do want to get to know him better. He's occupied a small percentage of my brain these last few years, lingering in the background, and it's time I push him to the front.

"Where are we going?" I ask, my coming out voice softer than I intended.

"You'll see. A place you've probably never been to before."

We drive for a few minutes before he parks outside an old arcade, which has kitschy Christmas decor stuck on the windows and a blowup reindeer out front. It's cute. Almost as cute as Fern.

"Have you ever been here?" he asks, scratching the back of his neck.

"I have not," I confirm.

A grin lines his features. "Good."

Fern takes my hand and leads me into the building, where we greet the woman at the front desk before getting out our phones. Each game takes one fourth of a dabloon, and we take turns paying for different rounds.

There's a giant metallic floor with light-up arrows on the ground next to a sign that says Dance Dance Revolution: 6000.

"This is my favorite game," Fern practically shouts, excitement sparkling in his eyes. He yanks on our already linked hands, pulling me onto the dance floor.

I pick a song I'm somewhat familiar with, and the arrows come onto the screen, telling us where to step.

"Hey, this isn't fair," I say, already breaking a sweat. "You have four legs. That's cheating."

"Don't even." In my peripheral vision, I watch as Fern turns his head to look at me. "You're much more limber and flexible than I am."

He didn't mean it in a dirty way, but my mind immediately tosses itself into the gutters. I'd like to show him exactly how limber and flexible I can be.

When he looks back on the screen, he must realize he missed a few arrows, because Fern starts cursing and trying to move his legs faster, his tail rapidly swishing through the air.

The game ends, and a scoreboard comes onto the screen, telling us our points for different categories. *Perfect. Great. Good. Boo. Miss.*

It's clear I've won, and I can't stop the shit-eating grin that possesses my features as I turn to look at Fern. I expect him to scowl or frown, but he's smiling back at me, his eyes scanning my body.

"Oh, it's on. Time for me to reclaim victory," he says and gestures towards the skee-ball machine.

I have never in my life played skee-ball, but I guess there's a first time for everything.

Fern throws the first ball, landing it in the fifty hole with grace. I try for the same hole, but my ball flies its way into the larger ten hole. Whoops.

"Well, you're no pro," Fern teases.

"And you are?" I say, quirking a brow.

"I really want to crack a corny joke about never missing a hole, but the pathetic look on your face tells me I should be gentle," he jests, and I cross my arms.

"What if I like it rough?"

It continues like this, Fern landing one hundreds and fifties, while the highest I score is thirty. Our banter continues as well, him managing to bully me while making me laugh the entire time. He makes me feel warm inside.

Strong arms come up from behind and wrap around me, Fern nuzzling into the crook of my neck. "Here, let me show you."

He takes my arms, holding onto them as he guides me to throw the ball, and we land perfectly in the fifty hole. "You were throwing too hard," he explains.

I breathe in his scent, relishing in his warmth and closeness as he kisses down my neck before releasing me.

Turning, I bite my lip and look down at his. "Thank you."

He kisses me slowly, and I yelp when a hand squeezes my ass through my pants.

"Let's go get some snacks before we go," he says, and we head for the ticket counter.

Fern counts our tickets and puts them together, preparing to exchange them for a sweet treat. The clerk takes the tickets and grabs the bag of peppermint bark he pointed to, and we take it as we head out of the arcade.

"Where to now?"

"Hmm." Fern scratches his chin. "You've seen my place, but I've never seen yours. Wanna go watch a movie and enjoy our treat?"

"Let's do it," I say. Thank fuck I had the foresight to clean my apartment just in case.

Fern drives us back to my apartment, and I stick my head out the window, looking at all the Christmas lights that already adorn everyone's homes.

When we get inside, my familiar, Edgar, greets us, flicking his tongue. He's laying on a branch in his vivarium, his fluffy leopard print fur tousled every which was as he slithers towards the glass.

"Hi buddy," I say and pull a frozen rat out of the freezer.

"Your familiar eats other peoples' familiars for dinner?" Fern asks, his eyes lined with fear.

"Not exactly," I say and shrug, turning to the kitchen sink to wash my hands. "But also, it's the circle of life."

"That it is."

I cross back into the living room and slide onto the couch and turn on the TV, flipping through channels while Fern's fingers linger on my bookshelves.

"Do you read a lot?" he asks. "Or have any other hobbies?"

"A decent amount. I like to read, play video games, and practice magic when I'm not at work. You?"

He shrugs. "This is going to sound stupid, but I mostly do what my friends do. I spend so much time studying, I feel like I can't even think about what hobbies I'd enjoy, so I just join them with whatever when I can."

"And what do they do?" I ask and pat the seat next to me.

"Iris likes to read and draw—oh! And she loves tattoos. Her boyfriend is a botanist, and we talk a lot about plants. Chrysanthemum and Daffodil are into roller skating and magic, and Basil and Saga are rugby players. I hangout with those two and Iris the most, so I've been working out a lot lately," he says, gushing about his friends. His hand is resting on my upper thigh, and it sends shivers down my spin.

I don't have many friends, as I mostly keep to myself, and a pang of jealousy hits me.

"Oooh! I should introduce you to one of Daffodil's partners. His name is Moss. Human dude, but super cool. He loves museums and nerdy shit. You guys would be swift friends. He's also trans, so maybe you two can relate in that way, too," Fern shares as if he could read my mind. His fingers make small circles on my legs, and although it's through the fabric of my pants, he might as well be touching my bare skin.

"He sounds great," I say. I hope he introduces me to Moss and all his friends. I'd love to find people I can hang out with whenever I have the energy to socialize.

"What are your friends like?"

I shrug, unsure of how to respond, before deciding self deprecating humor is for the best. "You met my only friend."

"The other paramedic?" he asks, red brows furrowing.

"No," I laugh. "Edgar!"

"Be serious. Do you actually not have friends?" Fern asks, concern sprinkled on his face.

I put my hands in my face and sigh before speaking again. *This might be the most embarrassing conversation I've ever participated in.* "Nope. I'm just a loser, baby. A hopelessly lonely person."

"I'm a hopeless romantic, so maybe the universe threw us together for a reason," he whispers, leaning close. "I can make you forget you ever felt lonely."

Grabbing me by my jaw, Fern kisses me with fervor, our lips pressing together. His words taste like candy as our tongues entangle with one another's.

Fern tugs at my sweater, pulling it off over my head before doing the same to his shirt. His abs might as well have been sculpted by gods, and I watch while he kisses down my chest, past my faint scars, and makes his way down to my stomach.

Where Fern is chiseled and strong, I am long and lean, and he takes his time as he strips off my belt and unbuttons my trousers. He continues to lick and nip at my inner thighs, and he grabs me by my hips, hoisting my legs over his shoulders.

Fern devours me like a man starved. He sucks on my most sensitive spot, stopping to let his tongue circle my cunt, and I whimper.

And he was right. There isn't a drop of loneliness in my soul as I let the warmth of his mouth envelop me.

My hips buck, the back of my shoulders pressing into the sofa as he eats me out until my muscles convulse and I'm bleary-eyed, my moans coming out louder than I expected. As I come down from climaxing, he slaps my cunt as he gently places me back onto the couch.

I flip over onto my stomach, already anticipating where this is going, and I look back to see Fern smirking down at me.

He gets behind me from where I'm bent over on the couch and pulls me back into him, his hand covering the front of my throat. I can feel his hard cock pressing against my backside, threatening to release.

"Can I ask a question?"

"You just did," he whispers, gliding his tongue along my ear.

"How big is it?"

Fern stifles a laugh, shifting his body down to where his front legs enclose my arms. I can feel his hard cock pressing against my backside, threatening to release. "Not at all what I expected you to ask, but alright. Around ten or so inches."

Holy *fuck.* I asked, not because I care about stuff like that, but because I wasn't sure if I *can* take it. And now I'm even less positive. I do the math in my head, figuring if I'm deeper than the average person with a vulva, he can come close to fully entering, but probably not all the way.

"I take contraceptives," I say, my voice practically squealing with anticipation and fear.

"Good, because I want to fill you until you're dripping with my seed." Fern's tone is husky. He pushes me onto the sofa, his body hovering above mine as his cock presses at my entrance.

Stretching me, he slowly fills me until I think I can't take any more.

"Yeah, just like that, sweetheart," he says.

I arch my back, and he pushes further inside me. I have to stifle a scream for fear I'll wake my neighbors.

"Take my cock like a good boy," he whispers, his voice low and full of heat.

His thrusts are slow and languid, his cock teasing me as I take nearly all of him. He's gentle, my cunt dripping as my body adjusts to his size.

"You don't have to be so gentle," I say. "I can take it."

And as if he were waiting for permission, Fern plows into me. His cock thrusts in and out, harder and faster than before.

"Fern," I moan aloud, praying my walls aren't as thin as I thought. All I can smell are his hormones, and all I can feel is his cock as he drills into me, his movements more and more rapid.

This is exactly what I needed. To be filled to the point where all I can remember is his name and the feel of his cock inside me. No loneliness, no critical patients, just me and another man.

We come at the same time, him panting as I feel his fluids bursting inside me. For a second I worry he'll collapse on top of me, crushing me instantly, but he gets down off the couch and pulls me into an embrace.

"I'd like to do this again sometime," I say, my cheeks flushing pink as I feel liquid drip out of me and down my thighs.

"I'd like to do you again sometime," Fern says and laughs. "Okay, not just the sex. Like—do—I'd like to take you out again." He stumbles on his words, and I think it's the first time I've actually heard him sound… nervous.

"What're you doing Christmas Eve?"

four

FERN

My eyes open just as the sweet scent of baked goods touches my nostrils. I know I made a pact with Saga and Basil to eat a fuck-ton of protein, but surely Christmas is an exception, right?

Oak's dad is a fancy pants baker, which must be why my kitchen smells like heaven. We opted to spend Christmas in the dorms, since almost no one would be here. That, and the walls aren't as thin.

Ring. Ring.

I pick my phone off my nightstand and lift it up, my eyes burning at the brightness level, but I click accept anyway.

A cacophony of greetings come as my friends' faces flood my screen before they realize they should probably talk one at a time.

"Merry Christmas, everyone," Saga says, her background making it clear that she's also still in bed.

Basil is in a room full of colorful decorations, but he waves his hand. "Happy belated Winter Solstice. I'm still with my parents, so I'm going to spend the day with them. Love you all."

He signs off, and Chrysanthemum blows a kiss at all of us, her pink hair tied up in a neat bow that wraps around her nubby horns.

"So, what are you all doing?" I ask.

Daffodil and Iris, who are usually the loudest, are awfully quiet and still. Daffodil shifts her phone down to two different arms that lay across her body.

I'm happy for her.

"I'm guessing Dr. Ali is still asleep," I say as pretentiously as possible while staring into Iris' purple eyes.

"No, I am not. Our familiars are still resting, and my farfora is being mindful of that," a deep voice comes from Iris' line.

"How cute," Chrysanthemum says, feigning adoration. "Okay, I'm sick of these lovebirds. Fern, Saga, what're you two up to?"

"Nothing," Saga says, her golden eyes squinting as she gives me a look. "Fern, you look way too fucking smug. Spit it out."

"Oak is here."

"Fuck yeah!" Iris squeals loudly, much to her boyfriends' dismay.

"Fern, would you come out here? I have a surprise for you," Oak's voice comes from the other side of the door.

"Speaking of, I've gotta go," I say and wink at the camera.

I'm almost jealous I don't get to hear what everyone says next. *Almost.*

Opening the door, I cross into the living room, but Oak is nowhere to be found.

"Oak?"

"Close your eyes," his voice sounds from behind me. "And get on your knees."

"My knees?" I ask, my tone teasing.

"Was I not clear?"

I kneel on the ground, as close to what I think he means, and I can hear crinkling sounds as Oak's warm body shifts closer to mine.

"You can open those emerald eyes of yours, sir."

And I do. Standing before me is Oak, wearing nothing but a small slip of wrapping paper on his lower half and a big red bow on top.

I bite my bottom lip, hugging his hips with my hands as I stare up at him. He's beautiful, probably the most gorgeous man I've ever seen, and he's all mine.

"Unwrap me, and do whatever you'd like," he whispers.

Merry fucking Christmas to me.

Orc's Midnight Kiss

orc's midnight kiss

RAEMOND

YOU CAN ONLY SCROLL ON KINK MEET-UP APPS WHILE YOU WAIT IN LINE FOR A WHALE watching tour so many times before even the captain and crew start to notice how lonely you look.

I'm a good fucking cambion. I'm also a good fuck, and I've got the illusionary magic skills to be able to change my form before someone's eyes. But love? That's a whole other issue.

Ring. Ring.

And there's Iris.

My two best friends—Erin and Iris—are trying to set me up, but it's no use. They both live on different islands than me. And besides, if I ever did find love, it's not like I could get married and throw an elaborate wedding.

Those bitches would fight so hard over maid of honor, I'd end up with no friends at all. Not to mention—I hate parties.

I sign up to go out, gaslight myself into thinking it's going to be fun and that I *need to socialize*, only to wind up hating whatever I'm wearing and feeling wildly overstimulated. I press to answer the call.

"Hey cutie patootie, what's up?" I say, forcing cheer into my tone.

I'm exhausted, but Iris is dealing with a whole heap of things over at Augury, so I'm trying not to worry her.

"Oh, you know. Creating potions and chaos. The usual," she says. "How was Christmas and Yule season? I'm sorry I didn't visit. Adeib doesn't really celebrate, and he wanted to take me sightseeing instead of visiting my family."

"It's okay. I was a little surprised Indigo didn't visit either, but I was really busy with the farm." My plant nursery, and specifically the Christmas Tree farm, really popped off this season. "We did a deal with a local welder that makes custom menorahs, and so many businesses and families took us up on the offer."

"That's amazing, dude. I'm so happy for you."

"So why did you call? If not to yap about work and Adeib," I say, and shift my phone to my other ear.

"I want you to come to Augury's New Year's Bash."

"That's in two days."

"Yep."

"I'd rather jump, thanks," I say.

I can feel Iris' glare through the phone. "Adeib is going to be super late. He has to meet with some guy about some business involving his twin sister. Apparently, some spacecraft from another planet is leaving soon, and he wants to contact her. It's a lot, but I'll be lonely until like... eleven."

I let out an audible sigh.

"Once Adeib shows up, I can cut you loose and you can go back to our apartment to crash, or you could find someone to kiss at midnight."

"Fine," I say. "But you're taking me to go pick out an outfit."

"Really? Yay!"

Welp. So much for avoiding parties.

One ferry ride, two shopping sprees, and a very busy day later, Iris and I waltz into Augury University's library.

Iris' gown is long and tight, with black fabric and silver sequins creating stripes down the skirt. I opted for a black romper to show off my legs. The sleeves are long, and the cut low. It's cute, but *very* sparkly. I was halfway afraid we looked like disco balls until we pulled up and everyone else was in silver and gold sequins.

Phew.

"I wonder why exactly we celebrate the New Year on this date," I ask as we take a seat at a small table.

Iris takes in a deep breath. "Well, it's partially because of the Roman god—"

"Hold on, since when do you know about Roman gods?" I ask.

"Since Alitha got a girlfriend who is obsessed with mythology. She talks about it every time she comes into the lab. It's so obnoxious."

"As opposed to you... who just talks... twenty-four seven regardless of the subject or topic and your knowledge base of it?"

She crosses her arms and shrugs. "Okay, point taken. But you love me."

"I must, but you're still insufferable."

A few hours and nearly a dozen mocktails later, Adeib arrives with flowers in tow.

The serpentine is dressed to impress in a fitted purple suit jacket, a purple iris in his hand to match.

"Good evening Raemond, good evening farfora," he says and kisses the top of Iris' head.

"And that's my cue to leave," I say, saluting them both.

Iris grabs my hand, holding me in place. "You should mingle."

"I would quite literally rather go to the dentist."

"That's a lie," she says, calling my bluff. "I'll call right—"

"Nope. No, I'll go mingle for a few minutes."

"Dentist offices are typically closed on New Years Eve," Adeib interrupts, and a wide grin spreads across my face.

"See? I'd rather go there."

Iris shoos me away, forcing me into a crowd of professors and other university employees. I take one of the tall, winding staircases up to a section with a balcony, and find a corner with standing space there.

Backing into a wall, I feel the rise and fall of someone's chest before I realize it's no wall, but a body. A very large, incredibly masculine body.

"Careful, I might start thinking you ran into me on purpose."

I squint. "That would imply I've run into you before, which I have not."

The orcling—actually, I think he might be just an orc—runs his hands over his face. "Apologies, I'm really bad at pick-up lines. You're very pretty, could we engage in polite but flirty conversation?"

"Proceed," I say with a giggle. "Also, I feel like it would maybe be helpful to address this..."

"Sure," he says.

"I'm genderfluid and polyamorous." "I'm an orc."

We look at one another, our brains catching up after having spoken at the same time.

"You go first."

"I was just going to say, I don't really care what pronouns you use for me, but I'm not a girl... and I'm definitely not a lady," I say with a wink.

"Got it. I am also not a lady, but I'd like to think I'm a gentleman," he says and winks in return. "I'm an orc. I know it's much more common to meet orclings, but I'm fully orc. Seven feet tall and all." He gestures to himself, and I use this as an excuse to get a better look at him.

This dude is... he's fucking hot. Wide, muscular shoulders. His hair is tied back in a low bun, and his biceps are practically rippling through his white, thin long sleeve shirt.

I thank my parents for my pinky red skin enabling me to blush without much notice by non-cambions. "Is that really... confounding? I mean, I don't like to make assumptions, but I was almost certain you're an orc."

"You'd be surprised. When it comes to orcs and serpentine—we get a lot more questions in this region. There's more orcs in Europa, and more serpentine in Arabia."

"Ah. Well, people are nosy as Hel about cambion, too," I say.

"Fair enough. Do you work for the university? I've never seen you before, but I don't get around much."

I shake my head. "Negative. I own a plant nursery on Octopus Island that I inherited from my Aunt Roxana. Christmas and Yule is our big season, so I'm *exhausted.*"

"Oooh. You like plants, did you study botanical magic?"

"Hel no. No. That's Adeib's thing. I'm actually an illusionary mage, I just really like regular plants. Most of my customers are human," I explain.

"Adeib Ali?"

Oops. Not really sure what's public knowledge or not, but there's no point in lying now. "Yes. He's my best friend's... boyfriend."

"Oh, so you're Iris Waton's friend?"

"Yes. Sorry, I realize I never introduced myself. I'm Raemond," I say, and reach out a hand.

"Chak Rokosmith. I'm the head librarian," he says, and shakes my hand with the largest hand I've ever seen.

He's beautiful. And he's probably smart. Oh fuck, I'm swooning.

"Head librarian, you say? Show me some good books."

He takes me by the hand and starts leading me through the crowd. "Pick a topic."

"Whales."

"Okay, do you want basic information on whales, or more interesting facts?"

"Interesting facts," I say and smile.

"How about... did you know humpback whales have patterns on their flukes that are as unique—"

"As human fingerprints," I answer, interrupting him. I think I might've just found my husband. Fuck Iris and Erin—we can elope.

"Okay, so it sounds like you need an *advanced* book on whales," he says, and pulls one off the shelf, handing it to me. "How does this one sound?"

"You can kiss me, if you want." The words tumble out of my mouth before I can second guess myself. Ultimately, at my core, I want to *feel* wanted. And boy do I want him.

Chak looks down at his watch. "It's eleven fifty-eight."

"Yeah, well." I shrug. "I said if you want."

"I'd like that."

I'm pulling him down to me by his tie before he can say another word, our mouths colliding. My skin feels hot, my heart racing as this orc's body melts into mine, his muscled frame hard against the softness of my curves.

He's so much taller than me, but our bodies somehow fit like puzzle pieces, clicking into place perfectly.

His tongue makes its way to mine, performing a song and dance, and I barely realize as the clock strikes twelve, the crowd erupting into cheers and laughter.

As much fun as I'm having, I'm emotionally torn. Chak and I will likely go back to his place and hook up, and my friends will tell me how proud they are of me, but I'm tired. Sex is wonderful, but the world can feel so lonely sometimes. I spent the holidays... alone. And for some people that's how they prefer it, and I'm happy for them, but that's not how I feel.

I want a boyfriend. Or a girlfriend or two. But being alone simply isn't for me, anymore, and neither is casual sex. I guess. I don't know, he's so hot he might just be the exception to my new rule.

"Do you want to get out of here?" I say, our noses still touching.

He lets go of my hair and stands at full-height. "No, I. Um."

Oof. With that kiss, I kind of assumed rejection wasn't in the cards. What an error.

"I'm sorry," I say. "Presumptuous of me."

He scratches the back of his neck. "No, I'm sorry. I'm quite shy, so it's hard to address you directly about this when you seem so chill and open."

"Oh?"

"You're quite attractive, but I'm demi. I don't really do hook-ups," he explains.

He's demisexual? Holy fuck. Did the universe send the potential partner of my dreams as a New Year's gift? I'm going to buy Iris some cute earrings or something tomorrow to say thank you for forcing me to come here tonight.

"I totally understand," I say, giving him a small smile.

"But I'd like to take you out sometime. If you're interested."

"I don't live here."

He smiles. "Yes, you said earlier you live on Octopus Island?"

"Yeah."

"When do you leave?"

"In two days," I answer.

Chak takes my hand and intertwines our fingers. "How about tomorrow, then?"

My grin spreads ear-to-ear, and I swear my heart grows in size. "I would love that."

He and I walk towards the ground floor, still holding hands, and Iris and Adeib are waiting at the bottom of the staircase for me. She sucks her lips into her mouth, suppressing her shit-eating grin.

"Mr. Rokosmith, it is a pleasure to see you," Adeib says.

"You as well, Dr. Ali," Chak replies.

Iris finally allows herself to smile. "Happy New Year, everyone."

Happy New Year, indeed.

Setting Up Love

I Am Not a Robot - MARINA
What Is This Feeling? - Wicked
Dirty Thoughts - Chloe Adams
Linger - The Cranberries
Valentine - Snail Mail
The Masochism Tango - Tom Lehrer
Good Luck, Babe! - Chappell Roan
That You Are - Hozier, Bedouine
What's It Gonna Take To Break Your Heart? - FINNEAS
Can't Explain This Love - Allen Stone

Setting Up Love

ROSE SANTORIELLO

prologue

WREN

Augury University can best be described as an ethereal, dream-like jungle of wonder. I have seen photographs, videos, and even 3D models, but nothing comes close to the real thing. It's breathtaking, really, the way the pod-like classrooms and offices are built into the branches of trees and how the jungle path snakes its way around campus, leading you in a multitude of directions.

Growing up, I always knew I was destined for this place. World-famous for its magical degrees, Augury was meant to be my home. And now, I find myself here on my first day of college, wandering about the courtyard, smiling like a fool. Utilizing my map, I make my way towards the History Tree, where History of Mages 101 is being held. I'm almost positive I won't be learning anything in this course, but it doesn't seem to matter. Excitement bubbles in my chest at the prospect of meeting my classmates and, more importantly, my future colleagues.

There are ladders and a lift system that lead up to the classroom pod, but I unfurl my wings and fly my way up into the doorway. I know every magical race has its perks, but I pity those without wings. They are my favorite part of my body.

Walking into the room, I quickly make note of my professor. She's petite and young, likely in her early twenties. Other than her white hair, which shimmers an iridescent purple, she's almost human. *Almost.* There's something quite magical about the way she scribes her name onto the whiteboard. Her handwriting is neat and feminine, but her fingers shake ever-so-slightly as she finishes.

Professor Watson.

I take a seat in the front row and pull out my notebook as other students pile in, when a very *familiar* familiar walks in with large black wings and a massive set of antlers, followed by a short, curvy satyr. Shock takes over my system as Zinnia Featherfields, my oldest crush and greatest nightmare, walks into the room.

"La—"

"Wren. I go by Wren, now," I say, cutting her off.

"My bad. It's a cool new name," Zinnia says as she takes the seat next to mine. "*Wren* Elric. It's been a while."

I'm surprised she'd say hi to me at all, let alone give me a compliment. There must be some ulterior motive at play. "Thank you. It just felt more genderless."

"That makes sense," she says and pulls out a notebook and pen.

"When did we see each other last... National Charmers?" I ask. I already know the answer. It was March 7th, but I am trying to be a good sport.

"I think so."

Though she is currently acting fairly polite, Zinnia Featherfields is my sworn enemy. We attended rival high schools and spent practically all of primary education competing against one another in local academic events. Even though I know she's smart enough to get into Augury, to say I'm surprised to see her today would be an understatement.

Zinnia's familiar—Nyxwing—sits down in the aisle next to us so his antlers don't obscure another student's view. My familiar squirms uncomfortably in my lap at the sight of him, but I pet the back of Liszt's head to remind him he's safe.

"Good morning, class. Let's get started." Professor Watson smiles. "A few thousand years ago, a massive black hole caused multiple galaxies to collide with one another, resulting in The Convergence," she starts.

She continues explaining the history of Earth and how all these magical species have come together to live in harmony. I sometimes like to picture my life without The Convergence. Would I be a demon on Hel or a human on Earth? I wonder what it is like to be without magic. In my research, I've learned about how humans favor technology, it acts as a sort-of magic for them, but I want to know more about the physicality of it all. How does it *feel* to not have magic?

Professor Watson continues sharing our history, and I watch Zinnia from my peripheral vision as she intensely stares at the woman. Her eyes burn so bright they could start a fire, and I know exactly what look she's giving. Determination. Oh, fuck.

"Welcome to The History of Mages 101. I'm Professor Watson, and it's a pleasure to meet all of you." Her voice sounds joyful, but there's a nervous undertone to her words, like she's not quite sure of herself. "I know that nobody really likes icebreakers, but could we do one anyway? Just something simple. Tell the class your name, major, and show us a magic trick."

Zinnia's hand shoots up into the air. Crossing over to the front of the class, her hooves make pleasant sounds against the wooden floorboards. "Good morning, y'all. My name is Zinnia, and I am double majoring in Creature Crafts and Botanical Crafts," she says.

Of *course* she's fucking double majoring. Just my luck.

Zinnia pulls a seed out of her pocket, showing it off to the class, and then snaps. Suddenly, a bright pink rose is nestled between her fingers, and she reaches my way as if to give it to me.

I open my hand to accept when I realize she's actually handing it to the elf seated behind me. The entire class claps and cheers, and the tall elf gets up to perform a trick of her own.

As I watch my classmates introduce themselves and perform their tricks, anxiety digs its claws into me. I have no idea what to perform. It doesn't matter, because this silly icebreaker doesn't have any effect on my academic performance, but it will create a perception of me. I'd like to say it's enough to just *be* smart, but a large part of me also wants to be *perceived* as smart. I'm sure a therapist would describe my need for academic validation as unhealthy, but it's all I've ever known.

When there are only a few students left, I rise and walk up to the front of the room, hopeful I can do something grand. Something to outdo Zinnia.

"I'm Wren, a potions major. Does anyone have any makeup with them? Or perhaps perfume?"

A faun unzips her bag and dumps the contents out onto the desk in front of her. There are all sorts of nail polishes and other liquids, most of which have some sort of residue on them, and I cringe internally as I grab a roller of perfume.

Rose scented. Perfect.

"Thank you," I say. I grab a bottle of enchanted water from out of my backpack and cross towards the windowsill, where I scoop up a small amount of dirt from one of the potted plants.

"And for the final ingredient, I'll need some pigment."

"Here," Zinnia says, handing me a small compact. "You're taking forever."

"Patience is a virtue," I say, taking the pink blush. I use a pencil to scrape a little out before I place the objects into a glass jar I keep with me.

I hand back the perfume and compact, giving Zinnia a malevolent smile as I place the blush in her hands, and work to clear my thoughts and focus.

After about a minute, a small glass rose emerges from the liquids, shimmering a pink-iridescent hue.

"How about a rose that won't die?" I say, handing it to the same elf as Zinnia.

The class cheers, many people in awe of my creation. I wasn't initially planning on one-upping Zinnia with this icebreaker, but after seeing the perfume scent, I couldn't resist.

I take my seat, smiling from ear-to ear.

Zinnia leans close to me and whispers, "That was a cute little show you put on there, but just remember—you've got *real* competition now. Don't expect me to go easy on you."

If I'm honest with myself, I'm not sure if she just terrified me or turned me on. A bit of both, actually. Bit of both.

Zinnia's not the only one up to the challenge.

one

WREN

Gold and blue shimmers of light flicker in from above as Liszt and I make our way through the library. It's a quiet, peaceful place, and I head up a flight of stairs until I find the table I reserved for the afternoon.

One *slight* problem. Someone is sitting at my table. Not only is she at my table, but she's in my seat. And not only is she in my seat, but she's my worst fucking enemy. My face flushes hot as I try to force myself to breathe. *Stay calm, Wren.* Find a way to tactfully inform her you reserved that table for the day.

I look Zinnia in the eyes and take a deep breath. "Get out of my fucking chair."

Okay, so, not what I had in mind, but it's too late now.

"Huh?"

I point to her chair. "I reserved this table, therefore that is my seat."

She lets out a chuckle before resting her chin in her hand. "Bless your heart, you can't be serious."

I sigh, not having the patience for this today. "I can go get the librarian."

"And say what, that someone sat in the chair you wanted before you?"

I rub my hands in my face. How is this the girl that beat or almost bested me at every competition in high school, who has been my only competition the last two and a half years? "Zinnia... There is a library app. Because they allow the public to access the space, students and staff are able to reserve specific areas. I reserved this table."

Zinnia picks up her book and huffs out a breath. "Fine then, sit down."

Part of me wants to argue with her—argue that she doesn't have the right to tell me to sit down, and that I should go to Mr. Rokosmith and ask him to have her escorted out, but part of me also knows she would just find another way to bother me.

Once, she signed me up for emails from some salesman, just so my phone would blow up during my study session. Another time, when I scored one point higher than her on a Botanical Magic test, which is supposed to be her specialty, she replaced all the jars of magic water in my room with moonshine. For someone who claims to hate me, Zinnia always seems to find a way to bother me with her presence.

I sit down at *my* table, right across from Zinnia. Her head is stuffed into her botanical magic textbook, her fingers skimming back and forth, highlighting different passages.

For the past two and a half years, Zinnia and I have been neck-and-neck for valedictorian of Augury University. It's been an uphill battle, but we're finally in our last semester, in which my current GPA puts me on top. I just hope I can remain here.

As much as I can't fucking stand her, I'm weirdly grateful for Zinnia. She has pushed me to be the best version of myself. Even studying can get competitive between us, especially because our methods are quite different. I have what's called an eidetic memory. Essentially, I have a near-perfect memory without needing mnemonic devices. The catch? I sometimes have to stare at pages or phrases for much longer periods of time. So whereas I take my time, carefully looking at every page, Zinnia has a tendency to skim and go over the same things again and again.

A loud smacking sound comes from a nearby part of the library, and I turn to see a pile of books stacked high. Shifting my body to peer behind it, I notice a beautiful, curvy satyr making out with an elfling that can only be described as resembling a historically accurate depiction of Jesus Christ of Nazareth.

Listen. I am all for getting your groove on wherever you please, but have some tact. This is a library, for Merlin's sake.

"Do you mind?" I say, nearly falling out of my chair to stare at them. I meant to whisper, but my voice comes out as a hoarse whisper-shout, causing Zinnia to look up from her frantic studying, her brows pulling together.

"Do *you* mind?" she mimics.

The couple breaks apart, and for a moment I think there's a shameful gleam in their eyes, before I realize that they're giggling. This is a game to them. Still staring, I notice the pink rose resting in her hand. It's almost fucking Valentine's Day; my least favorite holiday of the year. Everyone is a nuisance—it's not about romance; it's about capitalism, and yet everyone feels the need to put on a show to *prove their love.* It's so disingenuous, it makes me ill. I turn back to Zinnia, her face practically glowing as she finds an answer she was looking for.

"Zinnia," I whisper.

There's no reply as she puts the highlighter cap into her mouth and starts on another passage.

"Zinnia," I say and tap on the table repeatedly.

Still, she does not care. She had the audacity to commandeer my table, and now she feigns as though she hears nothing, continuing to 'study'.

"Zinnia Fucking Featherfields," I say through gritted teeth. It is in this moment I realize I actually don't have a clue what her middle name is.

I know so many peculiar facts about Zinnia: the way she drinks her matcha in the morning, how she changes her nails to match every season or holiday, and even how she acts when she's hungry or tired, but there's still so much more to uncover. I know her almost intimately, and yet not at all.

She removes the cap from her mouth, placing it back onto the marker in one quick motion. "What?" she asks in an exacerbated tone.

"It's almost Valentine's Day."

"Yes, Wren, it's February. What's your point?"

"All the couples are going to be unrelenting once again, ruining perfectly good walks through the courtyard and study trips to the library with their insensitive makeout sessions and grandiose public gestures."

She flicks her wrist, gesturing for me to continue. She doesn't look bored, but it's clear she's not sure where I'm going with this. Frankly, I'm not sure where I'm going with this, either.

"Well... I want to do something about it."

"Like what?"

I scratch the back of my neck, not having gotten this far in my head, when it hits me. "I propose an anti-Valentine's Day competition. Something that allows us to practice our magic, while also having some fun."

She squints at me and crosses her arms over her chest. "I'm listening."

"We utilize magic to create couples—they can be terrible, wonderful, whatever the case may be, but we cannot tell them anything about the competition nor can we directly mention anything about Valentine's Day or being asked on a date."

One small corner of her mouth ticks up. "I like it. What does the winner get?"

I tap my foot for a moment before answering. "How about a favor."

"Sure," she says almost instantly.

"Great."

"But nothing that can harm either of our academic standings," she says, reaching out her hand. "And no cheating." She gives me a warning glare.

I nod my head in agreement. "I've never cheated," I say.

"You cheated in 6001. At Magia Island's Charms Fair," she says through gritted teeth.

"I most certainly did not cheat," I say, appalled she would even imply such a thing. I won fair and square. "I'd love to see the evidence you have to back up this ridiculous claim."

"I don't have evidence from an event from when I was fifteen," she says.

"So you don't have any evidence?"

"Whatever, Wren. Do you agree or not?"

I take her hand and shake it, her skin warm and soft as it meets mine. "I agree."

Opening my textbook, I return to studying. There's a long chapter discussing the different properties of charming objects, and the levels of energy necessary for each type of object. Charming a gas, or a biological being, requires a substantially larger amount of magic and energy than inanimate objects. It takes a toll on both the mage and their familiar, but it isn't impossible.

There are also rules to charming carbon-based life forms. Laws based on the ethics of it, especially beings without magic, like humans or non-hybrid animals.

Warm fingers tap my wrist, and I put down the textbook.

"Yes?" I ask, as Zinnia watches me, a peculiar look in her eyes.

"I have more things I need clarified before we start the competition," she says, her southern accent like honey to my ears. Our fingers are still touching, and it does not go without notice on my part.

"Of course."

She smiles, her teeth perfectly straight and bright. "When does the competition end? And what qualifies as winning?"

"How about midnight, February 13th. Right when the clock strikes Valentine's Day. And great question; what do you think should deem someone the winner?"

She gradually pulls her hand back, and I fight my frown.

"Maybe most amount of couples successfully asking each other out?"

I shrug. "Works for me."

A tall orc—our librarian, Chak Rokosmith—walks by, and we're silent for a beat before continuing.

"Is anyone off limits?" she asks.

"I'd say friends and family. Too easy."

Zinnia smirks. "You don't have any friends."

My eyebrows raise at that. "And you don't have any family."

She flinches for a second, and I'm positive I'm a goner. My gravestone will say 'here lives Wren, the idiot that decided they needed to poke the bear,' when she lets out a loud cackle.

"Shh, quiet. It wasn't that funny," I say, jumping up to cross behind her, where I cover her mouth with my hand. The bright red of my flesh is in deep contrast with her light tan face, her freckles peeking out between the gaps in my fingers.

I release her, and she grins from ear to ear.

"It was pretty funny, but what was even funnier was your look of *instant* regret upon saying it. Did you think you were gonna hurt my feelings?" she teases. "Besides, my pa is alive and well. A workaholic, but still alive. I'm not a total orphan."

"And mine was true?" I ask, knowing that it is. I've never had a ton of friends. There's my cousin, Saga, and my parents, but generally, people aren't super fond of me. I'm pretentious, easy to anger, and I almost always have my head stuck in a book. I've accepted that I'm not easy to befriend, and I frankly don't care. I'd rather be teachers' pet than participate in petty, platonic drama.

"Maybe more people would be friends with you if you were actually likable," she says, and her words spit like fire, edging me on to fight back.

"Maybe your m—"

"So, when do we start?" she asks, changing the subject. I would have likely taken it too far, and I'm grateful for the interjection.

"Tomorrow. Let's begin first thing tomorrow."

"Sounds like a plan." Zinnia smiles and stands, and Nyxwing—a massive green and white elk with pitch black owl-like wings—gets up from where he was kneeling beside her. She collects her things into her hot pink backpack and makes her way down the path to the exit.

As Zinnia moves through the library, heads turn in her direction. Though I suspect some are because of her bubbly beauty, most are because of the beast that moves beside her.

Nyxwing makes most mage's familiars look pathetic in comparison. He is strong and large, but kind-eyed and wise. He's perfect for her.

Because she's perfect.

A perfect pain in my ass.

two

ZINNA

Every time I glance over at Dr. Ali, he looks madder than a wet hen. We're doing a botanical lab in his greenhouse this week, and whenever any of my classmates inch closer to one of his precious plants, I fear he'll finally snap and wrangle our necks.

And if I'm being real, I wouldn't blame him. He spends countless hours tending to this garden, only for some silly undergraduate student to ruin all his hard work? No, thank you.

I wouldn't say Dr. Ali and I get along. I think he sees me as an obnoxious try-hard, but I know he respects me. More importantly, he knows *I* respect *him* and his work, and that is why I have the courage to ask him for this favor.

"Dr. Ali," I say, keeping my tone neutral. "I have a request."

"What is it?" he asks, not looking up from his field journal.

"Could I—*safely*—remove a flower from the greenhouse?"

His golden eyes shoot up at me from where he rests, his long tail perched on the bench. "For what purpose?"

I figure honesty is the best policy. "There is another student who claims they are more knowledgeable than me, and we are... competing. I need the flower to..." I fumble on my words, unsure of how to explain this ridiculous bet.

"Is this student more knowledgeable than you?" he asks.

I shrug. "It's hard to say for sure. It's Wren Elric."

Dr. Ali's eyebrows furrow. "Dr. Taylor's research assistant? The cambion who shouts whenever they are frustrated, distracting everyone in the lab?"

"That would be the one."

One corner of his mouth ticks up in just a glimpse of a smile. "Take what you need."

I'm not sure what god or goddess to thank for Dr. Ali's random act of kindness, but I'll count my blessings for sure.

Taking my tools, I go to the enchanted carnations. I know that they have a long scientific name that's much more accurate, but, since nobody ever knows what I'm talking about, enchanted carnations it is. They're perfect for inspiring *new love*, and I clip a few before heading out the door.

Students are bustling about the courtyard. There's an orc couple cuddling on a blanket on the lawn, an elf is arguing with what looks like a TA about his grade, and countless other magical beings are roaming around. It's the perfect location for my most-perfect plan. All I need to do is find two individuals that look desperately single, and the first win is mine.

"You appear quite villainous right now. It looks like you're scheming," Wren says, staring at me from their seat on the bench. Their twin eyebrow piercings and matching gold septum twinkle in the daylight.

"That's because I am scheming," I say. My eyes catch on the tight fit of their black vest, and the way it cuts their figure nicely. Wren might be a royal pain in my ass, but at least they're pretty to look at.

I'm searching the courtyard as an elfling passes by, a sad expression on his face. He's walking closely to a girl, but she doesn't seem to notice him.

"Watch and learn, asshole." I blow a kiss towards Wren, and they pretend to wipe it off their cheek, a disgusted look on their face.

Stalking up to the elfling, I make my move. "Hey, I was just gifted a handful of flowers, but I'm having an allergic reaction to them. Would you be a doll and give them to someone else?"

"Oh," he says, and I can see the light bulb turn on in his eyes. "Of course. No problem at all."

He scurries over to the girl and taps on her shoulder, presenting the flower. She's leaning towards him, her body language clearly showing interest, and I watch Wren's jaw practically unhinge as she scribbles her number on the elfling's arm in pen.

"Zinnia one, Wren zero," I say with triumph.

"Why'd you keep one of the flowers?" they ask, their brow furrowing.

"For this," I say and walk straight towards Saga, Wren's cousin, who looks like she's headed straight to practice.

Saga is a hybrid. Specifically an orc and a cambion. She's big and red and muscular, but unlike Wren, she doesn't have wings. She's also our campus' finest enchanted rugby player and a total heartthrob.

"I think she dropped this," I say, pointing straight towards a pretty girl. My roommate, Aster. I don't know much about her, but she dances in a lot of the university's showcases, and almost everyone has a crush on her.

"I can return it to her, no worries. Thanks, Zinnia," Saga says.

When I cross back over to Wren, they look... pissed. Their eyebrows are raised so high they almost touch the long, black horns coming out from behind their bangs.

"What the fuck was that?" they ask, their voice upping in pitch.

"What?"

Wren sticks their head straight out towards me, like an angry little bird. "Don't fuck with me, Zinnia, you know exactly what you're doing."

"Winning? Yeah, thanks for noticing."

Wren shakes their head. "We agreed on no friends or family."

"I thought that meant our own friends and families. You didn't specify that your family was off-limits to me," I say, taking a seat next to them. I don't know what their problem is, but I'm over it.

"I did—I—didn't think I needed to, but let's clear things up. No, you cannot use my cousin to win," they say.

Whatever. I don't need this win to beat them. I throw up my hands in defeat. "Fine. No more using family. Now, I've got to head to class. I have a creature crafts lecture to attend."

"Enjoy crafting creatures," Wren says, sarcasm dripping off their tongue.

What a sore loser.

I head towards the Creature Crafts tree, Nyxwing clinging closely to my side as we get onto the lift. A charms mage moves us up, and, once we arrive at the right branch, we exit, crossing towards the classroom pod.

Dr. Aloe sits at her desk as the rest of my classmates pile in. When she stands, her hooves click against the floors, and it brings a smile to my face.

Satyrs aren't exactly the most popular creatures around. Elves practically run the world, orcs and cambion are the best with sports, and faun are popular for their cuteness. Satyrs? I don't know. I think we're cool. We're incredibly connected to nature, but a lot of us come from the rural, country parts of The Americas. The world has changed so much since The Convergence, but some ideologies—mainly capitalism and greed—unfortunately stuck. This doesn't bode well for people who just want to be one with nature. In fact, capitalism often destroys the natural world.

Dr. Aloe is a satyrborn though, and seeing someone like me be a popular professor brings me deep joy. Dr. McNab, the other creature crafts professor is fine, but Dr. Aloe has a way of captivating a class with her stories—and with her magic and familiar.

"I have a special guest for all of you today," Dr. Aloe announces once we're all seated. "But it will require a small... field trip, of sorts. Please follow me down to the enchanted rugby field."

Everyone stands, our familiars in tow, as we make our way down the lifts and ladders to the ground, crossing through the courtyard and down towards the sports fields.

Augury University is large and spacious, and it takes a while before we actually arrive. I don't see anything special, but knowing Dr. Aloe, she has to have something spectacular up her sleeve.

"Dr. Murphy will be joining us today from Aquatica Academy," Dr. Aloe says. "If you'd like to thank someone for this exciting opportunity, please express your gratitude towards Dr. Murphy, as well as our very own Dean Taylor. She coordinated this entire meet and greet."

A mermaid with long, green hair and light tan skin comes into view. There's a blue-haired kraken beside her, wielding her magic to create water that forms around them, allowing them to travel on land while still being partially submerged. There's a cat with a koi fish tail between them, and it seems to enjoy whatever is happening.

"Hello, Augury University students. I'm a Creature Crafts professor at your sister school. Aiding me today is Cordelia Tremblay, an Aquatica Academy graduate. And helping with my familiar is Nahla Aziz, Ms. Tremblay's younger sister, who is one of my current interns."

She goes on to tell us a little bit about her recent research, as well as some of the charity projects the professor and Ms. Tremblay are working on. Dr. Murphy brings up potential internships or job opportunities and tells us more about herself.

Everyone claps, and Dr. Murphy smiles widely at us. "My familiar is an incredibly rare one, and it is an honor to show you my beast of a friend. Come on, Sperm." She whistles, and a massive flying whale swims above us.

Did she name her sperm whale... Sperm? I'm not even gonna ask.

I watch in astonishment as the whale swims into the sky from somewhere hidden from view, its movement as graceful as a bird's.

I haven't learned a lot about aquatic familiars, especially because they're usually just a single unit within a class here, but I wonder what biological and magical mechanisms allow something so large to fly like that, swimming through the air with fluid precision.

Everyone takes out their phones and snaps pictures as the whale's fluke moves, steering the beast through the sky. It gradually ascends up into the clouds before descending back down, close to the ground, until we can almost touch it.

They held this here because otherwise the whale would've been obstructed by trees.

As much as I love reading and studying, these are the moments I truly yearn for.

"How was the circus?" Wren asks, knowing exactly how to push my buttons. "I heard you guys got to ride flying whales or some shit."

"It's familiar ethology, dumbo," I correct. "And it was quite fun. Arguably my favorite class. And we did not ride them, we just watched in awe."

"Isn't your goal to be an anthrozoologist? Why isn't that class your favorite?"

I shrug, walking side-by-side with them as we head out of the courtyard. "The professor is bland."

"Hmm. If I were you, I'd study multispecies ethnography. Comparing humans, elves, satyrs, cambions, all of us against one another as well as animals. That sounds truly exciting," Wren says, and it's possibly the first positive thing they've ever said about my course of study.

"Good thing I'm not you. Hey, how'd you do with cauldron class?" I tease as we continue walking through the jungle, though I know the joke doesn't land as hard.

"Great!" Wren beams and pulls a little vial out of their backpack. "I had extra time at the end to make this."

"What does it do?" I ask as we get closer to the dorms.

"Let me show you."

It's only the late afternoon, but there are already party-goers hovering around the outside of buildings, red solo cups in tow.

Wren walks over to a group of elves and slips the contents of the vial inside one of their drinks before walking away. They move close to me and watch as the elf begins behaving differently.

"That professor was such a douchebag!" he proclaims, and I realize it's one of the guys from my botanical magic class.

"Dr. Ali?" another drunk idiot asks.

"Yeah, the fucking snake-dude. He thinks he's hot shit because he's a thousand years old."

I'm pretty sure he's closer to seven thousand years old, but I remain silent as we listen in.

"I don't think he's that bad, but I haven't taken one of his classes since freshman year," another elf chimes in, shifting closer to the one Wren gave the potion to.

"Oh, and you!"

"Did you give him a *get angry* potion?" I whisper to Wren.

They put their pointer finger against their lips, gesturing for me to keep quiet. My gaze remains fixed, hovering on their lips for a second too long, before I look back at the crowd.

The two elves are kissing. What the fuck just happened?

"You can't create emotions that aren't there. I gave him a potion that helps release repressed emotions, hence the rage and... whatever this is."

"Lust? Love?" I offer.

Wren nods, one corner of their mouth perking up. "Something like that. It'll be more obvious tomorrow."

I smile in turn. "Congratulations," I say and lightly punch them on the shoulder. "You did it!"

"Did what?" they ask, their brows furrowing with confusion.

"Got your first and only win?"

Wren high fives the air. "Oh. Oh, yeah. *Fuck,* yeah! You're going down, clown."

I scowl. "Says the literal demon."

"*Half*-demon," they correct, flipping their long, pin-straight white hair. "I'll see you tomorrow."

Wren and I live in nearby dorms, and yet they still manage to feel a million miles away whenever we depart. What a nuisance.

three

WREN

"MAYBE IF YOU GOT THE STICK OUT OF YOUR ASS, YOU WOULD'VE KNOWN THE RIGHT answer," Zinnia mutters from the seat next to me, a punitive gleam in her eyes.

"Even if I had a stick up my ass, it wouldn't have affected my intellectual capabilities. It was actually your big, loud mouth that distracted me," I say, so sure it'll shut her up.

It doesn't.

"This big loud mouth got a 98 on our last exam; the same grade as you."

I smirk. "You received a 98.4, I received a 98.6. If you follow the basic rules of rounding, I essentially got a ninety—"

"Enough," Dr. Daelor says from the front, crossing her well-muscled arms. "If you two don't mind, I'm teaching a class."

Dr. Daelor is normally our most chill professor. She's a big, strong, kind-hearted orc who constantly gives our classmates extensions they don't deserve, so we know if she's irritable rather than sarcastic, we're *really* acting foolish. Zinnia huffs, but we nod at one another, simultaneously agreeing to pause today's debate.

When class finishes, Zinnia looks over at me, a massive grin smeared across her face. "You might have scored higher than me on the last test, but we're two to one on our Valentine's competition right now."

"We'll see how long that lasts," I say, one eyebrow raising. "And hey, no. It's one to one, asshole."

"Your win was ethically wrong, so really it should be one to zero," she shoots back.

We may have the highest grades of the school, but neither of us are winning any maturity contests. Popularity contests aren't doing us any favors either, and I think that's part of what keeps us going. If nobody's going to like us, we might as well be smarter than all of them.

"What're you doing after class?" I ask.

"Winning," she replies with a wink.

"Me too. I'll see you then," I say.

Zinnia walks away from me, her curves on full display. She's wearing what she calls a wiggle dress, and I understand how it got its name. I spent all of class trying not to make it obvious I was ogling her. I'm well aware that lusting after my worst enemy is a solidly bad idea, but nature does what nature wants. Besides, it doesn't hurt to look.

I fly over to my Intermediate Affective State Potion class. We mostly focus on mind-altering potions. It's similar to healing potions, but with more specific fixations on emotion and less on physicality. I'm hoping this class will provide me exactly what I need to make another proper love potion.

"Good morning, magical minds," Professor Watson says.

Class goes by in a blur, but it vaguely reminded me of my first day at Augury. Zinnia and I had already known each other—and known that we did not like one another—but half of our class schedules were the same.

Somehow that translated into spending almost *all* our time outside of class together, too. It wasn't purposeful, at least not at first. We'd be studying in the same section of the library, or discover the same quiet hiding spots, but now it feels like we've escalated to war. We are constantly at each other's throats, trying to throw one another off and commandeer the other one's study sessions. It's made things more interesting, but we're lucky we don't have a strong third competitor, otherwise they might've done us over by now.

Zinnia and I meet up in the courtyard, and I'm ready to watch her... lose. I'm anticipating coming out victorious in this match.

"Are you here to witness me defeat you firsthand?" I say as I approach her.

"No, I'm here to ensure you're not a snake in the grass," she says and huffs a green strand of hair out of her eyes. She fixes her hair, which parts on either side at the base of her deep brown ram-like horns.

"A what?" I ask, not sure of her meaning. I'm not a serpentine.

"A snake. A scoundrel?" she clarifies.

"Um..."

"Whatever, asshole. It's your turn." She rolls her big green eyes, crossing her arms as I maneuver around the courtyard, searching for my next victim.

I spot an elfling sitting on a blanket with a picnic basket and an e-reader and decide to make my move. Taking a seat, I charm her device to begin speaking to her. The goal is for it to repeat romantic things from her favorite novels, and in return, it'll inspire her to go find love for herself. Hopefully quick enough for us to catch it... and catch myself a win.

"My feelings will not be repressed," the device says in a low, sensual tone. "You must allow me to tell you how ardently—"

"So, what was your goal here?" Zinnia whispers.

"She's going to want to fall in love."

"It looks like she *is* in love. With her Kindle," Zinnia says before she huffs out a laugh. "Y'know, I'm starting to think you might just be a masochist."

"My sexual tendencies have nothing to do with this, Zinnia, but I'm glad to know you're thinking about me in those ways," I say boldly.

Her face flushes a bright pink before she turns away from me. I might enjoy getting under her skin even more than I enjoy academic validation, and that's truly saying something.

"Nyxwing, go for it," Zinnia says, and her familiar stalks towards two mages that are standing a little ways apart from one another.

He uses his antler to try to nudge one of the mages into the other. It's a cute idea, really, but it goes horribly when the mage turns around and sees the giant beast looming above them. The mage screams, and Nyxwing flaps his wings in response to the loud sound, suddenly shifting into a defensive stance.

"Hey," Zinnia shouts. "Down, boy. You're scaring them."

The two mages run out of the courtyard, and I have to stifle a laugh as Zinnia takes her familiar and drags him back to where we've been sitting.

"Well, that was a disaster," Zinnia says. "I'm plumb tired. Are you done for today?"

"Not hardly. I've still got another amory potion to test," I reply. And it's true. Love potions can take many forms, but this one is almost-perfect.

I stand and cross towards a vending machine before getting whatever electrolyte drink is the current rage. Energy and sports drinks change popularity every couple of years, and I tend not to pay attention to them anymore, because none of them are very healthy anyway. But all our student athletes love them.

This is why I know my idea is brilliant.

I open the bottle and pour in the contents of the love potion. Walking over to the nearest dude in a jersey, I gesture for him to take the bottle.

"Here, I'm allergic to this flavor," I say, borrowing that idea from Zinnia.

I look over to where she's seated. She looks pissed, but she says nothing. Her dress is short and tight, revealing the light brown fur of her legs. I stare for a moment too long when I realize the athlete is staring at himself in the reflection of his phone screen, admiring his jawline.

The universe is fucking with me. Just my luck.

My face flushes hot, my entire body buzzing with a quiet rage. I'm not mad at this jock, and I'm not mad at Zinnia; I'm just mad at myself. Liszt sticks his red, furry face out from my satchel and gives me a pathetic look.

"Urgh," I say, letting the emotion out so it doesn't fester. "I mean... he fell in love?"

"As much as I'm pro self-love, there is no way that counts. We agreed to create *couples.*"

"I'm aware. 'Couples' comes from the Latin word copula, which means bond."

Zinnia looks at me with a mock-empathetic smile. "What a strange way to cope with this epic loss. Want me to make you a little ribbon for second place?"

"Fuck off."

Thursdays always start out quiet for me. I work in the cosmetic lab on Tuesday and Thursday mornings, as well as Friday afternoons, but Thursday is particularly nice because Iris has her internship at the tattoo shop then.

Iris Watson is a brilliant scientist, but she's quite possibly the most chaotic individual I've ever met. She leaves research documents all over the lab, she never stops talking, and I'm pretty sure the only reason she eats every day is because Dr. Ali or one of his assistants brings her lunch.

The biggest catch of all? She claims *I'm* the distracting one.

On occasion, when I am extra frustrated, I admit that I have a tendency to shout or make disgruntled sounds, but let's be logical here. She is almost as annoying as Zinnia with the way she's constantly nosing about other's business, or asking questions she could easily search for online. Her manifestation ADHD and my autism simply do not mesh.

It's fine. Stop thinking about all the ladies that piss you off regularly, Wren, and just work on your magic.

Ring. Ring.

Dr. Taylor's button flashes on the desk phone in the office. I'm currently assisting her with a cosmetic project on shaping hair with magic. It's fun and intriguing, and I'm guessing the reason for her call.

"This is Wren Elric speaking," I say into the phone.

"Excellent. Please meet me in my office at 12 P.M." she requests.

I take in a sharp inhale. "Your office here...at the cosmetic lab?"

"No. In the Dean's office. I will see you then."

She hangs up the phone, but the handset remains in my grip as I'm unable to let go. My muscles refuse to relax, and I'm forced to replay our conversation over and over again.

Shit.

four
ZINNIA

I rarely break rules. As someone with near-perfect grades, I don't have time to be rebellious. Which is why the email requesting my attendance in Dean Taylor's office is sending me into a bit of a spiral.

I switch screens on my phone and dial my pa, just to double check. I'm sure he's fine, but the last time I was requested at the Principal's office, it was my fifth-grade principal telling me that my mom had passed. It's likely I haven't entirely healed from that trauma.

"Hey Zinn, everything alright?" he says, breathing heavily.

My pa is in his fifties, but he still works two jobs. One as a magical liaison at the airport, and another in construction. That's one of the reasons I work so hard—I don't want him to feel like he needs to keep at this for me. I have to prove that I'm fine, and that I can even provide for him, if he'd like.

I let out a sigh of relief. "Yep! Just checking on ya. I love you."

"I love you too, honey. I'm really bu—"

"I know, I know," I cut him off. "I hope you have a great rest of your day."

"See you later, alligator."

"After while, crocodile," I say before hanging up the phone. If it were up to me, he'd be wearing a heart monitor that sends me live updates at all times, but random check-ins will have to do.

Okay, so she's not calling me to her office to tell me my father died. Maybe she's decided that I'm Valedictorian—no, don't be delusional, Zinnia. What could this possibly be about?

Heading out of the greenhouse, I make my way down the path that leads to the Potions Tree, where Dean Taylor's office resides. Nyxwing walks closely to me, and I'm so tired, I almost consider seeing if he'll let me ride him half the way there.

Almost.

Nyxwing is a massive, strong beast. But for whatever reason, I think he's afraid of heights. It's kinda hilarious, honestly, the irony of a huge creature with large feathered wings being afraid to fly.

There's guilt there too, though. Maybe I didn't make him practice flying enough when I adopted him. Or maybe I was too harsh on him when he misbehaved. Either way, he's an incredibly intelligent, but equally skittish, being.

We cross through the courtyard and get onto a lift, which takes us up to Dean Taylor's office. As we walk over to reach for the door, I spot Wren flying up with Liszt in tow.

This is *really* not good.

Entering the office, I hold my breath as Dean Taylor gestures for us to take our seats.

"I am holding this meeting to ask you both some questions about an ongoing investigation I'm performing here at Augury University," she says. "Neither of you are in trouble, but as two of our brightest minds here, I figured you both might have some insight into what's been happening."

"Of course, Dr. Taylor," Wren says immediately, kissing up. It's bad enough they literally work in Dr. Taylor's lab.

"What's this about?" I ask, unsure of what she's investigating.

"There have been some... peculiar occurrences happening on campus. Mages feeling like they've been drugged, others sharing stories of giant monsters. The most recent incident was of a guy walking around staring at his own reflection, obsessing over himself for hours," she shares, and my heart sinks into my chest.

"Sounds like a total narcissist," Wren says, and I'm not sure if they're joking.

Do they not realize Dr. Taylor totally knows it's us?

"It does," she says, her tone coy. "Would you two happen to know anything about this?"

"No, but I'll definitely be keeping my eyes out," Wren says, and I step on their food with my hoof.

What an absolute idiot. Act a little more surprised than that, for fucks' sake. "Hmm. I did see the strange guy and his reflection obsession. I thought it was like... some artsy-fartsy way of expressing the greatest kind of love; self-love," I say, and I want to kick myself for how ridiculous I sound.

"Interesting," Dr. Taylor deadpans. "Well, if you see anything, let me know. Hopefully, these pranks cease, and we don't have to worry about it again."

She emphasized the word we, and I swear my stomach is as hollow as Wren's overconfidence.

Practically stumbling out of the Dean's office, I make my way back down to the courtyard, and Wren follows shortly behind me.

"Zinnia, wait," they call out to me, but I continue walking.

Maybe this was Wren's plan all along. To get me expelled so I can't be valedictorian.

"Zinnia." They grab the back of my arm, and I halt.

"What?"

"Why are you running?"

"Because." I turn back to them. "I'm not going to let you get me expelled."

"Expelled?" Wren's facial expression is pure confusion. "Zinnia, if anything, I'd be the one to get expelled."

That's a fair point. Wren has performed the riskier spells throughout this competition. Their long white hair is tied back in a low ponytail, and it flutters in the wind, back-and-forth like a metronome.

"Zinnia?" they say, interrupting my train of thought.

"Yes?"

Wren grabs my hand and squeezes it. "You're annoying as Hel, but I'm not trying to get you expelled, I promise."

I rip my hand away. "Whatever, just promise me we'll be more careful for the remainder of the competition."

"I can do that," they say with a smile.

"So say it," I demand.

Their golden eyes widen. "I promise. Damn."

After we got our subtle lecture from Dean Taylor, Wren and I went easy on each other for the rest of the week. We both lost. A lot. It's actually quite hard to make people fall in love, especially when you're working double time to avoid the wrath of the head of your university.

I finally manage to get another win, which puts me back in the lead, before I'm shortly bested by Wren yet again.

"Should I just take the win now and put you out of your misery?" they suggest with a cocky grin.

"Not a chance, hellion," I say.

By the time Friday afternoon rolls around, Wren and I are both four-to-four. A good way to end before the weekend, so we decide to call it there.

Clover and I sit at the barstools of our favorite brunch spot, and she watches as I annihilate this Sunday's crossword in the digital papers.

"Why do you do those, again?" she asks, sipping her chai.

"Honestly, I feel like this is something Wren does, which made me want to start doing them."

"Weird. Alright. How's it going with your competition, by the way?"

I shrug. "I'm not really sure. I mean, we're four-to-four, which is wild, but we might've gotten called into the dean's office."

"Zinnia," Clover says on a gasp. "I'm jealous. She's *gorgeous*."

"I know, I know, but she's also kind of terrifying. She's so...serious."

"Not as serious as fucking Avery."

Avery is Clover's ice skating partner, and also the bane of her existence. I swear I'll be at their wedding one day, but they claim to hate one another. "That bad, huh?"

"It's literally our final year—our final chance to win the big spring tournament against the other universities—and here's a picture of him out late last night. Probably partying," she shares and shows me a picture of him walking out of some skeevy looking club.

Avery is lean with long hair like Wren, but he's a taller hybrid and a lot more muscular. And Clover is a satyr like me, but she's even curvier and much, much taller. They're actually the tallest skating partners in competitive history, and it's impressive how many stunts they're able to pull off. It's a shame they don't give one another enough credit.

I take another sip of my blueberry matcha and wince when a pang of pain hits my lower abdomen. Here we fucking go.

"Hey, the red death is here. I'm gonna head back to the dorm and get ready to lay on a heating pad for the next 12 hours," I say.

"Oh no, I'm sorry, lovebug. I wish you didn't have to deal with fucking endo," Clover says, her red, long hair framing her beautiful face.

"Ditto to you and your PCOS," I say.

"Hey, at least I can still take an edible," she teases, and I scrunch my nose.

"Don't bully me."

Ping.

I look over at my phone on my nightstand and see it's only 6 P.M., but my body doesn't want to move.

WREN

Are you available tonight?

What on Earth could they possibly be texting me about on a Sunday night?

ZINNIA

Technically, yea

WREN

Come out with me. I'll meet you in the dining hall.

ZINNIA

what??

WREN

I want you to watch this match so you know I didn't cheat.

Oh. Wren isn't asking me out, thank goodness. They're just asking me to play a round. Got it.

ZINNIA

Omw!

I throw on a pair of high-rise leggings and a cute vintage pop art t-shirt and make my way to dining, where I can hear Wren singing an old love song.

Am I hallucinating? We're supposed to win the competition using magic, not our other personal talents.

Wren pops up from a corner and hails me over. I slowly walk towards them, staring as not one but two couples start kissing.

"Recording love songs doesn't count," I say. "That's not magic."

"Oh, but it is." They smirk. "I charmed the speaker. It's a voice modulation spell—should turn the singer into the voice of the person they care for. In the case of the two couples, they likely think this was personally recorded for them," they explain.

"Did you... who is singing?"

"I think his name is Michael Bublé. I don't know; I picked an old dead guy from pre-Convergence times. Felt the most ethical. Knowing you, though, you're probably hearing a KPOP singer or the guy who sings that beautiful Farsi song you love."

I smile at that. "Mohsen? Yeah, he's great." I try not to think about the fact that I could've sworn it was Wren's voice coming through those speakers. It's likely my pain and exhaustion getting to me.

"Well, thank you for joining me on this most incredible win," they say, grinning ear to ear. Their pearly whites contrast nicely against the bright red of their skin, and I smile back, though it's not nearly as bright.

"Good job. That was very clever. Now, let me let you go. I'm sure you're tired and could use some rest after using up all that magic," I say to Wren but gesture to Liszt, who looks tuckered out.

"Goodnight, Zinnia. I'll see you tomorrow."

"Bye." I yawn and head back down to the dorms.

My eyes shoot open, and I stifle a scream as agonizing pain shoots down my abdomen and back.

Fuck. My. Life.

five

WREN

Tick. Tick.

My eyes are glued to the clock as I wait for Zinnia to get here. Dr. Daelor starts going over our next chapter, instructing us on what passages to highlight and make notes on. I'm hardly listening though as I impatiently wait for my partner in crime.

The door swings open, and my heartbeat quickens, only to be let down when an orc walks through the door.

Where is she?

Many students would skip an 8 AM course on a Monday, sure. But not Zinnia.

Never Zinnia. She wouldn't want me to get an edge on her. Hel, she wouldn't want to miss Dr. Daelor's lecture. She has a thirst for knowledge that rivals even mine.

Tick. Tick.

I get out my phone and search for Zin.

WREN

Where are you?

Zinnia's text bubble pops up with three dots, and I wait for her reply. When nothing comes, I shoot out another quick text.

WREN

Proof your respiratory and cardiovascular systems are still working, please.

Still, no response.

I look up to see Dr. Daelor eyeing me curiously, before she gestures for me to leave. It's not an angry gesture, but gentle. Like she wants to tell me to *go handle it*, but doesn't want to draw attention to my likely frantic expression.

Dr. Daelor is the best. Emotionally speaking, that is. I'm not sure where she ranks in terms of overall magical capabilities, though I'd bet money it's fairly high.

I collect my things into my backpack and rush out the door. Letting my wings propel me, I fly through the trees until I see the clearing that leads to our dorms. There are birds and leaves flying through the wind, and I dodge a parrot as I let myself down to the ground.

I just hope she's here.

Making my way into our building, I quickly cross down a hallway until I'm at Zinnia's dorm. Our respective programs give us private or two-person dorms our senior year, and thanks to us both being soon-to-be graduating seniors, Zinnia only has one roommate for me to deal with.

Knocking on the door, I patiently wait for Zinnia to open up, but nothing happens.

"Zinnia?" I call, trying not to shout. It's still early, and other students might be sleeping.

I knock again. Nothing.

I walk down the hallway, searching every door until I find one that says RA in big, sparkly letters. I knock on the door, and it opens up almost instantly to reveal a familiar-looking satyr.

Oh fuck. Is that the girl from the library?

"Hey, how can I help you?"

"Zinnia didn't come to class, and she's not answering her texts or the door, and neither is her roommate. I just want to check on her," I say, hoping this RA can prove useful.

"Oh, fair. I haven't seen her today, but she doesn't hang around much. Let me check and see if this is something I'm allowed to do," she says and turns back into her room. Her hair is long and wavy, billowing down her back.

"Are you two siblings?"

I shake my head.

"Damn, dude. I don't know if I'm going to be able to let you in. Are you her significant other?"

I am significant. I am a cambion, which is something *other* than a satyr. *Close enough.*

"Yes," I lie, hoping she doesn't realize.

She gives me a look but grabs a ring of keys and starts towards Zinnia's door anyway. She puts in the key and unlocks the door, leaving it slightly ajar before backing up.

"Thank you..."

"Allie," she says and reaches out a hand.

I shake it, her hand cold against mine. "Wren."

"Good luck!"

Walking in, Zinnia's room is exactly like her wardrobe, all pastels and retro designs. There are no lights on, but the temperature is fairly cold for early February on a tropical island. The AC must be blasting.

"Zinnia?" I call into the dim space, but there's no answer.

I sort through all the floor plans in my mind before recalling Zinnia's, and find the door to her bedroom, which is closed. I turn the doorknob.

Okay. Closed, but not locked. I can work with that.

Logically, I should just go in and check on her, but I know there's an emotional component to all of this at play. I don't want to invade her priv—actually, I don't fucking care.

"Zinnia!" I shout while opening the door.

"What?" She sounds angry.

She doesn't just sound angry, though. She looks... unwell. The short green strands of her hair are unstyled, and there's not a drop of makeup to be seen. There are bags under her eyes, and she is wearing pajamas, huddled against what looks like a heating pad.

"Are you okay?" I ask, crossing over to sit on the edge of her bed.

"Do I look okay?" she bites back, and it's clear she's in a lot of pain.

I shrug. "I mean, you look half-dead, but do you need me to take you to the hospital?"

"Why, so they can tell me I'm being dramatic, give me some extra strength naproxen, and send me on my way?" She sits up, bringing her heating pad with her as rests her back against her headboard.

"If you don't mind me asking... what's wrong?" I ask.

"I have endometriosis," she shares.

I cock my head to the side. "And that does... what? The roots break down to mean inside uterus disease, but that could mean so many things."

She places a pillow against her face and screams, before gently placing it back down against her bed. "Have you ever learned about anything that doesn't directly pertain to you and your interests?"

"What?" I ask, somewhat shocked at this line of questioning.

"Have you ever even thought, *hmm, I should learn about people from different cultures than me, or maybe people with ailments who have different body parts than me?*" she asks.

I stop dead in my tracks. Because I have. Sort of. I've researched a little about other cultures, at least. But ailments? I've never really bothered learning about diseases that don't affect me. I've been hyper-focused on learning about what could benefit me, or the things I find intriguing. It's rare I take the time to appreciate much else.

"Have you ever thought about anything other than your overinflated ego?" she asks, temporarily breaking me from my train of thought.

Zinnia listens to music from all over the world. She clearly learned enough about gender nonconformity, because she's never said or done anything disrespectful since I came out as nonbinary. But wow, I can't say the same about myself. I haven't bothered to learn about the things that could possibly affect her. And I mean, why would I? Her reproductive system isn't really my problem; we don't even like one another.

But I have a mother. And an aunt. And a cousin. All with uteruses and could be affected by things like endometriosis.

Am I the asshole?

"You're right. I'm sorry," I say and exit Zinnia's room, because what else is there for me to say?

As I walk through the dorms, I search online and learn about endometriosis and shudder. She's likely in so much pain regularly—a type of pain I can't possibly fathom. *Fuck.*

I ponder what she said about pain meds and fly straight towards the cosmetic lab, my wings taking me faster than they ever have. I'm going so fast I consider signing up for one of those triathlons, but reconsider when I remember there's a swimming portion.

Once I'm finally at the cosmetic lab, the door swings open, and I shout. "Does anyone have any potions for period cramps?"

Professor Watson and Dean Taylor stare at me like deer in headlights.

"Wren, do you need some Midol or something?" Professor Watson asks, and I smile at her sincerity.

"No, it's not for me. And no, pain meds won't do. I need something stronger. It's urgent," I say.

Iris peeks her head out from her office, holding a glass vial. "I've been working on a potion on the side, but I have not taken it to clinical trials yet."

"Well, consider this your trial," I say, taking the potion from her.

"Wren, please be cautious. Make sure the person you are giving this to is aware that it hasn't been properly tested. It could make her as green as Piccolo for all I know," she says.

"Like the instrument?" I ask, unsure of her meaning.

"Like The Wicked Witch of the West," Professor Watson corrects and turns to Iris. "They don't get anime analogies; they're more into musicals."

"*Boring*," Iris replies.

"You know... both of you failed to recognize that you could've easily referenced something much less historical, like... Dr. Daelor, your literal fianeé?" Dean Taylor says to Professor Watson.

"Can I go now?" I ask, and the three of them nod.

"Please inform Zinnia that the cosmetic lab is not responsible for you and Miss Iris Watson's decision to give her this experimental potion," Dean Taylor says as I cross through the threshold of the front door.

Did I even tell her this is for Zinnia?

Entering Zinnia's bedroom, she groans as I turn her over to face me.

"I brought you something for your pain," I say, holding up the vial. "It's experimen—" She grabs it out of my hand and downs the whole thing.

"Zinnia! That hasn't been tested on anyone yet."

"Okay? I don't exactly care anymore. I'll let y'all know if it actually works," she says.

"Alright. Well, that was... I'm sorry, Zinnia. You were right. I should do some more introspection and improve myself—"

"Wren."

"Yes?"

"Do less introspection. Pay more attention to the people around you, and those you care about," she says, and it hits me straight in the gut.

"You're right," I say again. The words are bitter on my tongue, but they ring true.

"I know." She gives a small giggle, like she knows how much admitting that injures my ego. My apparently overinflated ego.

"Well, I'm going to go," I say, turning towards the door.

Something stops me, and I turn to spot Zinnia gripping onto my sleeve.

"Will you stay with me?"

"I have..." I trail off, because I have nothing Monday afternoons, and Zinnia knows it. We know each other's schedules by heart. "Yeah. Do you want to watch something?"

"Sure. You pick," she says before scooting over to make room for me.

"There's this musical called Magictown. It's about a dystopian future where corrupt corporations charge people to use their magic."

"Whatever you want," Zinnia whispers, her eyes flickering shut.

She's asleep before I even press play.

six

ZINNIA

My eyes flutter open, and there's a basket at the end of my bed. Inside it is a blanket, pain patches, chocolate, and pads and tampons in various sizes.

Did Wren make me a care package?

I vaguely remember being in too much pain to even go to class, then Wren showing up and me bitching them out, and then they returned with some kind of magical elixir.

Damn. Whoever created it is a fucking genius.

I wonder if Wren did all that because they care about me, or because they'd feel guilty winning Valedictorian against me because of my chronic illness. Or maybe curiosity finally killed the cat, and they just wanted to snoop in my bedroom.

Either way, even if their reasons were selfish, I'm still grateful. All of this is genuinely helpful, and maybe Wren can go on to help others, too. Although I doubt they made that potion by themselves. Wren is smart, but not *that* smart.

At least that's the lie I tell myself. Wren is a fucking genius. An evil fucking genius who doesn't have to study, but does just so they can do better than me. And I study late at night when nobody is awake in hopes I can get somewhat of an edge on them.

It isn't fair. But that's the thing; life isn't fair.

Alright, enough existential crises, Zinnia.

I stand up, determined to win today's match. I need a win. I need a win, a good fuck, and a large margarita. With a grade discrepancy of 0.0002 between Wren and I though, it doesn't look like any of that is likely.

Walking over to my closet, I grab one of my best *if looks could kill* dresses and put it on before heading out the door.

"I really wish we could bend time," Wren says, looking out into the courtyard. We're seated on the same bench, but as far away from one another as possible. "Can you imagine the possibilities?"

"Even if we could, it would be a major moral dilemma," I say, eyeing them warily.

Would Wren tell me if they discovered a new kind of magic? Probably not. It's not like we're friends or anything.

"Yeah, but it would be so easy. Someone could ask someone out a thousand different ways until they found a way to get them to say yes."

"Sure," I say. "Coerce people via time manipulation. *Or,* y'all could use it to...I don't know...stop someone from getting hit by a train or something. Use it for the greater good."

Wren sticks up a finger, ready to correct me like the petulant child they are. "I would do things for the greater good, just *after* I beat you in this contest."

"How heroic."

Wren shrugs. "I think so. Not that it matters. Unfortunately, I haven't made any cool discoveries."

"Not all discoveries have to be time-bending. Have you made any cool, but maybe basic potions discoveries?"

"Nope." They give a slight frown. "Not one. I guess the only thing I'm good at is being better than you."

An elfling walks by, her textbooks stacked up high in her arms. Wren flicks their wrist and her books go flying. I make to stand up and help her, but a nearby orcling is already coming to the rescue. Their eyes lock as they pick up the same book, their fingers brushing against one another's, and I can practically feel the sparks flying through the air.

"I cannot fucking stand you," I say, rolling my eyes. That was so easy, it's almost pathetic I didn't think of it first.

"But sweetheart, you're sitting down."

Another student walks by, and I attempt the same move as Wren without thinking, and her calculator crashes down, the plastic cracking as it hits the ground.

Her familiar, a golden retriever covered in flowers, helps her pick up her supplies. I watch in stunned silence, embarrassed by how bad this is. Wren's shit-eating grin says it all.

But unlike Wren, I won't give them the satisfaction of storming off angrily. I will take this loss with pride.

"Well, now that I've watched you thoroughly ruin a girl's day, I guess I'll see you after class?"

"No, thank you."

"What?" We both stand, and Wren adjusts their vest.

I look into their golden eyes. "I have no interest in spending any more time with you today. I'll see you tomorrow," I say, and gesture for Nyxwing to follow me as we head to the Creature Crafts tree.

Nyxwing gives me a look, and I frown. "I'm not trying to be a jackass, but I'm not in the mood for their shit. I'm bleeding, cramping, I just embarrassed the heck out of myself, and frankly, I just need some space."

He shifts a few feet away from me, and I shake my head. "Not from you, dummy, from Wren."

We continue onto the lift until we're back in Dr. Aloe's class. Today's lecture is about the emotions in familiars we tend to avoid or ignore—feelings like rage and fear. Funnily enough, they're the same negatives mages avoid in ourselves. I'm not scared of feelings like rage, but I am afraid of fear. Nyxwing, as big and strong as he looks, is full of it.

"I want you and your familiar to do something that scares you both. Right now it can be something small, something that maybe makes your familiar uncomfortable," Dr. Aloe says, and I flinch.

Everyone pulls out their phones, playing sounds and showing their familiars images that make them uncomfortable or scared. Some of the creatures balk or hide, while others shriek in fear. Dr. Aloe walks by slowly, watching everyone experiment with their familiars' behavior. Unlike regular animals and their human companions, familiars and mages are connected emotionally and physically. Our life lines are the same, so no one here is going to do anything awful to their creature, or take things too far. This is an exercise in trust.

"Zinnia, do you not know what Nyxwing is afraid of?" Dr. Aloe questions me as she comes by my row.

"No, I'm well aware, but I would prefer not to do it at this time."

"Oh?" Her eyebrows tick up in surprise. "I've never seen you refuse an assignment, but if you want the zero, I will happily oblige."

Dr. Aloe knows me well. Incredibly well. She has been nothing but kind and respectful to me my entire three years here. But she also knows what I'm capable of, which means we're going flying or I'm fucked—I can kiss first place goodbye.

"No. But we'll have to leave the classroom for this," I explain before cracking my knuckles.

"I love a good show-and-tell," she says with a sly smile.

Nyxwing and I cross the threshold of the room, and as I mount him, I regret wearing the dress I chose. Pants would've been so much better for this.

Nyxie's anxiety is a tangible entity as it tangles between us like reins, waiting for me to take charge. I tap my foot against his leg, and we take off, wings as dark as night gliding through the air.

All I can hear is wind, all I can see are blurred visions of trees and clouds, but I think my class is watching me as we soar to new heights. Nyxwing's heart rate is still accelerated, his breathing somewhat labored, but he's flying all the same. I have no talent for it, but I hum a soft lullaby in hopes it'll comfort him.

Once it feels like enough time has passed, we make our landing back on the Creature Crafts Tree, and I can hear an audience—my classmates—applauding from behind the window.

"That was excellent, Zinnia. Your bond with Nyxwing is incredibly strong. You should be proud of yourself," she says and pats my shoulder. "Alright class, here's your homework. I want you to do something you're afraid of, without your familiar, and write a short essay on the experience."

You've. Got. To. Be. Joking.

After my Wednesday morning class with Wren, I head to the Creature Crafts tree for Familiar Anthrozoology with Professor McNab. My head is pounding, my body drained of all energy, but here I am, desperately trying to perform better than my biggest rival. They're not even in this class, but they invade my every thought as Professor McNab goes on and on about a recent study of familiars compared to free-roaming animals on the continent of the Levant.

We pull out our computers and begin doing our own research, when my mind and search engine wander over to endometriosis clinical trials, menstrual cups, and period underwear.

Cursed fucking reproductive system. I don't even know if I want children, but even if I do, is it worth feeling like a tiny army is going to war inside my organs every month? I could be someone's legal guardian or foster parent one day. I could try to ethically adopt—I don't know. Can't I just get this shit ripped out already?

Sigh.

Clicking back into my research assignment, my thoughts scurry back and forth between the work I should be doing, my cramping abdomen, and the care basket waiting for me back in my dorm.

The care basket Wren, of all individuals, made me.

Double sigh.

seven

WREN

No good deed goes unpunished is a fucking understatement. I'm normally kind of a prick to Zinnia, and, in turn, she's kind of a prick to me. It's a give and take, but there's equilibrium. Ever since I was actually nice to her, she's been giving me the cold shoulder. She's somehow both bitchier and more reserved, and it's driving me nuts.

I don't even know what I want.

That's not entirely true. I think my deepest desire is to be valedictorian. Or maybe it's just general validation. I haven't fully fleshed out my feelings on the matter.

I have other desires too. I'm contemplating whether I want to run from Zinnia or get railed by her. *Or both.* Both is good.

"Do you have an extra pencil?" a guy asks from my left, breaking me from my Zinnia-induced trance.

Dr. Daelor is a great professor. Some semesters she's even been my favorite. But today? I am having a difficult time focusing. Especially when I expected to be interning in the cosmetic lab. I'd love to blame Iris, but apparently the class-day switcheroo was Professor Watson's fault. She sprained her ankle, and Dr. Daelor had to take her to the hospital.

I should write to President Bariel and suggest they develop an Augury University hospital. It would prevent situations like this from happening again and allow medicinal magic students to get more experience before residency.

"What do you think is the most efficient way to cast a charm?" Dr. Daelor asks the class, forcing my mind back to class.

A mage I don't know very well raises their hand. "Historically, it's always been wands."

Zinnia's hand shoots up, and all heads turn her way.

"Zinnia, did you have a counter to that statement?" Dr. Daelor asks, her golden eyes locked on the smart-assed satyr.

"Well, no offense," she says, looking over at the other mage. "But using a wand is wildly inefficient. You have to have a wand, or some wood that you can make into a wand available. You'd also have to know how to properly wield a wand, which is essentially a lost practice. Mages used wands on the planets Loria and Moonflower, but Hel and Barac never utilized them. We had a short era of wand use post-Convergence here on Earth, but it was never widespread."

I have to fight the smile that creeps across my face at the level of nerdiness Zinnia just committed.

"So what do you suggest?" the other mage asks in an irritated tone, crossing their arms.

Zinnia smiles. "Use your hands. I often snap my fingers."

"I wholeheartedly agree with you, Zinnia. I think using what you have accessible to you at all times is the best move for a charms mage," our professor chimes in.

The mage who originally answered gives Zinnia a pointed glare.

"Snapping your fingers is also inefficient," I whisper to where no one else can hear it. "Flicking your wrist is objectively the best choice."

I feel a slight pressure on my toes, and I look down to spot Zinnia stepping on my boots underneath the table.

Petty.

"Is that supposed to hurt?" I say in a hushed tone.

"It'll hurt if I step somewhere else," she whispers, her sharp tone matching her harsh words.

My eyes widen, and my brain and body can't seem to locate which emotion is resonating through my body. Fear, arousal, and anger all bounce about, fighting for dominance.

I need to take a walk.

After my afternoon class with Dr. Taylor, I received a text from Zinnia asking me to meet her by the athletic fields, so here I am, leaning against a fence. It's warm out, and the black long sleeves of my shirt are doing me no favors.

Zinnia comes into view and walks past a group of people in Augury University jerseys, her round ass and wide hips swaying in her dress as she moves. She heads up the bleachers, straight for where their familiars rest.

Why? I haven't the slightest idea what trick she has up her metaphorical sleeves, but there's a look of determination in those eyes that could scare even the bravest of warriors.

And definitely the wussiest of demons. *I'd know.*

Zinnia whispers something to two of the familiars, a rat and a flying pig, and they scurry down the bleachers and across the field, until they're close to their mages.

I watch as the oversized rat, colorful crystals growing out of its back, pushes its paws against its mage's shins, forcing him to move forward. The flying pig appears to be grabbing its mage's collar with his teeth, dragging him towards the other athlete. The familiars continue until the two athletes are face-to-face, breathing against one another.

So much for the expression *when pigs fly*....

I can't hear what they're saying, but it looks like the athletes are either going to fight or fuck, and I'm not sure which I'd prefer. If they fight, I'm most definitely winning this competition. If they fuck though... that'd be one hell of a win for Zinnia.

After a few beats of tension, the athletes' lips collide, and we have our answer. Un-fucking-believable. I'd punch a wall if there was one nearby. She might actually fucking beat me, or worse...tie.

Zinnia comes back over to where I lean against a fence. "I figured if using my familiar scares people away, maybe I could use their own familiars against each other," she explains. "You have six wins; I have five. It's improbable, but not impossible for me to catch up."

"There's only a few hours left," I say and shrug before knocking my shoulder against hers. "Besides, soon enough you'll be watching me take win number seven."

The cockiness I felt earlier dissipates when I realize I don't have a single plan for another win. I considered more potions, using someone's sight against them, and even baking something with magic, but every idea that populates in my brain gives me anxiety that we'll end up in the dean's office once more.

The food hall is quiet this late at night, just a few groups of mages hanging out.

"It's almost midnight, you win, Wren," Zinnia concedes, staring at the wall clock that reads eleven-fifty-seven.

"You're not going to try and best me at the last moment?"

"Honestly? I'm just about worse out." She yawns, stretching her arms up into the air.

Both corners of my mouth tick up in a devious grin. "I would like to humbly and selflessly accept this victory."

"Humble and selfless are not synonyms to any of the words I'd use to describe you, unfortunately," Zinnia quips.

"You sound like a sore loser."

"And you sound insufferable," she says, taking a sip of her milkshake. "Now, what's your prize? And don't you dare say an I.O.U."

Many prizes flash through my mind. I'd love to race Nyxwing. I'd love to feel her—nope. Push those thoughts down, Wren. There's a poster for a Valentine's Day Carnival on the wall behind her, and my grin widens.

"Go on a date with me," I say swiftly, before I can change my mind.

"What?" Her brows furrow in disbelief.

"We spend so much time together fighting, what's the harm in a little bit of fun?" I take the hair tie off my wrist and put my hair back in a low bun, getting it off my neck. I hate to admit it, but nervous energy settles in my gut.

"You want to go out with me? Like, you enjoy my company?"

I shrug. "I enjoy looking at you. And you're intelligent enough to keep things interesting. Albeit, you're quite annoying at times."

She squints, muttering *intelligent enough,* while giving me a nasty glare. "And you're attractive until you open your stinkin' mouth."

"So you think I'm attractive? Then it's settled. I'll meet you outside your dorm room tomorrow night at six." I stand and make to leave when she grabs my arm.

"I have a shift at the library until—"

"Five. You work from noon to five, I know. That's why I said six," I interrupt.

She lets go of me and crosses her arms. "Fine."

There's a flutter in my stomach, but I try not to show it as I walk out of the building. Once I'm in the cooler night air and out of Zinnia's sight, I fly up into the sky and do a triple backflip, my heart racing with joy.

eight
ZINNIA

Welp, I'm thoroughly fucking confused. I have tried my damndest not to spend all of Professor Hill's class staring at Wren, but I can't help it.

Why did they ask me out? And better yet, why did I say yes?

Truth be told, I *know* why I said yes. I want to use this experience for my essay in Dr. Aloe's class, to let this be the uncomfortable moment of vulnerability required of me. But that still doesn't answer my original question.

Does Wren have romantic feelings for me? Or sexual? If all they're looking for is a quick fuck, they're not getting that from me. I have *very* specific interests and desires in the bedroom, and I can almost guarantee Wren will not match up with those. There's just no way.

Besides, I don't have the energy for romantic relationships. Currently, I'm focusing on my academics and my career, and once I have my master's degree and I'm out in the field, maybe then I'll look for a life partner. But for now? It's much easier to plug all my kinks and requests into an app and find someone looking for the same things. Just for a night, or even a few, but it does *not* need to be the person I spend every fucking day challenging myself against.

I don't mix work and play. Especially not with someone so insufferable.

My shifts at the library can be pretty dull. Besides midterms and finals, nobody seems to want to spend their Friday afternoon at a library, or really at school at all, and I prefer it this way. I get to be in my own little bubble, and I spend a lot of time reading about things outside of magic. History, mythology, philosophy. All of it fascinates me, but especially other cultures. I love learning about life on earth before The Convergence, as well as life on Loria, Moonflower, Hel, and Barac.

Chak Rokosmith—the head librarian at Augury University—is a massively tall orc with a heart of gold. He prints out articles on different studying methods and gives them to me, knowing my desire to be valedictorian. He has also visited Barac, his ancestors' home planet many times, and I love to hear him recall his experiences.

If I could snap my fingers and go anywhere, it would be Moonflower. I love the diversity of Earth, but humans and elves are the majority. It would be fun to experience a planet full of mostly satyrs, fauns, and centaurs.

I wonder if anyone on Moonflower wears shoes. I bet they don't. I sure as heck won't wear them ever, even though it's the norm here.

Ring. Ring. Ring. Ring.

The clock chimes four. Just one hour until I'm out of here.

"Zinnia," Chak says, collecting some paperwork and placing it into his briefcase. "You can leave now, if you'd like. I'm going to be closing the library early tonight."

"My partner..." he starts, and my eyes probably bug out of my head. "Don't give me that look, this is a recent development. Anyway, my partner is in town, and I'd like to take them out. Don't worry about the end of your shift; you'll still get paid."

"That would be amazing, honestly," I say. "I have somewhere to be as well."

"Really?" His tone is one of surprise. "I thought you'd be upset and say you want to stay open late to study."

I let out a small chuckle. "Not tonight."

"Perfect. See you next week, kid," he says as I cross out of the building.

I walk past the full-body mirror in the shared space between my roommate and I's bedrooms at least six times. I love my body, and I love fashion—but there's something about getting ready for a date that really makes me fixate on my looks. Maybe it's this idea that you're supposed to look special on a date. But why? Why do we not just aim to look like our most authentic selves? Besides, Wren has seen me at my best and my worst.

There's a light knock on my door, and when I open it, my heart beats a tad too fast for my liking. Wren looks... well, like Wren, but somehow cuter.

They traded their typical all black, angsty look for something more academic. A white dress shirt and black vest, with black pants and knee-high leather boots. Honestly? They kind of remind me of the love interest in this steam punk-esque visual novel game I was playing.

My brain is at war with itself. Part of me thinks I need to avoid all of these emotions, and another part of me remembers that old adage *what happens in Vegas, stays in Vegas*. Whatever kind of place Vegas was is lost to time, but I've heard it was a lot like Hel—full of debauchery and fun—so maybe tonight can be Vegas.

One night of enough vulnerability to write this essay, and then we can go back to hating each other.

"Are you ready?" they ask, and I nod.

Once we're out of the dorms, my brows furrow when I remember neither of us have cars.

"Uh, Wren. How are we getting there? Please tell me we're not flying there," I say, thinking of how much time I just spent on my hair.

"No," they shake their head. "I called an Oovoo; it should be here shortly."

"Oh." I sigh in relief. "Perfect."

"Speaking of perfect, I have to apologize," they say as they grab me by my hand and lift up my arm, spinning me so my teal blue-colored dress twirls around me.

"For?"

"Not immediately telling you how splendid you look tonight."

I don't know whether I want to blush, roll my eyes, or punch them. Probably a little bit of everything, but I settle on something more normal. "Thank you."

"Thank *you*."

Ugh, gosh. I don't know what's worse... cocky, pretentious Wren or flirty, dreamy Wren.

The Oovoo shows up, and we get in, heading straight to the carnival, which is apparently in Sunspell City.

"I don't think I've ever been to a carnival," I admit as the car takes us out of the Illusionary Jungle.

"Really? I thought those were big where you're from," Wren says.

"Well, sorta. We have the Louisabama State Fair. I know, I know, states don't exist anymore, but the name stuck. They're really big on things like livestock animal showcasing, pie eating contests, and stuff like that. It's really competitive," I explain.

"Oh. Yeah, no. Carnivals are more about joy and satisfaction. Sugary sweets, exhilarating rides, and unique games are the focus here."

My knee brushes against theirs, and I scooch closer to the window.

"Hel, where cambion are originally from, is really big on hedonism. Carnivals, casinos, and nightclubs are all the rage there," Wren says.

I already knew that, but I give them the satisfaction of teaching me about their culture. They've never asked about Moonflower before, but maybe—

"Do you know much about Moonflower?" Wren asks, as if reading my mind.

I stammer, surprised at their sudden interest. "I've never been."

They shrug. "I've never been to Hel either, but have you researched Moonflower at all? It seems like something that would intrigue you."

"Yeah, a bit. Nymphs, as we're originally called, are very nature oriented. Moonflower is much more rural and natural than Earth or Hel."

"Perhaps that's why Augury is so bent on keeping everything with the university in tune with nature," Wren says.

The car pulls into a parking lot where everything is bright and covered in colorful lights and flowers. Everywhere I look things are pink and red, and there's a giant Ferris wheel in front of us.

"Here," the driver says from the front seat.

Wren helps me out of the car, and we hop in line for tickets.

"So, what's on the itinerary for tonight?"

Wren furrows their brows. "I don't have one; I figured we could go with the flow for once."

My stomach lets out an embarrassingly loud grumble. "I haven't eaten yet."

"We can get something to eat and then see a show? They have a few performers here. A juggler, a comedian, and some sort of dancer."

"Ooh! Let's go to the comedy show."

Wren gives me a small smile. "Sure."

After we grab our tickets, we head to the food stalls, where Wren orders a bunch of different things for us to try. Funnel cake, cotton candy, caramel apples, and other goodies.

Crossing through a heart-shaped archway covered in flowers, we make our way to wooden benches that sit in front of a small stage.

"This show is apparently called The Raunch Rump. It's an adult comedy show," Wren shares, reading the information off the pamphlet someone passed us when we walked over.

We take our seats in the third row, and other audience members file in. I take a handful of cotton candy and shove it into my mouth, enjoying the sweet flavor.

"Good evening, and welcome to the Tommy Phoenix show," the comedian, a human man, says. He's wearing a pair of tights and tall boots, and his shirt reminds me of something you'd see at Medieval Times.

This entire thing feels surreal. The fact that I'm on a date at all is strange, but especially that I'm somewhere like this with Wren, of all individuals. This place isn't educational—it's pure, silly fun, and so unlike both of us.

It's kind of liberating.

Tommy Phoenix makes a woman's panties disappear, and they end up on someone else's head. The entire audience laughs.

"Is that not unsanitary?" I whisper to Wren, who is laughing along, while also trying to finish our funnel cake.

"I mean, STIs were eradicated. The worst thing you could get is a bacterial infection or a cold or another virus. So while technically, yes, it is unsanitary; it is improbable that anything major would occur from this," they explain.

"Okay."

They nudge their shoulder against mine. "So it's safe to laugh, Zinnia."

The show continues, and an audience member consents to being spanked while reading a book. The guy desperately tries to read without making a noise, but the occasional gasp or giggle comes out, and Tommy forces him to start that page over again.

"I feel like we're simultaneously at a BDSM club and a renaissance festival," I whisper.

"BDSM club?" Wren whispers back, curiosity creeping into their tone.

"Yeah. Have you ever been to one?"

Wren's red skin flushes even more crimson. "No," they whisper-shout. "Have you?"

"Oh, yeah. I've probably been more times than I can count. My cousin owns one in Boca Raton," I share, and I swear those golden eyes of theirs are going to pop right out of their head.

An older woman shushes us, so we pause our conversation and watch as Tommy finishes out the show with some funny but sexual magic tricks. Everyone claps as he comes around with a QR code to tip him.

We exit down the aisle, and Wren stares at me silently until we're out of anyone's earshot.

"You never told me you go to sex clubs?!" they say.

"You never asked," I say coyly. Dr. Aloe wanted us to write about an uncomfortable, vulnerable experience. Discussing sex clubs with Wren is definitely top of the list.

"What on fucking Earth would make it acceptable for me to ask you about your sex education or sexual tendencies?" Wren asks, crossing their arms.

"You can discuss sex with others without making it weird, dude." Wren's eyes go wide.

"I don't like that," they say, and I frown.

"You don't like being sex positive?" I lift up my hand and flick my wrist, my palm facing upwards as we walk towards all the booths with different games.

"No, I don't like being called 'dude.' I know it's neutral for some people, but it makes me feel like you see me as a dude. I'm sorry."

My cheeks get hot with embarrassment. "Oh. Oh goodness, *I'm* sorry. I won't use that endearment with you anymore, my bad. If it's any consolation, I do not see you as a dude."

"Oh yeah, how do you see me?" they ask, tone suddenly flirty.

"Um. You're an annoying asshole, but definitely not a dude. You're like a genderless fairy creature that infected my brain and won't leave," I say without thinking. The loudest cackle leaves my throat at my brutally honest admission.

Wren chuckles. "A parasite?"

"Something like that."

All around us are different booths and smaller rides. There's one with water guns, and another where a human stands and tries to guess your age. We come up to a booth with bottles and plastic rings, and Wren stops in their tracks.

"Would you like to give it a shot?"

"I reckon I'll just make a fool of myself, but why not?" I say. Mentally, I give myself another gold star in vulnerability. "What do I do?"

"You get three throws per ticket," the man with a mustache says and hands me the plastic rings.

I throw the first one and nearly hit him in the head.

"I'm not the most athletic cambion on earth, but fucking Hel, Zinnia," Wren says as they laugh. "Here."

Wren comes up from behind me, their long limbs reaching down to guide me as we toss another ring, and it lands on one of the closer bottles. Their chest is pressed against my back, and I can feel their breath on my neck. "Good, now try on your own."

They let go of me, and I immediately miss the warmth of their body heat as I throw the third ring and make it onto another bottle.

"Attagirl," Wren says with pride, and electricity shoots up my body in waves.

I can feel myself smiling from ear-to-ear, but I can't seem to stop. *What happens in Vegas, stays in Vegas, right?*

Wren quickly tosses and makes all three of their rings in one go, and the man lets them pick out a prize. Pointing to a stuffed animal—a pink and red monkey—Wren hands the toy to me.

"Why'd you choose the monkey and not the bunny rabbit?" I ask, knowing Wren will have some smart aleck reply.

"Isn't it obvious? You drive me bananas," they say, and I almost snort.

Called it.

We continue walking, and Wren starts to take us towards the Ferris wheel.

"Isn't this where everyone kisses in the movies?" Wren asks, and my anxiety spikes, my heart lurching up into my throat. If we end up at the top of this thing, Wren is going to try and kiss me, and then I have to decide if I actually want to kiss Wren, which is *not* something I'm willing to think about right now.

Okay, Zinnia. You're fucking smart, think of something.

The boats! There's a boat ride, and they seem to be moving at snail-like speed. Wren and I could go on the little boat, I could be emotionally vulnerable about my dead mom or something, and then we could go home. It would be perfect fodder for this stupid essay, and the trauma dumping would ruin any romantic or sexual energy resonating between us. Bingo.

"Do you wanna go on the boat ride?" I ask, gesturing to the entrance.

"I am down for anything you'd like," they say and grab me by the hand, dragging me towards the line.

I can barely register the movement before I'm reading the sign on top of the dock.

Tunnel of Love. *Oh, fuck.*

nine
WREN

My head feels like it's going to implode with the amount of revelations I've had in the last two hours. Zinnia told me she goes to sex clubs, talked about being sex positive, and then asked me to join her for a ride in the Tunnel of Love.

Surely I'm not misreading these signals?

She even frowned when I backed away from her at the ring-toss booth. There's no way. She might not be as attracted to me as I am to her, but there's something there. I can feel the metaphorical spark.

We climb into the boat, and I realize we're still holding hands. She doesn't loosen her grip as I place my hands on the paddles, with hers resting on top. The worker releases the boat from the dock, and we row ourselves into the dimly-lit tunnel.

"Do you know why I want to be valedictorian?" Zinnia asks.

"Because you love to watch me suffer?" I tease.

"Yes, but no. It's because of everything my father went through to raise me after my mother died. Moving, working multiple jobs. He did everything in his power to ensure I had a safe and bright future. This feels like a way to tell him that his work paid off," she explains.

"That makes sense," I say, and I truly empathize with her situation. I honestly wish there was a way we both could get what we wanted.

"What about you?"

"The only positive attention I've ever received was academic. It's not as poetic or beautiful of a reason as yours, but my parents only really seem to care about what I'm doing when I'm on top."

"That's incredibly sad, actually," she says, and her face forms a pitiful expression, which is not what I want at all right now.

"It's not, because at least if I'm on top, I'm on top of you," I say and wink, trying to force levity into the situation.

She giggles, and I sigh in relief before we fall into an awkward silence.

Zinnia acts as if she's about to speak a few times, before I finally decide to speak my mind. As much as I want to be fun and flirty tonight, there's something that's been bothering me for weeks.

"Could I ask you something serious?" I say, breaking the silence as we continue rowing.

"Always."

"Why do you think I cheated on our first competition? Have you not learned by now that I'm intelligent enough to never *need* to cheat?" It comes out more arrogant than I intended, but I hope she knows my meaning.

"You don't remember?"

I shake my head. "No, because I didn't cheat. The judges never implied that I did—nothing about cheating was ever even brought up to me."

"Wren," she says and puts her hand on my knee. "No offense, but you don't exactly pay attention to everyone around you. Do you remember Susan Saffron?"

"The elfling? I vaguely remember her. She didn't go to either of our schools, right?"

"Right. Well, she saw you passing a note to a member of the audience, and pointed it out to me. I brought it up to the judges, but nothing was ever done about it," she explains.

This feels like the world's biggest joke.

"The note I passed to Saga, my cousin?"

"Is that who it was?"

"Yes," I say, looking into those big green eyes of hers. "My himbo of a cousin? I'm pretty sure she failed Composition One, Zinnia."

"Okay?"

"I wasn't asking Saga for information, I promise you," I assure her.

The tunnel is covered in lights, which all form different beautiful shapes. Roses, hearts, and little cupids. I barely take note as I stare at Zinnia's face. Her soft lips and rounded cheeks.

"So, what was on the note?"

"Um." I knew she was going to ask. I fucking knew it. I want to tell her, I do, but I am equally ashamed of the prospect of how she might react.

"If you weren't cheating, what was on the note?"

It's now or never, I suppose. "It was about you."

"What?"

I let go of the paddles and rub my face with my hands before looking back up at her. "Embarrassingly enough, I was telling Saga how pretty I thought you were and how I wanted to find out your name and number."

"Wren."

"Zinnia."

Zinnia sighs. "Don't piss in my ear and tell me it's raining."

I squint my eyes at her. "You know, you say a lot of peculiar southern slang, but that one definitely places at number one. Olympic Gold of weird idioms."

She crosses her arms. "I'm telling you not to lie to me."

"I swear on my fucking GPA I am not lying to you, Zinnia. You had this adorable pixie cut, and you were wearing a pink dress that I described, probably inaccurately, as a poodle skirt. I asked Saga for advice on how to get your name and number without, and I quote, *sounding like a total dorkus*." My face feels hot, and I wonder if Zinnia can feel the nervous energy vibrating off my body in waves. "I have always thought you were the most beautiful girl in any room. Even now."

"I—"

"And the most obnoxious. *Especially* now."

Zinnia lets go of the paddle and leans over the boat. For a second, I think she's going to fall off, but then she splashes water into my face.

I let go of the paddles and put the toe of my boot into the water, getting water onto her beautiful dress.

She gives me a glare. "You're such a kumquat." Zinnia goes to splash me again when she nearly tips the boat over, and I hold her by the shoulders, stopping her from ruining both our evenings.

Disney's *Kiss The Girl* starts playing over a loudspeaker as the boat exits the tunnel. There's a sign overhead that reads *Kiss Cam* and a camera next to it.

Zinnia and I are staring into each other's eyes, unsure of what to do or say next, when she grabs my face with both hands and pulls me in. Her lips slam into mine, the kiss both passionate and ferocious, and I allow myself to melt into her.

Her tongue parts my lips as it enters my mouth, swirling against mine in duel-like motions. We continue to kiss until I realize the boat has stopped moving.

"Hey," I whisper against her lips.

"What? Oh." She looks around. "We should probably get the boat back to the dock."

I look down at the paddles, which aren't moving, and give her a smile. "Actually, I've got this," I say, and flick my wrist. Magic swirls around the paddles, and in an instant, they're moving the boat without our help.

"I never think of using my magic for unnecessary things like this," she says as I lean back into her.

"Oh, it was *very* necessary." I hold the small of her waist, pulling her into me as I press my lips against hers once more. She's the definition of softness, and I revel in the feeling of her chest pressing up against mine.

"Welcome back, lovebirds," a masculine voice says, and it breaks us from our love tunnel-induced trance.

All of the color leaches from Zinnia's face as she processes that we've been caught. I think this must be some normal version of shame or embarrassment, because there's no reason we can't kiss, especially on a Valentine's Day ride that seems to be designed for precisely such an act.

As we get out of the boat and back onto the dock, the man hands me a photograph, which I tuck into my pocket without showing Zinnia, and we continue our way to the front exit.

The carnival is lovely, truly lovely, but I ignore almost every inch of brightly lit landscape as I watch her escort me out of here. The minty blue fabric of her dress sways back and forth, illuminating the light tan of her skin.

"Who do you think the best professor at Augury is?" Zinnia asks as I open my phone to the Oovoo app.

"Either Dr. Daelor or Dean Taylor," I say in earnest. Dr. Daelor is our most captivating professor, but Dean Taylor is one of the most brilliant mages I've ever seen.

"There's no way. It's definitely Dr. Aloe," she says, so sure of herself.

"Why?"

"She just is."

I shake my head, leaning against the fence that's attached to the front gates. "*She just is* isn't a valid reason to claim she's the best. Where's your evidence?"

"Where's yours?"

"Dean Taylor finished with her PhD at twenty-two years old, went on to become a full-time professor, move up to Department Chair, then start a cosmetic lab, and eventually become dean of the entire school, all before turning thirty. If she isn't one of the greatest mages of all time, I don't know who is," I say, defensive of Dr. Alitha Taylor, who is arguably my idol and epistemological frame of reference.

"Wow. I mean, she is amazing, but I don't know her well. Isn't Professor Watson incredibly young too?"

"Yeah. And she's great, but she's no Dr. Taylor." I check the app. Our ride is 3 minutes away.

"And why did you say Dr. Daelor?" Zinnia asks. Dr. Daelor and Professor Watson are the two mutual professors we've had.

"For the same reason you didn't say Dr. Ali," I jest. "You can't stand him, and I adore that orcling."

"She is pretty great," Zinnia admits. "And Dr. Ali is growing on me... he lent me a flower for our competition."

"Let me know how you feel about him when you have to break the news that you lost."

Zinnia scowls, and I let out a hearty laugh. A silver sedan pulls up, the doors swing open for Zinnia and I. Once we're in the car, I realize I'm having a physical reaction to being so close to her.

My palms are sweating, my heart is racing, and there's this funny feeling in my stomach that I've rarely experienced. It almost reminds me of the thrill before winning a competition, when you're not quite positive of the outcome.

Except touching her is better than any prize won.

She pulls out her phone, and I look out of the corner of my eye to catch her in a back-and-forth texting match with someone. I hope it's Clover, her best friend, but a small part of me is jealous at the possibility it could be someone she fancies.

I've never seen Zinnia out on a date, but I've seen her walk a few individuals towards or out of her dorm before. She and I are both more into casual sex than relationships. I've mostly slept with humans. I'm not more attracted to them than cambions or other magical races, it's just more convenient. They're outside my school and inner circles, and they find my magic knowledge to be fascinating instead of bumptious.

Once the car pulls up to our dorm buildings, I get out and swiftly move to open Zinnia's door for her, helping her out as we head towards her room.

She gets out her keys and puts them into the lock.

"So," I say, looking for any excuse to spend more time with her, even though I check my pocket watch to see Valentine's Day has come to an end. "What kind of toys do you have?"

Zinnia almost drops her keys, her head cocks forward, and her pretty mouth parts in a small gasp. "Did you actually just ask me that?"

"You said I could talk about sex with anyone, and that I should be more sex positive," I remind her. Placing my hand on the top of the frame, I lean towards her, pressing her back into the door. I place a finger under her jaw and tilt it up so that she has to look me in the eye. "So show me."

I don't know what has taken over me, but it's like my body moves before my brain can register, my emotions overriding all logic. And by the looks of it, she's enjoying every second of this side of me.

Still staring at me, she reaches for the door handle and pushes it open. I follow her through the shared space until we're in her bedroom, and my brain goes numb.

Her bedroom is not what I expected now that I'm actually *seeing* it in the light. The comforter is pastel pink, sure, but there's something sensual about it. The bed frame is black and metal, with many slits that I can imagine could come in handy, based on what Zinnia has already shared with me. There's a painting of three naked satyrs, their feminine bodies pressed against each other, hanging next to a small black vanity, with little pink flowers painted on the edges.

I gulp, still uncertain of how I've made it this far. Zinnia is both my rival and my fantasy.

"I can show you the toys I use on others, but I'm not willing to show you my personal collection. But if you can imagine, they're just dildos and vibrators of varying sizes and colors," she shares, her cheeks flushing pink.

"Sure. No, I totally understand. That would be incredibly intimate. Your toy collection you use with others, please." I've never sounded more stupid in my entire life, but curiosity is getting the better of me.

I've never used... any toys, actually. Not even the basic ones.

She bends over and pulls out a black bin from under her bed. I dip down and look underneath to see two other bins, one pink, and the other red.

"You have three bins of sex toys?"

"Yeah. The pink is my stuff, and the red is stuff I've never tried that I received at parties or were gifted by previous partners but never used. I'm pretty sure there's a sounding rod in there," she says.

"A what?"

"Nevermind. You're not ready for the red box."

"Okay," I say, throwing up my hands.

"Sit," she instructs me, and I sit down on her bed, the comforter soft against my hands.

She pulls out black leather cuffs, a strap-on, and a blindfold, and places them all on the bed beside me. All of these are things I've seen before, whether in books or other media, and I smile, happy she's willing to share this with me.

"So those are some of the basics, as you called them. And here are a few things you might be less familiar with," she explains, before pulling out a leather collar with a ball attached.

"And that is for?"

She lets out an incredibly loud giggle, snorting into her hand, before she places it down next to me. "Shutting you up."

Oh. My.

Zinnia pulls out rope, a small paddle, and a small thing that reminds me almost of a tail, attached to a whip-like handle.

"Okay, what is that?" I'm not sure I've ever even seen one of those before.

"The flogger?" she asks, pointing to the toy.

"Yeah, what does it feel like?"

She shrugs before picking it up. "I'm not really sure how to explain it."

"Could you show me?" I ask, before I quickly amend. "With clothes on, I mean. Just what it feels like."

Zinnia seems to blanch for a moment before she raises the toy and hits my arm with it. It barely touches me, and I give her a look that says *really*.

She hits it against me again, but this time it thuds against my inner thigh, the sensation sending jolts through me. It's a dull, concentrated sort of pain, and a smile spreads across my face as I sense the pheromones coming off of her. She's enjoying this.

"Did you like that?" she asks.

"Yes." I don't tell her that I know she did too.

"I bet you fucking did," she says as she presses the flat of her palm against my chest, pushing me onto the bed.

Without another word, Zinnia is straddling me, her mouth and tongue grazing down my neck. I find the zipper of her dress and pull it down before lifting it over her head to reveal a lacy red bra and matching underwear.

This is going to be fun.

"This is," she starts between kisses. "Going to be." Another kiss. "A one time thing."

"Sure," I agree. I doubt it, but whatever makes her happy. I just need her at least once in my life.

"I'm serious, Wren. You can't get in the way of valedictorian for me. Not anymore than you already have."

"I'm sorry I've been such a distraction," I say, and she rolls her eyes.

Zinnia unhooks her bra as she continues to kiss me, and her breasts drop into my hands as I squeeze her warm flesh. Her legs are covered in short fur, which grows up her body and stops before her soft belly.

I want to run my fingers through it all. I want to touch every inch of her.

ten

ZINNA

So much for not kissing Wren. Now, against my better judgment, I'm straddling them, kissing down their torso as they grab my ass.

I can't help it. You can't confess to me that you've always found me beautiful on a romantic boat ride, ask me to flog you, and not expect me to want to fuck. I'm not a saint.

I knew I shouldn't have let them in my room. On the way here, I texted my best friend and asked her how to avoid having sex with Wren. Not because I don't want to, because I definitely do, but because I don't need another complication or wrench in my plans.

Clover reiterated again and again that we could just have one night of fun and fuckery, and I hope she's right, because I'm about to let loose.

Fuck it.

Wren sits up against my headboard, unbuttoning their vest and shirt as I remove my underwear, and we toss our clothes to the ground. All that's left is their pants, and I pull them down to reveal underwear, which is incredibly similar to mine, the head of their cock sticking out from the top.

"I knew you liked lace," Wren says, and I laugh, not knowing what I expected.

"I never knew what kind of anatomy cambions have," I confess. I did know Wren has some sort of dick, them having mentioned it before in passing, but I never knew the specifics of cambion anatomy.

"Is this your first time fucking a demon?" they ask as they strip off their last article of clothing, and I place my left leg back over their hips, straddling above them.

"Yes, and I bet I can be the best satyr you've ever slept with," I say. Even in sex, I am competitive.

"First and best," they say with a grin. "If you want a surprise, move my cock so that your body is resting above it."

What I'd really like to do is spank and peg them until they can't see clearly, but I think that'd be a little much for them. I stare at Wren's thin, lightly muscled chest as I adjust on them before my clit finds something... interesting. It feels almost like a grinding toy.

"What is that?"

Wren pulls my face to theirs. "It's called a terefrico. It's meant purely for pleasure."

Their entire body seems to be built for my pleasure. From the way their hands grip me, to the warmth of their body heat, I'm enjoying it all.

With one hand resting on their chest, I grind against them, letting the friction propel my pleasure. I continue like this, writhing and moaning, before I'm nearly toppling over the edge.

"Put your cock in me," I demand.

"So bossy," they say. "But I'll do anything you ask me to."

At that, my eyes widen. They adjust their cock until their head is pushing at my entrance. "Anything?"

"Within reason," they say coyly, and I sink down onto them.

Wren's cock is hard and warm, and I snap my fingers, my magic swirling through the air, as I sit still, straddling Wren. All of the toys make their way back into the box, with the exception of the rope, and my magic charms it to wrap around Wren's wrists, before it ties them to the bedframe.

"I think that's within reason," I say, and Wren bites their bottom lip.

I let my inner walls pulse against Wren, but I don't move. They make to move me with their legs, but I snap my fingers again, and another rope snakes its way out of the box. My magic nearly sparkles as it wraps around their ankles, and suddenly I find Wren completely at my disposal.

The trick to sex magic is ensuring that consent is required for every spell. Whenever I wield a sex charm, I make sure to put the intention that if either participant no longer consents, the charm wears off.

"Did you just use a sex charm?" Wren asks.

"Did you just speak without permission?" I ask, and Wren shakes their head.

"Good," I say.

I continue to straddle Wren and slowly start to move. Ever-so-slightly, I add more and more friction, until Wren is writhing, clearly desperate for more.

They let out a soft whimper, and I allow my body to finally move.

I ride them, my shins pressing into the bed as my thighs move up and down. I sink down onto their cock, moaning with every bounce.

Whenever I feel that Wren is close, I stop. I want to edge them on as long as possible.

Their cock is thick and long, with rib-like texture towards the base of their shaft. My back arches as I pick up my pace until I topple over the edge.

I jump off of Wren, and put their cock in my hand before allowing them to follow after me. Their body jerks, fighting against their restraints, and I watch the face they make, which borders on agony, as I continue pumping their cock even after they've come.

"Please, Zinnia, stop," they beg, and I finally let go.

The ropes come loose, and I wipe Wren off with a towel before resting beside them. My eyes close for just a moment, and I can feel myself drift off.

Our limbs are still intertwined, my head resting on Wren's chest, when I look up to see their eyes are open.

"Good morning, beautiful," Wren whispers when they see I'm awake.

My hand is resting on their chest, and I draw small circles into their vibrant red skin. "Good morning."

"Can I ask you a personal question?"

"Sure."

They shift their head to make eye contact with me. "Have you ever considered taking an edible or something for your endometriosis pain?"

Have they been thinking about solutions for my reproductive issues? "Yeah, I used to all the time. Then I developed something called Cannabinoid Hyperemesis Syndrome, and now I can't take any at all without vomiting everywhere."

"Seriously? Does your body even fucking like you?"

"Nope," I say and sit up, covering my exposed chest with the sheet. "I'm pretty sure there's other things wrong with my body too, but I guess only time will tell."

"I'm sorry," they say and sit up beside me. Wren tucks a strand of hair behind my ear. "I really like your body."

"Wren," I whisper.

"Yes?"

"This can't happen again."

"Yeah, okay," they say in a disbelieving tone.

"I'm serious. I don't do relationships, and I definitely don't fuck my greatest rival."

They shrug. "You just did, sweetheart."

"And I will *not* be doing it again," I reiterate.

"Whatever you say."

I furrow my brows. "Wren, I'm so serious. We are not doing this again."

"I know," they say. "You established that from the beginning."

I sigh with relief. "Okay, good."

"It's totally fine. There are plenty of fish in the sea, I can assure you I don't need mine to be you. Thank you for the little lesson in... flogging?"

"You're welcome. Now get the fuck out of my dorm."

Wren stands up, their bare ass exposed as they bend over to pick up their clothes, and I watch their unearthly beauty as they dress themselves.

"Well, I suppose I shall see you around," they say, saluting me goodbye.

"This was fun," I admit. It's the last moment of vulnerability that I'll allow.

"Yeah, it was," they say as they cross the threshold of my bedroom door.

I head into my bathroom and turn on the water before jumping in, letting the warm feeling absorb me and melt away all my guilt and lingering feelings.

I don't know what's worse: the fact that I enjoyed spending time and hooking up with Wren, or the fact that I felt a little guilty telling them it can't happen again. This was a mutually beneficial exchange, and I have no reason to feel bad about it. We agreed both before and after that it couldn't happen again. A one-time thing.

So why do I kind of want more? Ugh.

Quickly, I shampoo and condition my hair and legs, slipping into something cozy and sitting down at my vanity.

Opening my laptop, I start to outline my essay. *The Vulnerability Date*, I title it. Typing away, I recount our date, how much fun it was, and the uncomfortable moments of vulnerability I provided. I call Wren ANONYMOUS, and even vaguely describe our sexual adventures–our sexual adventures that we are never. Doing. Again.

eleven

WREN

Oh, we're *definitely* doing that again. Time to bust out the mini-skirt.

twelve

ZINNIA

Having submitted my essay last night, I feel better about the whole *experience* with Wren, and I've accepted it was a one-time thing. Though sleeping with them was a ton of fun, and honestly a great stress reliever, I don't need to be dilly dallying with the half-demon. Even if said half-demon could be an incredible submissive.

Putting on my favorite vintage playsuit, I walk out of the dorms and head towards Dr. Daelor's classroom. Nyxwing heels beside me, and we cross down the tree-lines path until we're at the main part of campus. We take our time, slowly making our way up the Charms Tree. My period and star tracking app told me I'm in my follicular phase *and* something about the stars and how they align with my chart should lead to peak productivity for me this week.

Unfortunately, I am not feeling very productive. I am feeling like I want to go hide in my dorm to avoid Wren.

Walking into class, Wren is already sitting in the front row, so I sit three rows behind them. I prefer the front, but I can make do with this. I'm trying to send a message, even if I'm not positive what I want that message to be.

Dr. Daelor starts her lecture with the mention of permanent and indefinitely placed charms. She goes on to explain their importance in society, and how, if performed correctly, they can exist without draining anyone's magic.

"Alright annoyances, you are all going to partner up with someone for this project, and it will be a big chunk of your final grade, so choose wisely," Dr. Daelor says.

Everyone stands up, moving about the room to match up with someone they know, or the first person in sight. Clover isn't in this class—I don't have any other friends—so I just mindlessly wander, hoping to lock eyes with someone.

Just my luck. The pair of golden eyes I've been tediously avoiding, looks directly my way.

"It appears we will be partners for this project," Wren says, their voice oddly monotone.

"It appears so."

Wren scratches the back of their neck. "Is there a reason you're avoiding me? I mean, did you not think this through? If we partner with other people, and those people suck, it could tank our GPAs."

I hadn't even thought of that, but they're right.

"No, I'm not avoiding you," I say.

They cross their arms, sitting on the table, and unfurl their wings a bit to shield me from the class.

Are they wearing a mini-skirt? It feels like the oxygen has been sucked directly out of my lungs.

"So now you're a liar, too? Zinnia, we fucked. It's not a big deal," they whisper.

"Not so loud," I gulp, trying to avoid eye contact.

"How about we meet this afternoon to discuss our ideas?" they suggest, and I reach out a hand to shake on it.

Why am I being so fucking awkward? And why is Wren torturing me with the sight of their upper thighs?

"Sounds good."

Nyxwing and I head out of the room and towards the Creature Crafts Tree, where Professor McNab's class awaits. "When researching archeological digs of familiars' bodies, please keep in mind that things will be completely distorted from The Convergence..." she begins.

I almost fall asleep during Professor McNab's class, but force myself to stay awake as she drones on. When class finally ends, I grab my things and quickly exit the building, Nyxwing by my side.

Ping. Ping.

I somehow have notifications from both Clover and Wren.

CLOVER

how'd it go seeing your little friend after y'alls sleepover?

ZINNIA

hate you.

CLOVER

was it awkward?

ZINNIA

Definitely a little.

CLOVER

are you going to fuck them again?

ZINNIA

Nope.

CLOVER

are you lying to me?

ZINNIA

...

I click over to Wren and I's conversation.

WREN

Meet me at the cosmetic lab in 15, please.

ZINNIA

Okidoki.

Placing my phone back into my purse, I cross towards the cosmetic lab, which is located near Dr. Ali's greenhouse and the athletic fields, not far from our dorms.

The cosmetic lab is a large building, with many offices and individual workstations. I drop Nyxwing off in the room familiars hangout in, which is notably empty except for Wren's little red mushroomfox, Liszt.

"Wren?" I call out, walking through the clean, crisp space. It reminds me a bit of a dental office, but with beautiful artwork everywhere.

"Naming your dog is a complicated matter," Wren sings out from another room.

What are they on about?

"Names like Max, Fido, Sadie, and Milo," they sing, their voice resonating off the walls of the lab. "Bella and Bailey and Luna and Lacey."

"Are you okay?" I say, finally locating the door and crossing into the room.

Wren is standing on top of a desk, their boots on pieces of paper, as they dance while singing about dogs.

"What are you doing?" I ask as they jump down, sliding around the room.

"I was cast in Dogs The Musical," they say nonchalantly.

"What? We don't even have a musical theatre program." I sit on the desk and watch Wren twirl back and forth, their short skirt flipping up to reveal the shorts underneath.

I am no better than a man.

They shift so close they can almost kiss me, their elbows resting on my knees, and I see their eyes are incredibly dilated.

"Did you take something?" I ask, because there's no other explanation for this kind of behavior.

"I don't recall."

"Wren." They rest their head in my lap, and I tug on their arms, trying to lift them back up. It's no use, they're a dead weight, seemingly slumped against me.

Ring. Ring.

Whose phone is that?

"The Broadway Tour of Less Miserables is coming to town!" they shout, standing up and clicking their heels.

"Less Miserables?"

Wren slides their finger across their phone screen and answers it. "I can't get to the phone right now, I'm participating in hot nonbinary extracurriculars." They hang up. "You were asking?"

"What's Less Miserables?"

"Oh! It's a musical about the Dutch Revolution of 2085, when robots poisoned their potatoes, and everyone got Tuber Culosis," they explain. "It's potato poisoning."

"You just said—nevermind." I stand and grab Wren by the shoulders and lightly shake them. "Why are you acting like this?"

Wren wriggles out of my grip and runs over to the center of the room, where they bend over towards the ground, nearly touching their toes, before snapping back up to hip level, a ridiculous grin spreading across their face. I move towards them, and they push a chair into my path, avoiding me.

Are all theatre kids this fucking insufferable?

Wren flips their long white hair behind their back. "Do you think they'd cast me as Elsa?"

"Probably not," I say blandly, reaching for their hand. "You literally live on a tropical island."

"I can handle the cold," they say and bolt out of the door.

Fuck my life.

I run, faster than my goat legs have ever taken me, as I chase Wren through the empty lab. We round a corner into a room full of shelves and vials, and an icy chill runs down my spine as the door slams behind us.

I reach for the large, circular handle, but the door won't open.

"Will you help me open this door," I ask, turning back to Wren on the floor. "No, no. You do not get to lock us in a freezer and then go to sleep."

I shake Wren, this time almost violently, and their eyes slowly open, their pupils back to their normal size.

"Where are we?" they ask, their hands reaching down to touch their skirt.

"We're in some sort of freezer in the cosmetic lab."

They sit up, their eyes widening. "How did we get here?"

I cross my arms. "You were pretending to be—I don't know. A Broadway star? An Ice Queen? And got us trapped in here."

"That is quite embarrassing. Alright. Well, let's open the door."

"It's stuck."

They stand and swiftly reach for the door, trying to turn it, but it won't budge. "Okay. Okay. Where's your phone?"

"Back in the other room. Where's yours?"

"It's usually in my back pocket, but I wore this skirt today," they say, and I slump onto the floor. Wren sits down next to me, our knees touching.

"What did you take?" I ask, tone accusatory.

Wren looks down. "I was trying this potion; it's for a project in Professor Watson's class. It's all about changing your emotions. I thought I had perfected it, so I tested it on myself."

"That was incredibly irresponsible of you. Where is everyone else?" I'm starting to shiver, the biting cold of the freezer finally getting to me.

"Dean Taylor is busy, and Professor Watson is still out with her sprained ankle. Allegedly, her sister spilled a potion, and she slipped."

"I sprained my ankle, and I still came to school," I say. "You shouldn't have experimented like that with no one else around. What if you got sick or had a bad reaction to the potion?"

"Maybe she fractured her leg; I don't know the specifics. I would've thought you'd want me to make a mistake like this so you can get your wish." Their words are shaky as they come out.

"Of course not. I want to win, but I want to win fair and square," I say. "Lay down."

"Okay."

Wren lays onto the floor, and I get on top of them, huddling close for warmth.

"Give me a break, Zinnia," they say through gritted teeth. "You avoided me all morning—don't act like you suddenly care." Their words are like venom.

"Do you think I casually share bits and pieces of my life with people I don't care about?" I whisper.

"I don't know."

"No. And frankly, sometimes I think you don't know much of anything."

Wren's brows furrow. "That's quantifiably impossible, of course I know things. I'm speaking to you right no—"

"Shut the fuck up and kiss me you idiot."

thirteen

WREN

I sit up and unfurl my wings, wrapping them around us as I press my lips against Zinnia's. Her body is still warm, and I tuck her into me, her ass on my lap, both legs crossing over mine. Her hands press into my skin, pulling me deeper into the kiss. Zinnia's tongue dances against my mouth, asking to be invited in, and I allow her.

I'd give her the whole world if she asked for it. Or at least whatever I had in my power to provide.

"Heat," I say through clattering teeth. "I need friction."

I need something, anything to get this icy feeling out of my body. Zinnia shifts, now straddling me, and her fur-covered thighs provide much needed warmth as they squeeze against mine. She grinds down on my hardened length, and I moan out, not having expected the quick change in activities.

Zinnia's body is perfect. I want to see more, want to feel more of her, but I also don't want to be cold.

"Wren," she whispers into my ear, her breath hot against my neck. "I want you to fill me," she moans, running her fingers against the sensitive spot on my wing.

My dick strains against the fabric of my underwear, begging to be released, and as she rubs my wing, I can't help but wonder where she learned this evil trick. She continues to grind against me, and I don't want to ruin the moment, but I have information I need to share with her. It's now or never, I suppose.

"I feel like this is an important time to tell you I get those contraceptive shots," I say.

She gives me a pointed look. "Wren, I know. You whined like a baby about how bad the last one hurt."

"Oh. I apologize—"

"Stop talking and take my clothes off."

"Yes ma'am," I say and unzip her romper.

Zinnia isn't wearing anything underneath. Though her vulva is covered by her short fur, her breasts are on full display, and I pull her towards me, sucking on one of her beautiful nipples.

"Wren," she whimpers, her eyes fluttering closed. "I want..."

"Anything."

"I want you inside me."

I circle her other nipple with my finger, gently caressing her as I kiss her neck. "How do you want me? Tell me what you want, sweetheart."

Her eyes go wide, a devious grin making its way into her features. "I want you to pick me up and flip me over. I want you to fuck me until I can't see straight."

"Your wish is my command," I say and lift her up, pushing her against the cold metal laboratory table.

Pulling my skirt down, I angle my cock right at her opening and slowly push into her perfect pussy.

"Now," she demands.

"So bossy."

Gradually, I pick up the pace, thrusting into her. Sweat trickles down my neck as I slam my body against hers, the heat and sensation warming me up.

"Grab my," she says between pants. "Horns. Grab my horns."

Confused but intrigued, I take her horns in my hands and pull her back towards me, her body arching as I continue to pound into her.

I'm on the edge, but I want her to come first—so I hold it in as best I can, my mind circling with thoughts to keep me from my impending orgasm.

"Oh, fuck," she calls out as her body shudders, her muscles spasming as I let go of her horns. She perches on her arms and looks back at me, arching her back further. "Come for me."

And with that command, I completely let go, my cock practically vibrating as I slam inside her, completely absorbed into her warm wetness.

Removing myself from her, I watch as my fluids drip down from her entrance, onto her legs.

"I'm going to kill you," Zinnia says as she scans the room.

"Here." I open a drawer and throw her a towel, helping her wipe off her legs, before wiping off myself.

"We're going to die of frostbite in here, but at least we both orgasmed," she says with a small laugh.

"Probably not. It's 0 degree celsius in here, and we shouldn't be trapped long enough to get frostbite," I explain.

She does not look reassured.

Once we get cleaned up, I help her get into her romper. As I'm pushing up her back zipper, light streams into the room, illuminating us.

Iris Watson. Of *course*. And I am *entirely* naked. Correction... I might as well be Winnie the Pooh in just my shirt, no bottoms.

"Wow. Congratulations, intern," she croons from the doorway. "Now, please put your clothes back on. I'm pretty sure I have to report this to my sister *and* my therapist."

"As long as you don't tell your boyfriend," Zinnia says to Iris as she hands me my skirt.

"Okay, so about that. Wait. How does she know who my—you know what, I don't really care. Wren, put your junk away. Quickly," Iris says with urgency.

"Farfora, are you in here?" a deep, masculine voice comes from down the hallway.

"You're joking. That's Dr. Ali. Oh no," Zinnia whispers, and I use my hand to cover her mouth.

"Yes, sorry. I went inside to grab my things and got swept up in a thrilling conversation about pants—"

"Plants? What variety of plants?"

Iris lets out a quiet cough. "*Pants*. The intern got new pants." She looks down at me. "A skirt, actually, and I wanted to know what brand it was," she says, covering.

Iris gestures for us to follow her out of the freezer. Zinnia refuses to move at first, but I push her hooves with my boots, forcing her out of the cold room.

When Iris opens the main door, I stand in the doorway, and Zinnia hides on the wall behind the door.

"Is this the cambion that is always getting on your nerves, my love?" Dr. Ali whispers, though not very subtly.

"Yes, but we're getting along better now. They owe me a favor, anyway," she says smiling and takes her hand in the serpent's hand before walking off.

Zinnia lets out a deep sigh. "If we're ever alone together again, fear for your life."

I chuckle before grabbing the small of her waist. "I'm counting on it."

Zinnia and I both passed our midterms with flying colors, just as we predicted. The narrow gap between our GPAs has gotten even more narrow, with a high chance that Zinnia could actually beat me, even without a big mishap on my part.

She will just need to do a tiny bit better on finals, and I'm screwed.

Metaphorically, that is. Physically, she's already screwing me, and there's no complaints there. We have hooked up at least six or seven times in the last four weeks.

It was pretty cyclical, actually. We'd meet up to work on our project or study for midterms, get into an argument, and, like clockwork, our clothes would be on the floor.

Now we're almost to spring break, and I'm not sure what to do. Zinnia is preparing to go home for the week, whereas I've decided to stay on campus.

Do I kiss her goodbye?

My mind wanders, my heart racing as I head towards her dorm room to help her gather her things. Knocking on her door, a petite girl I recognize opens the door.

"Come in, Wren," she says.

"Are you dating my cousin Saga?" I ask, genuinely shocked.

"Yes," she giggles. "My name's Aster, nice to meet you." She places out a hand, and we shake before I cross towards Zinnia's room.

"Unbelievable," I shout as I practically kick open her bedroom door. "You set up your *roommate* and *my* cousin during the Valentine's day competition and had the audacity to accuse me of cheating at—" I stop in my tracks when I see Zinnia keeled over, a pillow to her stomach.

"Hey, hey, hey," I rush over towards her, and she rolls over, facing away from me. "Sweetheart. Is it your endo?" My hand finds its way to her back, and I sit down on her bed, drawing hearts on her shirt with my finger.

"Yeah," she whimpers.

"Is your dad picking you up or did you schedule an Oovoo?"

She groans. "I scheduled an Oovoo to take me to the bus stop, and then my dad will pick me up from there. It'll be here in fifteen minutes."

"Did you pack yet?"

"No."

Sweet Merlin. This girl is made of nightmares.

I rummage around her room, packing anything that looks useful into her suitcases. Study books. A few outfits. Period supplies. Toiletries. Her toothbrush. A phone charger. I pause for a moment when I get to her bra and underwear drawer. She won't be with me, and she's on her period, so I'm guessing she just wants to be comfortable.

I pick out the bigger and softer looking pieces in her collection and neatly fold them into the bag as well. Zinnia's eyes flutter as I scoop her up in my arms. I'm about to charm her suitcase to follow us, when Nyxwing gets out of his bed and pushes it using his horns.

Excellent.

Once we're outside the dorms, I place Zinnia down and let her lean against me.

"Hey, pretty girl. Your ride is almost here. I'll see you in a week? Call me if you want to discuss the final touches on the project. We'll finish it when we get back," I say, and she sniffs me. Why did she sniff me?

"Okay," she says.

A teal SUV with no top pulls up, and I place her suitcase into the trunk. The backdoor swings open, and Nyxwing crawls inside.

"Bye, Zinnia."

To my surprise, she reaches down and squeezes my dick and balls. "Mine," she whispers and kisses me on the cheek.

I help her settle into the backseat before closing the door and watching her drive away.

Did Zinnia just claim me as hers?

Professor Watson, Iris Watson, and Dean Taylor all sit in one of the common rooms of the cosmetic lab. I'm in one of the adjacent rooms, working on my big project with Zinnia and casually eavesdropping on their conversation.

"Indie, I'm so glad you're back. It was fucking creepy in here without you," Iris confesses.

"I'm glad to be back. Apparently, a bunch of people thought I had died or something. I was out with the sprain, and then I had already scheduled PTO for all my wedding appointments. With you and Alitha gone, students thought you guys were at my funeral," Professor Watson says in disbelief.

"That's absurd," the dean's voice chimes in. "Especially since Vega was still at work."

"Yeah, but not everyone knows V and I are engaged. We don't wear rings"

"Indigo," Iris says, her tone sharp. "Be serious, you two have matching snowflake tattoos on your fingers."

There's multiple laughs going on at once, and Dean Taylor's voice travels. "They literally sparkle."

I make myself busy, flipping through the closest textbook to me, as the footsteps draw nearer.

"Wren, what're you doing here?" Dean Taylor asks. "Students are not supposed to be on campus; it's spring break."

"I decided to stay for the week. I've got a lot of work to do."

She shakes her head, crossing closer to where I'm seated. "No, you don't. You're caught up on all your internship projects. You should be out with friends. Maybe not partying, but doing something fun."

"I don't really *do* fun," I confess. "I wanted to watch you and Professor Watson experiment this week."

"We were mostly going to do wedding planning activities this week, Wren. Why are you really here?"

I take in a deep breath. "I mean, my cousin and my... best and only friend went back to their families for the break. I wanted to stay here and soak up everything you and Professor Watson show me, because ultimately my goal is to work *with* you two one day." I just referred to Zinnia as my best friend. It was because I didn't know how else to refer to her, but I think it might be true.

"Alright," she says, looking me up and down. "Indigo, will you come in here?"

High-heeled boots clack against the shiny floors of the lab, and Professor Watson with her glowy white hair crosses the threshold into the room.

The dean gives her a wide smile before looking back at me. "What would you like us to teach you this week, Wren?"

fourteen

ZINNIA

The bus pulls into the station, which is connected to the airport my pa works at. I can see his yellow pickup truck waiting in the parking lot for me. He gets out, his hair visibly grayer than the last time I saw him. Picking up my suitcase, I get off the bus and run towards him, and my dress twirls as he spins me around. *Thank the gods and goddesses for pain meds.*

"Did you just get off work?" I ask, noting his uniform.

"Yeah." My father's southern drawl is a lot thicker than mine, and it's comforting. Feels like a warm hug after a long day. It's only been a few months since the last time we were together, but it feels like ages.

"Thank you for picking me up; I've missed you."

He grabs my suitcase, we get into his truck, and drive away.

My pa's house is on the outskirts of Florgia Beach, on the southwest side of Magia Island. It's a small, bungalow-style house, and nothing like the farmhouse from my childhood. This cottage is small and white, and the yard is tightly packed.

Before my momma died, we had lots of land and cattle in Louisabama, over in The Americas. After she passed, we struggled to care for the farm just the two of us, and my pa was offered better job opportunities on Magia Island. That's when we moved here. Florgia Beach is a coastal town, and all we could really afford to keep on our property were chickens and dogs.

And one pig. Patricia.

But it's home, all the same. I spent all my teenage years sneaking out of that bedroom window, and Nyxwing's horns got caught in the tree branches of that big oak in the front yard.

We walk inside, and I head into my room, where my bed is made. There's a basket sitting on top, neatly wrapped in a cute bow made of old fabric. In it are my favorite snacks and soda and a candle.

Nyxwing settles down in his old spot, huddled against a wall, which is still covered in different international popstar posters from all over the globe.

"Zinnia," my pa calls from down the hallway. "Would you like to come to work with me tomorrow?"

"Sure thing; I'd love to help."

How does my father work in these conditions?

The receptionist at Magia Builders quit a few months back, and they never hired another one. Instead, they charmed the phone to send text messages to whoever each caller was speaking to.

The results? There is paperwork everywhere. When I opened the bathroom door, bills fell out.

Bills that are unpaid and overdue.

I have spent the last two days completely fixing their lives. I worked with the owner to help them pay their unpaid bills, sent out invoices that never reached their recipients, as well as put all their files into folders with proper labels.

The office looks totally different. I even burned some incense, as well as made some affordable decorations to put around with some dried flowers and a hot glue gun.

I check my phone. No notifications from Wren, but one from Clover.

CLOVER

are you going to the spring fling?

ZINNIA

I don't know. Are you?

CLOVER

i think avery and i are required to attend together

ZINNIA

Oh boy. I wish y'all luck.

I'm sitting in a big leather chair, doing my nails while texting Clover, when my pa walks in. Sweat and dirt coat the skin of his face and arms, but his pants are thick enough to protect his fur.

"How's my sweet Zinnia doing? All the guys want to thank you again for organizing," he says, putting his hat down on the table.

"I'm good. I mean, the partner for my project hasn't called me all week, and I'm a little disappointed, but overall I'm great. Happy to be here."

He furrows his brows, blowing the green strands of his hair out of his face. "Have you tried calling him? Her?"

"Them," I correct.

"Have you tried calling them?"

I shrug as I finish applying polish to my pinky. "No."

"Why not?"

"I don't want to call them. Might give the wrong impression," I say.

"Why would calling your classmate give the wrong impression?" he asks, eyeing me suspiciously.

"It's complicated." I don't meet his eyes.

"I feel like this individual is more than just your class partner," Pa says, picking his hat up. "I'm not trying to pry, but I know you, Zinnia. You guard your heart too much."

"I don't guard my heart. I just don't fall in love. It's not like I'm avoiding it on purpose. I'm busy, and it's not worth my time." Everyone always dies or leaves.

"Estrella was worth all my time, even the time I've spent grieving her," he says before walking off.

I'm glad that's his truth, but I don't see it being mine. I truly am not avoiding love; I'm just not looking for it. Academics are my focus. I want to graduate, really grow in my career, and then maybe I'll find someone to spend my life with. I don't need to rush into picking a partner now, though.

Pa and I sit on the shore, the evening sky glowing vibrant shades of orange and red.

"Red sky morning, shepherd's warning. Red sky night, shepherd's delight," pa says, looking at the skyline.

There's the pitter-patter of footsteps against the sand, and I feel a slight breeze when Nyxwing soars over us.

"She's flying now?!" Pa asks, his eyes wide.

"Sort of. I made her fly in class once, but she hasn't since. She did okay then, though," I explain. "I was actually on her back."

"Do you think that maybe she feels safer doing it here because of the open air?"

"Maybe! Though she never enjoyed it much growing up."

"Hmm. Well, regardless, it's a beautiful sight. She seems happy."

"She does."

He leans his shoulder into mine. "I wish you seemed happier too."

"I am happy, I promise," I say, resting my head on his shoulder. I breathe in and let the salty ocean air fill my lungs.

"You are too absorbed in your studies—I reckon you don't do anything else," he says and places a kiss on the top of my head.

But my studies are all I have. I mean, I have Nyxwing and my pa, but after that... it's just me and my knowledge. My books. Should there be more to my life? Am I not well-rounded enough? Maybe I should try to go to the spring fling, or even pick up another hobby. Something, anything outside of academics.

Ping.

I get my phone out of my back pocket and see one notification from Wren. My heart practically leaps out of my chest as I click into the message.

WREN

I've been working on the potion that we plan to charm for Professor Daelor's assignment. It's almost ready.

Good. I'm glad they've been working on their half of the project.

Ping.

Another text comes in from Wren.

WREN

PS. I missed fighting with you this week. There's nobody else I'd rather be insufferable with.

Putting my phone down, I smile as the sun lowers until it's completely out of the sky.

The last month has been a series of strange events. Wren went from being my enemy and rival, to becoming my fuck-buddy and project partner, and then a week of almost radio silence. I don't know what to think or how to move forward, but studying for finals has me in a chokehold. There isn't time to be stressed over the cute half-demon I'm sleeping with.

And now I'm here, sitting in a chair in their dorm room, as we try and charm the potion they've made. Our goal is to create an infinity ring of water.

If we can get the spell right, it can be worn like jewelry, but is ultimately just constant flowing water. We used a potion instead of tap water to prevent bacteria and parasites from being able to infect it, but it looks the same.

"I think your intentions are off," I say as they flick their wrist for the hundredth time. "You're thinking of it like it's flowing water, but maybe you have to envision it as jewelry."

"That doesn't make any sense," Wren argues. "It's not metal. Envisioning the water as a metallic shape does nothing."

"It does... you're the one," I start, but stop myself. It's not that I don't want to argue with Wren anymore, I do, it's just that I don't want to argue if I'm not going to win.

And they're definitely right, but I won't be admitting that twice.

"Let's go get food, and then we can reconvene," I suggest, changing the subject.

"Fine."

The energy between us has shifted, but I'm not sure why. Did the time apart make it even clearer that we're better off as enemies than friends? Or did I upset or offend Wren in some way unknowingly?

We walk towards the food hall, and our hands brush against one another's before I pull away. Not a word is spoken between us as we grab our food and get seated. There's a poster that reads *Spring Fling* hanging overhead, and I sigh.

Going to a dance seems so fun. I love dressing up and wearing cute clothes, and I love dancing. Visions flash in my mind of movies where the love interest twirls the main character, dipping them before finally planting a kiss.

It's romantic and beautiful and wonderful, but it just doesn't align with my focus. I love my pa, I'm glad I spent spring break with him, but I spend too much time dilly-dallying, and not enough time studying. I can't afford another night of fun.

"What are you thinking about? Existential dread? The vastness of the universe?" Wren asks as they steal one of my french fries.

"Those aren't yours," I say, pulling the basket closer to me.

They smile and cross their arms over their chest. “What’s bothering you?”

My mom is dead. My dad is overworked and underpaid. Or I don’t know, the fact that I might’ve wasted all of college working towards a goal, only to not achieve it. Oh! And I have a total of two friends and practically no hobbies or social life outside of academics. Perhaps that’s what’s bothering me. “Nothing,” I mumble. Wren can’t fix all my problems.

My eyes trail back towards the poster on the wall.

“Are you considering attending the spring fling?”

“Yeah, but I’m not going to go.”

Wren’s eyebrows draw together, their mouth slightly agape. “Why not? I think it’d be good for you.”

More like good for them to get ahead of me. “I don’t have time. I’m busy studying.”

“You can take a break for a night.”

I shake my head. “It wouldn’t just be a night, though. I’d need to take the time out of my day to buy a dress. Pictures—I’d have to take some pictures to send to my pa. And what about hair and makeup? That takes time and energy. That’s hours that I’d be doing something frivolous, meanwhile you’re here, getting the better of me.”

“What if... hmm... what if I went with you?”

“To the dance?”

“To all of it.” Wren grins. “I could be your date, so to speak. We could ask my cousin and her girlfriend, your roommate, to tag along.”

If Wren goes with me, they won’t be able to study without me. This might be the perfect opportunity. “What about Clover, could she come too?”

“Sure. The more the merrier!”

fifteen
WREN

I've always been well aware of my connection to Zinnia. Even in grade school, when we were at each other's throats, it was an undeniable truth. As many times as I gaslit myself into thinking it was just sexual or platonic interest alone, I knew there was a romantic component.

What I didn't consider, however, was that Zinnia could feel the same way. That my fondness of her doesn't go unrequited.

I have always written off these feelings festering inside me, telling myself that she wasn't an option. Because she wasn't. We weren't even really friends, so how could we become something more?

But now that I see a chance for us, I can't stop thinking about it. I have to try. I'm pretty sure if I wanted to, I could scientifically or at least psychosocially prove that we're a good match. Can she deny us if it's fact?

Dating isn't something I've focused on, but it's not because I don't want to. I do; I've just spent so much of my life trying to impress my parents, rather than do anything that fulfills my own wants and desires. My parents rarely check in on me, except to see how my grades are. Now all I want to do is practice magic for my love of it. Knowledge for the sake of knowledge. And the only being other than myself that I hope to impress is Zinnia.

I'm sitting on my couch, Liszt by my side, as I wait for everyone to show up. I consider texting my therapist to inform him I think Zinnia is my special interest, but decide I better not. She's been the topic of half our sessions lately as it is.

Saga, Aster, Clover, and someone named Avery—who I've never met—are all meeting up with Zinnia and me to go to the mall and shop for outfits. It's been a couple of weeks since I asked Zinnia to go to the dance, and she apparently already found her dress online, but the rest of us are less prepared when it comes to fashion.

Bored, I pull out a pen and paper, and practice my potential graduation speech.

I was in a three year bachelors-to-masters program, which specializes in preparing future professors, I write.

Boring. I pick the pen back up.

My undergraduate degree is in Potions, with a minor in Charms, and my masters will be in Magical Pedagogy. There was no doubt in my mind that I'd be accepted into this prestigious program, I try, but scribble out. Why does everything I say sound incredibly self-absorbed and stupid?

The stairs we'll take next, nope.*The hard work we all put into,* Ugh.

Did I put in a bunch of hard work? If I'm being honest with myself, college has been a breeze. I've struggled with besting Zinnia, but the work hasn't been challenging. Exciting, sometimes, but not difficult.

My phone faintly rings, but I don't see it anywhere. Getting up off the couch, I move about my dorm, searching for the device. It's not in my back pockets, not in the key bowl next to the door. Nowhere.

Liszt is giving me a strange look, and I lift him up to find my phone hidden underneath him, buzzing.

Silly fox. "This is Wren Elric," I say.

"Hey, I'm downstairs in the car. Zinnia and Aster are already with me," Saga says, and I grab my boots off the shoe rack.

"I'll be out shortly," I respond and hang up.

I give Liszt a pat on the head before crossing out the door, into the hallway.

Saga and Aster sit in the front seats, so I hop in the back with Zinnia, who is wearing a frilly, short pink dress, showing off her gorgeous legs. Part of me wants to compliment her and tell her how great she looks, but I give her some space, since I'm trying not to come on too strong.

"Where's Clover and Avery?" I ask.

"Avery wanted to drive them himself in his fancy car. Plus, my car only legally fits five," Saga answers.

We pull away from the dorms and head out of the Illusionary Jungle, straight for Sunspell City Mall. Spring flowers are blooming everywhere, the colors vibrant and beautiful, reminding me a lot of Zinnia.

"What do you want to wear, baby?" Aster asks Saga.

"I want to match you, my love," my cousin replies, her hand resting on her girlfriend's upper thigh.

Zinnia and I exchange matching glances that scream *really? My love after a few months?* Ick. Why are people in love so sickly sweet?

When we pull up to the mall, Clover and who I can only assume to be Avery are standing next to one another, their arms crossed and their skins flushing red.

"They look redder than us," Saga whispers to me.

"Hey y'all, how're we doing?" Zinnia asks the pair.

"Fine," they both say in tandem.

"Good," Zinnia says and turns back, gesturing for me to stand next to her. I do.

As we walk through the mall, Aster and Saga hold hands, while Avery and Clover bicker quietly amongst themselves. I'm honestly not sure which couple is worse. Both pairs are insufferable.

We enter what might be the most high school prom store out there.

Aster zips up Clover's dress while the rest of us sit in the waiting room part of the dressing room. The two girls tried on close to twenty ball gowns. Aster picked a long, baby blue dress, and Clover is trying something red on now.

Avery has been complaining about the temperature in this store for the last twenty minutes. Saga reiterates continuously that it's likely much warmer for the two girls trying on outfits and that he should quit his bitching, but he's relentless.

"Do we sound like those two?" I whisper to where only Zinnia can hear.

"Who, Clover and Avery?"

"Yeah, are we that bad?"

Zinnia lets out a slight giggle. "No, we're worse"

"In our defense, our arguments are almost always academic."

"Are they, though? Sometimes I think the only reason we keep the other one around is to have someone to argue with," she says.

That might be true for her, but it's not true for me. It's so much more than that.

"I think this is the one," Clover says, smiling down at a softer, pink dress that reminds me of a mermaid tail.

"You look amazing," Zinnia says. She goes on to explain how it's similar to a famous dress worn by some model from a few hundred years ago.

I don't know what Zinnia's talking about, but everyone seems to agree it looks great.

"Okay, now that the girly-girls are taken care of, can we go get some suits?" Avery says after a long beat of silence.

"Um, I'm not sure. Wren, are you feeling a suit?" Saga looks over at me.

I shrug. "I want something different."

"I want something to eat," Clover says. "We can go to the food court, and then decide what we're doing from there."

Making our way down to the food court, we all split off to different restaurants. Saga and I end up at a sandwich shop, while Clover and Zinnia go grab smoothies. Poor Aster is stuck with Avery, as they both want feta wraps, and as Saga as I stand there in line, I watch everyone interact with one another. People watching has always been interesting to me.

"Aster is like a champion dancer," Saga shares.

"That's fantastic! Has she been in any musicals?"

Saga eyes me. "No, she does like... sexy dancing. Lyrical stuff."

"Musical theatre can be incredibly sexy."

"Don't start with me. Anyway, I've been practicing my moves so I don't embarrass her at the Spring Fling," she says.

My cousin has always been likable. A big red muscular hybrid, she's the product of one cambion parent—my uncle Steve—and one orcling parent, her mother Cai. Saga might not be the smartest person in any room, but she's athletic and charming. And kind to everyone, not just the people she likes or finds to be valuable.

"How... thoughtful of you," I say, unsure of how to reply. We order our food and take our numbers, waiting off to the side for our food.

"Do you plan on dancing with Zinnia?" she asks, one eyebrow raised.

"Absolutely not. I'm not making a fool out of myself in front of the smartest and prettiest girl I—"

"Hey," Clover says as she and Zinnia walk up from behind us, smoothies in tow.

"Where's Aster and Avery?" Saga asks.

"They're sitting at a table already," Clover says. "Avery is probably telling her about every time I've messed up a move while we're out on the ice."

"Don't let that prick bother you," Zinnia reminds her friend.

Once our food is ready, we all head back to the table and eat. The girls, Saga included, all chat about athletic competitions. Zinnia tells them a little about our Valentine's Day contest, conveniently leaving out the fact that I won, and I stay silent.

She can have this one.

"I want ice cream," Aster says suddenly and completely off topic.

We all stand and clear the table, and Clover gives Zinnia a look. "I'm going to take Aster to get ice cream while Avery and Saga go shopping for suits. Since Zinnia is our fashion expert, she can assist Wren in finding something unique."

I'm not positive if Clover is aware of what she's doing or not, but I don't say anything. I'm more than happy to have the time alone with Zinnia.

Everyone clears the area, and Zinnia lets out a small sigh. "Is it bad that I'm relieved our friends are gone?" She walks towards me, coming incredibly close, before she runs her fingers on my shirt and unpops my collar. "There. That was driving me nuts."

"Where should we go?" I ask, walking out of the food court. She falls into step beside me, and we go in the opposite direction of the rest of the group.

"Do you want to wear a skirt or dress situation?"

I shake my head. "Not really."

"Good. I'm not sure I can handle another mini-skirt."

I cock my head at her, one corner of my mouth ticking up. "You seemed to handle me just fine the first time."

Red seeps into her cheeks, her face and neck becoming flushed. "Okay. So no suit, no dress. A vest?"

"I want something weird," I share. "Something that screams *gender fluidity.* Not quite feminine, not quite masculine."

"Like a coat with a long fluttering tail, or maybe a jacket that ends in a skirt-like formation, maybe? Almost like a peplum top, but it's a jacket," she asks.

"I have no idea what any of those words mean in this context," I confess. "My vocabulary is expansive, but it's almost abysmal when it comes to fashion."

She links our arms and ups her speed. "I think I know just the place."

I half expected her to drag me to a cute store with rainbow flags and hair dressers with mohawks and tongue piercings. That seems like my vibe. Instead, she brings me to a place that looks posh, even for me. My parents aren't rich, but they're both financially successful individuals. My father is a surgeon, and my mother is a magical engineer. This place? This place feels like it's meant for celebrities.

It's almost too clean.

I bump my elbow on something as we're passing through racks, and I yelp. Zinnia quickly shushes me.

"Why did you pick this store?" I ask.

"Their designs are progressive and innovative. This isn't the regular store; this is the outlet version. The real store is way out of our price range," she shares. "But I thought they might have something on clearance that's your vibe."

Zinnia grabs a hundred different things, placing them up against me, and comparing them to one another, before she finally settles on three sets.

"To the dressing room," she quietly announced.

We cross through a small doorway and into the dressing room. Nobody seems to be occupying it, and there isn't a worker in sight, so I head into one of the larger stalls. Zinnia follows me.

"What are you doing?" I whisper.

"I'm going to sit in here and see how they look" she says, as if it's nothing. She places the outfits on the hooks and takes a seat on the bench.

"While I'm getting dressed?"

She crosses her arms. "Wren... we saw each other naked like two fucking days ago. Relax."

Somehow, this feels more intimate than sex in a way I cannot describe. Sex is often done in the dark, or for us, in a haze of rage. We have hate-sex. There's no hiding under these bright lights.

"What would you like me to try on first, the black or the blue?" I ask, holding up two different sets.

"The black."

I turn away from Zinnia and unbutton my jeans, quickly slipping them off and slipping into the trousers. I tuck in my shirt and put the jacket over top. It's a unique cut. One side of the jacket ends in pleated panels that emulate the cut of many skirts, whereas the other side stops abruptly like a shortened suit.

Buttoning the last button, I turn to Zinnia, whose eyes go wide.

"Oh my," she says. "Come closer."

I move towards her, my body between her legs, as she adjusts the coat.

"There."

Looking down at her perfect face, I can't help myself. I run my hands across her jaw, bending down and pulling her into a soft kiss. It's light and lovely, and I squat down so that I'm resting between her legs. She deepens the kiss, her button nose pressing against mine, as our tongues collide. Her fingers run through the long strands of my white hair, and I let out a breathy moan.

"Let me do something for you," I say, kissing down the side of her neck. "Don't say another word."

Sex with Zinnia is always fun and pleasurable. We get into some stupid argument, we start yelling at one another, and then we take it out on each other's bodies. We've fallen into a rhythm. Zinnia likes to dominate me, and, while I enjoy letting her, I don't want that right now.

I don't want her to tell me what to do—I just want to worship her.

"Okay," she says, her voice all breathy, and I'm shocked it was that easy to get her to give in.

I kiss her ankle and run kisses all the way up her calves until I reach her thigh. Once I'm there, I gently push the frilly fabric of her dress up, revealing her lower half.

No underwear today.

Pushing her back, I get onto my knees and spread her legs apart, using my fingers to part her lips for me. Zinnia lets out a quiet moan as I suck on her clit. I allow my tongue to dance over her most sensitive areas, watching her quiver and squirm with every movement. Nothing has ever turned me on more. There's nothing sexier than pleasuring this beautiful satyr. My dick hardens against the zipper of my trousers, but I carry on.

Gently, I push one finger inside her wet cunt, slowly moving in and out as her breathing gets heavier and louder.

"That's it, sweetheart," I whisper against her thigh. When I feel like she's ready, I push in another.

She grabs my horns, pushing my face into her skin, and I slowly move my fingers in deeper.

"Please," she begs breathlessly, her head craning back.

And that's all that it takes. I finger her with fervor, licking and lapping at her sweet pussy until she's a moaning, shaking mess.

"How's it feel to be a good girl for once in your life?" I tease.

"Shut the fuck up, Wren."

And there she is. That's my Zinnia.

sixteen

ZINNIA

When Wren and I get back to our friends, they don't say anything about our messy hair or disheveled clothes, thankfully. Clover eyes me in a silent *you're welcome* that I refuse to acknowledge. That was the first time Wren and I did anything sexual that wasn't sparked by an argument. It's also probably the first time, ever, that I let someone else take the reins in bed, and I actually liked it.

I think I'll always prefer being the more dominant partner, but it was nice to be cared for, and even nicer that I trust Wren enough to let them.

As we're walking, Aster starts jumping up for joy, and I realize there's a photobooth towards the exit of the mall.

"Let's all take a picture," she shouts, grabbing Saga by the hand.

The six of us pile in, all ready to make our poses. For the first photo, Saga and Aster make a heart, where Avery and Clover stand back to back behind everyone. Wren and I are the shortest coupling, so we sit in the front and smile. Right before the photo is taken, we both throw up peace signs.

Giggles erupt from the two of us as the next photo is taken: Saga and Aster are kissing, and I can't even look back to see what Clover and Avery are doing before the camera flashes a third and final time.

We all get out of what feels like a clown car and wait for our photos to print. Three prints come out. Aster of course takes one, Clover takes the second, and I'm handed the last copy. It's a cute set of photos. Saga and Aster look endlessly in love, Clover and Avery look like they want to kill each other, and Wren and I... Well, we look happy.

I've always enjoyed Wren's company. I like arguing with them; I think our banter is fun. They also challenge me in ways no one else can. It's clear those things are true, but I wasn't anticipating actually enjoying *Wren.*

Wren is an annoying, self-centered, pretentious, self-inflated butthead, and I think I actually like them for it. I think that I like even the things I don't like about Wren, and I don't know what I should do about that.

Clover squeezes me tightly, hugging me goodbye, before Wren and I climb into the back of Saga's car to head towards Augury. The Spring Fling is tomorrow night, and we're all excited for the experience.

Prom is something high schools always do, but universities don't all do dances or balls every semester. Augury University has apparently done one in the past. It's a magical competition that the professors put on against one another, and it's done on some sort of cycle, but that's all Wren could share with me. They claim it's top secret and that they only know because they're an intern at the cosmetic lab.

Not my place to pry, but I'm excited to see the magical showcase and everyone dancing and having a good time regardless. I think my pa is right: I need to have more fun.

Saga and Aster are singing along to the radio, when I glance over at Wren and realize I'm being kind of selfish myself. "Hey," I whisper.

They turn back from staring out the window to look at me. "Hello."

"Did you want the photo booth picture? I feel bad. I just assumed I could have it," I admit.

"No, thank you. I don't need a photo of us."

Ouch. Alright. "Oh?"

The corners of Wren's mouth tick up, ever-so-slightly, as they pull out their wallet and open it up. "I have one already," they say and pull out a small polaroid.

It's the photo of us kissing from the Valentine's Day carnival. I can't believe it. "How long have you had this in here?"

"Well, that was taken on February Fourteenth," Wren says and sticks up a hand, counting on their fingers. "March, April. A little over two months."

"Really?"

"Really, really."

My brain threatens to malfunction, but my heart melts at this new piece of information. Like a tornado, it whirls around, every memory flying by. The note when we were fifteen, the care package, the photograph. As much as I want to paint Wren as an asshole, and they definitely can be, they're also one of my biggest supporters.

And one of my closest friends. *Fuck.*

I have spent the last twenty-four hours accepting that I have feelings for the person I have spent all of high school and university loathing. Good and truly loathing. And now? I can't picture my life without them. There's not a single soul in the universe I'd rather spend my days bickering with, or just plain speaking to. And the worst part of it all is how much time I've spent convincing them I'm not interested. I told Wren I won't do relationships, that I'm too busy. I have sex with them and reiterate time and time again that it'll never be more than physical.

And now here we are.

I'm not even sure Wren will want anything to do with me after one of us is crowned valedictorian. But as I walk outside with Aster, knowing that Wren and our other friends are out there waiting for us, I tell myself it doesn't matter. Tonight is just about *tonight*, and we're going to have the time of our lives.

I'm not sure what you'd call the vehicle standing before me. It's not a limo, but it's not an SUV; it's some strange raised hybrid. It's big enough to fit the six of us, and that's all that matters.

Saga whistles at Aster, and they warmly embrace. Nobody, not even Clover, had seen my dress until tonight, and I swear I hear someone gasp.

"Where did you get that dress?" Clover asks.

"I made it myself," I beam. I designed it in two parts. There's a corset-style bodice with built-in cups and loose, draping sleeves that come off my shoulders and a skirt that's essentially just a long, giant pile of fabric layers. It's a light green, and I sewed on embroidered patches of flowers all over it after I sprayed it with glitter.

I'm actually really proud of it.

"You look stunning," Wren whispers and presses their soft, rounded lips against the top of my hand.

We all pile into the vehicle, each couple sitting together.

"I didn't know you sew. I'll have to get you to help me with my costumes at some point," Aster says.

"Anytime, roomie," I say. "Have y'all heard anything about a theme for this thing?"

"I believe it's just magic themed," Avery answers first.

Saga smiles. "I guess we'll just have to wait and see."

When the car finally pulls into the event plaza, which is in the heart of

Sunspell City, we see lights and magic everywhere. There are illusions lining the space. Magical rainbows coming out of potted plants, and sparkles floating through the air like bubbles. It's ethereal and beautiful and completely out of this world.

"Woah," Wren says as we walk in. There's a fountain in the center of where all the food tables are and what looks like liquid gold circulates over-and-over again.

"Who do you think did that one?" I ask.

"Dean Taylor, without a doubt," Wren answers. "Indi—Professor Watson wouldn't do something so front and center."

We take our seats, noticing the light fixtures hanging above us are floating seemingly out of nowhere.

"Professor Daelor," Wren and I say in tandem.

"What are you two babbling about?" Saga asks.

"They're guessing which professors did the magic for every piece of decor," Aster answers. "But I feel like the simpler answer is that they hired mages that do stuff like this for a living."

Avery points to the plants that are actively growing down one of the walls, their petals falling off and regrowing endlessly in a cycle. "I have to agree with the nerds. That plant wall *screams* Dr. Ali."

"They asked if we'd do an ice showcase," Clover admits. "But Avery refused."

"I did not refuse," he says. "You kept bringing up how badly you wanted to go to this dance, and I knew if we performed, you'd be too stressed to have any fun."

A pang hits my heart. Although I'm not Avery's biggest fan, I know that he cares for Clover, even if he rarely shows it.

An owl flies over where everyone is seated and transforms into none other than President Bariel. He grabs a microphone and introduces himself, as well as the staff, before passing it off to Dr. Aloe.

She walks in with a bunch of familiars, and they perform an interpretive dance. It's moving and exciting, and it's fun to see all the creatures move both in sync with each other as well as at separate times. By the end of it, Aster and I are practically in tears, while Saga and Wren poke fun at us. Avery and Clover don't say a word, but I can cut the sexual tension between them with a knife.

The dance floor clears, and Saga stands, grabbing Aster by the hand. "Aster Al Anzi, can I have this dance?"

"Why Saga Vo, I thought you'd never ask."

They run off, holding onto one another, and Avery awkwardly coughs. "Well. I'm parched. Clover, would you like a drink?"

"Actually, I'll go with you," she says, and gives me a wink.

And with that, Wren and I are alone once more.

They point to a table nearby and whisper. "Look, it's Professor Watson and Dr. Daelor."

"They're adorable," I say.

"They're getting married."

"Really? That's sweeter than cherry pie." I look over and notice Dean Taylor sitting next to them, as well as some other people I don't recognize. "Who are they?"

"The woman next to Dean Taylor is her life partner, and then the other girl is Professor Watson and Dean Taylor's best friend and her husband," they explain.

"That brings me joy."

"Me too," they say. "It's cool that all of these people are incredibly successful mages, but they also have social lives and romantic entanglements."

"Do you see that table?" I ask, pointing to where Dr. Ali sits.

"Yeah, that's Iris Watson," they say. "And Dr. Ali. How could I forget?"

I shake my head. "No, look next to them."

Wren squints. "Is that Mr. Rokosmith?"

"Yeah!" I squeal. "And his partner. But don't tell him I told you. It's kind of a new development."

Avery and Clover come back with food and drinks, and we fall into a comfortable silence, everyone snacking away. Aster and Saga are still dancing, and Professor Watson and Dr. Daelor have even made their ways onto the floor. I won't lie to myself, I'm a little jealous.

"What's wrong?" Wren asks, touching their hand to mine.

"Nothing," I swiftly respond. I overheard Wren tell Saga they don't like dancing, so I don't want to push it. Besides, it was nice enough of them to ask me to the dance at all.

"Do you want to dance?" Their cute head cocks to the side.

"I mean I do, but we don't have to."

"I want to dance," Wren blurts out.

I furrow my brows. "No you don't."

"Yes, I do," they say, standing up and reaching out their hand.

I sigh and take it, following them as they lead me onto the dance floor. Their hands make their way to my waist, and I rest my arms on their shoulders as we slowly rock. "Why did you do this?"

"Do what?"

"Wren, don't act stupid. Why are you dancing with me?"

"I told you, I want to dance."

"No you don't," I insist, my voice carrying. Aster looks over, and I grimace. "Sorry." I'm not trying to embarrass Wren, but I don't want them to dance with me out of pity, either.

"Why do you think you know more about my own feelings than I do?" Wren asks, frustration leaking into their voice.

"Because I heard you tell your cousin you don't want to dance with me."

Wren shakes their head. "I told my cousin I didn't want to embarrass myself in front of you."

"What changed your mind, then?" I ask.

"You. You clearly want to dance, and I want to do anything to make you happy," they answer. "Also, both Clover and Saga texted me last night telling me that they'd off me if I didn't."

I laugh at their confession. "Why do you want to make me happy?"

The music changes to a slow ballad, and Wren pulls me in close, tucking my head to their chest. "Because this is just an ounce of the joy you've given me all these years."

I have spent so much time setting myself up to become valedictorian, I never considered that I might be setting myself up to fall in love.

"Wren," I start, but they cut me off.

"I don't think about things the way I used to."

"What?"

Wren takes in a deep breath. "I used to see something happen, like a flower blossoming, and think... huh, I wonder what genus it's in. Now, I see them and I think wow, I wonder if Zinnia likes these. I do this with everything. You invade my every thought. The smell of your perfume has coated every inch of my mind; the feel of your horns in my hand is my favorite touch. You are the last thing I think about before I fall asleep, and the first thing I consider when I rise. I am more likely to remember any random fact about you than I am about magic at this point, and magic's kind of my whole field of study, if you haven't noticed."

"Wren." I lift my head up to stare into their eyes, which are somehow more golden than the fountain.

Their eyes are watering, distress lining their features. "You are both the most frustrating and most captivating part of my universe."

"Wren," I say again, this time a little louder.

"What?" A single tear falls down their cheek, and I wipe it with my finger.

"I love you too."

Their face softens, and they pull me in close, hugging me tightly to them. "I have fought these feelings for years."

"I know," I say as I reach up to kiss their forehead. "I'm sorry it took me so long to figure out my side of things."

"I forgive you," they laugh against my lips before kissing me.

I take back every time I said I was too busy for love. Nothing can keep me from this.

seventeen

WREN

"Is that your girlfriend? Or boyfriend?" the clerk asks Zinnia as she rings her up.

"Yes," I say before anyone can interject. "Yes, I am."

We grab our groceries and head out of the store. Zinnia and I are doing a dinner-study-date combination night, as finals start tomorrow. It's our last hoorah before one of us is named the ultimate victor.

"Why would you say yes?"

I shrug. "I'm not a boy, but I could be your boyfriend."

She lets out a little snort. "Smooth. What do you want to be called?"

"Valedictorian," I say. "And you?"

She squints and chucks the grocery bag at my chest. "Valedictorian would be nice. So would, oh I don't know, Mistress. Or maybe Queen. Oooh, no, I've got it. Goddess."

I get out my phone and text Saga, who should be grabbing us on her way back from meeting Aster's parents.

"She says they're three minutes away," I say.

"Perfect. Now seriously, what do you want to be called? Significant other?"

"Hate that," I admit. "I mean, it's fine, but it's not for me."

"Lover?" she questions.

"Virginia is for Lovers," I jest.

She blinks at me. "What?"

"It's an old historical phrase—nevermind. I don't like lover, either."

"Partner?"

Howdy Partner. I laugh. "Yes! It's even better in your accent."

"I feel like I'm more like your partner in crime," she says, letting out a giggle.

"Even better."

Saga's car pulls up, and Wren grabs the door, helping me in before scooting in next to me. We head back towards the illusionary jungle.

Wren and I hold hands through the entire car ride. It's nice.

"I'm going to stay at Saga's tonight," Aster says. "Have fun with your study sesh!"

"Thanks," Zinnia replies, and we head for her dorm.

Spreading the ingredients out on the counter, I start making the curry. We argued on whether to make curry or chili, as we wanted something that needed to simmer while we studied, but ultimately decided on the dish in front of us.

Zinnia claimed she needed to go get flashcards for our study session, and I whistle my favorite show tunes as I eagerly await her return.

Loud footsteps patter through the space, and I turn to spot Zinnia in nothing but a strap-on, her plump breasts bouncing with every movement.

My brain buzzes in my head, my mouth agape, as she stalks towards me.

"Get on the ground," she says, and I do, diligently listening to her next instructions. "And crawl to bed with me."

Zinnia walks back towards her bedroom. I follow shortly after on my hands and knees, leaving the food in the kitchen to simmer.

Once we're in her room, she shuts the door and sits on the bed, where she gestures for me to come join her. I climb on next to Zinnia, and she leans down to kiss my neck, slowly making her way up my face. She kisses up my jaw, trailing towards my mouth, before parting my lips.

I would gladly let her do whatever she wanted to me.

Grabbing a tub from her nightstand, Zinnia dips her finger inside and starts prepping me with the lube. Her tongue dances in my mouth as her finger rubs against the rim of my hole before slipping it inside, slowly stretching me.

I let out a soft moan, and after a few minutes, she sits up and pulls me towards her, angling the strap to enter me. It's not very large, but I gasp as it stretches me, filling me.

Slowly, Zinnia thrusts, getting deeper and faster each time. It feels like she's almost edging me until one of her hands makes their way towards my cock, and I absolutely melt with sensation.

Between the dick that fills me and her soft hand stroking my cock, I lose myself to her touch. To the power she holds over me. Both physically and emotionally, I am hers.

"Remember when I said these were mine?" she asks, using her other hand to squeeze my balls. "It's still true. Every part of you belongs to me, Wren."

"Yes," I let out.

She lets go of my cock, and I groan in frustration, missing the friction.

"Yes, what?" she says.

"Yes, my Goddess." I squirm, almost desperate for her touch to return.

"What are you saying yes to?" she asks, gently squeezing my tip, her other hand now twisting my balls.

"I belong to you. I'm yours. Completely yours," I whimper. "Please, Zinnia."

She continues to thrust into me while jerking my cock, stopping every so often around my head, playing with all the ridges until I can't take a second more and come toppling over the edge.

Zinnia kisses me as she pulls out. "You're perfect."

No, Zinnia. You are.

Finals week has been stressful, to say the least. I almost believed that Zinnia and I resigned ourselves to no longer caring—no longer stressing over who ends up on top. I was very wrong. While it's obvious to anyone with eyes that we both care for one another, that fighting spirit is still alive in both of us, and only the lords of the GPA know what's yet to come.

I'm currently number one, but it is so close that I'm actually starting to doubt it'll remain that way.

Dr. Daelor's giving my last exam. It's a charm exam, so each student has to take it separately. Zinnia has already completed her last finals. She did great, flying colors. We even received extra credit for our infinity ring. Ultimately, this exam will be the tie breaker between us.

My heart is racing, practically thundering in my chest as I finish up charming the final object. Dr. Daelor grabs her laptop, inputting my score into the system.

"When will we know who is valedictorian?"

"Patience, kid. Give the computer thirty seconds," she says. "Is it between you and Zinnia?"

"Yes."

"I'm guessing you hope to win."

"No," I blurt out without thinking.

"No?" Dr. Daelor examines me, and a ghost of a smile crosses her face. "You don't want to be valedictorian?"

"I do," I say and put my hands on my head, pulling my hair. "I don't know. Frankly, I think Zinnia deserves it more than I do. She's had to claw her way to the top, where everything comes more naturally to me."

Dr. Daelor clicks on her computer and a smile forms. "I'm glad you feel that way."

"Why?"

"Because she's valedictorian."

"Fucking shit fuck. Really?" I ask, standing up.

"Don't forget to invite me to your wedding," Dr. Daelor says as I start for the door.

"You first," I shout as I race down the hallway, Liszt tailing closely behind me.

I'm so proud of my girl. So endlessly proud. I don't even care that it's not me. My speech would've sucked anyway. Zinnia is fucking Valedictorian of Augury University.

Scrambling, I almost knock into a student as I race through the courtyard and haul ass towards the dorms. I just hope Zinnia is there.

I pass Dr. Ali's greenhouse, all the sports fields, and the cosmetic lab as I sprint to the dorms. Crossing the threshold, I run down the hallway.

"Watch it, buddy," someone says as my shoulder hits theirs.

"Sorry!" I shout, continuing towards Zinnia's room.

Once I get there, I slam my fist into the door. Rustling sounds come from the other side, and Aster opens the door.

"Hey, Wren," she says. Aster is petite, and I'm careful not to slam into her as I race to Zinnia's room.

"Sorry. Need. Zinnia," I pant. "Zinnia!"

Opening the door, I see a room empty of Zinnia. "Where is she?"

"I think she went out to get a snack," Aster answers. "Something about flowers and clearing her head."

I haul out of the building, my feet lifting off the ground as I take flight, my wings carrying me past trees and structures as I make my way back toward the greenhouse. Distantly, I see Zinnia walking my direction, and I charge towards her, scooping her into my arms.

Her squeals ring through the air. We're not far off the ground, but it's more than Zinnia is used to, and she kicks her hooves.

"You're valedictorian," I say, holding her tightly to me.

"What?! Really?"

Gently, I place us back down on the ground and grab her hand to twirl her around. "You did it! You're valedictorian."

Her face looks solemn. "Are you okay?"

My brows draw in together, forehead wrinkling, as I look her over. "Why are you not happy about this?"

"It's hard to be happy when I'm afraid my happiness is hurting you," she says, our hands still holding one another's.

"Zinnia. How could I be upset? You deserve this more than anyone," I say and pull her in close, kissing her forehead.

"Promise?"

"I promise."

She shifts from out of my arms and shakes her hips, her ass and short, fluffy tail wiggling with the movement. "I'm number fucking one, baby," she shouts, sticking her tongue out at me.

All's right with the universe.

Graduation is tomorrow morning, so we decided to go to one of the open fields and watch the sunset before Nyxwing and I have our race.

I'm sure the owl-elk is going to best me, as their wingspan is massive, but I'm still going to give it my all. Our wings are unfurled, and the big beast and I stand neck and neck as we wait for our cue.

"Three... two... one... go," Zinnia shouts from her lawn chair, Liszt seated on her lap, the two of them ready to watch the show.

The two of us take off, our wings flapping at ridiculous speeds as we soar through the air. Nyxwing thrusts in a downward stroke, the feathered tips making a loop as air flows over them. It's much different than my wings, which feel almost like my hands, as the flexible membrane of my wing skin generates lift, allowing me to swim through the air.

Nyxwing makes it to the end of the field first and lets out a loud victory huff.

"Yeah. I bet you're unable to do this," I say and shoot up into the air before doing three consecutive backflips.

"Of course they can't do that, they have antlers," Zinnia shouts as I fly towards her.

"I have horns," I protest.

She lets out a snort, followed by a long fit of giggles.

"What?"

"One might say you're... horny." Her cheeks are completely flushed, and I pull her in for a kiss, before tapping on one of her horns.

"Yeah, well, so are you."

I sit on stage beside Zinnia and all our professors, as we listen to President Bariel give the graduation introduction speech. He talks about the fundamentals of Augury University, and how it came to be, before Dean Taylor takes the stand and talks about how proud she is of each and every one of us.

Zinnia's name is called, and she stands, her hooves clacking against the floor as she makes her way towards the podium. Her perfectly manicured fingers tremble as she grabs the mic. She glances over at me, and I give her a wide smile and a thumbs up, probably looking foolish, but I don't care.

Be confident, Zinnia. You've got this.

"Fellow graduates," she begins, her voice exuding confidence. That's my girl. "It's an honor to stand before you all today at the prestigious and magical Augury University. Together, we all made it through one of the most challenging, mystical, magical, and equally rigorous programs, and we made it through without accidentally killing any of our professors. All of you managed to survive times like when Dr. Daelor accidentally charmed the rugby ball to fly at forty-five mile per hour speeds. Or when Wren, our salutatorian, put a love spell over the loudspeaker in the food hall." The audience laughs as we all start to recall our own memories with the many professors at Augury University.

She takes in a breath. "Y'all, when I first arrived at Augury, I had no idea what to expect. I was a country satyr, born in Louisabama and raised there and outside of Florgia Beach. I knew more about chickens and cows than I did magical plants. Sure, I was good with charms and great at creature crafts, but I didn't expect to be tested with acid-spewing sunflowers at eight A.M. on a Tuesday morning. However, Dr. Ali, as well as Dr. Aloe and many others, have taught me to expect the unexpected. It's where my love of botanical magic grew."

Zinnia gives the audience a small smile. "Spells and grades and magic are not what tested us, here. Individuals did. It was our professors and friends who pushed us to be the ultimate versions of ourselves, and in turn, the best mages we can be. Even when life got hard, or we accidentally turned our textbooks sentient. This school taught us more than magic: it taught us to utilize logic, challenge everything thrown our way, and how to view failure as an opportunity to summon something entirely new—pun very much intended."

Zinnia cracks her knuckles. "I could go on for hours about every single member of the Augury staff. From Professor Watson's kindness, to Professor McNab's unique perspective on whether familiars have separate magic of their own, there is something to learn from everyone here, and I couldn't be more grateful for the experiences they've given me. Augury University is one of the only places in the world where magical minds and monstrous hearts come together to create prophecies and potions. Charms and conjurations. Magic, but also mayhem."

Her grin spreads from ear to ear, and a single tear falls down my cheek. "Congratulations class of 6007! May your charms be successful, may your visions always be faultless, and may your potion bottles never break. Thank you."

I've never been happier to lose.

Augury University: Next Generation

augury university: next generation

WREN

In the year 6009

"SOMEWHERE BETWEEN THE YEAR 3005 AND 3017, A SUPERMASSIVE BLACK HOLE caused six galaxies to collide with one another, resulting in The Convergence. It was catastrophic and detrimental to the land, cultures, and infrastructure of over fifteen habitable planets. Entire segments of continents made their way to other planets, and pieces of other planets made their way onto Earth. Now, in the year 6009, you will find satyrs, cambion, elves, orcs, and many other species roaming the planet, all living in harmony. The Convergence is precisely how individuals like you and I came to be," I explain.

I have achieved all my greatest desires. I was salutatorian in my bachelor's program, and valedictorian of my Masters in Magical Pedagogy program. Did I mention I have the most beautiful fiancé in the world? I even got to witness history during my internship program when Dean Taylor and a few scientists invented magical teleportation.

And now? I'm a professor at Augury University, where Earth's most magical minds and monstrous hearts work, study, and experiment.

My first class feels so familiar, yet it's so strange to be on the other side. I can remember introducing myself to Professor Watson, and showing her my trick. I recall Zinnia too, and the way we were so determined to outshine one another.

She's still the brightest star in my galaxy. Metaphorically speaking, that is.

Once we finish with class, I head towards the quantumagic lab, which has become a second home to me. During undergrad, I spent most of my time in the cosmetic lab. My mentor, Dean Taylor, opened a new lab a few years ago dedicated to quantum magic, and that is where I interned during graduate school.

Dean Taylor, as well as a few other mages and scientists, were successfully able to create a method of teleportation, and my life has only continued to change and grow from there. When I am not teaching or cuddling—*and arguing with*—my fiancé, I am experimenting with potions to help their new research.

I love research.

If it weren't for the incredible risks posed on our lives, I would volunteer to be a part of the next round of teleportation trials. That, and I can't because I'm not human. Humans make better test subjects since they have no magic which could intervene with the circumstances. Our first subject, who we've nicknamed subject zero, never made it back to the lab, though her vital tracker shows she is very much still alive. We can't find her because she's off-world.

As much as I'm enjoying the quantumagic lab, I hope to move on soon. I have incredibly personal goals I intend to work on next. Luckily, I don't think they'll need me here much longer. We're *so* close.

Walking into the lab, I'm greeted by Dean Taylor and some of the other mages and scientists. Dr. Wyatt, Dr. Hoag, and their assistant Mrs. Palmer are all standing in front of one of the quantum forges, in front of a thick sheet of glass, staring at it as if they're expecting something.

"What's going on?"

"I've been in contact with someone on Hel, and they're attempting to send someone back through a forge of their own," Dean Taylor explains.

"Subject zero?"

"Negative." She shakes her head. "Subject zero has stated she has no interest in returning to earth. They're going to send someone who is actively seeking to travel here."

The quantum forge, which is now glowing an extremely bright light, begins to shake. The beams of light turn and twist, smearing space itself in front of us as the mirror-like forge transforms into a spherical wormhole. A body makes its way out of the tube. Light brown skin and striking eyes and a tail. A golden snake tail.

This woman—this serpentine looks identical to... Dr. Adeib Ali.

Fucking *shit,* this is amazing. I have never been more excited to see what the future holds. We've figured out teleportation, which means now I can move on to my next assignment at the medicinal magic lab.

We've eradicated STIs, and we're working on cancer—time to put an end to endometriosis.

Augury University Series Epilogue

augury university series epilogue

INDIGO

On my to-do list:

- Let Dahlia finish styling my hair
- Go over my vows again with Alitha
- Marry the love of my life

Not on my to-do list:

- Have an anxiety attack

Unlike many brides, I'm not anxious about the whole *getting married* thing. Vega is the best thing that's ever happened to me. If I could redo the past, I'd smudge my eyeliner in the bar every single time.

Augury isn't working on a time machine—though Alitha is buzzing about a secret project that involves teleportation—so I don't have to worry about all of that. I'm more nervous about things like *what if I trip and fall? What happens if Vega's dad shows up?* Or worse, he doesn't.

I also can't stop thinking about the proposal. Nobody knows this except Vega, Alitha, Adeib, and myself, but Adeib is going to propose to Iris today, and I am terrified.

My brain keeps coming up with endless visions of her fainting, throwing up, or... saying no. There's no reason she'd say no, she loves Adeib, but the idea keeps circulating like a pest, ready to ruin this beautiful day for me.

I won't let my anxiety get the best of me. Not today.

Dahlia stands behind me and pulls a chunk of my hair, which is freshly cut, towards the back of my head, looping the pieces through my veil. Vega nor I went for a traditional bridal look, but neither of us have a clue what the other one is wearing, and that's half the fun.

Vega could've gone with anything, really. Anything except a dress. I could see her rocking a vest, or maybe a jumpsuit? A tuxedo would be sexy as well. Whatever she chose, I'm sure it's perfect.

My sister straddles my lap in an awkward, bird-like pose as she applies eyeshadow to my lids. She completes the job and gives my face a once over. "You look... otherworldly."

It's a funny thing to say, given that our DNA is mostly human, and everyone else we know is *actually* otherworldly, but I get her meaning.

"Like something out of myth," Alitha adds. "You look divine."

"Thank you," I say and smile. "You both look beautiful."

The girls and I continue getting dressed, putting on the finishing touches for our jewelry and makeup. I kept my wedding party small. Iris is my maid of honor, and Dahlia is my bridesmaid. Alitha, of course, is the one marrying us. And I wouldn't have it any other way.

Our wedding is going to be an amazing day for everyone, but it's not the big bash that everyone always talks about. We have like fifty guests, mostly coworkers, but friends and family too. There are two people in each of our wedding parties, and we have no flower girl or ring bearer or any of that extra stuff.

We hired a photographer, but no videographer. I want to live in the moment, unbothered by what I will look like as I laugh or move. With photographs, we can just delete the bad ones, but videos live forever. I don't need to fixate on a misstep, or the way one of my eyes awkwardly blinked for the rest of my life.

"Alitha, it's time for you to head down there," my mother says, peeking her head into the dressing room.

Thankfully, Iris and I have mended much of our relationship with our mother. It isn't perfect, but she doesn't go out of her way to criticise me, and she's learned to see the flaws in Iris too. We no longer have to live and breathe under the pressure of her scrutiny. We can just be us, and she'll love us anyway.

"Iris, Dahlia, once Vega and her bridesmates get down there, it'll be your turn," my mother says. "And then myself, and finally Indie and her father."

The music changes to the song I chose, and my girls start their descent down the aisle. Taking in a deep breath, I try to calm my racing heart as my mom blows me a kiss goodbye.

Before I leave, I take one last look in the mirror. My wedding gown has a white base, with a sheer black layer overtop. There are black lace adornments on the waistline, as well as on my shoulders, and it matches the black of my veil. I feel like a bride.

I turn to my dad, who has tears in his eyes, and loop our arms.

We decided to have the wedding at the Sunspell City Fine Arts Museum, so as we cross down the aisle, there are beautiful paintings on the walls. There is a painting to my left of a human woman wrapping her arms around another woman, the two beautifully embraced, yet their faces are almost somber. A small faun sits in the background, and I stop for a second, taking the time to appreciate the artistry. This is a piece of sapphic history, and we are likely making history by getting married in the same room as it, though this will never be recorded.

It's something I will hold dear to me.

As I get closer to the makeshift altar, the tears begin to well in my violet eyes. Every memory of Vega and I flash before me. From our first encounter, to me dropping everything when I realized she was my new boss. I can see images and videos and stills in my mind of her and I in the bathroom at work, in our bedrooms, in the kitchen. Her defending me to my family, her comforting my anxiety, every little thing.

The snow globe. The hot chocolate and Christmas carolers and strap-ons and stolen glances. The way she's supported me through every project and endeavor and has cheered me on as I've taken over the cosmetic lab.

I love this woman—this orcling, *so* fucking much. She is everything I ever dreamed of in a partner and more, and every day I am so grateful she's mine.

Vega is wearing a black suit that forms to her body, showcasing her broad muscular shoulders and the strong muscles of her biceps. She looks truly handsome, standing up there waiting for me to walk down, and she winks, trying to disguise the tears lining her eyes.

My dad unlinks our arms and presses a kiss against my cheek before I take my place alongside Iris and Dahlia.

"In life, many individuals' goal on this earth is to find their person. Whatever souls are made of, you want yours and theirs to be the same," Alitha begins. I can feel the stares of the audience, but I don't let it bother me.

These are the people who love me. Love us. I see my parents and Raemond in the front row, Elorthiel and Archeron in the second, and many of our other coworkers fill the seats. I continue to scan the crowd, looking at all the familiar faces. Wren—Alitha and I's pesky, but brilliant young intern—is sitting in the third row with their girlfriend. And there's a... a man. A human man. He's muscular and broad, with strawberry-blonde hair and a nose that reminds me so much of Vega.

Oh my goodness. That must be Vega's father. Looking over, I see him and V have locked eyes, and he gives her a small smile. A single tear falls down her face; my insides feel like goo. I don't know what they're communicating to one another, but it's clear there's a mutual understanding in their expressions.

He loves her. He accepts her. I just hope he will continue to show up for her, because if anyone deserves it, it's V.

We exchange our vows with the microphones off. Only Alitha, our wedding party, and one another can hear, and it makes the moment just that much more intimate.

"You both have shared beautiful sentiments that are now woven into the fabric of your relationship. By the powers vested in me by the Elven Council, it is with deep joy that I pronounce you wife and wife. Indigo Watson-Daelor and Vega Watson-Daelor, you may now seal this life changing moment with a kiss," Alitha says.

Vega crosses towards me, and I wrap my arms around her neck as she grabs my face and kisses me deeply. Her tusks brush against my lips in the most familiar and comforting way, and for a moment I forget there's anyone else alive but us.

When we release from one another, I glance up to see mistletoe hanging from the ceiling, and my heart threatens to burst. My friends and family truly did right by me when planning this wedding, and it was so nice to allow them to do so much of the heavy lifting.

To be loved is truly to be known.

Our reception is arguably what I was most nervous for, even though I'm having a blast. We had our first dance, and then we danced with our fathers. Everything's gone just as we planned. Raemond, Alitha, and I ran through the list of events at least a hundred times, but as we get towards the bouquet toss, my hands grow clammy. I just want to make Iris happy.

It's V and I's special day, but it's her day too. Even if she doesn't know it yet.

Raemond makes a call over the speaker for all the unmarried women to gather around. Wren's girlfriend joins us, followed by Dahlia, though she and Elorthiel are engaged, and even Alitha and Cordelia—who never plan to marry, but simply live as life partners—make their way to the dance floor. Other friends and coworkers slowly join us, yet Iris is nowhere to be found.

My heart is beating in my chest as the minutes tick on.

"Hey, fucking wait for me," Iris shrills as a door swings open. She's flicking her wrists as if to dry them, and I can't help but laugh.

Of course Iris would be late to her own proposal.

She pushes towards the front and stands beside Dahlia. "You're probably going to be the next to get married, but it's worth a shot," she says and shrugs. Dahlia doesn't make a peep.

I turn around and make to toss the bouquet, my smile reaching from ear-to-ear as my cheeks flush pink. *This is it.* Turning, I lock eyes with Iris as Adeib slithers over to where we're all standing, and I hand her the bouquet.

"What?" she asks, her head cocked to one side, her dark brown hair beautifully draped down her back, all tattoos on display.

"It's your turn," I say and gesture behind her.

Iris quickly realizes that Adeib is right there, one hand holding an open box, while the other reaches for her. We all back away, and I can't hear what he's saying, but the tears in her eyes matched with their smiles on both of their faces tell me everything I need to know.

This man and my younger sister were made for one another, just as Vega and I were. The ring he got her is made of rubies, shaped into flower petals with a diamond in the center, and a shiny golden band. She nods her head repeatedly, and he places it onto her hand.

My heart is so full. They kiss, and everyone's cheering—but Iris runs up to me and grabs my face, smooshing our noses together.

She gives me a look. "This was supposed to be your day."

I hug her tight. "There is no me without you."

Only our closest friends and family members remain. We're all sitting in somewhat of a circle, everyone is tired or drunk, but everyone's still beaming with joy over our special day.

"We did a song at our wedding—a celtic folk song—and I'd like you girls to do it here," my mom says, and I vaguely remember watching the video recording as a young girl.

"Bog down in the valley?" Iris asks, her face lighting up.

"You know the one."

"What're we getting into now?" Vega asks, and I laugh.

"You'll see."

My dad starts us off, taking a deep a breath before he begins. "O-ro, the rattlin' bog, the bog down in the valley-o."

After he runs through the first verse, my mother comes in with the second. "On that tree there was a branch. A rare branch, a rattlin' branch. Branch on the tree and the tree on the bog and the bog down in the valley-o."

Everyone joins in. "O-ro, the rattlin' bog, a bog down in the valley-o. O-ro, the rattlin' bog, the bog down in the valley-o."

Vega, Alitha, Dahlia, and even Malik try, with my father's help, to say some of the later verses. It's embarrassing and hilarious and they struggle the entire time, but it's so full of joy and love.

I gesture to Adeib, who shakes his head no, so Wren takes his place, drunk off their ass as they mumble-sing the lyrics horribly.

Iris takes a shot before it's our turn for what'll be the final verse of the night. "From that bird there was a feather. A rare feather, a rattlin' feather. A feather from the bird and the bird from the nest and the nest on the leaf and the leaf on the twig and the twig on the branch and the branch on the tree and the tree on the bog and the bog down in the valley-o."

Vega kisses my hand, and we all sing the last chorus. "O-ro, the rattlin' bog, the bog down in the valley-o. O-ro, the rattlin' bog, the bog down in the valley-o."

"I love you," V whispers in my ear.

"I love you more."

pronunciation guide

Adeib Ali: uh-deeb ah-lee
Alitha Taylor: uh-leeth-uh tay-ler
Augury University: aww-guh-ree university
Aura Nguyen: or-uh win
Barac: buh-rock
Daffodil: daff-oh-dill
Dahlia Torres: dolly-uh tor-rez
Dean Archeron Bariel: dean are-chur-on berry-ell
Elara Lothial: e-lara loth-e-uhl
Fern: furrn
Florp: flore-puh
Freja: fray-uh
Hiro: he-row (flipped r sound; between an English R and an L)
Indigo Watson: in-dih-go watt-son
Iris Watson: eye-rihs watt-son
Liszt: least
Magia Island: ma (like mad)-g-uh island
Malik Hills: mal-ick hills
Momiji: mo-me-g
Moss: ma (like mom)-ss
Naiad Island: nye-add island
Nyxwing: nix wing
Oak: ohk

Raemond: ray-mohnd
Serenade: sarah-nayd
Torzu: tour-zoo
Vega Daelor: vay-guh day-lore
Wren Elric: ren el-rick
Zinnia Featherfields: zinn-e-uh featherfields

glossary

Terms/Places

Augury University: a university on Magia Island where mages can study and further develop their magic.
Aquatica Academy: Augury University's sister campus their magic.
Familiar: a mage's animal companion, and conduit for their magic.
Mage: a being who practices magic.
The Convergence: a magical collision of multiple planets (Barac, Earth, Hel, Loria, and Moonflower), resulting in changes to Earth, as well as those prospective planets, including magical beings living on Earth and shifts in our geographical and sociological features.
Magic types
Botanical Crafts: the ability to communicate with plants (hibiscae, hyndrangigus, murrseae, rosa aeternitas, etc.)
Charms: the ability to move and utilize an object, or alter it, without touching it.
Creature Crafts: the ability to communicate with animals.
Illusions: the ability to create and project illusions, or images, with your mind which look real to those around you.
Potions: the ability to create potions which can change objects, bodies, and other things, sometimes permanently.
Sight: the ability to see visions of the possible future, as well as glimpses of the past.

Magical Races

Cambion: half-human, half-demon from the planet Hel.
Centaur: half-human, half-horse nymph from the planet Moonflower.
Elf: a tall, magical race of beings with pointed ears and longer life spans from the planet Loria.
Faun: half-human, half-deer nymph from the planet Moonflower.
Kraken: half-human, half-octopus or squid. This magical race comes from the deep depths of Earth and other planet's oceans.
Merfolk: half-human, half-fish or fish-like creature. This magical race comes from the deep depths of Earth and other planet's oceans.
Orc: a tall and muscular, magical race of beings with green skin and longer life spans from the planet Barac.
Satyr: half-human, half-goat nymph from the planet Moonflower.
Serpentine: half-human, half-snake magical race whose origins are unknown.
Hybrid: a being descended from multiple magical races.
Orcling, elfling: a person born with one human parent and one orc or elven parent.
Elfborn, orcborn, merborn, etc.: a person who has some distant ancestry of magical descent.

acknowledgments

Although I'm a writer, it is still hard to put into words how grateful I am to have published this series. There are so many unseen aspects that go into writing, publishing, and marketing a book, even when you're indie.

I'd like to think that people buy my books because of my writing, and I think sometimes they do! But ultimately these books would hardly sell if it weren't for the beautiful covers by Fallnskye, and now the equally pretty cover by Eternal Geekery (who also did my map). Fallnyskye also did the omnibus chapter headers and other sketches and bits. This series wouldn't be what it is without these two women's artistry. I'm also grateful to Ram, who allowed me to put his lovely pieces into the book as well. I love art—please support real artists.

This book has many pieces of me. My ADHD and anxiety and autism and endometriosis and SPD, my family's Arab culture (if the Arabic is wrong, blame my brother), and all other little parts of me, but it also has much of my friends and their cultures and experiences as well. Thank you to my sensitivity and authenticity readers Ruthie (Stealing Elf Hearts), Rhys (Disco Spring Fever and Riding Centaur's Sleigh), and Lo (Haunt Me, Baby) for your expertise. Thank you to Heather and Emilee for lending me your very lovely lesbian eyes. And though I'm also genderfluid, thank you to Rae and Abby for being extra eyes and ears for the nonbinary experience. Lo, Ruthie, and my childhood friend Silvercloud allowed me to bug and consult with them many times when creating this world, as did my friend Alexis in regards to the disability representation within it. Endless thank you to all of you. Seriously.

Thank you to my many editors (in which I needed 3). Rae, Abby, & Heather, I could not do with without y'all. Rae is the other half of my brain, Abby is my cheerleader and wordsmith, and Heather is my final set of eyes. This book would've been messy as heck without you 3 wonderful humans.

Lastly, thank you to my readers. Although I don't always respond (blame the ADHD), I see all of your posts, shares, and comments and I'm forever glad

I could put out my very unapologetically queer romances, and that you're all enjoying them. Stay queer and stay weird.

Thank you.

about the author

Rose Santoriello is a non-human romance author that currently resides in the hellish swamps of Central Florida with their husband, dogs Luna and Blitz, and cats Storm and Millie. When Rose isn't writing, reading, or dealing with their menagerie of pets, they spent their time at Renaissance Festivals and Anime Conventions, cosplaying to their heart's content. They are looking forward to showing you their monstrously cute stories. You can find them @rosesantoriello on all socials.

www.ingramcontent.com/pod-product-compliance
Lightning Source LLC
Chambersburg PA
CBHW060818310726
48980CB00002B/338

* 9 7 9 8 9 9 2 7 2 5 5 0 6 *